When Darkness Falls

THE OBSIDIAN TRILOGY
BY MERCEDES LACKEY AND JAMES MALLORY

The Outstretched Shadow
To Light a Candle

ALSO BY JAMES MALLORY

Merlin: The Old Magic
Merlin: The King's Wizard
Merlin: The End of Magic

TOR BOOKS BY MERCEDES LACKEY

Firebird
Sacred Ground

DIANA TREGARDE NOVELS
Burning Water
Children of the Night
Jinx High

THE HALFBLOOD CHRONICLES
(written with Andre Norton)
The Elvenbane
Elvenblood
Elvenborn

When Darkness Falls

The Obsidian Trilogy, Book 3

Mercedes Lackey and James Mallory

A TOM DOHERTY ASSOCIATES BOOK   *New York*

WHEN DARKNESS FALLS: THE OBSIDIAN TRILOGY, BOOK 3

A Tor Book
Published by Tom Doherty Associates, LLC
175 Fifth Avenue
New York, NY 10010

www.tor.com

Tor® is a registered trademark of Tom Doherty Associates, LLC.

Library of Congress Cataloging-in-Publication Data

Lackey, Mercedes.
    When darkness falls / Mercedes Lackey and James Mallory.—1st ed.
        p.   cm.—(The Obsidian trilogy ; bk. 3)
    "A Tom Doherty Associates book."
    ISBN 0-765-30221-7 (acid-free paper)
    EAN 978-0-765-30221-2
    I. Mallory, James.   II. Title.
    PS3562.A246W46   2006
    813'.54—dc22   2005034506

First Edition: July 2006

Printed in the United States of America

0 9 8 7 6 5 4 3 2 1

When Darkness Falls

Prologue

The Surface of the Mirror

THE DAY OF the Working at the Allied camp outside Ysterialpo-erin dawned pale and overcast—and far too cold to snow.

None of the Wildmages was certain of what would happen when the spell to see past the wards of Armethalieh was cast. The spell itself could be as safe as a scrying spell, or as dangerous as the assault upon the Black Cairn; there was no way to know except by doing. But though the spell itself might be safe, its aftermath was certain to be dangerous, since a spell of such power would inevitably draw the attention of the Endark-ened, and even after centuries of fighting *Them*, all the Allies really knew about Demons was that *They* were evil, terribly powerful, immortal, could assume any shape, and fueled *Their* magic through the blood and pain of others. It was not impossible—in fact, it was highly likely—that *They* could sense things non-Demons couldn't.

Oh, Kellen could guess at *Their* tactics. Imagine *Their* strategy—some of the time. But truly think like one? No Creature of the Light could manage that.

What if this is a trap? Cilarnen is innocent—I truly believe that—but what if this is still a trap? The Demons have given us information before, knowing we would have no choice but to act upon it. If They arranged for Cilarnen to find out what he did, They would also know we would do everything in our power to investigate further. Making ourselves vulnerable . . .

And just as with the discovery of the Shadowed Elves, there was no way to turn away from such a task. If what Cilarnen said was true—if there was any possibility that there was a Dark-tainted traitor within Armethalieh—the Allies had to know.

They had to do exactly what they were doing now.

Someday, Kellen vowed grimly, *we will no longer dance to your piping, Shadow Mountain. Someday we will choose the battlefield—and the battle. And we will win.*

⟨≫⟩

IT would have been impossible to gather the Wildmages together properly for this work in any of the structures within the camp, so Jermayan and the black dragon Ancaladar had created an ice-pavilion for the work. Its polished surface—a faithful, though enormous, replica of a traditional Elven campaigning tent—was already crusted white with new-fallen snow.

Kellen and Cilarnen walked toward the pavilion, each occupied by his own sober thoughts.

The other Wildmages were already gathered here, though not all were yet inside. The Mountainfolk undoubtedly thought this was a fine calm day—even warm—and the Lostlanders were used to even harsher conditions. Some were gathered around a brazier, brewing their thick black tea and talking quietly. Others paced back and forth, their heavy furs dark against the snow.

It was the calm before battle.

Ancaladar was coiled around the pavilion, as immobile as if he'd decided to become a part of it. The dragon raised his head as they approached, his large golden eyes fixed on Cilarnen.

"This should be interesting," Ancaladar commented, lowering his head again.

They went inside. Idalia was standing near the mirror, talking intently to Jermayan. She looked up as Kellen and Cilarnen entered, and her violet eyes flashed dangerously. Cilarnen was a High Mage born and bred. He had been unjustly Banished from Armethalieh, yet somehow managed to retain his Magegift—and with it, a peculiar—and painful—sensitivity to the Wild Magic. This was the last place Cilarnen should be.

"He believes he has a good reason to stand in the Circle with us. I've heard his reasons, and I agree," Kellen said evenly. "I've told him it may kill him. He has still chosen to come."

"Cilarnen—" Idalia began.

"Idalia," Kellen said gently. "No one is asking your permission."

Idalia stared at Kellen as if seeing him for the very first time.

Jermayan appeared at Idalia's side. Even in plain sight, even in a crowd of people, the Elven Mage could appear and disappear with a silent grace that owed nothing to magic and everything to his Elven heritage.

"To know these reasons would make good hearing," Jermayan said quietly, putting a hand on Idalia's arm.

"I think . . ." Cilarnen faltered to a stop and started again. "I . . . *need* to be here. To help, if I can."

There was another silence. Idalia looked from Cilarnen to Kellen and back again. At last she nodded—not permitting but accepting. "As Kellen says, it's your choice."

"Stand where you like," Kellen said to Cilarnen. "I don't think it will matter."

"I'll want you in the center with me, Kellen," Idalia said. "Come on. I'll show you."

She took his arm and walked with him over to the space before Kindolhinadetil's mirror. Her stave leaned against it. There was now an iron brazier set before it—one of the largest the Elves possessed—filled with pieces of *namanar* wood. On a square of cloth beside it lay a small herb bundle that would also be needed.

The mirror was a perfect oval as tall as Kellen was, set in a wide standing frame. The frame was of a light-colored fine-grained wood, intricately carved.

But it was hard to say with what. Each time Kellen was certain he had identified an object depicted in the frame and the base—fruit and flower, tree and bird—it seemed to change. Was that a deer? Or a wolf? Or was it a vine?

He gave up.

But then he looked directly *at* the mirror.

It was made of a single thick pane of flawless rock crystal backed with Elvensilver, and the reflection it gave back was utterly perfect.

Kellen hadn't had much time for mirrors lately. There'd been none in the Wildwood, and he'd paid little attention to the small ones in the house in Sentarshadeen. Since then, well . . . he couldn't remember the last time he'd seen a mirror.

Was this him?

He was no longer the gawky, awkward, half-grown boy who'd been Banished from Armethalieh two seasons before, a child ill-at-ease in his own body.

In the mirror, Kellen saw a stranger. A man . . . and one he wouldn't want to face in battle, either. Curly light brown hair, long enough by now to braid tightly at the back of his neck, gray eyes. Broad shoulders, strong muscles honed by hours of sword-practice and long hours spent in armor. He towered over Cilarnen—even after several moonturns working in Stonehearth's stables, you'd never mistake Cilarnen for anything but one of the fine-boned and delicate Armethaliehan Mageborn. Kellen . . .

They'd call me a High Reaches barbarian trying to pass for an Elf, he thought with an inward grin. Well, if he wanted nothing to do with the City, the City had obviously returned the favor.

"It's certainly impressive," he said.

"It will serve our needs," Idalia said with a dismissive shrug. "Now. I'll stand here. You'll stand behind me. You'll see what I See—everyone will, I think, just like a regular scrying spell, but if this spell goes the way I think, I'm the only one who will Know whatever there is to know. But you should be able to sense how the spell is running, and . . . interfere, if it becomes necessary."

And hope the Wild Magic shows me what I need to do, Kellen thought soberly.

Idalia lit the brazier. As the ghostwood began to kindle, she took her staff and began to walk around the outer edge of the group of Wildmages, drawing a line in the beaten snow.

❧

SHE refused to let herself think beyond each moment, trying to make herself seem confident and assured. She'd refused to accept Jermayan's betrothal pendant for fear that it would establish a deeper form of just such a link as she was proposing to forge now, and allow him to see into her mind to glimpse her unpaid Price in its fullness. She could just hope that with so many minds joined, all focused upon their task, the secret of her unpaid Mageprice would remain unshared by Jermayan.

The circle drawn, she returned to her place in the center of the circle, between Kellen and the brazier. He stood as calmly as if he were already in deep trance, as alertly as if he might be called upon to fight at any moment.

Waiting.

Idalia knelt and took up the tokens needed to cast the spell. She slipped her dagger from her belt and scored a long line down her palm, then clutched the herbs and hair in that hand tightly, moistening both with her blood.

Then she cast them onto the brazier of burning wood.

The smoke coiling upward changed color abruptly, and Idalia felt the shimmer as the dome of Protection rose around them all, expanding outward to enfold the army that waited outside as well.

The Link formed, and the Power of the assembled Wildmages joined together, becoming one, becoming hers. She felt the spell uncoil within her as she inhaled the smoke.

She reached out toward the mirror.

Show me what I need to See: Tell me what I need to Know.

The spellbound mirror glowed bright as the moon, growing larger and larger until it was all there was.

❧

IDALIA was in the City.

Not *now*—but *then*. What she saw was in the past. For a moment she was puzzled, then realized she must need to See this as well as anything that might be happening now.

The Temple of the Light. The Adoption ceremony of a pale fair-haired man a decade—perhaps a few years more—older than Kellen. The spell let her Know the meaning of everything she Saw, and so she knew that what she saw was Anigrel—Kellen's former tutor, Lycaelon's private secretary, the Mage who had neglected to Burn the Magegift from Cilarnen's mind before Cilarnen was Banished—being adopted into House Tavadon. Later this same day Anigrel would be appointed to the Mage Council and take High Mage Volpiril's seat.

She knew that Mages Breulin and Isas had been forced to resign.

With dreamlike swiftness, the hours and days of Anigrel's life unfolded to her: the formation of the Magewardens and the Commons Wardens—the network of spies to inform upon the people of Armethalieh and sow terror among them. Every thread of unholy Darkness woven through the golden fabric of the City was spun from Anigrel's hands.

The conspiracy for which Cilarnen was Banished never existed. Anigrel started it all—

Idalia watched in sick horror as Anigrel murdered Lord Vilmos. It was worse than she had imagined—worse than anyone had feared. Anigrel was the Demons' creature—had been for years. And now he'd managed to reach a position where he would soon be able to strip away Armethalieh's defenses—and let the Demons in.

He was going to give them the City.

And all she could do was watch.

⤜⤛

DEEP in the darkness of the World Without Sun, the Demon Queen Savilla stood naked in her ivory chamber. Through the soul-deep link she shared with her Mageman, she felt the festering sickness of the Light approach him.

They will not!

The walls were spattered with blood, and the remains of half-a-dozen dismembered slaves lay scattered about, for she'd had no time to be neat or elegant. The obsidian bowl was filled to overflowing with hot fresh blood, and more pooled on the ebony table and ran down its legs to the floor.

Savilla's fury grew until it nearly choked her. How dare Wildmages meddle in her plans?

She bared her fangs in savage glee as she tested the power of their spell and followed it to its source. They'd worked so hard and so diligently to penetrate the human city's defenses.

But a breech for you is a breech for me, my darlings, Savilla purred to herself in sudden delight. In their desperation, they had made themselves vulnerable.

She struck with all her might.

❧

KELLEN Saw all that Idalia Saw—they all did—but without the Knowing, it meant little to him. He let the images go, concentrating on feeling the currents of power that flowed through them all—through the ring of Wildmages into Idalia; from the army into the ring of Wildmages—searching constantly for anything out of place.

The spark that was Cilarnen was like a bright ember; different, apart, but not wrong.

Jermayan . . . another sort of difference.

Kellen ignored them both.

Then:

"No!"

He sensed disaster—coming—already here—he didn't know which.

He reached out to Idalia. She had to end the spell.

He was too late.

Time seemed to slow. The surface of the mirror faded to darkness, and bowed outward as if its surface were not crystal but oil. It reached for Idalia.

If it touched her, they would all die.

❧

KELLEN saw Cilarnen fling Mage-Shield over Idalia at the exact moment Jermayan Cast his own Shield. But Cilarnen had only his own power to draw upon, and Kellen felt him reach the end of that power in seconds—

And felt Ancaladar bolster Cilarnen's power with his own.

"*Freely given,*" Kellen heard. "*Freely given.*"

Cilarnen's shield strengthened.

Held.

The two shields—one of High Magick, one of Elven Magery—sparked and boiled over each other, the emerald and purple refusing to blend. In moments they would fly apart, leaving Idalia vulnerable to the attack.

They have to hold!

Kellen felt as if the whole force of both forms of magic—neither his—was pouring through him, tearing him apart.

But the power of the entire Circle was his to wield as well.

He drew upon it, forcing the two Shields together. He felt as if he'd plunged both hands into a bed of live coals, but his pain was a distant thing. He forced it still farther from his consciousness, focusing all his intent upon holding the two Shields together. Now he could see them clasped in a faint blue tracery: his Will. The will of a Knight-Mage, which could not be turned aside from its purpose, save by death.

Time seemed to speed up again. The bolt of pure Darkness struck their combined Shield, and if he had felt pain before, it was nothing to what he experienced now. He heard Cilarnen scream; felt Jermayan's agony. Ancaladar bellowed in pain and outrage at the pain—and more, the *vileness* of the attack.

The Shield held. And Kellen held; though he felt as if every atom of his body was being torn asunder, he held, and held, and held, by will alone, as the Darkness hammered at their combined defense, and then as his will eroded, and he felt even that failing—

He was filled again with power, with a pure white power that held every color of magic there ever was within itself. And what little remained of his ability to think put a name to that power.

Shalkan.

This was why Shalkan had held back from the other workings, even when it was to heal one of his own kind. *This* was what Shalkan had been saving himself for, without knowing exactly what would be needed, only that it *would*. He fed the very essence of *unicorn* through the bond that tied him to Kellen, and into Kellen's Will, into Cilarnen, because Cilarnen was as virgin as Kellen, into the Shield, so that all powers fused into one color that held all—

With a lightless flash and an earsplitting shriek of backlash, the Darkbolt recoiled upon itself.

Kindolhinadetil's mirror . . . dissolved.

The Link was gone, and so was the Sphere of Protection. The two Shields vanished beneath Kellen's grasp, and with them, his need to hold them. Suddenly alone in his own skin, Kellen tried to take a step, and went sprawling. Without the spell to concentrate on, all that was left was the pain.

He felt drained—unnaturally drained—as if his body had given up more than it could safely give, and he *hurt* from the energies he had forced through himself.

I'll never be a High Mage . . . Kellen thought groggily.

He tried to get to his knees, but he was too sick and dizzy to move.

Cilarnen—Jermayan—I have to get up—

"Stay down. It's all right. I know what they want," someone—Idalia?—said. "I know what they're doing."

One

A Thousand Shades of Darkness

THE PRICE THAT the Wildmages, the Elves, and their Allies had paid to learn the plans of their Enemy had been high. Two-thirds of the Allied camp had shared in the cost of the Wildmages' spell, and lay now in their tents stunned into exhaustion, cared for by those who had been exempted from the Price of the spell.

No one had expected that the Price would be so heavy. If not for Cilarnen, Jermayan, and Kellen managing to blend their magics to shield Idalia from the attack of the Demon Queen Savilla and save the lives of the spell-linked Wildmages, the sacrifice would have been greater still: the lives of all the Elven Army's Wildmages, and perhaps the death of hundreds, even thousands, of fighters.

But with Shalkan and Ancaladar's help, Wild Magic and High Magick had worked together, though the effort of making them do so had cost Kellen dearly. And the spell had done what they needed it to do: Idalia had seen across Armethalieh's wards and decoded the cryptic warning that it had cost Cilarnen Volpiril so much to bring them. They now knew the specifics of the Demon's foothold in the Golden City.

Somehow, long ago, Savilla had touched the mind of the young Mageborn Anigrel, corrupting him utterly while he was still a child. All his life Anigrel had worked to one goal: to see the Endarkened gain ultimate power. Though Anigrel's father had been Commonsborn, Anigrel had risen above his lowly birth, becoming Arch-Mage Lycaelon Tavadon's private secretary and tutor to his son, Kellen, all the while worshipping his Dark Lady in secret. When Kellen had been

Banished for practicing the Wild Magic, Anigrel's fortunes had continued to rise: Lycaelon had relied upon him more and more, elevating him swiftly through the ranks of Magehood. To increase his clandestine power, Anigrel had invented a conspiracy against the Mage Council, which had resulted in the Banishment of High Mage Volpiril's son, Cilarnen, and the resignation of several members of the High Council. The Arch-Mage, knowing nothing of this, had appointed Anigrel to one of the new vacancies, and adopted him as his son and heir.

From his new position of power, Anigrel had continued his work, sowing fear and distrust throughout the City against the Elves and the Wildmages, and creating the Magewardens and the Commons Wardens to watch the High Mages and the Commons for any sign of further treason—treason he himself had created. And all along he moved closer to his ultimate goal: removing the ancient and complex wards from the walls of Armethalieh—wards which sealed the City against attack by Demonic magic. . . .

≈

IT was three days before Kellen was able to leave his bed, and at that, he was the first of the Wildmages—other than Idalia, who had not been touched at all by the spell's backlash—to be able to do so.

≈

HE guessed he was just stubborn.

All his life he'd been stubborn. His earliest memories—the ones he knew that were truly his, that hadn't been tampered with by Lycaelon to remove inconvenient memories of his sister Idalia—were of people telling him he was "too stubborn"—whatever that had meant in terms of life in Armethalieh. Too stubborn to learn his lessons by rote. Too stubborn to be a proper Mage-student and ornament to House Tavadon.

Later, of course, when he'd discovered that he was not only a Wildmage, but a Knight-Mage, he'd understood, because a Knight-Mage's most vital tool and weapon was his will. Once a Knight-Mage had made up his (or her—Kellen supposed the Wild Magic could make a female Knight-Mage if it chose, just as there were female Elven Knights) mind to do something, only Death could turn him aside from his purpose. If that wasn't being stubborn, Kellen didn't know what was.

Being stubborn had saved his life—and the lives of those around him and under his command—more than once since this war began. And it *was* a war. There could be no doubt in anyone's mind about that now.

When it had begun—it seemed so long ago, though the establishment of the Black Cairn to keep the rains from falling on the Elven Lands, which marked the first move in the Demons' strategy, could hardly have been more than a full turn of the seasons ago—no one had been sure of that. Even after Kellen had destroyed the Cairn, and the Elves had discovered that the Elven Lands were infested with a race of Dark-tainted beings that had lived there, unsuspected, for centuries, they had still not been sure.

After all, the Elves had fought the Endarkened twice before—the last time a thousand years ago—and each time it had been openly, on the battlefield. Only Kellen had been sure that this was war again, and though the Elves were polite, and certainly respected the fact that he was the first Knight-Mage born in a thousand years, they hadn't been willing to pay a lot of attention to the opinions of a seventeen-year-old boy. Even battle after battle with the Shadowed Elves—with Kellen proving himself in every one—hadn't really changed their minds. Elves lived a thousand years, and they did not hurry. Especially about changing long-held opinions.

But even before the Wildmages' spell, many of them had been changing their minds. Unfortunately, even if they did, it wasn't much help. You couldn't have a war if only one side showed up, and the Endarkened had shown absolutely no interest in taking to the battlefield. *They* were more than happy to cause droughts, to force the Elves and their Allies to expend their strength in things like cleansing the Elven Lands of the Shadowed Elves, to breed monsters in the Lost Lands and send them out to prey on anything they could reach, but as no one knew where Obsidian Mountain—the Demons' stronghold—was, or how to reach it, there was no way for the Allies to carry the war to the Enemy.

Leaving aside the fact that we're probably outnumbered, and we know that They're *more powerful than we are*, Kellen thought to himself. Demons were the most powerful Mages there were. All the Allies had to set against them was a handful of Wildmages, and no High Mages at all. In the last war, Armethalieh had fought on the Allied side. But not this time.

Despite that, the constant doubts and near-despair that Kellen had felt since the beginning were gone. With Idalia's discovery of the traitor within Armethalieh, and the discovery of the Endarkened's strategy, Kellen now knew why the Demons had been refusing to fight openly. *Their* intention was to subvert Armethalieh and make it fight against the Elves on behalf of the Demons—Light against Light. And then the Demons would destroy the winner.

Which means that powerful as They *are,* They're *still afraid of us. Which has to mean we have a chance of winning. All we have to do is figure out what it is—and use it.*

IT was more effort than he'd expected it would be to dress, and for the first time in ages Kellen actually noticed the weight of his Coldwarg-fur cloak when he settled it over his shoulders. But it was unthinkable to brave the outdoors without it—when he'd broken the power of the Black Cairn, ending the year-long drought, the weather-patterns had been violently unsettled, and were still returning to normal. One of the side-effects of that was the hardest winter the Elven Lands had seen in centuries—and the coldest and snowiest, too.

When Kellen stepped out of his pavilion, the cold bit into him like a sword, and he shuddered, pulling his cloak tightly around him. It was sheer stubborn restlessness, he admitted to himself, that had gotten him up and out—that, and the fact that he wanted to see how Cilarnen was doing for himself. Since the Golden City had sealed its gates against the "Lesser Races," its name, and that of the High Mages, had been a byword for stupidity and ignorance. Cilarnen had as much to do to prove himself in the wider world as Vestakia did, and in helping to thwart the Demon attack upon Idalia, he'd done much to enhance his reputation.

Cilarnen was still living in the Centaur camp. Idalia had been a frequent visitor to Kellen's bedside, and she'd told Kellen that Cilarnen had been taken back there to recover, since the Healer's Tents were still filled with wounded from the Battle for the Heart of the Forest. By the time Kellen had walked there, he considered himself well-served for his rash decision to venture out. He couldn't remember the last time he'd felt this exhausted—even poisoned and half-frozen, he hadn't felt quite this hollow-boned.

Fortunately, most of the rest of the army seemed to be in better shape than he was. Oh, the camp was a great deal quieter than he'd ever seen it, and he didn't hear the sounds of drilling on the practice-field, but Kellen merely had the sense that the army was resting, not mortally wounded. And since he had come into his power, he had learned to rely upon those instincts.

He reached the edge of the Elven encampment and passed over into the Centaur encampment.

The Elves had their elaborate pavilions, and the Mountainfolk had their sturdy domed tents, but neither design would do for the Centaurfolk. Though in their villages they lived in houses very much like those of the humans with whom they often shared their lives, on campaign, their physical needs were best accommodated by a series of large boxy tents, big enough to hold a dozen Centaurs at once.

The last time Kellen had been here, he had realized that Andoreniel's people must have constructed all of these tents specially when Andoreniel had summoned the Centaur levies, because the Elves never, but never, went to war in winter, and in summer, the Centaurs would probably simply have slept outdoors. But for a winter campaign—and a hard winter at that—different arrangements had to be made. At least this way, nobody would freeze.

He found the tent where Cilarnen was staying without difficulty, making a mental note to see about at least getting Cilarnen a pavilion of his own to pitch in the Centaur camp as soon as possible. They'd had so many losses, Kellen reflected grimly, that a spare pavilion and furniture wouldn't be hard to find.

He lifted the flap and ducked inside—no Elven formality here!—glad to be out of the wind. It was comparatively warm inside; a heavy clay pot filled with coals set in the center of the tent radiated warmth.

The Centaur Wildmage Kardus stood beside Cilarnen's bedside, dozing, the only person in the tent besides Cilarnen.

The Centaurs had no ability to do magic, so Kardus, as a Centaur Wildmage, was as much a rarity as Kellen himself. Kellen supposed Kardus's lack of innate magic was the reason he wasn't suffering the same aftereffects of the spell that the other Wildmages were.

Kardus wore his black hair as long as any Elf, and braided into it were a number of charms and ornaments. He carried more such charms on his necklace, and others upon the broad belt that lay upon his hips. Some of them were bespelled—gifts from other Wildmages—since if Kardus could not cast spells of his own, that certainly did not keep him from taking advantage of the magic others gave him. His horselike body—for the Centaurs only closely resembled horses, being actually smaller and stockier—was as black as his hair, and he had three white feet, a pattern Kellen had not seen in any other Centaur.

Kardus cast no spells, but like all Wildmages, possessed the Three Books of the Wild Magic and followed their teachings. Unlike all other Wildmages, Kardus's life was guided by mysterious Knowings and Tasks presented to him, so he said, by the Gods of the Wild Magic, which he dealt with in his own way.

It was one such Task and Knowing that had brought Kardus's path to cross with Cilarnen's for the first time at Stonehearth, and their ways had lain together ever since. Kellen was glad for Cilarnen's sake. With everything that was being thrown at him so abruptly, Cilarnen desperately needed a level-headed friend to support him.

There was a stool at Cilarnen's bedside—placed for the convenience of the human Healers who came to check on him, Kellen supposed—and Kellen moved forward and sat down on it heavily. Another few moments and he would have sat down on the floor. He'd overestimated his strength, he supposed, and right now he wasn't really looking forward to the long cold walk back.

Cilarnen was lying listlessly in his sleeping pallet. There were deep shadows under his eyes, and he looked ravaged, as if he'd been suffering from a high fever. But he opened his eyes when Kellen sat down.

"Kellen," he said. "Did we win?"

What? Leaf and Star, hadn't anyone told the boy? It didn't matter that Cilarnen was a full year older than Kellen was. In so many ways Kellen was older than Cilarnen was, and always would be—though Gods of the Wild Magic forefend that he ever call Cilarnen "boy" aloud.

But perhaps Cilarnen simply needed to hear it again. Certainly the stakes were high enough that the truth could bear repeating.

"Yes. You saved us all."

Cilarnen grimaced and turned his head away, as if Kellen were offering false praise.

"Cilarnen, it's true," Kellen said. "It wasn't your shield alone that stopped the attack, or Jermayan's. It was both together. I think that's the secret: High Magick and Wild Magic working together. I don't think *They* can stand that. I think it's how you won at Stonehearth—because you and Wirance worked together there."

Cilarnen took a deep breath, struggling to sit up. Kellen moved quickly to help him, feeling Cilarnen's muscles tremble with the effort. Even a season's hard labor in the stables of the Centaur village of Stonehearth hadn't done much to put muscle on Cilarnen's fine-boned Mageborn frame. Kellen took after his Mountainborn mother—after two seasons of Knightly training he had the muscles and the stamina for a hard winter campaign. For the first time, it occurred to him that Cilarnen simply might not be physically strong enough to survive out here.

"So all we have to do to defeat *Them* is convince the High Mages to fight for the Elves," Cilarnen said with a faint note of despairing humor in his voice. "Well, *that's* simple enough."

"Harder tasks have been accomplished, when one has set their feet upon the Herdsman's Path," Kardus said reprovingly, raising his head. "And now, since you will admit that you are awake, tea, and soup. I will fetch them." Kardus walked from the tent, collecting his cloak at the door.

"He nags me to eat," Cilarnen said with a sigh when the Centaur Wildmage had gone.

"Isinwen does the same to me," Kellen said. "You have to eat, though. You're going to need all your strength."

"For what?" Cilarnen demanded bitterly. "I'm a High Mage who can't do magick—unless you want fires lit or water boiled—because to cast any really powerful spells I need training I haven't got, tools I haven't got, and most of all, a power source I can't possibly get!"

"You've already saved us once," Kellen said, refusing to let Cilarnen give in to despair. "You know more spells of the High Magick than anyone else between here and Armethalieh. You can make the tools. As for the power source . . . don't just give up. Besides, you're more than just a source of spells. You're the one with the best idea of Armethaliehan politics. We'll need your advice."

Cilarnen stared at Kellen as if Kellen had lost his mind.

"Think about it," Kellen said. "I never paid any attention. Idalia left the city more than a decade ago. But you . . . you know the families, the people. If someone can figure out a way to get a warning to them that they'll listen to, it might just turn out to be you."

Cilarnen shook his head in disbelief. But he looked thoughtful.

⁓

KARDUS insisted that Kellen share Cilarnen's meal, and Kellen was grateful for the strength that it lent him, for he realized that he had another stop to make before he could return to the comfort of his bed.

Redhelwar, the Commander of the Elven Army, had shared in the spell-price for the Working, and like all the others, was still recovering from its effects. From Idalia, Kellen knew that Redhelwar already knew all that she had learned. But what Kellen did not know was what Redhelwar intended to do about it. When Cilarnen had first come with his cryptic warning, Redhelwar had set the Wildmages to discover what it truly meant before deciding what to do.

Now he knew.

If the Demons got Armethalieh . . .

They *have* everything They want. *Everything* They *were waiting to get before* They *attacked us openly. And if* They *can convince Armethalieh to attack us* . . .

The thought made him feel sick. Against Armethalieh—even with the power of the High Mages on the Armethaliehan side—the Allied Army would be fairly evenly matched. Which meant both forces would cut each other to pieces in a long, bloody, drawn-out war. Armethalieh would give no quarter. The Demons would see to that. *They* would make sure that the Golden City was convinced that the Elves, the Wildmages, and anyone who fought at their side had to be utterly destroyed.

And when it was over, no matter who won, there would be no victory.

So we can't fight them. We can't possibly surrender to them. There's no place we can run from them—I'm sure the Endarkened will see to that. We've got to keep that war from happening.

He walked up the slope to Redhelwar's scarlet pavilion. Ninolion, Redhelwar's adjutant, was waiting inside the doorway and ushered Kellen in out of the wind with the briefest of Elven courtesies.

Kellen stood inside the doorway, waiting to be noticed.

The Army's General was alone at his worktable, making changes to the great map that represented the eastern portion of the Elven Lands. Maps fascinated Kellen, though they were largely a mystery to him: In Armethalieh, the world had stopped at the City walls, so of course in the City, the creation and study of maps—aside from maps of the streets of the City—were among the many things that were strictly anathema, forbidden to Mageborn and Commons alike. Before Kellen had come to live among the Elves, he had never imagined that the world could be depicted as a series of marks on vellum. Well, actually, he'd never imagined the world at all, come to that.

Under Master Belesharon's tutelage at the House of Sword and Shield in Sentarshadeen, he had learned a little—a very little—of how to read them, and so he could tell that this one represented not only Ysterialpoerin and its surrounding forest, but the Army camped outside it. Its scale was such that it included even the two Elven cities to the north of Ysterialpoerin: Lerkalpoldara and Realthataladon, and the mountains that surrounded them.

But north even of them, Redhelwar was making careful marks upon the map, at various points along the Border.

At last Redhelwar glanced up. "I See you, Kellen Knight-Mage. Be welcome at my hearth. It is my hour to drink tea, and I would be honored if you would join me."

"It is always a joy to drink tea in the pavilion of a friend," Kellen answered. The proper response came easily to him now, though once finding the right words for the intricate verbal dance of Elven courtesy would have baffled and frustrated him. But Elves did not hurry—if there was one lesson that Kellen had had to learn the hard way, it was that one. They were creatures of age-honed ritual and politeness, and—except when actually using War Manners—sometimes maddeningly indirect speech.

But at the moment nobody was actually attacking, he'd be glad of a cup of tea, and he'd welcome the chance to collect his thoughts before finding out what Redhelwar was thinking—and figuring out if he had to try to change the Elven Commander's mind.

Redhelwar gestured him to a seat, and Kellen sank into it gratefully.

In the fashion that Kellen had become used to over the past several moon-turns, Redhelwar then began a seemingly-idle discussion of the weather—cold, though after the last series of severe storms, they could expect only moderate snow for the next few sennights—and the entertaining seasonal menu they had been granted through the generosity of Kindolhinadetil, Viceroy of Ysterialpoerin, who had made sure that the Army was well-supplied with both fresh and preserved food.

Apparently "entertaining seasonal menu" meant they were eating the greenneedle trees of the Heart Forest; Kellen tried not to think too hard about that, but he'd eaten a lot of things he never thought he'd eat since he'd been Banished from the City.

"One observes that the other Wildmages are still abed," Redhelwar remarked shrewdly when they both had full mugs of Winter Spice tea before them. "Even Jermayan, with Ancaladar's power to draw upon, has not ventured forth to taste the pleasures of the day." "The pleasures of the day" being a joke, or as much of one as Redhelwar ever made.

And Jermayan is probably the strongest of all the Wildmages, with Ancaladar's power to draw on.

"I was restless," Kellen admitted. "And I am well-served for my impetuousness."

"Nevertheless, you have come in a good hour, for matters have . . . progressed since *They* chose to move so openly against us, and I would welcome your counsel," Redhelwar said, allowing the conversation to turn to practical matters at last.

The Army's General gestured to the map spread out upon the table. "Scouts have come from Lerkalpoldara and Realthataladon, bringing news of the Borders. The Enemy sends its creatures to gather in strength—here, and here, and here—the Ice Trolls and the Frost Giants—and those who can pass through the Boundary-wards—the ice-drakes, the Deathwings, the Coldwarg, and others—freely do so in greater kind and number than have been seen since the Great War. *They* once used the Lost Lands as their nursery, but I think that now that time has passed. Now *Their* creatures will use the Elven Lands as a gateway to harry the Wild Lands to the west and south . . . and I do not think we can protect them."

"It's another feint," Kellen said slowly, reasoning it out. "*They* must know we've discovered *Their* agent in Armethalieh. Anigrel wants to open the City to *Them*. If he succeeds, *They* win."

"Yet we cannot abandon our allies to *Their* attack," Redhelwar said. "And those who might defend them are here, gathered at Andoreniel's word. I sent to Sentarshadeen as soon as Idalia told me the news from the City, and only this morning I have received Andoreniel's answering word to me."

Kellen was impressed. Even a unicorn couldn't cover the distance to Sentarshadeen and back in just four days, and that would have left no time for the royal Council to debate its reply. Though Andoreniel was the king of the Elves, he did not act without the advice and consent of his Council.

"It would be good to know how this was done—and to hear the words of Andoreniel," Kellen said carefully.

"You will wonder how word could travel so fast in winter, without magic to aid it," Redhelwar said with a faint smile. "Yet we have never relied upon magic as you humans do. The weather was calm enough to send birds; they flew to the signaling towers, and the towers passed the message along by means of sunlight and mirrors through the mountains until it reached a place where it must be transferred to the birds once more. Andoreniel's word to me returned the same way.

"As soon as Ancaladar has recovered enough strength to fly, I am to ask him to go to each of the Nine Cities in turn, starting with those closest to the Eastern borders, and carry all the women with child to the Fortress of the Crowned Horns of the Moon. Andoreniel says that we will open it to the children of our Allies as well—the Centaurkin, the Mountainfolk, and the Lostlanders who have come down into the Wild Lands so that their Wildmages may fight at our side."

It took Kellen a moment to understand what he was hearing. The Crowned Horns of the Moon was a fortress in the Mystral Mountains that dated back to the days of the Great War. It had never been taken by direct assault, and Kellen didn't think that even the Demons' trickery could manage to find *Them* a way in. When Andoreniel had first realized that Shadow Mountain might be moving against the Elves, he had ordered all the Elven children of the Nine Cities moved to the fortress, purely as a precaution, there to be guarded by a coterie of hand-picked defenders, Elven Knights and unicorns both. Elven children were few, and when Kellen had visited there, most of the Crowned Horns still stood empty.

But now Andoreniel was proposing to fill it.

And that told Kellen that Andoreniel was certain the Allies were going to lose.

Of course, if the Allies lost, nobody in the Fortress of the Crowned Horns was going to survive anyway.

But that's not right! Kellen thought angrily. *For the first time since this all began, we've finally got a chance of winning. We know what* They *want—what* They *have to have—and where it is. For the first time, we actually have a chance!*

"It won't work," Kellen said bluntly.

Redhelwar gazed at him, his brows raised in mild reproof. Kellen knew he'd been rude—much more than rude, by Elven standards—but he couldn't help it.

"Knight-Mage wisdom?" Redhelwar asked, dropping into War Manners.

"Simple common sense," Kellen answered. "They won't all fit. The pregnant women and the children of the Herdsfolk, the Centaurkin, the Mountainfolk . . . humans and Centaurs live shorter lives than Elves. I don't know about Centaurs, but humans certainly breed faster. You're talking about not a few dozen children and women, or even a few hundred, but a couple of thousand at the very least, and probably more, scattered throughout the Wild Lands and the High Reaches. If you choose to do this, you can't leave anybody behind. And if you *do* choose to do this . . . Redhelwar, it is as good as saying we have already lost. There will be panic. And . . . how are they to get there? Ancaladar can bring the women of the

Nine Cities, I guess, but the others? If they have to come overland, in winter . . . either the Army will have to protect them—and we can't split the Army—or they have to come unprotected. Either way, anyone on the ground is a feast for anything *They* want to throw at them."

The longer he spoke, the more problems crowded into Kellen's mind. Getting word to everyone. Preventing panic. Gathering them for the journey. Protecting them at every stage—keeping them from freezing would be the least of everyone's problems; these were *children* they were talking about.

Kellen shook his head wordlessly. It wouldn't work. It was well-intentioned, but it wouldn't work.

"Surely Andoreniel has thought of this," Redhelwar said, sounding puzzled and weary.

"The message came very fast," Kellen suggested tentatively.

"I will send again," Redhelwar said after a long pause. "This time, the message will go by Unicorn Knight. Meanwhile, of your courtesy, perhaps you will oblige me by thinking of some way to protect the children of our Allies that does not involve feeding them to a pack of Coldwarg."

❧

IF only I could think of one, Kellen reflected sourly, leaving Redhelwar's tent. The problem was the same one it had always been—the Demons wouldn't stand and fight. Although of course if they did, they'd probably slaughter the entire Allied Army . . .

The trouble is, we need all our strength, and our Allies, to have any hope of winning. And why should they stay here in the Elvenlands if the Demons are attacking them at home?

Kellen sighed. The weariness he'd held at bay in Redhelwar's tent had come sneaking back, making it hard to think clearly.

❧

ISINWEN, Kellen's Second, was waiting for Kellen when he got back to his tent, and the look of disapproval on the Elven Knight's face made Kellen wish—just for an instant—that he'd stayed out in the wind.

"I observe," Isinwen said quietly, "that many would lose heart should we lose you, Kellen."

The oblique rebuke cut more sharply than any outright scold could have. Kellen shook his head, acknowledging the barb, and allowed Isinwen to help him off with his cloak.

"I will not die of a walk around the camp, Isinwen," he said gently, sitting down on a stool to pull off his boots. "I wanted to test my strength. From what I have learned today, I can tell you that we will not have Wildmages to support us for a sennight, perhaps two."

The sudden feeling of a key turning in a lock made him blink.

Yes.

He'd wanted to know that. The army needed to know it. And there was certainly no way to find it out other than taking a stroll himself.

Sometimes he wished the Wild Magic could be—well, more *obvious* about things. But it never was.

"Then . . . I suppose it is for the best. Providing you do not take a lung-fever and end up in bed for a moonturn," Isinwen said, still sounding faintly exasperated.

Kellen laughed, though there was no real humor in the sound. "I don't have time." He set his sword beside his boots. "It would please me greatly if you would present this information to Ninolion at your convenience."

He yawned; he couldn't help himself.

"Get back into bed," Isinwen said firmly. "I will make known to Ninolion what you have learned, so he may advise Redhelwar. And we shall all hope that their services will not be needed."

Kellen nodded in acknowledgment, pulling off his heavy outer tunic. Weariness pulled at him like heavy chains; he had only a moment to hope that he'd find some more of the answers they needed in sleep before it claimed him.

⁂

THE cost of attacking the Wildmages—and defending her creature within the Golden City—had been high. It had cost Queen Savilla dearly, both in the drain upon her power—for when the Wildmages had turned her Darkbolt back upon her, the backlash had depleted her of as much power again as it had cost her to cast it—and in the knowledge it had given to her son Zyperis, for it had been he who had found her in her ritual chamber, and he who had nursed her back to strength in secret.

Among the Endarkened, knowledge was power. Now Zyperis had seen her humbled; weakened nearly to death. Now he knew a secret lost for a thousand years: that the magic of Mage-man and Wildmage, working together, could end the eternal lives of the perfect creatures of He Who Is.

Zyperis was ambitious. He was her son, after all. He knew he could never hope to rule the World Without Sun while she lived—and the Endarkened lived forever.

He would want to use what he had learned. If not at once, then soon.

And meanwhile, the cursed Light-begotten had almost certainly discovered the existence of her Armethaliehan slave and learned his intentions.

Let them, Savilla thought, regarding her reflected image in the mirror of her Rising chamber. Around her, well-cowed slaves from the World Above scuttled, bringing jewels and perfumes and cosmetics to ornament the Queen of the Endarkened to properly appear before her subjects once more. *It is too late for them to use what they have learned. I have won. Anigrel sits upon Armethalieh's High Council. The reins of power are in his hands. Soon the City of a Thousand Bells will be mine to turn against my enemies.*

And meanwhile . . . I shall distract my son and lover as easily as I have distracted my enemies. He is young. Let him think I fear him. For now.

Until it is too late for him as well.

As always upon her Rising, there were the Petitions of the Grooming Chamber to be heard. It did not matter that there was a war to conduct; the petty squabbles of the Endarkened nobles must always have first claim on Savilla's attention, for centuries of rule had taught her that over time quarrels grew into vendettas that spread until they drew everyone into them, on one side or the other. And eventually Savilla would be forced to take a side—unless the matter, whatever it was, was settled before it had truly begun to fester, while the grievance was still a matter of a favorite slave or a bottle of spilled perfume.

Fortunately, these days such matters were few, for this was a time of such splendor and abundance as the Endarkened had not seen in centuries. Slaves and prey were available in plenty—and Savilla intended to open new hunting grounds very soon, which would distract her restless quarrelsome subjects further.

When the last of the lesser nobles' petitions had been heard, she beckoned her son forward.

Zyperis had been waiting with uncharacteristic patience while the others were heard. As always when she beheld her son, Savilla felt a pang of delight. So bold, so handsome, so much her match in cunning and daring. Time would make him her equal, and inevitably he would challenge her, for that was the way of the Kings and Queens beneath the Earth.

In that way Savilla had taken the throne from her own father, Uralesse, lulling and beguiling him over the centuries. Uralesse would never have had the patience and the vision to take this long subtle path to destroy the Children of the Light. He had spent too many centuries mourning his own shattering defeat on the battlefield in the Great War. Yet Savilla, who had fought at his side, had not despaired as he had. In that defeat she had seen the need to begin anew in a new way.

First she had needed to kill Uralesse, to gain the power to put her plans into motion. Then it had been necessary to move with maddening slowness, for the Endarkened had been weakened nearly to destruction by their last defeat at the hands of the Light-spawn, and should they have realized they had not truly won, all Savilla's plans would have been as a quenched candle-flame. For centuries, as generations of the race of Men lived and died, and the long-lived Elves turned back to harp and loom and forgot them, Savilla had worked through her human agents to unbind the great Alliance that had proved the undoing of the Endarkened. The human city raised its walls and closed them tight. The Elves forgot war and thought only of peace.

And Savilla had planned.

"MAMA?" Zyperis asked.

Savilla blinked slowly. Her son was kneeling at her feet, the picture of perfect humility. It was not precisely feigned . . . but it was something Zyperis granted, not something Savilla took. It was a shift in the balance of power, and both of them recognized it.

But it is only temporary, Savilla vowed.

"I was contemplating the great favors I shall bestow upon you," she said. "We have all worked hard for this day—you with your agents among the humans most of all. Now it is time to move forward. . . ."

Savilla spoke long and persuasively, mantling Zyperis with her great scarlet wings—a token of great favor. The Endarkened Prince's face glowed with delight, for he had long chafed at inaction—and at being excluded from her plans.

"Oh, Mama, how wonderful!" he said, when she had finished speaking. "Surely the Elven King's allies will desert him to look to their own once we begin to act in the Wild Lands! But . . . you have always said . . ."

"Oh, my son," she said, stroking his cheek fondly, "it will not matter soon. Just go slowly, as I have told you. Stay far from any lands the Mage-men have ever claimed as their own, for it would not do for them to suspect that their ancient enemy is anything but an ancient myth."

Zyperis drew himself up proudly. "You will see, my sweet Crown of Pain. I shall do all as you would do it yourself. They will sicken, sorrow, and despair—and barely know at first that it is we who are to blame for it all. You shall feast upon unicorn and dryad, wood-nymph and selkie: I shall bring them to you with my own hands!"

"I shall rely upon you," Savilla purred, stroking his long black hair as he knelt at her feet. "Sow dissention in their ranks, fill their homelands with sickness and blight, drive the game from their hunters' nets, and all the time let them wonder if we are to blame, or if it is terrible coincidence. . . ."

"Because they dare not ignore either one," Zyperis said happily. "Whether the cause is an enemy's hand, or simple misfortune, the result is the same."

"Our victory," Savilla agreed.

Zyperis raised her hands to his lips and kissed them. She felt the touch of his fangs upon her skin and closed her eyes momentarily in pleasure.

She would bring him to heel. And his anger and frustration would make his utter and inevitable submission all the sweeter.

When Zyperis had gone, Savilla accepted a spangled cloak of gossamer spider-silk from one of her attendants. Draping it loosely about her shoulders, she left her private chambers.

THE World Without Sun was vast, extending far beneath the surface of the earth. Let the Light-begotten think their world was vast: That of the Endarkened was vaster still, so enormous that there were few indeed who knew every chamber and pathway of it.

It was a place of secrets, for the Endarkened treasured secrets as much as they cherished the pain and death of others. It took Savilla more than half of her Rising-cycle to reach the place she sought, a chamber of incalculable age, deep in the living rock. Its very existence had been forgotten by most of the Endarkened. Uralesse had not known of it.

Savilla had come here once before, long ago, and learned the magics that would one day allow her to pierce the wards of Armethalieh and make a young boy her servant. When she had first come here, the walls of the Golden City had barely been begun. It would be centuries before she dared to try the spells she had learned that day.

The cost to her of forging that tiny chink in Armethalieh's defenses had been great. It had taken her years, as the World Above measured time, to prepare the spell, years more to fully recover from the casting of it, as her human catspaw grew from boy to man.

Now she meant to cast a spell more subtle still.

Uncounted thousands of years ago, when the Elves were a hundred scattered warrior tribes who fought against each other as often as they fought together, and humans were no more than grunting brutes yet to find their magic, the Endarkened and the Elves had fought for the first time. In those days, there had still been Elven Mages, and the most powerful of these was Vielissar Farcarinon, whose name was still a curse among the Endarkened.

It was she who had united the Elven tribes beneath her rule, she who had brought the dragons to be their allies, increasing the power of the Elven Mages a thousandfold.

It was Vielissar Farcarinon who, through the power of the Wild Magic and the power of the dragons, had forged the bargain that would keep He Who Is from acting directly upon the world for ever after. To win that boon, the Elves had given up their magic.

Wounded nearly to death in that war, maddened with grief by the casting out from the world of their Creator, it had taken the Endarkened millennia to re-cover from their defeat. When they had next struck against the Children of Light, they had expected their victory to be quick, for though He Who Is had been barred from the world, the Endarkened were still creatures of magic, and the Elves now had none.

But while they had slept in the World Without Sun, a new race had risen in the World Above. Humans had aided the Elves, and with them had come the Wildmages. Though human magic was a subtly different thing than the Elven Magery the Endarkened had faced before, the Endarkened had still been defeated.

But now they are weak, all of them. They have forgotten. And I . . . I shall call He Who Is *back into the world again. His presence will assure our victory. I shall become first among His children, and none of my subjects will ever challenge my power. And all this world will at last become what He willed that it should be, what He intended it to be when we were first created.*

Changeless.

Perfect.

Eternal.

Savilla drew a deep breath, readying herself for what she would do next. Later would come the sacrifices—and there would be many of them, until she had filled this chamber once again with blood, as she had done once before, so many years ago. But now, to begin, simple intent was enough. In a sense, a promise.

To any senses but those of the Endarkened, the chamber would have been unremittingly black. Savilla saw, not colors precisely, but a thousand shades of darkness, hues that no other race had words for. The darkness showed her a chamber carved of the living rock. Every inch of the walls and ceiling was cov-ered with deeply-incised symbols in the ancient Endarkened script. They did not run in neat rows, but swirled along the rock, dipping and arcing, as if per-haps they had once been straight, and Time itself had bent the lines of writing, while leaving each etched symbol sharp and clear as the day it had been cut into the rock. As if what was written there was too horrible for even Time to touch it.

In the center of the chamber there was a long hollow spike of obsidian that stood as high as Savilla's heart. It tapered to a needle-fine point, and looked as delicate as any of the glass knives in Savilla's own torture chamber, but she knew from experimentation that nothing she could do would chip or break it.

There were a hundred ways to kill someone with the obsidian spire.

Impale a victim upon it, and they could die as quickly or slowly as Savilla wished. The chamber enjoyed the slow deaths, as was only to be expected. But most of all it enjoyed the deaths she brought about when, as a living victim writhed, impaled upon it, she struck the obsidian shaft with one of the round smooth black stones that lay scattered about the floor of the chamber.

Then the entire chamber rang like a crystal bell, the glyphs upon the walls blooming into dark fire. The victim died at once—but not painlessly. No. That death was the most agonizing of all, as if every iota of pain it was possible for one frail mortal shell of flesh to experience were somehow compacted into one single moment.

Those bodies simply vanished.

But those executions were not without cost to Savilla, for when she engineered such ultimate communions for her victims with the obsidian spire, she felt everything her mortal victims did.

A high price.

But it will be worth it, to allow He Who Is *to return to the world once more.*

The last time Savilla had left the chamber, it had been littered with bone and decaying flesh. All that was gone now, dissolved by the strange alchemy of the Black Chamber. All that remained were the scattered stones upon the floor, the spell-runes upon the walls, the obsidian spire itself.

Once begun, once promised, Savilla could not stop or turn aside. At best, she could delay, and delay would come at a price.

But she did not wish to delay.

She would prepare the way. She would gather the power.

He Who Is would enter the world once more, and reward the one who had made it possible.

And destroy all His enemies.

Savilla placed her hands atop the obsidian spire, and pressed down. The point pierced both her hands. She saw the glistening black point break through her scarlet skin, and saw the dark blood well forth around it. Her body shuddered faintly with pain, her great ribbed wings trembling and unfurling.

All around her, the chamber sang faintly in approval.

Two

Against All Odds

N O MATTER HOW desirable it might have been to keep what the Wildmages had learned confined to the High Command alone, Kellen quickly discovered that wasn't possible. Almost the first thing he'd learned when he'd first met the Elves was that they gossiped as naturally as they breathed, and that gossip flew through an Elven city—or an Elven war-camp—as swiftly as summer lightning.

"Everyone knows," Idalia said succinctly.

She'd come to his pavilion the morning after he'd seen Redhelwar. Isinwen had undoubtedly asked her to come—at the moment, Idalia was the only Wildmage Healer they had.

Kellen had slept for the rest of the day and through the night as well, and awoke feeling much stronger. Not fully recovered, of course, but if the Gods of the Wild Magic—and the Enemy, of course—allowed him another sennight of rest, he knew he'd be back to his old self.

"I'm fine," he'd said hastily, the moment he'd seen her. Idalia's strengthening cordials were notoriously unpalatable.

She'd laughed, seeing his expression. "Then I'll just make tea. That way I can tell Isinwen that I've seen you, and that you're *not* at Death's Gate."

Kellen made a rude noise. "He's seen me at Death's Gate. He should know the difference."

Idalia glanced over her shoulder, in the middle of kindling the brazier for tea. "But this time it's more than a matter of a few Shadowed Elves, and an Enemy who may not come for decades . . . or centuries. Tell me, when you saw Red-helwar yesterday, how did he seem to you?"

"Not very happy." Quickly Kellen related the details of his conversation with the Army's General—and the strange orders that had come from Andoreniel.

Idalia set the pot on the brazier to heat and squatted beside it. She shook her head ruefully. "Well, Andoreniel has to do something. The whole army knows what we saw in the mirror by now—and that includes the Centaurs, the Herds-folk, and the Mountainfolk. They don't have Elven land-wards to protect them. And the Mountainfolk trade with Armethalieh. They know how powerful the High Mages are. The idea that Armethalieh could come in on *Their* side . . ."

"That doesn't mean we just give up!" Kellen protested.

Idalia met his eyes. There was no despair in that violet gaze, but there was no hope there, either. "Can you tell me Armethalieh isn't going to fall because of Anigrel? Can you tell me we can convince the High Mages to fight on our side? Can you think of some way we can protect our Allies? You said it yourself—even if they try to move in winter, the weather will kill as many of them as *They* will. And winter's only half over."

"So we need to give them hope," Kellen said stubbornly. "Idalia, I don't have answers—not all of them, anyway. Most of the time I just seem to know when something's a bad idea—and giving up and trying to fight a defensive war against *Them* is a really bad idea.

"And I know—and so do you—that if *They* didn't think we could defeat *Them*, *They* wouldn't be working so hard to weaken us instead of attacking us directly."

The water had boiled, and Idalia sifted loose tea—Armethaliehan Black, Kellen's favorite—into the waiting pot and filled it. While the tea steeped, she and Kellen sat in silence, listening to the wind whistle over the heavy silk of the pavilion.

When the tea was ready, she filled two mugs, added several honey-disks for sweetening, and passed one to Kellen.

"You know Redhelwar values your advice," she said at last. "What will you suggest?"

Kellen ran his hand through his hair, raking it back out of his eyes. It hadn't been cut since he'd left the City, and it was long enough now for some of the shorter Elven styles—though no Elf would ever have to contend with Kellen's mop of unruly light-brown curls.

"Right now two-thirds of the army isn't fit to fight, and we've got a lot of wounded. On top of that, we still need to locate the other Enclave of Shadowed Elves that the Crystal Spiders told us about. And . . ." Kellen hesitated. "An-doreniel is the King. Redhelwar will follow his orders, not my suggestions."

"Then we'd better hope you come up with some good suggestions," Idalia said. "And that Vestakia can locate that other Enclave."

⚊⚊⚊

BECAUSE of their Elven blood—no matter how debased and Tainted—the land-wards surrounding the Elven Lands did not recognize the Shadowed Elves as enemies, and while any yet lived, they could use that weakness to bring other ancient foes of the Elves into the land, bypassing the protections of the land-wards, as they had done when they had helped the Frost Giants and Ice Trolls to attack the caravan bound for the Fortress of the Crowned Horns.

When Kellen and Idalia had gone down into the caverns where the Shadowed Elves laired, they had found allies, for not all creatures who lived in darkness were of the Dark. The Crystal Spiders had suffered greatly from the Shadowed Elves' encroachment, for the Dark-tainted Elven hybrids had preyed cruelly upon the gentle unworldly arachnids, taking their webs to make hunting nets, and feasting upon their eggs and their young. When the Elves had liberated them, the Crystal Spiders had promised to help them in their fight in any way they could.

In communicating with them while cleansing the Further Cavern of *duergar*, Kellen had discovered that the Crystal Spiders shared a sort of group mind—and that furthermore, they also seemed to be in contact with all the other Crystal Spiders in the other caves across the Elven Lands, no matter how widely separated. That was how Kellen had discovered that there was at least one more Enclave of the Shadowed Elves.

But attempting to communicate telepathically with a race so alien was a long and exhausting process. The Crystal Spiders neither saw nor thought as humans—or even Elves—did. It was Vestakia who had realized that if the Crystal Spiders could sense the presence of what they called "Black Minds," possibly they could tell the army where to search for them. Vestakia had volunteered to take on the task of attempting to figure out what the Crystal Spiders were trying to tell them.

It was a suggestion motivated by something very near to desperation. Vestakia was the daughter of the Prince of Shadow Mountain. Her mother, Virgivet, had been a Lostlands Wildmage, who had worked a powerful spell, so that even though Vestakia had much of the outward appearance of a Demon—*Their* ruby skin, yellow eyes, fangs, and even a pair of tiny golden horns upon her forehead—her heart and soul were as human as her mother's. She had been raised in hiding, for no one in the Lostlands who caught sight of her would believe she was not the monster she appeared to be—nor had her father ever stopped searching for her, to drag her back to Shadow Mountain. Yet the Gods of the Wild Magic had granted her a second boon besides her human spirit.

Vestakia could sense the presence of Demons and their magic, and had used that gift to hide herself from them in the Lostlands until the day Kellen had rescued her from a thieving goatherd. As her powers grew, Vestakia came to be able to sense all forms of Demonic Taint, and that was how she had discovered the first three Enclaves of Shadowed Elves.

But she had to be nearby for her powers of detection to work—within a few miles of the source at the outside. Earlier in the winter, Jermayan had taken her on patrol with Ancaladar. They had covered hundreds of leagues, searching for Shadowed Elf Enclaves. But the weather was much worse now, and that method wouldn't work any longer.

A few days ago, Redhelwar had re-established a secondary camp at the mouth of the farther caverns, so that Vestakia could go down into them to work with the Crystal Spiders no matter the weather.

It was the first time she had seen him in many days, for Kellen spent little time in her presence, and none of it alone with her. Vestakia understood the reason for this very well. It wasn't because Kellen didn't like her quite as much as she liked him. Entirely the opposite, she suspected—and hoped. But Kellen was a Knight-Mage, and he was vowed to a year and a day of chastity and celibacy, the price Shalkan—and the Wild Magic—had required for rescuing him from the Outlaw Hunt. Her own mother had given up twenty years of her life to pay the Mageprice that had given Vestakia a human soul. She knew Mageprices could be harsh things.

So when Kellen came to escort her down into the caverns to meet the Crystal Spiders for the first time, Vestakia did her best to pay as little attention to him as she would to any of the Elven Knights who were her nearly-constant companions.

✤

EVERY day was shorter than the last, and colder, and darker. Idalia said this was normal, and had nothing to do with Demon sorcery; Kellen, raised in a city where Mages had controlled the weather, was dubious, but supposed she must be right. As Redhelwar waited for the Unicorn Knights he had sent to Sentarshadeen to return, the army began to resume its normal activity. As they had planned before the spell of Kindolhinadetil's Mirror, arrangements were made for Vestakia to go down into the cavern to try to communicate with the Crystal Spiders. As they were shy and timid creatures, Kellen went with Vestakia to perform the introduction.

He hadn't seen her since Cilarnen's arrival in camp, and was alarmed at how tired she looked.

"You work too hard," he blurted out before he could stop himself. "Are you sure you can do this?"

"I suppose you'd rather do it yourself," Vestakia shot back. "Keirasti told me how much you both enjoyed the caverns."

Kellen forced himself to look away. No. He mustn't tell Vestakia not to do something because he was worried about her—any more than he'd tell Keirasti, or Isinwen. Or Idalia.

Kellen grinned to himself, imagining how much luck he'd have telling Idalia not to do something "for her own good."

"They're cold and damp and very uncomfortable," he said, forcing a light tone into his voice. "But Redhelwar tells me you won't have to sleep down there. He's established a secondary camp at the cavernmouth, so you'll have all the possible comforts of, ah, camp."

Without waiting for her reply, he swung into Firareth's saddle. Isinwen assisted Vestakia into her palfrey's saddle—a courtesy only, as by now Vestakia had gotten enough practice to become quite a good rider.

Kellen's troop rode toward the farther caverns, along the well-marked track made by the supply-wagons that had gone on ahead of them to set up the camp. A light snow was falling, but by now hardly a day passed without some snow, and Kellen barely noticed it.

When they reached the caverns, Kellen dismounted and chose six of his troop to accompany them into the cavern. Such caution was automatic by now— even though the caverns had been thoroughly cleared of Tainted creatures, there was always the possibility that something might have crept back in.

Supplying themselves with lanterns—Kellen didn't want to count on his ability to cast Coldfire just yet—they entered the caverns.

It was a long walk, and one that brought back unpleasant memories for all of them.

"Not much farther now," Kellen said, when they'd passed through the cavern where the Shadowed Elf village had once stood. Little remained to show what it had once been; the Elves had scoured the place thoroughly in the aftermath of the battle, and even taken down most of the crude stone huts that the Shadowed Elves had constructed.

Kellen reached the place where he'd last encountered the Crystal Spiders. The cave was so vast that their lanterns gave very little light, and even with their superior night-sight, Kellen doubted that the Elves could see much more than he could.

"I'm sure they know we're here," he told Vestakia. "But it may take them a little while to show up. We should move away from the others a bit—I think they're sort of shy."

Vestakia made a stifled sound that might have been a giggle. "I suppose they have every right to be—with odd-looking strangers barging into their home at all hours! Come on, then."

The two of them walked a few yards away from the others and stood, waiting. Kellen set his lantern down on the cave floor and rested his hand on the pommel of his sword.

He didn't feel nervous, precisely. He felt some of the same keyed-up energy that he did when he was about to go into battle, but it was an energy without an outlet. There was no battle to fight—not an immediate one, at any rate. And there were far too many problems that had to be solved.

He'd learned enough since the day he'd ridden out from Sentarshadeen to join the army at Ondoladeshiron to know what most of them were, unfortunately for his peace of mind.

They had to keep their Allies in the field and with the army. The Herdsfolk and the Mountainfolk were their Wildmages and their mountaineers and light infantry; the Centaurkin were their heavy infantry. Right now humans and Centaurs made up about a third of the army; in the spring, when the full levies arrived, they would make up two-thirds of it. According to the Teaching Songs he'd learned at the House of Sword and Shield, maintaining the Alliance had always been the main difficulty for the Allies, and one the Demons always exploited. If they left to protect their own lands, the Demons could destroy all of them piecemeal.

If they stayed, it would be to watch their loved ones die while they did nothing, for even if he wanted to, there was no way Andoreniel could protect all the Wild Lands, the High Reaches, and the Elvenlands at once.

Even though everyone knew the stakes if the Demons should win, it was a hard thing to ask someone to let his family, his village, everyone he knew fall prey to Demons and their creations—especially when it was clear that the Elves were not suffering the same losses.

It hasn't started yet, Kellen told himself. *I know it will—if I can think of it, They certainly can. But we still have time to come up with a countermove. I'll ask Jermayan's advice. He's older than I am—a lot older. And he's trained for this all his life, even if he never expected it to happen. . . .*

Just then he became aware of a faint scuffling sound.

"They're here," he said quietly.

A vast living carpet of spiders was moving across the floor of the cave toward Kellen and Vestakia. Each of them was the size of a large cat, and their bodies were covered with thick transparent bristles, giving them something of the look of puffballs. Both Kellen and Vestakia could see them clearly, because the Crystal Spiders radiated their own light in a rainbow of pastel colors: green, pink, violet, yellow, blue . . .

"They're beautiful," Vestakia said in surprise.

"I guess they are—for spiders," Kellen said, trying not to grin. He knelt down and pulled off one of his armored gauntlets. Contact with bare skin made it much easier to communicate telepathically with the creatures.

The Spiders clambered up over his body. Their legs made a faint scritching sound as they passed over his armor. One of them settled into his hand, and its bristles tickled his skin. As always when he was in contact with them, a sense of peace and warmth filled him like phantom sunlight.

:Welcome,: the Spiders sent. :You have brought the one who will help to fight the Black Minds?:

"Yes," Kellen answered. He spoke aloud—it was easier that way to focus his thoughts for the Crystal Spiders to hear. "This is Vestakia. She helps us fight the Black Minds."

Vestakia had already knelt down and removed both her gauntlets. More Spiders appeared out of the darkness, and clambered up her body.

"Hello," Vestakia said, more calmly than Kellen would have under the circumstances.

Something happened then that he hadn't expected—though he *should* have expected it. He knew the Crystal Spiders were telepathic, and seemed to function as a group mind. The whole basis of his and Vestakia's plan relied on the hope that the Crystal Spiders here were in touch with their brethren elsewhere—in all the caves everywhere across the Elven Lands—and would be able to tell Vestakia the location of other Enclaves of the Shadowed Elves.

It simply hadn't occurred to Kellen that the Crystal Spiders would put them in touch with *each other.*

For a moment the cold dampness of the cave fell away. Instinctively Kellen reached out toward the warmth—*human* warmth—and love embedded in the web of the Crystal Spiders' linked minds—

No!

He lunged to his feet, hastily dislodging several Crystal Spiders. They scuttled backward, and Kellen strode quickly away into the darkness, gripping the haft of his sword until his fingers ached.

Gods of the Wild Magic, what had he almost done? He had a Price to pay! Break his vow, and Shalkan would have no choice but to exact the penalty.

"Kellen?" Vestakia said uncertainly.

Kellen's face burned hot with shame. She'd been able to sense, to feel, the same things he had—

He cut off the direction of those thoughts with painfully-acquired discipline.

"Just ask them what you need to know," he said harshly, willing himself to pretend that the last few minutes hadn't happened. "They know what Black Minds are, and they know we need to find the others."

After a moment, he heard Vestakia speaking in a low voice to the Spiders, but the eternal background noise of the deep caves blurred her words, and he couldn't make them out. He didn't try very hard, either. For the first time, Kellen blessed the fact that his hearing wasn't as sharp as the Elves'. He didn't *want* to know what she might be saying right now.

Her voice stopped, and when the silence stretched, Kellen risked a glance over his shoulder.

She was covered in the Spiders, the outlines of her slender body completely obscured beneath the round furry forms. In the faint luminescence from their bodies, he could see that her head was thrown back and her eyes were closed, as if she basked in sunlight.

At least, Kellen thought ruefully, he didn't seem to have offended the Crystal Spiders *too* badly.

Making a careful detour around the Spiders and Vestakia—though he doubted that just now she'd have noticed him if he'd jumped up and down and shouted—he walked back to where Isinwen and the others stood, waiting patiently.

"It would be good to know how long the Lady Vestakia will remain," Isinwen said when Kellen had joined him.

"I'm not sure," Kellen admitted. "I know—from my own experience—that the Crystal Spiders don't think the way we do. And they don't have anything like the same sense of time. I do know that they won't hurt her."

"Then we must wait," Isinwen said inarguably.

It was something Kellen had become fairly good at over the last several moonturns—the life of an army seemed to involve a great deal of waiting, far more than it did actual fighting, and eventually Vestakia heaved a deep sigh and lowered her head. A few seconds later, the Crystal Spiders began to move, picking their way delicately down along her shoulders and arms. Kellen was always impressed by how gracefully they moved. Next they began flowing in a tidal motion across the floor of the cavern, until their glow was lost in the shadows. Vestakia stretched—much as if she were rousing from a deep sleep—and began to get stiffly to her feet.

Ambanire—one of the new recruits who had been added to Kellen's troop after the Battle of the Further Cavern—moved forward (quickly, yet seemingly without haste, in the fashion of the Elves) to assist her. This time, the aid was more than simple courtesy. Kellen knew from his own experience how sitting motionless for an extended period in the frigid damp of the deep caves made one stiff and sore. Vestakia actually tottered a bit, clutching at Ambanire's arm for support.

"I *had* hoped it was going to be easier than this," she said when she rejoined the others. Reyezeyt passed her a flask of cordial—it wasn't warm, but it was sweet, and certainly better than nothing. Vestakia took it and drank gratefully.

"There *is* another Enclave of the Shadowed Elves—as we already knew," she said when she'd finished drinking. "The Crystal Spiders are eager to tell me all about it." She uttered a stifled giggle. "If I could just figure out what they were saying! A realm of ice and jewels—what does that mean?"

"Understanding will surely come with time," Isinwen answered when Kellen said nothing. "And from all you have said, the caves, damp and cold as they are, are far better than flying about in the heavens at this time of year."

"Oh, yes!" Vestakia agreed fervently. "I like flying—but I am very tired of snow!"

⧢

KELLEN saw Vestakia to her tent at the new camp—she'd be staying here, well-guarded, for the immediate future. Until matters changed—or until she managed to figure out what the cryptic pictures the Crystal Spiders were putting into her mind meant.

He sent the rest of his troop on ahead, saying he'd follow shortly. He suspected that Shalkan was out here somewhere, and if the unicorn wanted to scold him for his near-miss, he'd prefer it was done with as much privacy as possible.

There were only a couple of hours of light left by the time Kellen left the camp, having spoken at length to Ercanirnei, the Elven Knight who commanded Vestakia's camp. Ercanirnei was from Lerkalpoldara, one of the two northern-most of the Nine Cities—where, he assured Kellen, the winters were nearly as long and as harsh as they were in the High Reaches, so there was little he did not know of the ways of snow and ice. Kellen need have no fear that Ercanirnei would fail in any attention to the safety and well-being of the Army's Treasure.

Kellen supposed he would have to take as much comfort from that as he could. Because he was going to have to make very sure that his path and Vestakia's didn't cross for a very long time.

At last he turned Firareth's head in the direction of what, for lack of a better word, had to be called home. The only sounds were the crunch of the war-stallion's hooves through the icy crust of the fresh snow, the creak and jingle of

Firareth's harness and Kellen's armor, and the sound of the wind. The winter twilight seemed to reverse the natural colors of the world: The sky and the clouds were dun with flashes of gold where the slanting winter sun managed to peek through; the trees, the ground, and the shadows were all in shades of blue; even the snow looked blue, even if a very pale blue.

If it had been a picture, Kellen would have thought it was very pretty. While he was riding through it, all he could think about was how cold it was. His breath froze in his nostrils as he inhaled, and each exhalation made a cloud of steam, quickly whipped away by the wind. That had picked up, so even if it wasn't snowing any harder, there was a lot more snow in the air. It was going to be a long cold ride back.

But not really a lonely one. As Kellen left the cavern-camp, he felt his Knight-Mage senses spread out across the landscape. There behind him was the cavern-camp, all quiet. Ahead, a larger presence, was the main camp outside Ysterialpoerin. Everything was quiet there as well. Around it, like spokes spread out from a wheel, were the pickets and the sentries, and beyond them, the scout parties. Farther ahead, he could sense Ysterialpoerin itself.

No immediate danger.

"You managed to stay out of trouble today," Shalkan said, coming up beside him.

"Just barely," Kellen answered. Since he'd been expecting Shalkan, he managed not to jump out of his skin at the abrupt arrival, but it took a bit of effort. No matter how finely-tuned his Knight-Mage senses were, a unicorn was as stealthy as the falling snow itself. "I should have seen it coming, though."

The unicorn dipped his head in acknowledgement. While Firareth forged through the drifted snow, Shalkan trotted along daintily atop it, barely leaving a trace of his passage.

"You can't foresee everything," the unicorn said.

Kellen bit back the immediate—and obvious—reply. The fact that Shalkan was right didn't make it any easier to hear. *If I can't manage something as fundamental as figuring out how to keep from breaking a simple vow, how am I ever going to manage to figure out something really hard—like what it will take to save Armethalieh and defeat the Demons?*

"Don't be so hard on yourself," Shalkan said. "Just because you can manage to drag yourself into the saddle and ride around the landscape doesn't mean you're completely recovered. You're tired. It's affecting your judgment."

"Just what I needed to hear," Kellen muttered under his breath.

"I suppose you'd rather go on riding into disaster as if nothing were wrong?" Shalkan asked sweetly, since he could hear Kellen perfectly well.

Kellen winced at the sarcasm. "I'd rather nothing *were* wrong," he answered honestly. "Instead of so many things being wrong I hardly know where to start worrying."

"Start in the obvious place, then," Shalkan advised. "With something you can fix."

"And what . . . ?" Kellen began, then blinked. Where Shalkan had been a moment before was nothing more than a unicorn-sized hole in the air.

It was obvious that Shalkan had meant him to solve that puzzle on his own, and it occupied Kellen for the rest of the ride back to the main camp. Thinking things over carefully, Kellen had to admit there were very few things he could actually control just now.

With enormous reluctance, he came to the very conclusion Shalkan had meant him to reach: that the best thing he could do right now was rest.

⟿

HE left Firareth at the horselines. The ostlers would make sure that the destrier's coat was toweled dry where it had been under the harness and that Firareth got a good warm feed before he was turned out into the near herd. Kellen was hoping for much the same treatment himself, as he headed through the darkness to the main dining tent. There he could be sure of a hot meal—even if it did involve greenneedle leaves—and several mugs of hot cider to wash the taste of the caves out of his mouth. Maybe a night's rest would give him some fresh ideas, and in the morning he could talk to Jermayan.

To his surprise, when Kellen walked into the dining tent, Cilarnen was there. Though it would be days, or even sennights yet, before the army's Wild-mages could call upon the Wild Magic again, nearly all of those who had participated in the spell of Kindolhinadetil's Mirror had left their beds by now, but as of this morning, Cilarnen had not. Though Kellen had tried hard not to think of it, he had worried that the intense exposure to the Wild Magic had been as inimical to the young High Mage as they had originally feared, and that Cilarnen would simply waste away, one of the hidden casualties of the war.

But now, Cilarnen was sitting at a table in the far corner of the tent with Wirance—the High Reaches Wildmage who had accompanied him from Stone-hearth into the Elven Lands—beside him. Cilarnen looked alert and vigorous—and actually more cheerful than Kellen could remember ever having seen him. The table before him was heaped with books—bound books, not the cased scrolls the Elves preferred.

And the books looked oddly familiar. . . .

"Kellen!" Cilarnen called out excitedly, seeing him. "You missed all the excitement! Come and see what Kindolhinadetil has brought us!"

"Brought to *you*, you mean," Wirance growled good-naturedly, as Kellen reached the table.

"They were a gift to all of us—to the human mages—" Cilarnen said, trying—and failing—to sound apologetic. "I don't really think Kindolhinadetil can tell humans apart very well."

"Or one kind of magic from another," Kellen agreed, puzzled. "Except for Jermayan, who's Bonded to Ancaladar, all the Elves have is what they call 'small magics,' and I have no idea what . . ."

In the middle of his sentence, he looked down, and completely forgot what he'd been about to say.

The books were from his father's library.

Or—they could have been. Lycaelon Tavadon's passion was rare books, and it would have been amazing indeed if the Arch-Mage of Armethalieh did not own a number of rare and ancient books on the Art Magickal.

"What—" he sputtered. "Where—"

Cilarnen laughed. "I wanted to know the same thing—but you're the one who told me that it's very rude to ask Elves questions, Kellen! And anyway, I wasn't here when they came—so if you want to know, you'll have to ask someone else. All I know is that they're a gift from Kindolhinadetil's library."

Kellen sat down slowly opposite Cilarnen. He picked up a book at random and opened it to a middle page. There were no words—it was a table of complicated symbols, arranged in a grid. He turned the page. More symbols, this time arranged in a circle.

Meaningless.

He set the book down and tried not to look as baffled as he felt.

"They're books of High Magick, Kellen," Cilarnen said, his voice filled with excitement and delight. "Spellbooks. Glyphs—sigils—seals—wards—that one is for the wand; this one here is for the sword—these have spoken spells and conjurations—it is everything a Master Mage would have in his personal library! Kellen, with these I can finish my training—back home I was ready to test for Full Apprentice; Master Tocsel taught me well—I know I would have passed, and once you have made Apprentice, progress through the grades is mostly a matter of power and mastering the spellwork—oh, that and patronage, but that doesn't matter here!"

Cilarnen was practically babbling, his voice filled with relief. Kellen felt a pang of sympathy—as much as he was a Knight-Mage, or Idalia was a Wildmage, Cilarnen was a High Mage, and his unjust Banishment had cut him off from the only life he had ever known—or wanted.

"But . . . how did Kindolhinadetil . . . ?"

Wirance snorted. "Who knows what the Elves may choose to do or predict how they may choose to do it? A man might grow old wondering. For my part, I have heard that the library here in the Forest City is an amazing thing, containing books from many lands. It is plain that it also holds books from your Armethalieh as well, and that Kindolhinadetil decided to make you a present of them."

"I'm sure he meant them as a present to all of us," Cilarnen said, though it was obvious from his expression that it would take a more than a Wildmage—or several Wildmages—to get him to give them up.

"I have all the books I need—and so does any Wildmage," Wirance told Cilarnen. "Look at them! You'd need a packhorse just to carry them—and from all you've said, that's barely the beginning of what you need for that High Magick of yours. *Faugh!* Keep your bloodless nonsense, and welcome."

But though his words were rough, the Mountainborn Wildmage's expression was kindly. He had fought beside Cilarnen at Stonehearth, and though he understood High Magick as little as Cilarnen understood the Wild Magic, he respected Cilarnen himself.

"I shall keep my 'bloodless nonsense,' old man," Cilarnen answered lightly. "And you may go on babbling to empty air and burning wet leaves—and reading blank books—and I shall do nothing to stop you. Light knows, the world is big enough that I think there is room for us both in it."

"Then I shall leave you to it, and take my old bones to their rest," Wirance said, getting to his feet. "Mind that you do not do too much too soon."

"As if I could do anything at all," Cilarnen said, when Wirance had gone. His good humor had vanished as if it had never been, and the abrupt change startled Kellen. "I had nearly forgotten . . . seeing all this . . . what good will all the knowledge in the world do me without the power to cast my spells? I cannot forever be relying upon Ancaladar's power."

"No," Kellen agreed. The dragon had loaned his power to Cilarnen's Shielding spell to save all their lives, but Ancaladar was understandably touchy about being regarded as nothing more than a living storage battery. And besides, so far as Kellen knew, Ancaladar was only supposed to be able to express his magic through his Bonded—Jermayan. They had all been linked together in the Spell of Kindolhinadetil's Mirror, which explained, Kellen supposed, why Ancaladar had been able to loan Cilarnen his power. But that would hardly work as a regular solution.

"But the Wild Magic has arranged for you to gain the spellbooks you need to study the High Magick," Kellen said, "so obviously it wants you to be a High Mage. And that means you will find a way to power your spells, when the time comes."

Cilarnen regarded him as if he'd lost his wits. "'The Wild Magic has arranged,'" he quoted. "The Wild Magic didn't arrange *anything*. Kindolhinadetil made the Wildmages a gift of books from his library."

"Which only you can use," Kellen pointed out. "And which are exactly the books you need. That's how the Wild Magic works."

Cilarnen shook his head, plainly unconvinced.

"Have you eaten?" Kellen asked, changing the subject. "Because I haven't, and I'm hungry." Without waiting for an answer, he got to his feet and headed for the kitchen.

The kitchen staff knew him by sight; he'd barely opened his mouth before he was handed a heavily-laden tray. Hot cider, hot stew, several stuffed buns, and a large mug of Winter Spice tea as well. He took the tray back to the table.

Cilarnen was being as stubborn as . . . as an Elf. Why wouldn't he admit what was so obvious to Kellen—that the books were here because the Wild Magic willed it so? The Elves of Ysterialpoerin understood humans about as well as a cat understood maths; it was highly unlikely (in Kellen's opinion) that Ysterialpoerin's Viceroy would have simply decided to empty his library of every book Cilarnen would find useful and hand them over without the Wild Magic being involved *somehow.*

And it wasn't as if Cilarnen had never seen the Wild Magic at work. He'd seen Wirance casting spells at Stonehearth. He'd been part of the Spell of Kindolhinadetil's Mirror. He knew it was real.

But it functions very differently from the High Magick he's used to, Kellen reminded himself. *The High Magick is mechanical, like—like a machine. The Wild Magic is alive; we speak to it, and it speaks to—and through—us. You remember when the Books came to you, and you felt the difference for the first time. But Cilarnen is not called to the Wild Magic. He cannot feel what a Wildmage feels.*

He set the tray down on the table.

"Do you really think your—the Wild Magic arranged for me to have these books?" Cilarnen asked doubtfully.

"Yes, I do," Kellen said honestly, picking up a bun and biting into it.

"I think you're mad," Cilarnen said simply. "A magic that thinks—that *wants* things . . ." He took a deep breath. "But I know there *is* a Wild Magic. And you haven't been wrong so far. And the books are here, and they're what I need. I suppose it doesn't matter what I believe about how they got here. Now all I have to do is study them. And learn in a few sennights what ought to take me years."

There was a grim note in his voice, and that made Kellen take a moment to think about what Cilarnen was intending to do.

The study of the High Magick was dangerous and fraught with peril. All of his Mage-teachers had said that so often—and in so many different ways—that

Kellen had simply started ignoring it years before he'd been Banished. His own lessons had been merely boring, not particularly hazardous.

Of course, he'd never gotten beyond Student Apprentice work.

The look he must have had on his face made Cilarnen laugh out loud.

"Oh, Kellen, if you tell me it will be dangerous I promise I will get Kardus to throw you into the nearest snowbank! I am not planning to practice in the middle of the camp, I promise you—I think that might only do The Enemy's work for him! No, when the time comes I will find a place that is safely out of the way—I think that ice-house your Elven Mage built for your working will do, as I am sure it is not going to melt any time soon. And wards are simple, and can be built up over several days.

"But there are things I must know, especially now that we know that Anigrel is *Their* agent. He meant me to escape my Banishing alive, and with my Magegift intact. Why?"

"I don't know," Kellen said slowly. It was a puzzle that needed more thought than any of them had been able to devote to it. "You aren't Tainted in any way. Shalkan—Idalia—Vestakia—they all agree on that. And I would trust any one of them with my life. With all our lives."

"But there are other ways of tampering with a mind—as you well know," Cilarnen answered bleakly. He would not meet Kellen's eyes. They were both thinking of Magecraft that owed nothing to Demontaint—the High Mage's ability to remove memories, and even implant false ones, seamlessly and undetectably. It had been done to Kellen when he was a child, to erase his memories of his sister.

If Anigrel had done it to Cilarnen—with the High Magick—there was no way for either of them to know. Wild Magic would not detect the alteration.

"I know my Magegift was suppressed, until seeing that *Thing* at Stonehearth made it come back. I want to know why—and what else might have been done to me. And I will discover a way to be of some use to you all—without taking that which can only be freely given. I swear it by the Eternal Light," Cilarnen vowed.

"If anyone can—in or out of Armethalieh—it's you," Kellen said.

He was sure of that—Cilarnen had abandoned none of the good things about Armethalieh, but somehow he seemed able to cast off much of what was hidebound and bad. If anyone could manage to look at the High Magick in a new way, and find some way to use it, even here, it was Cilarnen Volpiril.

"Now eat something." Kellen pushed one of the stuffed buns across the table.

AFTER they'd both eaten—Kellen bullied Cilarnen into making a proper meal—he helped the young High Mage carry his library to his new quarters.

Cilarnen was still living in the Centaur encampment, but now he had what Kellen unconsciously thought of as "proper" accommodations: one of the Elven pavilions. It looked as if it had formerly belonged to one of the Healers, for even in the dark and the snow Kellen could see that its surface was covered with some sort of design, though he could not make out precisely what it was.

"Well, come in," Cilarnen said when Kellen automatically stopped at the threshold.

I've spent much too long with the Elves, Kellen thought ruefully to himself. Their ways were starting to seem automatic to him, to the point that it did not occur to him to enter a dwelling-place without being expressly invited. He followed Cilarnen inside.

The interior of the pavilion was much like his own—though of course, having been a Healer's pavilion, it was slightly larger. A brazier had been left burning, and it was . . . well, it was as warm as the pavilions ever got.

Cilarnen set his armful of books down on the nearest chest and motioned for Kellen to do the same with his own burden. He kindled a spill from the brazier and lit the hanging lamps by hand, shrugging apologetically.

"I'm no better off," Kellen told him. "I couldn't even cast Coldfire in the caverns today."

Cilarnen smiled in acknowledgment. "What will we do, Kellen?" he asked seriously.

There were too many possible answers to that question.

"The best we can," Kellen answered. "There *is* hope, you know. *They* would not be working so hard to convince us there was none if that was not the case."

"I think you truly believe that," Cilarnen said after a moment. "And, for what it's worth, I think . . . I don't care whether you're right or not. I'm going to believe you."

"Thanks . . . I think," Kellen answered. "Now you should get some rest. I certainly intend to."

Cilarnen looked longingly toward the pile of books, then sighed. "I suppose you're right. I won't become a Master Mage in one night."

"Sleep well," Kellen answered, stepping from the tent.

⁓

THE next morning, after checking with the Captain of the Day Watch to see what duties might be required of his troop, Kellen saddled Firareth and went in search of Jermayan. Though the Elven Knight had quarters within the camp itself, he rarely used them, preferring to spend his time with Ancaladar, in the ice-pavilion he had built near the edge of the forest to shelter the great black dragon from the wind and the storm. Kellen was fairly sure that Ancaladar didn't feel the cold—at least not the way he did, or even Shalkan did—but nobody liked to be crusted in ice and buried in snow if there was any way to avoid it. And Jermayan and Valdien certainly did not.

But when Kellen reached the ice-pavilion, it was deserted. Nor was Valdien awaiting his master's return in the stabling Jermayan had built to shelter the Elven destrier from the storm. That implied to Kellen that wherever Jermayan was, he did not expect to return soon.

He glanced up at the sky, squinting against the ice-laden wind. Not the best weather for flying, and the clouds were low; he doubted that the two of them were on patrol. To see the ground, Ancaladar would have to fly beneath the cloud-cover, so low that he'd be constantly at the mercy of the strong winds of the lower air.

Perhaps Idalia would know where they were.

Kellen turned Firareth's head back toward the camp.

❧

"HE has gone to Lerkalpoldara to begin the evacuation that Andoreniel ordered," Idalia said when Kellen finally tracked her down. "They left last night, when the winds dropped. I do not know when he will return—sennights, perhaps, as Ancaladar cannot carry very many passengers at a time, but no other way is actually safe."

Kellen took a deep breath. He hadn't realized until just this moment how much he'd wanted to talk things over with Jermayan and get his opinion of how matters stood.

"You look like you've just lost your last friend," Idalia said. "Anything I can do to help?"

Kellen shrugged. "I'd wanted Jermayan's advice. We can't move all the Allied women and children to the Crowned Horns, and if they can't all go, moving any of them there is going to open a pretty ugly can of worms, as the Mountainborn say. But we can't just leave them without protection, especially when we have some. So I was going to ask Jermayan what he thought."

Idalia considered for a moment. "Well, you're right," she said after a pause. "And they can't move in winter anyway, but that isn't the point, really. They need to know we're trying to help. That will give them—everyone, really—the courage to hold out until spring, when they *can* move."

"Idalia, when *is* spring?" Kellen asked. He knew how long a year was, of course, but seasonal changes were still largely a mystery to him.

Idalia laughed, reaching out to ruffle his hair. "I sometimes forget what a sheltered life you've led! The Longest Night is less than a moonturn away—that's the midpoint of winter, though really, there are more cold days after it than before it. But four moonturns after that—at least in Sentarshadeen—the trees will be setting new leaves and it will be the middle of spring plowing season in the Wild Lands." Her expression turned dark. "At least, it will be if the weather runs the way it has in previous years."

And assuming any of us is there to plow. Kellen didn't say that aloud. Four moonturns—almost five? If the war went on that long, he hated to imagine what they'd be doing then.

Would it take that long for Anigrel to persuade Armethalieh to open its gates to the Demons?

And if, against all odds, they could convince the City to come in on the Allied side . . .

Then the war might be considerably longer than a few moonturns. According to what he'd learned at the House of Sword and Shield, the Great War had lasted most of a century, from the first Endarkened attacks to what everyone had thought was their ultimate defeat.

"Well, that's not so long to wait," Kellen said, trying to put a good face on things. "I'm sure the Mountainborn and the Wildlanders can hold out where they are against whatever *They* intend to do that long if we can convince them we have a plan to help them as soon as the weather turns." *All I need to do is come up with one.*

"If anybody can think of something the Elves are likely to miss, it's you, brother mine," Idalia said reassuringly. "Now scat—unless you want to help me roll bandages, count out medicines, or deal with the rest of the decidedly nonmagical scutwork that goes with being a Healer." She grinned impishly. "Or you could go help Cilarnen study to become a High Mage."

"Gods of the Wild Magic forefend!" Kellen swore feelingly. "That idiocy makes my head hurt! If you want to do magic, why not just *do* it, instead of consulting a bunch of books about the right time and hour to do a spell, and locking yourself away from everything in the world that's truly magical?" He knew he sounded just like Cilarnen when Cilarnen was talking about the Wild Magic, but he couldn't help it. Even the thought of High Magick made him want to run away and bury his head in the snow.

"If I knew the answer to that, Kellen, I'd probably be a High Mage—assuming, of course, I'd had the great good fortune to be born male, since 'everybody knows' that women can't do magic," Idalia said. "Now scat. I have work to do, and I'm sure you do, too."

And on that note, Kellen had no choice but to take his leave.

⁓

THIS was the work he'd been born for.

Cilarnen barely noticed the cold, or the moan of the wind whipping around his pavilion. He'd been appalled by it when he'd first seen it—pale yellow, and covered with an intricate design of birds and flowers that made it look like nothing in the world so much as a vulgar serving woman's shawl. Now the only thing that mattered to him was that the color let in a lot of light.

The books Kindolhinadetil had sent were spread over every available surface. He'd discovered that he only had to ask for things to be given them—providing they were available in the camp, of course—and so he had a thick sheaf of loose sheets of vellum on which he was making careful notes, both of things he would need for the work to come, and of notes from his reading.

He had so many questions! But there was no one at all to ask. If the answers could not be found among these books, he must do without them.

And he could not do without them.

I cannot do the Great Conjurations—they require a full working Circle of thirteen High Mages all performing their parts—but there are so many other spells I can do. Or I could do, if I had the power!

And, strangely, there were other spells that he thought he could manage now, spells that only seemed to require a Mage's own personal power, but that were in the books among advanced—and even proscribed—magicks. Spells of scrying and divination.

Why? Because whoever did them would see things that the High Council didn't approve of? Or because they're dangerous? The books don't say. They expect you to know. And I don't . . .

He'd awoken early that morning, too excited at the prospect of study to sleep. He'd dressed quickly, lit the lanterns and the braziers, and begun. Several hours later, hunger had driven him from his pavilion long enough to seek breakfast—though it was nearly midday by then—and he'd ensured that wouldn't happen again by stuffing his tunic as full of rolls and pastries as he could.

Everything was here. *Everything.* There was even a copy of the Art Khemitic—there was no way now to gather the necessary materials, but if they only could, they could probably make enough *umbrastone* to destroy all the magick in Armethalieh.

Kermis said that what the Art Khemitic was best for was getting blown up. I won-der if that would be useful?

The thought of his friend—of all his friends—brought a momentary spasm of grief. What had happened to them? Were any of them still alive? If they were, did they even remember him? Or had their memories been edited—as Kellen Tavadon's had once been—"for the good of the City"?

Cilarnen set the book on the Art Khemitic aside. He would never know what had happened to them.

Because of Lord Anigrel.

Who had left him alive, his Magegift intact.

Why?

I have to know.

A sharp and all-too-familiar stabbing ache began behind his eyes. He'd thought the headaches were gone forever when his suppressed Gift had resur-faced, but they'd returned as soon as he'd gotten to Ysterialpoerin.

Maybe I'm just allergic to large quantities of Elves.

Or maybe something else was trying to happen to him.

Whatever it is, I'm not going to let it happen. Not if I have to find the spell that burns my Magegift out myself.

Grimly, Cilarnen reached for another book.

The answer was here somewhere.

It had to be.

Three

The Winter City

ERKALPOLDARA WAS THE northernmost of the Nine Cities, held in the icy grasp of winter for more than half the year. It lay between two mountain ranges, upon a vast tundral plain within the valley of Bazrahil that woke to fierce beautiful life in the short seasons of warmth.

In those seasons, the Elves of Lerkalpoldara roamed the plains with their vast herds of horses and livestock—for Lerkalpoldara was a city only by courtesy. When the snows came, the Elves retreated to their Flower Forest, pitched their tents one last time, and constructed, as the winter deepened, elaborate walls of ice behind which to live until the spring thaws came.

The drought that had lain heavy on Sentarshadeen had taken an even more brutal toll upon Lerkalpoldara. When the snows had melted, and the spring rains had not come, Chalaseniel and Magarabeleniel, Vicereigns of Lerkalpoldara, had driven the vast majority of their livestock south, hoping to find water for the animals there, for they knew that without the rains, it was only a matter of time before the streams and springs of Lerkalpoldara failed and the animals would be too weak to make the journey over the mountains.

They had not even kept horses for riding. As Magarabeleniel had said when she reached Windalorianan and had been able to pass the task of driving the herds on to others, horses, as the riders of Windalorianan knew best of any in the Nine Cities, drank a great deal. If the Lerkalpoldarans could not even be sure of providing water for their goats, their cattle, and their talldeer, how much less could they expect to water horses?

And so, after leaving the herds in the south, Magarabeleniel had gone back across the mountains with her people on foot.

When the drought had broken and the rains had come, Gaiscawenorel of Windalorianan, the Viceroy's son, had gone himself over the mountain pass, returning Lerkalpoldara's horses and her herds. The herd had been gathered from across half the Elven Land, for while much of the livestock had been sacrificed when there had been no water to keep it alive, to the Elves, their horses were as precious as their children, and to keep them alive in the drought-time they had taken them to wherever there was water to keep them.

When he had reached the top of the pass that led down into Bazrahil, Gaiscawenorel had seen that the lands belonging to the City-Without-Walls had been terribly injured. The plains had gone tinder-dry with the lack of rain, and somehow they had been set ablaze. As he had looked down from the pass, he saw a black scar of burning that stretched a thousand miles. It was only by the mercy of Leaf and Star that Lerkalpoldara's Flower Forest had been spared from the fire.

⁓

THE spring to come would have given Chalaseniel and Magarabeleniel a chance to rebuild the herds and the flocks, Jermayan thought grimly, as he and Ancaladar flew through the mountain pass on their way to Lerkalpoldara. But almost as soon as Gaiscawenorel had delivered the horses, and the sibling rulers had gathered up what they could of their scattered and winnowed herds in the teeth of the autumn storms to drive them home again, Andoreniel's summonses had come, and they must send, first their children to refuge at the Fortress of the Crowned Horns, and then their warriors forth to face the malice of Shadow Mountain.

A sudden gust of wind flipped Ancaladar over and spun him around like a child's toy. Jermayan had never been so grateful for the straps that bound him to his Bonded's saddle. Without them, he would have been dashed to the ice and rocks below a thousand times since they'd begun their flight: The winds were so strong and so unpredictable here in the east that he didn't think that even a combination of his spells (assuming he could actually manage to cast any yet, though the prospect of imminent death was a great incentive) and Ancaladar's speed and strength could save his life if he fell.

The dragon could read weather as well as Jermayan could read the pages of a scroll. Better, in fact, as Ancaladar could see not only what was, and for hundreds of miles around, but tell what was to be for several days' distance. They had left on Andoreniel's errand in the middle of the night (skulking out of the camp like thieves, as Jermayan thought of it) because Ancaladar said it was the time that the air would be most quiet for hours to come. But if this was quiet, Jermayan would hate to see turbulent.

They had flown above the clouds, and dawn had come as they flew. Normally, the high sky was quiet, but this time the rivers of air were not going where Ancaladar wished to go, and the dragon had been forced to leap from one to the next like a salmon in spring, sometimes dropping hundreds of feet with a bone-rattling thump, sometimes being swept a thousand feet into the sky so swiftly it took Jermayan's breath away. And though they crossed the land below faster than the fastest running unicorn, Ancaladar had been forced to fight for every mile of distance.

"Fear not," Ancaladar said aloud, sensing Jermayan's unease through their Bond. "The journey to the Fortress of the Crowned Horns will be far easier—for us, and for our passengers. The wind-rivers run more comfortably in that direction."

"For their sake, I hope so," Jermayan said feelingly.

ANDORENIEL'S decree should already have been passed to all of the Nine Cities by the signaling towers, and in case that had failed, Jermayan's own word would certainly be enough, especially with Ancaladar to back it up. But if they were not already expecting him at his various destinations, he suspected valuable time might be wasted—especially at Lerkalpoldara.

The journey into the east itself had been bad enough, but when it came time to descend into the valley that was their goal, the passage down into the more turbulent air made all the flying Jermayan had ever before done a-dragonback seem like the most gentle excursion he had ever taken with Vestakia. The mountains did the same for the winds that rocks would have done to the waters in a rushing stream—and finally, in a desperate attempt to seek shelter from at least some of the winds, Ancaladar flew so low that he was *below* the mountaintops.

Here the winds were fierce and cold, carrying a brutal burden of snow and ice. But they were funneled by the towering granite peaks surrounding them, and they only blew one way.

Three times Ancaladar aimed himself at the pass into Bazrahil that the Elves called the Gatekeeper, only to pull up at the last moment, beating desperately at the air as he drove himself up, away from the sheer granite cliffs that flanked each side of the western side of the pass. The pass was sealed to ground travel this deep into the winter—especially a hard winter like this one—and the only way in or out of Lerkalpoldara's valley until the spring thaw was either for a few Mountain Scouts on foot, which would be wildly dangerous, or for someone like Ancaladar.

The fourth time, as Ancaladar prepared to dive at the pass, Jermayan felt the great black dragon summon all his skill and determination. Ancaladar forced himself higher into the churning air than on the previous three attempts, and this time thrust himself down through the winds with the fury of a striking thunderbolt.

There would be no turning aside this time, Jermayan realized. They would either make it through the pass, or he would discover which was harder—frozen granite or a dragon's head.

The wind whistled over armor, harness, and dragonhide with a sound Jermayan had not known it could make. It was louder than a whistle; it was a scream such as the Stone Golems Kellen had told him about might make, assuming such creatures had voices: wholly inhuman, wholly unalive, utterly dispassionate, yet somehow filled with intent and purpose. It made a stabbing ache in Jermayan's jaw and made his eyes water; the tears were instantly turned to ice, and crumbled as he blinked them away.

The mountains appeared as they shot through the clouds; drew closer. The gap between them, its size difficult to judge, appeared from among a hundred scattered mountains, and in an instant was less than a hundred yards away. Then the granite wall filled the world.

Their force and speed was all that saved them. Suddenly they were through. The scream became a muffled boom—Jermayan winced, as air with nowhere to go pressed against his ears—and he heard a shrill painful grating sound like sword-upon-sword that he identified, after a moment, as the grating of Ancaladar's belly-scales over pack-ice. There was nothing to be done about it: The pass was too narrow for Ancaladar to spread his wings.

Despite that, they shot forward at a speed nearly as fast as Ancaladar's fastest flight. The walls of the pass, crusted in ice, sped by above them, so fast they were no more than a blur of white.

Then they reached the top of the pass, and Ancaladar shot off into space.

It had not, perhaps, been the dragon's intention. He began to tumble, his wings flapping as he desperately strained once more for height. They had left the pass behind, but not the mountains, and at any moment the wind might sweep them back against the rock and ice once more.

At last Ancaladar found the air-current he sought, and veered off and up into the sky.

"It will be easier next time, Bonded," he said, a faint note of amusement in his voice.

"It would be . . . interesting to learn how it is that you have come to such a conclusion, should it please you to share such information," Jermayan said, after a very long pause. By the time he had found his voice, they were away from the walls of the mountains, and could dare to fly above the clouds again.

"Of course," Ancaladar replied. "You wingless ones make trails upon the ground, and having once made them, can follow them easily, though the creation of them is a difficult matter, needing much thought. So it is with finding a path through the air. It is true that these change, with the day and the season, but that means only that more of them need be learned to a single destination. Yet all the sky-paths to one destination are but variations upon a single theme, as it is in music. You are a musician, Bonded. You will understand this well. I have now written my theme—and a difficult one it was—and now I can create variations upon it."

"As you say," Jermayan said, not entirely convinced. Knowing where to go was one thing. Being able to go there was quite another.

After a few more minutes' flight—and compared to what had gone before, it was actually quite smooth—Ancaladar began his descent to the Flower Forest of Lerkalpoldara.

They landed in a snowstorm. The wind blew with such stunning force that even Ancaladar—who had been prepared for it—skidded several feet before he dug his claws into the ice beneath the drifting snow and anchored himself.

Jermayan knew it could not be truly cold—the coldest days of all were too arid to allow snow to fall from the sky, and on those nearly as cold, what rained down from the heavens was not snow, but a sort of ice dust. But even so, he felt as cold as if he were still in the upper air.

Ahead was the Winter City of Lerkalpoldara, nearly invisible in the snow.

Its walls towered higher than the roof of the House of Leaf and Star. Were the weather better, Jermayan knew he would see breathtaking beauty, for all life among the Elves was art, even the building of a city of ice that would be swept away with the flowers of spring. As it was, centuries of experience had allowed the Elves to sculpt the snow around the city into structures to direct the wind so that it kept a path leading up to the walls clear.

"Go," Ancaladar said. "I shall be fine here."

Stiffly, Jermayan dismounted from the saddle. Fortunately, they had not needed to recreate an entire pack-harness for this mission, as Ancaladar's original harness had taken a fortnight to make: Artenel had simply needed to come up with some way of attaching new carry-baskets to Ancaladar's existing harness, a quick and simple matter. As for the baskets themselves, they could be provided at the departure point. Which was just as well, Jermayan reflected, as he walked toward the city, as the baskets would surely not have survived the journey here. . . .

As he drew closer to the walls of the Winter City, he could see them clearly, and he frowned in confusion. The wind-cleared path led forward, but to a stark and utterly featureless wall of ice that looked as if it owed its sculpture less to Elven hands, and more to wind and snow. It was crude, perhaps even ungraceful in places, and Jermayan's heart ached with sudden fear: Had the Enemy's agents penetrated the Elven Lands as far as Lerkalpoldara?

But the head that appeared over the top of the ice wall was reassuringly Elven, cloaked in the white furs and artfully-tattered silks of a Scout-sentry.

"It is a strange bird that flies in winter," the woman observed, "yet we would recognize Ancaladar and his rider anywhere. I See you, Jermayan, Elven Mage and Knight."

"I See you, Magarabeleniel, Vicereign of Lerkalpoldara," Jermayan responded, gazing up. "We are grateful that you recognized us, for I have no doubt that if you had not, our welcome would have been colder than the snow."

"Maiden Winter is more than playful this year," Magarabeleniel agreed wryly. "But come. Be welcome in our city and at our hearth."

For a moment Jermayan wondered how that was to be possible, for he saw no sign of a doorway in the wall, but a second head appeared beside hers, and a ladder of rope and bone was lowered down to him.

He expected to climb up it, but as soon as his hands and feet were securely in place upon its rungs, unseen hands within Lerkalpoldara pulled him quickly up the wall, and guided him over the side, until he was standing on a ledge a few feet below the top. From here he could look out over the valley—just now, though it was near midday, the twisting veils of hard-driven snow obscured everything. Even Ancaladar was invisible, though Jermayan knew the dragon must be where he had left him, and something of Ancaladar's size and color would be difficult to miss.

He glanced around. Below him stood Lerkalpoldara's Flower Forest. Even in winter he could smell the life of the forest, and it warmed him as no fire could. Surrounding the forest were the tents of the Elves of Lerkalpoldara. They were made of heavy wool, dyed and woven in elaborate patterns—heavier and sturdier than the campaigning tents of the Elven Knights, for these were not a temporary accommodation, but the only home of the Elves of the Plains City.

Lerkalpoldara had sent many of her young men and women to Andoreniel's army to fight—and many more had gone to tend the cows and horses, the sheep and pigs and goats, to repair armor and harness, to mend old tents and to make new ones, and to cook—for Lerkalpoldara's people lived all the year in tents and under sky, and no one in all the Nine Cities was more expert in making and holding camp tidily and well.

Of those that had not gone to war, not all would be here within walls at this time, for the herds that were the life of the Plains Elves must be husbanded, even in winter, and her people took turns to care for the central herd.

But only a handful of the people did this, and even accounting for those who were riding herd, and those who were away at war, Jermayan saw too few tents erected here within the Winter City, and too many sentries standing upon the walls, even in the midst of a storm.

This was a city at war.

But with what, or whom ? And why had word not come to Redhelwar, or Andoreniel?

Questions it would have been the height of rudeness to ask—even if Magarabeleniel had not far outranked him—crowded Jermayan's thoughts, but the Elven Knight held his tongue. There was yet time.

Magarabeleniel led him down from the walls and into the streets of the Winter City. Here the air was comparatively still, the winds blocked by the walls of the city.

Together they walked among the tents to The House of Sky and Grass. Jermayan saw no one else as he passed between the tents, not even the street-sweepers who would normally be about in this weather, for even though the ice-walls blocked most of the falling snow, it did not block all of it. But word of his arrival had obviously gone ahead, and the inhabitants of the Winter City were doing him the courtesy of ignoring his presence entirely.

The House of Sky and Grass was no larger than the largest of the other tents they passed—perhaps the size of Redhelwar's pavilion—and there was nothing to mark it as the Vicereign's House save an elaborate braided knot of dried summer grass that hung beside the door. Magarabeleniel stopped beneath the canopy.

"Be welcome in my home and at my hearth, Jermayan son of Malkirinath, Elven Knight, Ancaladar's Bondmate. Stay as long as you will, and when you go, go with joy."

"To be welcomed at the hearth of a friend is to be made doubly welcome," Jermayan answered formally. "I accept with thanks." He followed her into the tent.

The floor of the tent was covered with rugs that matched the weaving of the tent's walls, and here the air was so warm that the ice on Jermayan's heavy stormcloak actually began to melt. There was a rack near the doorway to hang outdoor garments, and after Magarabeleniel had pulled the door curtains snug against the outside air, they both removed their outer layers—and Jermayan his armor—and spread them to dry, Jermayan accepting a houserobe and boots from his hostess.

Though there seemed to be no one else present, someone had obviously been here recently, for the braziers and the lanterns were lit, and someone had prepared the tea things. The kettle was boiling, and a low table was prepared with what looked to be a rather more substantial meal than Jermayan was used to taking with his tea.

"You will discover that you do not hunger, here in the Great Cold," Magarabeleniel said. "But one must eat, all the same."

She seated herself upon a cushion upon the floor, and motioned for him to do the same. She filled the teapot, and as the tea steeped, they began with a thick soup, and talk of the weather.

They did not speak of the sentries upon the walls, or why those walls were so stark and plain.

Over several small courses—all very rich—and several pots of tea—they discussed many things, though never, of course, the reason Jermayan had come. The weavers had produced some truly splendid work recently. The autumn flowers had been less extravagant than usual, but some beautiful specimens had still been seen. The herds were as well as could be expected, and in ten years or so would have been restored to their former size. The burn which Gaiscawenorel had remarked upon the Plain, of course, would be gone long before that; in a growing season, or perhaps two, no trace of it would remain. Grass fires were a fact of life, and easily dealt with; it was only the Great Drought that had made this one so very difficult.

At last Magarabeleniel allowed the conversation to turn to the progress of the war—though still, of course, not to the reason that Jermayan had come.

"I regret that my brother is not here to greet you as well, but he is riding with the herds and will not return for at least a fortnight. Were he here, he would wonder how it goes with our folk who answered Andoreniel's call, if there were anything you cared to tell of that."

"Were Chalaseniel here, I would have much to tell him," Jermayan answered, and spoke at length of the army's recent battles. Of the Shadowed Elves, and their fight against them. Of their victory in determining the Demons' ultimate strategy: to gain the human Mage-City for their own. And of Redhelwar's recent discovery that the Demons were now massing their forces to send what creatures they could into the Elven Lands, as well as along their borders, using the ways the Shadowed Elves had prepared.

There was a long silence after Jermayan finished telling this news, and in it he came to realize that whatever message Andoreniel might have sent, it had not reached Lerkalpoldara. Well, that was only to be expected. And so Magarabeleniel's next words did not surprise him.

"Andoreniel knows we will fight the Shadow to our last breath, as we did in the days of old, no matter how unlikely the chance of victory," Magarabeleniel said at last. "Should the City of a Thousand Bells fall—and forgive me for speaking bluntly, cousin, but what you tell me does not make me think it will long stand, with this canker in its heart—then I cannot think where in all the forests or beneath all the stars the Children of Leaf and Star may find shelter from the Shadow's hunger. We will stand against it, and fall—and unlike the Seven, no victory will rise up from our slain bodies. But no one can truly know how the game will play before the stones are laid upon the board, as Master Belesharon has told us all, so we will not think of that yet. What is in my mind now is of a more practical nature. It is in my mind to wonder at your purpose in traveling to tell me of these things now, with so much of winter yet to run, for you have seen the Gatekeeper, and know he is not to be traversed for many moonturns yet—later this year, we think, than in other years. We would have sent word of this, but the ice has claimed our signaling mirrors, and those who would care for them are with the army. All who remain must look to the herds, and to other difficulties of which you do not yet know."

Though the tone of her voice had not changed, there was a faint note of warning there.

"I would hear of these difficulties, if there were anything you cared to tell," Jermayan said mildly.

"You have said that the Ancient Enemy wishes to send its forces into the Elven Lands, to strike and harry. I say to you that they are here *now*. Some we have faced of old, and know. Others we have never seen before, but know now to our cost: the great white bats that fly by day and night.

"These monsters drove the wolf and tiger down upon the herds, for anything that lives will run from a Coldwarg pack. The Coldwarg followed them to slay, first the predators and then the herds. Yet were it Coldwarg alone, well, we have slain Coldwarg before. They make a fine cloak-lining—yes, and a saddle-cloth, too!" She smiled, faintly and without mirth. "Yet there are others, and worse. After the high passes froze, but before the Great Cold set in, we saw signs of shadewalkers and even the hint of an ice-drake lair, though that we are not sure of, for it is not cold enough yet to bring the creature out to hunt. But to know that the war against the Shadow goes badly makes ill hearing, for I think our own war for the Eastern Plains is that one in small, and I tell you plainly, cousin, the walls of the Winter City shall not rise with next year's snow."

Because there will be no one left alive to build them again, Jermayan thought to himself. The Lerkalpoldarans could fight—indeed, they were fighting—but without magic and without Elvensteel. And against the monsters of Shadow Mountain's brewing, it was a battle they could not win.

In such a position, a prudent general called for retreat, and Jermayan was certain that Magarabeleniel had thought of that a thousand times over, but from the high plains of Lerkalpoldara, in winter, they could not retreat. The Gatekeeper was the only pass of any size out of the mountains, and Jermayan and Ancaladar had flown through it on the way in. Even if the Lerkalpoldarans were willing to abandon all of their livestock and everything they owned, they could not make it through that ice-choked pass on foot. They were trapped here in the northernmost east, with their numbers slowly dwindling day by day against the assaults of the Shadow.

"And now I would hear what message you bear from Andoreniel," Magarabeleniel said, when Jermayan had sat silent for a very long time.

"In autumn, you sent your children to the Fortress of the Crowned Horns, where, by the grace of Leaf and Star, all arrived safely. Now, as the Enemy grows bolder, Andoreniel has sent me to bring all women with child to the same safety upon Ancaladar's back. It is his decree."

"So badly as that . . ." Magarabeleniel whispered, bowing her head. "It goes so badly as that. . . ."

After a moment she straightened, composed again. "Indeed, I am desolated to be forced to bear words of rebuke and refusal to Andoreniel in this time of his difficulty, and were matters otherwise, I would have found it a restful thing to have visited the Fortress of the Crowned Horns, for I have never seen it, and it would have been a pleasant thing to see my nephew Rierochan again. Yet I cannot leave my people, no matter what Andoreniel's decree, nor is any woman to be so ordered, as if she were herself a child, but given a choice to go or to stay. There are four here who must choose. I have chosen. Three have yet to choose."

She regarded him steadily, her black eyes unyielding.

"I thank you for your courtesy," Jermayan said, bowing his head. It had not occurred to him that the Lady of Lerkalpoldara might be among those affected by Andoreniel's decree; in the face of what she had just told him about Enemy forces drawing closer around the city, it made sense that she did not want to leave her people, whatever the cost.

"But come. I believe our cloaks are dry now. Let me show you the walls of Lerkalpoldara, though they are far from what they should be. And I can make you known to the rest of the folk, before they burst with curiosity," Magarabeleniel said.

✥

THOUGH Lerkalpoldara's normal population was greatly diminished, those that remained were filled with lively curiosity about Jermayan and his errand— and about Ancaladar as well.

Jermayan's mind was in turmoil. It had never before occurred to him to disobey a decree of Andoreniel's, yet how could he rescue a handful—at most—of the people here and leave the rest to die?

What if none of the other three women wanted to come? How could he order them if Magarabeleniel refused to order them?

The city that had been so empty when he and Magarabeleniel had walked
through it a few hours earlier was now bustling with life—paths being swept;
snow being carried away, and the walls being repaired or added to. Magarabeleniel took Jermayan on a leisurely tour of the city, stopping to speak with everyone, and by the time they reached the Flower Forest—which Jermayan had
slowly come to realize was their eventual destination—the inhabitants of
Lerkalpoldara knew a great deal about dragons.

"Your dragon can come in here to spend the night. He will be warmer—and
safer as well," Magarabeleniel said. "*They* mean to show us our fate by slaughtering everything that lives here upon the plains, everything wild and tame. It is
how we have escaped death so far, for *They* will happily slaughter cows and
talldeer instead of us—the bodies just lie there and freeze, now, for there is nothing left to eat them. The wolves are gone, and the foxes, and the weasels . . . the
ice-tiger is gone, though we saw too many of them while they were being starved
out. The owls are gone . . . everything that flies in the air but one."

She took a deep breath. "We have made a promise to one another, my people and I. In the spring the wind sets east and blows over the pass until summer.
The grasslands bloom and flower—I think that even this year they will flower.
The rivers roar with melt and all the springs are full. But in summer the wind
shifts away from the passes. The grass turns from green to gold. The rivers wane
to streams and no rain comes in any year. And when that time comes, whoever is
still alive will take a torch and a string of fast horses and ride into the wind, and
set the Plains alight so that the fires kindle like a chain of pearls. If he cannot
ride he will run; if he cannot run, he will walk; if he cannot walk he will set the
Plains alight where he stands. But we will burn it all this time—every leaf, every
seed, every blade of grass, the Flower Forest itself, so that *They* gain no foothold
here, nor anything *They* can use."

It was as if Jermayan had opened a door and stepped back a thousand years,
to the time of the Great War. Such desperate bargains, such terrible battles, had
been commonplace then, and the land still bore their scars.

There must, there must be another way!

"I hear your words, Lady, and will bear them to Andoreniel with all you
have said. I thank you for your courtesy to Ancaladar; he tells me he does not
feel the cold, but there are times when it makes my heart ache with cold to look
upon him."

"The forest is warm," Magarabeleniel said, and indeed, it was warm enough
that Jermayan had removed his heavy fur-lined mittens and thrown back the
hood of his heavy fur cloak. "And he need not fear to fly over our walls in the

storm, for the winds will drop soon, the better for him to see his way. Nor will we fire upon him, for we have had time to learn our Enemy by now."

Though Jermayan doubted that even the heavy shafts of the Elven hunting bow could penetrate Ancaladar's scales, the barbed quarrels could certainly tear the membrane of his great wings, and Jermayan was not yet certain of his power to repair such damage. Though he had Ancaladar's inexhaustible power to draw upon, he was the one who must do the drawing, and that part of him which was an Elven Mage had been taxed to the uttermost by the spell of Kindolhinadetil's Mirror. Like Kellen and the other Wildmages—and the High Mage Cilarnen— who had played their parts in that spell, the longer he could go without doing magic, the better it would be for him.

"And so I shall tell him," Jermayan said. "In truth, he is quite timid, and will welcome the reassurance."

Magarabeleniel made a faint noise that might, months ago, have been something as undignified as a laugh. "Perhaps you think I will believe any nursery-tale you care to sing, Jermayan, but *I* have been to Sentarshadeen, and am no child at her first Spring Foaling. If you can fight as well as you can dance, your dragon cannot be timid. But refresh yourself here in our forest, if you will, and perhaps you will rejoin me and my advisors for the evening meal."

"It will be my pleasure," Jermayan assured her, bowing as Magarabeleniel turned and walked away.

The shadows lengthened as he walked deeper into the forest, and over the sound of the wind he heard a wild deep-chested howling.

Coldwarg.

Tainted, creatures of the Shadow, created specifically to hunt and kill unicorns, but willing, even eager, to kill *anything*; they lusted for the pain and fear of their victims even more than for their deaths.

And they were only one of the monsters that plagued the High Plains, if what Magarabeleniel said was true.

Coldwarg could be slain. Deathwings could be slain. Even shadewalkers could be slain. But it had taken Ancaladar to kill the last ice-drake they had seen, and the ice-drake had very nearly killed *him*. If there were indeed an ice-drake here, lairing until the winter had deepened further, when it finally emerged and began to hunt, the Lerkalpoldarans would have no defense against it.

What was he to do? Jermayan knew he must not stay longer than needed to complete his mission—or acknowledge failure. He must press on to the other Eight Cities. And then he must return to the army, for the power he could lend to the battles it had yet to fight could be vital.

And what then, Son of Malkirinath? Were you to level the Golden City, slay everyone within it, guilty and innocent alike, you would not win this war. You would only deny Them *a tool to* Their *using. The war would go on, as your friends die about you, until there is nothing left. . . .*

Perhaps the destruction of Armethalieh by the Light would buy time, but at a price no one of the Light would be willing to pay. There was always the danger, in fighting the creatures of the Shadow, in being tempted to use *Their* methods in order to win, but all that was, was a sort of surrender to *Them.* No one thought it was better to lose cleanly than to win with the Shadow's tools: It was simply that it was impossible to win with the Shadow's tools. No victory for the Light could be gained by using the tools and the methods of the Shadow—once they were taken up, they began to twist the wielder, changing him or her bit by bit, moment by moment, until he or she no longer recognized the original purpose for which their side had once fought. They began to make changes, compromises, disastrous alliances—until soon they were the Shadow's pawn in all but name.

Was that what had happened to Anigrel, in Armethalieh?

Or was he one of the rare ones who stared the Darkness unblinkingly in Its eyes, and flung himself into Its embrace, knowing full well what it was that he chose to serve?

How could any creature, mad or sane, do such a thing?

Jermayan shook his head, a human gesture he had picked up from Idalia. He did not know, but as Master Belesharon was fond of saying, all answers are to be found in the Circle, or else you have asked the wrong question.

It did not matter how Anigrel had come to do such a thing.

What mattered was how what he had set in motion could be stopped.

❧

THOUGH it had seemed unlikely that afternoon, when Jermayan had landed in the full strength of the snowstorm, as the shadows of evening fell, the temperature dropped sharply, and the snow stopped falling.

Earlier, Jermayan had passed Magarabeleniel's message on to Ancaladar through the Bond they shared, and now Ancaladar descended into a clearing at the forest's heart—though leaving the forest again might be a more difficult matter.

Snow, leaves, and loose branches cascaded to the forest floor as Ancaladar settled to the ground, folding his wings warily, for his flanks pressed against the trunks of the trees at the edges of the clearing. Jermayan wasn't at all sure of how the dragon could possibly move without knocking trees over.

"So this is a Flower Forest?" the dragon observed. "It is very nice."

"Yes," Jermayan agreed. "I think . . . I think we will be leaving here soon. And without what we came for."

"Indeed," said Ancaladar, sounding maddeningly calm. "I believe you must reconsider."

Jermayan stared at his friend in surprise. Of all the things he had expected to hear from Ancaladar, this had not been among them.

"While you spoke with the Lady of Lerkalpoldara, I flew over the valley, for I did not feel comfortable upon the ground," Ancaladar said. "And I saw many distressing things. Coldwarg packs—flights of Deathwings—creatures such as I have not seen"—the dragon shuddered—"in a thousand years. They have come over the northern border, I think; over the mountains, from the High Desert beyond the Elven Lands. I believe there is even another ice-drake such as the one I slew here. One does not forget that smell easily, I promise you.

"They will slay everyone here. And then, perhaps, they will seek fresh game, for I do not think that the closed passes will stop any of them, and they are all creatures of the cold and the dark."

The dragon regarded Jermayan steadily from its great golden eyes.

"It would interest me greatly, of course, to hear your thoughts on the matter of how to prevent this, should you choose to share them," Jermayan said.

"I have given it consideration," Ancaladar said, sounding faintly amused. "You must open the Gatekeeper. The people will go through and seek refuge in Windalorianan, with as much of the stock as will travel fast. The creatures will follow them, so you must fly ahead and warn Windalorianan as well. But Windalorianan would have suffered attack in any event, whether you unsealed the Gatekeeper or not, so you must not feel that by doing so you have exposed them to peril they would otherwise have escaped."

It took a moment for the full impact of Ancaladar's words to sink in.

"You cannot mean for me to bespell the ice and snow of the pass," Jermayan said, unable to believe what he was hearing. Even if he could clear the Gatekeeper—something that would not be a certain thing even if he were entirely rested—the Lerkalpoldarans must reach it and get through it, which the Enemy would not wish to see happen. Most of all, he was not completely certain that Magarabeleniel would not wish to remain behind and fight.

"Of course I mean nothing," Ancaladar answered, rather tartly. "After all, I cast no spells, wield no magic. *I* am no great Elven Mage, who calls storms and builds palaces out of ice! It is of course for you to decide what you must do."

"I am sorry, my friend." Jermayan reached out and placed a hand upon the dragon's head. Even through the armored gauntlet he still wore, he could feel the heat that radiated from beneath the dragon's skin. Ancaladar was always warm.

"If it can be done . . . then surely they would come south to the plains of Vardirvoshanon if they could. And once they had done so, surely then Magarabeleniel and the others would be willing to leave for the Fortress of the Crowned Horns."

"Perhaps you will ask them tonight, at dinner."

Jermayan considered the possibility. But no. It would be too cruel to hold out the hope of life and freedom, only to deny it to them in the end. He would speak to them of leaving *after* he had opened the Gatekeeper.

If he could.

He shook his head. "Tomorrow morning, my friend, you and I shall see what we can do about that matter. And then we shall speak to Magarabeleniel again."

THAT evening Magarabeleniel's tent was filled with guests: all the Council elders who remained in Lerkalpoldara, those who were being considered to replace the absent Counselors, and those others who might have a particular interest in the news from Outside. All in all, if the entire city was not here, a good portion of it was, with the rest gathered upon the walls.

"Not a night goes by that *They* do not try our walls," a woman named Elodiane grumbled dourly. She was the chief of the weavers—or of those who remained in Lerkalpoldara. "We have built them thicker than ever before, and on the outside they are as smooth as Elvenware, yet it does not stop the creatures from trying to climb them. Each morning we melt away the damage they have caused, and rebuild the walls anew. They will not break them down."

But some of them can fly over your walls, Jermayan thought bleakly. And he had seen what an ice-drake could do: If it did not simply slither over the walls as if they were not there, it could smash right through them.

As if to underscore the truth of Jermayan's grim thoughts, the Coldwarg howling, which had been intermittent through the late afternoon, began again in earnest, rising and falling like cresting waves. It was as bad as he had ever heard it when the packs had followed the army, looking for any opening to exploit.

Magarabeleniel had made certain that all of the pregnant women were present that evening, and that each was given the opportunity to speak with Jermayan. He was not in the least surprised that all of them refused to obey Andoreniel's decree. Here, knowing that their city faced extinction at the hands of creatures of the Shadow, to save themselves must seem faithless and cowardly.

Though it was impossible not to hear the howling of the Coldwarg, it was possible to ignore it. There was even music during the meal—not to mask the sound, precisely, but to transform it into something else: The sound of harp and flute, blending with the howling of the Coldwarg and the moaning of the wind, made a strange sad melody that was perfect for this time and place.

"And now that you have spoken Andoreniel's word, and heard the word of the Vicereign of Lerkalpoldara, you are naturally welcome to remain in the

House of Sky and Grass for as long as may please you," Magarabeleniel said. "Though I fear we cannot offer such rare sport as you may have lately been used to."

"I would say that you hold yourselves too lightly here in the Winter City, Lady, and that it is possible that I may yet linger a few days. Come the morning, should Ancaladar be able to manage it, I believe I should like to fly once again over the valley."

"Tanarakiel tells us that the weather should remain calm for the next sennight—unfortunate, in a way, as the Deathwings prefer to fly when the air is still, and no walls will keep them out. Still, they dare not try the Flower Forest, so we will move beneath the canopy until the winds bluster again. And in doing so, we will make the space for you and Ancaladar to go forth in the morning."

"It will be as you say, Lady," Jermayan said, inclining his head.

"And perhaps, should you see my brother upon your journeying, you would be so good as to tell him that it is not convenient for me to await him a fortnight from now, but that I should prefer him to return to the city at once."

<hr />

AN hour before dawn Jermayan was awakened by his hostess, and assisted her and several others in collapsing the House of Sky and Grass and rolling it into a neat bundle about its poles. A few of the smaller tents would be taken into the Flower Forest until the danger of attack from the sky was past, but the majority of the tents and furnishings that made up the Lerkalpoldarans' possessions would remain tidily bundled against the walls.

By an hour or so after dawn, the entire city was packed and ready to move, and the entire space within the walls of ice had been emptied. Only the marks in the packed snow, the sculptures of ice, and the gently-meandering trails darkened with ash gave any hint that a city had once covered the several acres enclosed by the gleaming wall of ice.

The day was free of snow, and the air was still, but though it was clear, the day was far from bright: There were high clouds in the sky, and the light was gray. Still, the day would serve for flying.

When the preparations had all been made, and the city had been cleared away, Ancaladar emerged from the forest. Kellen had described the dragon's uncanny ability to insinuate his massive form into the tightest of places, and now Jermayan watched the same process in reverse, as the dragon seemed to ooze from between the trees as if his great scaled form were liquid, not flesh. If Jermayan had not removed Ancaladar's harness last night, he doubted the trick would have been possible now, so tightly did the dragon seem to be wedged among the trees.

Yet Ancaladar extracted himself from the forest without dislodging a single trunk.

Jermayan could feel his Bondmate's relief to be done with the delicate operation, however, and once he was free of the forest Ancaladar shook himself all over, rattling his great wings like half-unfurled fans.

Now Jermayan came forward carrying Ancaladar's flying harness—or, as the dragon insisted, *Jermayan's* flying harness, as Ancaladar had no need of a saddle and straps to fly. First Jermayan wiped away the last of the quickly-melting snow with a soft cloth, then buckled the flying harness into place with the swiftness of long familiarity.

But though there was more than enough room here outside the Flower Forest for Ancaladar to stand and even to spread his wings, there was far from sufficient space within the walls of Lerkalpoldara for him to launch himself into the sky.

"It is not such a high wall," Ancaladar said, peering over it. "And I think, if I am careful, I can climb over it without damaging it. Mount up, Bonded, and we will see if I am right."

"By all means, do as the dragon says," Magarabeleniel said to Jermayan, a stifled note of despairing amusement in her voice. "I am sorry that we could not make the walls higher, Ancaladar, but if they were very much higher, they would fall down, and then we would have no walls at all."

"If the walls were higher, I could not climb over them," Ancaladar said soothingly, crouching down so that Jermayan could step up to the saddle upon his neck. "And most creatures will not be able to climb over even these."

By now Jermayan had buckled himself into place in Ancaladar's saddle. He raised a hand in salute to Magarabeleniel, and Ancaladar got to his feet once more.

A few steps brought them to the wall itself. The portion they faced had been prudently cleared of sentries; now Ancaladar reared up on his hind legs, spreading his great wings wide for balance. Jermayan was grateful, once again, for the straps that held him firmly in the saddle no matter what position Ancaladar assumed.

Jermayan had expected many possibilities from his friend in scaling the wall, but he had not expected Ancaladar to simply hop. Ancaladar furled his wings, gathered himself, and sprang strongly upward off his haunches, bounding into the sky as if he were a giant hare.

Though he spread his wings as soon as they had cleared the top of the wall, nothing could prevent a bone-jarring landing. Still, Ancaladar sounded pleased with himself as he said:

"The wall remains undamaged. As I promised."

"Let us only hope there will be no need of it soon," Jermayan said.

Ancaladar dropped to all fours and began to canter forward, then to run, and soon had launched himself into the air. As Tanarakiel had promised, the air was entirely still, and the clouds were so high that for Jermayan and Ancaladar's purposes they might as well not have been there at all. As a result, of course, the air was far colder than it had been on the previous day, so cold that there was hardly any difference between the temperature on the ground and in the high sky.

As they rose in a long flat spiral, Jermayan could look down and see the whole of the valley—an unbroken sweep of whiteness save for the Flower Forest and the Winter City now falling far behind them. Moving dots on the landscape below resolved themselves into herds—of horses, cattle, talldeer—some with accompanying riders.

But less congenial things roamed the landscape as well. Jermayan saw the faint gray shadows of prowling Coldwarg, and lean dark slashes that Ancaladar identified as shadewalkers. As Magarabeleniel had warned him he would, he came to a place where he found the snow stained with the blood not of simple kills, but of mass slaughters, and that place was ringed with tracks unlike those of any animal Jermayan had ever seen. Ancaladar told him that the tracks belonged to a herd of serpentmarae. They had undoubtedly run their prey to exhaustion, and then kicked and trampled it to death with their sharp cloven hooves.

They flew on.

If he could not do this thing, Jermayan knew, some day a few moonturns from now, all in Lerkalpoldara would share the fate of those unfortunate beasts below.

And if Kellen could not—somehow—find a way to save them all, it would be very little longer until all the Elven Lands—in fact, all the world—shared Lerkalpoldara's fate.

It was a heavy burden to place upon the shoulders of a child—for Kellen was young even by human standards—but it was no Elf or human who had placed it there, but the Wild Magic itself, which had made Kellen Tavadon a Knight-Mage.

They approached the Gatekeeper.

This close to the mountain wall, on even the mildest day, the air was unsettled, and only speed could make their passage smooth. Jermayan had only a few moments to regard the pass before Ancaladar had soared past it in a wide circle.

He would be near the pass for seconds only—but time enough to set the spell, if he could set it at all.

The Elves had given up their share in the Great Magics in the time of Great Queen Vieliessar Farcarinon, at the time of the First War. It was she who had learned the secret of Bonding with dragons, and so had gained the power for the Elven Wildmages to defeat the Endarkened, long before humans had been much more than a particularly promising sort of animal, far less civilized than the fauns of the forest.

But all the Wild Magic was based on prices and bargains, and so in exchange for that victory, Vieliessar Farcarinon, in the name of her people, had surrendered the Elves' share in the Greater Magics, in exchange for peace and long life. The Elven Mages lived out their brief lives—as the lives of the Elves had been in those days—and died, and no more Wildmages were born among the Elves, though the Elves' lives could thereafter be measured in centuries. The Children of Leaf and Star taught the arts of Civilization to the brief bright humans, and when that race was old enough to understand, the Elves taught the humans about the Wild Magic as well, for they had never ceased to revere it, and to follow its teachings. And soon magic flared bright among the humans—and just in time, by Elven standards, for a scant few thousand years later, the Enemy struck once more.

That war the Elves had fought without Greater Magics of their own, for in that time the last Elven Mage was ten thousand years dead. Yet they had fought beside allies in whom the Wild Magic burned brightly, and thought that they had triumphed, thinking themselves as secure in their victory as the Great Queen and their ancestors once did.

Now the Great Enemy gathered once more, and Jermayan found himself resurrected, a creature out of legend, with powers that had not been seen since the ancient days of Elven civilization, powers subtly unlike any others those of the Light could claim.

The human Wildmages' magic was that of what *could* be. However unlikely it appeared to a non-Mage, its workings were merely improbable, not impossible.

The High Magick—which Jermayan understood much better now that Cilarnen had come to live among them—was also a magic of change, but of tiny changes layered one upon another like coat after coat of lacquer. The end result was often profoundly startling, but not to one who truly saw how it had been accomplished. And so, though the High Magick did not work closely with the natural world as the Wild Magic did, each individual change it made in the fabric of the world's being was not large.

But an Elven Mage, especially one Bonded to a Dragon . . .

Elven Magery was the magic of Transformation. One thing became another, without regard for what it had once been: Fire burned upon ice, stone became water, air became ice.

Perhaps that was the deeper reason for Vieliessar Farcarinon's bargain. With such power, might not the Elves, in time, have become no different than the Enemy they fought? Perhaps Men would never have risen up at all if the Elves had not renounced their Magery. And there would never have been any Wildmages.

"Are you ready, Bonded?" Ancaladar asked, breaking into Jermayan's thoughts.

"It is now, or not at all," Jermayan responded with grim humor. It was a favorite expression of Kellen's, and one that had always puzzled him. For the Elves, there was always another time one could do a thing.

Until *They* had returned. And at last, "now" was the only time there was, for all the races of the Light.

He concentrated his mind upon his purpose, and let it fill with the unnamable colorshapes that were the forms of the spells of Elven Magery.

To do even that much filled him with pain, but Jermayan had felt pain before. He gathered up the spell waiting in his mind, and struck.

The snow and ice of the pass suddenly glowed as brightly as if the sun had suddenly come forth from behind the clouds, and for a moment that was all.

Then suddenly the pass itself began to boil with mist, as the ice and snow, down to the bare rock of the mountainside itself, began simply to waft away.

Jermayan felt as if he could not breathe. His heart hammered in his chest, the air darkened in his vision, as if Ancaladar had unwarily flown too high. He felt the power of the spell flow from him as if it were the blood from his veins. Each beat of his slowing heart bound the magic more firmly to its course—and drained away more of his life with it. A spell was only as strong as the focus of its power—while Jermayan's power was the limitless power of a dragon's magical might, his focus was the mortal power of an Elven Knight.

But he did not die. He *would* not, for if he did, Ancaladar's life would be extinguished with his own, for the Bond that was the source of the Mage's great power was also the dragon's greatest weakness.

At last the spell was run, and Ancaladar carried them gently to the ground, and Jermayan roused himself to gaze up at his handiwork.

The mountains that ringed the valley of Bazrahil were white with snow, save for the few patches of gray where a snow-spill had ripped the burden of snow and ice from the face of the rock—in every place but one. The pass the Elves called the Gatekeeper was now a dark scar against the whiteness, its rock as bare as it would be at summer's height.

"One obstacle gone," Ancaladar said, both relief and satisfaction in his voice. "Now all that remains is to convince the Vicereign of the wisdom of abandoning her city."

Four

The Smoke of That Great Burning

B UT IN THE end, that was far easier than casting the spell had been—easier, in fact, even than the return to Lerkalpoldara itself, for with the clear weather, the Deathwings were out in force, hunting for any prey they might find, and Jermayan was in no condition to offer battle. It was left to Ancaladar to outfly them, which was a long and delicate matter. The dragon's one advantage was that he could fly far higher and faster than his enemy, and unlike in his previous clashes with the Deathwings, he did not have to worry about protecting the army from aerial attacks. In the end, Ancaladar carried Jermayan high above the clouds, where the creatures could not follow.

"This," Jermayan observed, gazing down at the tops of the clouds speeding by below them, as Ancaladar made a wide circle about Lerkalpoldara far below, "may provide the two of us with a temporary respite, but it does nothing to accomplish our return in safety."

And in fact he was not certain how safe Ancaladar would be once the dragon was on the ground, even if he could land within the walls of Lerkalpoldara. The Deathwings' favorite tactic, as they had seen so far, was to swoop upon their victims and carry them off into the sky. Obviously that would not work on Ancaladar—but it was always possible they might have another form of attack held in reserve.

"If we are quick, we can land before they are aware of us. I can see them through the clouds—they circle the city like ravens over a battlefield. I will take off again to draw them away, and return again at nightfall. You need not fear for my safety—they are nasty and foul-tasting, but their claws cannot pierce my hide, and I will take care to fly high."

Jermayan knew that Ancaladar was being optimistic for his benefit, but he also knew they did not have the luxury of waiting out the day in the hope—no more than that—that the Deathwings would leave with the darkness. The creatures had flown by night before, and Ancaladar's presence might incite them to do so again.

"Very well," he said.

"Then we go—now."

Ancaladar folded back his wings, and for a moment he hung weightless in the sky. Then he began to fall—no, more than that, to dive, his long sinuous neck extended, the wind whistling along his neck-barbs as he arrowed head-first toward the earth. Even through his armor, the saddle-straps cut into Jermayan's shoulders and torso; he hung against them rather than being pressed down into the saddle.

They flashed through the clouds, and now Jermayan could see the Winter City far below. Gray-white shapes circled above it, seeking for some unwary victim to snatch, but everyone had retreated within the Flower Forest, and the Deathwings dared not venture too close to its protection.

Then they plunged through the flock of Deathwings. Pain lanced through Jermayan's head as the creatures shrilled their soundless cries. Ancaladar spread his wings with a boom like distant thunder, his body jerking itself level with a whiplash crack that rattled Jermayan's teeth. The Elven Knight had been waiting for that part of the maneuver; the moment it was done, he began loosening the buckles and straps of the flying harness. A fall from this height would not kill him, and it would save precious moments on the ground.

Even though he was expecting it, the jarring shock when Ancaladar dug all four sets of claws into the ice to stop himself flung Jermayan from the saddle. His training in the House of Sword and Shield stood him in good stead, however, for he converted the motion to a forward roll and came up running, fleeing for the safety of the Flower Forest as if his very life depended on it. Behind him he heard the hiss and squeal of the ice as Ancaladar sprang to his feet and turned, bounding toward the wall and then over it as lightly as a unicorn could leap a hedge.

Jermayan did not stop running until the green shadows of the Flower Forest had replaced the bright glare of the Winter City outside.

"One hopes that your flight this morning was all that you hoped for from it," Magarabeleniel said, stepping out from behind a tree. Here in the Flower Forest, she had exchanged her furs and robes of winter's white for garments that echoed the browns and greens of the winter forest—for the Flower Forest was in leaf at every season.

"I did what I had intended to do," Jermayan said, "but it is with regret that I must say I was unable to bear your word to Chalaseniel, for Ancaladar and I found ourselves to be of unbearable interest to those flying rats that plague your city."

Unexpectedly, Magarabeleniel laughed. "Jermayan, you malign rats! Their skins have a hundred uses, they are loyal, they make good pets—and one may even eat them if one is starving. None of these things is true of those creatures—even when we kill them, the stink is nearly unbearable, no matter what we do, so that even in death they strike at us. As for Chalaseniel, I shall send riders to him tonight, if I can."

"Perhaps you have more to tell him than you know," Jermayan said.

"The Lady of Lerkalpoldara knows all that transpires on the Plains of Bazrahil," Magarabeleniel assured him. "It was my nurse's first teaching, when I was scarcely old enough to follow the talldeer. Come. We will take tea, and you will tell me what I am presumed to know already."

⌖

SOON Jermayan was settled in her tent—a much smaller tent, tucked among the trees, but no less the House of Sky and Grass for that—with a cup of hot tea in his hand. It smelled of honey and new-mown hay—an odd tea to drink in the depths of winter, but no one in the Winter City thought that they would live to drink the teas of summer in their rightful season. They spoke for a few minutes about the weather—not idle pleasantry for a tent-dwelling people—and Jermayan learned that Tanarakiel believed that the clear weather would hold for some days yet. How long she could not say, though surely four or five.

"A blessing and a curse, that, both—but clear weather for your flight, at least," Magarabeleniel said.

"A flight I must make soon, but before I go, I would see you safely upon your way. This morning I have opened the Gatekeeper, and the road to Windalori-anan lies clear. I would counsel you to take it while you may, and if you would take it, you must go soon."

There was a long pause after such blunt speaking. Magarabeleniel gazed off into the distance, seemingly entranced by the muted glow of light on the bronze trunk of an alyon, and the winter-gold carpet of moss at its feet. In spring the bronze of the alyon's bark would warm to copper, the moss brighten to green, and the forest waken to even more vibrant life.

Were any of them here to see it. If, in fact, the forest itself were here at all.

The death of a Flower Forest was rare, but not unthinkable. The Flower Forests themselves were but the remnants of the great Elven Forests which had once covered the mountains of the east, where now there was little more than sparse grass and a few stunted trees—where anything would grow at all. The forests had been re-seeded before—and could be again, if Lerkalpoldara's was lost.

But the thought of destroying it lest it be defiled by the Enemy was heartbreaking.

Jermayan realized that without noticing he had been straining to hear the sounds of birds, for even in winter the Flower Forests were filled with them. Many had no other home. But there was silence in the trees.

"There are no birds, Jermayan," Magarabeleniel said softly, seeing his face. "Even here." She took a deep breath. "This is my word to you: We will cross the pass. I do not know how many of us will survive the journey, for I know the creatures of the Enemy will not wish to lose their prey, but it is a chance at life, at least for some, and we will take it."

⁂

THE winter days were short this far north, and a few hours after dark, Ancaladar returned.

He was not alone.

"Ancaladar has told me that the Gatekeeper is clear and we may all leave— if we do not mind fighting off Coldwarg, shadewalkers, and herds of serpent-marae," Chalaseniel said, appearing in the doorway of the House of Grass and Wind. He did not sound as if the prospect dismayed him particularly.

Though he had been dressed for riding with the herd, it was still not sufficient protection from the cold of the high sky, but though he looked chilled through, he also looked like someone who had received unexpectedly good news—as indeed he had.

Chalaseniel was co-Viceroy of Lerkalpoldara, Magarabeleniel's brother— reckless where she was prudent, optimistic where she was dour, impetuous where she was cautious, cheerful where she was bleak. Or so the Elves judged them; Jermayan suspected that humans would see little difference between the siblings' behavior at all.

"I have sent the word among the herd-riders. They must bring the talldeer and the horses here as fast as they can, as many as the can manage and still come quickly. We will go as soon as they arrive and the beasts can be set to harness."

If Magarabeleniel was surprised at her brother's unlooked-for arrival, or at his presumption of knowing her mind, she did not show it. "We will burn the forest before we leave," she said calmly, as Chalaseniel went to change his wet and frozen riding leathers.

When he returned, she poured tea, and Chalaseniel seated himself beside Jermayan.

"I See you, Jermayan, son of Malkirinath, Elven Knight, Ancaladar's Bonded," he said formally, now acknowledging Jermayan's presence.

"I See you, Chalaseniel, brother of Magarabeleniel, Viceroy of Lerkalpoldara," Jermayan returned, equally formally.

"You have our gratitude for this," Chalaseniel said simply. "And now, there is much to do."

"Much has been done," Magarabeleniel said. "Elodiane and Tanarakiel oversee the preparation of sledges to carry the tents. Lauryoneth and Sarimarel check to see that the harness is strong and will not break, for we dare not stop to mend it this side of Windalorianan. If we can pass the Gatekeeper, the Enemy can do so as well, unless he is sealed again."

She glanced at Jermayan, the unspoken question plain in her eyes.

"Sealed or unsealed, Lady—and I confess, I am not certain if I am able to seal the pass again—your mountain passes will not stop the creatures of the Enemy from going where they will. They are creatures of Shadow, who thrive upon the dark and the cold."

Magarabeleniel gave a faint shrug. "Then we shall pray for Leaf and Star to favor us, and hope that Windalorianan will look favorably upon us, despite the plague we bring with us."

"It is a plague that will be everywhere in the Elven Lands soon," Jermayan said grimly. "The ancient subject-races of the Enemy—Ice Trolls, snow giants, *duergar*, goblins, and the like—might need the help of the Shadowed Elves to cross the ancient Elven land-wards, but either the monsters of the Enemy's breeding needed no such aid, or they had been smuggled in long since."

"Three days to reach the mountains, another day to reach the pass itself," Chalaseniel said, and now the lightness was gone from his voice. "I think they may toy with us at first. That will give us a day, perhaps two. Then they will begin to attack in earnest. Shadewalkers do not range so far from their home dens, but neither Coldwarg nor serpentmarae have dens, and both will be eager to hunt us."

"If they hunt us, then we shall hunt them," Magarabeleniel said grimly. "They are beasts out of Shadow, but they can be killed, and we have arrows enough for all of them. The weather will hold—Tanarakiel says it will, if the herds arrive no later than tomorrow night, and hard cold makes good running. A chance for any is better than no chance for all."

There was no possible argument with that.

⋙⋙

THE herds of which Chalaseniel had spoken arrived in the middle of the next day. Their arrival was heralded by a great disturbance among the Deathwings, which dove upon them, over and over, in an attempt to pluck the riders from the saddles, or, failing that, blind the herd animals so that they would panic and become easy prey.

But the Elves of Lerkalpoldara possessed many moonturns of experience with their winged enemy. The herd-riders swung from their saddles to the sides of their mounts, firing upward past their horses' shoulders with the short horseman's bow as they clung to their saddles with crooked knees.

Those on the walls fired the Elven longbow, and behind the head of each arrow was a round ball of oil-soaked wool. These they lit from a brazier just before launching their shafts, and shot flaming arrows into the sky. The Deathwings dissolved instantly upon death into a puddle of foul-smelling liquid—and in life, as Jermayan discovered now, they burned like dry hay, if you could only set one properly alight.

Jermayan stood just inside the wall, waiting.

It would do the herds no good to arrive and be trapped outside the walls. Nor would the walls be of any use for protection against the four-footed enemy if they had a hole knocked in them.

"Now," Ancaladar said, his voice a whisper in Jermayan's ear though the dragon soared far above.

Jermayan cast his spell. Several yards of wall . . . vanished.

The herd-riders surged through with the mixed herd of horses and talldeer—quite enough animals to fill the empty enclosure that had once held the Winter City, but, as Jermayan knew from talking to Magarabeleniel and Chalaseniel, many of the animals were intended as bait, to draw the attentions of packs that would follow them for as long as possible.

When they were all through the gap, Jermayan cast another spell, and the wall remade itself again. The two simple spells rippled through his mind easily, and though they were followed by a surge of weakness, it was not as bad as Jermayan feared it would be. His strength was returning rapidly, and with it, he gained new hope for victory in the fight to come.

His task complete, Ancaladar soared off above the clouds, where the Deathwings could not follow—for there certainly was not room for him and the livestock within the walls below.

<hr />

IN the wait for the animals to arrive, much had been accomplished, most of it unthinkable in any time other than this. Many of the smaller trees of the Flower

Forest had been cut down to clear a space for the Lerkalpoldarans to work. The carts which carried their tents in summer had been converted to sledges to move the same tents over winter's ice, for they would need their protection on the journey. Everything that was not essential would be left behind, to be burned along with the Flower Forest. But that left an entire city of clothing, food, tents, and weapons to move.

Chalaseniel and Magarabeleniel had decided that their best hope of avoiding immediate ambush was to leave at dusk. The Deathwings would probably depart then, and even starlight on snow would give the Elves enough light to see by over the first part of their journey.

But many will die. Perhaps all, yet with more hope than if they did not make the attempt. And there is no chance to fly anyone to the Crowned Horns now, even if they would go, for the baskets for the journey were to have been made here, and now there is no time for that, Jermayan thought.

Talldeer, Jermayan discovered, were not quite like deer at all. They were beasts nearly as large as horses, superbly adapted for the cold. They had the split hooves and small flat heads of deer, but their antlers were enormous, far heavier and thicker than those of the small red deer of the south. They produced wool like sheep, which was the majority of the wool the Lerkalpoldarans used for their rugs and tents.

The talldeer were also the primary draft animal used on the Plains of Bazrahil, and now, as Jermayan watched, the Lerkalpoldarans began to harness them in hitches of twelve. No reins or bridles were used, only traces and collars. Normally the talldeer wagons followed the rest of the herd, or if necessary the hitch could be led by someone holding the headstall of the leader.

"Oh, they will run when the herd runs—and the herd will run, with riders to goad it," Elodiane said, seeing Jermayan's expression. "You should be grateful you will be in the heavens far above, on the back of a nice, safe dragon."

It was hardly the way Jermayan would think of it himself, but at the moment he was grateful that he would not be either one of the sledge-drivers or one of those who were mounted. That would be most of the Winter City's population, whose task it would be to drive the supply wagons and the herd of remounts onward as fast as possible, across a landscape which afforded no cover, no place where they could rest and recover from the assaults that would surely come.

The herd-riders switched their saddles to fresh horses as the talldeer were harnessed, and more horses were saddled. These were not Vardirvoshan-bred destriers, but they were magnificent animals for all that, strong and fast, bred to work and to run beneath the sky.

Many of them were carrying packs as well, for the co-Viceroys had made plans within plans, and in the ultimate extremity the Lerkalpoldarans would flee on horseback, abandoning the talldeer and the sledges as a further sacrifice to the Coldwarg, carrying with them nothing but food for the horses. It was better to arrive in Windalorianan starving and in rags than not at all.

By sunset everything was ready, and the space within the walls of the Winter City was uncomfortably crowded. The life of an entire city had been packed into thirty sledges, and its citizens, save for those who still watched the walls, sat their horses like the most disciplined of cavalry.

"I shall remain to light the forest," Magarabeleniel said, her voice soft with grief.

"No," Jermayan said. "I shall do that. And if you are prepared, I shall open the wall once more."

"I think it would be best," Chalaseniel said. "It grows . . . crowded here, cousin. And I have never liked walls overmuch!"

With a gesture, Jermayan caused a section of wall to vanish. It was only a small spell, and he was grateful to see that each time he called upon his Magery it came more easily. Riders began streaming through the gap at once, followed by sledges and the herd of free-running talldeer and horses. As soon as there was space, the sentinels came down from the walls to claim their own mounts, and followed the others. The cries of encouragement and whistles of the herders were soon dimmed by the wind.

Jermayan looked up into the sky. The clouds had fled with evening, and the sky was dark blue, showing the first stars of night. A darker shadow blotted out those stars, and then Ancaladar landed.

"Mucky," the dragon said fastidiously, lifting first one foot then the next.

"It was a great many animals in a very small space," Jermayan said apologetically, gathering up Ancaladar's harness. Once the dragon was harnessed, they were quickly aloft.

"So far, so good," Ancaladar said, glancing down at the refugees. They formed a dark line against the snow, nearly a mile in length, and were obviously running flat-out. He'd better tell Chalaseniel and Magarabeleniel to rein them in soon, or they'd simply exhaust their beasts now, and they had scores of leagues yet to travel.

But there was another task to complete first. He and Ancaladar turned back toward Lerkalpoldara.

Fire was the simplest and easiest spell, the first learned by any Mage, no matter what Path they followed. With Ancaladar's power to draw upon, Jermayan could burn air, or rock.

How much simpler, then, to burn that which was meant to burn?

He reached down.

The entire forest came alight at once, every tree bursting into flame in the same moment. The heat rolled out from it in every direction, melting the ice around the forest and exposing the winter-parched grass on the ground beneath. It was brighter than the sun of the dull winter's day; it was summer ripped out of its proper season and chained to earth, and it roared with the injustice of it, a constant sound almost like falling water. The heat created an updraft that Ancaladar had to fly around, just as if the furnace air were a pillar of marble that had suddenly sprouted out of the ice.

In moments the grass exposed by the melted ice had baked dry and begun to kindle, though the melting snow around it would keep the grass fire from spreading far. The constant trickle of melt into the fire made steam, and added a high hissing sound to the deep roaring note of the burning. The wind blew the smoke sideways, but the steam swirled above it, the two billows silver and black.

But no amount of snowmelt could save the forest from its fate. The trees were blackened now, their leaves gone, their remaining branches skeletal. It was impossible to tell what had been vilya, what alyon, what *namanar* and orchad and lemuri. The forest floor was ash that swirled and danced in the wind caused by the burning. All that existed was the red-gold of fire.

The radiant heat had begun to melt the walls of the winter city as well. They glistened like soft custard, running with water, their tops already humped and shapeless. The inside of the walls curved outward now, as if they, too, were attempting to escape the heat of the burning forest, and a fan of water poured out through the gap that Jermayan had made in the wall, softening the riders' tracks in the snow. The water froze again to ice as it spread farther from the fire.

As Jermayan watched, a portion of the standing wall around the Winter City collapsed under its own now-uneven weight. Now more and more of the wall began to collapse, melting away from the edges of the central gap.

The trees of the Flower Forest, wasted away to cinders by the conflagration, began to fall into the flame. The sound of their collapse was not audible above the roar of the burning, but each one that fell released a dense cloud of gold and white sparks that swirled on the updraft. They fell into the ragged pennon of smoke and steam. The center of the forest, where the heat had been greatest, was already gone entirely, and the trees that surrounded that center had been sharpened by the flames to spearpoints. Their crowns were gone, toppled away into the inferno. Their smaller branches had been burned away entirely and the larger ones had been set afire, burning where they grew until they were consumed entirely or had burned through close to the trunk, leaving the weight of the branch to fall free into the fire below. Now all that was left was a ragged forest of spikes, their broken and uneven points jabbing into a sickly orange sky.

Another section of the wall collapsed, caving mushily, as if it were made of wet sand.

Satisfied at last that the forest was dead beyond all rescue, Jermayan and Ancaladar flew after the others.

⬱

THE first attack occurred at dawn a day later.

They were given that much grace at least: a night and a day and a night to race across the snow toward the Gatekeeper, knowing every minute, every mile, was precious ground gained. They did not stop, though after the first exodus from Lerkalpoldara the convoy moved only at the walk. Riders stopped to change for remounts and rode on. At slightly longer intervals, one of the sledges would change its team, releasing its exhausted animals into the larger herd. That was all.

Though it was seemingly effortless, and hardly faster than the pace an Elf on foot might keep, the toll it took on both beast and Elf was brutal, for there was no rest for either. Many of the animals fell behind—too tired to go on, or simply unwilling to be driven further; they fell to their knees in the snow or simply stood, heads hanging, staring miserably after the retreating herd.

Water was the most precious commodity, for one of the things that had to be left behind in Lerkalpoldara was the bulky collections of mirrors and catchbasins that melted snow and ice and turned them into warm, drinkable water. And there was no time now to stop and build a fire to melt snow.

There at least Jermayan could aid them. The spell that would temporarily unfreeze a mile or so of river as they passed, so that the animals could drink and be on their way again quickly, was a simple one and did not drain him. His Mage-strength grew with each passing hour; when the time came, his power might, perhaps, be enough.

The convoy lost animals at the rivers as well. Some waded out to where the river turned icy again and drowned, some drank so much they made themselves sick, some simply refused to leave the riverbank, for the talldeer were not used to being driven this way.

The main force went on.

Jermayan and Ancaladar flew above the long column, watching for pursuers. They'd expected trouble at the dawn of the first day, but not even Deathwings were visible in the sky, and no Coldwarg were to be seen upon the ground. Even the smoke of the burning Flower Forest had long since blown away, and when Jermayan and Ancaladar returned to overfly the site of the city, they saw that the trees themselves, and such things as the Elves had left behind, had been reduced to cinders and ash at the center of a glistening disk of flawless ice. The melted snow had re-frozen as smoothly as a mirror around the ruins of what had once been the Winter City.

All through that day their luck had held, and on into the night. Another day and night would see them into the foothills and forests at the base of the mountains, where Magarabeleniel hoped to rest the animals before beginning the climb to the Gatekeeper. Though Jermayan had cleared the pass itself, the road to the pass was still choked with ice. He had not tampered with it yet, knowing he must save his power to help the Lerkalpoldarans deal with what might be following them.

As it developed, he was grateful that he had.

At dawn of their second day on the march, Jermayan heard a distant chorus of howls greet the rising sun. Those below him heard it as well: From his vantage point high above, Jermayan saw a ripple of movement pass through the animals below, as horses that had been plodding through the snow a moment before were now lifting their heads to sniff the wind nervously. The talldeer jostled for position, preparing to fight.

It was not coming from behind them—*No*, thought Jermayan wearily, *that would render things far too simple*—but from in front. The long absence of the Coldwarg from their trail was now explained: They had been making a great circle around the convoy, a circle so wide that Jermayan and Ancaladar had not seen it, and now they were attacking from directly ahead.

The wind was blowing toward the convoy, and the pack was still several miles off. The Lerkalpoldarans' animals could hear them, though were not yet sure where they were.

"Magarabeleniel—Chalaseniel—the Coldwarg pack lies ahead," Jermayan said, using a simple spell to carry his words to their ears alone.

"There is worse," Ancaladar said tersely.

Without pausing to consult Jermayan, the black dragon wheeled around, carrying Jermayan back along the way they had come. In a moment, Jermayan saw what Ancaladar had seen.

A herd of serpentmarae was following them.

Serpentmarae were often used as riding animals by the Creatures of the Dark. They vaguely resembled small misshapen horses, but with cloven hooves, wolf-yellow eyes, and the sharp fangs of flesh-eaters. Their mottled mud-colored skin was hairless, as were the long whip-like tails that had given them their names. Their preferred method of killing a group of victims was to trap them in the center of the herd and then trample them to death, but their sharp fangs were just as effective as a means of killing their victims.

With a gesture, Jermayan summoned lightning down from a cloudless sky. The bolt sizzled as it split the air, and struck the herd dead-center with a bright flare of light. Bodies—and charred pieces of bodies—flew in all directions. The handful of survivors staggered slowly away from the crater Jermayan had made and then began to flee from the convoy.

Though the attack had not pained him, a few more such would truly weaken him, and he could not afford that so early in their flight. As little as he liked the idea, Jermayan must hold back from doing all he could, for if he exhausted himself here, there was no chance of resting this side of Windalorianan, and his magic might be even more vital later. He unwrapped his Elven Bow from its protective covering as Ancaladar turned in the direction of the Coldwarg pack.

"There are more serpentmarae," Ancaladar said, resignation in his voice, "but they are several hours away."

"We will deal with them when we must," Jermayan said. "The Coldwarg pack is here now."

Coldwarg were difficult to kill. They were nearly as large as serpentmarae, and far more savage, for they had no other purpose in the world than to kill any creature they could clamp their jaws around.

Ancaladar flew low over the pack, and Jermayan fired. Every arrow hit its mark, but he quickly realized that unless he managed to take one of the creatures directly in the heart, he could expend an entire quiver on one of them without killing it, and flying over the pack the angle was such that a heart-shot was difficult to get. He continued to cast spells upon the pack as much as he dared—Fire was one that did not strain his resources, and it would kill as well as any other.

But he could not kill them all.

Ancaladar's approach was more direct. He simply dipped low enough to seize the creatures in his foreclaws, one by one, and twisted them in half.

A few miles behind, the Lerkalpoldarans had made their preparations as well. They well knew that their convoy could not outrun the Coldwarg pack, nor outmaneuver it—the creatures had been bred to take down unicorns, after all—so their only hope left was to outthink it.

The riders of the sledges abandoned them and mounted horses. They separated out the horses from the talldeer herd; if it were possible afterward, they would reclaim the talldeer herd and their possessions.

By now the animals had caught the scent of what hunted them. Without the horses to hold them back, the talldeer turned in a body and began to veer away from the horses, picking up speed as they saw they were not stopped, until they were running as fast as they could.

All of the riders strung their bows and nocked arrows, bunched their horses and the unsaddled stock, and waited. And a few—a very few—of the bravest of the Elves dismounted and prepared to do battle on foot, for the Elven longbow could not be used from horseback.

Not all of Ancaladar's depredations upon the pack, nor Jermayan's careful sparing spells, had discouraged the pack's survivors, who seemed to understand that the inhabitants of an entire Elven city were attempting to escape the wrath of their Endarkened allies. Even while the convoy was settling itself into position, the first Coldwarg appeared.

The convoy was not an army, and they had no true leader. A human city would at least have had a city Militia, and even a city guard, but Elven cities had no such things, for to offend against good taste and good manners was unthinkable. Their Knights and their Scouts defended the Elven Cities from danger arising from without: Lerkalpoldara's Knights were all away at war, and her Scouts were used to acting independently.

It was almost enough.

The archers shot at whim and random, without plan. The first Coldwarg died under a longbowyer's arrow, for the range of a longbow was farther than that of a horseman's bow, but she was only the fastest of a pack that still numbered in dozens. Others followed, and the archers did not slay them all.

Jermayan and Ancaladar were busy enough. They were circling the bunched Elves from above, firing down at the Coldwarg.

Though Jermayan could call down Fire, he could not be everywhere at once. And so he was helpless to do much more than watch as one of the Coldwarg eluded death at the arrows of the archers and reached the Elven band. It broke through the line, followed by half a dozen of its fellows, snapping and slaughtering in a mad frenzy as the horses nearest to it plunged madly to escape.

The convoy was ringed by the Coldwarg pack. Any of the horses that tried to bolt through the ring of circling Coldwarg would be instantly cut down.

The Elves frantically tried to destroy the predators in their midst. They succeeded, cutting the Coldwarg down with axes and spears, but the cost was high: ten or a dozen Elves slain for every Coldwarg life ended. Beyond the immediate range of the herd, Jermayan and Ancaladar did all they could to ravage the pack, decreasing its numbers as best they could. Jermayan had discovered that an arrow fired from directly above would pierce a Coldwarg's heart and kill one of the beasts, but to make the shot required perfect timing and absolute concentration, and as good as he was, Jermayan often missed.

The pack had quickly learned that the vast black shadow in the sky meant danger, and scattered quickly the moment Ancaladar swooped down from above. But such momentary intermissions in their attacks gave little respite to the

Lerkalpoldarans. Jermayan's only hope was that together he and Ancaladar could kill enough of the Coldwarg to make the creatures break off their attack and flee.

As the dragon and his rider pulled up from one such dive, they saw movement in the sky from the east. Flying toward them, their motion a ponderous parody of that of their smaller cave-bat cousins, were several score Deathwings, as many as had circled the Winter City two days before.

They could not be allowed to reach the convoy. They would swoop down among the massed Elves, pluck riders from horseback, and toss their victims to the waiting Coldwarg. Jermayan did not know who they took their orders from here— he hoped there was no Enclave of the Shadowed Elves this far north—but from all Chalaseniel and Magarabeleniel had told him, these Deathwings behaved much as the ones that followed the army had, whether they were following orders or not.

He must abandon the Elves on the ground to fend for themselves against the Coldwarg to deal with an enemy only he and Ancaladar could fight.

In moments they were close enough to see the glitter of the pale winter morning sunlight on the Deathwings' flat black eyes. The Deathwings bore a faint resemblance to Coldwarg, with their long canine muzzles and sharp carnivorous teeth. They might deliver prey into Coldwarg jaws, but they would probably quarrel over the remains later.

You should not have come, Jermayan thought toward them grimly.

In the south, they had not known how easily the Deathwings burned. Now Jermayan set the nearest ones afire with a thought.

The winged monsters burned like pitch-soaked torches, keening wild soundless death-cries that made Jermayan feel as if some invisible force was pressing his head between two giant hands. In their death-agonies, they veered wildly in circles, some crashing into each other before they plummeted to earth.

Weariness pulled at him like quicksand, warning him to cease his labors— Fire was a simple spell, but he had been casting it for what seemed like hours— but he dared not stop. Now he and Ancaladar were the pursuers, hunting the Deathwings across the sky with merciless ferocity.

When they were gone, he saw no more.

They turned back to the convoy, scanning the ground below as they flew. Riderless horses—both saddled and unsaddled—fled from the battle; Chalaseniel had released the herd, maddened to panic by the presence of so many predators, hoping to draw off the pack. A few Coldwarg loped after them, harrying their heels, but the main body of the pack remained with the mounted Elves. The snow around the Elves was churned to red mud. Coldwarg bodies lay upon the snow, and living Coldwarg toyed with the bodies of the dead and—horribly—the dying. The screams came faintly to Jermayan's ears.

He set another arrow to his bowstring and carefully took aim at a new target.

It was brutal, agonizing work; not quick, without easy victory. Hundreds of Elves died to kill a pack of less than three-score Coldwarg.

When the last white-furred body lay dead upon the snow, Jermayan made a broad circle to look for the talldeer and the horses.

He came upon a slaughter.

The talldeer, fleeing from the Coldwarg, had blundered directly into the following serpentmarae. The talldeer that were running free had been able to make their escape, but those yoked to the sledges had been easy prey.

Terrible as it was, the beasts' sacrifice had bought the fleeing Elves time, for the serpentmarae had lingered over their kills, and lingered longer to feed. Now they wandered slowly in the direction of the convoy, but almost certainly would trail the convoy without attacking until hunger—or superior numbers—made the thought of attacking attractive once again.

Jermayan returned to the convoy to replenish his supply of arrows and give what aid he could to the wounded.

HE was able to report what he had seen to Chalaseniel and Magarabeleniel, who made the decision to try to recover the sledges and round up what talldeer and remounts could be gathered quickly.

Only twenty of the sledges had usable harness. Salvaging what harness they could, and rounding up the herd animals, took precious hours they did not have. But there was no choice. The supplies and the remounts were as precious as sleep. Or water.

There was no room to carry their dead with them. They could lay them out decorously in the clean snow before they left. That was all.

IT took twice as long as they had expected to reach the Gatekeeper—a full sennight. As Tanarakiel had foreseen, on the fourth day out from the Winter City, the weather had failed, bringing heavy snow.

It was that, paradoxically, that had saved their lives. The Coldwarg and the serpentmarae had harried them across the plains—though the Deathwings had not returned after Jermayan's first decisive victory over them—winnowing their numbers slowly but inexorably.

The hellbeasts had been no more bitter an enemy than the cold. The Lerkalpoldarans said it was cold enough to freeze fire, though Jermayan did not put the local saying to the test. It was the cold that made leather brittle and delicate, no matter how lavishly it was greased, and when enough pieces of a harness broke, the sledge its talldeer were pulling had to be abandoned.

Night and day, they did not stop. Every hour, every mile, was precious. They made camp only to brew tea, to allow the animals with them to eat and drink, before moving on. True children of the Plains, the Elves slept in their saddles and wagons. For food, they butchered the animals that dropped from exhaustion on the long march. When they had left Lerkelpoldara, they had packed little food for themselves, knowing this was what they would do. Nearly all the space they could spare in the sledges was packed with fodder for the animals. But even so, they drove the talldeer onward in nearly starving condition; a mark of their true desperation.

When the snow came the harsh cold lessened, the temperature rising nearly to freezing. The serpentmarae fled for shelter and even the Coldwarg dropped back out of sight.

It had taken them five days to reach the foothills, when it should have, by Chalaseniel's estimation, have taken three. But they had reached them at last, and there was wood to burn and shelter from the wind and the snow.

In summer this would be the foot of the trail that led over the mountain, and the trail would be clearly visible. Now, in the middle of a winter snowstorm, with their horses floundering through snow to their withers, to believe that there was a path here at all required an act of faith.

Jermayan did what he could to clear it. His spellcasting against the Death-wings had tired him, and that strength had not been easily regained, here in the High Cold. But it was enough to ease their way.

They had paused in the foothills long enough to eat, and to make a final disposition of the nine sledges that still remained, and to rest a few hours.

Then they had begun the ascent to the Gatekeeper itself.

The combination of the storm and the air-currents near the mountain wall were such that scout-flying was now impossible for Ancaladar and Jermayan, and would have been even if Jermayan had possessed the full resources of an Elven Mage to wield. They could wait behind, or wait ahead, but they could do nothing else. In any event, they would not be able to see the Lerkalpoldarans through the trees and the blinding snow. Jermayan left them Coldfire to light their way, and he and Ancaladar went on ahead.

If he had not, none of them would have reached the summit.

⁓

"I smell something," Ancaladar said.

They stood within the pass itself. Bare rock it might have been a sennight before, but it was already filling with snow that would soon pack down to ice. Fortunately the constant winds at this altitude blew most of it away. The Gatekeeper would remain passable for some days yet.

Without Ancaladar, Jermayan would have frozen where he stood, but the dragon's body radiated heat like a furnace. Jermayan stood beside him, within the shelter of one half-spread wing. It was, he reflected, the first time he'd been truly warm since they'd left Lerkalpoldara.

"It cannot be good," Jermayan said uneasily.

"Magarabeleniel said the city's scouts thought there was an ice-drake somewhere on the plains, did she not? And indeed, I thought I smelled one as we landed."

"It is true that they suspected the presence of one, though they were not certain."

"It is not on the plains—not anymore," Ancaladar said with certainty. "I believe we should find it before it finds her people."

Wearily, Jermayan mounted once more. Ancaladar folded his wings tightly against his body and trotted down out of the pass, until there was space to launch himself into the air.

The Lerkalpoldarans were still in the trees below, invisible. The ice-drake's lair would probably be above the tree-line, where it was colder. But it would be quickly drawn to the heat of prey.

Even if he were at the height of his powers, no spell Jermayan knew had any effect upon an ice-drake, and Ancaladar had barely defeated the last one they had encountered.

But we do not need to kill this one, Jermayan realized. *We only need to keep it from killing the Lerkalpoldarans.*

⚒

"THERE," Ancaladar said at last, indicating a cave in the ice below. Even without his Bonded's heightened sense of smell, Jermayan would have known that *something* laired there, for the path to the entrance was polished smooth by the passage of a long heavy body. "I would never be so slovenly in leaving a path to my lair," the dragon said disparagingly.

"It is not as if anyone wishes to seek out ice-drakes," Jermayan answered soothingly. "There is no reason for it to hide as you were forced to. But now we must draw it out."

"That is a simple matter, simply done," Ancaladar said. He landed on the slope below the cave, and waited.

They were only on the ground for a few moments before the ice-drake appeared. A wave of bone-numbing cold preceded it, and at that warning, Ancaladar flung himself into the air—not a moment too soon, for the long ice-white serpentine body whipped out from its hole with stunning speed, a fog of poison breathing from the ice-drake's jaws as the creature swung its head about, looking for its prey.

Ancaladar landed again, farther down the slope, luring his enemy onward, and the ice-drake obligingly rushed forward. This time, the black dragon barely made it into the air in time to evade the creature's attack. It rose up on its coils, exhaling a thick fog of poison.

Ancaladar wheeled around and struck the ice-drake from above and behind, seizing it, as he had the other he had fought, just behind the head.

This time he did not waste time in trying to kill it, nor did Jermayan spend any of his own energy on anything but Healing spells to save his friend from the worst of the monster's cold-damage. This time Ancaladar simply flew as high and as far as he could, doing his best to keep the wildly-thrashing serpent from striking his wings, or from coiling itself around his body.

"I see a lake," Ancaladar gasped, when they were well across the valley.

"Yes," Jermayan said, understanding what was in his Bondmate's mind.

With a groan of relief, Ancaladar released the ice-drake.

It plummeted through the air, thrashing helplessly, and Ancaladar spiraled down after it to watch its fall. They flew beneath the low clouds, to where they could see the dark star of water in the center of the frozen lake where its impact had shattered the thick sheet of ice.

But the lake was already freezing again—this time from within, frozen by the ice-drake's radiant cold. The ice-drake's head appeared above the surface as it churned the freezing slurry in its frantic attempts to escape, but though it thrashed madly, it could only get a small portion of its length near the surface, and was unable to pull itself out onto the unbroken ice. Jermayan and Ancaladar could see that the lake was obviously freezing faster than the creature could pull itself free of the water, and in a few moments it would be held fast beyond all escape.

The lake itself would entomb the creature until it melted in the spring—if a solid block of ice with an ice-drake at its heart ever would melt—when the very warmth that had liberated the ice-drake might do what magic could not. Assuming of course that the ice-drake did not starve before then.

At the very least, the east was safe from this ice-drake for now.

"Let us return and tell the Lerkalpoldarans of their good fortune," Ancaladar said, with a sigh of relief.

"It will be a pleasure to have good news to share, for once," Jermayan agreed.

OVER a thousand souls had left the walls of Lerkalpoldara's Winter City. A few days later, just under three hundred stood at the top of the pass with Jermayan and Ancaladar. It was only by the grace of Leaf and Star that among their number could be counted all of the women with child whom Jermayan had originally come to Lerkalpoldara to bring away.

They had succeeded in keeping six sledges out of the original thirty with them, though they no longer had any draft animals running free. There were no spare horses left, either; the remount herd was gone, most ridden to exhaustion or death, the few survivors abandoned in the foothills.

Magarabeleniel ruled alone now. Last night, as Jermayan had fought to protect their rear guard from Coldwarg following them across the ice, Chalaseniel had died among those fighting a shadewalker. There had been no time to stop to mourn him; no chance to recover his body, just as there had been no chance to honor any of the seven hundred who had died, whether by the jaws or hooves of monsters, or from cold, frost-burn, or simple exhaustion.

"Now you must leave us," Magarabeleniel said to him simply. "You have Andoreniel's work to do, and we must go to Windalorianan, to tell Vanantiriel and Leamrainsia that Lerkalpoldara is fallen, and we are all that remain. The fortune of Leaf and Star go with you and with Ancaladar on your journey."

"And with all of you. And may Leaf and Star grant that we see you again on a happier day," Jermayan answered.

"Let it be so," Magarabeleniel said. She turned her horse's head and rode to the top of the column, and the riders moved slowly off through the blowing snow.

⇌

BEFORE he left the Gatekeeper, there was one last task Jermayan wished to perform. He was not sure if he could, but he wished to try, for the sake of Magarabeleniel and her people.

And here and now it should not be so difficult.

He stretched out his hands toward the pass.

A shimmering curtain of ice began to form in the air, soap-bubble-thin at first, then becoming thicker. It spread to the walls of the pass, and rose to the very top, in moments becoming a wall thicker and higher than those that had circled the lost Winter City, sealing the pass against anything that might wish to follow as unequivocally as a wall of solid rock.

If the monsters that now roamed the Plains of Bazrahil wished to cross the pass, they would have to work for the privilege.

Five

The Best of All Beginnings

O UTSIDE YSTERIALPOERIN, A fortnight after Jermayan's departure, the army held a council of war.

They were still awaiting new orders from Andoreniel, and the silence was beginning to worry all of the Senior Commanders, Redhelwar most of all. His forces were still not yet fully battle-ready, though another fortnight, at most, should see the majority of the Allies prepared to fight.

Most unsettling of all, they had no clear idea of *who* to fight. Vestakia had still not been able to discover from the Crystal Spiders where the next—and Leaf and Star grant, the *last*—Enclave of the Shadowed Elves lay, nor did Redhelwar dare move his army against any lesser threat.

❧

IT was not a small group that was gathered in Redhelwar's tent, though since the Battle of the Further Caverns, and the Battle for the Heart of the Forest, some long-familiar faces were absent from the strategy meeting, and would be forever. Nor was it restricted entirely to the Elves, for the Allied Senior Commanders were there as well.

In addition to Padredor, Adaerion, Arambor, Belepheriel, and Ninolion, Rulorwen, Master of the Engineers, had been newly raised in rank. Though he and his command were not mounted Knights, Rulorwen's quiet promise was that if something held still long enough, he and his people would destroy it, tunnel beneath it, dismantle it for the army's later use, or build a bridge across it.

There were also two Elven sub-commanders present, for their specialized work for the army was vital: Artenal, Master of the Armorers, whose work it was to come up with new weapons and armor to deal with the evolving threats that the army faced; and Riasen, who had become captain of the Unicorn Knights upon Petariel's death.

Idalia was there both as Wildmage and as chief of the Healers, who were drawn from every race that marched with the army.

Kerleu, Wirance, and Kearn attended to represent the High Reaches Wild-mages and the Mountainfolk, including the farmers from the Wildlands who had fled to the High Reaches when Armethalieh had expanded her borders and had answered Andoreniel's call for levies instead of returning home, adding their numbers to the small but valued cadre of Mountainborn foot troops. At home the Mountainfolk were organized first by families, then by clans, and at last the clans were gathered into houses. To an outsider, the Mountainborn organization looked like anarchy at best, madness at worst, for it was a structure designed to acknowledge the harsh realities of life in the High Reaches, where at the beginning of winter, no man—or woman—might be sure they would see the spring.

As such, though they were fierce warriors, who did all and more that Red-helwar asked of them, they simply did not have the same sort of organization that either the Elves or the Centaurs did. What Kerleu, Wirance, and Kearn heard here would be carried back to the Mountainfolk camp to be discussed among them all, with a final decision reached only after hours—perhaps days—of arguing.

Atroist was here for the Lostlander Wildmages, and Feyrt was here as the leader of the Lostlander fighting men. Though the villages were autonomous at home, here Feyrt had been elected absolute leader of all the warriors—Belrix, or War King—in a move unprecedented in Lostlander history. Though their numbers were small, they had already proven to be terrifyingly expert fighters, adept with their ancestral weapon, the *murragh*, or steelbride—a massive sword which, blade to pommel, stood taller than a tall man. Razor sharp and heavy as a war-axe, the *murragh* took much training to use properly, but it was said that an expert wielder could behead a running horse or slice a lightly armored man in half with one blow.

Feyrt deferred to Atroist in all matters where the Wild Magic chose to give counsel, of course, for the Lostlanders lived more closely than any other folk with the power of the Wild Magic, since it had been their only defense against the constant raids of the Dark Folk, as they called Demons.

Kellen was there; that went without saying. He was the army's only Knight-Mage; the only Knight-Mage there *was*, so far as anyone knew, and the only one born in the last thousand years. This particular form of the Wild Magic gave an instinctive understanding of battle and war. Which didn't mean Kellen always knew what he knew. Or that other people believed that he knew it.

Cilarnen was there as well, though he had no true right to be, being neither a fighter nor one whose work was to support the fighters. But of all of them— even Kellen—he was the one who best understood Armethalieh, and he was the one who could best advise Redhelwar and the others in how to deal with her.

And dealing with Armethalieh was one of their many priorities.

Kellen had not seen Cilarnen since Kindolhinadetil had made his odd gift of books, and he was shocked at how changed Cilarnen seemed. The boy had lost weight—his skin was tightly drawn across the bones of his face and there were dark shadows beneath his eyes. He wondered if Cilarnen was still having his headaches, and if the Healers had discovered the cause. He promised himself he would make time to see Cilarnen after this meeting was over, and find out how his work was progressing.

The traditional Elven formalities were shortened—out of respect to the humans and the Centaurs—to a single ceremonious round of tea.

"We begin by hearing reports and sharing information in this informal manner," Redhelwar said. "I regret to inform you all that fresh word has not yet come from Sentarshadeen."

There was a moment of dismayed silence as those present heard Redhelwar's news.

"Vestakia is making some progress in her task at least," Idalia said with a rueful sigh. "She has ruled out the north and the east as locations for a Shadowed Elf Enclave—the lands around Windalorianan, Deskethomaynel, and Lerkalpoldara. Unfortunately, with the new encroachments, she's starting to get, well, *interference* from the increased Enemy activity along our Borders and within the Elven Lands themselves. So far it isn't bad, but if it gets worse, opening herself to link to the Spiders will become difficult, if not impossible."

"So we had better have an answer before then."

Kreylmedd was the warchief of the Centaurs, Redhelwar's liaison to the Centaur camp, here with his lieutenants Siust and Truanolm. The three of them, between them, spoke for the Centaur army. In times of peace Kreylmedd was a landholder and a council member in the village of Mossmeade, and the beer he brewed was famed throughout the Wild Lands. Siust was a blacksmith said to be able to work iron fine enough to shoe the wind, whose forge held many fine young apprentices and journeymen, and had produced more than one master smith. Truanolm was a miller, whose eight sons and five daughters held much of the land between Merryknoll and Greenlaw, and whose fields kept his grindstones turning constantly.

But fifty generations ago their ancestors had fought beside the Elves against Shadow Mountain, and if the Centaurs had forgotten much else about that time, they had not forgotten the need to be ready. Each generation they trained and prepared their Centaur warriors, even though they saw no more of battle than keeping the peace at country fairs and occasional run-ins with bandits and outlaws.

Now the Centaurs were the backbone of Redhelwar's army, for the Centaur nation was more numerous than the Elves. They fought as his heavy cavalry—infantry: slower-moving than an Elven Knight mounted on a destrier, but massive and unstoppable.

"We will hope that she does, for if she does not, we will not be able to strike at the next Enclave of the Shadowed Elves. But whether we can do this or not, we must also find a way to warn the human city of the treachery she nurtures within," Adaerion said.

"Tell Armethalieh anything? Herdsman guide you," Kreylmedd said with a cynical snort.

"To warn the City of a Thousand Bells is only one of many priorities," Redhelwar said, summoning the meeting back to order. "The Frost Giants are gathering beyond Deskethomaynel, and in a moonturn their shamans will be able to batter through the land-wards and the Frost Giants and their kindred will walk the Elven Lands unopposed. There is plague in both Deskethomaynel and Windalorianan—it brings fever and delirium, and many are stricken. There have been no deaths yet, but they are expected.

"And this day, at last, riders have come from Deskethomaynel, bringing terrible news. Lerkalpoldara is no more. Its Flower Forest is gone."

There was a moment of stunned silence from the Elves in the tent.

"They were besieged by the beasts of the Shadow, their passes sealed by winter, their numbers too few to defend themselves—not that any defense would have been possible against *Them*."

Kellen groaned inwardly. This was hardly the sort of talk he wanted to hear from the army's general, especially when he was talking to his senior commanders.

"When Jermayan went to the Winter City upon Andoreniel's orders, he saw how it was with them," Redhelwar continued. "By the grace of Leaf and Star, Jermayan and Ancaladar were able to unseal the pass leading out of the valley and help in the evacuation, but losses were yet heavy. At the pass he had to leave them to make their own way to Windalorianan while he flew on to Deskethomaynel, from which he sends this message, so he knows not how many of the three hundred survivors of the city reached their destination."

"Leaf and Star deliver us," Belepheriel said softly. "One of the Nine is gone."

"Believe me, I share your grief," Kerleu of the High Reaches said, "but before I came to this council I spoke over distance with my home village. My wife tells me there is sickness there as well—perhaps of the same sort that has stricken your cities—and in the other villages nearby. She says that the Forest Wife has warned her that sickness will soon come to the plants of the forest as well, and the Huntsman warns that the monsters our cousins of the Lost Lands have long feared and fought are now moving into our domain."

"They can be fought," Feyrt said simply. "But your losses will be heavy. The story-songs tell us that the first year the Dark Folk came to ravage us, after we had gone to live in the Lost Lands, half of all the Folk died before we learned how to fight them and win."

"That is no comfort," Kerleu snapped, "when we have stripped the High Reaches of her Wildmages and fighting folk to come here and die in Elven Lands! We'd meant to draw the Enemy to us, but instead *They* seem to be every-where but here—in our homes, and at our children's throats!"

"What are we to do?" Redhelwar said aloud, as if he were alone in the tent.

Everyone, including Redhelwar, looked toward Kellen.

When he had first ridden off to war—it seemed like a century ago now!—Kellen had been the only one who knew it really *was* a war, and that Shadow Mountain was as serious about destroying them in the here-and-now as it had been a thousand years ago. Then, he had realized that the only way to get the Elves to believe him—and to follow a battlefield strategy that had any hope of winning—was to teach them to trust, not Kellen-the-teenager, but Kellen-the-Knight-Mage.

Apparently he'd succeeded.

He took a deep breath.

"*They* want us to scatter our forces," he said, beginning with what they all knew. "*They* want us to try to hold the whole of the Elven Border against *Them*, and it can't be done. *They* are trying to pull us in every direction at once. Warning Armethalieh has to be our highest priority—*not* because it was once my home, and still is Cilarnen's, and not because it is the largest human city, but because if *They* take it *They* will become too powerful to be stopped. If warning Armethalieh won't work, we have to keep *Them* from taking it by some other way."

The others regarded him intently, the humans and Centaurs nodding but still not yet convinced, the Elves gazing at him alertly.

"As for the Frost Giants . . ."

Kellen took a deep breath.

"Lerkelpoldara is gone. That can't be changed. Evacuate Windalorianan and Deskethomaynel as well. Bring the inhabitants here to help hold Ysterialpoerin—perhaps the sickness Jermayan mentions will decrease once the inhabitants arrive here, and if not, Ysterialpoerin has fine healers.

"I know travel is hard in winter, especially this winter, but those who can should travel farther into the south. Ondoladeshiron, Realthataladon, Thultafoniseen, Valwendigorean, and Sentarshadeen are all to the south and west of here, and as yet they are some distance from the encroachments. It should be spring before they are in real danger, and many of the Enemy's creatures will simply retreat into the north in the warm seasons."

"So you would simply abandon the east to our enemy," Redhelwar said, and his voice was so inflectionless it did not even hold a question.

"I think these attacks are a feint," Kellen answered. "If we do not take their bait, they will withdraw, and concentrate their forces elsewhere. But whether they do or not, we cannot hold all the Elven Lands with the forces we have. Your cities are small and widely scattered. The Endarkened use that against you, concentrating their forces against each city one at a time and destroying it before moving on to the next. And I think that once they see that we don't mean to turn our forces east to fight them, they'll stop provoking us there and move on to another attack point." *Probably in the west,* Kellen thought bleakly.

"Concentrating their forces in the High Reaches, where they only dally with us now," Kerleu said, echoing Kellen's unspoken thought.

"It's possible," Kellen said, keeping his voice even. "You all know: We are almost certainly outnumbered by the Enemy. They have resources we don't know about. They are more mobile than we are, and they have more power. Without a doubt we will take losses, and heavy ones, before this is over.

"But remember this as well: If the Enemy did not think we had a good chance of defeating them, they would not be wasting so much time on us. We know what they need in order to win, and what they're doing to get it. Stop them, and this becomes a different war entirely."

"Brave words for the long view," Kearn said. "But how does that help the High Reaches now?"

"From what we saw in Kindolhinadetil's Mirror, Anigrel expects to get the High Mages to turn control of Armethalieh over to *Them* willingly, as Allies, by convincing them that we—the Elves and the Wildmages—are the true threat to their safety, not *Them.* What I believe that means is that *They* will have to work hard to disguise *Their* true nature from the High Mages, to aid in that masquerade. Since the High Reaches trades with Armethalieh, and the Mountainfolk have right of passage through Armethaliehan lands, I don't think *They* will dare risk making as much trouble in the High Reaches, where the High Mages are likely to notice and ask questions."

"You don't *think,*" Wirance said.

"I know they remember the De—*Them* in Armethalieh," Cilarnen said. "It's true that most people only think of *Them* as a nursery tale, but I'm sure the Mage

Council knows that they're real. I've been doing a lot of reading lately, and I'm pretty sure that if they saw anything that looked like *Them* around, all the High Mages would ride out in a body to attack it—even if it meant leaving Armethalieh."

Kellen flashed Cilarnen a grateful look. Cilarnen shrugged and smiled faintly.

Now came the crux of the matter, and the part Kellen was pretty sure the Elves wouldn't like. He'd hoped to have had word from Andoreniel before going into this, but it was something that had to be dealt with. Kerleu, Wirance, and Kearn could no more *make* the gathered Mountainfolk do something—or not do it—than they could influence the path of the wind. They were here because of treaties between their people and the Elves, but it was, as it had always been, a fragile alliance, and they would resent seeing their families left unprotected.

Feyrt and Atroist ruled the Lostlanders more decisively, nor were the people they had left behind in danger—yet. The Lostlanders had been settled among the Centaurs and humans of the Wild Lands, which the Lostlanders thought—even in winter—was a very pleasant place in comparison to their own harsh homeland. But the High Reaches were the road to the Wild Lands, and no one could doubt that the farmers, Herdingfolk, and Centaurs of the Wild Lands would be next in the Endarkened's plans.

Kreylmedd, Siust, and Truanolm knew it as well—they had all taken the Siege of Stonehearth to heart, when only one of *Them* had nearly destroyed an entire Centaur village in just a few moments. Centaurs had no magic at all to protect them; they were incapable of using it. And while more than half their fighting strength was still at home, to arrive in the spring—(if any of them, Kellen amended mentally, were still here in the spring)—even the fact that their villages were currently well-defended would not protect them from the sort of threats they would face.

Kellen only hoped that the Elves' trust in him was as great as he thought it was.

"You know that Andoreniel has offered the protection of the Fortress of the Crowned Horns to the pregnant women and children of all who fight beside us. But even if there were any way to get all of them there, there's no point in pretending there's room for all of them."

Redhelwar cleared his throat meaningfully. Adaerion, Kellen's direct superior in line-of-command, had developed a rapt interest in the carpet. Of all the Elves, only Belepheriel, who had conferred upon him the third degree of Knighthood, and Riasen were watching him with interest and confidence.

"But the Elven Lands themselves *will* offer slightly more protection than either the High Reaches or the Wild Lands, so we'd better find someplace in the southwest for the noncombatants to stay."

"You don't do anything by halves, do you, brother mine?" Idalia muttered, low enough that Kellen was fairly sure he was the only one meant to hear.

"Bring them here?" Redhelwar asked, stunned, direct to the point of rudeness.

"It is what Andoreniel meant to do, after all," Belepheriel pointed out inarguably. "Save that this is more practical than attempting to barrack them all in a fortress where they will not fit. Where will you put them? In the Elven Lands, yes, but not among us. That will not serve."

"Nor would we wish it to," Kerleu said. "Fight beside you, gladly. Live among you? A man would cut his throat in a week. I say this as fact, not insult."

"Fact *or* insult," Kreylmedd said, "the question stands: Where? Not that there isn't plenty of time to argue about it, as nobody can stir a stump until spring, and I expect there will be plenty to do to get whatever place you choose ready."

"A cave would suit all of your purposes," Rulorwen said suddenly.

For a moment Kellen thought the Master of Engineers was joking—so far they'd found nothing but incredible danger in caves, as well as plenty of Shadowed Elves—but searching the Elf's solemn face he realized that Rulorwen was perfectly serious.

"It would be good to know what lies behind your thoughts," Kellen said, falling into the everyday form of Elven politeness entirely without thinking.

"What is in my mind, Kellen Knight-Mage, is this: The Caverns of Halacira are near Sentarshadeen, which is near our southeastern border, which has so far been safe. They are extensive, and fairly well explored: We mine many of our gemstones there, and as a result of that work, many of the cavern spaces have been finished into rooms. It would be easier than many other places to convert into a defensible stronghold: simply seal off all but one or two entrances. Best of all, the Jeweled Caverns have a constant source of water in Angarussa the Undying, which flows through the caverns."

The name was vaguely familiar, and suddenly Kellen remembered. He'd ridden past Angarussa the Undying—or more precisely, *over* it—on his second day out from Sentarshadeen, when he and Jermayan had been riding in search of the Black Cairn.

"It would be good to know that it would fulfill all the requirements of the situation," Kellen suggested.

"Anyone who has seen the Jeweled Caverns of Halacira would be easy in his mind upon that matter," Rulorwen said, "for he would know that the caverns are quite vast, and should the finished areas be insufficient to the necessity before us, further areas could be finished and put to use."

"I am instructed," Kellen said, borrowing one of the favored phrases from the House of Sword and Shield. "Good. We'll use that, then. A nice homey cave."

Idalia kicked him under the table, her face studiously blank.

Of course that was not the end of the matter, but after an hour and more of debate, no one—not Lostlanders, not Wildlanders, not Centaurs, not even the Elves themselves, could find something to truly object to in the proposal. The caves could be made safe and comfortable. That they were located within the borders of the Elven Lands was the best hope of protection that the Elves could offer to their Allies.

Kellen remembered the horror with which Jermayan had once reacted to the suggestion that humans even *cross* the Elven Lands. The war was changing everything. He only hoped that even if they won, enough of the good things survived.

"I shall send to inform Andoreniel of your decision," Redhelwar said, with only the faintest of ironies in his voice. "Meanwhile, you may take a force to Halacira, to scout and secure the caves, as well as blazoning our line of march as far south as Ondoladeshiron, should word come from Andoreniel that we be permitted to withdraw to the Gathering Plain."

⥿

KELLEN caught Cilarnen's eye as the meeting came to a close, and after making an appointment to meet with Redhelwar on the following morning to discuss the disposition and selection of the force that would be dispatched to Halacira within the next sennight, he caught up with Cilarnen outside the pavilion.

"I haven't seen you around lately," he said.

Cilarnen smiled wanly. "Not *quite* as indirect as one of the Elves, Tavadon, but it will do, believe me! You haven't seen me because you've been at the other end of the camp. And I've been studying. Light deliver me—if I'd studied half this hard back in the City I'd be sitting on the Mage Council right now, I swear it!" He rubbed his forehead wearily. "Oh, don't fear I've neglected Anganil. He gets a good ride morning and night if I can manage it—which means assuming the weather cooperates. Weather! If I never see any more weather I shall be well pleased," he muttered darkly.

"They tell me it is worse this year than it has been before," Kellen said, as they began to walk slowly in the direction of the Centaur encampment.

"It is uncivilized. I am tired of huddling in a freezing tent like an animal," Cilarnen said with a shuddering sigh. "I am tired of strange clothes and strange food and not having my own bathroom. I know it sounds petty, when we are all—when the world itself—is in so much danger, but I want to go home. And the worst of it is, I know home isn't even there. That damned Dark-tainted traitor Anigrel has ruined everything we in the City took centuries to build, and if we cannot stop him, he will smash it completely."

Cilarnen caught himself with an effort, and took a deep breath. "But it hasn't happened yet, and will not, by the Mercy of the Light, and just now you heard about a whole city of your friends that *has* been destroyed. For that I am truly sorry. I should like to see an Elven City someday."

If there are any left standing soon, Kellen thought. "I hope you will," he said. "Thank you for your kindness."

"And you will want to know if I've gotten anywhere with turning myself into a useful High Mage. I think so. But I think . . . I think I need your help."

⸎

THE last time Kellen had seen Cilarnen's tent it had looked very much like his own, with the addition, of course, of a double armload of books.

Since then, the tent had exploded into chaos. Kellen only hoped that Redhelwar did not order the main force of the army to move out on short notice, because he was certain that the contents of Cilarnen's pavilion could not be packed for moving in anything less than two days. Cilarnen's sleeping pallet was crammed off in a corner, a table and stool had been added—both were heaped with papers—and in addition to the books, several scrolls had been added to the disorder.

Now that was puzzling. The scrolls could only be written in Elven—the older the book, the more likely it was to use the older alphabet—and Kellen was pretty sure that Cilarnen didn't read Elven.

In addition to the scrolls and the new furniture, Cilarnen's tent now also contained a stave cut precisely to Cilarnen's height, a broadsword—which did not seem to be intended for what Kellen would consider practical use—and a set of shelves crammed into a corner and filled with pots, bags, jars, and boxes.

There was barely room to move.

Cilarnen set the lamps and braziers alight with a gesture as the two of them entered—perilous, that, with the amount of loose vellum, scrolls, and bound books the pavilion contained, the pavilion was a tinderbox—and as the air began to warm, Kellen could smell that the air was redolent of oddly familiar scents.

"Light-incense," he said, surprised.

"Well, the ingredients for it, anyway," Cilarnen said. "Or most of them. You can't do a conjuration without it. Fortunately I found the recipe in one of the books, as Armethalieh is hardly likely to send me some if I ask. All I have to do now is figure out a way to get my hands on either oil of cassiar, or cassiar bark, and I can compound as much as I need."

"Ask Kindolhinadetil," Kellen said. "Or, properly, ask Redhelwar to ask Kindolhinadetil. He might have some. Cassiars probably grow in the Flower Forest."

"If he has given me all these books, I suppose he might let me harvest a bit from his trees," Cilarnen said, sounding faintly baffled.

Moving carefully, Cilarnen consolidated several piles until he had cleared space atop the storage trunks for them to sit. Their cloaks hung in the one corner of the tent not filled with papers—Cilarnen had that much practicality—slowly dripping melting snow onto the carpet.

"I can offer you tea—if I can find the tea-brazier and the pot," he said. "Of course, I don't have any decent tea, but still . . ."

"I'll take the thought for the deed," Kellen said. "So what did you want my help with?"

"What, should we not discuss the weather for at least half-a-bell?" Cilarnen teased. Then he sobered, settling to business.

"I think I may have figured out how to power my magick, Kellen.

"You know how they do it in Armethalieh. Because Power is something that everyone has in tiny amounts, though only those with the Magegift can use it to fuel their spells, long ago the High Mages decided that they would harvest and store the power of the unGifted citizens and use it for their spells, adding it to their own natural power. If I have to rely on nothing more than my own innate power, there are very few spells of the High Magick that I will ever be able to successfully cast, but outside of Armethalieh, with its elaborate system of Talismans and—probably—greater reservoirs, there is no mechanism for harvesting and storing Power."

Kellen nodded. Cilarnen was telling him nothing neither of them didn't already know, but he was obviously working his way up to something.

"But Armethalieh didn't always exist, and for the High Mages to create their system, they had to have a power source before they discovered that one, or else they wouldn't have been able to cast spells in the first place and invent the High Magick, do you see? These books that Kindolhinadetil gave me are very very old, Kellen—I studied one or two of the same ones back in the City, and in the copies I saw there, everything was slightly different. As if they'd been rewritten here and there over the centuries. So I wasn't surprised when I finally came across references to the original source of the High Mages' power—something that, needless to say, is certainly nowhere taught in the City today.

"It seems that the High Mages once harnessed Elemental energy directly to fuel their spells. Apparently it was very dangerous—the one book I have that talks much about it goes on and on about how the Mage must be careful not to cast too many spells, and to rest frequently, lest he burn out his Gift and his life. And apparently you couldn't do it for long—the book talks about High Mages 'retiring if they can' after seven years—as if that ever happened. That part just doesn't make sense!"

It might not make sense to Cilarnen, but it did to Kellen. If Cilarnen was talking about High Mages from before the founding of Armethalieh, then he was talking about High Mages who were still fighting Demons—for, he now knew, Armethalieh had been founded shortly after the end of The Great War, when the High Magick came to declare the Wild Magic anathema. High Mages who fought for the Light would almost certainly die young, burning out their Magegift on the battlefield fighting the Endarkened.

"Anyway, I'm not exactly ready to evoke an Elemental and try to figure out how to take away its power in order to use it myself," Cilarnen said. "I'm barely used to the idea that the Elemental Powers are something—things—you might actually meet, and not abstract concepts used to balance out the design of a spell. I keep thinking of them as a different kind of Illusory Creature, and then my mind stops working entirely. But whatever they really are, I'm certainly not going to kidnap one of them and steal from it. And even if I could figure out how to ask for its permission, I think the arrangement of taking its power might kill it—assuming they can be killed."

Kellen was sure by now that Cilarnen was taking as long to get to the point as any Elf ever had. But he could also see that whatever conclusion he had reached was a troubling one for the young High Mage, so he supposed that it was just as well to let Cilarnen reach the point in his own way.

"But the Elves guard their land through the land-wards, which are also linked—according to these scrolls—to the Elemental Powers. Oh, I can't exactly read them, of course, but Kardus can, and I think I am learning to puzzle out a word or two. At any rate, I think I could adapt the High Magery spell to link with the land-wards and draw on the Elemental Powers through that. I wouldn't be tapping into the energy of any specific Elemental Creature, so there would be no danger of harming any of them, and I do not think I could draw enough power off the land-wards to affect them. At any rate, I could easily do a divination to make sure."

Cilarnen seemed to be finished talking, and so far he had not raised any points, as far as Kellen could see, that would require Kellen's help.

And if what he had said he had learned from the ancient texts was true, even if Cilarnen knew precisely what he was doing, it would be more than dangerous. And he was talking about *adapting* a spell that hadn't been cast since the last time there were Knight-Mages—and if there was one thing Kellen knew for sure, it was that playing fast-and-loose with the rule-bound High Magick wasn't simply dangerous. It was disastrous.

"Cilarnen . . ." he began uneasily.

"You think I don't understand the consequences?" Cilarnen asked. "Or just the magickal theory involved? At heart it's a simple substitution of Powers of equivalent class: every Mage learns it in order to adapt spells to specific functions. Otherwise you couldn't—oh, Preserve a specific loaf of bread instead of *all* bread within the range of your spell."

It's just like Maths. At heart, the High Magick is just like Maths, Kellen realized with a stunning sense of sudden insight.

Of course, he'd always *liked* Maths. And he doubted anything was ever going to make him like—or really understand—the High Magick.

"This is a lot more complicated than loaves of bread," he pointed out. "And even if you get it exactly right, it could still kill you—which I know you know. But mainly, you said you needed my help, and I know it can't be in the spellwork."

Kellen's comment startled a sharp laugh from Cilarnen. "As if I would have you anywhere near any proper Working Circle! Precious Light, Kellen, I would as soon Work without a Circle at all as have your help! And you would be just as pleased to have me guard your back in battle, I imagine. Whatever it is that you do, I suppose you do it very well, but you are even less of a High Mage than I am. No, it is the matter of permission. If I am to try to take power from the Elven land-wards, I must have permission. But whose? And how do I ask for it?"

KELLEN raised the matter with Redhelwar the following day, when he met with the Army's General to plan his own journey toward the south.

"In a matter such as this, affecting the whole of the land, it is Andoreniel who is the voice of the land," Redhelwar said, after a long hesitation. But his voice was troubled.

"Yet Andoreniel is silent," Kellen said, forcing himself to remain calm. "As is Ashaniel. And we are far from Sentarshadeen. I do not believe that we may let this matter lie until Cilarnen can go in person to Sentarshadeen. Jermayan and Ancaladar could make the journey quickly and safely to bring Cilarnen there, it is true. But we do not know when they will return to the army, and while they are on the wing, flying between cities, there is no way of getting a message to them quickly, so the same problem applies. If I take Cilarnen with me, we will be several moonturns on the road. It is time we cannot afford to waste. We know that a High Mage and a Wildmage combining their powers can slay *Them*—and the High Magick has other spells that the Wild Magic does not."

"I cannot speak in Andoreniel's name," Redhelwar said. "But Kindolhinade-til is the Voice of Andoreniel. We must go to him and ask for his counsel."

THERE are so many ways this can go horribly wrong, Kellen thought a sennight later, and magic was the farthest thing from his mind.

He, Cilarnen, Redhelwar, and several others were on their way to seek an audience from Kindolhinadetil at the House of Bough and Wind.

And Kellen was very much afraid that Cilarnen was going to have to speak for himself.

Kellen had taken every spare moment he had in the past several days—and there weren't many—to give Cilarnen every warning and piece of advice he could think of about how to behave when he met the Viceroy of Ysterialpo-erin. Cilarnen thought the Elves he'd met so far were bizarre and mysterious, but they were nothing compared to the Elves who lived in the Heart of the Forest. Jermayan had once told Kellen that the Elves of Ysterialpoerin were the ones who lived as closely as possible to the way Elves had lived before there were humans. Isinwen, Kellen's second in command, had left Ysterialpoerin, the city of his birth, because he found the people stultifying formal. If they were so formal that even other Elves wanted to leave, Kellen couldn't imagine them having any patience at all with humans. The one time he'd been there, he'd kept his mouth shut and his head down, and hoped they hadn't noticed him too much.

He'd told Cilarnen all that, of course. But he wasn't sure he'd gotten through to him. And he hadn't really had the time to figure out a way to *get* through, because the preparations for his own departure were taking up all his attention.

When Redhelwar had said he was giving Kellen a "force" to take to Ha-lacira, Kellen had imagined it would be something small—perhaps his own troop with a few supply-wagons added.

Instead, Redhelwar was placing a full third of the army under Kellen's direct command.

There were ways in which it made sense. Two sets of messengers had failed to report back from Sentarshadeen; Kellen might need to fight his way into the southwest and be able to send back word with a heavily-defended force to the main army without weakening his own forces. Artenel and several of Rulorwen's people were accompanying Kellen in order to begin the assessment of the cav-erns, and Engineers do not travel light; there would also need to be enough mounted troops to protect the Engineers' equipment.

Pack animals, destriers, and draft animals—and their riders and handlers—all had to be fed and sheltered, which meant supply and equipment wagons, which in turn added to the number of draft animals. . . .

And Kellen was in charge of all of it.

In part this indicated a vote of confidence from the Army's General. Partly it was—Kellen sighed inwardly—another test. Being placed in charge of this portion of the army meant he was being placed in charge of commanders who were—except for Artenel—his equals in rank, and certainly his seniors in age and possibly experience. Redhelwar would wish to know if Kellen could command them.

What Kellen wanted to know was if he could keep them alive. The continuing silence from Sentarshadeen worried him desperately. Perhaps Cilarnen could find out what the problem was there.

If today's meeting went well.

If Cilarnen didn't manage to offend Kindolhinadetil completely.

And, of course, don't forget, if this is something Kindolhinadetil can even grant. Redhelwar only said we could "ask his counsel." He didn't say what would come of it.

"Will you stop twitching?" Cilarnen whispered beneath the steady crunch of their horses' hooves through the snow-crust. The day was clear and bright—for a change—one less thing to worry about in a day that held far too many things to worry about. As much as Kellen had needed to leave Isinwen behind to oversee the work of departure, he'd felt he'd needed him with the embassy to Kindolhinadetil even more. Ysterialpoerin was Isinwen's birthplace, and Kellen's Second might be able to help keep Cilarnen from unwittingly giving grave offense. Isinwen rode silently behind Kellen, dressed, as Kellen was, in the best their clothes-chests had to offer after a season of hard campaigning.

"I'm worried enough as it is," Cilarnen went on, in an undertone that was—nevertheless—perfectly audible not only to Kellen but to every Elf there. "You've already made it sound as if everything I know about Elves is true."

"That they never lie, and they never tell the truth." Kellen didn't even need to look around to know that Isinwen would be wearing his blandest expression. Kellen forced himself not to think of the consequences if Cilarnen said something so shatteringly tactless in front of the Viceroy. Dammit—*Cilarnen* was the one who'd grown up being successfully groomed for a Council seat until Anigrel had maneuvered him into plotting treason. Why couldn't he remember something as simple as how acute Elven hearing was?

I'll only have to hope he remembers it when it really *counts,* Kellen thought gloomily. Then a new thought struck him. Just what *did* Cilarnen really know about Elves? The proverb he'd just quoted to himself was from the oldest Proscribed Histories of the City. He'd learned it from Idalia, who'd been using it to teach him quite a different lesson. What Cilarnen would have been taught, as Kellen had been—back in the City—was that Elves were fatally beautiful, treacherous, and incapable of telling the truth at all.

He only hoped experience—and familiarity—had been a better teacher to Cilarnen than the City Histories had been.

Kellen forced a smile. "The truth is, I don't know what to expect in Ysteri-alpoerin. I don't like that."

"Well, who does?" Cilarnen said crossly. "But from what you say, the Viceroy is the only one who can give permission for me to try this experiment, so . . ." he shrugged helplessly, the gesture muffled by the heavy cloak he wore.

Kellen nodded. Outnumbered as they were in this war, they could afford to overlook nothing that might give them the edge in battle. No matter what risk it involved.

❧

THE High Reaches had a stark beauty in winter. It was a land of dark forests and deep valleys nestled among the mountains that had given the area its name. It marked the border between the Elven Lands and the Wild Lands, and its people loved it fiercely. Centuries ago, in the aftermath of the Great War, humans had come to these high hills and mountains seeking one thing: freedom and peace, and they had found it here. They traded with their neighbors—the Centaurs, the lowlanders, even with Armethalieh in the West—and went their own way, holding to their own customs as they always had, for as long as they could remember.

They followed the teachings of the Huntsman and the Forest Wife, who taught them to live in harmony with their land, taking only what was needed, and always returning gift for gift.

And so they had prospered.

No longer.

Death came to the High Reaches on silent scarlet wings.

❧

PRINCE Zyperis stood in the middle of the forest. He could barely contain his glee. Where to begin? The best part was that the foolish Lightborn would not know that he had been here . . . oh, not for a moonturn at least. It would all be done in secret.

And sometimes secrets could be the highest form of *Their* art.

He spread his wings wide and shook them, and a fine black mist drifted from them on the cold still air. It settled on the trees around him, and wherever it touched, the greenneedle bark began to whiten, just a little.

Within days, the tree would be dead.

The blight would spread throughout the forest, spreading from tree to tree upon the wind, to everything that grew. The winds would carry it beyond the High Reaches, into the Elven Lands and the Wildlands as well. It would begin slowly—that was its beauty—but within one turn of the moon that the Light-born used to mark Time, it would have spread so far that all who lived here would know of it . . . though they would not know its source.

Zyperis walked on, pausing now and again to seed the forest with blight.

And that was not all.

As he walked, he transformed himself, taking on a form he had often used: a shape pleasing to the Lightborn. There were many wanderers these days, and even if someone should see him, out here in the deep woods, it would not be that unusual.

As he walked, he scattered grain upon the snow. It glowed faintly, but the hungry animals—hares, deer, birds—who came to feed upon it would not notice.

All of them would leave their feast carrying plague.

As would those who fed upon them.

And those who fed upon them.

Plague and blight, the surest, most stealthy weapons of the Endarkened. They would spread through the High Reaches—oh, not necessarily to kill. That would not be sufficiently elegant. But to starve, to weaken, to cripple.

To call the Elves' troublesome Allies home.

⁂

AS on his last visit, Kellen felt entirely out of place in Ysterialpoerin, and the idea that the Elves—any Elves—could consider the city homelike and inviting was disturbing to him in some way he couldn't entirely articulate.

It wasn't as if they were simply living in the woods. Kellen had done that—with and without a roof over his head—and while he preferred to be comfort-able, he could understand people (like Idalia) who'd rather live in the forest than in a town.

But in Ysterialpoerin, the Elves had taken a city and made it look like a for-est. Only not like a real forest—by now Kellen had seen plenty of those—but like a *dream* of a forest, so that the longer you were in Ysterialpoerin, the more you felt as if you were asleep with your eyes open.

It was . . . perfect. Every snow-covered branch, every drooping bough, even the shadows on the glittering surface of the snow were . . . perfect.

It made Kellen feel as if he were suffocating. In a strange way, it reminded him of the City. But at least if you were born in Ysterialpoerin and didn't like it,

there was somewhere else you could *go*, since in the Elven Lands, nobody ob-
jected to your leaving the place where you had been born.

He glanced over at Cilarnen. Cilarnen looked as if he'd been hit over the
head with a very large hammer. He was staring around himself, eyes wide, and his
lips were pressed together in a tight line.

At last they reached the House of Bough and Wind. Kellen was pleased to
see that its beauty had brought Cilarnen out of himself. So far as he knew, it was
the only building in Ysterialpoerin that looked like a conventional house, and it
was as beautiful as all things Elven, though thankfully in a way humans could
appreciate.

This time they were making a formal visit, so Kindolhinadetil and Neishandellazel were not waiting for them on the steps of the House. Instead there were
six servants waiting—one for every rider—all wearing long gray hooded cloaks
precisely the color of the House. The cloaks were stitched all over with tiny col-
orless crystals that precisely duplicated the pattern of the carving of leaf and
vine that covered every inch of the structure, and when they came silently down
from the steps and across the snow to take the horses' headstalls, the fabric shimmered in the pale sunlight as though stitched in flame.

They did not speak, so Redhelwar and the others did not speak either. When
the riders had dismounted, and their horses had been led away, the door of the
House opened, and a woman appeared.

To Kellen's great surprise, he recognized her. It was the Lady Arquelle, the
Elven Healer from Ysterialpoerin who had aided the Unicorn Knights after the
Battle for the Heart of the Forest.

"In the name of Kindolhinadetil, Voice of Andoreniel in Ysterialpoerin, in
the name of Neishandellazel, Lady of Ysterialpoerin, we See you, Redhelwar,
General of Andoreniel's armies; Adaerion; Dionan; Kellen Knight-Mage; Isinwen; and Cilarnen High Mage of the City of a Thousand Bells. Be welcome in
the House of Bough and Wind, branch of Leaf and Star."

As was traditional among the Elves, she had put the most important name
last; Kellen wasn't sure whether to be pleased that Kindolhinadetil knew that
Cilarnen was important or just continue to worry about all the ways this meeting
could go wrong.

"We thank the Name of Kindolhinadetil for his welcome," Redhelwar responded gravely, "to find sanctuary in the home of a friend is to be doubly
blessed."

Arquelle stood aside, holding the door even wider, and the six of them entered.

Kellen was glad he'd warned Cilarnen what to expect, because even having
been here before, even knowing what he was going to see and knowing that it was all
an illusion, crafted not by magic but by simple skill, it nearly took his breath away.

As soon as he crossed the threshold of the doorway into the House of Bough and Wind, he was standing in a summer forest. The snow might be melting on his boots, but the melt was trickling away into thick green moss. Trees stretched away as far as the eye could see—it didn't *matter* that he knew he'd walked into a perfectly house-seeming house on the outside: In here there was a forest. He could smell flowers and feel the warm summer breeze, and as he looked up into the golden light of the forest canopy, he could see butterflies flitting back and forth among the leaves. He wondered if the forest outside looked anything like this when it was summer, and if so, did they make the House of Bough and Wind look as if it were a *winter* forest then? Interesting thought.

More servants appeared to take their hooded cloaks and fur-lined gloves, and the party followed the Lady Arquelle farther into the House.

❧

HE wasn't sure how or when it happened. He'd been lulled by the beauty of the forest, even if it wasn't, in any true sense, "real"—but when they arrived in what, for lack of a better term, his mind insisted on thinking of as the "clearing" where Kindolhinadetil and Neishandellazel were waiting for them, Adaerion, Isinwen, and Dionan were no longer with them. He, Redhelwar, and Cilarnen were the only ones following Arquelle.

Kellen blinked, running the last few minutes through his mind. Adaerion and Dionan had been ahead of him; Isinwen had been behind. No, at one point Adaerion and Dionan had simply stepped aside, going around a tree in one direction while Redhelwar went around it in another. They'd gone off somewhere else then, and probably Isinwen with them.

Obviously they'd been told to somehow—possibly even by something as obvious (to Elven eyes) as the message-wands Elven scouts used to mark trails and leave messages. But compared to Elves, humans were nearly color-blind, and there were a number of things that Elves saw that Kellen simply couldn't see.

Yes, that was the simplest explanation. After all, it couldn't be magic.

And, if that was how it had to be, there was no point in complaining. But it only underscored the fact that Kellen had no idea of how the Ysterialpoerin Elves' minds worked. And he'd been counting on Isinwen to smooth things over, if need be.

❧

THE last time they had come this way, the "clearing" had been filled with what Kellen had assumed then was the Viceregal Court—or at least Kindolhinadetil's Council. This time it was empty except for the Viceroy of Ysterialpoerin and his

Lady. They were seated upon the same ornately-carved chairs in the center of the clearing, but to Kellen's faint surprise, three more chairs stood empty facing the others, obviously meant for him, Cilarnen, and Redhelwar. The inevitable tea-service was also there, set beside Nishandellazel's chair.

I will never understand the Elves, Kellen thought ruefully. This was all a great deal more . . . informal . . . than what he'd been led to expect from his last visit to the House of Bough and Wind.

Arquelle led them to their chairs and then knelt beside the tea-service, beginning the protracted preparation of tea. Apparently this was to be conducted entirely in silence. Maybe Kindolhinadetil and Nishanellazel wanted to see how long the two humans could go without saying anything.

But as Kellen sat there in the warm silence, listening to distant drone of insects and the sleepy calling of birds—all illusion, but how did they manage it?—he felt himself begin to relax in a way he had not in a very long time. Even his toes started to warm up. If they wanted to sit here for the next three hours and not say a word, fine. He'd just watch the butterflies. He wondered if they were real butterflies. Idalia would probably know if there were any way to keep butterflies alive in winter. Maybe the Elves kept them as pets, the way some people kept birds. And the forest truly seemed to go on for miles, though it couldn't possibly, even if this were the only room in the entire House of Bough and Wind. He'd seen the outside of the House. It was big, of course, but not *that* big. . . .

Arquelle handed him a cup of tea and Kellen took it, lost in thoughts that, for the moment, had nothing to do with the war or his problems.

❦

"NOW, perhaps, if it were to find answering agreement in your hearts, would be a good time to begin," Kindolhinadetil said a while later, setting aside his cup. "In repose is found the best of all beginnings."

"Your words are indeed wise," Redhelwar said. "And so it is with a glad heart that I turn to the Voice of Andoreniel for wise counsel."

It all sounded to Kellen—who'd heard hours of similar exchanges in his time with the Elves—like meaningless interchanges of empty flattering phrases, made doubly ridiculous by the fact that he strongly suspected that Kindolhinadetil already knew every single detail of why they were here and what they'd come to ask, and, further, had known them a sennight ago.

But you did not rush Elves. Not unless somebody was actually about to die.

He slanted his glance sideways to see how Cilarnen was taking all this. To his relief, Cilarnen looked calm, even faintly detached. Well, Kellen supposed

that *good* High-Mages-in-training got used to being bored. And good at concealing their boredom.

". . . then perhaps it would be well did the High Mage speak upon his own
behalf," Kindolhinadetil said eventually.

Cilarnen rose to his feet and bowed deeply, first to Nishandellazel, then to
Kindolhinadetil.

"Lady Nishandellazel; Kindolhinadetil, Voice of Andoreniel, it is my honor
to speak before you. Hear my words, though I am but a poor speaker, unused to
your ways. I am Cilarnen, son of Setarion, of the House of Volpiril, of
Armethalieh, called among many names the City of Mages. The secrets of the
High Mages are many, but here is one: that the power that we use to fuel our
spells is present in every person, though it can only be turned to magick by those
with the Magegift. For centuries the High Mages of Armethalieh have harvested
and stored that power without their citizen-subjects' knowledge, and thus have
become powerful and feared. Without access to such a store they—we—are
nearly powerless, yet there is another way to fuel the Magegift. In ancient days,
at the dawn of the City and perhaps even before, the High Magick was given
strength by Elemental energy, just as your Elven land-wards are now. It would be
dangerous, I believe, to an Elemental Creature were I to attempt to use its power,
nor do I know how to speak with one to make such an arrangement. Yet I believe
I could draw on the power of the land-wards without harm to the creatures that
power them, did I have permission of those in whose keeping such wards are.
And so I come before you in petition. With the power to cast the Greater Spells
of my Art, I could learn more, and faster, of the ways of the High Magick than I
could ever learn without. And I could be of aid to Redhelwar as well. The High
Magick holds spells for speaking over distance, for augury, and for war that
are . . . different in inclination from those of the Wild Magic. It has other powers
as well. Some I know now, some I can only learn once I have the full powers of a
High Mage.

"I know such a request should properly be put before the King, but . . . I do
not think we have time to wait."

Cilarnen bowed again and stood silently, waiting.

Despite himself, Kellen was impressed. Cilarnen's speech had taken careful
planning.

He knew, of course, that Cilarnen's speech would certainly be considered almost offensively concise just about anywhere in the Elven Lands, doubly so in
Ysterialpoerin. But he also knew that Andoreniel did not choose fools to reign
over the rest of the Nine—now Eight—Cities. Kindolhinadetil might never have
seen a human in all his long life before he'd seen Kellen, but before he'd come to
today's meeting, he had undoubtedly studied their ways as thoroughly as Cilar-

nen had been studying those books. The wise did not take offense casually; Cilarnen had made a great effort to be polite, and that was what Kindolhinadetil would see.

The silence lengthened, and both humans waited, betraying no sign of apprehension. Kellen had been trained in the House of Sword and Shield not to waste his energy in anticipating an encounter, but simply to respond to it when it came; Cilarnen, he was coming to realize, had skills honed equally sharp, though for a different battlefield.

At last Kindolhinadetil spoke.

"You speak of what will be gained, not what may be lost. Speak now of these things, of the harm that might come to the land-wards . . . and to yourself."

Kellen saw Cilarnen hesitate, then take a deep breath.

"Viceroy, I do not know. The Elementals' first duty is to the land-wards, and all that I have read tells me that such creatures have a sort of consciousness. I believe they would know if what I intend would harm the land-wards, and either stop it before it began, or break the link afterward. I am told they are a sort of living creature, with the power to act in their own interests, or in the interests of those they serve, which implies to me that they would choose to preserve the land-wards at their traditional strength rather than aid me, if they had to choose between the two. Further, once I have the power to do so, if I do indeed gain such power, I shall do a divination to be quite certain that the link is harmless to the land-wards, so that even if the Elemental Creatures are incapable of making such an assessment, the High Magick will make the determination, and if it is wrong to continue, I shall stop immediately.

"As for harm to me . . ." Cilarnen hesitated again. "Attempting this may kill me outright. Using my Magegift in this fashion will certainly cause it to be Burned from me over time, and perhaps I will die then. Beyond that, I do not know."

Again there was silence, save for the sound of the wind through the trees. It made Kellen think, with regret and something oddly like homesickness, of the only true summer he'd ever known, the one he'd spent with Idalia in the Wildwood, and wonder if he, if anyone, would live to see another one.

"A fair answer, human child," Kindolhinadetil said at last. "If you had lied to me about any part of it, even the danger to yourself, I would have forbidden it outright. But as you have trusted me, may Leaf and Star guide us all to true wisdom."

He and Nishandellazel rose to their feet. Apparently the audience was over.

⤬

ARQUELLE conducted the three of them back through the "forest" to the front door of the House of Bough and Wind. Though Kellen could have managed to find the way himself—no Knight-Mage could truly be "lost," since the Wild Magic gave him the innate ability to exactly retrace his steps—it would have taken quite a bit of effort on his part.

He wasn't at all surprised to see their horses waiting for them, with Adaerion, Dionan, and Isinwen already mounted. The other three looked very much as if they had just awakened from a dream—even Isinwen, who must be used to things like this.

Pleasant as it had been (in an odd way), Kellen didn't really think he wanted to come back to the House of Bough and Wind any time soon. If ever. What he thought of as "normal" Elves were hard enough to deal with for a simple round-ear. The Elves of Ysterialpoerin were downright spooky.

⁂

"SO was that a 'yes' or a 'no'?" Cilarnen asked once they'd left the city and were riding through the Heart-Forest in the direction of camp.

Kellen glanced sideways at Isinwen. His Second gave no indication that he had heard anything at all.

"I have absolutely no idea," Kellen said with a deep sigh. "It would be good to know how to find out—without, of course, offending anyone," he said, gazing pointedly at Isinwen.

The Elven Knight abandoned his pretense of polite deafness.

"The Lady Arquelle will have made clear to Kindolhinadetil, as a member of the Council, the most desirable way to phrase things to avoid misunderstandings when one is conversing with humans," Isinwen began. "Certainly since the attack on the Heart of the Forest, Kindolhinadetil as much as anyone knows that there is a need for decisiveness and speed in making decisions related to the conduct of the war. But this is not a decision he should be asked to make, and he knows it. He will certainly consult his Council before proceeding.

"I still have family here," Isinwen said. "Kindolhinadetil, of course, is aware of this. It is possible he will pass word of his decision to me privately, knowing I will pass it on to you. That way he may render a judgment without making it a matter for—too public—comment."

"If that's what he intends, he'll have to be quick about it," Kellen said. "We leave in four days."

⁂

BUT the days leading up to Kellen's departure passed without any word from Kindolhinadetil, through official or unofficial channels. Nor did word come from Sentarshadeen, or from Jermayan.

Kellen could not delay his departure, no matter how much he wanted to know what Kindolhinadetil's decision would be. No matter how important Cilarnen's work, the young High Mage was still only one *xaique*-piece on the board, and the winning play—if it could be made—involved many others. With the continuing silence from the south, Kellen's mission took on added importance. Once he had reached Halacira and established a presence there, Redhelwar told him he was to take a force on into Sentarshadeen to discover the reason for the continuing silence from Andoreniel.

For without word from Andoreniel, the army could not move.

Six

The Stars and the Light

THE MORNING OF Kellen's departure was much like any other; light snow and bitter cold. The Wildmages traveling with his convoy predicted a sennight of calm weather, with snow no heavier than could be expected at this season, but there was a mountain range to cross between Ysterialpoerin and Ondoladeshiron, and they could be certain of heavy weather in the higher altitudes. If they were not unreasonably delayed by the weather, they should be at Ondoladeshiron within the moonturn, and from there, the rest of the journey should be somewhat easier. The trek between Sentarshadeen and Ondoladeshiron had only taken ten days when he'd come up from Sentarshadeen to the Gathering Plain with the army the first time—but Kellen suspected that there'd been a great deal less snow on the ground then. Not to mention the fact that he'd been traveling with a smaller—and more lightly-burdened—force.

They'd just have to do their best, though. Even if Redhelwar hadn't impressed upon him the need for haste—and an Elf counseling hurry was impressive enough—it didn't take a Knight-Mage's special senses to know that they had no time to spare. Anigrel wasn't going to be wasting any time in bringing Armethalieh's wards down—and once the Demons could actually get *into* the City . . . well, Kellen knew from bitter experience how persuasive the Endarkened could be. They'd be able to convince the High Council of anything they chose—and have the Mageborn to feed off of as an added bonus. The sooner he got to Sentarshadeen and found out why Andoreniel had fallen silent, the better.

Amid the last-minute bustle as troops, horses, mules, oxen, and sledges found their places in line, his friends had come to bid him a private farewell. Idalia was there, of course, and Vestakia had come down to the main camp from the caverns to be there at his departure as well.

Kellen had not seen her for nearly a moonturn, and only the self-discipline he had learned over the sennights of this long hard winter war kept him from showing how shocked he was to see her. She looked thin and worn, almost haggard, drained by the twin struggles to understand the Crystal Spiders' Otherworldly minds and to withstand the growing sense of Demontaint in the Elvenlands. Vestakia looked a little more than Otherworldly herself, despite the bright red and gold velvets she wore.

"Take care of yourself," Idalia said, giving Kellen a quick fierce hug. "Don't make me regret staying here instead of going with you."

"I'm sure I'll see you soon enough—just as soon as the Crystal Spiders manage to tell us where the last Enclave of the Shadowed Elves is. And besides, I'll feel much better knowing that you're here to keep an eye on Cilarnen," Kellen said.

He kept his eyes on his sister, not looking at Vestakia. He would give Vestakia a warrior's courtesy of ignoring her wounds—for they *were* wounds, as much as any sword-cut taken in battle—but it was hard to see her this way.

It was harder still to know that he could stop all her pain with a simple request to Redhelwar to remove her from the caverns, and that he wouldn't. Vestakia wouldn't thank him for saving her life when there was a chance her sacrifice could save others—in fact, she'd despise him for even suggesting it—but it was more than that. He knew, down in a part of himself he didn't like to look at too often, that even if she asked, no, even if she *begged,* to be sent away to safety, he'd do his very best to find some way to keep her here where her talents could be used. Because winning this war was more important than preserving any single life, and he knew it. He'd learned that about himself, and the knowledge wasn't a very pleasant thing.

It wasn't that he didn't love his friends. Kellen hadn't had many friends—*any* friends, he corrected himself—until he'd been Banished from Armethalieh. Somehow the war—knowing when you got up in the morning that they—or you—might not be there by nightfall—made friendships forge faster and burn brighter. Leaf and Star, he was willing to call *Cilarnen* a friend, something he would once have sworn would never happen!

But he would use them all ruthlessly when the opportunity came, if it would grant the Allies a chance of victory. He, and the Wild Magic that worked through him.

He only hoped he could live with himself afterward if it worked. If it didn't work, living with himself wasn't something he'd have to worry about.

"I'm far too old for nursemaids," Cilarnen said firmly, startling Kellen out of his grim thoughts. What had they just been talking about? Oh, yes—he'd said Idalia should keep an eye on Cilarnen. As if any of the Mageborn would tolerate that for an instant! Kellen smiled to himself. Cilarnen had Centaurs for friends and had made great strides in learning to deal suitably with the Elves, but compared to the brainwashing the Mageborn received about women, what they were told about the Other Races and the Wild Magic was just a mild suggestion, really. Kellen was a little surprised Idalia hadn't poisoned Cilarnen by now for his unconscious attitude toward her.

"But I wish I were going with you," Cilarnen added with a touch of wistfulness.

"Leaf and Star—why?" Kellen demanded, honestly surprised. "There won't be time to open a book—or wave a wand—between here and Sentarshadeen. And I'm sure you'd freeze, besides. I know I'm going to."

"I don't know," Cilarnen said pensively. "I just wish I were."

Idalia shot Cilarnen an odd look. "Well, you can at least ride a little way with him. Anganil will enjoy the exercise."

"And you'd meant to do that anyway," Vestakia pointed out, with a small smile.

It was inarguably true, as Anganil stood tacked-out and ready beside Firareth, his breath steaming in the cold shadows of morning.

"If you're going, go," Idalia said. "The day isn't getting any younger."

"I'll see you all soon," Kellen said, swinging up into Firareth's saddle. *Whenever that will be. If we're all still alive.*

He waved, and Isinwen lifted a horn to his lips and blew a complicated series of notes. It echoed up and down the line as the horses and the baggage-train began slowly to move.

◈

CILARNEN turned Anganil back an hour later—even though they had seen no sign of Tainted predators anywhere near camp since the Battle for the Heart of the Forest, there was no sense in exposing a lone rider to danger. Cilarnen was in high spirits, looking forward to the prospect of a good fast gallop over the cleared and trampled trail that Kellen's people had left.

When he was gone, Kellen felt oddly alone, although he was precisely as *un*alone as he had been the moment before. Isinwen and the rest of his troop rode behind him; to his left Keirasti's people did the same.

Because of the heavy wagons, they were taking a course that would circle around the forest as much as possible, keeping them on the open plain. But for that same reason, their path lay where the snow was heaviest.

Like the others, Kellen wore a thin veil of gauze over the eye-slits of his visor to provide protection against snow-glare. It was not especially needed today, when the sky was overcast, but he already knew from experience that bright sun on a brilliant snowfield could give you a memorable headache.

This particular snowfield looked as if it might be especially brilliant if the sun ever came out from behind the clouds. It stretched as far as Kellen could see, snow that was as flat as still water, though here and there it had been shaped and sculpted by the wind into odd dunes and ridges, a surface of powdered ice that chilled the cold wind even further as it blew across it, freezing exposed skin instantly and slowly numbing even the best protected flesh as the hours passed. Occasional animal tracks were preserved in the surface, though the wind had scrubbed at them until they were hard to read: Kellen recognized hare, bird—hawk? owl?—and something that was neither one, weathered away to an anonymous line of dots in the snow. Probably a fox after that hare.

The snow was also exceptionally deep: certainly up to the shoulder of an Elven destrier, and out here, sun and wind had turned its top layer to a crust of ice thick enough to cut flesh. If the cavalry had to make its own way through the snow, they'd be lucky to manage five miles a day, and the army wouldn't reach Sentarshadeen until Midsummer, if that.

But if the Elves preferred not to fight in winter, that certainly didn't mean they didn't know how. At the head of the column ran a large sledge drawn by twelve patient oxen. The oxen were hitched in single file, so that except for the first beast, its chest well protected by a shield of studded leather, none of the animals actually had to break through the icy crust of the snow, and only the lead animal had to struggle against an unbroken trail. All their enormous brawn could be concentrated on pulling the prow-shaped sledge behind them, and its only purpose was to turn the snow out of a wide enough path for a sumpter-wagon—or four destriers riding abreast—to pass.

Kellen had never seen anything like it before. The snow had not been deep enough when the army got to Ysterialpoerin to require it, he supposed, or else there hadn't been time to build one along the way. But it was very much like an odd Elven sculpture; as the oxen dragged it forward, the snow slid over its curves and angles, pressed into two high mounds several feet apart with a flat firm packed-down area between. If he had not seen it himself, Kellen would have been willing to swear that the trail it left could only be accomplished by magic—and a very powerful spell besides—but it was nothing more than Elven ingenuity. Though every few hours they had to back the team up and change out to fresh animals—and though the whole army could only move at the oxen's walking pace—they were still making far better speed than they would have been did they have to break their own trail through this snow, and without overtiring the horses, or taking any injuries.

And we have absolutely no room to maneuver. If something hits the column, and we have to leave the path, we might as well be riding through shoulder-deep mud. And no Ancaladar to look down and tell us what's coming from miles away.

Was that why the Scouts had never reported back? Because they'd never reached Sentarshadeen in the first place? But they'd been riding unicorns. The snow would have presented no difficulty for them.

Coldwargs would. Or Deathwings. And if either of those come after us . . .

It was something he'd rather not think about, but now he had no choice. He was the leader of his own small army. He had to think about *everything*.

A bright dazzle on the snow ahead—as if the sun had broken through, even though Kellen knew it hadn't—caught his attention. Kellen relaxed fractionally. Shalkan. If there were anything really bad out there, Shalkan wouldn't be cavorting around. He'd be crying *havoc* at the top of his lungs, and Kellen knew from experience just how loud a unicorn could yell.

So they'd have that warning, at least. And the horns could pass messages up and down the line faster than speech—complicated ones, too.

What then?

Kellen spent the rest of the day making plans for every imaginable possibility.

⸻

BEFORE the first sennight was over, he learned the trick of sending the ox-sledge off in the morning with an armed escort before breaking camp. The army easily caught up to it within an hour, but it gained them valuable time. In the evening, he did the reverse: stopped to make camp, sending the sledge on to break as much more trail as it could while there was still light, while the camp was being set up at the same time.

"You're learning," Wirance said approvingly, as they shared tea in Kellen's tent one night.

"I'd better be," Kellen answered grimly.

While there was very little the Mountainborn Wildmage could teach Kellen about the Wild Magic—their styles were much too different—and nothing at all that Wirance could teach Kellen about war—since the Wild Magic was doing that in its own way—no one born and bred in the High Reaches was a stranger to cold and snow, and there Kellen eagerly absorbed everything Wirance was willing to teach.

In the cold, every motion, every act, must do the work of two. Food was sleep, and sleep was food—and your body would lie to you in strange ways, telling you that you needed neither one, telling you that you weren't thirsty when you were, keeping you from being hungry until you starved to death.

Kellen had thought he had gotten used to the cold and winter back in Ysterialpoerin camp. On the march he realized how pampered he'd been, with relatively little exertion, abundant fuel and food, and a comparatively sheltered campsite. Out here there were none of those things. Thanks to the Wildmages, they had water in abundance, from melted snow—but if they didn't reach Ondoladeshiron within a sennight or so of their timetable, there would be no fodder for the animals—which would hardly matter, as Kellen and the others would have been reduced to eating them to stay alive.

One more thing to worry about.

The other thing to be concerned about was the weather, and there Wirance was more than valuable. He could not only tell Kellen how the weather was going to run—just as any Wildmage could—but tell Kellen *about* weather: what was normal, what was unnatural, how long winter would run . . . while the Elves were willing to talk endlessly about the weather, the great disadvantage there was that they couldn't easily be questioned about it, and Kellen needed to repair the ignorance of growing up in a city where the weather was controlled by magick.

Mud and springtime, now. If they all survived that long and the Demons ever actually fought a pitched battle against them, that would all be pretty interesting. He remembered when the Rains had started after he'd destroyed the Black Cairn, and everything had turned to mud. Apparently, it did that every year, though most years on a slightly smaller scale. Still, mud was mud, slippery and inconvenient. And this spring the mud wouldn't be on a small scale at all, since all this snowmelt was going to have to go somewhere, just as Belepheriel had said once.

He frowned. Wirance said you couldn't move sledges through mud, and he knew from his own experience that you couldn't move wagons through it. What that meant was that by spring the army had better be where it needed to be, because it wasn't going to be able to move its supplies.

And who's going to be handling Spring Planting while every able-bodied fighter from Ysterialpoerin to Armethalieh is fighting Demons? Cilarnen said the Delfier Valley lost most of the fall harvest because of the rains; Belepheriel was saying that they won't be able to plant some of the usual crops this spring in the Elven Lands because of the weather. If all of the farmers are with the army, nobody's going to be planting anything at all, though. When the stores run out, we'll all starve unless everyone can put a new crop in the ground this spring.

A chill that owed nothing to the snow passed over Kellen. He knew their resources were slender, but he'd been thinking in terms of troops and magic. For the first time he realized the stark truth: If they were going to win at all, they had to win fast.

Very fast.

AGAINST all odds, Kellen's force continued to be free of Shadow-borne attack. Kellen wondered if it was because the creatures he associated with Shadow Mountain were massing on the northern border to support the Demons' Allies, or if, as Redhelwar had feared, they'd left the Elven Lands entirely for easier prey elsewhere.

But if the Coldwarg and their cousins were absent, that did not mean the convoy was safe from attack.

Wolves, panthers, and lowland tiger prowled the upland plains and the foothills, just as ice-tiger patrolled the higher peaks. Normally the predators shied away from Men and Elves, coexisting peacefully on the abundance of wild game available.

But not this year.

First the Great Drought had come. It had hit the smallest animals first and hardest, killing many and driving others from their usual homes. The larger animals had followed—the predators in search of prey, the grazers in search of grass that was not burnt and withered, and all of them in search of water. The rains had come at last, but not soon enough to save many of them.

By the time the herds and flocks had begun to return to their accustomed ranges, followed by their hunters, winter had begun, bringing with it war, and the predators of Shadow. They had destroyed everything that might be of use to their enemy—slaughtered the deer-herds and the wild cattle and left their carcasses to spoil in the cold; dug up warrens of rabbits; killed the wild boar and even dug the squirrels out of their winter nests.

Little escaped them.

But they had spared those creatures who preyed on the deer and the wild ox and all the others, and moonturn by moonturn wolf, panther, and tiger grew more ravenous, and more desperate for prey.

THE wolfpack began trailing the army at the end of the first sennight, drawn to them by the scent of food. Reyezeyt reported that the pack was unusually large; he told Kellen his guesses as to the reason, and Kellen saw no reason to doubt him. Reyezeyt had been from Lerkelpoldara; before he had come to the House of Sword and Shield to train as an Elven Knight, he had never slept a single night beneath a roof of stone or wood. He understood the tides of the natural world in a way that no one else—not even other Elves—could.

And he—and everyone else who came from the northernmost Elven City—now had a greater reason to hate Shadow Mountain than ever before.

There was little for Kellen to do against the wolves. Some of the Wildmages traveling with the army were skilled in animal communication, but what point was there in telling a starving animal to forsake the only source of food it could see? All he could do was increase the sentries and make sure the horselines and the ox-herds were especially well-guarded.

The wolfpack shadowed the army for another sennight before it finally attacked.

The attack came just at dawn—always a vulnerable time for the camp—when the oxen were being hitched to the snow-sledge and the escort was saddling up their destriers.

The day was overcast, with a low heavy sky that hid the mountain peaks in the distance, and a fine powdery snow fell nearly straight down, for the wind had dropped just before dawn.

"Kellen!"

Shalkan's distant shout was the first warning he had. Kellen was in his tent, awake but only half-armored, when he heard Shalkan's call. It was almost immediately followed by a volley of horn-song: They were under attack.

He grabbed his helmet and his sword and flung himself out of his tent.

In the wild, Reyezeyt had told him, wolves would run their prey down, taking the weakest member of the herd while the stronger ones escaped. Here they were desperate enough to dash into what they saw as a standing herd and attempt to drag their prey out—or eat it where it stood, dead or alive.

They'd gotten past the sentries with few losses to their numbers, and the animals, scenting the wolves only when they were almost upon them, were reacting violently. The normally-stolid oxen were bawling in alarm, jostling one another in their fear: If they took it into their heads to stampede, they'd do far more harm to the camp than the wolfpack ever could.

The destriers, on the other hand, were obviously looking forward to a good fight. Ears back and teeth bared, they rolled their eyes and stamped their feet, looking around eagerly for the enemy. The ostlers had already seen what the true danger here was, and were moving the horse-herd as far from the oxen as possible. At the same time, Elves were moving over the snow, attacking the swarming pack with sword and bow.

Kellen ran toward Shalkan.

The unicorn was standing on top of the snow, watching things from a safe—for him—distance. Kellen floundered through the snow toward him and dragged himself up over Shalkan's back.

"Of all the things that are happening in this war, I think this is the saddest," the unicorn remarked in conversational tones. "They're just animals. They haven't got any choice."

"Neither do we," Kellen said grimly. "We have to get to Halacira in one piece. Let's go."

With a bound, Shalkan sprang off across the surface of the snow, moving faster than the fastest wolf. He circled around the convoy and came upon the wolves from the back.

Kellen showed no mercy. With the deer gone, the wolves would begin to prey on the domestic herds next—if they hadn't already. And the Elves were already facing famine.

Light At The Heart Of The Mountain—the thousand-year sword Belepheriel had given him—did her work incomparably. Each stroke severed spines, limbs, heads. The wolves were considerably easier than Coldwarg to kill.

But he did not accomplish his objective. He did not drive off the pack.

In the end, it was the oxen themselves that did that. With the wolves diving among them snapping at their legs and flanks, no power on earth could keep them from stampeding, but Kellen and the Knights were able to buy the ostlers and the Wildmages enough time to bunch and turn the ox-herd so that when it did bolt, it went exactly where they wanted it to go.

Right into the wolves that were harassing them.

Most of the wolves were able to get out of the way. A few of them were trapped in the middle of the herd and were trampled underfoot. And Kellen was quite impressed at how fast a herd of thoroughly maddened oxen could manage to gallop across a fresh snowfield.

The surviving wolves fled, pursued by archers, who managed to take down a few more before they were out of range.

Then all that was left was cleaning up and resuming the interrupted morning routine.

"You know they'll be back, don't you?" Shalkan asked, as Kellen slipped from his back and prepared to walk down into the camp.

"Not the ones we killed," Kellen pointed out reasonably. Though there would be others, he was certain, unless the Wildmages could come up with some way of arranging things so that the wolves looked elsewhere for prey. "I'll see you later." He began wading back through the snow toward the camp.

⟡

WINTER was as much an enemy as a wolfpack, however, and one that never went away. It was a relief to reach a wind-scrubbed streambed and to be able to trot the horses along it for a few miles, but such reliefs were few. Possibly on the other side of the mountains the snow would not be as deep. Kellen hoped not; as it was, he could not imagine how anyone following them along the trail they blazed would ever be able to find the trail-wands they were leaving behind to mark their passage, even with the carefully built-up snow-cairns to help.

Kellen had once speculated that winning a battle with a sword in one's hand was very little like commanding an army, and on this journey he proved himself right a dozen times over. He gave thanks to the Gods of the Wild Magic each time that he didn't have to figure out how to fight a battle in addition to simply learning how to move an army. It seemed to him that he spent his days riding from one end of the caravan to the other sorting matters out: scouting, patrols, halts for repairs, changes to the marching order, and endless administrative details. Without Isinwen and Wirance to remember everything he forgot, or that he simply didn't have time to hear—as not even a Knight-Mage could manage to be in two places at once—things would not have run nearly as smoothly as they did. It was a full sennight before Kellen felt he was truly beginning to properly *understand* the fighting force Redhelwar had placed at his disposal.

It's not enough to know them as people and to have fought beside them. Redhelwar's done that, and so have I. I have to know what they can do, and what they're best at.

And how to use them . . .

Despite the fact that every moment not actually spent asleep seemed to be spent solving problems, Kellen also somehow seemed to have a lot of free time to think. When he'd entered the Elven Lands for the first time it had been late summer, and even though the land had been drought-parched and suffering then, Kellen had been struck by its extraordinary beauty, and, despite everything, its vitality. Now it was deep winter, and you couldn't see the *land* at all—unless you counted the mountain peaks in the distance—but that sense of vitality he'd taken for granted was gone.

"SOMETIMES I forget that you are a Knight-Mage, and not a proper Wildmage," Wirance said when Kellen mentioned it to him that night.

"So this is something you've noticed all along?" Kellen said. *Nice of everybody to mention this to me.*

Wirance shrugged eloquently.

"The land . . . ails," Isinwen said, sounding uncomfortable.

Kellen sighed and rubbed his forehead. "It would be good to know if anything Cilarnen wishes to do will make a difference to the land." *And if Kindolhinadetil will give him permission to do it, since the land is "ailing."*

Isinwen looked at him blankly. "That is in the hands of Leaf and Star," he said at last.

There was a sudden commotion outside Kellen's tent, and the entry-bells jingled. "Enter," Kellen called.

Keirasti entered the tent and nodded. "The latest scouts are back. You'll want to hear what they have to say."

⁓

AFTER the first sennight had passed with no attacks, at least from the Enemy, Kellen had felt confident enough to begin sending out scouting parties. He also sent messengers back to the army, for even the information that they'd traveled a sennight without incident was valuable, and the broken trail would be fairly easy for riders to follow back to the main encampment.

Though Kellen had gotten the vague impression that all Elves lived in one of the Nine Cities, his troops assured him this was not so. There were small villages and even single dwelling places scattered all across the Elven Lands (though considering the size of an Elven city, Kellen privately reflected, he could probably fit the entire population of a "small village" into his tent and still have room to sleep comfortably). And while they were undetectable for all practical purposes, that didn't mean they were actively hidden, or even hard to find, at least for other Elves. Kellen had instructed his scouts to seek out as many of such houses and villages as they could reach, to give their inhabitants the news about Lerkelpoldara, and encourage them to seek shelter in Ysterialpoerin.

⁓

BECAUSE of the continuing danger from wolves and other natural predators, he sent the scouts out in groups of four. This group had included Nironoshan, and he was the one making the report.

Kellen had put Keirasti in charge of the scouts, and so Nironoshan was waiting in Keirasti's tent, a mug of tea already in his hands. Kellen accepted his own mug of Winter Spice tea gratefully and hunkered down on his heels, waiting for Nironoshan to speak.

Elves never made a point of displaying their emotions at the best of times, but Nironoshan was a member of Kellen's own troop and had been with him from the day Redhelwar had first given Kellen a command of his own. As much as Kellen could read the expressions of any of the Elves, he could read Nironoshan's, and he could tell that something had upset the Elven Knight greatly.

"Commander," Nironoshan said simply. "We have returned from the village of White Spring. There is no one there left alive."

⟡

THE scouting party had begun with the outlying steadings along the path of march—single dwellings in the vicinity of White Spring. All were empty, but Nironoshan and the others did not find that entirely unusual. The inhabitants might have left because of the unusually hard weather. They might be serving with the army. They might be off on an extended hunting trip. There might be any number of reasons for the houses to be vacant, and he and the other scouts had seen no sign that the dwellings had been left in haste, or that the inhabitants had been forced out by violence.

On the chance the inhabitants might return, they had left warnings to evacuate, and continued on to White Spring. Though they had looked to see signs of game along the way, there had been none, confirming Reyezeyt's theory that the Coldwarg and other creatures of the Enemy had slaughtered or driven off most of the wild creatures in the area.

As the scouting party approached White Spring, they had seen the plague flags.

The yellow banners on their tall red-painted willow poles were ice-crusted and tattered by weather. They had obviously not been recently tended. The scouts approached cautiously. The small village was silent.

"Not even the animals were left, Kellen. I think they had turned them loose to fend for themselves at the last, when they could no longer care for them, and of course the wolves took them." Nironoshan shook his head sadly. "Better they had killed them themselves, but perhaps they were too ill to think of that."

"Perhaps," Kellen said. "Or perhaps someone had already taken them away."

Nironoshan shook his head again. "No. We searched the village. Everyone who belonged there was there."

⟡

THEY had entered the village, hoping against all evidence that someone might be alive. They did not find the orderly stillness they had seen in the single houses. Wolves had been here, wandering through the streets and pawing at the doors. The beasts had not been able to enter, but they had gotten into the now-empty stables and byres and coops, picking them clean of whatever they had held and destroying everything they could not eat.

Nironoshan and the others had done what the wolves could not, opening the doors and entering the small cluster of houses one by one.

The first house, he told Kellen, had apparently been used to hold the earliest plague cases until they could be taken to the trees. Those bodies were neatly wrapped and laid out. But the sickness had obviously spread quickly after that. The disposition of the rest of the bodies told the grim story far too plainly: Some lay in their beds, as if they had been tended in their illness, but far more of the bodies had been found, Nironoshan reported, sprawled upon the floors of their houses, as if Death had come upon them and struck them down where they stood. It was obvious that from the first deaths to the death of everyone had been only a matter of days; long enough for the people of White Spring to set out the plague-flags, but not long enough for them to understand how serious the situation was and to decide to send a messenger to Ysterialpoerin for help.

"None of us touched anything," Nironoshan said, sounding uneasy. "And we did not stay long. But that the Shadow's Kiss should come again . . ."

"Again?" Kellen asked, before he could stop himself from asking a direct question. "What do you mean 'again'?"

"I saw the bodies," Nironoshan said. "It is just as it was in the time of the Great War. *They* send sickness to do their foul work. It is *Their* doing."

And sickness was an enemy no armor—or shield—could defend against.

⁓

IT had now been a full moonturn since Jermayan had begun his latest series of flights to the Fortress of the Crowned Horns, and a few more sennights—he hoped—would see that mission complete.

From Lerkelpoldara he had gone to Deskethomaynel, where he had been able to make use of the signaling mirrors. He had finally been able to send a report to Redhelwar of all he had done on the Plains of Bazrahil, and of the tragic fate of the Winter City. He had ferried his living cargo to the fortress of the Crowned Horns, and then gone to Sentarshadeen to bring the news there in person.

Among those who needed to leave Sentarshadeen for the Fortress of the Crowned Horns was the Queen herself. Andoreniel's decree made more sense now that Jermayan knew of her condition, for Andoreniel certainly could not send Ashaniel to safety and leave the other Elven women unprotected. There were already reports of plague in the human lands—sent by the Enemy, both Andoreniel and Jermayan were certain—and it was only a matter of time before it crossed the borders into the Elven Lands themselves.

From Sentarshadeen Jermayan had returned to Windaloriannan, where he discovered, to his relief, that the ragged band of refugees from Lerkelpoldara had arrived at the city without any further losses. Magarabeleniel greeted him there, and at last agreed to accompany him to the Fortress of the Crowned Horns, having left the remains of her people in the safekeeping of Vanantiriel, the Viceroy of Windaloriannan.

"Though it seems that we are all to become refugees," Vanantiriel told Jermayan. "The signaling mirrors have sent word from Redhelwar. He tells us we are to prepare to cede the north to the Shadow, and move south as far and as fast as we can. It will be a difficult thing traveling in winter, and with so many sick, but we shall do what we must."

"In Sentarshadeen, we had reports of sickness in the human lands," Jermayan said uneasily.

"Our old enemy is here among us as well," Vanantiriel said with a grim smile. "And the Knight-Mage warns that *Their* Allies seek to broach the land-wards besides, destroying us in our cities one by one, just as they did at Lerkelpoldara."

"It is the sort of tactic *They* would find appealing," Jermayan admitted. "It is a hard thing to leave one's home, knowing that it may be overrun and spoiled by the Enemy, but Kellen has told us over and over that *Their* strategy is always to entice us into splitting our forces and our attention so that we can be more easily destroyed. And I have never found him to be wrong, when he speaks as a Knight-Mage. *They* attack our homes, certain that we will not be able to resist defending them, when to defend them is to lose all. And so I said in Deskethomaynel as well."

"Then I shall expect to see Arelin Viceroy in Ysterialpoerin, where we can finish our game of *xaique* face to face," Vanantiriel said with a deep sigh. "And that shall be some compensation for leaving the Fields of Vardirvoshanon and moving all of our horses in this weather—for when your Knight-Mage suggested we move, I am certain he was not suggesting that they be left behind."

I am certain, Jermayan thought, *that it did not occur to Kellen that the Fields of Vardirvoshanon were here, with their thousands of mares, stallions, and yearling foals. Nevertheless, he is right: Windaloriannan is vulnerable, and the Enemy will strike at it next. With one of the Triad of the North fallen, it is logical that the other two should be* Their *next targets. And he is also right that we must save the Triad of the Heartland—Ysterialpoerin, Ondoladeshiron, and Valwendigorean—by sacrificing the north. But it is not easy. . . .*

⤫

"WE'RE nearly done," Ancaladar told him consolingly, as they flew from Realthataladaon toward the Crowned Horns. Ondoladashiron was next, then Ysterialpoerin, then they would be done.

They had swept back and forth from city to city—through what remained of the North Triad, through the Heart Triad, and among the close-held cities of the

Southern Triad—Sentarshadeen, Thultafoniseen, and Realthataladon—gathering their precious cargo and bearing it safe to the Fortress of the Crowned Horns. Once he brought the women from Ysterialpoerin to the Crowned Horns, Master Tyrvin would seal up the doors of the fortress for the last time, perhaps never to open them again.

Jermayan forced his mind away from such thoughts. He must believe they could find their way to victory yet a third time. But in the First War, they had been . . . perhaps more evenly matched against their foe, neither side having yet fully taken the measure of the other, and in the Great War they had had the full strength of the humans, in arms and magic, to draw upon, rather than dreading every moment to see it turned into a sword for their throats.

Better that the sea had claimed Armethalieh before the first stone of her walls had been laid upon the next, than that the world should see this day.

"I think you underestimate the humans' resiliency of spirit," Ancaladar protested softly. "They will see through Anigrel's tricks, given time."

"Time!" Jermayan said. "When have humans ever had enough time? And especially now—when none of us has enough time!"

❧

"I must say, they took their time giving you their answer," Idalia said tartly, as Cilarnen peered distractedly out through the tent-flap. "There's a messenger from Ysterialpoerin for you waiting with Redhelwar."

She'd been in the dining tent that morning when the messenger had come with a scroll for Cilarnen, more than a sennight after Kellen's departure with his convoy. Ninolion had come to the dining tent looking for him, and Idalia had attached herself to the search. After all, Kellen *had* told her to keep an eye on Cilarnen.

He was easily found in his tent in the Centaur encampment, looking precisely like a wondertale depiction of a High Mage: vague, irritable, and decidedly unkempt. Idalia doubted that he'd either eaten or slept recently, and his pavilion reeked of the most interesting collection of herbal smells to be found outside of Healer's Alley. For a brief moment she wished that Shalkan hadn't gone off with Kellen—she was sure that the unicorn could manage to talk sense into the boy, even if no one else could.

Cilarnen stared at them both in blank incomprehension, definitely with no idea of why they had come and possibly with no idea of who they were.

Men and High Mages, Idalia thought irascibly.

"A messenger has come from Kindolhinadetil," she repeated. "The Viceroy of Ysterialpoerin. For you. He's waiting in Redhelwar's pavilion. To see you. It would be helpful if you were a little more presentable when you went." Idalia spoke slowly and plainly, giving Cilarnen time to return to the here-and-now from whatever dream-world he'd been wandering in.

Abruptly Cilarnen's eyes snapped into focus and he seemed to come to himself. He sketched a barely-correct bow and withdrew into his tent like a snapping-turtle retreating into its shell. More quickly than Idalia would have thought possible, he emerged again: tidied, hair brushed, and in a fresh pale blue tunic, fastening a white fur cloak about his shoulders and pulling on his gloves. When he bowed again, his bow was correct and flawlessly executed.

"Idalia. Ninolion. My regrets that my present accommodation forced you to await me in the street; it was especially unfortunate in view of the weather." It was, as usual, snowing. "Equally unfortunate in that I was unable to offer you tea, a lapse which I hope to repair at your earliest convenience."

Now it was Idalia's turn to stare. She'd been quite certain—well, fairly certain, anyway—that Cilarnen was not twins. Yet the young man babbling inanely (and urbanely) along at her side just now bore very little resemblance to the intense wild-eyed young mystic who had answered Ninolion's summons to the door of his tent.

"I, too, look forward to such an occasion," Ninolion said blandly. "I believe that to take tea with you would be highly entertaining."

"One regrets, of course, that one's library of tea is not large, nor all that it could be were matters otherwise. I possess some Armethaliehan Black, and naturally some Winter Spice; I've recently been able to acquire some Phastan Red, though unfortunately it is in block form, not leaf. Phastan Silvertip, is, of course, the preferred growth, though somewhat common; connoisseurs favor Phastan Gold, which is quite rare. And naturally, as my own knowledge runs more in the line of the cured-leaf teas, I would welcome instruction and advice in those areas where my understanding should prove deficient."

At least, thought Idalia, Cilarnen seems to have taken to heart all of Kellen's instructions on making small talk and not trying to hurry an Elven conversation along. Though he must have been bursting with impatience to find out what Kindolhinadetil's messenger had to say, he and Ninolion were happily chattering along about the sorts of tea that might be available in camp for Cilarnen to add to his collection, and the possibility of him getting his hands on more cured-leaf varieties, which most Elves found so bitter as to be unpalatable. Both of them were in complete agreement that the High Reaches Smokeleaf was utterly undrinkable—which only went to prove, Idalia supposed, that she would never be a true connoisseur of tea.

This conversation continued all the way to Redhelwar's tent and well inside. The messenger, Enolwiar, was introduced, and gave Cilarnen the message. It was in the form of a thin scroll in a golden case, with the implication of this particu-lar form of delivery being that the messenger himself would not be privy to the information he conveyed. He, too, was solicited for his opinions on the matter of tea, which he was, of course, perfectly happy to provide.

The entire Shadow army might be waiting outside . . . and they'd have to go on waiting while the Elves finished their tea. Little brother, you had much more patience than I ever gave you credit for, Idalia thought crossly.

When he had finished his tea, Enolwiar thanked Redhelwar for his courtesy and hospitality, and left. But Cilarnen still made no move toward the scroll-case.

"Well?" Idalia demanded, after a pause. "Are you just going to stare at it? Or are you going to open it and see what Kindolhinadetil's answer is?"

"I'll assume he's made the right choice," Cilarnen said, in a somewhat stifled voice, reaching for the scroll. "Since it took him this long to do it. Saying 'no' wouldn't take very long at all."

It took him a few moments to figure out how to work the catch, but at last the case opened, and the inner spindle slid free. Cilarnen pounced on the curl of vellum and scanned it eagerly.

"Perhaps I spoke too soon," he said, sounding puzzled and faintly hurt. "I can read it, but I can't tell what it says."

"Let me try," Idalia suggested. Cilarnen handed the sheet to her, but she found herself in much the same situation: staring at a page of beautifully-calligraphed and illuminated text that seemed to be . . . a poem. About astron-omy, as far as she could tell.

It might, of course, be something else. In fact, it almost certainly was. But if it was a personal message from Kindolhinadetil to Cilarnen—and she supposed it really had to be—she had no idea of how to interpret it, either. Wordlessly, she passed the page to Redhelwar.

The army's general regarded the page for only a moment, and both the hu-mans sensed that he was trying *very* hard not to smile.

"'To Cilarnen High Mage, of the Golden City of Armethalieh, from Kindol-hinadetil Viceroy, of the House of Bough and Wind, Greetings. In this dark time, when our great Enemy attempts to quench not only the stars but the light itself, we must act in ways that in times of peace and serenity would seem to be not only madness, but treason. Therefore I counsel you to do all that you can to come into your power, to use it as a sword and shield in battle against our great Enemy. In which matter I as the hand and voice of Andoreniel urge you to do what you will do for the good of the land unless the King himself should unspeak these words.'"

Redhelwar curled the sheet around the spindle again and closed the scroll-case, passing it back to Cilarnen.

Even more-or-less translated, Kindolhinadetil's message made hard going. Idalia and Cilarnen looked at each other, and Idalia was prepared to say that Cilarnen looked as confused as she felt.

"I think he said I can try to tap the power of the land-wards, at least unless—or until—the King says I can't," Cilarnen said hesitantly.

"Indeed, to be exceptionally brief, that is the gist of the Viceroy's message to you," Redhelwar said kindly. "It is written very much in the old style, and I thought perhaps you would be unfamiliar with the conventions of the form," he added gently. "It would be good to know what it is that you will do, now that you have heard his word to you."

"I'm going to have to go and see if I can do something that I'd always been told—back in the City—couldn't be done. I'm going to make a pact with Elemental Forces. And see if I live through it," Cilarnen answered with grim cheerfulness.

⁂

KARDUS and Idalia had said goodbye to him as if they were sending him off to war. In a way, Cilarnen supposed they were—the only kind of war he was equipped to fight. Not a war of horses and armor, but a war of spells, of Illusory Creatures and Elemental Beings. Of dragons and unicorns.

And, yes, of Demons.

High Magick could find them. High Magick could kill them. True, it had to be done in concert with a Wildmage, but the Allies seemed to have plenty of those, and he was the only High Mage there was. On their side, anyway.

For now.

The Allies talked about finding more Wildmages. They even talked about finding and training another Knight-Mage like Kellen—everybody said he was a different kind of Wildmage, but nobody had ever explained the difference to Cilarnen in any way he understood. But they all overlooked one thing.

If this worked, Cilarnen could find and train more *High Mages*.

Everyone had the power that fueled the High Magick, the power that the High Magick burned the way a lamp burned oil. The difference was, the High Mages could *use* that power, not merely create and horde it. What made them re-spected (*feared*, a small part of Cilarnen's mind traitorously supplied) was that they had found a way to harvest (*steal*) a lot of that power, so they would have a lot of it to use. They had found that way because that method was safer, easier, and more comfortable than the method Cilarnen was about to try.

But with everyone having the power—and that meant Wildlander farmers and High Reaches families, too—that certainly meant that there were people

born into those families who could use the power just as those born into Mageborn families did. It had just never been awakened in them, the way the power
naturally awoke in the sons of Mageborn families from close proximity to all the
magick in Armethalieh.

There might not be many, but they were out there. They had to be.

Cilarnen could find them and train them.

If this worked.

And if the Demons would give them time.

Idalia, Kardus, and Cilarnen's other friends among the Wildmages had spent
the whole morning moving his tent and everything he owned up to the ice-pavilion
that was going to be his new home. That way, when (*if*) he made a disastrous mistake with his spellcraft, the only person he'd blow to Darkness would be him.

Idalia had worried about how far he was from the main camp, since now the
patrols were starting to see wolves in the Heart-Forest, though the Ysterialpoer-
ines said that this was rare this early in the season (and thus a cause for even more
concern than it would be normally), but Cilarnen had assured her that if his plans
worked as he hoped, he would have nothing to fear from wolves. And if they did
not, he would have nothing to fear from wolves for quite a different reason.

He had been very nearly rude, shooing them out of his new camp as quickly
as possible, ignoring their offers to stay and help him finish setting up, or—worse
yet—stay the night. But he could not afford the presence of the non-Mageborn.
He had gained Kindolhinadetil's permission at last, and this was the last day for
nearly a moonturn upon which he could perform the Summoning Ritual. He had
an enormous amount of work to complete before the appropriate half-bell.

There were five wandering stars in the night sky over the City: Metwoch,
Gwener, Tienstag, Dediau, and Shanbe. Each one governed a day of the sennight; the two leftover days were governed by the sun and the moon. In addition, the seven heavenly bodies, plus the four Magickal Elements, plus the
Eternal Light, were paired to govern the ritual bells that marked time in
Armethalieh in its twelve daylight aspects and twelve nighttime aspects. The
Summoning Ritual must be performed under a waxing moon, upon the day and
the portion of the bell of Metwoch dedicated to it. If he missed tonight, the day
and half-bell of Metwoch under a waxing moon would not come again for an
entire moonturn.

And that was only the beginning of his preparations.

There were braziers in the Number of Metwoch which had to be set out in
precisely the right directions, the Seal of Metwoch to be inscribed upon the floor
of his working area with his ritual sword, the proper incenses to be compounded
and burned at the proper times leading up to the casting of his Circle, the preliminary prayers and ablutions to take care of—because contacting an Elemental

was a potentially-dangerous business and he did not wish to scrimp on any part of the procedure and cause himself unnecessary risk due to sloppy preparation and having allowed his attention to wander at the vital moment.

Normally a Mage would have an apprentice—or a number of apprentices— to do most of the scutwork while he concentrated on those tasks that only he could do. Cilarnen had to do it all himself.

He couldn't remember the last time he'd been so happy.

Cilarnen vaguely remembered Kellen from Before. In those days Kellen had been a sulky gangly boy who stank of the Commons and radiated misery like heat. Lord Lycaelon must have flinched every time he'd laid eyes on him. So much had changed! Now Kellen was happy, having apparently found something that he understood.

He'd obviously never understood the High Magick, and so he'd hated it. From the little he'd said since Cilarnen had met him again, Kellen still thought of the High Magick as really only a way to get the unGifted to grovel to you. But what he had never understood—and what Cilarnen had always known too well to even be able to articulate it—was that the High Magick was always so much more than that.

It was beauty. It was an end in itself. Cilarnen could have found true joy in spending his entire life serving its exacting specifications.

At its heart, the High Magick was a map to the way the world worked. Describe something exactly, know it utterly, and you could change it in any way you desired. How could anyone want anything more than this? Not the power—but the knowledge! See into the heart of a tree, and you could create anything you wanted, from furniture to a forest. Or you could just see the tree, and have the knowledge that it could be either one at any time you wished. Because you understood the tree from its first seedling bud to the ash of its burning.

Spells could be elegantly simple, such as the ones that made fire or heated water—or turned water to ice. Or they could be brilliantly complex, like the spells that stopped Time in order to preserve food and strengthen walls. Or they could be created from layers of several different classes of spell together to produce an effect which seemed—on the surface—to be nothing like any of them. Like Mageshield, which was at root a stasis spell combined with several other simple spells, including the spell of levitation that moved it through the air.

Once, Cilarnen's highest ambition had been to become an arcane experimenter, one of those Mages who worked day-in, day-out with the simple homely building-block spells, trying them in new combinations in an attempt to produce a useful new spell for the good of the City.

Such a possibility now seemed as unlikely as that he would live until summer.

Or that Kellen Tavadon would ever understand how purely glorious the High Magick could be.

Because he's all caught up in his Wild Magic, I suppose. Wild? Lunatic, is more like it! Truly, I've heard more sense from the headsick people my masters were called upon to cure when I was an Entered Apprentice. But it does not mean there is harm in them . . . so why not leave them alone instead of condemning them to death and pretending they are agents of Demonkind? It's just that their magic seems so . . . untidy.

Untidy or not, Cilarnen did have to admit that it took far less time: He'd never seen a Wildmage cast a spell that took more than half a chime, if that. As for him, it was mid-day when he began working, and five bells later when his preparations were complete.

It lacked a bell of midnight, the second half of which was Metwoch's time, so Cilarnen allowed himself a chime of rest before beginning the last series of invocations and prayers. By now his workspace shimmered with the wards he had set, and he was feeling the tug of exhaustion, for he had used up nearly all his own personal reserves of power as the bells moved from Dediau to Shanbe and on to Metwoch.

⁓

THE glyphs he traced hung before him in the air. He whispered their names under his breath, and the air was so cold that steam rose to swirl amid the traceries of colored light.

Soon. It would be soon.

He had never done anything like this before.

The High Magick taught that any creatures the Mageborn might see in their spells were only hallucinations—one of the first things a young Apprentice studied was the types of Illusory Creatures he might expect to see during his working life, and how to ignore them. They were, so he was told, only the symbols of the power he commanded by right of his training in the High Magick.

But Cilarnen knew now that they were not symbols, but *real*.

And he had not come to command, but to *ask*.

I ask not for myself, but for the good I might do with any Power You would loan me, he recited in his mind. It was only the truth, but he wondered if, when the time came—*if* the time came—he would be calm enough to say the words aloud.

"Come to me, Powers of the Elven Lands. I co— I *ask* that you come to me. In the name of those who rule these lands, I summon you—I request that you come before me to hear my words."

He drew the last of the sigils in the air before the eleventh brazier. It was the most complicated of all, and he was sweating before he had finished. For a moment it hung in the air, perfect, and Cilarnen let out the pent-up breath he had been holding in a long sigh of relief.

But then it began to blur and change, swelling and growing brighter. If it had been badly done, it would simply have faded away.

Something must have gone dreadfully wrong.

He clutched his wand tightly, scouring his mind for some counterspell to contain the damage. But he had stretched his resources to their uttermost simply to cast this spell. He could not do so much as light a candle now.

The glyph became a ball of light, then an oval, then a cylinder. All its colors faded into a pale blue-white, as it slowly settled to the ice, balancing on its end. It began to melt into itself as Cilarnen watched in horrified fascination, slowly taking on something like a human form.

By the Eternal Light. It's worked. I called it here.

And now it's going to kill me.

He'd done nothing to protect himself from what he'd intended to summon—he'd had barely enough energy to cast the most basic of wards and then to cast the Summoning Spell itself. All he could do was watch.

It was like seeing something come from far away, as the manikin took on form. The glow resolved itself into flame—blue flame—racing all over its body. It was small and slender, the humanlike form inches shorter than Cilarnen himself, and somehow Cilarnen could see eyes, a nose, a mouth in that burning face of flame, although he was not certain of how he could make them out.

He had not known what would come to his Summoning—the land-wards which protected the Elven Lands were made up of a blending of all four Elements—but it seemed that the Powers themselves had chosen.

And what they had sent was a Salamander, creature of Elemental Fire.

"You have Called Me, Cilarnen Volpiril. For what task?" Its voice was blurred and hard to understand, like the roaring of a large fire, and he could smell an odd scent that he could not quite describe. Something burning, he decided. But not wood. It smelled like fire itself, burning without fuel.

"I need your help. The Elves need your help."

"We already aid the Children of Leaf and Star."

Cilarnen sensed rather than saw the strange drawing-inward, as if the Salamander was preparing once more to depart. And he knew he did not have the strength to cast this spell again.

"No! Wait!"

He did not know what he said then. He'd had a speech carefully prepared, but he'd forgotten it. He babbled like a fool, telling the creature things he was certain it already knew—about the Demons, and the war. About the High Mages, and their ancient source of power, and what they had taken to use instead. And how he hoped to fight the Demons, but he needed . . .

"Help," the Salamander finished for him. "Our help."

He felt the creature look into him, as if only now was it seeing him for the first time. A terror he had not known he had the energy left to feel gripped him. Cilarnen had not felt so afraid when he and his friends had been discovered by the Stone Golems in the City, or on the night he had thought his Magegift stripped from him. He had thought he had been afraid when he had seen the Scouring Hunt for what it truly was, or when he had seen the Demon's face in Stonehearth.

All those moments were pale echoes of this. Each of those times, Cilarnen understood now, he could only have died. The force he confronted now was raw Magick Itself: It had the power to unmake him, as if he had never been at all. No one would remember him—that he had been here, that he had cast this spell . . . in Armethalieh, his family would forget his very existence. . . .

The Salamander smiled sadly, and Cilarnen's terror faded. No, it would not do that. It had such power, yes, but for all its inhumanity, it was a Creature of the Light. It had come at his call.

Did he have the courage to accept the help it might offer?

He'd thought he'd understood what that would mean. He'd had *no* idea. This was Death, as certain as any a warrior faced upon a battlefield. Yes, he could gain the power to cast any spell he needed, but it would be like carrying the sun itself within the marrow of his bones. Such power would waste him as surely as if he consumed a slow-acting poison, and in the end it would kill him. *"The life of a Battle-Mage is bright and brief,"* the old books had said. Well, now he understood why. The Mages had not changed their ways for no reason. They had changed in order to live.

"Help me," he whispered.

"Take my hand, Cilarnen Volpiril," the creature of blue flame said, "and be one with the land."

He hesitated at the thought of plunging his hand into that conflagration. The ice-pavilion was filled with heat. His clothes were steaming with it. The only oddity was that the wards and the circle stopped the heat precisely, so that the circle itself was wet with water, but the ice outside it was dry with cold.

But he had called it, and now it had agreed.

And if this did not work, he did not know what else to try.

He reached out, and took its hand.

The Salamander flowed into him through their clasped hands. Fast enough that Cilarnen didn't have time to think of ways to stop it, slow enough that he knew what was happening and had time to think of the precise word to label the sensation.

It was intolerable.

That was what it was.

It was intolerable.

He was being stretched from within, his lungs pressed against his ribs so hard he could not take a breath, and the same cloying unclassifiable burning scent was all around him now, except now it was coming from inside: It was on his breath, in his nostrils, on his tongue. He felt light filling his brain and shining out through his eyes, blinding him; he gagged on thick radiance filling the back of his throat and he tried to cough it out, to empty his throat and his stomach and his lungs, but he couldn't. It was there, stretching him until he thought his skin might tear like a too-tight glove. But what would spill out?

Slowly all of it faded away: the light, the smell, the gagging pressure. He was alone in the ice pavilion, and suddenly he was shivering with cold.

He felt a faint numbness in his hands and lips, like frostburn or poison, but in a few minutes that faded, too, and Cilarnen realized he was cold because all of the braziers in the ice-pavilion had gone out and he was standing in four inches of cold water.

The Salamander was gone. Cilarnen felt as if he'd just suddenly awakened from an odd dream. As if the spell had been a dream. It had all seemed very logical and even compelling at the time, but now that he was awake, its events seemed peculiar, even absurd, and the more time that passed, the more the events of the dream became vague and unreal.

He knew from his reading that the Great Spells were often like that, but he had never cast one before and didn't know if this experience was what it ought to feel like. He simply felt as if he ought to be terribly frightened, and for some reason his body wouldn't cooperate.

He stepped carefully to the edge of the circle—there was more ice beneath the water, and a scrum of ice was already re-forming at the edges of the circle— and stepped out onto the ice. As he walked toward the braziers, his shoes began to stick to the ice as they froze.

With a gesture, he lit the braziers.

All of them.

He shouldn't have had the power to do that after the ritual, but he did.

He felt the Salamander's ghostly presence as it shifted beneath his skin. It wasn't there, not of itself. That would kill him in truth just as he had feared during the ritual. But he was now linked to the land-wards of the Elven Lands, and through them, to the Elemental Powers that gave them life: sylph, gnome, undine, Salamander.

He had the power he needed.

⟨≈⟩

HE completed the ritual—the prayers and glyphs that ended it were simple, compared to the preparations—and spent the rest of the night reinforcing the wards around the ice-pavilion, making them as strong and complex as he could. Now that he could practice—*really* practice—there was a lot more potential for disaster than ever before.

Warping a Mageshield, or . . . some of the spells for summoning lightning, or a rain of fire . . . I don't want to even try those without the best damping wards I can possibly cast. Layers of them.

And if he meant to go viewing over a distance, the most important thing was that no one he chose to look at be able to look at *him*.

Cilarnen knew that both Idalia and Kellen thought that the High Magick contained no spells for seeing things at a distance. He smiled. As if no High Mage had ever wanted to see something on the other side of the City without leaving the comfort and privacy of his own chambers! The City might not be as vast as the Elvenlands, but it was the whole world to its inhabitants, and contained the world in miniature. Of course, the spells of Far-Seeing were not made available to every Apprentice or Journeyman who might be tempted to misuse them. It would be as unfortunate to look in the wrong window as to look beyond the bounds of Armethalieh, and it was much better for all if the Lower Grades were not tempted. But that didn't mean such spells didn't exist, and they were in the books that Kindolhinadetil had provided him with. It would be simple enough to adjust the parameters of the spell to compensate for the increased distance from the place he wanted to view, and he could visualize *where* he wanted to see very clearly.

The Council Chamber of Armethalieh.

But not now. Now he needed rest, and sleep, and food. The sun was rising, the traditional signal to the end of the labors of a High Mage.

Cilarnen doused the braziers, wrapped his cloak tightly around himself against the morning chill, and headed for his own tent.

Seven

The Sword of the City

I F ARMETHALIEH WERE known anywhere outside her own walls—
a matter of supreme indifference to both her inhabitants and her
rulers—she was known as the City of Mages. Wildly inaccurate tales
were told about Armethalieh in the lands beyond the sea, but one thing
known about her was the simple truth: Mages had built her and Mages
ruled her, for Armethalieh was a city of magick.

The ultimate authority in Armethalieh was the High Council: twelve High
Mages ruled over by the Arch-Mage, the ultimate authority in the City.

At least, that had been true once.

Three High Mages—Lords Breulin, Isas, and Volpiril—had left the Council
under mysterious circumstances to retire into private life.

One had died during a ritual that he had been far too old and frail to partic-
ipate in—Lord Vilmos.

Two—Lords Arance and Perizel—had been murdered by evil Wildmage
magic, that much everyone in the City knew.

Only one of the six empty seats had been refilled, and that by the Arch-
Mage's own adopted son, Anigrel Tavadon.

The High Council had once debated strongly and at endless length over
every facet of the numerous laws that governed every facet of life in the Golden
City, for as well as being a city of Mages, Armethalieh was a city of Law, and the
High Council was the ultimate expression of that law. Now the only voice heard
within the Council Chamber was Anigrel Tavadon's.

Had it not been Anigrel's idea to set a group of Wardens over the Commons to report all suspicious activity, so that never again would treason be attempted against the Mageborn? And because the Wildmages were so viciously clever, extending their taint to the Mageborn themselves, there were Wardens to watch over the Mageborn themselves. For their own protection, of course.

But Anigrel's reforms had not stopped there. Since the ranks of the High Council were now so sadly depleted—by treason and murder within their very ranks, proof of the growing Wildmage menace—had not Anigrel drawn from the ranks of the Magewardens a group of loyal young acolytes to take over some of the most important spellwork involved in running the City itself, so that the Council could expend its own resources on only the most vital matters?

Indeed, as the sennights stretched to moonturns, the High Council found—with varying senses of relief and unease among its members—that more and more of its magickal work was turned over to the Magewardens. And there was less of it to do than ever before, for at Anigrel's urging, the Council had reinstated a series of ancient taxes on the citizens of Armethalieh for the privilege of calling upon the Mages for magick at all.

The Great Spells of Protection and Preservation were still cast, of course: Food was preserved, fires were quenched, walls were strengthened, the bells that kept time in the Golden City continued to do so. And most of all, the Great Wards that strengthened the high stone walls of Armethalieh against any assault, magickal or physical, remained firm.

❦

OR *so they believe.*

Anigrel Tavadon—he had possessed another name once, but it was quite unimportant to him now—stood in his private robing chamber, preparing to take his place in the Circle. Though his rank—entirely unofficial, to be sure, but influential just the same—would have allowed him to delegate this task to his subordinates without eliciting any comment, Anigrel always attended the Warding Circles.

It was the most important thing he did; the keystone of his secret life. Long before Anigrel had pledged his service to the City, he had sworn his allegiance to an older, darker power. From earliest childhood, Anigrel had served the Queen of the Endarkened, and everything he had done in life looked toward the day when he could lay the Golden City at her feet as her prize.

The City Wards were centuries old, layer upon layer of protective spells to ensure that nothing that was not human could enter the City of Mages, that no spell of Darkness, that nothing Tainted, that no creature of baneful intent, could pass its gates or soar over its walls to imperil those who lived within. Any who had attained the rank of High Mage could read these wards as easily as one of the unGifted could read a book of wondertales, and would instantly recognize any change in them.

That was why he had needed to be so very careful.

Every change he had made had been insignificant in itself. And at the same time he worked upon the wards, he had changed the City, creating such a climate of fear among the Mageborn so that by the time the changes could no longer be hidden—and that time was very near, perhaps even tonight—anyone who could see the changes to the City Wards, and who dared to speak of it, could easily be arrested and condemned as a traitor.

Anigrel smiled. But the time in which any *would* see the change to the City Wards would be very brief, for when the changes became visible, it would be the signal that his Dark Lady's powers could reach within the City at last.

Oh, she would not yet be able to enter in person. Much more work would still have to be done. It was no light thing to dismantle the spells of centuries: he did not have such power. But when the wards had been transformed, her influence would be able to extend within the City openly and easily—not along the tiny thread he had nurtured all his life, but as a rushing torrent of blessed Darkness. She could protect him from any who opposed him, erase the knowledge of his tamperings from the minds of those who discovered it.

And help him winnow the High Council still further.

Once Lycaelon had dreamed of ruling Armethalieh alone and unopposed. Perhaps, before the old man died, Anigrel would grant him his wish. Meron and Harith were annoying old fools, and once Anigrel had the power that compromising the City Wards would grant him—the power to conceal his own dark magic—he could ensure that even more members of the High Council met with unfortunate . . . accidents.

He finished robing—only the sheerest of gray linen would do for this most important of the City's rituals—picked up the Sword of the City, and walked from the chamber.

⤝

THE long and elaborate ritual was completed without a flaw. The Magewardens were all young and ambitious; they saw Anigrel as the very embodiment of Armethalieh, and were personally loyal to him. Through him, they had gained power and rank that would not otherwise have been theirs for years, if not decades, and all of them were ambitious enough to do nothing to risk it. Anigrel had chosen and promoted his Magewardens on the basis of ability alone, advancing them through the ranks far more quickly than tradition would have permitted. The men who stood in the Circle with him, who carried out his orders and spied upon their fellow Mageborn "for the good of the City," would have been mere Journeymen without his patronage, and every one of them knew it. The black badge and tabard of the Magewardens allowed them equality with the most exalted of the High Mages—equality, and even superiority, for no High Mage was safe from what Anigrel's Magewardens might report to him under the veil of strict secrecy and anonymity, and every one of the Mageborn knew it.

When Anigrel left the Circle, Lycaelon was waiting for him.

As always, the Arch-Mage wore his gray Mage-robes, with their embroidered tabard of rank over them. One who was experienced in Mage-heraldry could read from the symbols upon a Mage's tabard not only a Mage's House and lineage—for the tabard was naturally embroidered in the Household Colors of that Mage—but his rank, his position, and the Great Workings to which he had been called. A Mage's tabard held the entire history of his life in service to the City, and it was a constantly-changing tapestry, for those who had the eyes to see.

Though Lycaelon had other garments, of course, Anigrel had rarely seen him wear them. Lycaelon's identification with the City—and his Art—was utterly complete. Long ago, the distinction between the private man and the Arch-Mage of Armethalieh had been utterly forgotten. Lycaelon Tavadon *had* no private life.

That Lycaelon should be up and about at this hour was in and of itself not unusual, for the High Mages were as much creatures of nighttime as daylight. Spells might be cast at any bell, but the Great Workings were best accomplished during the bells of night, when the City was at its quietest, and the intrusive clamor of waking minds was stilled by sleep.

But the peculiar look of worry upon the Arch-Mage's face was something Anigrel was not used to seeing. It was no part of Anigrel's plans that his adoptive father should find things to worry about. Anigrel spent precious bells of his time ensuring that Lycaelon believed that the City was running more smoothly than it ever had before. What had the old man found to worry him now?

"My son," Lycaelon said, "I know you are weary, but I felt you should know of this at once—before the Council session tomorrow."

"Later today, surely?" Anigrel said, with a gentle smile, for the Council House rang all the bells of the night, and he had heard First Dawn Bells just as the ritual ended.

"The Council will know you have been in the Circle tonight, and so will wait until Noontide Bells to convene, but I had thought it best to prepare you now. There has been another attack upon Nerendale. The farmers there petition to leave their village, and move closer to the City."

"The Wildmages grow bolder, Father," Anigrel murmured, putting a soothing hand upon Lycaelon's arm.

Of course he'd already known about this. His spies were better than Lycaelon's—or anyone else in the City's. The trouble was, Lycaelon should not have known about it at all.

"Tell me everything, Father," Anigrel said soothingly.

⫘

NERENDALE was at the far edge of the Delfier Valley. Before Lord Volpiril's disastrous decision to reduce the bounds of the City lands, it had been a large and prosperous farming community, one which had also contained a trading outpost since the decision to bar the Mountain Traders from the City over a decade before. Since that time, the trading caravans from the High Reaches came only as far as Nerendale to exchange their freight of furs and cloth and medicinals—and sometimes even precious Elvenware—for grain, cloth, produce, and Golden Suns.

But hard times had come to Nerendale, as to all the villages that had once prospered under Armethalieh's care, and now, for the first time in centuries, the farmers suffered disaster after disaster, barely understanding why.

When the Bounds had been restricted, at first they had rejoiced at the cessation of tithe and tax. But then torrential autumn rains had fallen heavily upon all the villages of the valley, destroying the crops in the field and bringing famine to the land. The Bounds had lately been restored—and with them, the taxes and tithes—but too late to save this year's crops.

And now a new scourge had come to trouble the farmers of the Delfier Valley: Not only their herdbeasts, but their people were vanishing mysteriously in ones and twos, always without a trace. It was always the outlying villages—such as Nerendale.

So far.

As a Trading Post, Nerendale naturally had a High Mage in residence, for there was no other way to determine the suitability of the trade goods offered by the Mountainfolk. This year, Lycaelon had taken the unprecedented step of sending High Mages to many of the other villages as well, for without doing so, it might have been impossible to bring the villagers to heel in the spring, and without the fruits of their labors, Armethalieh would begin to starve in earnest.

The High Mages, naturally, had been the first to vanish when the raids on the villages began, for as Anigrel knew—though Lycaelon certainly did not—it was the servants of Anigrel's Dark Lady, not Wildmage terrorists, who raided the villages of the Delfier Valley.

The time was near when the Endarkened would be able to walk openly through the streets of Armethalieh, but so that time could come, the High

Mages must be utterly convinced that the Wildmages and the Other Races were a great threat, and one that drew ever closer with each passing day.

Anigrel listened intently as Lycaelon told him the news from Nerendale—of the inhabitants of an outlying house taken in the night; the terror of the village headman—and nodded, as if he were weighing the matter carefully.

"Truly, Father, I believe you are right. The farmers must leave Nerendale. It would be cruel to ask them to remain when they are so frightened. We will show the people we can be merciful as well as just. Perhaps the Council will agree to send the Militia to escort them to the nearest suitable village, so that they can feel perfectly safe. I will go myself."

"No—no, you must not do that," Lycaelon said, shaking his head. "You are far too selfless—what if the Wildmages lurking in the forest should manage to bespell you? You must think of the City! Armethalieh needs you more than ever—far more than a few farmers ever could. No, no, my son. Your place is here. I will insist that the Council send the Militia, and I will have them choose suitable Journeymen to accompany our soldiers. It is a fine idea to show how Armethalieh cares for her dependents, providing it is not taken to extremes."

Anigrel forced himself not to smile. Lycaelon had responded just as Anigrel had known that he would. And Lycaelon would always remember that Anigrel had offered to go to Nerendale.

"Of course, Father. Your wisdom is an inspiration to me," Anigrel said, lowing his eyes modestly.

And when his friends had feasted upon all of them—villagers, Militia, and Mages all—Lycaelon would be nearly ready to listen to his suggestion of . . . an alliance.

⟨❧⟩

HE saw everything.

He'd had to make do with a bowl of water instead of the sphere of flawless crystal the High Mages normally used for the work of seeing things from afar, but the books were clear. *Any transparent substance*, they said, could be used as a medium to summon the Visions of Far-Seeing.

Cilarnen knew, of course, that none of the Wildmages had been able to see into the City, but they always spoke of the Wild Magic as though it were a living thing—like Anganil, or Shalkan, or the Salamander that had come to his call. If that were so, then the Wild Magic could decide whether or not to do what they asked it to do.

The High Magick was not like that. It was without mind and will. It was a tool, nothing more—an extension of the High Mage's mind and will. There was not the slightest possibility that a spell of the High Magick could ever control its caster, nor require him to do something against his wishes.

And therefore—so Cilarnen believed—the wards *They* had put in place against the Wild Magic would be useless against the spells of a High Mage.

And he was right.

Two days after he had linked his power to that of the Elven Lands, Cilarnen was ready to cast the Spell of Far-Seeing.

He had spent the previous day preparing a number of useful spells so that they could be triggered with nothing more than a single keyword—High Magick was a slow and painstaking process, though it could be made to *seem* rapid to the uninitiated—and practicing others. The last time he had cast Mageshield he had done so out of desperation and in a blind panic; thank the Light—and Shalkan and Ancaladar—it had held, or they would certainly all be dead now, and the Allies would know nothing about Anigrel and his plans to destroy the City.

Now he practiced it carefully, building it up layer by layer, just as Master Tocsel had taught him, until he was satisfied that his old facility with it had returned. A student first learned the glyphs by studying them in a text, then to draw them upon the air with a wand. Next came the spells of wand and glyph, and the summoning of Fire, which was essentially a matter of visualizing the proper glyph, though that almost always came as a surprise to students when it was explained to them.

The second Spell of Visualization every Student learned was Mageshield: Those who did not learn it did not live to learn any other spells.

Once Cilarnen was satisfied that he could once more Shield himself instantly against any attack, he was ready to look into the City.

He prepared his working area carefully, making it as much like a High Mage's workspace as he could, given his circumstances; lit the lamps on his newly-erected Altar to the Light and recited the whole of the Litany of the Light, then prepared his Circle. *That* was easy enough, as the Salamander's visit had left a geometrically-perfect ring melted deeply into the floor of the ice-pavilion.

The Elvenware bowl he placed upon his worktable was as white as the snow that covered the ground outside, and so delicate that it was a miracle of a sort that it had survived unbroken through all of its journeys, for Isinwen, who had provided it for him several sennights ago, had said it had come all the way from a city called Sentarshadeen, from the workshop of an Elf named Iletel, who was a master craftsman among their kind.

Gazing upon its simple beauty, Cilarnen could well believe that. Only the wealthiest High Mage in Armethalieh could afford to purchase such a substantial piece of Elvenware to grace his collection, and he had never seen any as fine.

You know, I never thought of it before, and I would certainly never have dared to question Father about it, but . . . we despise them as a mockery of the Light and bar them from even setting foot within the City, yet the Elves make some of our most eagerly-desired trade-goods. There's not a Mageborn family in the City that doesn't have at least one piece of Elvenware on display.

Well, he shouldn't be surprised. Kellen had told him that Armethalieh was built upon a firm foundation of hypocrisy.

But now it was time to clear his mind for the spell he wished to cast.

He picked up a homely wooden jug and poured the bowl full of melted snow. He could only tell it was filling by the glints of light on the surface of the water, sliding and breaking apart as the water rocked and jounced off the walls of the bowl. Once it was full, the surface slowly stilled, the waves slowing and disappearing, the bubbles in the water rising to the top. When the water was completely still, the bowl looked in fact as if it truly was filled with the finest crystal.

Cilarnen took his wand into his right hand, and sketched the first of the glyphs of the spell.

When the spell was complete, the glyph doubled itself, one copy of it rushing through the wall of the ice-pavilion, speeding in the direction of Armethalieh, while the other half continued to hang above the Elvenware bowl. In a few moments more the absent copy reached its destination, and the glyph blurred into images. The images did not appear in the bowl, as Cilarnen had vaguely expected, but above it, like mist hanging above a lake.

As he had planned, Cilarnen was looking upon the Council Chamber. The High Mages had no notion they were being watched: The copy of the glyph that was there was heavily Warded, wrapped in every spell Cilarnen could devise.

And if someone *did* happen to notice it . . . well! It certainly wasn't a *Wildmage* spell. It was nothing more—or less—than their own High Magick. He thought they'd be so busy accusing one another of treachery that he'd have plenty of time to cover his tracks.

And after looking through Idalia's eyes at what Armethalieh had become, he wanted to see for himself how the City was being run these days.

As he had hoped, the Council was in session, but only seven of the thirteen seats were filled. Cilarnen recognized every face from the old days but one; the slender blond young man who sat in Cilarnen's father's own seat. That one he only knew from Idalia's spell. Anigrel the secret Darkmage: the Mage with a Commons-born father who had been Lycaelon's secretary and Kellen's tutor. Lycaelon thought his own son a traitor, but his adopted son had betrayed the Tavadons more terribly than the Arch-Mage could possibly imagine.

He tried to remember what he could about the political alliances among the Council. His father had certainly spoken to him of them often enough, preparing him for the day when he might join them, and would certainly serve them.

Arch-Mage Lycaelon Tavadon. He looked far older than he had the last time Cilanen had seen him, on the night of his Banishing, as if all the cares of the City weighed deeply on his shoulders these days. Cilarnen felt a pang of pity for him. It must be hard beyond words to have lost both his children to what he must believe was something worse than Demon magic, and now be facing the worst threat to face his beloved City since the days the first stones of her walls were laid. And he did not even suspect that the worst threat of all sat beside him in his own Council chambers, sat at his table in his own home. . . .

Cilarnen turned his attentions to the others.

High Mage Harith had always been Lycaelon's political crony; he would support any decision the Arch-Mage made without bothering to think for himself. Harith had no hope of ascending to the ultimate power himself; he was an old man, and had already climbed as high as he would ever reach. He would die where he was, in service to the City and the Arch-Mage.

High Mage Ganaret was ambitious, but not for himself precisely; Ganaret was always willing to endorse any project that involved exalting the power and prestige of the Mageborn, even at the expense of the other classes who shared the City with them—and so, Cilarnen's father had said, Ganaret was easily swayed in some matters.

High Mage Lorins he knew very little of, save that his father had always said that he was ambitious, and sought to become Arch-Mage himself.

High Mage Nagid; an excellent Mage, but interested most of all in his own comfort. That made him one of the most conservative voices on the Council, unwilling to consider change unless it was forced upon him. That, too, Lord Volpiril had said, could be useful when properly manipulated.

High Mage Dagan. Dagan was old and fearful, and Cilarnen saw marks of strain and sleeplessness etched into the old man's face. It was odd to think of any of the High Council as being old men, though no one ascended to that post except after attaining the rank of High Mage and devoting years of service to the City in addition before being proposed for membership when a vacancy arose. And in normal times, vacancies on the Mage Council were rare things.

Anigrel Tavadon.

In the presence of so many elderly High Mages, his youth stood out like a beacon; he was less than twice Cilarnen's own age. He had used the High Mages' fear, their love for the City and their desire to protect Armethalieh, to set himself on the High Council. To destroy it from within.

Just as—in the disguise of "Master Raellan"—he had used Cilarnen's own love for the City to lead him into the pretend conspiracy that had begun it all.

Cilarnen listened as the High Council debated a measure to send the Militia to Nerendale to evacuate the village's survivors and settle them among the inhabitants of the nearby villages such as Greenmile, Overlook, and Long Walk. The reason, Cilarnen inferred from the Council's long-winded speeches, was that the village's inhabitants were too fearful of the continuing murderous raids of the Wildmages on Nerendale to remain where they were.

That's the most preposterous thing I've ever heard! Certainly a Wildmage would kill someone—Kellen has killed lots of people, and he's a Wildmage—but not innocent helpless farmers! Someone else is doing this, and I'm sure Anigrel knows who.

Cilarnen made certain to note the time that the Council said that the Militia would arrive at Nerendale. He was almost certain he knew who was truly behind the attacks, but it wouldn't hurt to see if he could get proof.

The Council then began a long debate on the structuring of a new series of taxes on magick. Cilarnen doubted he could learn much more here—and besides, there were other places he wanted to see in the City. And he didn't want to press his luck by remaining in the Council Chamber too long. He was fairly certain they'd know someone had been spying on them. What he was counting on was that they wouldn't know who it had been.

HOUSE Volpiril still looked the same. The green-and-copper banners—their house colors—still hung on either side of the front door; the forbidding statues of snarling winged lions that flanked the walkway out by the street—all were as familiar to Cilarnen as the fingers of his own hand. As he regarded the front door, Vedhin, their formidably-correct butler, opened it, ushering his mother, two sisters, several maids, and a phalanx of menservants through the portal. Since it was his mother and his sisters, Cilarnen had literally no notion whatsoever where they might be going, as well as the feeling that it might be impertinent to try to find out.

He sent the Glyph of Far-Seeing on into the house.

Here, too, nothing had changed—but then, each piece of furniture had been in precisely these positions in his grandfather's day, and if he had inherited, Cilarnen would never have thought of changing a single thing.

He had to force himself to follow the stairs to his father's study.

Setarion Volpiril sat behind his desk, writing a letter. Cilarnen felt a clutch of joy at the sight of his father, and firmly suppressed it; strong emotion of any kind would break the spell.

His father seemed to have aged decades since the last time Cilarnen had seen him; the auburn hair of the Volpiril line had paled and was thickly streaked with gray, and new lines etched his cheeks. Even more shocking than this, Lord Volpiril's gray Mage-robes were flung carelessly over a chair—ready to be donned at need, it was true, but Cilarnen beheld his father in ordinary clothing such as any wealthy fashionable noble might own. He couldn't remember seeing his father in anything but his gray Mage-robes and rank-tabard before, at any time in his entire life.

It gave Cilarnen an odd feeling, as if his father's life must have changed as profoundly as Cilarnen's own.

But Lord Volpiril was alive. Alive! Idalia had sworn to Cilarnen that he was, that Anigrel had lied to Cilarnen in the punishment cells, but all along Cilarnen had never quite dared to believe it. In this moment it didn't matter to him that he'd been condemned as a traitor and that his father surely believed in his guilt. They were both alive, and while that was true, there was a chance for him to let his father know the truth.

Strong emotion, as Cilarnen well knew, was the enemy of magick. The intense joy he could no longer suppress upon seeing his father disrupted the spell at last. The images faded until once more Cilarnen was staring at nothing more than a bowl of water.

He drew a deep breath. It didn't matter. He'd learned what he needed to know.

And in two days, he would see what there was to see at Nerendale.

❧

TWO days later he cast the spell again.

This time it was much harder to find what he sought.

He'd never been to Nerendale, and knew nobody who had. If his life depended on locating it, he only hoped he'd have plenty of time to look.

But today he had one particular advantage, because he'd heard in the Council Chamber that the Mage Council intended to send High Mages with the Militia.

One of the things the High Mages were asked to do most often in the City was to find lost objects: a necklace, a key, a favorite pair of gloves. Almost always the object could be found using an Affinity spell, since the object and the person seeking it would have been in close contact very recently. But they were also sometimes asked to find objects for which an Affinity spell would not work: a will, a lost pet, a family heirloom only rumored to exist. For such circumstances, one of the High Magick's many different Seeking spells must be used.

What Cilarnen intended to do now was to Seek all High Mages outside of Armethalieh, using himself as an example of what he wanted the spell to find. It should lead him directly to Nerendale.

If it led him to some other group of High Mages, well, that at least would be interesting. Very interesting indeed . . .

⁓

THE wondertales that were popular within the City created images of the farming villages that were wholly unlike real life. The "cottages" the wondertales described were as spacious as a merchant's townhouse; the work of tilling and planting and harvest was neither arduous nor time-consuming.

Having lived for several moonturns in Stonehearth, Cilarnen knew what a farming village looked like; and though he had not been there in spring to see the planting begin, he had no doubt that the work was even more strenuous than the winter's work he had been doing in the stables.

He was surprised at how very much Nerendale resembled Stonehearth, though the one was a human village under the protection of the City of a Thousand Bells, and the other was a city inhabited only by Centaurs in the midst of the Wild Lands. In fact, Stonehearth was by far the more sophisticated of the two, with two-story houses, a village wall, stone-paved streets, and, Cilarnen suspected, other refinements that Nerendale did not have.

But the village square of Nerendale looked essentially the same as that of Stonehearth, save for the fact that Stonehearth did not have a Temple of the Light. There was even a well in just about the same place, and, standing around the well, two score *very* bored looking members of Armethalieh's Militia, mounted on fine chestnut horses.

Or at least Cilarnen would have thought them fine once, before he had seen Elvenbred animals. Now they seemed to him to be weedy, narrow-chested, second-rate animals, without either style or stamina.

The two Mages' animals were no better. Both were riding grays—undoubtedly borrowed from their fathers' stables, since journeyman Mages such as they both were certainly were not keeping horses of their own. The grays were skittish high-bred young animals who wanted nothing to do with the Militia's chestnuts, even as tired out as they must be after the long ride here from the City, and so far the Mages had not bothered to set a spell of Control over them.

He had not thought he would recognize either of the Mages, but he did. One of them was Juvalira, a Senior Journeyman with whom Cilarnen had served during his Apprenticeship. The other was Juvalira's usual partner, Thekinalo. Both were of middle-level Mage families, without close ties to the Council, as Cilarnen remembered, though Thekinalo had a cousin who was secretary to Lord Harith. Both had older brothers who were Undermages—Juvalira's brother was an Apprentice Undermage; Thekinalo's brother had attained Mastership the last Cilarnen had heard—and both of whom served on two of the many Councils that kept the City running smoothly. Juvalira's brother was Assistant Private Secretary to the Master of the Vermin Control Board for the Seventh District, and Thekinalo's brother served on the Water Purification Council. Both families were realistic, and neither looked as high for their sons as a seat on the High Council. Undoubtedly Juvalira and Thekinalo expected to follow their brothers into lives of service to the City, marry well when the time came, and bring honor to their respective family names.

And they were both going to die today.

Cilarnen listened as the Captain of the Militia troop argued with the village elders. The Captain wanted to leave immediately. The headman, who had petitioned for help but had received no advance word of their arrival, wanted time for everyone to gather their possessions for the journey. And everyone was gathered around the Captain, shouting about how vital those possessions were—everything from skeps of dormant bees, to foraging pigs, to scattered flocks of sheep and goats, to lost chickens.

A year ago, Cilarnen would have just thought it was funny.

Now he wished Kellen were there with them.

Cilarnen wasn't really sure how he felt about Kellen Tavadon—whether he liked him and wanted to be friends; or was so jealous of what Kellen could do and the way everybody seemed to adore him for it that he just wanted to strangle him (as if he could); or still felt the simple soothing contempt for Kellen that he had had when the two of them were boys in Armethalieh, and Cilarnen was the envied success, and Kellen was just . . . pitiable.

But what he did know for sure was that if you dropped Kellen in the middle of the situation in Nerendale, he'd somehow manage to get everyone to stop shouting, and also get everybody organized and moving almost immediately. Because Cilarnen didn't think they had the time to waste arguing about what to bring, and neither Juvalira nor Thekinalo were doing anything to help.

Cilarnen could have wept.

He was far from knowing all the spells that made up a High Mage's repertoire, but by now he knew *about* them. The two Journeymen could have been searching for danger—they knew there was danger around, even if only from whatever was killing the villagers. They could have been calling in the livestock with cantrips of persuasion. And even if they chose to do none of those things, they could have used the inbred reverence of the villages for the Mages of Armethalieh to quell this squabbling and make everyone understand that the village must be evacuated at once.

But they did none of those things.

I remember back in the City, they found it easier to laugh at the disaster my father caused than try to do anything to fix it. By the Light, can all the High Mages be so self-obsessed?

It was earlier in Nerendale than where Cilarnen was; he could tell by the way the shadows lay on the walls of the huts that in Nerendale the sun had not yet reached midheaven, while here near Ysterialpoerin it was already a bell past midday.

He watched, helplessly and in growing despair, as the soldiers shouted and the farmers argued and the blurry winter shadows grew shorter.

This time *They* came in the light.

Because this time it wouldn't matter who saw *Them*, because *They* meant to leave no one alive.

⁕

CILARNEN was the only one who saw *Them* come. He had drawn the Glyph of Far-Seeing back to high above the village, where he didn't have to listen to the tragic circular arguments between the villagers and the Captain. From there he could see the whole of the village: the roads, fields, and woods beyond, and the sky above. Because of the Mages' newly-restored weather-spells, the sky was a pale glassy blue; a color he remembered seeing often enough in winter growing up in the City. Until he had left, he'd thought it was normal for the sky to be that color throughout the winter, but since he'd left, he'd barely seen blue sky at all.

They came from the east. At first he thought the dark shadows upon the horizon were a flock of birds, but only for a few seconds. No flock of birds would fly so fast, nor be so misshapen.

Demons.

Four . . . six . . . a dozen. And even one would be enough to kill everyone there.

"Run, you fools! There are Demons attacking!"

He dropped the wards that hid his glyph from detection for long enough to shout that warning, knowing even as he did that it would be useless. Thekinalo and Juvalira heard him—he wondered if they recognized his voice—and began looking wildly around for the source of the outcry.

In doing so, they saw the advancing Demons.

They flung Mage-Shield over the square, shouting orders for the villagers to take shelter, to bar their doors against the mysterious attack. Their voices came to Cilarnen with faint yet unmistakable clarity through the lens of his spell.

The first of the Demons landed atop the shimmering violet Mage-Shield as if it were a dome of glass. As if it were ice, not glass, Cilarnen saw the protective barrier melt away to nothing, absorbed by the Demon's own magic. The Demon

It sprang to the ground, crouching for a moment on bare hands and feet, and gazed up at Juvalira with glowing yellow eyes.

Cilarnen saw the expression on the Mage's face when he realized what it was he was facing. Childhood nightmares come true. Bad dreams and Commons' nursery tales brought terrifyingly to life.

It straightened to its full height, and even though Juvalira was mounted, *It* was able to look him in the eye. Juvalira's horse skittered wildly sideways, but that did not save him. The Demon plucked him from the saddle as easily as if he were a small child and sprang into the sky with him, unfurling *Its* great scarlet wings with a snap.

It had only taken seconds.

Juvalira screamed, but his screams were lost in the other screams of men and horses, for the other Demons that had flown behind the first had landed.

One landed on the back of Juvalira's now-riderless horse. It was trapped in the midst of two-score other horses, all of which had only one thought in their minds: run. Those of the Militia who were still mounted—for many had been thrown in the first seconds after the Demons made their appearance—had no control over their panicked animals at all. Cilarnen heard the screams of those who had fallen beneath the trampling hooves and knew, miserably, that those who died in this way were the lucky ones.

What happened next maddened the terrified animals even further. The De-mon that had landed on the gray's back reached forward. *It* dug its fingers into the base of the animal's neck—impossibly, they seemed to sink in, as if they were knives.

Then *It* gave a savage yank, and the horse's head and neck parted from its body as easily as a man might tear soft fruit into pieces. Blood jetted from the wet red stump, and the Demon bounded into the air again as the dismembered body collapsed to the earth.

Cilarnen should have felt rage, despair, horror, but he knew that if he felt any of those things it would break the spell. And the most important thing of all—far more important than his own feelings—seemed to Cilarnen to be that he should see and remember what happened in Nerendale today, so that some-one, somewhere, would know the truth. Though he knew that what he had seen was only the beginning of the horrors to come, he forced himself to continue watching.

Thekinalo's horse had thrown him when the first Demon had landed, and he had run into the village's small Temple of the Light. The sacred enclosure gave him no protection from the Demon that followed him. *It* killed the Light-priest packing up the sacred objects in the shrine with one backhanded blow.

Thekinalo's face was chalk white with fear, but he had enough courage to try to fight. He summoned up a spell and cast it at the Demon.

There was a bright flash, and the Demon was enfolded in light. At first Cilarnen thought it must be Fire. But then he realized, as the light grew brighter and brighter still, that Thekinalo had prepared a cantrip for Lightning—a dangerous spell, one a Journeyman should not, by rights, know.

Cilarnen held his breath, hoping it would work.

But the light faded, and the Demon was still there, untouched. *It was laughing.* All around it, the Temple was burning, as if the lightning had sprayed away from its body like water to kindle everything it touched.

The Demon grabbed Thekinalo. His robes smoked and began to burn where the Demon touched him. The Lightning spell had blown away a large section of the roof and wall; the Demon rose up through the opening, not using its wings at all. Only when they were level with the roof did Thekinalo seem to notice what had happened and begin to struggle.

As if that were some sort of signal in the Demon's mind, the entire Temple became a roaring blaze, as if it had been suddenly soaked in oil. Thekinalo struggled to throw himself down into the blaze, but it was no use. The Demon, its wings beating strongly now, bore him off into the sky.

They're taking Juvalira and Thekinalo away alive so that they can torture them to death. Because they're Mages. Because pain and death fuel the Dark Magic. And if They can get into Armethalieh, They'll have a whole city full of Mageborn to fuel Their magic. And who knows how strong that will make Them?

In the square beside the village well, Demons barred the way to freedom. Some of the Militiamen had tried to fight, but their only arms were sword and truncheon, and Cilarnen was willing to bet that they had never used either one in actual battle. They were soldiers of Armethalieh, after all. Who could there be to fight?

The Demons had torn those few who had dared to oppose them apart with their bare hands. *They* hadn't even bothered to use spells.

The surviving members of the Militia were as willing to flee as their horses, only there was nowhere to go. The alleyways between the small stone huts that ringed the village square were narrow, and the Demons had blocked them with the bodies of dead horses. The Temple of the Light was burning, blocking that avenue of escape. And Demons barred the road out of the village.

A few of the soldiers were still in the saddle, though by now most were on foot, in nearly as much danger from their terrified horses as from the Demons. Now the Demons began to move in, perhaps jealous that anyone else should kill today. *They* began at the edges of the mass of milling animals, disemboweling horses with one swift swipe of their claws and spreading the entrails in glistening ropes across the ground, leaving the wounded dying animal to thrash and scream in agony as *They* moved on to the next victim.

Cilarnen forced himself to look around, to see what else was happening here, and that was when he saw four Demons crouched quietly on the roofs of nearby houses. *Their* wings were folded and *Their* shoulders were hunched; in *Their* stillness, *They* bore an eerie resemblance to the Stone Golems of Armethalieh.

Why are They *just watching?*

Curious and disgusted all at once, Cilarnen moved his glyph farther away, until once more he felt as if he were hovering high above the village.

When the two Mages had ordered the villagers into their houses, the farmers had not each run to their own homes, but had all crowded into the nearest available shelter: the houses immediately around the village square. Now the children—and the smallest and slenderest of the adults—were climbing out through the windows at the back of the houses and running in groups of two and three down the narrow lanes that led to the fallow fields and the trees beyond.

The Demons on the rooftops were watching with interest.

They *cannot mean to let the villagers escape . . . not now that they have seen the sort of creature their enemy is!*

He was right.

The first of the fugitives was at the edge of the fields when the first of the Demons lofted *Itself* into the air. *It* soared like a great and terrible carrion bird over one small band of refugees, and as *It* did, their bodies burst into flame.

It seemed to be a contest among the four as to which could kill most inventively with *Its* spells. Cilarnen saw flesh liquefied, bodies erupt into hideous boils which burst in fountains of blood and pus until the victim had wasted entirely away, saw bones distort and grow through flesh, saw living men and women turned inside out with a gesture.

And when *They* had killed everyone who had fled the village, the Demons returned to the houses still sheltering survivors, and took on the forms of four of those who had fled, and climbed in the windows.

Cilarnen steeled himself against imagining what would happen next, and looked back into the village square.

It had been perhaps a chime, if that, since he had last looked, but there was nothing left alive. The body parts of the men and the horses had been mixed together into one red jellylike mass. It covered the ground evenly around the fountain. In places blood had pooled in a declivity in the meat, and the blood sparkled in the sun.

It was hard to imagine that men and horses had been here and been killed. Looking at this strange mess, too horrible for the mind to make sense of, it seemed so much more logical that they had just vanished, somehow, and this . . . stuff . . . had been transported out of some other reality to take their place.

Then Cilarnen saw a hand, perfect and unmistakable, still clutching a cavalry sword, and it took all of his training to hold his emotions at bay.

He managed.

Master Tocsel would have approved.

His father—

No.

Cilarnen forced himself to watch, to note every detail, to record all he saw and not to care. Not yet. Strength, insight, dispassion—these made a High Mage. He would master himself. He would master his Gift.

For the good of all the land.

The Demons were playing amid the . . . mess, jumping up and down in the remains to see the blood splash, just as a child would play in a mud puddle.

They thought it was *funny*, Cilarnen realized, with a distant sense of discovery. They thought mortality was amusing, they thought pain and death and suffering was entertaining. It was obvious from their behavior that they didn't think of the humans who had died here today as enemies, nor did they even grant them the basic dignity that the Wildlander farmers gave to the animals they slaughtered for their dinner tables.

No.

The longer he watched, the more obvious it was to Cilarnen that the Demons thought that anybody who died was simply *stupid*. Because if they weren't stupid, they'd be both immortal and invulnerable, as Demons were. And obviously the feelings of something stupid enough to get itself killed weren't even worth considering.

He felt bile rise in his throat, and swallowed hard, willing himself to have the detachment he needed to maintain the spell.

Control. Detachment. Power.

One of the four that had been in the houses stalked out into the square. It had resumed its own form.

It wore a human skin like a cape.

It looked upward, to where the Glyph of Far-Seeing was.

And smiled, baring long bloody fangs.

It knew I was here all along—they all knew! They wanted me to watch—or let me watch—because—because—

It was, at last, too much. With a cry of horror Cilarnen struck out at his worktable, knocking it sideways. His wand, a jar of incense, the small brazier, the Elvenware bowl, were all swept from its surface. The vision vanished like smoke as the bowl spun to the ice. The sound it made when it hit and shattered had a horrible flat finality, like snapping bone.

The terrible spectacle Cilarnen had forced himself to watch unfeelingly came cascading back into his mind, and this time he did not have the needs of the spell to protect him. He staggered out of the ice-pavilion, and the unfiltered light of day struck his eyes like a blow. The normalcy and familiarity of his surroundings should have been soothing, after what he had watched happen in Nerendale, but they were not. Cilarnen looked at the wide expanse of gray sky above, the luminous white of the untouched snowfield below, the green-shading-to-black of the forest's edge in the distance, and he could see none of these things as themselves, only as what they were not.

Not the sky filled with Demons.

Not the ground soaked with blood, covered with fragments of men and horses, each piece reminding him, as if a story were being spoken aloud in his head, of how some living thing had died in agony at the hands of Demons.

Not the houses that had become killing-pens for the last of the villagers, who had died at the hands of those they thought were their own kin.

Knowing these things at all was like poison. To know the Demons had *let* him see them . . .

It was as if he had been a willing participant in what *They* had done.

Cilarnen fell to his knees in the snow, gagging. Of course he had fasted in preparation for the spell, so there was nothing in his stomach to bring up, but that only made things worse. He felt as if while he had been watching the Demons, somehow *They* had been looking into him as well. He felt unclean—Tainted—and try as he might, he could not spew up that foulness, make it a thing outside himself.

He felt the old pain return behind his eyes as he scrubbed at his face with snow. Tainted. Somehow he was Tainted, in a way none of them could find the answer to. No one could see it—not Shalkan, not Vestakia, but more than ever Cilarnen was certain that somewhere deep inside himself there was a trap cunningly laid by Master Anigrel when he had sent Cilarnen's Magegift to sleep.

The thought dissolved before he could fully grasp it, swept away by exhaustion and urgency. The others would want to know all that he knew, and he must tell them immediately.

He forced himself to his feet, shaking with cold and everything he had forced himself not to feel while the spell was running. Tears froze on his face as he stumbled across the snow toward his sleeping pavilion. He would need his warmest clothes for the walk back to the main camp.

⤜⤛

MENERCHEL and Hindulo were the ones that found him. Hindulo had scented strange magic on the wind, which was what had brought the two of them so far from their assigned patrol area in the first place. The chestnut unicorn lowered his golden horn to touch the fallen body in the snow experimentally.

"This is not good," Hindulo pronounced, as Cilarnen stirred only sluggishly. "We need him."

"Fool of a human and a child!" Menerchel burst out in exasperation, going to his knees beside Cilarnen and lifting Cilarnen to his feet. The boy blinked at him groggily, obviously unaware of how close he had come to death out here in the cold. Cold stole one's wits, encouraging even adults to believe that they could lie down for a few minutes rest in the snow and arise safely. "Though even children know better than to wander in the snow at night," Menerchel added.

"Proper children do not come from the Mage City, where they do not have weather," Hindulo reminded his rider.

"I wasn't wandering," Cilarnen protested. His voice was hoarse and slurred. "I must see Redhelwar. Or Idalia."

"An odd selection of choices," Menerchel observed. "But Idalia you must certainly see. And quickly, I think."

"Come—I shall carry the two of you as close to the main camp as I can, and you will take him the rest of the way. Be sure and find out what he thought was so important that he forgot everything he'd learned about weather," Hindulo added.

"I *can* hear you," Cilarnen said, sounding faintly irritated. It was still difficult to understand his speech, but Menerchel could tell he was making a great effort to be understood. "I could tell you now, if you like." He took a deep breath and began to cough.

Menerchel picked him up and set him on Hindulo's back, then mounted up behind him. Cilarnen slumped forward against the unicorn's neck before he could stop himself. He struggled to sit upright; the warmth Hindulo radiated was enough to thaw him to the point his teeth began to chatter violently.

His shivering passed after a few minutes, and Cilarnen began to talk, his voice stronger now, and clear. His speech was as blunt as a sword-cut, but Menerchel was not offended. It would be foolish to hold Mages—especially young human Mages—to the same standards of conduct as his own people. Different peoples had different customs, after all. And Mages were different from everyone.

"There is—there was—a village called Nerendale in the Delfier Valley, where the Mountainfolk come—came—to trade with the City. The—*They*—came there, and killed them all. And the men and the horses—*They* took the Mages away with *Them*—Juvelira and Thekinalo—I knew them—I worked with them at home. . . ." The boy's voice faltered, catching on a sob.

"How could you see this?" Hindulo demanded, not pausing in his easy trot across the surface of the snow. "The Wildmages have not been able to see what goes on in the City."

"I am no Wildmage. The High Magick does what I tell it to do," Cilarnen said, his voice going hard. But Menerchel could feel his body shaking beneath the heavy cloak with something that was more than cold.

"No further," Hindalo said regretfully, stopping.

The edge of the main camp lay just ahead. In the darkness, the pavilions that had their lanterns lit glowed as if they themselves were enormous colored lanterns, and the sound of laughter and even music could be heard across the distance. Near the camp the deep loose snow had been cleared from the ground so that the Centaurs and the various mounted units could drill; what remained was hard-packed and easy to walk upon.

"Menerchel will wish to know if he must carry you," the unicorn added for Cilarnen's benefit, tossing his head.

"I can walk!" Cilarnen said instantly. "But . . . I will be grateful if you will come with me, Menerchel. And I thank you—both—for being there tonight."

"It is a small matter," Menerchel said. "Do not think of it."

He swung down from Hindulo's back, and helped Cilarnen to dismount. The boy was a little unsteady on his feet, but in much better shape than he had been when they had first found him.

"I will wait for you at the edge of camp," Hindulo said, turning and springing away. His body was a golden gleam against the snow as he sprang through the darkness.

Cilarnen turned to watch Hindulo go.

"They are the most beautiful things in all the world," he said, as solemnly and intensely as if he were passing judgment.

"In that matter, you and he are in full agreement," Menerchel said with a smile. "And I as well, for that matter. Come. It is not far."

Hasty and strange the young human Mage certainly was, but anything that loved unicorns as Cilarnen High Mage so obviously did was certainly of the Light.

A High Mage was something Menerchel only knew of from the oldest of Master Belesharon's Teaching Stories. He had never expected to meet one—in fact, if anyone had asked him five years ago, he would have solemnly assured them that it was far more likely that he would meet a Knight-Mage first—even though as far as anyone knew at that time, there were no Knight-Mages at all, and there was an entire city of High Mages at the other side of the Wild Lands.

But to meet a High Mage—if he had been foolish enough to attempt it— Menerchel would have had to leave the Elven Lands (and he had been entirely happy in Thultafoniseen, working in his family's tea business, when he and Hindulo were not engaged in other duties), cross the Wild Lands, and successfully enter Armethalieh, something his friend Hyandur had not been able to do—

doing much to prove, in Menerchel's mind, that the thing could not be done save by overwhelming force.

And since Menerchel had thought in those days that he would be unlikely to leave Thultafoniseen for long, and never leave the Elven Lands at all, and he knew that he was certainly incapable of overwhelming Armethalieh by himself, and the High Mages *never* left their city, it seemed far more likely that, of the two possibilities, he would see a Knight-Mage first, since a Knight-Mage was a kind of Wildmage when all was said and done, and they were not in the least uncommon in the Elven Lands.

And in fact he *had* seen a Knight-Mage first, but to add rarity to improbability, a High Mage had left the City of Mages and traveled across the Wild Lands and into the Elven Lands, so now Menerchel had seen a High Mage as well.

I must stop wishing to see things—unless it is our victory, and all of Them vanished. I am certain Hindulo would agree. And yet . . . it seems very odd to me that such brief and hasty people as the High Mages should have such power as Kellen and Cilarnen have both spoken of. Perhaps they have such powers precisely because there are creatures such as Them in the world. In which case, if all of Them were destroyed, would the High Mages lose their powers as well?

It was a riddle that could not be solved tonight.

Healer's Row was near the middle of the camp, where the most vulnerable of the camp's inhabitants—the sick, the wounded, and the Healers, who rarely wore armor, at least while treating patients—could be sheltered in the event the camp was directly attacked. Because it was early in the evening, Menerchel looked for Idalia first in the sick-tents, and not at her own pavilion.

⚓

CILARNEN sat on the long bench in the outer room with Menerchel while another Elf—Yatimumil, he thought his name was—went off to get Idalia. The setting bore an odd resemblance to the day he'd met Kellen, and Kellen had dragged him off to the Healer's tent.

His head had hurt then, too. Thank the Light it wasn't summer; he felt as if the cold was the only thing keeping the pain at bay. He lowered his head into his hands and squeezed his temples. It didn't help.

There were Healing Spells in the High Magick, of course, but nowhere in all the Art Magickal had a time been foreseen when a Mage might have to heal himself. Wildmages might wander the earth like solitary lunatics, so Wirance had told him, never seeing another of their own kind from the moment they embraced their magical destiny till the day of their death, but High Mage worked in

Circles, in Colleges, in Councils . . . Cilarnen could *be* a solitary High Mage much easier than he could imagine one.

"I See you, Menerchel."

When he heard Idalia's voice, Cilarnen raised his head.

Menerchel bowed. "I See you, Idalia. The blessings of Leaf and Star be upon you this night. I bring you Cilarnen High Mage, whom Hindulo found asleep in a snowbank, though not for long enough to take much hurt from it, I think. He brings grave news of a place called Nerendale, and he would have you know of it. I regret such rudeness and brevity, but the Unicorn Scouts ride picket tonight, and I am needed elsewhere."

"Then you must go at once, Menerchel, and give my thanks to Hindulo. The blessings of Leaf and Star go with you also."

She waited until Menerchel had left, and then turned to Cilarnen.

"Of all the stupid, half-witted, inconsiderate—" she began furiously.

Cilarnen laughed, though it turned into a groan of pain halfway through. "'Stupid' and 'half-witted' I will grant you, Lady—Idalia—though by the Light, I could not bear to be alone tonight—but how 'inconsiderate'?"

Idalia stared at him for a moment, then took a deep breath. "To begin, once we noticed you missing, we'd have to go looking for you. And then, once we found you dead, some of us would be sorry. And even those who did not mourn your loss would worry that your death meant that some enemy had managed to get close to the camp to kill you."

"I see," Cilarnen said distantly. "I apologize for troubling you, Wildmage. Nevertheless, my news is urgent. Perhaps you will hear it and give your opinion as to whether Redhelwar should hear this at once."

⸙

IDALIA sighed inwardly. She'd managed to forget what Kellen had been like at the very first—in feverish high spirits one moment and brooding in corners the next, wearing his feelings on the outside of his skin and as volatile as only a teenaged boy could be.

Though he did his best, Cilarnen was a thousand times worse, adding to Kellen's mix the sensibilities of a pampered aristocrat and the arrogance of a High Mage. That they *all* hadn't been tempted to murder him a thousand times over was a tribute to the fact that somehow Armethalieh hadn't managed to ruin him.

But tonight he was tired, and he *knew* he'd pulled a stupid stunt trying to walk down from the ice-pavilion in the dark. It was a long walk even in the daylight. Too long, unless the air was absolutely still and the sun was out.

And he looked ill. Feverish.

Let the plague not come here. Gods of the Wild Magic, is that too much to ask? So many people gathered in one place, it would go through the camp like fire through a standing grain field at harvest.

"Cilarnen?" she asked quietly. "Are you ill? Is that why you came?"

"No." He sounded very positive, but she had never seen him look less well in all the time she had known him. "My head hurts again, but that is not why I came. *They* have killed everyone in Nerendale, and the Militia, too. Anigrel sent them to Nerendale—I think he sent them so that they would be there to be killed. Perhaps it was a sort of sacrifice. Or perhaps he does it willingly. *They* have two High Mages now as well—they were not friends of mine, but they were men I knew. Middle Houses, of course. Not well-connected. Or else they would not have been sent, you see." His tone was reasonable, but his pupils were widely dilated, and his words made no sense at all.

"Cilarnen," Idalia said carefully, "you can't know what's going on in Nerendale. That's inside the Bounds, and none of us can scry inside the Bounds."

"The difference between your magic and mine," Cilarnen said dismissively, "is that mine does what I tell it to, and yours does what it thinks you should do. Today I saw Nerendale. I wish I hadn't," he added, as if to himself.

"You made your magic work," Idalia said, realizing what Cilarnen was not saying.

Cilarnen nodded, and then winced. "I can cast any of the spells of a High Mage. I haven't practiced most of them, and I don't understand them, and I still don't have a lot of the equipment and materials I need, and some of the spells just require more than one person, but as long as I'm within the Elven Lands, I have the power." He took a deep breath, and seemed to consider the matter carefully. "I think I'd rather have a dragon."

Idalia shook her head, exasperated with herself. Shock. He was in shock. She hadn't seen the symptoms because she hadn't been looking for them and they were masked by the magic, but they were there, now that she was looking for them.

Curse every High Mage back to the founding of Armethalieh for the way they raised their sons! Cilarnen was no Elven Knight, but it looked like the Mage College could show the House of Sword and Shield a thing or two about stoic endurance.

And possibly pure stupidity.

"First I'll get you the cordial for your headache. Then I'll get you a mug of hot sweet cider and a little soup. Then you can tell me about Nerendale from the very beginning. If you *can* look into Armethalieh, there are some things I'd like to look at."

❧

SHE sent a runner to the Centaur camp for Kardus, then she had Yatimumil get Cilarnen into dry clothes and wrapped in blankets and settled between a pair of warming braziers. Once she'd dosed him with the cordial and gotten some food and drink into him, his color improved, and he seemed to be tracking better.

By that time, Kardus had arrived.

"You have seen *Them* again," the Centaur Wildmage said without preamble.

Cilarnen nodded, looking very much as if he wanted to cry. He nodded. "Like Stonehearth. Worse. Anigrel . . . he knew *They'd* be there. I know he did. He sent the Militia right to them. And two High Mages. *They* took them away alive. *They* killed all the others."

"Cilarnen," Idalia said gently, "will you be able to tell this twice?"

While nothing that had happened several hours ago in Nerendale could be urgent enough to justify rousing Redelwar for in the middle of the night, he would certainly need to be told, and it would be best if he could be told by the one who had actually witnessed the events.

Cilarnen nodded shortly. He seemed to draw on his resources, pulling the facts together in the proper order. Then he began.

"As you've guessed by now, the spell to gain a power source worked. The Elven Elementals sent help. As soon as I had a source of power for my spells, the first thing I did was to cast the Glyph of Far-Seeing upon the Council Chamber of Armethalieh."

Cilarnen said this as if it were the most logical—and reasonable—thing in the world. Idalia supposed a High Mage might think it was, and silently cursed herself for not sending someone to check on Cilarnen every single day—but the army's resources were still stretched far too thin since the Battle for the Heart Forest and the Spell of Kindolhinadetil's Mirror. He'd been sure he'd be fine, and was so insistent about being left alone—to study, she'd thought—that she'd simply let the matter drop. The ice-pavilion had been within range of the farthest-out of the patrols, after all, so it wasn't as if nobody at all had been keeping an eye on him.

Just not, apparently, a close enough one. She'd been going to ride up there tomorrow, since it would have been four days without word.

She sighed. She should have gone sooner. She knew how single-minded Cilarnen had become once he'd gotten the idea that getting his magic back was possible. It probably hadn't even occurred to him that he should let someone know what he'd done and what he was about to do.

And he'd made fun of the Wildmages for being solitary!

"There are only seven on the High Council now," Cilarnen went on. "Lord Anigrel—*Lord* Anigrel, oh, that is a mockery! House Anigrel was never particularly high among the Mage Houses; when Ceonece Anigrel married Torbet Dusaynt there was a great scandal, as he was a commoner, like poor Tiedor, but he had a strong Gift, and House Anigrel fostered him. . . . Anyway, Lord Anigrel proposed sending the Militia to evacuate Nerendale. The villagers had petitioned for relief. According to the Council, the Wildmages were raiding in the Valley and killing villagers, and they were afraid to stay."

"Wildmages!" Kardus said in disbelief. "But that's—"

"Part of Anigrel's plan," Idalia said bitterly. "So the Council—which apparently means Anigrel these days—sent a detachment of the Militia to move them."

"Yes," Cilarnen said. He pulled his blankets more tightly around himself, staring down at his empty cider mug. "I knew when they would arrive, and I knew there would be Mages with the Militia, so I sent out my next Far-Seeing Spell two days later to find any Mages outside the walls of Armethalieh, since I didn't know where Nerendale was, or what it looked like. And I found them. Forty soldiers and two Journeymen, Masters Juvalira and Thekinalo. The villagers didn't know they were coming, and they'd made no preparations to leave. They stood around and argued about what they needed to take. Juvalira and Thekinalo could have made them stop, but they didn't.

"Then six of *Them* came." He stopped, staring at something only he could see.

It took little effort for Idalia to imagine what had happened next, however, and then it did take an effort to keep from grabbing him and shaking him until his teeth rattled. They should never have left him to himself for so long without checking on him. He might have listened to her, or maybe not, but he would certainly have listened to Vestakia or Kardus.

What he would *not* have done was gone looking for Demons while he was all alone, no matter how much the Allies needed to know what he might learn.

"*They* saw you, didn't *They?*" she said quietly.

Cilarnen jerked as if he'd been stung by a wasp, and stared at her in startled surprise. Then understanding grew in his expression as he realized how she must know. She'd faced the Demon Queen through Kindolhinadetil's Mirror.

"I thought I'd been careful enough. I'd shielded the glyph. It went undetected in Armethalieh—if it had not, the Stone Golems in the Council Chamber would have alerted the Mages. But *They* knew I was watching all along. *They wanted* me to watch, as *They* . . . played with the people there."

"That is *Their* way," Kardus said gravely. "*They* wish to spoil everything *They* touch. *They* are the enemy of all who walk in the Light."

"And now all those people are dead," Cilarnen said, a despairing note in his voice. "And Anigrel will make it seem as if the Wildmages are responsible, and make everyone in the City even more terrified of Wildmages, if that's even possible. Idalia, you'll never get an alliance now. He's seen to that."

She wasn't going to let him talk himself into a complete blue funk.

"Unfortunately, *They've* made one huge mistake. You saw what really happened at Nerendale—and you can testify to that before the High Council under Truthspell," Idalia said.

Cilarnen stared at her, hope and confusion mixed in his expression. "But . . . I've been Banished," he said blankly.

Idalia laughed shortly. "Somehow, Cilarnen, I think the entire Elven Army at your back might just be able to reverse that decree. But what you need right now is a bowl of soup and a warm bed. I'll inform Redhelwar about this now, but I don't think you'll be making your report to him until sometime tomorrow, because horrible as this news is, it isn't urgent.

"But once you've recovered, if you *can* use the High Magick to see places that we can't, don't be surprised if Redhelwar has a long list of tasks for you."

Cilarnen drew a deep breath, obviously at the end of his strength. "If I'm all that Armethalieh can send to help, be sure that I will do all I can."

Eight

Hare and Hound

THERE WERE TEN women in Ondoladeshiron who must be taken to the Crowned Horns. This was Ancaladar and Jermayan's second trip.

He'd grown up with Caronide, Heryelion, Miranaya, and Firetaldo, just as he had with Amentiel, Missondore, Estauril, Viranarya, Aryante, and Ingaruuile. Aryante was the youngest—she had been a child when he had left Ondoladeshiron—while Missondore was nearly four centuries his elder. Estauril and Heryelion were close enough to his own age for the three of them to have played together as children.

But they were all part of the fabric of his life.

The fabric that seemed to be unraveling so drastically now.

The people of the War City were careful and practical. Sentarshadeen was the City of Peace, and Ysterialpoerin was the City of History. But Ondoladeshiron, the War City, was where the armies mustered in time of danger, and it was always . . . watchful.

Jermayan had been saddened, but not surprised, to see the changes war had brought to the city of his birth. Of course many of the city's inhabitants were away with the army, since Ondoladeshiron sent more students to the House of Sword and Shield than any other of the Nine Cities, and so he had been prepared to see much of the city deserted, but Rochinuviel had asked everyone to move their dwelling-places to the district nearest the Flower Forest, in many cases occupying the homes of those who were away.

It had seemed to Jermayan as if the city had shrunk.

There were many practical reasons for the Vicereign's request, of course. If the people were gathered close together, they could watch over one another. There was less chance that any of the Dark-tainted creatures who now roamed the Elven Lands might attack a lone dwelling at the edge of the city and over-whelm its occupant. And the nearness of the Flower Forest provided its own subtle protection from Taint, as well as raising the spirits of all who gazed upon it.

But the sight of the streets of empty shuttered dwellings at the outskirts of the city had brought home the reality of the war to Jermayan as nothing else had, despite the terrible battles he had fought, despite seeing Windalorianan de-stroyed. Watching Ondoladeshiron quietly dwindle, without fire or battle, was like watching a loved one slowly die of a long wasting illness. It had a silent hor-ror that struck him to the roots of his being.

Even if we win this war, nothing will ever be the same again.

"They said that a thousand years ago," Ancaladar said for his ears alone, breaking into his reverie as they flew toward the Crowned Horns. Jermayan was never quite certain whether the dragon read his mind, or was simply an uncan-nily accurate guesser. It would certainly take no great sorcery to guess the direc-tion of his mind lately, Jermayan thought ruefully. He had been all but rude ever since they had arrived in Ondoladeshiron. Fortunately the mirror-relays had been working well between Realthataladon and Ondoladeshiron, and everything he and Ancaladar had needed had been waiting for them, so their wait there had been brief, giving him less time to brood over the changes to the city. All they'd needed to do was await the break in the weather that Ancaladar had said was coming.

"And you see? The world went on. Different, and also good," the dragon continued insistently, finishing his argument.

Yes, my friend, but we won that war, Jermayan answered silently.

Ancaladar snorted explosively. If they had not been carrying passengers, Jer-mayan was certain he would have been treated to some spectacular aerial acro-batics to jar him out of his mood. Ancaladar said nothing, but he did not need to. Jermayan could easily imagine the dragon's reply:

"If you do not win this war, you will not need to worry about the state of the world at all."

Jermayan sighed. He wished he could share Kellen's faith that matters had taken a turn for the better, but Kellen was the only one who seemed to think they had. For all their sakes, he hoped Kellen was right, but he simply lacked a Knight-Mage's vision.

A movement on the snow far below caught his attention.

A pack of Coldwarg was loping across the snow in search of prey. They were difficult to spot, being nearly the color of the snow, and it was motion more than color that had attracted Jermayan's eye.

Some of the pack looked up as Ancaladar's shadow passed over them. But the dragon did not attack, and they ignored him as they ran on.

So many . . . Jermayan thought. *A pack of such size would make trouble for even the army, should it encounter them. No lesser band of travelers would be safe. They seek to tighten their grasp upon us by proxy, isolating us from each other through weather and* Their *creatures.*

Finally the Fortress was once more in sight. Today it gleamed like the bright crown of the mountains it had been built to be, in those ancient days.

⤜⤏

MASTER Tyrvin had not been pleased to hear he must open the doors of his fortress again, and not once, but more than a dozen times so that Jermayan and Ancaladar could bring the women of the Nine Cities to him. When Kellen had visited here earlier in the winter, he had convinced Tyrvin of the need to keep the fortress sealed against any who might be a Demon in disguise. Only Andore-niel's decree, made for the most logical and compelling, if not the best, of reasons could have convinced the Fortress's master to obey.

Fortunately I need endure my old friend's silent reproaches only once more after today, for there is only one at Ysterialpoerin who must come here, and then this task is done.

As he landed, Ancaladar broke through the ice-crust on the snow at the foot of the causeway with the sound of an axe biting into wood. Where the crust was unbroken, it was thick enough to bear Jermayan's weight, and he quickly moved around Ancaladar, helping his passengers from the carrying baskets and then cutting the baskets free of the harness the dragon wore, for they would only hinder Ancaladar on his flight to Ysterialpoerin, and at any moment they might need to fight.

By the time Jermayan was finished with his task, the Knights waiting on the narrow causeway that provided the only access to the Fortress had reached the dragon's side and were shepherding Jermayan's charges up the causeway. Jermayan prepared to follow.

"Will you be long?" Ancaladar asked, turning his head to look directly at Jermayan.

"I must see Ashaniel; she left word last time that she wished to see me, but she was asleep when I came, and they would not waken her. But I will be brief."

Ancaladar snorted gustily. "Brief for Elves," the dragon sighed. "I will wait." He spread his wings to catch as much of the sun's rays as they possibly could.

⌐⌐

BY now the narrow halls and corridors of the Fortress were as familiar to Jermayan as the back of his own hand, but the Fortress had been designed to confuse intruders, and he was pleased to have an escort as he followed Shentorris to Ashaniel's chambers. The colorful and elaborate murals on the walls looked even more battered than the last time he had inspected them; the inevitable result of the corridors being used as battlegrounds for active children.

For battlegrounds and not playgrounds they had now become. Now every child here, not just those who had been students at the House of Sword and Shield, was learning everything the Knights had to teach. It did not matter if they were barely old enough to walk, like Kalainia, or nearly old enough to take the field outside, like Alkadoran, who had been nearly ready to enter the House of Sword and Shield to begin his Knightly training when he had come with the caravan from Sentarshadeen: Each learned all he or she was capable of, whether it was simply to run and hide, or the dancelike moves of swordless fighting, or how to attack with club, stave, bow, sword. . . .

As he and Shentorris moved down the hall, two Elven children ran the other way. The elder could have been no more than five, her companion at least a year younger, and their faces shone with delight at the wonderful game they were playing. Hands over their mouths to stifle giggles, they dodged down the cross-corridor.

Behind them came Alkadoran, his face grim. In his mind, at least, this was no game, for he was one of the children who had been captured and held prisoner by the Shadowed Elves, and more than many here, he knew the true horror that they all faced. He did not give the two Knights a passing glance, but continued down the corridor after the two children at a measured pace, his lips moving as he counted off seconds.

Hare and Hound, a game all children play . . . but if it is ever played out in earnest in this place, the stakes will be far higher than the forfeit of a sweetmeat or a hair ribbon. Leaf and Star, if the day comes that the children must fight because we have failed to defend them, I think it would be much better for us, and for them as well, if this place had been sealed up so tightly that they had starved to death instead.

And that is yet possible. Tyr says the food supplies here will not last much past late spring. We must find some way to resupply. . . .

After several more twists and turns—corridors were short on purpose, and there were many ways to reach every destination—Shentorris stopped before a door. "Come and see Master Tyrvin before you leave. Sandalon will bring you." He tapped at the door.

A voice from within bid them enter, and Shentorris opened the door.

Few of the rooms of the Fortress of the Crowned Horns had windows, and Ashaniel's chamber was no exception, though the walls had been painted to make the room seem as if it were a tower room, with paintings of pretended windows on all four walls looking out over the Mystrals in high summer, when the meadows below were green and starred with flowers.

Sandalon and Lairamo, the Elven woman who was nurse to the young Elven Prince, were with the Queen. Jermayan was sorry to see that Sandalon still looked hollow-eyed and unnaturally aged. Idalia had told him that Sandalon blamed himself for being the cause of all the deaths in the caravan that he had been a part of. Idalia had said that he'd told Lairamo that it was his fault because the caravan had only been taken because of him.

It was a terrible weight of responsibility for a young child to carry. They'd all told him it wasn't true, that he wasn't responsible for the deaths, or for the capture of Alkadoran, Kalainia, and all the rest.

But of course, in a way he was right: The Endarkened had struck at that caravan precisely because Sandalon was traveling with it. But to say the boy was responsible for the attack would be as if one were saying he could accept responsibility for what *They* chose to do. And he couldn't.

It was a difficult concept to explain to a five-year-old child who knew only that some day he would be King, and that being King meant taking responsibility.

Jermayan entered, bowing very low.

"Oh, come, Jermayan, there is no need for such formality here. It was I who asked to see you."

Jermayan raised his head, and then rose gracefully from his bow. "I shall do whatever my Queen desires."

Ashaniel chuckled, low in her throat. "You are *just* as mannerly as Sandalon, you know, Jermayan—and *just* as hard on your clothes."

"It is difficult to follow the fashion in the field," Jermayan said ruefully, settling himself beside her, at her gesture, on the low padded bench. "But naturally such matters are meaningless to you. As always, you neither set nor follow fashion, but transcend it."

Ashaniel wore a simple gray gown beneath an open fur-lined robe. The lines of the gown were loose, designed to conceal much, though she was not yet halfway through her pregnancy. But unless there were stores of unfinished cloth here in the fortress, the gown she had arrived wearing was the only clothing she had. Ancaladar could carry passengers, but not baggage.

"Were it the season to carry a fan, I would strike you with it to remind you of the utter foolishness of that remark," Ashaniel said serenely. "Lairamo, perhaps you would find it appropriate to distract our guest with tea before he says something even more foolish."

Lairamo went to the cabinet at the side of the room and brought out the tea-brazier and a pot.

AS the water heated and then the tea brewed, the three of them spoke of inconsequential things: the weather, the people now living in the Fortress. Both Jermayan and Ashaniel encouraged Sandalon to talk about how he found things here in his new home, since for the first time in his life, there were children his own age around for him to play with. But he was difficult to draw out, as if he were struggling with ideas that he simply did not have the words to express. What he wanted to know about was Kellen, and Shalkan, and Vestakia, and Idalia. In order to save the child from enumerating the entire list of people he had known back in Sentarshadeen, Jermayan told him all that he knew about all of Sandalon's friends as he had last seen them. He was glad he was able to say that they were all alive and well.

He hoped what he told the boy was still true.

When the tea was poured, and a cup of cider had been mulled for Sandalon, Jermayan sensed that they would soon be coming to the reason that Ashaniel had summoned him.

Sandalon seemed to sense it, too. He finished his drink in a few inelegant gulps and looked appealingly at his mother. She smiled and reached out to ruffle his short dark hair.

"I think it is time for you to go and play *gan* with Lairamo for a little while, my heart. And then Jermayan will need you to show him the way back to Master Tyrvin's chambers, or else he will wander here for a very long time."

Sandalon actually looked grateful to be excused, while the boy Jermayan had known of old would have teased to be allowed to stay and listen in on the conversation of the adults.

"Do you rea— I mean, thank you for allowing me to be of service to you, Jermayan." The boy made a deep and surprisingly-practiced bow.

"It is my honor and my pleasure as well, Sandalon," Jermayan replied.

Lairamo took Sandalon's hand and led him from the room, through a door that was not the one through which Jermayan had entered. The door was flanked by tall painted windows showing a vista of imaginary rooftops, mountains, and a long sweep of flower-starred green. Spring.

Jermayan hardly dared to imagine what horrors this spring would bring.

Ashaniel settled herself more comfortably and refilled both their cups.

"Now," she said, a hint of winter's ice in her voice. "Truth will make good hearing."

Jermayan stared at her in surprise. Ashaniel raised her eyebrows.

"Master Tyrvin assures me that we are all quite safe. One presumes that he is training children of six to wield a dagger because we are all quite safe. One presumes also that he must think that Magarabeleniel has suddenly been wreft of the power of speech—oh, she is no fool, as you know, to spread her news everywhere, but certainly she spoke to me. And so has every woman from every city that you have ferried here."

"Perhaps," Jermayan said quietly, "you know more than I."

"Perhaps," Ashaniel said unrelentingly. "And if you tell me what you know, we may be certain of it."

Jermayan bowed his head, acknowledging defeat. "I think I may not know as much as you, Lady Ashaniel, since for nearly two moonturns Ancaladar and I have been flying among the Nine Cities, and our only news is fragmentary and long out of date. Of Lerkalpoldara you know as much as I. You know, too, that Deskethomayel and Windalorianan have been evacuated, their inhabitants sent south. I know that none of them went to Ondoladeshiron, for I have just come from there, and I only hope they reached what destinations they chose safely. There was fear of both plague and blight in Windalorianan when I was there, and also of ancient Allies of the Enemy breaching our northern borders. Because of the Shadowed Elves, *Their* creatures already roam our land freely: serpent-marae, ice-drakes, and Coldwarg, despoiling the land of both game and herd, and tainting what it feeds upon. Coldwarg I saw myself on our flight here."

Ashaniel nodded in reluctant approval of this summary. "It is much as I have heard. And so we fall back upon our young cities in the west, and surrender the north to the darkness. Victory, it seems, lies outside our borders, in who claims the allegiance of the Mage City, and when. But I must know what lies within your thoughts, Jermayan, and if it seems to you that it is possible that the High Mages will come to listen to us in time to save themselves and us."

Jermayan hesitated. He wanted to tell her that certainly Armethalieh would come to its senses and ally itself with the Children of Leaf and Star as Men had with Elves in the last Great War.

But not even Kellen had faith in that, though Kellen believed the Light would win this war.

"Perhaps yes, perhaps no," Jermayan said at last. "Kellen believes that whatever path the Golden City chooses, the Light can yet prevail."

"But I would hear your thoughts, not what Kellen believes," Ashaniel reminded him softly.

"It is . . . too soon to say," Jermayan said, after a long silence had grown between them. "The human High Mage Cilarnen reminds us of something we had nearly forgotten—that Armethalieh, too, remembers the ancient Enemy. The war has not yet touched the human city. When it does, it may well be that they awaken to their true danger and fight, for all that Anigrel High Mage has done to make them blind and unaware."

"So . . . 'the Wild Magic goes as it wills'?" the Queen quoted with a faint smile.

"Kellen Knight-Mage has often been right before. And he feels we are closer to victory than we have ever yet been," Jermayan said honestly.

"But all know that Kellen has two selves," Ashaniel said, touching once again on many of the Elves' greatest worry. "It would be good to know which speaks: the human boy or the Knight-Mage. We all hope. But I must *know*."

Jermayan shook his head decisively. "Once, at the beginning, before Kellen knew what it was to be a Knight-Mage, before any of us knew what the cost of this war was to be . . . yes, then he had two selves and either might speak. But the fires of war have burned the boy to ash, and only the Knight-Mage speaks now."

"Then the Knight-Mage believes there is a chance for victory," Ashaniel said, resting her hand lightly against her stomach.

"One thing Kellen has never done well is evade the truth. It is wholly entertaining to watch him try. The Wild Magic speaks to him. If he believed anything other than what he has said, I would know. And I would not have come to see you at all."

His words caused Ashaniel to go completely still for a moment. Then she smiled—the first genuine peaceful smile Jermayan had seen since he had entered her chamber.

"Then fare you well, Jermayan, and a swift and serene journey to you. May our victory come swiftly, and at a price no higher than any of us can bear."

"May Leaf and Star grant that it be so," Jermayan said, getting to his feet.

⟨≋⟩

SANDALON escorted him through the labyrinthine corridors of the Fortress of the Crowned Horns. In contrast to his earlier silence, the boy chattered along now, pointing out landmarks of his games and—now—talking about friends and playfellows.

"Aralmar is very slow. She is in my group—we're the Badgers—but she never hides fast enough, and Master Tyrvin says we are not to help each other hide lest we be caught ourselves."

He looked at Jermayan questioningly.

"I suppose if those are Master Tyrvin's orders, you must obey them. He was my master once, and he is very wise. Still, if you can help Aralmar so that she can hide faster, and keep anyone from catching you at it, that would be a very clever thing to do. And since Master Tyrvin is teaching you to be clever, it would be hard for him to object."

Sandalon beamed, and even skipped a few steps. Then he slowed again. "Mama is very sad," he said.

"I think perhaps she will be less sad now," Jermayan said. He only hoped Kellen never found out that he'd told Ashaniel that they were going to win because Kellen said they were going to win. He wasn't entirely certain how Kellen would react.

"Because we're—" Sandalon began excitedly, then managed to stop. "I mean, it would be good to know how much longer we'll have to remain here."

"I'm sorry, Sandalon," Jermayan said. "I truly don't know."

⤨

SANDALON stopped before a familiar door. "I will leave you here, of your courtesy," he said, with carefully-acquired manners.

"I thank you for your company on the way," Jermayan answered, equally formally. He waited until the boy was out of sight before knocking at Master Tyrvin's door.

After a moment, Tyrvin opened it. "Enter and be welcome," he said, stepping aside to allow Jermayan to pass.

"I will not keep you overlong," Tyrvin said without preamble, "for I am certain Ancaladar will not thank me for it. Yet I will be grateful for all that you wish to tell."

Jermayan bowed in acknowledgment. "You will rejoice, I am certain, to know that you will only see me once more. I fly once from Ysterialpoerin, and then you may seal the Fortress until our victory."

"I do not doubt this to be a matter much upon Ashaniel's mind," Tyrvin commented.

"I hope I brought her comfort. I could say to her only what I have said to you, and what Kellen Knight-Mage has said to Redhelwar: that he believes we may prevail."

"Let our victory come before high summer, then," Tyrvin said bluntly. "We are adequately provisioned, but we cannot hold out past that. And from all you have told me of what roams the land, it will not be possible to resupply us."

Jermayan shook his head in reluctant agreement. "No supply caravan can reach you safely overland, even in the spring. The Coldwarg will retreat with the snows, but *They* have other creatures who do not fear the warmth. And you will not dare to unbar your doors lest any who come be the Enemy in disguise."

"True enough," Tyrvin said. "You and Ancaladar I know cannot be impersonated by *Them*. But few others."

There was a long moment of silence, filled with the things neither Knight wished to say aloud.

"You must go now," Tyrvin said at last. "I will walk you to the gate."

⌘

"BRIEF, were you?" Ancaladar scoffed. He got to his feet and fanned his wings, shaking nonexistent drifts of snow from them.

"As brief as was suitable," Jermayan said. He brushed crusted snow from the stirrup and vaulted into Ancaladar's saddle, pulling the riding-straps into place with the ease of long practice.

Ancaladar lumbered through the snow, bounding down the long slope that led away from the Fortress, his wings folded tightly against his back as he built up speed. Snow and shards of ice-crust sprayed up around him to either side in wide fans.

When he was running flat-out, he spread his wings with a sudden snap, and was pulled from the ground. For the first few yards, the dragon struggled for height, wings fanning, but then he found the wind he'd been seeking and gained height quickly in a series of sharp zig-zagging motions, until he'd reached what he considered a safe height above the ground.

"And now?" Ancaladar asked, once he was soaring smoothly through the sky.

"Ysterialpoerin," Jermayan answered. "But I wish to go to the camp first, and speak to Redhelwar."

"And Idalia," the dragon said smugly.

⌘

KELLEN'S scouts had brought more reports of plague in the days that followed, until he ordered his scouts to stay away from settlements entirely. He dared not risk losing any of his troops to sickness out here in the cold waste, especially with the mountains still to cross.

They lost a fortnight camped at the foot of the Mystrals as a winter storm raged over them. To attempt to ascend the mountains in such weather would be purest suicide, but though the delay was unavoidable, it gnawed at Kellen's nerves. At least they'd be able to stop at Ondoladeshiron to resupply, and to get out of the weather for a day or so, and from there the journey to Halacira and on to Sentarshadeen should be fairly easy going. The weather should be milder too, at least by comparison.

At last the weather broke, and the army moved on.

When they entered the mountains, Kellen rode far ahead of everyone, for Shalkan, sure-footed as a mountain goat and light-footed as only a unicorn could be, blazed the trail through the passes for the snow-sledge to follow. The unicorn was able to tell where the ice would bear the weight of the carts and horses, and where it would crack and fissure, trapping the heavy, slow-moving oxen. The two of them searched the slopes above for the treacherous, precariously-balanced weights of snow that might at any moment cascade into a deadly snow-spill, crushing men and animals beneath tons of snow and ice.

Most of all, both Knight-Mage and unicorn strained their senses to detect the Enemy's creatures. The high cold realms were their natural habitat, and the narrow mountain passes were the perfect spot for an ambush.

"ARE you sure this is the smartest thing we've ever done?" Kellen asked, trying to keep the uneasiness out of his voice.

It was their seventh day in the mountains, and so far they had encountered no living things at all. Kellen distrusted the quiet; in his time with the army, he had gained the soldier's dislike of too much good fortune. It always seemed to mean that some particularly bad stroke of luck was about to fall.

And so far, they'd been far too lucky. Only a few cases of frost-burn, some snow-dazzle, and a bit of mountain-sickness, all of which the Wildmages—all from the High Reaches—had warned him to expect. They'd run out of fresh meat during the storm, but they still had enough provisions to make Ondoladeshiron.

Much too easy, Kellen thought grimly. *And I know* They *know we're here. Why aren't* They *trying to stop us?*

He had the sense that *Their* attention was elsewhere, that *They* weren't paying attention to him because *They* felt *They* didn't need to. Either *Their* attacks and defenses had been put into place long ago, or *They* were concentrating *Their* attentions on something *They* thought was far more important than destroying a third of the Elven Army.

And if that was the case, Kellen desperately wanted to know what it was.

Kellen's force was several hundred yards behind him, and the whistling of the wind over the ice-covered rocks drowned out any sound they made. Though he could sense their presence through the Wild Magic, his eyes and ears insisted to Kellen that he and Shalkan were completely alone in a frigid gray and white wilderness. He hadn't really liked the idea of riding out with him and Shalkan so far ahead of any possible support—or rescue—but they were the only ones who would be able to find any traps before the army did. He really had no choice.

"Oh, let me see . . ." Shalkan appeared to actually be giving Kellen's question serious thought. "We faced down several Outlaw Hunts clumped together armed with nothing more than a big stick. We attacked an Endarkened stronghold with only Jermayan and Vestakia for company, and then you defied the Queen of Shadow Mountain in your underwear. You challenged Belepheriel and disobeyed Redhelwar and entered the Shadowed Elf caverns with only Idalia to accompany you. This is probably not the most ill-considered venture of your career."

"You know, that makes me feel a lot better," Kellen said.

"It should," Shalkan said sweetly. "Since you survived all those things, you'll probably survive this, too."

" 'Probably,' " Kellen muttered.

"Well, there are no certainties, of course," Shalkan drawled. "I just think you ought to bear in mind that if you don't survive, this army you're leading probably won't make it to the banks of the Angarussa, and if Redhelwar loses a third of his Knights and his Knight-Mage, I don't think he can win the war. And now I think it's time for you to dismount so we can fight for our lives."

The last sentence was delivered in the same light conversational tones as the rest of Shalkan's speech, so it took a moment for the sense of his words to penetrate.

Kellen didn't waste a moment in foolish questions, but flung himself from the unicorn's saddle. The quiver of trail-wands at his hip spilled onto the ice as he drew his sword.

Light at the Heart of the Mountain glowed, even in the dull winter's light. Kellen knew his sword had no magic—the Elves were not Mages, to craft magic swords—but the blade had a perfection that was nearly Otherworldly.

As if the flicker of light on steel were a signal, a thunderous roar filled the air, coming from farther up the narrow pass. Kellen knew instinctively—a Knight-Mage's gift—that the passage opened out ahead. They could use the room to fight, if they could reach the open space before whatever had made the sound reached them.

Something strong enough to stop us, he thought as he ran. *Don't bother with arrows, then. Cut it to pieces. And stay out of its reach.*

That wasn't going to be easy.

All at once the walls of the passage ended, and Kellen was standing at the entrance to an ice-field that slanted down and away from him. It was one of the landmarks he and Shalkan had been told to look for; it meant they were near the top of the pass and would be starting down soon. It would also give the army a place to stop and rest for a few hours.

Just as he reached the open air, he saw something come charging up the slope. When it saw him, it skidded to a stop. Kellen sensed he'd disappointed it: He should have been terrified of its bellowing, and cowered in the narrow pass until it could reach him and tear him to pieces.

It reared up on its hind legs.

And up—

And up—

"Shadewalker," Shalkan said tersely from behind Kellen's left shoulder. "Though usually they come in black," he added in something closer to his normal conversational tones.

Atroist and Jermayan had said that Shadewalkers looked like giant bears. When Kellen had lived in the Wildwood, Idalia had told him to be wary of bears, but Kellen had never seen one. He decided now he didn't want to.

The Shadewalker was as tall as three men standing upon one another's shoulders, and so massive that it actually looked squat. It was covered in thick dirty-white fur. It had a flat triangular earless head that reminded Kellen of a snake's—and Kellen hated snakes—and beady blazing red eyes. Long curved yellow teeth protruded from both its upper and lower jaws, distorting its rubbery black lips. It had narrow sloping shoulders, and its long arms dangled. Against the whiteness of its fur the long black claws that studded its paws glistened like glass knives. Its hind legs were squat, bulging with muscle.

It will try to get past me and reach the convoy, Kellen thought. Then there was no more time for thought as the Shadewalker dropped to all four legs again and charged.

If he had not been a Knight-Mage, trained in the House of Sword and Shield, it would have been fatally easy for Kellen to misjudge the scale of his attacker and the seeming slowness of its attack, and not gotten out of the way in time. But as if Time itself had stopped, Kellen knew where the blow would strike. He dug his heels into the treacherous ice beneath his feet and sprang backward at the last moment, striking downward with his sword as he did.

The claws missed him by inches, and his sword did not cut as deeply as he'd hoped. But it drew blood, and the Shadewalker recoiled, bellowing in outrage.

Kellen was already running down the slope, away from the entrance to the pass. Shalkan danced over the ice, circling in the opposite direction. Both knew that the Shadewalker would not dare turn its back on them while it was uncertain of how much of a threat they represented.

It reared up, slapping at the shallow cut on its arm, trying to keep both of them in sight at once. Certain now that he had the Shadewalker's attention, Kellen stopped and turned, concentrating upon the enemy he must kill.

For Kellen, the world became stark and vivid, as he automatically dropped into Battlesight. The Shadewalker's enormous muscled form was overlaid with a vivid tracery of red and blue images, showing Kellen where best to strike, and how the beast would attack, but how he could land a blow upon an enemy with a reach more than three times his own was a problem never addressed within the Teaching Circle at the House of Sword and Shield.

He must find a way.

Half a dozen times Kellen began an attack, only to break off at the last moment as the Shadewalker moved to block it. The only parts of it within his reach were its enormous arms, and while he could hit them, he was not completely sure he could do enough damage. The only thing he succeeded in doing was in luring it farther out onto the snowfield, where he and Shalkan had more room to move.

He was afraid for Shalkan.

He pushed that fear aside.

He was afraid for the Knights who would be hurrying to help.

He pushed that fear aside.

Only the Battle-mind could help him now.

Once, in the House of Sword and Shield, Kellen had sparred against a dozen Knights. Then, the object of the exercise was to move through them neither striking nor being struck: Master Belesharon had called it "Water Mind," and it was one of the gifts of a Knight-Mage. It was also the hardest thing Kellen had ever achieved, for Water Mind showed him the course of the unfolding battle as if it were the water through which a fish swam, and as the fish sensed obstacles in its path, so Kellen could sense how the fight would move, and he could move with it, or around it.

Or into it.

Water Mind was dangerous, for it drained energy, strength, reserves, far past the point of exhaustion. But he had no choice now.

Kellen felt the utter peace of Water Mind enfold him, and suddenly he had all the time in the world. The tracery of light over the Shadewalker's body dimmed and vanished, for Kellen no longer needed it. He stepped forward, bringing his sword up in a drawing cut beneath its arm, and stepped back.

It was as if he and the Shadewalker no longer fought, but cooperated in the deadly dance of its destruction. Kellen never shifted more than a few steps to avoid its wildly-thrashing arms; when it lowered its head to snap at him, his dagger was already in his hand. He drove it through the bottom of the jaw, spiking the creature's tongue to its soft palate and making it keen in muffled agony.

Shalkan darted in behind, stabbing with his horn. The Shadewalker swung around on all fours, slashing at the unicorn, then turned back to confront his chief tormenter, pawing at its chin and finally tearing the dagger free in a spatter of blood.

Kellen cut again, this time across the ribs. He reversed his blade and brought it down hard across the Shadewalker's foreleg. He felt the blade grate against bone, but the limb remained intact.

The Shadewalker reared back, taking its wounded head and arm out of Kellen's reach, but as it did, it exposed its belly.

Kellen feinted toward it with his sword—

Swayed backward out of the way of the slashing blow the creature aimed at him—

And struck with all his might in the moment it was off-balance.

It tumbled forward, its weight ripping its flesh along the edge of the blade. Kellen let the momentum of his strike carry him in the opposite direction, so that he would not be beneath the Shadewalker's body when it collapsed. Its belly tore open with a foul-smelling gush of entrails; it collapsed into them, releasing a wet stench. Almost instantly frost began to form on the exposed gray-pink surfaces.

It struggled to get to its feet for a few seconds longer, then something else tore inside it, and dark red blood came squirting out over the mass of pale intestines and onto the snow, causing a cloud of steam to rise around the still-twitching body.

Seeing that, Kellen knew his work was over, and Water Mind left him.

The floating peace he had felt only an instant before deserted him. Suddenly he felt as if he couldn't breathe—or as if he hadn't taken a breath in far too long. He took an unsteady step backward, and sat down—hard—on the ice. The world darkened, and all he could see were sparkling lights before his eyes.

"Kellen?" Shalkan's voice, sounding very far away.

"*Kellen!*"

Isinwen dragged him to his feet. Though Kellen's vision was still hazy, he could see Rhuifai, Seheimith, Janshil, and the rest of his troop crowded in behind his Second.

"I'm fine," he said unconvincingly.

"You're hurt," Isinwen said, sounding worried.

"No," Kellen protested. But a deep breath brought a sudden soreness in his right side, and when he reached down, his fingers encountered roughness instead of the glassy smoothness of his armor's enameled surface.

He looked down. There were three long furrows across his ribs, where one of the Shadewalker's blows had come a little too close. He would have an excellent set of bruises to show for this encounter.

"Nothing that Allheal won't cure," Kellen said, feeling stronger now.

"You take too many chances," Isinwen said, a note of exasperation—and relief—in his voice.

Kellen nodded. There was nothing to say. He knew it was wrong to hazard himself this way when he was responsible for the lives of his entire force. But he also knew that no one else could do what he had done, and if he had not done it, his command would have perished.

"Go back to the convoy and bring them up. Pass the word that we will stop here long enough to drink tea. I could do with a cup myself," he added. He felt thirsty—unusually so. Undoubtedly it was more of the aftermath of Water Mind. The floating state was a potent tool, but just like his own sword or dagger, it did not care what it harmed, and could destroy him as easily as an enemy.

Isinwen sent the others went back to their waiting destriers, and, with a last glance around the snowfield to make sure that no other danger lay in wait, followed. A few moments later six of the Knights mounted up and headed back toward the rest of the convoy. The rest settled down, spreading their cloaks to form a windbreak, and prepared to brew tea.

When they were thoroughly engaged in the activity, Shalkan trotted back to Kellen's side.

"Not that I had any doubts, of course, but it was interesting to watch," the unicorn said.

"Even more interesting to do," Kellen said, stretching tentatively.

He realized that the blood from the kill had frozen along the surface of his blade and sighed. It would take warm water and oil, then a session with a sharpening stone, before the blade was at its best again.

It took him three tries to summon Fire into the small block of charcoal that he laid inside his shield—he could have gone and gotten Fire from Isinwen but it would have meant leaving Shalkan alone—but once it was burning, it gave off enough heat to melt the ice beneath it sufficiently that he could begin to clean his sword. Once it was clean enough to sheath, Kellen tipped the charcoal out onto the ice and set the shield aside.

"There's something here you should see," Shalkan said, prodding at the body of the Shadewalker.

"What?" Kellen asked.

"Figure it out for yourself," Shalkan said, twitching his tail. "I'll be around."

Kellen sighed. It was awkward having to divide his time between Shalkan and the army, but there really wasn't any way for him to have specified that all members of his command be chaste virgins. It simply wasn't practical.

Keirasti and her troop rode out onto the ice-field, passing Isinwen and the others with a casual salute. She swung down off Orata's back and walked over to the body of the Shadewalker.

"That is a very ugly bear," she announced.

Kellen walked over to join her. "Shalkan said it was something called a Shadewalker."

"And it seems we are not the first to try its mettle recently," Keirasti continued. "It bears wounds of recent fighting—sword wounds—less than a sennight old, I judge."

She pointed.

"But . . . those are mine," Kellen said, dumbfounded.

He realized suddenly just how lucky he'd been to strike the fatal blow that he had. The Shadewalker's earlier injuries had already partly healed by the time he'd struck the blow that killed it—in fact, the first wound he'd given it was entirely gone. Even the deep cut to its foreleg was more than half healed.

The wounds Shalkan had given it were still raw and fresh, however, which made Kellen wonder. He knelt down beside it and investigated the body carefully, parting the fur to inspect the hide, and found several more wounds, these old enough to have healed over into angry raised knots in the Shadewalker's black skin.

"The scouts Redhelwar sent to Sentarshadeen came this way," he said.

"It is the main road to the King's city, and the fastest way," Keirasti said, puzzled at the seeming change of subject. "It is the way I would have gone, were I sent."

"Then they met this . . . thing," Kellen said. "And from the look of these wounds, they didn't get farther than this, either."

Fighting against an enemy who could heal anything but a mortal wound a hundred times faster than normal, the messengers must have been unable to kill it. And it had undoubtedly made sure to catch them in a place where their unicorn mounts couldn't simply outrun it. That trick would have worked again, on Kellen, if he and Shalkan had been a few seconds slower reaching the ice-field.

Keirasti made a quick gesture over her heart. "Gone to Leaf and Star," she said quietly.

"But never again," Kellen said grimly.

⤛

THEY saw no further evidence of the Enemy in their descent from the Mystrals, which made Kellen brood over their continuing good fortune. Their losses continued to be light, but descending a mountain presented more hazards than going up one—they lost wagons and teams of oxen down the sides of cliffs, along with supplies they could ill-afford to lose. It was up to Kellen to make the decisions that had to be made with the loss of supplies, and he chose to divert the remaining food, as much as possible, to the horses and oxen. The Knights could manage on shorter rations than their animals could, and Ondoladeshiron was less than a moonturn away now, depending on the weather.

But if the Enemy left them alone, the winter weather nearly made up for *Their* absence. Just after the army crossed the top of the peaks, the weather turned unexpectedly bad, making their descent through the mountains slow and miserable. Kellen and his Seconds pushed everyone as hard and as fast as they dared—they *had* to get down out of the mountains before they froze, starved, or were simply buried in snow.

⤛

THAT'S *it*, Kellen thought, patting Firareth's neck. Leather glove met padded crinet-cover with a dull wet sound, but Firareth seemed pleased. *I'm not going over those again—not even at high summer.*

It was early morning, barely light enough to ride. For a few hours, the Wildmages had promised them a break in the weather, and Kellen meant to take full advantage of it. For the last several days the army had been making its way through a series of mountain valleys, each indistinguishable from the last— or the next. But now they could fairly say that the mountains were behind them at last.

And if Redhelwar was to follow them, the Army's General would have to take the same route—and Redhelwar had most of the army's heavy equipment— the large tents, the main horse herds and remounts, the Centaur cavalry. And half again as many souls to move.

But he'll have *to move south to Ondoladeshiron. Five of the six Elven Cities that remain—if Deskethomaynel and Windalorianan were evacuated—are south of the Mystrals, and he has to be in a position to defend them if that's what Andoreniel decides to do. The only one north of the Mystrals is Ysterialpoerin, and the Elves won't leave that.*

But that makes it such a perfect target. . . .

Kellen sighed. He knew there was no point in worrying about that now. His job was to scout Halacira as a refuge for the families of the Elven Allies, and then go on to Sentarshadeen. And then, yes, report back to Redhelwar, which would probably mean crossing the Mystrals again—though fortunately *not* with a full army this time. Fortunately, they didn't need the snow-sledge here on the plains, and their progress would be faster.

❧

BUT after the first sennight, Kellen realized he had no choice but to send an ad-vance party ahead to the city. They'd simply lost too much of their supplies crossing the mountains.

It was the hardest thing he'd ever had to do. He wanted to lead the advance party himself, and knew that as the commander he had to stay with the main force.

But to send them off alone, knowing that the relative peace of their journey so far might simply be a subtle trap of the Enemy, knowing the advance party might never reach Ondoladeshiron at all . . . who, could he send?

He agonized over his choice, knowing it was obvious. The party should be made up of Knights from the skirmishing units, used to traveling light and fast and fighting independently. Keirasti should be in command; he knew she'd lead them well. They'd need Reyezeyt, who was one of the best trackers he had.

No matter who he sent, he'd be sending friends.

But that's the problem, isn't it?

He was alone in his tent, looking down at the scroll that carried the tally of his command. Outside the wind howled, making the heavy fabric of the tent shudder. He huddled next to a single brazier, using a ball of Coldfire for light. Charcoal and lamp oil were only two of the things they were running out of, and everybody was sleeping four and five to a pavilion for warmth, but he'd needed to be alone right now. There was nobody he could really talk to about this, nobody who could make these decisions for him. Tomorrow he had to make the selec-tions and send an advance party to Ondoladeshiron in hopes they could bring back supplies. He probably should have done it yesterday.

This isn't like a battle. There isn't one right answer. I don't even know that they won't get through and get back. I just have to be willing to send them, and know, if they die, that I'm the one who sent them to their deaths.

And that was why he hesitated.

Not because he wasn't willing to do that.

But because he was.

Long before he'd become a Knight-Mage, before he'd really understood what the Wild Magic was, Kellen's greatest fear had been that he would become a tool of the Dark. Though he'd realized his original fear was unfounded, the more he'd come to learn about the Demons, and how they corrupted Wildmages to their use, the more he worried—about his actions, and their consequences, and his reasons for doing everything he did. Ancaladar had said that in the Last War, the Bonded had taken their dragons with them into the service of the Demons out of love—the desire not to see their dragons die at the end of a human lifespan.

So the path into the Dark can begin with good intentions, and the desire to do good, even if it's wrong and misplaced. And if I'm willing to sacrifice lives in a good cause, am I going to know when to stop?

And if I don't, is anyone going to be able to stop me?

He took a deep breath.

If I do nothing out of fear of what I may do, They win anyway.

He unrolled the scroll and began to choose.

⌒⊰⌒

A sennight later Keirasti met them on the road—if you could call it that—coming up from Ondoladeshiron. All thirty of the Knights Kellen had sent were with her, and she had six sledge-wagons of supplies.

Even though they had encountered Keirasti's trail-wands along the way—each cluster proof that the party she commanded was still alive—Kellen did not relax until she had rejoined the main force.

Even as he gave the orders to make camp, and as the army surrounded the wagons and began unloading them, Kellen realized he'd been expecting the very worst up until the last moment—for Keirasti and her people to be ambushed within sight of the army, or . . .

Or things I can't imagine until the moment they'd happen. But manage to worry about anyway, Kellen realized with a rueful grin.

"It would be good to know what you can tell about the journey," he said, bringing Firareth up beside Orata.

"We brought tea," Keirasti said, pushing her fur-lined hood back from her helmet and starting with what she obviously considered the most important matter. "Grain, charcoal, oil, trailfood. Rochinuviel says not to come into the city when you get there—they have plague. It's in Sentarshadeen as well—everywhere in the south—the mirror-relays are up south of the Mystrals, and they have fresh news. And some Darkspawn blight is infesting the forest and killing the trees around the city, though it hasn't attacked the Flower Forest. Rochinuviel worries that they may not be able to plant in the spring, if what is affecting the trees spreads. She thinks the Deathwings bring it—they were certainly too busy with *something* to bother us, though we saw enough of them. No Coldwarg bothered us either, for which Leaf and Star be thanked, though I shot enough serpentmarae to make myself a new pavilion, if I'd stopped to skin the damned things."

Kellen grinned, too relieved to see her to worry about the bleak news she'd brought.

"I'm glad you're back."

Keirasti snorted. "As if I'd leave you to wander around out here all by yourself. As soon as we've unloaded everything, we'll all have a proper hot meal, and then I can make a full report."

❧

THAT night, well-fed and reasonably warm for the first time in sennights, Kellen took the opportunity to discuss what Keirasti had told him with Shalkan. He'd had a spare pavilion pitched at a suitable distance from the main camp for the unicorn's comfort—he wouldn't risk spending the night here, but he could certainly afford a few hours, now that they had the charcoal to spare to keep him from freezing.

Keirasti hadn't had much to add to her initial report—only more details of the journey to Ondoladeshiron, and more information about what she had heard from the Vicereign.

"You were expecting plague," Shalkan pointed out. "And they're having more success in treating it in Ondoladeshiron, according to Rochinuviel, than they did at White Spring."

"Yes . . ." Kellen admitted slowly. Once Reyezeyt had reminded him that plague was mentioned in the Teaching Songs about the Great War, he'd spent a lot of time going over what he remembered of them, and asking Isinwen to fill in the gaps in what he remembered. "The stories about the Last War mention sickness . . . if it's following the same pattern now as it did then, it will spread from the people to the animals—or maybe there are different kinds, and the animals just haven't started getting sick yet. And *They* certainly used some kind of crop-blight last time: It's one of the reasons so little grows in the Lostlands. But there are remedies for it, too. And if *They* sent the blight this early in the winter, it isn't going to affect very much, and we'll know we need to be ready for it in the spring."

If, he reflected, there was anyone available to plant crops in the spring. He ruffled the unicorn's fur, wordlessly seeking comfort. Shalkan leaned into him.

"So it doesn't make sense for them to use it now," he went on, following the train of his own thoughts. "It seems as if they're throwing everything at us here in the Elven Lands that they can get over the Borders. And why would they bother if they were certain they were going to win?"

"Well, they haven't got Armethalieh yet," Shalkan agreed. "And even if *They* can weaken the Land-wards to the point where Frost Giants and Ice Trolls can cross them, instead of just being brought in by the Shadowed Elves, *They* still won't risk crossing them *Themselves*. But that doesn't mean that enough High Mages working for them can't destroy the Land-wards."

"Or strengthen them," Kellen said. "Maybe Cilarnen can tell us if that's possible. But the point is, if *They* were so certain that winning was just a matter of time—taking Armethalieh over to the Dark and using it—why bother about us at all?"

"Knowing the answer to that is not the same thing as being able to use it," Shalkan said.

"Not yet," Kellen answered grimly.

⥈

WITH the additional supplies that Keirasti had brought, the last sennight's journey toward Ondoladeshiron was nearly easy.

As Keirasti had warned, herds of serpentmarae roamed the plain for hundreds of miles around the city, and along the way Kellen got his first look at the creatures.

The sight of the herd of dun-colored beasts pacing the convoy—they resembled giant rats as much as anything equine—was deeply unsettling to Kellen, for it brought back sharp memories of the vision he'd once had of a battle of the Great War, in which he'd seen these things being ridden into battle against the forces of the Light. For now, the serpentmarae herd simply followed at a wary distance, hoping to pull down stragglers—or, as Reyezeyt informed him, to attack the other creatures of the Plains who also followed the convoy, hoping for food.

He did what he could: assigned several skirmishing units to ride up and down the column, making sure that nobody fell behind, even by so much as a few hundred yards; posted additional guards at every night camp. And always he worried about what he might have left undone, and if he might be overlooking something vital.

⥈

IT was with both relief and an odd sense of loss that Kellen finally sighted the Gathering Plain outside Ondoladeshiron. The first time he'd seen it—was it only a few moonturns ago?—he'd been a different person entirely.

The Wild Magic is a magic of change, and change isn't always pleasant—or easy, he reminded himself. He'd known then that he would have a crucial part to play in the war to come, and knew that he would have to change if he was to play it. But he'd never suspected how much he'd have to change, or what that change would cost him.

I've killed more times than I can count. I've lost friends. I've seen friends die. And maybe worst of all, I've learned to see my friends as pieces on a xaique-board, and I know that I'll do what I have to do to win.

Because not to win, when the stakes were this high, was unthinkable.

There were more supplies waiting for them on the Gathering Plain—cairns containing more fuel, fresh meat, blankets—and Kellen set his people to the task of making a more permanent camp. They'd all earned a rest—even if only a few days.

And he wanted to talk to Rochinuviel, if that were at all possible.

⟿

"THE messages left with the supplies say that the sickness is under control in Ondoladeshiron," Isinwen reported, holding out a handful of long slender sticks to Kellen. Kellen could see that they were ringed with bands of color, but Elves saw far more colors than humans did; one of the few skills Kellen had been unable to master in the House of Sword and Shield was that of reading the trail-wands that the Elves used to leave messages in the field.

"Read them to me, of your courtesy," Kellen said.

"The Vicereign still does not wish us to enter the city, but there is a place outside where the foresters will check for messages, and where they will leave fresh supplies for us. She says that the mirrors say that the serpentmarae have not been sighted south of here. Which means that the rest of our journey should be a simple matter indeed."

"Oh yes, very simple," Kellen agreed ironically. "I hope to speak with Rochinuviel while I'm here, if that can be arranged."

"I can ask if she is willing. Artenel already has a long list of items that he wishes to acquire, so you would need to send someone to the message-cairn in any event."

Redhelwar had been unable to spare Rulorwen to send with Kellen, since the Master Engineer's skills would certainly be needed to get the bulk of the army over the Mystrals. But the Chief Artificer possessed many of the same skills, and in company with several of Rulorwen's most promising apprentices, should be able to do everything necessary at Halacira.

"I'll go myself," Kellen decided. "If it's between here and the city, it isn't far, and if I take Shalkan, we can outrun anything we can't outfight. And I should be able to sense trouble, which would be a good thing to know about anyway. Naturally, I expect you to let me know if you don't think this is a good idea."

Isinwen bowed. "If I did not, Kellen, Shalkan certainly would. But as you say, we are near the city, and Rochinuviel says it has been quiet here. I shall see what else we need to replace, and I should have the tally for you sometime tomorrow."

"Thank you," Kellen said, bowing in return. "That's certainly soon enough. And now, I believe there was a *gan* board included among the fresh supplies, and I believe Nironoshan has challenged you to a match. For myself, I shall merely watch, and learn."

⚗︎

COMPARED to the weather on the other side of the Mystrals—and in them—the temperatures here on the Gathering Plain were almost what Kellen was prepared to consider balmy, though he was also sure he'd quickly get tired of the wind that never seemed to stop blowing. He supposed if you had wings, though, you'd like a lot of wind; he remembered that Ondoladeshiron was where Idalia had come to when she'd transformed from a Silver Eagle back into a human. He glanced up at the mountain peaks, wondering if there were any Silver Eagles left.

Catching the direction of his thoughts, he firmly banished the speculation. He was going to enjoy the day as much as he could—the weather was clear, the sky was actually blue, and it was a grand day for a ride.

Despite the fact that he'd gone off to bed long before Isinwen and Nironoshan had finished their game of *gan*—games could take hours, even days, to play out, and both Knights were master players—by the time he'd awakened in the morning, the list he'd asked for was nearly complete. In addition to Artenel's mysterious list of requirements, the Wildmages and the other Healers were running low on supplies as well. Nothing absolutely vital, as he understood it, but it would all be nice to have.

The morning had been spent in meeting with his subcommanders—Artenel, who had assured him cheerfully that in a day or so, he could have bathing facilities set up, as well as a sheltered cooking area—Anindetiel the horsemaster and Thinelel the wagonmaster, who reported on the health of their respective charges—Wirance, who promised him detailed information about the weather as soon as possible—and several others. When Isinwen had presented him with the supply list, Kellen had told him that they would stay at Ondoladeshiron for a full sennight.

He didn't want to lose the time, but the horses and oxen had been pushed hard over the mountains, and deserved a full rest before they went on. Wagons and gear needed mending. And from here, Kellen could send scouts to cover a good distance of the trail ahead, which would save time later. South of the On-doladeshiron plain, they descended into forest, and while there was a broad high road through it—which should make moving the wagons a simple matter—the storms of winter might have felled trees or created other obstacles which they'd have to move.

It was best to be prepared.

And for now, having spent his morning making decisions and giving orders, he had nothing to do with his afternoon beyond riding over to the rendezvous point at Ondoladeshiron with Shalkan and leaving the scroll with the list of the army's needs. Fortunately, the unicorn's armor hadn't been in one of the wagons they'd lost. He was sure he'd never have heard the end of it.

⟿

"YOU should add honey-cakes to that list," Shalkan said musingly, as Kellen swung into the saddle. "People like honey-cakes."

Kellen laughed. "It was the first thing I wrote down," he assured the unicorn. "I'm sure Rochinuviel will be able to find some for you."

"Firareth likes them too," Shalkan said piously. "I'm not just thinking of my-self, you know."

"Certainly not," Kellen agreed, as the unicorn trotted off. "I hadn't thought so for a minute."

Honey-cakes would be nice, he thought. And pancakes with jam, and fresh butter. Milk. And proper tea, brewed strong and hot. "We'll see what they have."

In only a few moments, they were well beyond the perimeter of the camp. It was quiet out here, Kellen realized with a sense of peaceful discovery. Shalkan's hooves made no sound at all as the unicorn trotted over the surface of the snow, and the bustle and constant noise of the army was far behind him. For the first time in sennights nobody needed anything from him. There were no decisions to make. He could just be.

"You needed a rest," Shalkan observed, after they'd ridden along in silence for several minutes. "You were worrying too much."

"I hope it didn't show." Redhelwar never seemed to worry—the only time Kellen had seen the Elven General truly off-balance was when Kellen had brought him the news that the Shadowed Elves had turned their caverns into a death-trap for the army.

"Not much. I suppose people would rather have their commander worrying about things than taking everything too calmly. But they trust you. You're Kellen Knight-Mage, you know," Shalkan said.

As if I need reminding. Kellen made a rude noise. "I'm seventeen, and half a year ago I'd never held a sword in my hand in my entire life. And when I think about it that way, it seems like any moment I'm going to wake up in Idalia's cabin back in the Wildwood, and all of this is just going to have been a crazy dream."

"If you'd known this was where you'd end up, doing this, would you have left the City?" Shalkan asked, his tone idle.

"That's a dumb question!" Kellen burst out, stung. "I mean, yes, of course I would. Hell, I'd probably have left *earlier.* This is what I'm good at. It's what I'm supposed to be doing. And . . . it *needs* to be done. And there's nobody else."

"Good," the unicorn said, sounding satisfied. "Just remember that when you worry about not being good enough, or getting things wrong."

"Everybody gets things wrong sometimes," Kellen protested automatically. But his heart wasn't in it. He'd known before he started that it didn't matter if he *was* seventeen and had barely discovered his life's purpose, that to get done what the Wild Magic needed him to do he *had* to be good enough. And to get the Elves to see that, he had to be right—not some of the time, but all of the time. He couldn't afford mistakes. The people depending on him couldn't afford his mistakes.

It was a heavy burden to carry, all the more because most of the time he didn't think about it at all. He just did what he had to do.

And I'll keep doing it for as long as it takes. I just have to remember that I'm not alone. I have the Wild Magic to rely on. It made me a Knight-Mage. It won't let me fail.

"Come on," Kellen said aloud. "Is this as fast as you can go? I could *walk* to Ondoladeshiron faster."

"Well," Shalkan drawled, flicking his ears back, "since you ask so nicely . . ."

Kellen barely had a moment to gather himself before the unicorn was off, bounding at top speed across the snow.

⊸⧽⧼⊸

UNICORNS didn't gallop like horses, they bounded like deer, and a unicorn's top speed was very fast indeed. The wind whipped through every slit in Kellen's helmet, blasting his skin like liquid ice, and his Coldwarg-fur cloak streamed out behind him as if it were made of nothing more substantial than thin silk. He laughed aloud for the sheer joy of it.

But too soon the run was over. Ahead he saw what looked like nothing more than a natural outcropping of stone and scattered boulders—the city of Ondoladeshiron, hidden in plain sight by Elven artifice that was, to Kellen, far more wonderful than simple magic. Beyond the stones—even knowing that they were really houses, he could not make himself see them as such—Kellen could see the dark green of Ondoladeshiron's Flower Forest. The trees at its outer edge were snow-crusted, but still flourishing.

Shalkan slowed to a trot, then a walk, but didn't stop.

"Aren't we almost at the city?" Kellen asked. "I thought Rochinuviel said we weren't supposed to go into the city."

"The city has become appreciably smaller," Shalkan said, stretching out his long neck and sniffing the air. "The Elves that are still here have moved closer to the Flower Forest. These houses are deserted now."

Kellen wondered how he knew; Keirasti hadn't mentioned that, and she would have told him if she'd known. But he'd long since resigned himself to the fact that Shalkan—all the unicorns, in fact—simply had sources of information of their own.

"And we have company," Shalkan said. "Someone is waiting at the rendezvous for us."

When they came closer, Kellen could see a banner on a pole set outside of one of the houses—that must be what marked it as the rendezvous, but it was obviously much more than that. A design flashed on its surface, silver on white—the same design as on one of the banners that hung in Andoreniel's Council Chamber.

"Huh," Kellen said. "The Vicereign came herself? How did she know I'd be the one to come?"

"Maybe it was a lucky guess," Shalkan said. "Maybe when you get to be as old as Rochinuviel some things aren't hard to predict."

⋙

WHEN Kellen reached the place where the banner stood, a door opened in the side of what looked like a tumble of snow-covered stone. Suddenly Kellen's perceptions shifted, and what had seemed to be only a pile of rock a moment before was now—obviously—a house.

And Rochinuviel herself was standing in the doorway. The Vicereign of Ondoladeshiron looked very much as she had the last time Kellen had seen her—a graceful, androgynous figure dressed in white, her furs and jewels as elaborate as if she sat in her own Council Chamber. But unlike Ashaniel, whose Elven beauty had dazzled him from the first moment he'd seen her, there was something so remote and unyielding about Rochinuviel that she made him think of a piece of sculpture crafted by some unknown race that had absolutely nothing in common with humans.

"I See you, Kellen Knight-Mage. Be welcome at this hearth. We will drink tea," Rochinuviel said.

"I See you, Rochinuviel, Voice of Andoreniel," Kellen said, dismounting. "I am welcomed."

To Kellen's faint surprise, Shalkan followed him inside, as if it were expected. He remembered that at the Mustering of the Armies, Rochinuviel had greeted the Unicorn Knights personally, so obviously her presence didn't cause Shalkan any discomfort.

The house looked very much like the one he and Idalia had shared in Sentarshadeen, except for the fact that not only was this one empty, it hadn't even been prepared for occupancy. A carpet had been spread on the floor of the Common Room, with cushions for seating, and several braziers gave the room a pleasant warmth, but except for the stone walls and glass windows, it might have been Kellen's own tent.

As before, Rochinuviel had a companion with her, already seated upon one of the cushions, another Elf garbed almost identically to the Vicereign, but in shades of palest gray. Kellen wondered what the woman's function was. Adjutant? Chaperone? It was impossible to imagine Rochinuviel needing one, any more than it was possible to imagine being rude or boisterous in her presence.

The traditional Elven tea-service was set out in the center of the carpet. Rochinuviel seated herself gracefully upon one of the cushions and began to prepare tea.

Kellen removed his cloak and gauntlets and bundled them neatly, setting them aside before selecting a cushion opposite her and sitting down—passably, but with quite a bit less grace. Shalkan folded himself neatly beside him, still in his saddle and armor.

The silence unfolded. Once it would have bothered him, but now he was content to let matters proceed in their own good time. There was no reason just now to rush things, after all.

When the water had boiled and the tea was steeping, Rochinuviel spoke.

"My heart rejoices to see your company arrived in such good order. When Keirasti came to us a fortnight ago she was most vigorous in her requirements and in her need for haste," Rochinuviel said.

Well, that could mean nearly anything. And it certainly sounded as if Rochinuviel wanted to get right down to business. "I trust all went as you would have it go," Kellen said, after a moment's thought. "Our passage over the Mystrals was not without . . . moments of unusual interest . . . and unfortunately we lost several wagons of supplies in the crossing."

"So I was given to understand," Rochinuviel said, with a faint enigmatic smile. "I am not unaware of the needs of an army in the field, nor the disadvantages that come with a winter campaign. You may give your current list of requirements to Sherediel."

The woman in gray held out a slender gloved hand. After a moment's fumbling in his tunic, Kellen produced the scroll. Sherediel tucked it neatly away into a fold in her robe and folded her hands again, apparently content to take no part in the conversation at all.

"I wished to see you so that I might give you news from the south, as Keirasti tells me that you will go to Sentarshadeen," Rochinuviel continued. "But first we will drink tea, and perhaps you will oblige me in telling me the current news of the war, for Jermayan's news was many sennights old when he came here."

Kellen must have looked more confused than he intended, for she explained.

"He was here and gone before Keirasti arrived, to take the women with child to the Crowned Horns, as Andoreniel commanded. I do not say I agree or disagree with his decision. It is what it is. But had any of us been able to see the future, it might have been a different one."

Now this was odd speaking indeed from the Vicereign, and all of Kellen's senses strained to understand what it meant. Rochinuviel seemed to be attempting to tell him something without actually saying it outright, but while her implicit meaning might have been plain as day to another Elf, he was baffled. Maybe she'd speak more plainly soon. Or maybe Shalkan knew what she was talking about and he could ask him on the ride back.

"Not much has changed for us with the army between the time he left and the time I did," Kellen said, both responding to her desire for information and playing for time. "The Allies of the Enemy push against the land-wards to the north. Redhelwar believes they will break through the land-wards, but our forces are not great enough to defend the north and also meet the greater threat the Enemy poses in the south and west. We were able to cast a spell to see into Armethalieh, as perhaps Jermayan will have told you, and we now know that the Enemy has an agent there who is working to open the city to *Them*."

Rochinuviel pursed her lips. "Indeed, Jermayan said as much. He said you believed *Their* work in the Mage City to be the greater threat to us—and so we must abandon our northern cities to the Shadow."

"If—" Kellen began, but Rochinuviel held up her hand.

"The tea is ready."

It was a tea he had never tasted before—Rochinuviel told him the name was Ironwind—and with the first sip, Kellen wasn't sure he cared for it at all. Unlike most of the Elven teas he'd tasted, its flavor was intensely bitter. But it was also warming, seeming to burn all the way down his throat and into the pit of his stomach.

Cilarnen, he knew, would be able to go on for at least half an hour about its qualities. Kellen thought it was about as close to drinking a sword blade as he'd like to get.

"And with the bitter, the sweet, for balance," Rochinuviel said. She opened a diminutive box containing small round objects in pastel colors.

Following her lead, Kellen took one and put it in his mouth. The candy was creamy and grainy at the same time; it was also intensely sweet—without the tea, it would have been much too sweet—and tasted of honey, flowers, and, he suspected, some of the same spices that were in the tea. He took another sip of the tea—he found that mingled with the aftertaste of the candy, its flavor was much improved—and then selected one of the candies and offered it to Shalkan. The unicorn crunched it greedily, looking pleased.

"I haven't had these in far too long," Shalkan said. "Thank you."

"If they please you, I shall be certain to send a package of them to you," Rochinuviel said, smiling with genuine warmth this time. "But I have interrupted the guest, and for that, I beg pardon."

Kellen wracked his brain to remember what they'd been talking about before the tea had been poured. Oh yes, nothing important. Merely matters of life and death.

"It was nothing. I only wished to remark that if *They* should gain control of Armethalieh, *They* will have a great store of . . . food . . . at *Their* disposal, as well as access to wielders of the High Magick. Control of the City will provide *Them* with an advantage that we dare not let *Them* have. Further, I believe that *Their* tactics up until this point have all been misdirection, to keep us from seeing that this was *Their* ultimate goal, and to keep us and the Armethaliehans from uniting against *Them*, our common enemy."

Rochinuviel bowed her head, acknowledging the argument, and poured more tea into the tiny Elvenware cups.

"And here we come to the matter that I wished to speak to you of—a matter that I judge is best held closely and not scattered to the winds of gossip."

Kellen sat up straighter. This was important—important enough that the Vicereign of Ondoladeshiron had made a shrewd guess that he'd be here today and come to meet him, so that they could talk in what amounted to total secrecy.

"I had wished to speak with you to see what news you could give me of the south," he answered, feeling uneasy.

"Perhaps you already suspect what I have to tell. I warn you that it does not make good hearing. My grandfather was General of the Armies also, and fought at the direction of the King when last the Shadow walked the land. And so I know that if the King cannot say what shall be done, it is a grievous thing."

Is Andoreniel dead? Automatically Kellen reached out a hand and laid it across Shalkan's neck.

"I have said before that there is plague in Sentarshadeen. Now I add what I have just learned but long suspected. The King lies ill—too ill to make the decisions that must be made. Ashaniel cannot speak for him—she lies at the Fortress of the Crowned Horns, with the Crown Prince, who is but a child."

"But—But Andoreniel's Council . . ." Kellen stammered.

"Counsels the King," Rochinuviel finished. "As do we, when times are otherwise. None of us speak in his name. And those who might, in Sentarshadeen, perhaps lie ill as well. Or judge that it is best to watch—and wait."

Kellen felt as if he had just been hit very hard in the stomach. Andoreniel ill? But the army needed *orders*.

Who was going to make the decisions?

"Redhelwar—" he began, struggling to form the sentence politely.

"The Army's General does not know of the King's indisposition. Had I known earlier, I would have sent word with Jermayan. Word has just now reached us, by unicorn rider—they hoped he would rally, but he does not."

"If the King should die—" Kellen said, still trying to grasp the enormity of the disaster.

"Then Sandalon becomes King, and Ashaniel rules for him for many years yet. And we are no better off," Rochinuviel said inexorably. "I do not say what transpires in Sentarshadeen, for I do not know. But I imagine that those of the Council who are still in health are doing what they can to act as they believe Andoreniel would have them act."

Kellen's experiences of Andoreniel's Council had not been pleasant ones. He didn't doubt the truth of Rochinuviel's words, but he also knew that the Council took far too long to make up its mind about anything—and now, more than ever, speed and decisiveness was needed. That, and more—breaking with the traditional Elven way of doing things.

Andoreniel could do it—had done it. But not his Council.

"I thank you for sharing your wisdom with me," he said automatically. "And I am grateful for your words."

"Use them carefully," Rochinuviel said. "For it is in my mind that if Andoreniel's plight should come to be widely known, that knowledge would be more dangerous than plague."

❧

HER words echoed in Kellen's mind as he rode Shalkan—at a sedate walk—back to the Gathering Plain.

Part of him wanted to race there at top speed and start shouting orders, but he knew he needed time to think.

Redhelwar had to be told at once. That was imperative.

He couldn't just send Shalkan with a message—Kellen's Mageprice kept Shalkan with him. And Kellen couldn't go. He had to stay with the army—if he simply took off with Shalkan, no matter what story he gave for doing so, he'd start precisely the kind of panic he needed at all costs to avoid.

And there was still the mission to Halacira and Sentarshadeen. More than ever, Kellen wanted to get to Sentarshadeen and see for himself what was going on there. But if they didn't secure the caverns as a possible refugee camp, there was a strong possibility there wasn't going to *be* any army to worry about.

He groaned aloud. "Leaf and Star, what a mess!"

"To put it mildly," Shalkan said. "What are you going to do?"

The moment Shalkan asked the question, calm settled over Kellen. "I'm going to think," he said quietly.

～⁂～

WHEN he got back to camp (carrying Shalkan's armor, as he certainly couldn't ride Shalkan into camp), he was able to greet his people as if nothing had happened. The short winter day was already drawing toward dusk, and nobody found it unusual for Kellen to go off to his pavilion once he'd checked with Isinwen. Isinwen could run the camp, barring emergencies. As Kellen's Second, that had become part of his job.

But Kellen breathed a deep sigh of relief once he reached his pavilion and pegged the door shut behind him. Instinctively, he knew he'd convinced his Second that all was well and that nothing out of the ordinary had happened, and what Isinwen believed, the others would believe as well. But to keep up that deception—and it was a deception, Kellen acknowledged to himself—he needed to find a deeper measure of peace within himself, and find it quickly.

He lit the lamps and the braziers, took off his armor, and rummaged through his packs until he'd found his three Books.

He hadn't had much time for studying them lately, and he really doubted that the answer to his current dilemma was to be found in any of them—not *The Book of Moon*, which addressed the "how" of the Wild Magic, nor *The Book of Sun*, which mostly addressed the "when," nor even *The Book of Stars*, the most abstruse of the three, which was essentially about the "whether or not" of the Wild Magic— when it was best to intervene, and when it was best to just leave well enough alone.

Although if this is "well enough," I'd hate to see a really bad situation, Kellen thought with a sigh, opening the third Book. He guessed he was looking for peace of mind and calm as much as anything—he couldn't make any good decisions while he was chasing himself in circles, much less act as if he hadn't just received what was almost the worst possible news the Allies could have gotten. So he might as well improve his mind. *The Book of Stars* always managed to make him feel better, even when he didn't understand half of what it was saying.

What if Andorieniel dies? Ashaniel and Sandalon can't rule the Elven Lands from the Fortress of the Crowned Horns, and they can't come back. So the Council will have to make the decisions. And that just won't work.

Because the Council would probably—even now—still want to want for the Endarkened to fight a "traditional" war. And the Endarkened weren't going to do that—or weren't going to do that until the probability of victory was overwhelmingly on *Their* side.

Would Redhelwar act without waiting for the decisions of the Council? Did he even know what needed to be done next?

Do you?

Kellen took a deep breath, feeling as if he stood on the edge of a very high cliff. A rash decision right now would do nobody any good. Master Belesharon always said that to make a decision before it was needful was worse than making no decision at all.

Kellen put all thought of the future from his mind and settled down to read *The Book of Stars.*

As always his Book seemed to be speaking directly to him.

"Do nothing in haste, and everything in its proper time."

"What will be, is. And what is, will be."

"A Knight-Mage changes his surroundings by his very presence. Sometimes his presence is enough."

He read until a grumbling in his stomach told him that it was far past dinnertime, and closed his Book with a sigh, feeling better.

Nothing was any different than it had been this morning. And as much as the leisurely Elven way of doing things drove him crazy sometimes, right now he had to admit that as bleak as things were, the best thing to do was stick to his original plan. As urgent as matters were, the army needed rest before anyone went anywhere. And that would give him the time to think carefully over who was going where.

⤞

"THIS had better be good," Keirasti grumbled, though Kellen could tell her heart wasn't in it.

"I thought you'd like to take Orata for a ride," Kellen said, with as much innocence as he could muster. "She's getting fat and lazy sitting in camp, and so is

Firareth. And we'll be moving out day after tomorrow. Which is why I wanted to talk to you now."

"Privately," Keirasti observed, nodding at the emptiness surrounding them. "Which will be remarked, if not overheard."

"Then it must be remarked," Kellen said. "And not overheard."

He'd thought long and hard about this. He'd spent the last several days writing up a full report of everything that had happened so far for Redhelwar—the scroll was a fat one—and he'd already chosen the people he intended to send back over the Mystrals. But he hadn't yet told them they were going, intending to leave that for the last minute. Keirasti would be leading them—she'd handled the other mission to Ondoladeshiron well, and Kellen knew that she could do this just as expertly.

And he'd decided that she would need to know *why* she was going—all of it. So that in case disaster happened, the party was attacked, the report was lost, she would understand that she *had* to get through and deliver the gist of Kellen's message personally, no matter who and what she had to sacrifice to do it.

"I wish to lay a very heavy burden upon you," he said, beginning slowly and carefully. "Before I can tell you what it is, and why, I must tell you that it might require you to . . . throw away . . . hundreds of lives and save your own. I must know if you can do that."

"Leaf and Star," Keirasti whispered, reining Orata to a halt. "Kellen, I do not yet understand."

"Keirasti, can you let everyone under your care die to save yourself just because I tell you it's necessary? Hundreds of people?" Kellen asked bluntly.

The Elven Knight stared at him for a long moment, her dark eyes wide and unseeing beneath her helm. At last she nodded slowly. "Yes, *komentai'i*. I can do this."

Kellen let out a shuddering breath. "Leaf and Star grant you will not need to. You must tell no one—*no one*—of what we speak of here today. *Ever*."

Keirasti nodded again. "I understand."

"Tomorrow I am sending you and four hundred of my command back over the mountains. You must find Redhelwar wherever he is and deliver my report to him. It must reach him at all costs, no matter what you must do to get it there, no matter what sacrifices you must make. You must go as fast as you can."

Which meant risk, for her and all he would send with her, and though he could spare her two of the Wildmages to accompany her party, they would not be enough to protect her force from a magical attack, or to heal her injured swiftly.

"I . . . hear and obey, *komentai'i*," Keirasti said.

Kellen smiled unhappily. "If that were all, I would not have sworn you to secrecy. My report may be lost . . . and . . . I think you need to know why I am sending you." He took a deep breath and continued.

"Rochinuviel has had word from Sentarshadeen. Andoreniel lies gravely ill with plague, too ill to give orders. The Healers do not know when—or if—he will recover. Redhelwar doesn't know that he is sick; Rochinuviel found out too late to send a message with Jermayan when he came to Ondoladeshiron. This information is too . . . sensitive . . . to trust to the signaling mirrors—even if they did work across the Mystrals."

And Rochinuviel doesn't think the Council has sent word to Redhelwar. That was clear enough from what she said to me. If they had, we would almost certainly have met up with the rider. And I think Shalkan would have known, somehow.

Keirasti actually rocked in her saddle. Orata took a nervous step sideways in the snow, and tossed her head inquiringly. "The King . . ." Keirasti said.

"Ashaniel and Sandalon are safe at the Fortress of the Crowned Horns," Kellen said, reminding both of them. "And Andoreniel could recover. I will go to Sentarshadeen as soon as I am finished at Halacira, and see him myself."

Keirasti nodded, still looking stunned. Kellen waited, giving her time to take in what he had just told her. He'd had several days to get used to knowing that the Allies were essentially without a leader, after all, and when you came right down to it, Andoreniel wasn't *his* King. It was different for Keirasti.

After a few more moments she blinked and nodded, signifying that she was ready to go on.

"Knight-Mage, what are your orders for the Army's General?" she asked simply.

There it was, right out in the open, the one thing he'd been avoiding for days.

No, not avoiding. Setting aside until the proper time.

An irresistible sense of Presence filled him—the same calm that came with casting a Healing spell, or sinking into Water Mind. He knew the words he had to say, just as if he'd rehearsed them for sennights—or remembered them from an old Teaching Song.

"Say to the Army's General all that I have told you, and that it would please me greatly if he would bring the Army to the Gathering Plain to hear the news from Sentarshadeen," Kellen said firmly, and without a trace of doubt.

The sense of waiting Presence lifted.

What have I done? Have I just taken command of the Army? What if Redhelwar says no and stays in Ysterialpoerin?

There was no answer to that, nor would there be for quite some time. But he'd done all he could.

Keirasti sighed. "It shall be done. And now . . . if we are to depart tomorrow, there is much for me to do tonight."

"Travel safely," Kellen said.

"*Komentai'i,*" Keirasti answered uncompromisingly, "We will travel *fast.*"

Nine

A Lifetime in a Moon

IT HAD BEEN nearly three moonturns since Vestakia had begun her attempts to communicate with the Crystal Spiders, and the knowledge of failure was growing in her soul like a poisoned wound she could not heal.

If only she could make sense of what the Crystal Spiders were trying to tell her!

Since she had begun her work, she had risen each day at dawn, breakfasted, and gone with her guards down into the caverns. She was grateful for their presence, for Vestakia never forgot, not even for a moment, that her Endarkened father would do anything to get her back—and the Endarkened had many allies.

For the last several sennights she had divided her time between the Main Camp and the caverns, for with the steady influx of refugees from the now-abandoned Elven Cities farther north—and the outbreak of plague both in the temporary city and in Ysterialpoerin itself—every Healer was needed to tend them. And though Vestakia preferred not to go among strangers who would be shocked by her Demonic appearance, her assistance in the Main Camp could free another Elven or Wildmage healer to go among the sick and injured civilians—and skilled hands were always needed to compound medicines.

And her work here at the Further Caverns seemed to be going nowhere.

Though both Kellen and Idalia had spoken of how confusing communication with the Crystal Spiders was, Vestakia had hoped her Wildmage heritage—and the odd gifts it brought with it—would make things easier for her, but her hopes had been dashed on the very first day, when Kellen had brought her down into the caverns.

Of course she had learned much about learning to communicate with an alien mind, and even see through its eyes. Linking with the Crystal Spiders was an easy thing now, and sorting through the mind-pictures they sent her no longer caused Vestakia the sickness and disorientation it had at first. And oddly enough, though no magic was truly involved, the skills at perception and concentration that she honed in the caverns were useful elsewhere: Not only had she become far more expert at diagnosing the ills of her patients—or telling the minds of most of the people around her, in fact—simply from the way they looked and held themselves—but she could read the mood and intention of the mute beasts around her, and even her equestrian skills had improved remarkably as a result.

There was no doubt about it. When all of this was over, she would be an *excellent* goatherd, if that was what she chose to do. That was how she had begun her life, after all: as a goatherd, tending the herd of goats her mother Virgivet and her aunt Patanene had taken away from their home village with them into exile deep in the Lost Lands to provide them—and later, Vestakia—with food, shelter, clothing, and even trade-goods. Until Kellen, Shalkan, and Jermayan had found and rescued her, the goats had been her closest companions, and though she had learned much since of Healing, it was always good to know that she still had her first skills to rely on.

Assuming, of course, that all of this was ever over in a way that allowed for the herding of goats.

But no matter how much work there was for her at the main camp, her sense of duty drew her back, over and over, to the Further Cavern, and her frustrating communion with the Crystal Spiders.

By now Vestakia felt she knew everything about the location that she sought except where it *was*. The mind-pictures the Crystal Spiders sent her during their communications were still blurred and fragmented, the kaleidoscopic images of a world seen through eight eyes multiplied dozens of times over, but by now she was used to that. She was even used to seeing images of things that could not be, for by now she knew that the Crystal Spiders could create artificial images to communicate, as well as simply transmitting images of things they had seen.

Jewels and water. Jewels and water. A riddle she could not solve.

Even Cilarnen could not solve it with his Armethaliehan magick. They had all hoped, once he had found a source to power his spells, but . . . not only did the High Magick require a great deal of *preparation* for many of its spells, but they had to be done at specific times as well. And if that were not enough complication, the divination and scrying that Idalia and the other Wildmages took so much for granted was nearly absent from the High Magick, or so Cilarnen said. The forms of distance-seeing the High Magick did possess required that the Mage already have a link with what he wished to see, either of familiarity, or through a tangible object.

And what use is that? If you already know what it looks like, or where it is, why do you need magic to take a look at it? Vestakia had wondered irritably when he'd explained. But she hadn't said anything aloud. Cilarnen was already doing everything that he could—and much more than he safely could—to help their cause.

But it *was* frustrating.

Late this morning Vestakia had returned from three days spent at the Main Camp. The Healers were desperate to keep the plague from spreading to the army—or from claiming any more lives than it already had among the others—and though a Wildmage-infused cordial was having a certain amount of effect in treating it, a great deal of the stuff was needed, and preparing the cordial for charging was painstaking work.

But it was also vital work.

The Elves called the plague Shadow's Kiss, from the characteristic dark scars it left behind on all of its victims. If one survived most diseases, Vestakia knew, one was safe from them forever—that had been true of the goat-pox she had contracted as a child.

But if one survived Shadow's Kiss, it was still possible to get it again, and no one who got it a second time survived.

Or perhaps, Vestakia thought with a sigh, the second plague was a completely separate disease that only struck those who had been exposed to the first plague. The symptoms were very different: a quick high fever lasting only a day, followed by death. Unlike the original plague, it didn't seem to be contagious.

They had no way of knowing.

All they knew was that they had no way of treating the second plague. It seemed to be new—the Elven Healers said it wasn't mentioned in any of the Story Songs of the Last War.

Despite the fact that they were their main source of information on how to treat many of the diseases they were facing now, both Vestakia and Idalia were getting very tired of the Elven Story Songs.

Very nearly as tired as they were of seeing people die because their medicines simply weren't working very well.

⤙⤚

WHEN she'd gotten back to the smaller camp at last, the only thing she'd wanted was to throw herself down on her bedroll and sleep, but a sense of duty drove her down into the caverns.

There she had tried, yet again, to extract the information they all desperately needed from the Crystal Spiders' completely willing yet utterly alien minds, working until Khirethil—the captain of the troop who watched over her while she was beneath the mountain—had finally insisted that she stop.

"You gain nothing by forcing us to carry you to your bed, Vestakia," Khirethil had said, her black eyes uncompromising. "And in working yourself into exhaustion, you waste time in the end."

It was good advice, and kindly meant, and Vestakia had forced herself to take it.

In camp, under Khirethil's steady gaze, Vestakia also forced herself to eat, though the food lay heavily in her stomach. Afterward she had excused herself quickly, and gone to her pavilion.

Until she had started working here, she had not had a pavilion of her own, but shared Idalia's tent—for warmth and companionship far more than safety, for among the people of the Allied army she felt accepted and, yes, *cherished* as she had never expected to find herself in all the years of her life. From the moment she had been born, Demonic in form but human in soul, her mother and her aunt had taught her and warned her: *Trust no one. Show yourself to no one. No one will look beyond the surface and dare to believe in the human soul within.*

But Kellen had. Even now, tired and miserable as she was, the thought of him brought a warm glow of happiness to Vestakia's spirit. From the first moment he had seen her, Kellen had trusted her, believed in her, without question. What had grown between them—or might grow between them—was very awkward, given the Mageprice that Kellen paid, but Vestakia's own mother had given up twenty years of her life so that Vestakia could be human, and Vestakia was familiar with Mageprices. And a year and a day was not forever.

But even constrained as they were—not to look, not to touch, barely to take notice of one another save as comrades in the field, Vestakia wished Kellen were here now.

How he would laugh to see her pavilion!

She'd known, of course, that the Elves tended to choose a "signature" color for a person—Kellen's was a very pretty green, just the color of Shalkan's eyes—and she should have had fair warning when the armor that Artenel had produced for her had been enameled a cherry-red the exact shade of her skin, but she really hadn't expected to be presented with a matching tent.

It was quite a lovely color, really. And it certainly stood out against all this snow.

But since the Elves did things very thoroughly, and very single-mindedly, it turned out that nearly all of her clothes were red as well. And that made them rather hard to find, sometimes, in a red tent.

Yes, Kellen would definitely laugh.

Making certain that the braziers were filled for night, Vestakia got out of her armor and into a sleeping tunic and leggings. Curling up beneath several layers of blanket and fur coverlet, she pulled the one remaining lantern over to her and blew it out, then lay shivering in her bed as she waited for her covers to warm. Her muscles were filled with tiny tremors, and there was a nauseated, metallic taste in her mouth; she knew she was far too exhausted for sleep to come easily, no matter how badly she needed it.

Tomorrow she would think of something that would work. She *had* to.

The army can do nothing until it knows where the last Enclave of the Shadowed Elves is. In the dark, her mind returned to the problem that obsessed her. It did not help matters to know how much they were all depending on her to find the key. Like the other Healers, Vestakia had dealt with the Allied wounded after the two battles for the caverns, and the horrific Battle for the Heart Forest. She knew what a terrible enemy the Shadowed Elves could be. And if that weren't bad enough, the Shadowed Elves could bring other Allies of the Endarkened into the center of the Elven Lands without breaching the land-wards, as well as causing monsters such as the Deathwings and Coldwarg to do their bidding. If they were not stopped, they might attack Ysterialpoerin again—or one of the southern cities.

South.

Vestakia felt a faint spark of recognition. She *felt* that the last Enclave must be somewhere south of here, but she couldn't say why she felt that, and she could ask no one to act upon such a vague disorganized feeling. Certainly the Crystal Spiders had no sense of direction that she'd ever figured out. So the feeling couldn't come from them.

And if it didn't, it couldn't be allowed to count.

She sighed in frustration, pulling the blankets up higher. Jermayan and Ancaladar would be rejoining them soon—a sennight or two at most, Idalia had said—and if nothing else, the three of them could try flying a search-grid again, though in the winter storms it would be almost impossible for Ancaladar to fly low enough for her to sense a Shadowed Elf Enclave.

But they had to do something!

SLEEP came at last, and with it, vivid disjointed dreams that verged on nightmares.

Caverns . . . but caverns so much vaster and deeper than the ones Vestakia had spent so many hours in that it was impossible to compare them. She sensed that these caverns were utterly without light, yet somehow she could see, and all around her were the creations of a civilization far older and far more inhuman than that of the Crystal Spiders, one whose works made her dream-self shudder as she glimpsed them.

Thoughts that were not her own crowded her mind. For now they were still distant and indistinct as faint whispers in a noisy room, yet they terrified her with the possibility that she might come to hear and understand them clearly. As if the whispered thoughts represented a physical danger that she could escape, Vestakia tried to run, but only succeeded in entangling herself deeper in the dream-stuff clouding her mind.

SHE was in a garden, but this was no garden that had ever flourished beneath the rays of the sun. Everything here was cold unliving stone, yet she could sense that each stone cried out in pain, as if it were a living suffering thing whose torment would continue forever.

There was someone standing beside her, someone whose face she dared not raise her eyes to see, for if she looked, it would shatter her mind forever. She heard a voice:

"Do you love me, my own?"

And she heard her own voice reply:

"As I love power and pain, my mother, my heart . . ."

WITH a choked scream, Vestakia awoke. She was sitting bolt upright, her fists crammed into her mouth, heart hammering so hard her whole body shuddered with its force. Her whole body was covered in clammy, greasy sweat, and before she was quite awake, violent nausea overcame her. She barely made it to the slops bowl in time to deliver up her evening meal—and, it seemed, everything she'd ever eaten—in a foul-smelling rush of bile. She gagged and heaved over the vessel long after there was anything in her stomach to void, knowing as she did that what she really wanted to rid herself of—her dream—would not be so easily banished.

At last she sat back on her heels, panting and gasping, and reached for her water jug. The water was ice-cold, but she relished the shock, rinsing and spitting until she'd cleared her mouth.

She had a blinding headache, and she felt weak and ill. Her tunic and leggings were clammy with sweat, and she hardly had the strength to change them. But the thought of summoning Khirethil to help her—she was sure the Elven

Knight was awake; Khirethil's pavilion was pitched right next to hers, and Vestakia knew from experience that Elves slept lightly—galvanized her, at least as far as dragging the sodden items from her body and wrapping herself in her fur-lined cloak.

That would have to do for the moment.

Blessed Goddess, what is happening to me? Is it plague? The bruising that was one of the earliest symptoms probably wouldn't show on her cherry-red skin. But she had no sign of fever, which was one of the next symptoms. And Idalia had been fairly sure that her half-Demon heritage would protect her from catching it at all.

She forced herself to take several deep breaths. *You know it isn't plague.* She'd only been hoping it was. Plague would have been a kinder answer than what Vestakia suspected to be the truth.

Ever since she had begun to become a woman, she had known she was linked to the Demons—she could sense *Them*, and *Their* magic, and use that gift to hide from *Them*. Lately, the scope of her power had grown, so that she could sense not only *Them*, but what *They* had touched. It was a fortunate gift, for it had allowed Vestakia and her friends to track the Shadowed Elves in the first place, and rescue Sandalon and the other children they had captured, as well as finding their other Enclaves.

But it wasn't something she could just turn off when she didn't want it. And she didn't need to hear the reports from Redhelwar's scouts and patrols to know that *Their* Allies were broaching the boundaries of the Elven Lands to the north. Even though it was hundreds of miles away, Vestakia could feel it like a sore tooth—even more so when she was linked with the Crystal Spiders.

The work she was doing with them—concentrating so hard, sennight after sennight, on seeing things unseen—had opened up her Gift in a way it had never been opened before.

And now I can feel my father's mind as well.

Tears sprang to Vestakia's mind, and she hugged herself tightly. It was the very last thing she wanted. Her father was the Prince of Shadow Mountain, and he had doomed her mother and her aunt to a life of exile and caused them both to die years before their time. He had hunted Vestakia her entire life, and—until Kellen had rescued her and she had come to live in the Elven Lands—every waking moment of her life had been lived in fear either that her father would find her, or that one of the Lostlanders would accidentally see her face and kill her for the Demon she appeared to be. When Kellen had brought her into the Elven Lands, she'd thought she was safe from that forever.

But now that temporary sanctuary was gone—or nearly so. Tonight's bad dream wasn't the first she'd had, Vestakia sensed; simply the first one she managed to remember. There would be more, and worse ones, and if—when—if—the power of the Demons grew, the nightmares would invade her waking mind as well.

There were things she could do to stop that; potions that blocked Gift and allowed the minds of Mages and Healers to rest. She had taken one of them before. It would block her ability to sense *Them*—and probably her ability to link her mind with the Crystal Spiders, as well.

No.

The Allies needed to find the last Enclave of the Shadowed Elves.

And any possibility, however faint, that she might be able to give the Allies insight into what the Enemy thought and planned was something too valuable to throw away, no matter what it cost her.

South. The Crystal Spiders do not know where the last Enclave of the Shadowed Elves is, but he *does. It is from* him *that my belief comes, not what I take from their minds.*

Vestakia blinked back tears of acceptance and relief. It was not much, but it was something. If they must search for the last Enclave upon the wing, at least the area they had to search would be that much smaller.

Moving slowly and painfully, she crept to her clothes-chest and began to rummage through it for something dry and warm to wear. She thought she had slept only a few hours, and she was sure sleep would not return tonight, nor did she really want it to. Far better to let the images from her nightmare fade than risk renewing them—and at any rate, the slops-bowl certainly needed emptying.

Besides, her head throbbed, and her bones ached, and she was thirsty. At least in an Elven camp, one could always be sure of getting a hot cup of Allheal tea.

⋙

AT last Jermayan returned to the war-camp outside Ysterialpoerin, after nearly three moonturns of absence. And he saw why there were no refugees in Ondoladeshiron.

They had all come here.

Though it was counted as one of the Heart Triad, Ysterialpoerin was nearly as far north as Deskethomaynel. It only made sense that instead of risking a dangerous mountain journey in the depths of winter, the refugees of the Northern Triad would head for the only remaining city north of the Mystrals: Ysterialpoerin.

Lerkelpoldara had fallen, and left behind only a handful of survivors, but Windalorianan and Deskethomaynel had been fully inhabited, save for those they had sent to war, and the women and children who were now at the Fortress of the Crowned Horns. Both cities had evacuated in good order, bringing all that they could safely carry—and Windalorianan had brought every single mare, stal-lion, yearling, and foal from the Plains of Vardirvoshanon, as well—for to leave the Elven horses behind would be as unthinkable as leaving Windalorianan itself behind.

All were here.

As Jermayan and Ancaladar circled the Heart Forest on their way toward the camp, they could see that a vast second city, many times the size of Ysteri-alpoerin, had now spread around it, filling the Heart Forest and spreading out onto the plain beyond. The Windalorianan herds were dark clusters against the snow, and riders circled them on constant guard. Prowling over the snow at a safe distance beyond, Jermayan could see the dark shapes of wolves.

We will have to move, Jermayan thought, considering the army. Even if Win-dalorianan and Deskethomaynel had been able to bring every scrap of stored food in their winter larders with them—and he doubted that had been possible—Ysterialpoerin's resources would still be stretched to the utmost feeding the population not of one city, but of three, and there was no hunting to be had. To ask them to feed the army as well would be . . . impractical.

❧

ANCALADAR landed just outside the Unicorn Camp. No one walked farther than they had to in winter, and while Jermayan was certainly no fit company for unicorns, there was no place closer he dared land, and Valdien would be down at the horselines, not stabled up at Ancaladar's ice-pavilion. The Windalorianan herds were not at all familiar with dragons, and no one would thank him for caus-ing the stock to bolt.

"I will come to you as soon as I can, my friend," Jermayan said, dismounting and unbuckling Ancaladar's saddle. For all its size, it was surprisingly light.

"Bring Idalia," Ancaladar said. "I have missed her."

"So have I," Jermayan answered.

He left Ancaladar's saddle with Riasen, who promised to see it taken into the main camp, and began his long walk.

Idalia met him just inside the main camp.

"I See you, Jermayan. You look cold," she said, offering him a flask.

"I See you, Idalia. It is good to look upon you again," he answered, taking it. The warm cider it contained was highly-spiced, banishing some of the cold in his limbs. "Ancaladar sends his regards, and hopes for your company tonight."

"I trust he is not the only one," she answered, smiling.

"He is not," Jermayan said. "It cheers me to find the army in such good order, but I confess myself also . . . puzzled."

Idalia sighed. "Well, it's not as if we haven't had plenty to do here, with all the refugees arriving. And I can't say I'm unhappy not to have been dealing with casualties. The plague cases are bad enough."

"They had hoped, in Ondoladeshiron, that it had not crossed the mountains," Jermayan said.

"Jermayan, it *came* from the north," Idalia said. "And—" She stopped. "Never mind. Redhelwar wants to see you as soon as you arrive. It's his bad news to tell. Don't worry—Kellen's all right. At least, we haven't heard from him since he left."

"And we must assume that he would have sent word—or the Wild Magic would have—if ill fortune had befallen his mission," Jermayan said, finishing her unvoiced thought.

Idalia nodded. "I'd know if something happened to him," she said. "I know I would."

"As would I, should harm come to you," Jermayan said quietly.

NINOLION quickly admitted him to Redhelwar's tent. Over tea, Jermayan told the Army's General all that he had seen and heard in the sennights he had been away from the army.

"It surprises me to see the army still here," Jermayan said cautiously. "All was well when I left Sentarshadeen, though it was one of the first cities to which we flew. Ashaniel was well when last I saw her, though she is anxious to leave the Crowned Horns and rejoin Andoreniel."

"There has been no word from Sentarshadeen," Redhelwar said bluntly. "No word—and no orders. Nor has any messenger that I have yet sent returned from there.

"I have done all I can, save act without orders," Redhelwar continued. "The Wildmages cannot advise me. Even Cilarnen cannot, though he has found a way to use his power. Though the High Magick can see things that the Wild Magic cannot, it has its own limitations, and as Cilarnen has neither been to Sentarshadeen nor seen a Shadowed Elf, he can neither See Andoreniel nor where the last of the Shadowed Elves may be hiding."

"Then it is plain that I must go to Sentarshadeen, and seek out Andoreniel at once," Jermayan said.

"As much as I would wish this, I cannot counsel you to act against the last orders Andoreniel *did* give you," Redhelwar said heavily. "The women of Ysterialpoerin have yet to be transported to the Fortress of the Crowned Horns. That task must come first."

Jermayan shook his head in frustration, though he knew Redhelwar was right. "It will be a matter of but half a day, and then we will fly for Sentarshadeen, and end this troubling silence. And, further, I am moved to speak as Kellen would, in his absence."

Redhelwar smiled faintly. "I admit, I have missed his bold counsel. It has been . . . quiet . . . since he left."

Jermayan inclined his head in agreement. "It is true that, as Idalia tells me, we are needed here, and I am troubled at the thought that our absence might invite an attack upon Ysterialpoerin by those whom we oppose. Yet it is also true that our presence is a great drain upon the resources of the Forest City, especially now that she has so many other calls upon her substance. It is in my mind that Kellen would say that you must prepare the army to move south to Ondoladeshiron, even though Andoreniel has sent no word, lest the army become too great a drain upon Ysterialpoerin. I wish I could say that the Wild Magic speaks in this, but I cannot."

"We are not humans, to depend upon magic for everything," Redhelwar answered slowly. "It is good counsel—yet I fear, as you do, to leave them undefended."

"I have no resolution for you," Jermayan said unhappily.

"And so it must be my decision. Go. Rest, for both you and Ancaladar are to weary to fly again before morning, even if you would. I shall see you again when you have returned from the Crowned Horns. There are messages that must go to Sentarshadeen."

Jermayan left Redhelwar's pavilion, his steps heavy. Idalia was waiting for him.

"And now you know everything I do," she said, tucking her arm through his.

"Tomorrow I make my last flight to the Crowned Horns—and then Ancaladar and I must go to Sentarshadeen, to discover the reason for Andoreniel's silence," Jermayan said.

"I'd go with you," Idalia said wistfully, "but there's so much work to do here. Vestakia's been wearing herself to a frazzle trying to be in two places at once. She had such high hopes of getting information from the Crystal Spiders. They *want* to help, Jermayan, but Vestakia says she just can't understand what they're telling her."

Jermayan regarded her quizzically. Idalia sighed heavily.

"She says they're trying to communicate symbolically. Showing her pictures of a cave filled with water. And jewels. The same image, over and over, for sennights. But that doesn't mean anything to her, and she can't get them to make it any clearer."

They had been walking in the direction of Healer's Row, where Idalia's pavilion was. When she said those last words Jermayan stopped in mid-step.

"A cave marked out by water and jewels. It would be good to think that there were two such places in our land. I know of only one, and in it these things are not symbols, but reality."

"Jermayan! You know where it is?" Idalia demanded.

"Perhaps I am wrong," Jermayan answered, though not as if he thought he were. "But a cavern with water, and jewels . . . that sounds as if the Crystal Spiders speak of the Caverns of Halacira, through which runs Angarussa the Undying."

"Redhelwar sent Kellen there," Idalia said, her voice emotionless. "He might already be there."

"Perhaps," Jermayan said gently, "you might ask Vestakia to come to us, to see if she has more to tell."

⁓

THAT morning, Vestakia had entered the caverns filled with a grim determination. She would have an answer she could use this time no matter what she had to do to get it, Vestakia vowed. After a mostly-sleepless night, she and Khirethil and Khirethil's troop went down into the caverns once more. After so many sennights, the preparation for communicating with the Crystal Spiders had become almost a ritual. They came down into the caverns, she laid a heavy fur robe on the floor to protect her as much as possible from the chill of the stone floor, lay down upon it, and waited.

Soon the Crystal Spiders appeared, moving over the floor in a softly-glowing wave of many-legged bodies. They looked very much like the lanterns the Elves lighted outside their homes back in Sentarshadeen—assuming, of course, that those lanterns could walk.

The Crystal Spiders settled over her body, touching her face and hands with their stiff feathery bristles.

:*Once more you come to us,*: she heard in her mind.

"Yes. I still haven't found what I need. You have to show me . . . show me something about this place that makes it special to the Elves."

There was a long pause, during which she felt the pressure of the Crystal Spiders' thoughts like a background chorus of whispers in her mind. Though it was nothing like the experience of her dream, it reminded her of it, and she could not help shuddering, just a little.

:*You touch the Dark?*: came the question, clear and strong in her mind.

"Yes," she answered without hesitation. "I think I am beginning to see into my father's mind. I think it can be a weapon to help in our fight."

:*Darkness swallows Light. Be wary.*:

There was silence then—not even the whispers—and Vestakia began to believe the Crystal Spiders might have nothing to tell her. She was shaping another question for them when the images began.

Fast—too fast for her to "see" any of them clearly—they appeared inside her mind in quick flashes, changing so swiftly she began to grow sick and dizzy. She closed her eyes tightly, willing herself to endure. She sensed that whatever was taking place, the Crystal Spiders were making a greater effort to communicate in a way she could understand than they ever had before.

On and on the dizzying kaleidoscope of images went, until at last one held. Steadied.

She was looking at a vast cavern, like one she had seen here with her own eyes. The same conical pillars of stone extended from ceiling and floor, except here, some of them had been carved into familiar shapes.

Xaique-pieces.

The images withdrew from her mind, and Vestakia blinked, forcing herself to breathe normally. Her head pounded, as if it had been forced to hold far more than it ought. But her sense of triumph was so strong she almost didn't care.

A cavern filled with giant *xaique*-pieces? Surely *someone* would recognize that description!

"Thank you," she said to the spiders. "I think this is what we need."

:*We thank you for battling the Dark Minds. We hope we did not damage you, but we sensed your need was great.*:

"Oh yes," Vestakia said. "Yes, it was."

❧

WHEN the Crystal Spiders had retreated, and she tried to get to her feet, she discovered that she was as weak as if she'd lain long abed with a high fever. Khirethil had to help her to her feet.

"It would be good to hear that your work has prospered. It is nearly noon."

"So long?" Vestakia gasped. They'd come down to the caves just after dawn, and she'd thought only a few minutes had passed.

"I . . . think I have the answer now. We need to ride back to the Main Camp and find somebody who will know."

"We need to ride back to the Main Camp," Khirethil agreed. "But to place you beneath the eye of the Healers, were I to be consulted."

"There's no time for that!" Vestakia said impatiently. "Though I suppose Idalia would be a good place to start." Idalia knew as much about the Elven Lands as anyone Vestakia knew. If she didn't recognize Vestakia's description of the caverns, she might know someone who did.

❧

JERMAYAN and Idalia were just preparing to send a messenger up to the Further Cavern when Khirethil's troop rode down to Healer's Alley with Vestakia—chilled, shivering, and wrapped in several fur cloaks in addition to her own.

Khirethil and Idalia both insisted on putting Vestakia into a warm bed at once, while Vestakia was equally adamant that she must deliver her news: The Crystal Spiders had *finally* provided her with a landmark that someone would be able to use to identify the last of the Shadowed Elf Enclaves.

"Tell me, then, of your courtesy," Jermayan said, bowing slightly. "I do admit, that while Idalia is an admirable woman, there are times when she does not listen as well as she might, especially when one is attempting to tell her something important." There was a faintly teasing note in his voice.

"This news will wait," Idalia snapped. "The fact that Vestakia is freezing will not."

"But I am not freezing now," Vestakia said pleadingly. "I am perfectly warm, truly I am, Idalia. And I have worked so hard to find this out, and I am so tired. I want to tell someone. And I am sure that Jermayan must know."

"Very well then," Idalia said grudgingly. Her gruffness, both Vestakia and Jermayan knew, was caused by very real worry over Vestakia's health. "*You* may talk to Jermayan. *I* shall go to prepare you a sleeping cordial. And when I come back, you will drink it."

"I see our speech is to be brief," Jermayan said. "Then let us begin."

Vestakia drew a deep breath. "From the first, the Crystal Spiders have been showing me pictures of water and jewels—it is their way of making names, I think, because they do not talk in words. Sometimes they would show me actual pictures, but they were just the same: water and jewels. It made no sense to me!"

"It makes sense to me," Jermayan said. "But you have said that today they showed you a different thing."

"Yes!" Vestakia said, her voice vibrant with relief. "Today they showed me a great cavern carved to look like a giant *xaique* board, with all of the pieces in place, and the floor inlaid as well. Surely someone must know of such a place, Jermayan!"

"Indeed, and this confirms my deepest fears, for you have just told me that the Crystal Spiders say that the last lair of the Shadowed Elves is at the Jeweled Caverns of Halacira."

"But . . . Kellen is going to Halacira," Vestakia said numbly.

"He is," Jermayan said. "But he will not reach the caverns for some time yet, I am certain. When I return from the Crowned Horns, I will take your warning to Kellen, and he will be grateful to receive it, you may be sure."

"But—" Vestakia said.

"No buts—" Idalia said implacably, returning with a large steaming mug. "We now know where the last Enclave is, which is a lot more than we knew this morning. Kellen has been fighting these things all winter and doing just fine. And he certainly wouldn't thank me if I let you wear yourself to a frazzle worrying about him after you'd done your part. Now drink, and get a good rest. You've spent far too much time in those damp caverns."

Meekly, Vestakia did as she was told.

❧

JERMAYAN and Idalia waited until Vestakia was asleep, then left the Healer's Tent. Khirethil would stand guard over Vestakia, making certain she remained where she was supposed to even if she woke up. A nice warm sleep would be the best thing for her.

❧

WHILE they waited, Jermayan wrote out the details of what Vestakia had learned and gave them to a runner to deliver to Redhelwar, so that the Army's General would have the latest information—though there was little more that Redhelwar could do about it than what—as it turned out—he had already done.

No one knew better than Jermayan how well Kellen fought. And Kellen had as much experience as any of them against the Shadowed Elves. Further, Kellen was a Knight-Mage, the first in a thousand years. The Wild Magic often worked with great subtlety; it was not impossible that Kellen's being sent to Halacira was part of the unfolding of a pattern of the Wild Magic too vast and enigmatic for either Elves or Men to see. If there was one thing Jermayan was certain of about his young human friend, it was that Kellen would not go charging blindly into anything without making certain that it wasn't a trap.

And yet . . .

"It would be reassuring if we could warn Kellen immediately," Jermayan said aloud, when he and Idalia left the pavilion. He had told Vestakia that Kellen was days away from reaching Halacira, but in truth he was not certain of that at all. Distance was a variable thing in winter, depending much upon weather conditions. It was possible that Kellen was already there—or if not actually there, then certainly close enough that the Shadowed Elves might venture out of their stronghold to attack him.

Idalia made a rude noise. "If your magic can't reach him, mine certainly won't. But we can try Cilarnen. It's a lovely day for a ride, I think."

They turned and headed back in the direction of the horse-lines.

※

VALDIEN was delighted to see his master after such a long absence, and Cella had not gotten as much exercise as Idalia would have liked, with all the work she'd had to do in both camps. The two animals were quickly saddled, and Idalia and Jermayan set out.

"Cilarnen is living up at the pavilion you built for the mirror-spell now," Idalia told him as they rode. "He says he needs the quiet to work. Kardus visits him—daily, since a problem we ran into earlier—and I think the unicorns are fascinated by the High Magick, but otherwise he pretty much keeps to himself."

"I do not know that I would think that entirely wise," Jermayan said slowly.

"He says it's safer," Idalia said. "I'm not sure for whom. There's a lot he isn't telling us, but it's only common sense that you can't cram a lifetime of training and study into a few moonturns without serious side-effects. And I don't know much about the High Magick, but I do know it isn't meant to be worked by just one person alone, even if he does have . . . help."

"Redhelwar said that he has found a source of power for his spells," Jermayan said doubtfully.

Idalia made a face. "He's gained the consent of the Elementals to draw on them directly. Don't even ask me to explain how that works."

※

SOMEONE was coming, but he would be finished long before they were close enough to be a nuisance.

It had taken him a long time to build up this most dangerous of spells, but it was vital. He had told Kardus what he must do; the Centaur Wildmage, understanding the necessity, had promised to cease his visits until Cilarnen was finished. Cilarnen understood why Idalia thought they were necessary, and Kardus was his friend, but the constant fussing and interruptions annoyed him. To do what he must do, to learn what he must know, he needed privacy and solitude. A lot of it.

If he could not do it, there was always the possibility that he would be the traitor within, the Endarkened's weapon to use against the forces of the Light at the moment of their greatest weakness.

He knew that Anigrel had tampered with his mind.

He knew part of what the Tainted Darkmage had done: He had suppressed Cilarnen's Magegift when he should have Burned it from his mind.

Why?

And what else had he done?

How did it aid Anigrel—and the Demons—to have Cilarnen—whole, and in possession of his Magegift, alive and among Anigrel's enemies?

He must know.

He had told the Elves truly that he was no Mindhealer, and even now, with infinite power to draw on, and a High Mage's library at his disposal, he could not claim such skills, for those healing arts took a lifetime of practice to master.

But to find a compulsion set in his mind . . .

Perhaps he had the skill for that.

For the past three days he had been sitting in the center of the ice-pavilion, his sword across his knees.

Sifting through things that had no name in words.

All of his early training was there, laid down like layers of rock in the earth, or the densely-colorful weavings of a fine tapestry.

He touched each piece. Each was as it should be. Harmless. Innocent. He left them alone.

It took time—days—to work through all the years of his training. It took a lifetime to make a High Mage, or it should. What he was now, what he was making of himself in sennights instead of years, was something different, as different from a High Mage, he imagined, as Kellen Tavadon was from a Wild Mage. Something created to burn brightly in time of war.

At last he reached the place where things . . . stopped.

There it was. Alien magic, twined through his own. No wonder he'd been having headaches, Cilarnen realized. The only wonder was that he'd been having so few of them.

It lay dormant, glowing an ugly blackish-red to his spell-sight. It took him hours to work it free, setting layer upon layer of wards around it as he went. It was the most delicate and painstaking magick Cilarnen had ever performed—in a sense, in that moment he took and passed the test for Master Mage.

Once he had removed it from his mind, he was able to trigger it harmlessly, examining it in the moment that it expended itself fruitlessly against the wards he had created around it.

As if in a dream, he saw what might have been. Himself and Kellen, standing beside each other. There was no magick involved in the two of them seeking each other out: That had been inevitable from the moment Cilarnen had been Banished—and lived. Even without the Demons' raid on Stonehearth, it would have happened eventually.

And Anigrel's spell, lying dormant—not even a spell, as such, for the unicorns and Vestakia could have detected that—but a receiver for a spell, waiting for the moment when Anigrel would be invested with his full power as a Darkmage, and trigger it. . . .

And Cilarnen would strike at Kellen with all a High Mage's power.

Killing them both.

Cilarnen smiled grimly as the spell-construct fizzled away in a tiny flash of light. He carefully banished the wards he had constructed to contain it, and got stiffly to his feet, rubbing his head.

No more headaches around Kellen. Maybe no more headaches around Wildmages in general, although that might be too much to hope for. Their magics were as different as fire and water.

Which was why, together, they could slay Demons.

Cilarnen stretched, groaning as muscles too long unused protested. He was light-headed from long fasting, and dizzy from lack of sleep.

But company was coming, and it was time to go and greet them.

⤙⤚

THEY were within sight of the ice-pavilion when the snow rose up to bar their way.

Valdien stopped dead. Cella shied, and danced nervously.

The snow fell away, revealing the form of a man, carved entirely in ice.

"Very pretty," Idalia said dryly, patting her palfrey's neck soothingly.

The creature stood motionless in the snow.

"I wonder what would happen if we just rode around it?" Idalia said to no one in particular.

"I'm afraid it would try to stop you," Cilarnen called, walking toward them.

The young High Mage was unkempt and unshaven. His short red-gold hair was as rumpled and disheveled as if he'd been running his fingers through it in lieu of a comb, and he didn't look as if he'd slept for days.

He'd obviously dressed in haste to greet them. The pale-blue tunic and trousers he'd dragged on were meant for sleeping, not for a walk in the snow, and he was holding his heavy fur cloak closed with bare hands. But whatever he'd been doing, it seemed to have gone well, for despite his obvious exhaustion, he looked triumphant.

He paused a short distance away and sketched a quick glyph with his wand. "I'm sorry—you got here sooner than I thought you would. It's all right now. I've put it to sleep."

Valdien regarded the ice-statue—which looked no different now than it had a moment before—suspiciously, then took a step forward and nosed it. It remained unmoving. The destrier flicked his ears and apparently dismissed the strange object from further consideration.

"You didn't come all this way just to admire my ice-golems," Cilarnen said, walking the rest of the way up to them. "Though I do admit I'm proud of them." He rubbed his forehead.

"Are you still having headaches?" Idalia asked.

"I think that was the last of them," Cilarnen answered cryptically. "But if you'd like to stable your horses, I'm sure Anganil won't mind sharing. And even if it is the servants' day off, I can certainly offer you tea."

⁂

SINCE the last time Idalia had been here, Cilarnen had constructed a stabling area for Anganil—not as elegant as Jermayan's ice-pavilion, but sturdy and warm. They left Cella and Valdien there, and shortly the three of them were seated in Cilarnen's painted pavilion, waiting for the tea to brew.

He'd lost weight, Idalia judged critically. And he reminded her, oddly, of Kellen. It wasn't so much that he'd gained in self-confidence—Cilarnen Volpiril of Armethalieh had always had that—as that in the last few sennights he'd acquired a kind of *certainty*. He knew what he had to do, and how he had to do it.

No matter how high the cost.

"We've come because we need you to do something," Idalia said, bypassing the courtly Elven dance of politeness. Cilarnen wouldn't expect it, and they didn't have time for it anyway.

She hated to ask him for anything at all right now—especially now that she saw how tired he was—but this matter was beyond urgent.

"Of course," Cilarnen agreed. He glanced at Jermayan. "But with the most powerful Mage in the Elven Lands sitting beside you, you'll forgive me for being . . . worried."

Idalia smiled faintly. "We've discovered that the last of the Shadowed Elf Enclaves that Vestakia was searching for is Halacira. Kellen is going there. We need to warn him at once. Can you do it?"

"Probably not," Cilarnen said lightly. He looked at their faces. "As you knew," he added doubtfully.

There was a long moment of silence, and then Cilarnen spoke again, in the tone of one repeating a much-given speech.

"Kellen is a sort of Wildmage. The High Magick is innately incompatible with Wildmagery. I can bespell a Wildmage, assuming I use a large destructive spell, like Lightning, but something subtle, like speaking over a distance, or Far-Seeing . . . no. And I *have* tried. Redhelwar wanted me to send messages to you, Jermayan, and that didn't work at all. Look how hard Kellen had to work to hold your power and mine together in the mirror spell, and it took Shalkan to help. Whoever designed the High Magick did not design it to be compatible with the Wild Magic, the Eternal Light knows why."

Idalia's shoulders drooped. Jermayan put a comforting arm around her.

"Then he'll have to manage on his own," she said bleakly.

"Wait," Cilarnen said. "There's something else I can try. The Glyph of Far-Seeing can find things I have seen, and I have seen Kellen's army. I can't see *him*, but I can see them. I don't know if anyone without some sort of Gift could hear me through the Glyph, but I could try. Would that help?"

An angry retort sprang to Idalia's lips, but she bit it back. Cilarnen was already exhausted to the point of foolishness, yet he was still offering to help.

"Yes," she said gently. "That would help, Cilarnen."

He sighed and nodded, eyelids drooping before he caught himself. "Then give me the exact message you need to send. And then go away. I don't wish to be rude, but it's a delicate spell, and you're both powerful Wildmages. If I discover anything urgent, I'll send one of my ice-golems to the camp. Come to me then."

Idalia nodded. "Tell Kellen the Shadowed Elves are in Halacira. He'll know what to do."

⌘

"HE has changed a great deal," Jermayan said to Idalia, as they rode back to the camp to pick up a few things before heading up to Ancaladar's pavilion for the night.

"He's trying to do in sennights what takes years," Idalia said. "I think he's trying to make up for the fact that Armethalieh is refusing to honor the ancient treaties. All by himself."

⌘

IT was near dawn when Ancaladar awakened Jermayan.

The Elven Knight came instantly awake.

"Cilarnen is coming, Bonded," the dragon said softly.

"Coming? Here?" Jermayan reached for his sword and began to dress, tucking the furs around Idalia again in a futile attempt to keep from waking her, though he knew from experience that she slept as lightly as he.

"He seems very upset," the dragon said mildly, peering out through the doorway of the tent. "Shall I go and see why?"

"Better not," Idalia said, sitting up. "I don't think he's slept in days, and the last thing we want is for Anganil to pitch him off into the snow."

"The news can't be good if he's come himself—and come here," Jermayan said grimly, continuing to dress.

"I'll make tea," Idalia said pragmatically.

By the time they were both dressed—and the water had approached the boil—Cilarnen was in sight. He had not bothered with either saddle or bridle, riding Anganil tackless and bareback over the snow, lighting his way with a great globe of Magelight that followed him like a captive moon. It turned the snow azure in the predawn gloom. He looked like something out of one of the ancient story-songs; almost like an Elemental creature himself.

He slid from Anganil's back as he reached the pavilion, and staggered a couple of steps before sinking to his knees in the snow. Jermayan caught him and steadied him on his feet.

"There's news," Cilarnen gasped. "I didn't see Kellen. It's bad, though."

"Come in and get warm," Idalia demanded. "It will wait a second or two."

"It won't," Cilarnen insisted, trying without success to shrug Jermayan off. "I Saw—I Saw *some* of Kellen's people—only a few hundred—heading *back* across the Mystrals. Toward Ysterialpoerin. I don't know who they were, and I couldn't talk to them, but I recognized the horses. I'm sure they were with Kellen's people when they left."

Without a word Jermayan passed Cilarnen to Idalia, and strode into the tent. Cilarnen leaned against her heavily; she could feel him shaking with cold and exhaustion.

"Cilarnen, are you sure?"

"Idalia, who else would be crossing the Mystrals at this time of year? I can't tell one Elf from another, especially in armor, but I do know horses. Those horses went out with Kellen's party. I'm sure of it. And Kardus and I came through those mountains to get here; it's not as if I'd forget what they look like."

The speech had drained the last of his strength; she nearly carried him into the pavilion. There, Jermayan had finished putting on his armor and had picked up Ancaladar's saddle.

"I must go and see," he said simply.

Idalia nodded. There was nothing else to say.

"I'm sorry," Cilarnen whispered.

" 'Sorry'?" Idalia demanded, lowering him to the floor of the pavilion and wrapping him in the heaviest of the discarded sleeping furs. "Sorry for bringing us what might be vital warning? It's true, then, what the Wildlanders have always said—that they are all mad in the City. Now, you will drink a cup of tea, and eat something, and then you will sleep—here—or I promise you, by the Gods of the Wild Magic, I shall Heal the abuses you have heaped on your body myself!"

"Anything . . . but that . . ." Cilarnen said faintly.

Outside the ice-pavilion, Idalia heard the booming sound of Ancaladar taking flight.

⇜

IT had been six days since she had left the Gathering Plain and Kellen, and Keirasti had pushed her people mercilessly into the mountains.

If the weather favored them beyond all reason, it would be four sennights, perhaps five, before they saw Ysterialpoerin again.

Too long, with the urgency of the news she carried.

There was no way to go any faster. Horses were not unicorns, to outrun the wind, and they could not travel without the supplies the carts carried. And even if the mirror-relays were reliable, Kellen was right: The message she carried was not one that could be trusted to the mirrors. It was one she wished she did not know herself.

Once they reached the far side of the mountains, however, they would abandon the wagons and the heavy equipment, and go on with just what they could carry themselves, using their remounts as pack-horses. They would make better time that way. A sennight outside of Ysterialpoerin she would leave most of her command behind and take a small force, with several remounts for each Knight, and ride as fast as she could for the camp.

And pray to Leaf and Star that they met nothing to oppose them along the way. Her command was already suffering, from frost-burn, snow-glare, and the persistent cough that settled in the chest in the High Cold. Rest and warmth would soothe these ills, but there was no time for either. Each morning she had begged the gods that no horse would fall lame from the punishing pace she set, for they could not spare even an hour to stop to tend it, and Keirasti would leave no animal behind to starve and die, or be killed by predators.

"Keirasti! In the sky! Something comes!" Reyezeyt called, pointing eastward.

Keirasti looked, but could see nothing. Her heart sank in her chest. The Deathwings had found them, and as Kellen had warned her, she must leave her people to die, so that his message might get through.

"Archers!" she shouted. "Prepare for attack!"

⤫

JERMAYAN and Ancaladar flew westward, following the route Kellen's army had taken nearly two moonturns before. The dragon's sharp eyes picked out the ice-cairns and clusters of trail-wands that marked their path, though all other trace of their passage was erased by wind and fresh snow.

What can have happened? I have been through the Southern Triad not a fortnight ago, and seen no sign of the Enemy. I cannot believe they have destroyed all but a few hundred of those Redhelwar sent.

I cannot believe that Kellen is dead.

Idalia said she would know.

"Do not anticipate the day, Beloved," Ancaladar said softly. "Soon we will find what Cilarnen has Seen, and we may ask them ourselves. Have patience."

Jermayan smothered a curse. He knew his Bonded was right, but . . .

But Kellen had said, over and over, that to split their forces was arrant folly. He would never divide a force under his command.

Unless he faced a disaster beyond Jermayan's ability to imagine.

As they reached the mountains, the winds grew more turbulent, and Ancaladar fought and strained to follow the army's course. Again and again Jermayan was flung against the straps of the riding-harness, until he was as bruised as if he were still a novice Knight standing in the practice-Circle. He barely noticed, straining his eyes to pierce the blowing snow that covered the ground below.

"There," Ancaladar said.

In one of the narrow mountain valleys at the western side of the Mystrals, Jermayan saw what Cilarnen had undoubtedly Seen: a small party of Knights—a scant handful in comparison to what had been sent—with only half-a-dozen wagons accompanying them.

"Land," he said tersely.

⤫

SHE would not give the order to desert her command until the last moment. Her people would obey her without question—that much she knew—but she would carry the shame and horror of it to her grave, for she did not know if the reason for what she did would ever be known.

And she did not even know if abandoning her comrades would work, or if the skyborne enemy would simply kill them all.

"Keirasti! It is Ancaladar!" Reyezeyt said.

They must stop. Gods send that they will stop.

"Archers, light arrows and loose," she ordered.

The first rank of archers set fire to their arrows and loosed them into the sky, signaling the oncoming dragon and his rider. Even as Ancaladar circled to land, Keirasti had vaulted from Orata's back.

"Maredhiel," she said over her shoulder to her Second, "it would please me greatly if you were to make camp here until I return."

"It would please me greatly as well," Maredhiel said, relief in her voice. She raised her horn to her lips and blew the signal to make camp.

ANCALADAR had barely settled into the snow by the time Keirasti reached him.

"Jermayan, I know not where you fly, but you must take me to Redhelwar at once. Kellen has ordered this, and it is more vital than any other purpose you may have that I reach him at once."

"He is riding into a Shadowed Elf trap at Halacira," Jermayan said. "When did you leave him—and where?"

"On the Gathering Plain, six days past," Keirasti said promptly. "He will not reach Halacira for another four days yet, by my judgment; we would have reached it a fortnight ago, save that weather delayed us on the road. But my message will not wait even an hour."

"Then come," Jermayan said. "We will talk upon the wing."

As soon as Keirasti had strapped herself into place, Ancaladar began his larruping run upslope to gain the necessary speed for takeoff. After a few moments he had gained the necessary momentum, and bounded into the sky.

THIS time there was no need to fly close to the ground to try to track a warband that might be lost or injured, and Ancaladar was able to take advantage of every current in the high sky to ease their flight. It also meant that they flew very high, and Keirasti's teeth were quickly chattering, even with the heat the dragon's body radiated to warm her.

"Of what I carry I may not speak," she said. "But Kellen and all who travel with him were well when I left him. We have had no casualties and few injuries—more than I can say for the Shadewalker we encountered in the pass, which Kellen slew. No more messengers will find their deaths trying to reach Sentarshadeen, I think."

"So much makes good hearing," Jermayan said. But why Kellen felt it so vi-

tal to send Keirasti back from Ondoladeshiron with a message for Redhelwar—
and apparently a message of such terrible urgency—was a puzzle of grave importance. "Yet I would hear more."

"And I would tell it to you," Keirasti said, her voice tight with frustration.
"Yet Kellen swore me to silence, that the information I carried, and that which I
know, be given to the hand and ear of none but the Army's General."

"Now *that* is disturbing," Ancaladar said mildly. "I really do think we'd better
go ask Kellen about this ourselves."

"So do I," Jermayan said. He gritted his teeth, duty warring with the inclination of his heart. "Unfortunately, there is one thing we must do first."

"I would be grateful, if it is possible, if you were able to return me to my people on your way to speak to Kellen, of course," Keirasti said. "Maredhiel will wait
there until spring, otherwise, and once I have delivered my message, there is no
reason my troops should not return to Kellen."

"That I may promise with a full certainty of accomplishment," Jermayan
said with relief. "Once I have delivered you to Redhelwar, I must make my last
flight to the Fortress of the Crowned Horns, to discharge the last of my duty to
Andoreniel. Then I shall return you to your people, and join Kellen by sunset,
long before he has reached Halacira."

⁕

JERMAYAN landed as near the horse-lines as he dared. He helped Keirasti unbuckle the unfamiliar straps, and as soon as she was safely clear, Ancaladar began
his takeoff run again. It was only a short flight to Ysterialpoerin, but he would
have to choose his landing-place carefully.

Jermayan only wished he could afford the time to stop and speak to Idalia,
but now he grudged every hour that must elapse until he could fly to Kellen. If he
knew his heart's twin, she would already have brought Cilarnen down to Healer's
Row, where he could be tended more efficiently, and news of his and Keirasti's arrival would already be spreading through the camp. Soon Idalia would know that
Kellen was alive and well.

Or had been six days ago, at least.

Keirasti must have pushed her small band like Maiden Winter Herself to
have gotten so far into the Mystrals in only six days; whatever message Kellen
had entrusted her with must be of a terrible urgency.

*And you will know what it is soon enough. By this evening's sunset, if fortune fa-
vors you.*

⁕

KEIRASTI presented herself at Ninolion's pavilion shaking with cold and weariness. Redhelwar's adjutant shot to his feet, looking as if he beheld a spirit risen out of the earth itself.

"I come from Kellen Knight-Mage with urgent information for Redhelwar Army's General," Keirasti said, holding herself upright with great effort.

She'd thought she'd been cold, crossing the Mystrals, but the flight back to Ysterialpoerin on Ancaladar's back had introduced her to realms of cold she had never before imagined—and unnatural conditions of height and speed, as well. If that was what being an Elven Mage entailed, she was thankful that the Gods of Leaf and Star had seen fit to make her a simple Elven Knight.

Ninolion rose to his feet and bowed. "I will inform Redhelwar. And I will bring tea."

LESS than half an hour later she was seated in Redhelwar's scarlet pavilion, drinking yet another mug of tea. The potent liquid was rich with Allheal and honey, the brewing nicely judged to her weary state.

"I know already how you have come here, for all saw Ancaladar overfly the camp," Redhelwar said. "And you have said that Kellen sent you."

"He wished me to give this dispatch into your hand as fast as possible, and at all costs," Keirasti said, untying the scroll-case from where it lay against her armor and placing it into Redhelwar's hand. As she did, she felt a great burden ease. "In case it was lost, or had to be destroyed, he told me what it contains, but I am sworn never to speak of it, save to you."

Redhelwar broke the seal and began to read. As he read, a greater stillness descended over the tent, as if the air itself grew heavier.

At last Redhelwar finished reading.

"When you left Kellen, where was he?" Redhelwar asked bluntly.

Keirasti had been expecting this. If there were ever a time for War Manners, it was now.

"He continues on to Halacira. I left him six days ago; it will be four days more at least, I judge, before he reaches there. This is good, as Jermayan tells me that the Shadowed Elves lair there, and he flies to bring Kellen warning as soon as he returns from the Crowned Horns."

"As I too have heard," Redhelwar said. He sighed, shaking his head. "I am grateful that our passage through the Mystrals will be peaceful, at least. You will wish to return to your command, and I believe Jermayan will wish to accommodate you. I will ask that you inform Rochinuviel to expect us."

Redhelwar would do as Kellen wished, and bring the army to Ondoladeshiron. Keirasti's emotions were in turmoil. She was certain that Kellen had been sent by the Wild Magic to aid them in this time of their greatest need, but part of her felt a strange disquiet that the orderly arrangement of things that had stood unchanged for uncounted centuries was being blown away as abruptly as blossoms in a sudden storm. If things could change so suddenly, who could say what the future might hold?

"It shall be as you say, Redhelwar," she said, bowing her head.

"Now go. Rest and eat. There is much to do to prepare the army to move, and for the sake of Kellen's warning, it must be done with speed. I will send someone to you when Jermayan returns."

Keirasti stood. "I thank you for that kindness."

Redhelwar smiled. "Some would say it is no kindness, to send you back out into the cold and the snow. But I know it is what you would wish."

Ten

The Xaique Board Underground

THE FOREST LOOKED different in winter. Or it might only be he who'd changed, Kellen thought. The first time he'd ridden through these trees, searching for the Black Cairn, he'd had no idea of who he really was. Now, he was . . . whole.

The winter weather, comparatively mild south and west of the Mystrals, continued to favor them, though the Wildmages said another storm was coming. That was one of the reasons Kellen had pushed the army as hard as he had—that, and his desperate need, now, to reach Sentarshadeen and Andoreniel. Once he was in Sentarshadeen, he could send a message by unicorn to Redhelwar, and recall Keirasti. With luck, the riders could catch her before she reached the mountains themselves. He'd left her barely six days ago, but his troops had gotten a good rest at Ondoladeshiron and he'd pushed them hard through the lowlands. He didn't intend to tarry at Halacira, either—a quick check to make sure the caverns were safe, then he'd leave Artenel and a reserve force there to begin the work of readying them to become a fortress, and move on to Sentarshadeen. In summer, the caverns were a day and a half's ride from the Elven royal city—the journey might take twice that time in winter.

What he would do once he reached Sentarshadeen, he wasn't sure yet. He wished Idalia was here. He was no great Healer, and that was what Andoreniel needed most of all.

If the Elven King weren't already dead.

If he was, it would be a disaster for the Allies. Kellen could not imagine the Elven Council acting with quick decision, and Ashaniel wasn't here. He didn't know if Redhelwar would act at all without orders, nor could he imagine the El-ven Lands divided by civil war.

The Wild Magic will not let that happen, he thought to himself, and even he was not sure whether that thought was a certainty—or a prayer.

❧

THE last time Kellen had come this way, he had not approached the caverns themselves. Umerchiel, who knew this area well, led the army off the War Road—through the high road leading between Sentarshadeen and Ondoladesh-iron was not really as wide or as flat as some of the larger avenues in Armethalieh, it counted as a main thoroughfare in Elven terms—in the direc-tion of the caverns.

Before they reached the caves, they came to the Angarussa.

Even at the height of the Great Drought, the river had still run strongly, and with the torrential rains it had once more become one of the greatest rivers of the Elven Lands. But the cold that had followed the rains had been long and bit-ter, and the river that Kellen now saw was completely concealed beneath a thick shield of ice.

He called for Artenel.

"It would be good to know if the ice will bear our weight," he said to the El-ven Artificer.

Artenel nodded, and rode out onto the middle of the river. There he dis-mounted, and peered down into the ice. Next he took a slender metal rod from his horse's pack and knelt upon the ice, tapping at it gently and listening in-tently. After a few moments he rode back.

"The ice is quite thick," he reported. "The army may cross safely. But not all at once, and not all in one place. It is my recommendation that you choose sev-eral crossing-places."

Kellen nodded.

He prepared to give the order for the first units to cross, and stopped.

This was where he'd seen the Tainted starflowers, the first time he'd been here.

"Get the maps of the caverns."

❧

PART of him seethed with impatience at wasting precious time—he was almost entirely sure that there was nothing at Halacira besides the jewel-mines Jer-mayan had once described to him. But another part had learned hard lessons in too many battles. Those starflowers *had* to have been a warning.

And for once, going into a cave, they had complete and accurate maps. The Elves had been working the caves at Halacira for centuries.

"Churashil, Thenalakti, Arvaruth, Farathirian, Merioniach—I want you to cross first. Take your troops and ride ahead to these secondary entrances that I see marked on this map. Guard them closely. I wish nothing to escape from these caverns. If you see any sign of movement, sound your horn, but no one is to leave his position. I will leave a reserve force outside the main entrance that will come to your aid."

Although how quickly such a force could reach the trouble spot, when the entrances his sub-commanders must guard were scattered over several miles, was a troubling question.

"If it is possible, and seems good to you, block the entrances that you find."

"Yes, komentai'i," Churashil said. The others nodded.

The Knights began to move off. By the time the rest of the army was across and in position near the Main Entrance, the five groups guarding the entrances should be in position.

He turned to his Wildmages.

"Wirance, Kerleu, you must go to the others and tell them I need enough Coldfire to crown at least two hundred Knights. I would also like some of you to follow us into the caverns and cast Coldfire on the walls as we go."

Wirance regarded him, eyebrows raised. "Expecting trouble, are you?"

Kellen smiled without humor. "No. I'm just planning for it."

He wished—and not for the first time since he'd left Ysterialpoerin—that Vestakia were here. Not simply because he missed her company, but because right now she would have been incredibly useful to have around.

He didn't *know* that he was facing trouble across the river. In fact, it was likelier than not that he wasn't, and he was wasting precious time here when he could have been doing a quick reconnoiter of the caverns and heading quickly on to Sentarshadeen.

But he couldn't—he wouldn't—let his impatience cost lives. His information from Rochinuviel was already more than a sennight old. Whatever would happen in Sentarshadeen might have already happened. It was beyond his control. This wasn't.

He owed all those who had already died, and those who trusted him now, his very best efforts.

And part of him—a very tiny part, all things considered—felt a spark of pride. Even a moonturn ago he would not have had the experience—and, yes, the *wisdom*—to organize something like this. To think three and four steps ahead of the enemy—even an enemy he wasn't quite sure was there.

Why, he might even be able to beat Idalia at *xaique* now.

IT was a couple of hours past noon by the time the sledges crossed, the last elements of the army. By then the surface of the ice was starting to show signs of strain, though Artenel assured Kellen it would hold.

He waited on the far bank, watching as the slow heavy sledges made their way, one by one, across the surface of the frozen river.

"Fun, isn't it?" Shalkan asked.

"In a weird way," Kellen answered honestly. "It would be a lot more fun if there were no possibility that anyone could get hurt."

"I suppose that's why the Elves have Flower Wars," the unicorn said thoughtfully.

"I don't suppose you could go on to Sentarshadeen and see what's going on there?" Kellen said hopefully.

Shalkan snorted rudely. "And leave you here to fend for yourself? You'd probably get lost in the caverns and never come out. Though I understand they're worth an extended look."

"Yeah, well, it's not like I have time for sightseeing," Kellen grumbled. "I just wish I could be everywhere at once."

"That, unfortunately, is beyond even the power of a Knight-Mage," Shalkan said repressively. "Though you might manage something close to it if you Bonded to a dragon."

"No thanks," Kellen said briefly. Leaving aside the fact that there weren't any dragons either available or willing, the idea of shortening the lifespan of an immortal creature to a few brief decades would make him feel horribly guilty. It seemed utterly unfair. At least with Jermayan, Ancaladar would have centuries.

"It's time to go," Shalkan said.

"Wish me luck," Kellen said.

"Good hunting," the unicorn replied.

FIRARETH quickly passed the ox-drawn sledges as Kellen rode up to the head of the line. Pale nimbuses of Coldfire shimmered around the heads of many that he passed, testament to the Wildmages' tireless labors. Around him, units reorganized into marching order as the remains of the column reformed, several groups dropping back to guard the vulnerable supply-carts. Just because they hadn't been attacked yet didn't mean they weren't going to be. Both unicorns and scouts from Sentarshadeen should be patrolling the woods this far east, but by now Kellen took nothing for granted.

Another hour's march brought them in sight of the cavern's mouth.

Even if he had not known what this place was, there would have been no mistaking it for anything but an ancient and well-loved place of the Elves.

The opening of the cave had been shaped. Not made perfectly symmetrical—that wasn't the Elven way—but improved, so that it was somehow more vivid than something that had been left untouched. In contrast, the rock face that flanked the entrance had obviously been painstakingly engineered, for in this season, the cavernmouth was surrounded by a lacy webwork of ice, as delicate as spun sugar, created when streams of water arching into the air had frozen. They sparkled in the sunlight, giving back all the colors of the rainbow.

I wonder how they managed that? Kellen thought. *And why?* Surely no one came to the Caverns of Halacira at this time of year to see this. He wondered what the cavern face looked like in summer.

He'd made most of his dispositions while the army was waiting to cross. He took care of the last-minute details now. He would lead the first group into the caverns; after half an hour, Umerchiel would follow with a second force. Another party would stand ready to ride to the aid of those barricading the cave-system's other exits.

That accounted for the disposition of nearly all of his command, save for a skeleton force remaining behind to guard the supply wagons and begin the work of setting up the camp, since Artenel's forces would be settling into a permanent camp here, and he'd be leaving the oxen and the heavy equipment behind with most of his people while he headed on to Sentarshadeen.

And whether there was trouble in the caverns or not, he simply couldn't take his entire force down with him. It was bad enough—from a tactical standpoint—that he'd be leading them, but that was something he simply couldn't forgo. As a Knight-Mage, his battle-sense would give them the advantage that could spell life or death.

Assuming there was anything here at all.

Warily, Kellen gazed at the cavernmouth, shifting with the ease of long practice into battle-sight, but there was nothing to see, and his Wildmage senses brought him no trace of warning.

He blew out a deep breath, watching it turn to a plume of fog on the winter air. As was so often the case, the only way to know was to go and see.

He cast his own globe of Coldfire over his head and loosened his sword in his sheath. Isinwen handed him one of Artenel's glass shields. Just in case, everyone was carrying them now.

He gave the order to advance.

⊱⊰

THE passage into the caverns bore the same resemblance to the caves he had been in previously as a garden did to a wild woodland. He realized that subconsciously he'd been expecting something a good deal cruder. Hadn't Jermayan said that these were mines?

If the Elves *did* mine here, they did a good job of concealing it.

Some of the things he saw were patently artificial, like the twining pattern of Greet-the-Day vine that curled along the top edge of the walls, though it took him a few seconds to realize that the plant, with its delicate bell-shaped flowers, was carved out of the stone itself. As they got farther from the entrance, he saw that there were small niches carved into the walls, each one a perfect miniature copy of an Elven house-front, and obviously designed to hold lanterns. Every few yards there was a step down, so instead of a long steep slope into the earth, they descended by means of a series of short level terraces.

It would not be pleasant to have to retreat up these long shallow steps fighting a holding action against an enemy, Kellen thought soberly. Nor would it be an easy matter to get carts, either on wheels or sledges, through this passage. He hoped one of the other passages was better suited for moving heavy equipment in and out.

As they moved deeper into the earth, he ran through the details of the cavern map in his head. After the entry passageway, there was a large open cavern. Galleries led off that to the left and right, and directly ahead the main passage continued onward to the point about half a league farther on to where the Angarussa flowed through the caverns. Beyond that was one of the other exits from the cavern system.

The caverns had several levels, and Umerchiel had told him that there were staircases between the upper and lower galleries in many places, as well as pumps, carts, and equipment to lift ore from the deepest levels of the cave systems. Without Vestakia, the caverns would take at least three days to search thoroughly, but it was a task he dared not slight. Perhaps tomorrow, if all went well today, he would bring more people into the caves to search and clear them, but for now Kellen wouldn't be easy in his mind until he had overlooked as much as he could himself, searching with battle-sight for obvious traps.

When they entered the first open space, he received another of those odd surprises that one had to get used to when dealing with Elves. Though the walls of the cavern had been left pretty much untouched—aside from carved niches for lanterns, now empty—the entire stone floor of the cavern had been carefully inlaid to mimic one of the carpets Kellen had seen covering the floors of the House of Leaf and Star. He glanced back toward the entrance, and saw, as he'd expected, that whatever craftsman had laid down the design had even created the tasseled fringe at the edge of the carpet, making it slightly mussed, as a real carpet's fringe would be by the passage of feet over its surface.

Elves. They're just, I don't know . . . different.

There were four galleries on each side of the chamber. After checking each entrance for traps—or any sign that something *bad* had passed this way—Kellen left sentry-parties at each entrance, with orders to call for help—or simply fall back—if anything did appear. When Umerchiel's force arrived, it would relieve Kellen's all along his line of sortie. They needed to secure the topmost levels of the cave system before descending deeper. Fortunately, not all of the cave system involved multiple levels; the Elves had probably been worried about disturbing the Angarussa too much and ending up with an underground ocean instead of a jewel mine.

⸎

ONCE it would have been easy to fall under the spell of this place. If he hadn't seen Sentarshadeen, or Ysterialpoerin. Or the Fortress of the Crowned Horns. Or Pelashia's Veil. They entered a cavern that seemed to stretch on for miles, its vaulted ceiling stretching off to the distant horizon. But his senses told him that the space he and his troops stood within was small. It was only that the walls were carved in the semblance of distant caverns, the imitation so perfect that it could fool the eye, but not the body. Only the fact that their Coldfire illuminated the deepest "depths" of the carven caverns hinted at the artifice. Kellen paused to run his fingers over the carving, almost unable to believe what his senses told him even as he broke the illusion.

They moved on.

As they passed into the next chamber, the temperature dropped sharply, and the air began to feel much damper. Kellen inhaled deeply. They must be nearing the Angarussa, which meant they could start to clear some of the side-passages soon. After so long in the arid cold of winter, the dampness felt good.

This chamber, unlike the one they were leaving, was large in truth. The Coldfire illumination they all carried seemed to shrink back, burning brightly in a tight ball above their heads, illuminating the floor, but not reaching out to the walls or the ceiling.

The floor was inlaid in a pattern of green and white squares.

A few steps farther into the chamber, Kellen understood why.

Here, the action of rock and water had again created tall columns of stone that stretched from floor to ceiling. But these the Elves had not left untouched. Though they remained where the random action of Nature had deposited them, of the partial columns that had been allowed to remain, each one had been carved into the likeness of a *xaique* game-piece. It was as if some giant unfinished game of *xaique* were being played out on the floor of this chamber.

The moment Kellen approached the first of the carvings, he felt a thrill of unease.

Something is wrong here.

He did not know where the conviction came from. He had never seen Halacira before. But the feeling was strong, and he trusted it.

And a moment later, he understood.

One of the *xaique* figures—a delicate little dancer, her arms raised to offer a garland of flowers—had been smashed. The inside surface of the stone was paler than the outside; the mutilations to the statue seemed to glow in the dimness, and the chips and fragments that lay scattered on the stone floor glittered almost like ice.

At his shoulder, he heard Isinwen draw breath sharply, and heard a low susurrus of speech as word was passed back through the waiting Elves.

No Elf would have done this. No Elf *could* have done this.

Show me, Kellen said to his magic.

But instead of the clear vision of what-had-been that he had come to expect, it was as if a fog descended over his vision. He did not see what had gone before, nor did he see the utter darkness of the cavern without Coldfire. Instead he saw twisting shadows that slithered over each other like ink poured into water. He knew something had been here—and something Tainted, it was easy to guess—but precisely what it had been, he could not see.

He blinked his battle-sight away and turned to Isinwen.

"We know now that there have been trespassers here. But when they were here, and whether they remain, I cannot tell. You will oblige me by asking everyone to remain alert. And send someone to warn the sentries and Umerchiel."

"*Komentai*," Isinwen said, turning away to pass the order.

A lot of Shadowed Elves had escaped after the Battle for the Heart of the Forest. No one knew how many, but enough to cause serious problems for the Allies. They could be here. Something that hated Elves certainly was. If the Shadowed Elves were, it seemed to Kellen that they did not want to fight another losing battle. Perhaps they had learned wisdom in their earlier defeats. Or perhaps they knew that they were the last of their kind.

But from everything he'd learned of them previously, he thought that if he offered them a great enough prize, and a tempting enough target, he could lure them out. The Shadowed Elves seemed to be incapable of avoiding battle when their enemy came close enough.

"I need a few volunteers . . ." Kellen said, turning to his sub-commanders.

WITH fifty chosen Knights at his back, Kellen moved deeper into Halacira. Since everyone with him had volunteered to go, the difficulty had been in picking the best people for the task, not in finding ones willing to go.

He chose Knights that he could afford to lose.

There was every possibility that he was leading them into a trap. It was, after all, partly his intention to spring a trap. But he accepted the grim possibility that the trap's jaws might close on them all with lethal effect.

He had no choice but to place himself at risk. Of everyone there, he had not only the best chance to keep the warriors with him safe, but to provide an irresistible target for any enemy within these caverns. He knew, without false pride, that Shadow Mountain desperately wanted to get its hands on him, both because of his past victories over it, and because he was a Knight-Mage. If a Wildmage represented a source of both power and food to the Endarkened, he knew that a Knight-Mage must represent even more enticing bait.

As he and the Elves accompanying him moved across the enormous *xaique* board and toward what the maps had marked as the Southern Promenade, they saw that more and more of the carven *xaique*-pieces had been marred in some way, though none as thoroughly as the first they'd seen. There were no traps that he was able to detect, though now Kellen traveled a zig-zag course across the cavern floor, sweeping every inch of it himself. His sense of unease deepened. Beyond the Southern Promenade—another series of linked caverns, with galleries leading off them; the perfect place for an ambush—they should reach the banks of the Angarussa Underground, and beyond that a long, comparatively narrow passage leading up to the surface again. If they were allowed to traverse that entire distance unchallenged—it was at least a mile, if he was reading the maps at all correctly—then there would be no choice but to try another sweep, and another, through different parts of the cave-system, until they were absolutely certain they had secured every last square inch of it.

It might take sennights.

And meanwhile, what would be happening in Sentarshadeen?

They left the *xaique* chamber.

The next chamber's walls had been extensively carved—into the semblance of a Flower Forest. Kellen realized he would search the caverns of Halacira in vain for signs of mining; it had slowly dawned on him that the elaborate stone-carving was the way that the Elves disguised—or at least made up for—their mineworking activities. But the chamber seemed completely untouched by any activities of the interlopers.

The next chamber was carved with scenes of . . . mining. Stone scaffolds covered the walls, with stone figures climbing upon them, stone tools in their hands.

Still nothing.

He wondered what it was about the *xaique* board that had roused someone's anger to smash it and reveal their presence.

Xaique is about war. The figure with the garland . . . Master Belesharon told me she has something to do with the Flower Wars, which aren't actually real wars. Whoever is here is sending a sort of message to us—they want to be found—though I think only Master Belesharon could understand the whole of it.

I understand enough. I understand that there's someone here who needs to be gotten rid of.

The mining-cavern was long and comparatively narrow, its floor sloping very slightly downward. Suddenly Kellen's armored sabaton skidded on the smooth stone floor.

It was wet.

He knelt down and touched the stone. A distinct sheen of moisture clung to the stone, heavy enough to make it slippery. He raised his fingers to his nose and sniffed. Water.

"Be careful," he said aloud. "The floor is wet."

And why was it wet? It was true that the Angarussa had undoubtedly been running very high in its bed this season—both above and underground—but if Kellen was certain of one thing, it was that the Elves would have made certain that the caverns would not flood. And if for some strange reason they did not choose to do that, Umerchiel would have mentioned the possibility of flooding.

But if there was a trap, they were supposed to be walking into it. Gritting his teeth, Kellen gave the signal to advance.

The floor in the next cavern—its walls, suitably, as this was the last one before they reached the Angarussa, were carved with a frieze of selkies at play amid the currents of a river—was also slick with moisture, but no wetter than the floor of the one before.

At the end of the cavern, they came to a wall.

It was nothing the Elves had made. It was well-built, of blocks of shaped stone obviously cut from someplace here in the caverns, but compared to the workmanship of the Elves, it was as crude as a child's mud-pies. It blocked the opening to the next cavern, the one that led to the Angarussa. It was not quite finished, at least if it had been meant to seal the opening completely; there was still an opening at the top, where a few courses of stone had yet to be laid.

Umerchiel had described the chamber beyond to him, and it was clearly indicated on the map. A long low transverse gallery, the Angarussa ran through it at the bottom of a deep gorge: This chamber was actually entirely artificial, created to expose the river where it traveled beneath the earth. A stone bridge crossed the river at the top of the gorge, level with the floor of the gallery, and led to the passageway to the surface, where Churashil was waiting with his guard-party.

Kellen regarded the wall with his battle-sight. Not the trigger to a trap, but part of one. He pulled off his heavy leather glove and the armored gauntlet beneath it and touched the wall with his bare hand.

The stone was damp, beaded with water.

Holding his breath, he tapped it experimentally—and very gently—with his sword. The stone gave back a dull thudding sound. The wall was very thick, or else the chamber beyond had been filled in completely.

"I'm going to see if I can see over the top," Kellen said.

"*Komentai*, let me go," Ambanire said urgently.

"No. This is a trap. I need to see more."

Replacing his glove and gauntlet, and sheathing his sword, Kellen began to climb.

He reached the top, and sent the ball of Coldfire hovering over his head out into the chamber.

For an instant he could not believe what he saw.

Water. Black and still and smooth as glass, it filled the chamber beyond to the level of the retaining wall, a vast underground lake extending into the passage to the surface.

Suddenly there was a booming crash, and Kellen saw the level of the water in the lake begin to drop sharply.

"Ambanire, sound the alarm," he said, dropping back to the ground. Whatever had been meant to kill them, he'd just found it. He drew his sword.

⁘

UMERCHERIEL'S forces had reached the *xaique* chamber a little after Kellen's party had gone on ahead. Isinwen showed him the mutilated statues, and they settled in to wait.

It was hard to calculate time so far beneath the earth, but Isinwen thought that no more than three quarters of an hour had passed when he felt a long rumbling shake the rock beneath his feet.

A roaring sound built, as if suddenly they stood beneath an enormous waterfall, and a strong wind began to blow from the direction they had come.

He heard the sound of running—no, *splashing*—feet.

The orderly ranks of waiting Knights parted to allow the passage of the guards Kellen and Umerchiel had left on the side-galleries of the first cavern. They were as wet as if they'd fallen into the Angarussa itself.

"Isinwen! The caves fill with water!"

The ground shook again, and over the roar of water, Isinwen heard the distant notes of Ambanire's warhorn.

The water was to his ankles now, rising with a relentless surging motion. It came from the direction of the cavern's mouth.

"Follow me," Isinwen said. "Quickly!"

⤳

A strong steady wind began to blow toward Kellen, and he felt the rock beneath his feet shudder, as if the subterranean earth were some nightmare beast attempting to cast off unwelcome vermin. He risked one more climb up the wall. It was just as he'd feared. The water was already level with the surface of the bridge, and whirlpools eddied in its surface as the artificial lake was sucked elsewhere into the caverns. Suddenly the water that had been seeping toward them slowly but steadily began to pour into the chamber with the steady force of the Angarussa itself. When Kellen dropped to the floor again he was standing ankle-deep in a river that poured inexorably through the caverns with the steady force of a rising spring.

Dams. It was why the Angarussa had been so easy to cross. It had been frozen nearly solid because there hadn't been much water in its bed. Kellen knew from bitter experience that the Shadowed Elves were master engineers; they must have constructed a series of dams and spillways down here somewhere and diverted the Angarussa to fill them. Now they were pumping that water back up into the upper caverns, trapping Isinwen and the rest of his force.

As Kellen stared out at the rock it was as if, for a moment, it turned to smoke. He could *see* the dam-mechanism; the series of side and lower galleries painstakingly bricked up and outfitted with a complex mechanism of pumps and conduits over the last three moonturns.

There was no way he could reach them to disable it.

And there was worse. The vibrations he had felt were the sound of several of the side-galleries collapsing. The water roaring into the Caverns of Halacira would have even less space to fill than otherwise, and so it would fill it faster.

But though the work of the Shadowed Elves was brilliantly-conceived and sweeping in scope, it had been hastily-executed and would not hold for long. Already Kellen's battle-sight showed him that the damming and pumping mechanisms were buckling under the strain of operation and the new walls designed to seal up caverns as artificial dams were crumbling under the weight of the water pressing on them. Soon all the Shadowed Elves' careful work would give way and nearly everything would return to normal within the Caverns of Halacira.

But before that happened, Kellen and the people he had led down here would all be dead. If he could not get his army out before the water trapped them here, two thirds of the force Redhelwar had sent with him would drown beneath the earth.

And there was only one way out.

Across the bridge.

"We've got to get this wall down," he told his men. "This is the way we're going out."

He began to hack at the wall with his sword.

THE stone was soft and water-soaked; the wall was not something that was meant to hold for long. Ambanire shoved him rudely aside and began chipping at the mortar between two stones with his dagger; Kellen quickly switched to the smaller weapon and applied himself to the softer bands between the stone as well.

The water was rising around their legs.

Cilarnen or Jermayan could summon a lightning bolt to blast the stone to ash. As far as Kellen knew, he had no such abilities—even if he could call up a thunderstorm out of season, he couldn't bring the lightning *here*—and if he could, it would be far more likely to strike Elven armor than inert stone. He hammered harder at the wall, fury and frustration lending him a strength nearly that of his companions. He had not led them this far just to let them die.

"*Shield—and push.*"

It was not his own thought. It seemed to come from outside him. It was almost Shalkan's voice, and yet not.

But I don't Shield—I can't!

Shield was a spell no Knight-Mage cast, or needed.

But he wasn't going to let his people die simply because he wasn't willing to try.

"Stand back," he told the others.

The water was to their hips.

When Idalia had thought he was going to be a regular Wildmage, she'd told him about casting Shield-spells. A Wildmage Shielded naturally when Healing, though that wasn't quite the same thing. And of course, in his lessons in the High Magick, he'd had the principles of Mage-Shield dinned into him by Anigrel morning, noon, and night for almost a decade.

He did his best to forget all of it.

He placed his hands flat against the wall.

I need this, he said to the Wild Magic. *I need this for my people. They trust me to keep them alive. I will pay any price—anything!*

He felt the Presence descend.

"When the time comes, you must . . . let go."

Once he would have thought of that as a light Price. Now he thought it might be the highest Price of all.

Yes, he thought.

The sense of listening Presence departed.

His hands began to glow—brighter than the Coldfire above his head, until he had to close his eyes. Not the green glow of Healing—that he had seen before. Nor was it the blue light he had unconsciously expected—the first voice in his mind had sounded a lot like Shalkan. Instead, it was almost a blend of the two, a deep blue green, a color he had never seen in Nature. Even with his eyes closed, he could still see what the light was doing. It spread from his hands over the wall, and where it touched, the red glow of Taint vanished like smoke, until the entire wall radiated with the Shield he should never have been able to cast.

He pushed.

The stone resisted, but now it was soft and rotten, almost like chalk. His hands went through, pushing a large chunk of the center of the wall with them, and he pulled back just in time to keep from getting hit by the top of the wall as it fell free.

Water began to rush through the gap.

"Come on," he said to the others, his voice ragged with the exhaustion that came with summoning the Wild Magic. "Tear it down. Quickly."

⊷

A mile was a variable distance.

It was one thing if you were walking through the woods on a warm spring day. Another if you were riding—or walking—through a winter blizzard.

Yet another trying to move through waist-deep water in a cave beneath the earth.

Moving at the head of the Knights, Isinwen splashed forward as quickly as he could, though the waist-deep water slowed his steps and those of his men as if they moved through thick mud.

His heavy fur cloak was a sodden weight; he unclasped it and let the water pull it away. Though his heavy wool surcoat was also soaked with as much water as it could hold, and clung heavily to him, he did not consider removing it: That would require unbuckling his swordbelt, and he dared not take the time. Every item of clothing he wore was designed to withstand the cold of winter and the subterranean chill of a winter cave; it provided no protection at all against the icy water that he waded through, and the fur, thick weaves, and heavy leather soaked up and retained water, adding to the weight he carried.

The weight that would hold him down, hold every one of them down, and drown them when the waters reached above their heads. He could—they all could—strip off their armor and swim for it, but they would be miles from their supply wagons when they reached the surface.

And the exit they were heading for was narrow and steep, a small staircase.

It would take so many a long time to ascend by such a narrow passage.

❧

THE cave-opening was clear, and the water was pouring through it, back into the bed of the Angarussa. The level of the water here in the selkie-cavern had dropped to their knees, though the force of the current, as it foamed through the narrow opening, had increased. Kellen was glad to see that the river was running swiftly through its channel—which meant that at least some of the water in the caves should be draining away—but the water level was beginning to rise again as well—swiftly—it was possible that this gallery might refill, even with the constant drainage, cutting off their only way out. If these caves were flooded, then any chambers below this level were also flooded. Since the cave floors were both level and even, the water was almost certainly the same depth everywhere in every one of the surviving chambers.

They were running out of time.

Had he made the wrong decision, to go deeper into the caves with only a skeleton force? He knew he hadn't. If he had proceeded with his entire command, they would have been trapped here when the Shadowed Elves opened the spillways, with no time to open a line of retreat.

"Ambanire, it would please me greatly should you desire to take the Knights and cross the bridge to join up with Churashil's force immediately. Direct him to send messengers back to the main force: We will need our horses brought to this entrance."

The bridge itself was not trapped. Perhaps the Shadowed Elves themselves needed it. Perhaps trapping it was something they hadn't gotten around to. Or perhaps they'd realized that if they left it alone, it would be a lure he simply couldn't refuse.

"At once, *komentai*."

Ambanire turned and began to wade out toward the bridge, through the rushing water.

Now Kellen could see the steady glow of Coldfire that meant the approach of his main force. He felt a wave of relief. Isinwen wasn't an idiot, after all, needing Kellen to direct his every move. By the time the water had reached his ankles, he would already have begun to move the forces Kellen had left with him, and gathered Umacheriel's men with him along the way—whether he had heard the horn-call or not.

Suddenly, from the darkness ahead, came the gutteral barking yelps of the Shadowed Elves.

There were no other exits from this gallery on the maps. They had been hiding in the darkness. Waiting.

Ambanire's men had just reached the middle of the bridge. It was a narrow strip of smooth stone, just wide enough for two Elves to cross side by side. In normal times, the surface of the Angarussa ran several feet below it. Now the swiftly-rushing current was nearly level with the bridge's surface. The wet stone was slick as ice. Any armored Knight who slipped from it would drown beneath the surface of the icy water before he had the chance to struggle free of his armor.

The Shadowed Elves came swarming out of the darkness, too many to count. They held the far side of the bridge, but they did not need it to cross. As their archers began firing, more of the Tainted creatures began climbing across the walls of the cavern, heading toward Kellen.

"Back!" Kellen shouted, drawing his sword. If they could hold them in the doorway, they might survive the assault. But survival wasn't enough. They had to get across the bridge while they still could—and it was obvious that the Shadowed Elves intended to hold them here until the water did its work. They didn't care whether they lived or died—only that they killed Elves.

Shadowed Elf archers ran out onto the bridge, pressing their advantage. Though the glass shields Kellen's force carried provided more protection than the shields the Knights normally carried, some of the arrows still found their mark. Kellen watched helplessly as Elves staggered and fell, plummeting into the black water. Even though the wounds might not ordinarily have been fatal, they were enough to send their victims over the side of the bridge.

And there was no way he could get to them.

He waded through the rising water, out into the river gallery. The Elves who had not yet begun to cross had retreated to the bridgehead, forming a guard for those still on the bridge, but that wasn't enough either. How many Shadowed Elves had escaped Ysterialpoerin?

They needed the bridge. They needed the Shadowed Elves to come through. All of them.

Kellen grabbed the shoulder of the nearest Knight.

"Back!" he shouted, over the howls of the Shadowed Elves, the clash of steel and the roar of the rising water. "Back into the other cavern! Tell Isinwen to retreat!"

The Knights at the bridgehead began to back away, turning to head for the doorway.

It was blocked by a party of Shadowed Elves. They wore no armor, but every one of them carried an Elven-forged sword.

With a roar of anger, the Elves moved to engage their enemy.

It was almost a parody of a battle. Every move was slowed by the rising water, making the normally-graceful Elves clumsy and slow. The numbing chill of the caves penetrated their sodden clothing. Cloaks and surcoats wound around them, dragging them down and fouling blows.

But still, against this smaller, unarmored enemy, the conclusion of the battle was not in doubt. The water swirled with Shadowed Elf blood, its color impossible to tell in the azure Coldlight, and the bodies of their dead floated away from the battle, sliding down into the Angarussa.

Kellen glanced back. The last of the survivors were off the bridge.

More Shadowed Elves should have been crossing. More should have been swarming over the walls and the ceiling toward the embattled Elven Knights.

Instead, they . . . waited.

He could See the way the battle would go, See the Shadowed Elves' intention. This time they did not mean to follow their prey into the caves, as they always had before. This time they would wait, holding the cavern until the waters rose again. They would send a few attackers to convince him otherwise, but somewhere, in their last battles, they had learned patience and restraint. It could be a fatal lesson for the Elves.

He splashed back through the current after the others, cursing at his slowness. After a seeming eternity, he reached the others.

"The Shadowed Elves are holding the bridge. They aren't going to attack, and they aren't going to let us cross," he said shortly. "What about going back to the main entrance?"

"The water is even deeper there," Isinwen said. "It jets from the side galleries with the force of the river itself, making a wall we cannot breech."

It was only what Kellen had expected.

"Where's Wirance?"

The water rose several inches before Wirance arrived at his side, and while they waited Kellen removed his cloak and surcoat, and ordered those around him to do the same. He inspected his bow with resignation. The Elven bows had greater range and force than those of the Shadowed Elves, but by now their bowstrings were soaked. Useless. He tossed his bow and quiver into the water in disgust.

"Some of the archers string their bows with silver, Isinwen said. "The range is not as great, but—"

But silver would not stretch to uselessness in the damp.

"I want every one of them here. Now."

Isinwen moved off to pass the word.

As Isinwen departed, Wirance arrived. The Mountainborn Wildmage's leather armor was black with water, and his lips were blue with cold.

"I hope you have an idea," he said when he saw Kellen.

"The Shadowed Elves have built pumps and dams to flood the caverns. They'll fail soon. They'll fail *now* if we can jar them enough. I need you and the other Wildmages to come up with something that will shake these caves—hard."

If they saw that their plan to drown Kellen and his army had failed, the Shadowed Elves might revert to their old tactics and commit to an all-out attack. If not, at least Kellen's people would escape drowning, and be able to scour the caves for them afterward.

Wirance considered for a moment. "There is a spell. It will take time to cast. And it might just seal us in."

Kellen grimaced. "It's not as if we have a lot of choices. Do it."

Isinwen was struggling back toward the front of the army, staggering through the heavy weight of water and clutching the Elves around him for support as he moved. "Come on. We're going to try to take the bridge the old-fashioned way."

Kellen made his dispositions quickly. Umerchiel's force would remain to protect the Wildmages. Kellen, Isinwen, and the rest of the first force would do their best to cross the bridge and establish a bridgehead on the far side, so that they could protect more of their force in the crossing.

It would not be the easiest thing they'd ever done.

They made their way—once more—back to the river-cavern. Several times Elves fell, disappearing beneath the surface of the water to be dragged to the surface again by the Knights around them. Kellen only hoped that Isinwen had been right about the bows—part of his plan relied on being able to drive the Shadowed Elves back from the far side of the bridge.

The water poured with increasing force through the opening between the two caverns, white crests of foam upon its top.

As they reached the cavern's mouth, Kellen once again passed the word of his plan to all his commanders. A good General, he'd learned, did not keep his plans to himself. Others must be ready to carry them out if he was unable to.

And unlike a proper story-song General, Kellen would be leading this engagement, not directing it.

"It doesn't matter if some of them get past you. In fact, we want as many of them to get past you as possible. The more that attack Umerchiel's force, the fewer there will be holding the bridge. That's what we have to secure. If we can take the far side, we can bring enough of our force across to take the fight to them."

"So we begin," Isinwen said. "Leaf and Star guide us this day."

Kellen nodded. The Elven archers who were still able to loose arrows readied their bows.

Kellen raised Light At The Heart Of The Mountain in salute and slogged forward.

The water level dropped sharply once they were in the river-gallery, but Kellen saw, with a sinking heart, that the river now ran across the surface of the bridge itself.

He began to run. Master Belesharon had made him run through snow. This was not much harder.

He reached the bridge. It was as slick as glass, but he had fought in a Circle whose floor was oiled glass.

He ran faster.

Behind him, the Elven archers began to attack.

He'd caught the Shadowed Elves off guard, but it gave him no advantage. They would recover long before he could reach the far side of the bridge. Already their archers began to loose their deadly poisoned darts. Kellen ducked as far behind his shield as he could—it seemed to weigh far more than it had this morning; the subterranean cold and the cost of the spell he had cast were telling on him. Behind him, more Knights followed.

The world dimmed and brightened, in the peculiar vividness of battle-sight. He could see in every direction at once. The Elves behind him were moving away from the cavern opening as fast as they could, moving along the sides of the cavern walls. Fortunately the Shadowed Elf bows did not have the range of their Elven cousins, and they were out of range of the poisoned arrows.

Ahead, the Shadowed Elves were starting across the bridge, while others began, once again, to swarm the cavern walls, this time carrying the flasks of acid and poison that could kill instantly. Male and female were mixed equally in their ranks, and Kellen *Knew* that these were the last survivors of the Enclaves they had destroyed farther north.

The first of the enemy reached him. Kellen slashed at the body with his sword, the blow carrying the Shadowed Elf into the water.

On the far side of the river, several of the Shadowed Elves flung themselves into the water and began swimming toward the bridge.

The cold doesn't bother them. And the current will sweep them toward *the bridge. Which is exactly where they want to go . . .*

He banished the thought from his mind. There was no time to think now, or to change his plan. He had made the best possible plan that he could. It would work.

Or they would die.

It was a nightmare battle in the icy darkness, with only the globes of Cold-fire to illuminate the scene. The enemy came from in front—behind—beside—slowing their passage across the narrow bridgeway, and the water rose, threatening to do what even the Shadowed Elves could not: sweep them from the bridge and drown them in the depths of the river.

Worse, though the Angarussa had been running free before, the bodies of the Shadowed Elf dead did not sink, but floated. They had been pulled by the current toward the exit-passage of the river, and now blocked the outflow completely.

He drove all those thoughts from his mind.

All that existed were the targets for his sword.

Light At The Heart Of The Mountain rose and fell like a breath of wind, severing heads, arms, legs. The faceted jewel in her pommel glowed an eldritch blue in the reflected Coldlight, sparkling in the darkness. Each step Kellen managed to take forward was bought at the cost of a death—Shadowed Elves', Elven Knights.

A furious anger possessed him, banishing pain and weariness. He slammed his shield into the face of his next attacker, then tossed it aside. Spinning, turning, *dancing* through the river water as if it were the dry stone floor of the House of Sword and Shield, he hammered not only his sword, but his very will against the Shadowed Elves before him, daring them to stand and fight.

The press of the enemy before him broke. The Shadowed Elves were backing away, the ones facing him clawing their way over the ones behind them to escape his sword. The push of bodies drove many of them down into the river. The current was sluggish now, and they were not swept away, but they didn't seem to know which way to swim.

He felt a spell begin to build, jarring him momentarily from the battle-trance.

"Off the bridge! Off the bridge—*now!*"

He'd nearly reached the far side. He gained it in a few jumps, Isinwen just behind him. Sometime during the crossing the Shadowed Elves had stopped firing. They pushed forward.

The Elves still on the bridge crossed it at a splashing run, single file, hacking at the hands of the Shadowed Elves who lurked in the water trying to drag them from the bridge. The water was knee-deep above the causeway now, and rising. It would be even higher where Umerchiel was.

On the far side of the bridge, the Shadowed Elves seemed to go insane, throwing themselves on Kellen and the others with even greater ferocity than before. There was no thought of restraint now, of tactics. All they wanted to do was kill. Instead of facing them in ones and twos, Kellen was covered with clawing stabbing creatures attempting to tear his armor from his body.

Suddenly the cavern rocked.

He'd felt the shaking in the caverns when the Shadowed Elves had opened their dams. That had been nothing in comparison to this. It jarred him to his knees, and it didn't stop. Wirance had been right. The Wildmage's spell would do the Shadowed Elves' work for them.

The Shadowed Elves howled in terror at the quaking, breaking off their attack and turning to flee. It saved Kellen's life—if they had taken advantage of the moment, he'd surely be dead.

But they hadn't, and even while the aftershocks still shook the gallery, Kellen rolled to his feet and ran after them.

The Angarussa was running backward.

The river's level was dropping as fast as water draining from a bathtub, and the river was flowing in the opposite direction that it had been before. Already the causeway was exposed again, and the rest of the Elves running across it took full advantage of the moment.

⤜⤛

VESTAKIA slept through the rest of the day and into the night, repairing much of the damage she had done to herself in the long struggle to understand the Crystal Spiders. Her sleep, thanks to Idalia's cordial, was without dreams.

She was awakened, very early the following morning, by the arrival of Idalia and Cilarnen.

⤜⤛

SHE had seen little of Cilarnen over the past several sennights. Even when she had been down at the Main Camp, he had been in seclusion up at his ice-pavilion, engaged in his mysterious researches. When Idalia first brought him into the pavilion, for one horrified instant, Vestakia thought he had succumbed to the Shadow's Kiss; his eyes glittered fever-bright, there were hectic spots of color in his pale cheeks, and he reeled and staggered on unsteady feet as if he were drunk.

"Cilarnen!" she gasped.

"Another casualty of war," Idalia said ruefully. But the mockery in her tone could not disguise her concern. She lowered him gently onto a bench.

"I'd throw up, I think, if I'd eaten anything much lately," Cilarnen said, bending over to rest his head in his hands.

"What have you been *doing* to yourself?" Vestakia demanded fiercely.

At her words, he raised his head and smiled at her charmingly.

"Only magick, Lady Vestakia. It is not the simple business for High Mages that it seems to be for Wildmages. Hence, you see, the large city, the many servants . . . all the things I don't seem to have at the moment."

His tone was light, despite his obvious pain, making her smile despite herself.

"Vestakia, since you seem to be feeling better this morning, perhaps you could tend to our latest patient," Idalia said. "Sweet gruel for his tender stomach, I think, then into bed with him. Keep him warm. And stay with him—or I shall put you back into a bed again as well."

Vestakia simply tossed her head.

"Some people, Cilarnen, think that others can do nothing without constant supervision. Shall we show them that they are wrong?"

"Indeed, Lady Vestakia, I would be honored to assist you."

⇌

WHILE he ate and drank—the light breakfast was really all he could manage just now, after so many days of fasting—Cilarnen told Vestakia of his night's labors, and that Jermayan had gone in search of those he had seen in his vision.

Her teasing mood instantly sobered.

"But . . . what could have *happened?*" she asked in bewilderment.

"That I do not know. But Jermayan has set out to find them and see. Vestakia, there cannot have been a battle. I saw no wounded at all. And . . . these are the Elven Lands. You've said yourself that the last Enclave of the Shadowed Elves is at Halacira. They were nowhere near that. Certainly it is troubling, but Jermayan will find them soon, and bring news. We shall just have to wait until then."

⇌

BUT it was not Jermayan who entered the Healer's Tent to join them, a few hours later, but Keirasti, accompanied by Idalia.

The Elven Knight looked exhausted, and stunned with cold. Vestakia jumped up immediately from her place by Cilarnen's bedside, and went to fetch her a large mug of soup. Soup and tea were always ready and waiting in the Healer's pavilion.

"Before anyone asks, Kellen is alive and well," Idalia said. "At least he was six days ago, when Keirasti left him. And he was nowhere near Halacira."

"Well, there's some good news," Cilarnen said, lying back against his pillows again.

"Indeed it is," Keirasti said. "I judge he is yet a sennight from Halacira. When Jermayan returns from the Crowned Horns, he will take your warning to Kellen, and he will be grateful to receive it, you may be sure."

"I must go with Jermayan," Vestakia said, coming over and handing Keirasti a large mug of thick soup. "I can help."

"No," Keirasti said. "Jermayan has promised he will return me to my command. They await me at the foot of the Mystrals. Ancaladar can only carry two at speed."

"He can take your warning to Kellen," Idalia said gently. "That will be what Kellen needs now. He'll probably send for you anyway very soon, to make sure the caverns are clear."

❦

AND it would be just as well, Idalia reflected, for Vestakia to have a day or two to rest and compose herself before she saw Kellen again. The way she looked right now, the poor girl would probably throw herself into Kellen's arms the moment she saw him, and though her brother might have a head made of wood sometimes, he wasn't made of stone. But he did have a vow of chastity and celibacy that had some moonturns yet to run, and Idalia doubted it would be the easiest thing in the world to remember with a weeping Vestakia in his arms.

"And you'll have plenty to do here before you go. Redhelwar has given the order to move the army south."

"South? We're to move?" Cilarnen sat bolt upright. "But I—"

"Must stay right there and rest," Idalia said inexorably. "You will have plenty of time later to pack that mare's nest you call a camp. Which you cannot do if you are facedown in the snow, asleep with exhaustion."

Cilarnen subsided, grumbling.

Just then one of the other Healers entered the tent.

"Ancaladar is flying over the camp. Jermayan will be here soon."

"I must prepare," Keirasti said, setting down her wooden mug. "And hope not to freeze on the return journey."

She got to her feet, picking up two bulky packs that lay at her feet. "I thank you for these, Idalia. Our Healers were running low on supplies."

"At least you won't have to cross the Mystrals on horseback again soon," Idalia said. "Safe journey to you."

"Leaf and Star be with you all."

～

IDALIA and Vestakia rode out to see Jermayan and Keirasti off. Jermayan had ridden down into the camp on Valdien, who was once again stabled up at Ancaladar's ice-pavilion. Keirasti was riding pillion behind Idalia, since her destrier was still with her command.

"Be safe," Idalia said to Jermayan.

"I shall keep him so," Ancaladar promised.

"It should be a simple matter," Jermayan said. "At least as simple as anything involving the Shadowed Elves is."

"If only I had known sooner!" Vestakia said.

"Then all would have happened just as it has," Jermayan told her. "We must clear those caverns to fit them to our own use, and we would have sent just such a force to do it. Kellen is hardly a novice at this work. I will bring him your warning, and he will proceed with care."

Vestakia nodded, looking miserable and unconvinced.

Jermayan stepped up into Ancaladar's saddle, and reached down to help Keirasti into the saddle behind him. The packs she was taking back to her command, which had been lashed to Valdien's saddle, were already tied in place. The two riders began to buckle themselves in.

"Come on," Idalia said, setting her foot into Cella's stirrup and taking Valdien's reins with her. "The horses won't like getting a faceful of snow when Ancaladar takes off, and neither will we."

The two riders backed off a little distance as Ancaladar began his takeoff run. In moments the dragon was skyborne, circling over the camp in an ascending spiral and then heading westward, his black wings outstretched.

"Back to camp, then," Idalia said.

～

WHEN they returned to the Healer's Pavilion, Cilarnen was up and dressed.

"By your leave," Cilarnen said, when he saw Idalia. "I'd better go back to my own camp. Since we're moving, I have packing—a lot of packing—to do. And preparations to make. And there's no one to do it but me."

Idalia regarded him critically. Rest and food had done much to restore his vitality. The trouble was, she didn't really trust him to take care of himself.

"If you work yourself until you drop, you'll be no use to anyone. And I'll have no choice but to treat you to a selection of my strengthening cordials. And I warn you now, they taste incredibly vile."

"Your point is well taken," Cilarnen said with a faint smile. "Still, the work must be done, or I will be of no use to the army anyway. I promise to be careful. Elven tea is vile enough. I would hate to risk the experience of any more of your cordials. Kardus will help me. And perhaps Vestakia will come also."

"Fine. She can keep an eye on you. If she agrees?"

"If you don't need me down in camp, I'd be happy to keep an eye on Cilarnen," Vestakia said, with a faintly wicked smile. "And he can tell me more about Armethalieh."

Cilarnen bowed again. "That I shall be more than happy to do. It was once the most beautiful place in the world, and the Eternal Light grant that it shall be so again."

Eleven

To Live in the City of Distance

ANCALADAR SPED THROUGH the great halls of the upper air, his wings barely moving. The wind whistled over the armor of his two riders, making a monotonous, atonal song.

"Redhelwar orders the army south," Jermayan said.

"Yes," Keirasti agreed.

"So Kellen would have advised him, and so I said to him," Jermayan said. "And yet I wonder at the timing of it."

"And so you must, until you speak with Kellen," Keirasti said implacably.

Jermayan sighed. "And so I shall."

And when he spoke to Kellen, he would discover what Kellen had learned that was of such terrible urgency that he had needed to send Keirasti north to deliver the information to Redhelwar at all costs.

Though the flight back to where Keirasti had left Maredhiel and the rest of her command was just as long as the one away from her, it seemed shorter, for this time they knew exactly where they were going, and Ancaladar had no need to search every inch of the crags below for traces of a party in distress.

The site was easy to spot, for in the handful of hours—less than a full day—that Keirasti had been gone, the Knights had set up a full camp and picketed the horses. Ancaladar banked once over the ring of tents, the looked for a suitable landing place. It was easily found, for the mountain valley was filled with sweeps of smooth snow.

"Easy enough to land," the dragon grumbled, as he set his wings for his final descent. "Harder to get airborne again."

Jermayan patted Ancaladar's neck in sympathy. Left to himself, the dragon would make his flights from high places, such as the tops of mountains, where he had strong winds to bear him up, and hundreds of feet of free air below him in which to maneuver. Though he could take off from a level plain—and had, many times—as Ancaladar said, it was more work.

The landings were not things of ease, either.

At the last moment, Ancaladar fanned his wings backward—hard—and stood almost upright in the air, hitting the deep snow hind feet first. The backwinging in the air slowed his already greatly-diminished forward speed, but not enough to keep him from digging a deep trench through the heavy powdery snow. On solid ground, draconic landings were light and elegant things, but the uncertain surface of the snow often did not permit such grace.

At last Ancaladar settled his belly into the snow and folded his wings.

"We're here," he said unnecessarily.

Keirasti began to unbuckle her straps.

Maredhiel was already riding out toward them, leading Orata.

Keirasti glanced toward the sky. "You have only an hour of light more at best. It would please me should you choose to stay with us for the night and journey on in the morning."

"This is familiar territory to us," Ancaladar replied. "And the winds over the plains ahead present no challenge. If my Bonded agrees, we will fly on."

"Then let it be so. When you see Kellen, tell him I will be with him before another sennight passes."

She slipped down from the dragon's back, grunting as she found herself waist-deep in snow, and began untying the nearer pack from Ancaladar's saddle. Jermayan reached back to loose the one she could not reach, handing it across to her.

By the time they were both free, Maredhiel had reached them.

"Alas that you rejoin us so speedily," the Elven Knight said cheerfully. "I had thought we were to have at least a moonturn's recreation here in this garden spot."

"So much for your dreams of ease, lazy one," Keirasti said to her Second. "Take this pack up with you; it is filled with Idalia's medicines. Tomorrow we begin to rejoin the army."

Whatever message Keirasti had carried, Jermayan reflected, Maredhiel obviously had no inkling of it. She accepted her parcel readily, with no indication that she was burdened by more-than-ordinary cares.

He waited for the two Knights to ride away.

"Soon we can ask Kellen," Ancaladar said.

"Yes," Jermayan answered. "Soon."

IN the end, it came down to the simple work of butchery.

They outnumbered their enemy ten—a hundred—to one, and the Shadowed Elves had no place to run to. Some of them fled through the passage that led to the surface; Kellen's battle-sight showed him that Churashil's force made short work of them there.

But far more remained in the caverns below. Some had managed to evade Kellen's force, but Umerchiel and the others waited in the chamber beyond, and there were no other exists from it. So they, too, were accounted for.

Many of the Shadowed Elves in the river gallery had thrown down their weapons when the caverns began to shake; it became a matter of finding those that were still alive, driving them up against the walls of the gallery, and cutting them to pieces.

Sometimes the Shadowed Elves would hide among the mounds of their dead. After the first one had attacked from such a hiding place, Kellen ordered all the Shadowed Elf corpses checked. They found more survivors. Two Elves would hold the victim while a third slit the captive's throat.

None of the swimmers reached the far shore alive.

By the time the Elves had finished their bloody work, the Angarussa had begun to run normally, washing the bodies of the floating dead that had fallen into its waters away with it.

After he had disposed of the Shadowed Elf sortie that had reached the surface, Churashil had sent scouts down into the caverns, and received new orders from Kellen. Braziers had been brought to warm the river-gallery, and a steady stream of wounded were being evacuated to the main camp.

There weren't many. Only a tiny fraction of the company of Elves Kellen had brought into Halacira had actually engaged the enemy in the Shadowed Elf attack.

And most of them had drowned.

Eventually Kellen's people would have to try to dredge the river to recover the bodies.

Kellen tried to think of what he could have done differently, had he known Halacira had become an Enclave of the Shadowed Elves before he'd entered the caverns. But he could think of nothing. He would still have had to go down into the caves with his Knights to find them. The caves would still have been entrapped. The Shadowed Elves would still have flooded the caves.

If he had gone alone, he might have gotten out the way he'd come. Or he might have died. If he'd come down with a smaller force, they might all have died, for it was their overwhelming numbers that had kept so many of them alive today.

As brutal as it was, despite the losses they had suffered, this was the best outcome they could have hoped for.

It didn't feel right.

And they were *still* going to have to search the caves thoroughly, because they could not allow even one of the Tainted creatures to survive.

"Did the day go as you wished it?"

Wirance walked over to the nearest brazier and held his hands out to its warmth. The Wildmage looked exhausted. Lines of weariness etched his weatherbeaten features.

"What are you still doing here?" Kellen demanded. "I told Umerchiel to send all the Wildmages up to the Healers as soon as the passage was clear."

"Aye, well, as to that . . . I stayed with Kerleu. I have to say, I thought we were going to bring the whole place down on us when the spell ran. But the mountain's bones run deep."

Kerleu stayed too? But all the wounded should have been evacuated hours ago.

"He's dead, isn't he?" Kellen said.

"A life was the Price, a life freely given," Wirance said. "We all agreed to pay it. He had a valiant heart, but crossing the Mystrals too often will weaken it. It could well have happened without the spell."

But it didn't.

Kellen drew a deep breath. "He is no less a casualty of war than Ambanire, or any other who fell in battle here today. He will be so honored."

Wirance clapped him on the shoulder. "All goes as the Huntsman wills, lad. Kerleu goes to the Forest to be born again to the Wife. He'll be back, sure as flowers in the spring."

Kellen nodded, though spring—and Wirance's easy certainty that it would come—seemed very far away.

"And the day?" Wirance said again.

"We won," Kellen said slowly. "In a day or two, I suppose we'll know whether the caverns are clear. And Artenel and his people can get to work rebuilding them to make them into a fortress."

"So no one who died here died for nothing," Wirance said, sounding satisfied. "And now that I've got a little heat in these old bones, I'll get back to Kerleu."

"I'll go with you."

⁓≋⁓

MUCH of the main force of the army was still in the selkie-chamber and the mining-cavern beyond it. Kellen searched until he found Isinwen. His Second was battered—and, of course, soaking wet—but alive and well.

"It's going to take forever to move everyone out across the causeway," Kellen said once greetings had been exchanged. "Is there any chance now of getting out through the main entrance?"

For one thing, it was closer to the camp. That meant dry clothes, fires, and food—something all of them needed. Churashil had brought horses and wagons around to the river cavern entrance to transport the wounded, and the Knights that had so far made their way to the surface through that exit, but the sun was setting, and to move all the horses around to that entrance and ride back again would take a long time—and they'd be even colder than they were now.

"The main entrance should be clear by now—if damp," Isinwen said after a moment's thought.

"Take a party and see."

THOUGH several of the side-galleries had collapsed—due to either the Shadowed Elves' work or the Wildmages' spell—the route to the surface was clear, and Kellen immediately began evacuating his army through the larger entrance. He would leave no one behind in the caves tonight, not even the dead. Guarding the exits would have to be enough.

Leaving the caves went a good deal faster than entering them had. He was glad of that much. There were a number of blessings to be counted, if he cared to: no *duergar* had lurked anywhere in the unlighted depths of the caves to draw any of his troops farther in. The Shadowed Elves had not summoned any of the Shadow's other allies to aid them—if the Elves had faced Frost Giants and Ice Trolls here in Halacira, as well as Shadowed Elves and rising water, their situation would have been unwinnable.

But the Shadowed Elves had been willing to die to the last soul to destroy their enemy, and perhaps their allies had not. Or perhaps they simply had not been able to reach them in time.

Finally the last band of Elves prepared to ascend to the surface. Kellen wrapped his borrowed—dry—cloak around him and followed.

AS the day dimmed, Jermayan and Ancaladar saw no trace of Kellen's army, though as they neared Halacira, they saw signs of their passage in plenty, for the trees had kept the snow from eradicating the marks of the horses and wagons completely.

"He cannot have moved the army this fast," Jermayan groaned.

"He has," Ancaladar answered simply.

It was—barely—possible. For a master general, in complete command of his forces, driven by a necessity Jermayan could only wonder at. He could only hope that Kellen had stopped to rest for a day or two in camp before going down into the caverns.

But in his heart, he began to suspect he might already be too late.

When they flew over the Angarussa, he saw that its surface was cracked and marred by the passage of thousands of Elven Knights. His worst suspicions were confirmed when he reached the camp. It was fully set, but not fully tenanted. There was a deep path beaten in the snow between the campsite and the main entrance to the caverns. Near the trees, he could already see a few bodies wrapped in white.

"I will find a place to land," Ancaladar said.

The clearing Ancaladar found was a little distance from the main camp. After unsaddling Ancaladar, it took Jermayan a good half hour to make his way through the snow to the edge of the camp.

Artenel greeted him.

"I See you, Jermayan."

"I See you, Artenel. I expected to find you still upon the road for Halacira."

"Come, take tea. We might well have been, but we have made good time. And just as well, else the Shadowed Elves that Kellen encountered in the caverns below would have had more time to complete their work, and the day would have gone more wretchedly than it has. I would have welcomed the opportunity to have studied the engines they used to flood the caverns, but I believe they have now been smashed beyond all discerning."

"It will please me to hear all that you can tell. I came to warn Kellen that there was an Enclave here—but I see my warning comes too late."

If he had flown here directly the moment Idalia had told him of Vestakia's visions—

If he had not stopped to bring Keirasti back to Redhelwar, or put off his flight to the Crowned Horns—

"Our losses were light, so I am told," Artenel said simply. "The Wild Magic warned him that there was Taint in the caverns below, but we did not suspect that our poor brothers would be able to call the river into them. Umerchiel believes we have slain them all this time, but it will be many days before we are certain."

Artenel's words did much to reassure Jermayan, but little to comfort him. He had simply forgotten how fast Kellen could move when he decided there was a need to hurry.

And Jermayan still didn't know what it was.

"I am grateful for your offer of tea, but I must speak with Kellen as soon as I can," Jermayan said.

"Then you should go to the cavernmouth. Go first to the horse-lines. Casanilde is there, and will find you a mount to take you swiftly."

"My thanks to you," Jermayan said.

⨌

A few minutes later Jermayan was riding toward the horse-lines along the beaten path through the snow. Along the way he passed groups of weary riders heading back from the cavern mouth, and Elves leading more strings of horses back to the entrance to mount those yet to depart.

When he reached the cavernmouth, Jermayan saw that a series of hasty shelters had been erected, offering shelter and tea to those who had just come up from the depths. Kellen stood beneath one awning, holding a mug of tea in one hand and leaning over a flaming brazier.

Jermayan felt a deep pang of relief. Kellen looked exhausted, but uninjured.

"You'll burn yourself if you stand any closer," Jermayan said.

Kellen glanced up, first looking pleased to see his friend, then wary at the possibility of bad news.

"I bring no ill tidings," Jermayan said quickly. "I came to bring you warning. I see now that it is too late."

Kellen shook his head slowly. "I made too many mistakes. I can't think of anything I could have done differently, but . . ." He stopped. "I sent Keirasti back over the Mystrals with a message for Redhelwar. Jermayan—"

"I have already brought her and her message before the Army's General, and returned her to her command. She asks me to tell you she will be with you soon."

Kellen smiled at that. "I just bet she will."

"It would please me greatly to know what news she carried that was of such urgency," Jermayan said.

Kellen looked around. "I don't see Ancaladar."

"He is there." Jermayan pointed in the direction of the clearing where he had left the dragon.

"Let's go."

Kellen paused to give last orders to a few of his commanders, then mounted Firareth, and the two of them rode off toward Ancaladar's clearing. When the two of them were out of sight of the cavernmouth, Kellen spoke again.

"When we were at Ondoladeshiron, I had an audience with Rochinuviel. She'd had a private message from Sentarshadeen just after you left. There's plague in Sentarshadeen, and Andoreniel is very ill. Too ill to give orders. She didn't think a messenger had been sent to Redhelwar, and even if one had, nothing was getting through the pass. There was a Shadewalker."

Jermayan barely heard the rest of Kellen's words.

"The King is ill?" he asked, with blunt rudeness.

"I don't know what will happen to the army if Andoreniel can't give it orders," Kellen said, sounding as close to despair as Jermayan had ever heard him. "I asked Redhelwar to move the army to Ondoladeshiron, but . . . I don't know if he will."

"He is doing it now," Jermayan said. "Though to move an army across the mountains in the depths of winter is no quick matter."

"DON'T I know it," Kellen said.

A combination of uneasiness and relief filled him. He knew it was the right thing to do, but having Redhelwar take his advice . . . well, that only meant that he'd have to figure out what to do once the army had reached Ondoladeshiron, that was all.

"This speaks to why you moved in such haste to reach Halacira," Jermayan went on. "Sentarshadeen was your true destination."

"I wanted to see for myself what was going on there—and help Andoreniel, if I could. And I thought I might be able to send back Unicorn Scouts to the army. Even with Keirasti's head-start, they'd still get there faster than she would."

"But now that need not be done," Jermayan observed. "And there is news from Ysterialpoerin that you do not know, for much has changed since you left."

By now they had reached the clearing where Ancaladar waited.

The dragon's radiant heat—though Ancaladar swore he had no control over the magic for which he was such a mighty reservoir of power, he did seem to be able to control the amount of heat he radiated—had melted the snow around him in a wide circle, and steam rose from the bare ground in plumes. Kellen dismounted and moved forward gratefully into Ancaladar's pocket-summer.

"Kellen," the black dragon greeted him. "I am glad to see you safe. We were worried about you."

"Not as worried as *I* was about me," Kellen said fervently.

"There is bad news, Bonded," Jermayan said. Quickly he related what Kellen had told him.

"Bad news indeed," Ancaladar said, stretching out his long neck so that Jermayan could rub the sensitive skin beneath the hinge of his jaw. "Perhaps you can Heal him. But there is good news as well. The people of the Northern Cities are safe among the trees of Ysterialpoerin. Further, Cilarnen has discovered a source of power, and masters the spells of the High Magick."

"It worked?" Kellen asked.

"It did indeed," the dragon agreed. "Without Cilarnen's spells, we would not have found Keirasti. He recognized her horses, you see."

It was the first remotely funny thing Kellen had heard in far too long, and he laughed. Cilarnen could honestly not tell one Elf from another, but oh, horses were an entirely different matter. . . .

"But why were you looking for Keirasti?"

"In truth, we were looking for you," Jermayan said, "because Vestakia had received visions of a cavern of *xaique*-pieces, and when she told me what the Crystal Spiders had shown her, I thought to warn you against the Caverns of Halacira. But the High Magick and the Wild Magic do not marry well together, and Cilarnen could not see you. His Far-Seeing spells can only seek out what he knows, and so they showed him Keirasti's horses. When I went to her, she demanded to be taken to Redhelwar at once. Both she and I thought you still some days from the caverns. I thought there was time."

Kellen put a hand gently on his friend's shoulder. "Jermayan, it wouldn't have made any difference. In fact, if I'd *had* warning, it might have made matters worse. I went down into Halacira expecting, well, some kind of trouble, because we'd seen Taint there before, when you and I rode in search of the Black Cairn. If I'd known that the Shadowed Elves had an Enclave there, I might have chosen different tactics. And . . . I think the tactics I chose were the best ones for the situation."

Even as he said it, and hard as it was to say, Kellen knew it was true. He'd fought a battle in the Caverns of Halacira, and in every battle there were deaths. If he was too cautious, refusing to fight in case some of his troops might die, he would never be able to win a battle.

It was another lesson, and a hard one.

"The Wild Magic goes as it wills," Jermayan said. "It would be good to know what you propose to do now."

"I need to be sure the caverns are clear. For that I need Vestakia. I need to get to Sentarshadeen and see if anything can be done for Andoreniel, and Idalia is the best Healer I know. And Cilarnen . . . maybe the High Magick can do something where we can't."

"Then tomorrow I will bring them to you," Ancaladar said. "Along with the many things that Cilarnen will swear that he needs to be of help. I have become quite resigned to being a pack animal in the last few moonturns, I promise you." The dragon snorted gustily. "But I am hungry."

"That I can take care of," Kellen said. "We were going to slaughter one of the teams of oxen tonight. We need the fresh meat, and we're running low on fodder anyway."

<hr>

THE next morning, as Kellen's encampment began the sadly-familiar process of recovering from a battle, Ancaladar took wing northward again.

Along the way they sighted Keirasti's troop far below. Ancaladar soared above them as Jermayan used a spell to cast his voice down to her, telling her that Kellen had already met his enemy at the Caverns of Halacira, and that he had prevailed.

He saw her brandish her sword at him in salute and acknowledgment, standing high in her stirrups, and they flew on.

<hr>

AS they flew over the camp at Ysterialpoerin, it was already obvious that it would be moving very soon. Rows of wagon, still without teams, stood in lines of array, slowly taking on loads. Several streets of tents were already gone. The outlying herds were being brought into a semblance of order.

"I shall miss this." Ancaladar sighed, as he settled into his ice-pavilion once more and rested his jaw on his forelegs.

"I believe that within a day or two at most, you will be back in your canyon in the meadows beyond the House of Sword and Shield," Jermayan said. "I am certain Kellen intends to go there as soon as he feels he may leave Halacira safely."

"No one may know what the future holds," Ancaladar said somberly. "Not even Mages."

<hr>

IDALIA had left Valdien at his accustomed stabling with food and water for several days—though it was unlikely in the extreme, Jermayan thought, that she did not intend to visit every night to make certain of the destrier's comfort. Having unsaddled Ancaladar, he immediately saddled Valdien and rode down toward the camp.

The weather was starting to turn for the worse. In less than a sennight it would be Midwinter, and after that, if the weather ran at all true to previous years, the really hard part of the winter would begin, the weather getting bleaker and more foul until Kindling, the point that marked the halfway point between winter and spring. In some years, Kindling had marked when the very first snow-flowers appeared in the Unicorn Meadow. Jermayan did not think that would be the case this year.

⤙⤚

JERMAYAN went first to Redhelwar to report on what he had learned at Ha-lacira. Despite everything, the news he brought was good, and Redhelwar agreed that Vestakia, Cilarnen, and Idalia should accompany Jermayan back to the Cav-erns, and then on to Sentarshadeen to provide what assistance they could to Andoreniel.

Having Redhelwar's blessing, Jermayan had next gone to the Artificers, for if Ancaladar must carry three in addition to his rider, plus the working equip-ment of a High Mage, the carrying-baskets and harness that Jermayan had used so many times before would be needed. Mirqualirel, who had ascended to the post of Chief Armorer for the army now that Artenel had departed with Kellen, promised Jermayan that the items he required would be but the work of a few hours, and that Ancaladar would certainly be ready to fly again before nightfall.

Jermayan vowed that this would be the last time his patient friend would be called upon to do something he disliked so very much, but at the moment he could see no other way to get the others there as quickly as Kellen needed.

With the rest of his preparations made, he went to seek out Idalia.

Healer's Row had become a scene of controlled chaos. Though the Healers knew their duty lay with the army, it could not be denied that there was work aplenty for them in Ysterialpoerin and the Forest City that had grown up around it, and in the sennights that had passed, many of the Healers had become very attached to those people in the tent-city whom they had labored to save from the ravages of cold-sickness and plague.

Now, on the eve of their departure, the Healers struggled to be everywhere at once, and to pack for the journey as well. The complicated mechanisms of brewing and distilling that had been set up to take advantage of the long sen-nights of a permanent camp must be taken down and carefully packed away against the day when they could be set up once more.

Remedies must be decocted into unbreakable containers and carefully la-beled, as the next person who reached for them might not have a full Healer's training. Field aid kits must be prepared, and those that had been used must be restocked against need. There were a thousand tasks to perform before the mo-ment Redhelwar gave the order to march.

Jermayan moved carefully among the hurrying bodies until he spotted the flash of Vestakia's scarlet skin. She was helping to take down one of the large Healing pavilions—with their double walls for added warmth, and many inner partitions, this was a complicated process, and must be overseen carefully, so that the pavilion could be erected quickly—either at a new campsite, or—Leaf and Star avert—in the middle of some disaster so that the injured could be quickly and safely seen to.

Once the great mass of cloth lay flat upon the ground, and the others moved in to begin folding it into a tiny parcel so that it could be placed upon one of the wagon, he moved in to touch her arm. She spun around, obviously having had no idea he was near.

"Jermayan!" she gasped. Her whole face was a question.

Even after another day's rest and care, the marks of strain and exhaustion were still clear on her fine-boned features. This was something more than the effect of days and nights of trying to talk to the Crystal Spiders, Jermayan sensed.

"I rejoice to tell you that Kellen is alive and well," he said quickly. "The casualties at Halacira were light, for the Wild Magic guided his hand."

She frowned as the sense of his words reached her.

"Then . . . he has already reached Halacira."

"And the battle has been fought, and we have been victorious. Do not think that your warning has been in vain, for without it we would not have attempted to search him out, and would not have brought Keirasti back to deliver her message to Redhelwar—nor would I have gone on to speak to Kellen. It has all worked out for the best, even though the results have not been . . . quite as we expected."

Vestakia grimaced, but her worried gaze did not leave his face.

"And as the Crystal Spiders showed you, the Shadowed Elves were indeed there. Though Kellen believes the Shadowed Elves are no more, to be certain, he wishes you to come to him."

"But of course I will! Did he think I wouldn't?" she demanded indignantly. "I just have to tell Idalia that I'm going."

"Indeed you do not," Jermayan said. "He has asked for Idalia as well—and Cilarnen, too. I am to bring all three of you as fast as I can."

Vestakia's lips formed a silent "o," beginning a question that she steeled herself not to ask.

"Well!" she said instead. "I am not certain that Ancaladar will ever forgive you for making him carry such a heavy load—for I do not think you will get Cilarnen to accompany you if you ask him to leave even one book or brazier behind."

"I must ask him if they are *all* entirely necessary," Jermayan said, "or if some of his supplies may be sent with the army. But first, I must find Idalia and see if she will consent to accompany us."

"But of course she will!" Vestakia said. "Oh, Jermayan, I am so glad I said my goodbyes to the Crystal Spiders this morning! I would hate to simply have left them without thanking them for all their hard work. And I am certain they are glad that they have their caves back at last."

Jermayan only hoped that the Crystal Spiders that had been at Halacira had survived the deluge that had nearly drowned the army there, but saw no reason to tell Vestakia about that now. She would discover the full details of that battle soon enough.

"Then we will find Idalia," Jermayan said, taking her arm. "And hope she does not slay both of us for our presumption in hoping to remove her when there is so much work to be done here."

≈

IDALIA instantly guessed from their faces that the news was good.

"Oh, Idalia—Kellen has already fought the Shadowed Elves—and he has won!" Vestakia cried in relief. She ran across the tent to Idalia and flung her arms around the taller woman's neck.

Idalia was standing in the tent where the Healers kept their stores. Trunks and baskets of supplies stood everywhere, with half-empty shelves a mute testimony to what she had been doing when Vestakia interrupted her.

She hugged Vestakia in return, then placed her hands on her hips and regarded Jermayan.

"He must have had some excellent reason for shaving half a sennight off the time between Ondoladeshiron to Halacira—and in this season," she said.

"And he looks forward to telling you what it is," Jermayan agreed. He had no intention of spreading the news about Andoreniel about the camp here, even if it had been his secret to tell. "He has asked me to bring you—and Vestakia, and Cilarnen—to the camp at Halacira as soon as I can. Mirqualirel is having carrying-baskets made, so you will be able to bring more than your clothes, though not a great deal, apparently. Vestakia tells me that the High Magick requires many . . . objects."

≈

IDALIA shook her head, torn between the vast burden of work she would have to leave undone here, and the certain knowledge that Kellen would not have asked her to come if his need of her were not great. It was plain that Jermayan now knew the full content of whatever message Keirasti had brought—but Elves' ears were sharp, and he certainly wouldn't blurt it out in the middle of the camp. Not when Keirasti had gone to such agonizing lengths to keep it secret.

"He has not yet told Cilarnen that he must leave his precious library and all his toys and fly over the mountain, has he?" she said to Vestakia, nodding toward Jermayan.

She saw Vestakia's face light with a flash of inner mischief, and rejoiced inwardly. Since Kellen had left, and Vestakia had taken on the burden of trying to discover the location of the Shadowed Elves, Vestakia had been wearing herself down to nothing but a haggard shadow of her normal self. Now, at least, that was over.

Though apparently they now faced an even more appalling problem.

"He has not," Vestakia agreed. "I think he hoped you would help."

"I suppose I must," Idalia said, with an exaggerated and very theatrical sigh, the behavior assumed for Vestakia's benefit. "Elves are very timid creatures, you know. Timid, and . . . shy."

CILARNEN stared at the three of them as if they'd all gone mad.

The ice-golem had not appeared this time as they rode up to the mirror-pavilion, and Idalia could only assume that he'd already disenchanted it. If he'd had more than one, disenchanting all of them might take a lot of work, nor could he leave his protective wards standing in place. Those without any trace of magic might never notice them, but for Elementals and the many Brightfolk races that made their homes in the Elvenlands, Cilarnen's wards might as well have been stone walls. Depending on how they were constructed, innocent creatures of magic might become trapped within them and die. So he must remove them all, and Idalia suspected it might be a long process.

It certainly explained why he was not farther along in his packing.

An entire half-wagon had been reserved for Cilarnen's use. He would need all of it, between his pavilion itself and all of the equipment he had collected. So far it stood completely empty, though with Kardus and the driver's help he'd gotten as far as removing all of the trunks from its bed.

"Leave?" he said. "Now? With Ancaladar? But . . . Ancaladar can't carry all this!"

"Kellen wouldn't have asked for you if it wasn't important," Idalia said gently. Vestakia had gotten another good night's rest, but it was clear that Cilarnen hadn't. He'd told her he'd rest better behind his own wards and shields, but it was plain that the moment he'd heard that the army was to move, he'd begin dismantling his temple, working through the night.

He ran a hand through his hair. "How much can I take?"

Vestakia looked at Idalia.

"I'm sure Kellen has nearly everything I need," Idalia said. "I'll want to take a chest or two of medicines. Nothing more."

"And I don't need anything," Vestakia said. "I already have more than I ever had in my life, right now."

Cilarnen smiled. "I'm sorry, but . . . I'm sure Kellen doesn't want to see me just so he'll have someone to beat at *gan*. So I'll need my spellbooks. My workbooks. My robe. My sword, my wand, my staff. My scrying-crystal. All my incenses and herbs. I imagine he can provide braziers and candles, so I suppose I can leave those." He groaned. "I won't be able to take my *tabulum*. I might not be able to take my floor-cloth, either."

He ran a hand through his hair again, causing it to stand up in short auburn tufts. "I suppose it's just as well I hadn't really started packing yet."

"I can help," Vestakia offered. "I would have come earlier, but . . ."

"I'll need your help—and Kardus's, too," Cilarnen said simply.

WHILE Vestakia and the Centaur Wildmage helped Cilarnen separate those items of his Art that were absolutely vital from those that were merely desirable to bring along, Idalia and Jermayan occupied themselves in preparing soup and tea to keep everyone going, and in packing those items of a nonmagickal nature that would have to be sent with the army.

"I must say," Idalia said, bundling and tying a roll of blankets, "being a Wildmage seems much easier somehow. Cilarnen has said that he thinks the High Mages fought in the Great War—but frankly, I can't see how they would have managed it."

"Perhaps their spells were less elaborate then," Jermayan answered. "Or perhaps they had the luxury of preparing them in advance. I have heard all my life of what grim and terrible days those were—but at least that war was fought openly, against an enemy willing to challenge us upon an honest battlefield."

"Yes," Idalia answered tartly, dropping the bundle atop several others and kneeling to roll the first of the carpets beneath. "And we all know how well *that* worked out. Most of the land scoured to bare rock where nothing still grows a thousand years later. Half the races of the Light destroyed completely, and the rest slaughtered to a tenth of their populations. The Great Flower Forest of Ulanya, burned to ash. And we *still* didn't win."

"Idalia, my heart," Jermayan said, dropping an armful of Cilarnen's clothes into a open chest and coming to kneel beside her. "It is only simple truth that our circumstances are worse now than ever before. We do not know what the future may hold, save that we may only hope that we may all stand together to welcome victory. And I would be greatly honored, in such uncertain times, were you to consent to wear my betrothal pendant now."

Once before Jermayan had offered her his betrothal pendant. And Idalia had refused, because to accept it would form a link between them that might allow him to see into her mind, and know the secret she dared not let him guess.

The magic she had used to keep the rains from destroying Sentarshadeen had come at a very high Price.

Her life.

The Price was yet to be paid, but Mageprices always came due. Idalia did not know when it would be, but the knowledge of it was a burden she would not add to the ones Jermayan already carried.

"At the proper time," she said. "That time will come, and we will both know when it is. That much I promise you."

"Then I will take your promise," Jermayan said. "And only remind you of it on those occasions when you say to me that it is the Elves who delay when matters could profitably proceed with more . . . swiftness."

⁓

BY the time everything was ready, it had been dark for several hours, but by now Ancaladar had made this flight several times, and he assured Jermayan that even with the additional burden, he did not mind flying at night.

"Besides," the dragon told Cilarnen, "you won't be able to see the ground that way."

"I think that's probably best," the young High Mage said nervously. He didn't look at all pleased with the idea of going up into the sky, though the others knew he had gotten a dragon's eye view of the ground many times with his magick.

Of course, it was different if you were actually there.

"I am afraid the flight will be neither smooth nor short," Ancaladar went on, sounding concerned for his young passenger's nerves, "yet the weather will get no better over the next several days."

"I'm not complaining," Cilarnen said, with stubborn bravery. "I'm just not going to enjoy it. But I'm sure you'll get me there alive and safe. Just don't expect me to be of any use to anybody for a few hours after we land."

"Well in that case," said Idalia, who had come prepared, "you might as well drink this. It's a sleeping cordial. I don't think you'll actually sleep, of course, but it might take the edge off. Don't worry, there's not a drop of magic in it, just herbs and a touch of dream-honey."

She held out the tiny glass vial to him. Cilarnen drained it quickly, without a single word of complaint.

Mirqualirel had provided six baskets, as many as Ancaladar could carry attached to his flying harness. The other four had already been packed with what they were taking with them, most of it Cilarnen's supplies, all of the pieces thickly-wrapped, most of them first in bespelled silk, and then in leather. Now Vestakia helped Cilarnen into one of the two remaining baskets and assisted him as he pulled the straps tight. Once he was secure, she climbed quickly into her own.

"I feel like a basket of cheeses set to go to market," she commented as Jermayan checked her straps.

Idalia was settling into the saddle behind Jermayan's, pulling her own belts tight. If the journey was to be as cold and bumpy as Ancaladar claimed, she wanted to run no risk of falling out.

⤔

AFTER Jermayan left that morning, Kellen turned to the work he had come here to do.

The secondary entrances to Halacira must be sealed. Later, the passages could be filled in from within by quarried stone, but for now, wooden doors would serve. He set Artenel to the task of designing them, and sent work-parties into the forest to fell the trees that would be needed, with others to guard them. Felling trees was hard work in winter, but it must be done.

Still other parties were sent out as scouts, to make sure the area was clear of enemies. After his experience in Halacira, Kellen took nothing for granted.

They would need a bridge to cross the Angarussa as well, as soon as Artenel could build one, for the Wildmages' work beneath the earth had shattered the river's thick covering of ice, and the river ran freely in its bed. There was no safe passage across it now. The only bridge across the river lay several miles closer to Sentarshadeen, and it was a narrow one, unsuitable for cavalry or wagons. To get to Sentarshadeen from Halacira now, he would have to take the forest road—or fly.

Which meant, Kellen realized with an inward sigh, that when Keirasti arrived with her troops in a sennight, they would be trapped on the other side of the river.

Maybe Jermayan could build them a bridge.

He thought of the power Jermayan could command as an Elven Mage—magic bordering on the unbelievable. Surely there had been Elven Mages in the Great War?

If there had been, why had the Demons ever gotten as far as *They* had?

He had no idea.

He did his best to delegate as much as he could, wishing with all his heart that Adaerion were here—or Belepheriel. As soon as Vestakia arrived and the caverns were pronounced clean of Taint, he had to go on to Sentarshadeen to see Andoreniel, and that meant leaving someone else in charge here—but who? Redhelwar had sent him out with a force of sub-commanders of his own rank; though all of them were decades, many of them centuries, older than he was, none of them had a Knight-Mage's intuitive ability to command an army in the field. If they were attacked . . .

If there is any possibility of that, you cannot go.

He could not abandon his command to danger simply because he thought he had something better to do.

Then Idalia will have to do it for me, he thought grimly. *And Vestakia. And Jermayan. And Cilarnen.*

It was why he'd called for them, after all.

❧

WHEN he'd given every order he could think of to give, Kellen took Isinwen and twenty others and went down into the caverns again. Of his own twelve, Ambanire, Nironoshan, Seheimith, and Sihemand had perished in the caverns; he would have to go over the rolls and reorganize several commands. He wanted to talk to Shalkan about that—not because he thought the unicorn would have any particular ideas about troop formation, but just because talking to his friend always helped to clear his head. When they had been on the march, it had not often been possible to find the time—or the place—to talk safely with Shalkan, but here at Halacira, things were different, and Kellen intended to take full advantage of that, for what small comfort it could give him.

One of Master Belesharon's favorite sayings had always been that a commander of armies lived in a city of distance, and more and more these days Kellen was starting to understand what that meant. He was the one who had to make the decisions. There was no one else who could. And nobody he could share them with. He could ask for advice, and even take it, but the final responsibility for every decision was his.

As much as he hated the comparison, he supposed it was a little like being High Mage of Armethalieh.

❧

THE caves were still very damp, and in places there were pools of water on the floors, but now that the series of dams and pumps that the Shadowed Elves had built had been smashed, most of the water had drained back into the bed of the

Angarussa. Much of the Coldfire that the Wildmages had cast on the walls of the main galleries still glowed, and Kellen added more where he could, though he still felt the aftereffects of the spell he'd cast the day before to break down the dam-wall the Shadowed Elves had built. Still, Coldfire was a simple spell, one that asked little more than a payment of personal energy on the part of the Wildmage.

They inspected as much of the cave as they could, cautiously exploring the lower levels. Those, too, were damp but free of standing water, and Kellen's spell-sight enabled them to stay out of the areas where the rock was now dangerously unstable. He'd had the foresight to bring chalk, and marked those places when he came to them, as Artenel would certainly want to know.

There was so much to do here.

There was so much to do *everywhere*—and all of it vital.

If they held off the Enemy until Planting—six moonturns from now, as Kellen reckoned the Elven calendar—Halacira would have to be ready to welcome refugees. The Allies wouldn't fight if it meant abandoning their families to the Enemy, and even if Fortress Halacira were largely symbolic, it would keep them going now.

A few moonturns ago you would have thought something like that was dishonest, Kellen realized. Building a fortress—holding out a hope of safety—that he thought would never be used.

Now he only thought of it as a practical way to keep the army going.

And they'd use it if they could.

He just didn't think they'd get the chance.

What am I becoming?

He knew what he was becoming.

A Commander of Armies.

❧

BY the time Kellen had finished his preliminary survey of the caverns and returned to the surface, the sun was setting. Jermayan had not yet arrived. Kellen dismissed his men to a well-earned rest, heard brief reports from his commanders, stuffed his tunic with meat-pasties and honey-disks, and took a covered mug of tea out beyond the horse-lines to think.

"Are we having fun yet?" Shalkan asked, joining him.

Kellen drained his mug in a few gulps—it was almost cold, anyway—and sat down on a nearby pile of logs. It looked as if Artenel's men had managed to fell a good part of the forest today, which was just as well. He knew the Elves hated to do it, preferring to harvest trees only according to a careful plan, but right now they needed a lot of timber in a hurry.

He dug in his tunic for the honey-disks, and offered them to Shalkan.

"Sure we are," he said unconvincingly.

"You did the best you could," Shalkan reminded him.

"I know," Kellen said. "Jermayan says that Andoreniel's . . . sick."

"So Ancaladar told me."

"All *They* have to do is take the City—finish taking the City. And sit back and wait while the plagues wipe us out. Even before I left, Redhelwar heard it was starting to take hold in the High Reaches. Not just among the Mountainfolk, but in the forests. That means it will reach the Wildlander granaries soon, if it hasn't already. And the herds."

"I know," Shalkan said.

"And I'm sitting here thinking about how to reorganize the units that took losses at Halacira."

"That has to be done, too," the unicorn said inarguably.

"And building a fortress nobody will ever use."

Shalkan rested his chin on Kellen's shoulder. "Are you sure?" The unicorn's breath was warm in Kellen's ear. It smelled of honey.

"I'm sure it has to be done anyway," Kellen said with a long sigh. He reached up to stroke Shalkan's neck.

"Then do it. No one can see all of the future. Only their own part in it. And . . . Wait." Shalkan looked up, gazing at something Kellen couldn't see.

"They're coming."

⋙

WHEN he'd left that morning, Jermayan had lit the landing-grove with Cold-fire. Beneath their coverings of snow, the trees at the edges of the clearing glowed an eerie spectral blue, as if they were not honest wood and greenneedle leaf, but some strange glass copy made by the Elves and set in their place.

Which was not, considering what Kellen knew of the Elves, something he wasn't entirely certain he'd never see.

The Coldfire rendered the grove nearly as bright as day, and made the clearing easy for Ancaladar to find.

By the time Kellen rode into the clearing on Firareth, leading a string of horses—he'd gone back to get mounts for the new arrivals, and tell Isinwen to make arrangements to send a baggage cart, as it would have been a long walk in the night cold otherwise—the four of them had already dismounted. Vestakia was on her knees in the snow, hugging Shalkan, while Jermayan and Idalia hung back, giving Shalkan the space he needed to approach Vestakia in comfort.

They were supporting Cilarnen between them.

"Is he all right?" Kellen asked.

"Doesn't like to fly," Idalia said, doing her best to suppress a smile. "I gave him a soothing cordial."

"I am *never* doing that again," Cilarnen said fervently, raising his head with an effort. His speech sounded slurred. "If we were meant to fly, there would be spells for it. I'm sorry, Ancaladar, but I am *not* a dragon."

"I take no offense, Cilarnen," the dragon said kindly. "Many people do not like to fly."

"I am so glad you're all right, Kellen," Vestakia said, getting to her feet and brushing snow from her knees. She walked over to Kellen. "And I'm glad you won't have to fight the Shadowed Elves anymore. I tried so hard to find out what you needed to know in time!"

"Well I think they're all gone now," he said soothingly. "But I won't mind having a second opinion. Maybe tomorrow you can go down and look around. The caves are safe in most areas."

He'd spoken without really looking at her, as he'd trained himself to do. But there was something . . . different . . . in her voice, and without thinking he took a good look at her face.

She looked . . . old.

No, not old. *Haggard.* Worn, feverish, her cat-gold eyes with their slitted pupils blazing bright with fever—or the edge of madness.

For an instant he forgot his Mageprice, the battle, everything but taking her away somewhere where she'd be *safe*—

Shalkan cleared his throat.

Kellen stepped back.

No.

"We'd better get back to camp," he said.

VESTAKIA rode behind Cilarnen, helping him stay in the saddle. Jermayan had remained behind to oversee the unpacking—Cilarnen had refused to leave until he had been told that his precious baskets would be removed just as they were and transported to his tent untouched.

"I think I would rather travel with an entire Ladies' Academy than one High Mage," Idalia scolded him, once the three of them were heading in the direction of camp.

"Wildmage Idalia, you would rather not travel with a High Mage at all," Cilarnen corrected her grandly. "We are most inconvenient."

"But sometimes useful," Idalia said. "As long as you don't try to do too much."

Cilarnen waved that aside.

Kellen thought that Cilarnen must have been doing far too much, Elemental power-source or not. He looked to be as exhausted as Vestakia did, and his condition could not be entirely accounted for by the effects of whatever Idalia had dosed him with.

He'd said the magick he was working with was dangerous—to him.

How dangerous?

And would it matter? They needed all the help they could get right now.

No matter the cost.

With a day's warning of their arrival—and the knowledge that, on dragonback, they would of necessity be traveling light—Kellen had been able to assemble accommodations that provided not only shelter, but clothing and other basic necessities as well. He'd set aside an entire tent for Cilarnen's use, and helped Idalia and Vestakia settle him in. Cilarnen refused everything but a cup of heavily-sweetened tea.

"I promise you, Idalia, I'll eat an entire roast ox in the morning, so long as Kellen doesn't need any spells cast."

"Not tomorrow," Kellen said. He thought Idalia might slay him on the spot if he said anything else.

"Fine," Cilarnen said, thrusting the empty mug back at her, and throwing himself down in his blankets. "Now go away."

"Ah, the courtly manners of Armethalieh," Idalia said mockingly. But her voice was gentle.

"He seems very tired," Kellen said, when the three of them stood outside Cilarnen's tent.

"You don't look that much better," Idalia said tartly. "But yes. He's been wearing himself to a frazzle doing all that Redhelwar asks of him—and more. But let's go somewhere warm where we can talk. I think you need to know about Nerendale."

When the three of them were gathered together in Kellen's tent, she told him about the night Cilarnen had seen the massacre at Nerendale.

"The Bounds stop our scrying, but they cannot keep a High Mage out. Cilarnen has been able to look into Armethalieh, and tell us what goes on there. *They* are raiding freely within the Bounds—after what happened at Nerendale, you may be certain Cilarnen stays away from *Them*, but it's not hard to figure out from listening to the Council sessions—and he's been doing quite a bit of that. 'Lord' Anigrel has convinced the Arch-Mage that Wildmages are responsible for every single death."

"How close is Anigrel to taking down the City Wards?" Kellen asked.

"Cilarnen says they're more complicated than Anigrel thought. He thinks they've been seriously tampered with, but that the Demons still can't cross the City walls physically. He says something about the Light Itself working to Heal the wards."

Kellen shook his head. "Maybe he can explain it to me, but I doubt it. It would be nice if it were true. If *They* can't get in, *They* can't get their hands on the High Mages. Or the rest of the people."

"Unless *They* make them come out," Idalia said.

"Or someone orders them to come out, the way they were ordered to go to Nerendale," Kellen said. "But I don't think *They'll* risk doing anything in sight of the walls. As much as I loathe them, the High Mages do remember . . . *Them*. If the High Mages knew who Anigrel *really* served, who their real enemy was, I don't think they'd sit by tamely and let him hand them over to *Them*."

"So they're safe—or almost safe—for now," Idalia said. "I never thought I'd be glad of that."

There was a jingle of bells outside the tent.

"Enter and be welcome," Kellen said automatically.

Jermayan walked in, shaking the snow from his cloak, and settled himself beside Idalia.

"Cilarnen's baskets reside with Cilarnen. You will have to await the morning to retrieve your medicines, Idalia, for I fear I would rather face an Enclave of Shadowed Elves than hear what I would hear did I tamper with his spellbooks."

Despite the gravity of the situation, Kellen smiled. He could imagine as well as Jermayan could what Cilarnen's reaction would be, though it baffled Kellen what possible harm could come of just touching the volumes. It was not, after all, as if they had any innate magic—unlike, say, a Wildmage's Three Books.

"And now," Idalia said, breaking into his thoughts, "maybe you'd like to tell us why we're here? Vestakia's here because of the caverns, and she needed Jermayan to get her here, but Cilarnen isn't going to be that much use to you as far as I can imagine here, and do you really need another Healer?"

"No," Kellen said. "I need you to go to Sentarshadeen, and tell me if there's anything that Cilarnen can do there. So that means you and Jermayan and Ancaladar. Of your courtesy, Jermayan."

"It is my pleasure," Jermayan said. He paused for a moment, sipping tea. "Redhelwar has told me all that you gave Keirasti to tell him."

Kellen nodded, understanding the oblique remark. Idalia and Vestakia looked puzzled. Obviously Jermayan had not shared the news with them.

"I think that's enough plain speaking for now," Kellen said slowly. If they spoke of the matter any further here, it would be all over the camp in a matter of minutes. Tent walls were thin, and Elven ears were sharp. Even if nobody spoke of the matter openly—and the rituals of Elven politeness would ensure that—they'd still all know.

"Then let it remain so," Jermayan agreed.

"I suppose you'll explain things eventually," Idalia muttered darkly.

"Tomorrow," Jermayan promised. "Upon the wing."

"But aren't you going with them, Kellen?" Vestakia asked, obviously puzzled.

"Ancaladar can only carry one passenger," Jermayan said. "And Kellen must remain to give orders to the army. If there is true need of his presence, or Cilarnen's, in Sentarshadeen, I will leave Idalia there and return."

It was a hard choice, but Kellen knew it was the right one for him to have made.

"There's just one thing I'd like you to do for me before you go," Kellen said.

"It would be interesting to discover what that thing might be, should you wish to tell it," Jermayan answered, both his tone and his words overly-formal to the point of subtle Elven humor.

"Build me a bridge, of your courtesy," Kellen responded in the same vein.

Twelve

To Build a Bridge

THE FOLLOWING MORNING, Kellen, Jermayan, and Ancaladar stood at the edge of the Angarussa.

Kellen had explained what he needed: a stone bridge, suitable for cavalry and heavy carts. By the time Keirasti got here, the bridge would be covered with snow and probably ice as well, so the sledge-wagons should pass over it easily enough.

He'd almost thought Jermayan would refuse flat out.

"Kellen, there has *never* been a bridge over the Angarussa here," the Elven Knight said, shaking his head.

Idalia had made a small sound of exasperation, throwing up her hands. "Perhaps you will tell Keirasti that, when she arrives, Jermayan. I'm sure that will impress her."

"A bridge of ice—" Jermayan had suggested.

"Isn't strong enough. Will melt in the spring. Won't handle the traffic to the caverns once they've been turned into a fortress," Kellen had pointed out, sounding exasperated.

"Beloved, it is time to try new things," Ancaladar had said gently, settling the matter. "I am sure it will be a fine bridge."

"Very well," Jermayan said, acknowledging defeat. "I should know better than to argue with a dragon."

"Indeed you should," Ancaladar agreed. "Riddles are far more effective."

THERE was an interested party of observers standing a little distance away, including Vestakia, Idalia, and Cilarnen. Jermayan walked to the very edge of the river, gazing down into the water.

The edges had begun to freeze, though it would be moonturns yet before the whole river froze again. As Kellen and Ancaladar watched, Jermayan paced back and forth through the snow, his eyes half-closed, until Kellen began to wonder if anything were ever going to happen at all.

Suddenly the air began to shimmer.

Beneath their feet, the ice creaked and groaned as it split. Kellen jumped back out of the way. The mantle of snow and ice had been pushed upward several inches in a wide fan extending several dozen yards in every direction on this side of the river, as if by something suddenly appearing beneath.

Stone began to form in the air.

At first it was like fog, and Kellen doubted his eyes. But no, it was truly there, growing outward from this side of the river, low and wide enough for two ox-carts to cross side-by-side. As the fog drifted out over the river, the parts at the near bank became solid; Kellen could see that Jermayan's bridge was made of granite.

There was a subtle pattern of river currents etched into the stone, mimicking the currents beneath. The texturing of the stone would also keep the granite from becoming too slippery in the rain, of course; the Elves were nothing if not practical.

More fog swirled up, forming a railing along the sides of the bridge. Tall river rushes, a leaping fish silhouetted against them, here an angular river-bird—Kellen knew without being told that its long beak was meant to hold a lantern to light the bridge in the dark—there an otter, jumping up in play to snatch at a hovering dragonfly . . .

In moments, the fog-turned-stone had reached the far side of the river. There was another crackling and buckling of ice as it sunk stone roots deep into the earth on the far side.

Kellen regarded the result in awe.

It was a bridge that looked like . . . water.

But the more he gazed at it, the less it looked as though it belonged here. Unlike every other creation of the Elves', it did not fit. It seemed as if it intruded on the landscape, instead of growing out of it. It demanded the attention immediately, instead of revealing itself slowly, in a series of unexpected yet pleasant surprises.

It was . . . intrusive.

Jermayan took a deep breath and opened his eyes.

Kellen turned to him and bowed, very deeply.

"I think you've won the argument," he said. "A bridge does not belong here. But we need one. And it *is* beautiful."

Jermayan regarded the bridge, obviously still unreconciled to it.

"Perhaps, some day, it can be swept away again," he said.

"I believe it is time to go," Ancaladar said.

⁂

THE flight to Sentarshadeen was short—a good thing, as the heavy weather that the Wildmages had predicted was already starting to set in. This far to the south and west, the snow was wetter and heavier than what they had been used to north of the Mystrals; even on the short flight, it caked both Idalia and Jermayan's flying-furs, until they resembled snow-figures.

On the journey, Jermayan at last told her the contents of the message that Keirasti had brought to Redhelwar.

"Leaf and Star," Idalia groaned, after sitting a long time in silence. "Jermayan, this is . . . This is the *worst* possible time. . . ."

"Yes," Jermayan answered simply.

There was no need to say anything more.

⁂

ANCALADAR landed near the house of Leaf and Star. A curious herd of unicorns, their coats fluffed out against the cold and caked with falling snow, quickly gathered at a safe distance to observe this interesting sight.

Once they had dismounted, Jermayan quickly unbuckled the straps of Ancaladar's flying harness. There was no point in making his friend wear the saddle any more than he had to, and there was no way of telling how long they would be staying.

"I shall go off to my den," Ancaladar said once that had been accomplished. "Perhaps there will be . . . food . . . soon," he added hopefully.

"I shall bring you bullocks from my herd as soon as I can," Jermayan promised. He hefted the saddle to his shoulder; though it was comparatively light, it was bulky, and he was glad it was only a short walk to the House of Leaf and Star.

"Then I shall leave you now," Ancaladar said. He rose to his feet and trotted away. The unicorns followed, pacing him until he took off.

Jermayan and Idalia gazed up at the House of Leaf and Star.

"At the very least, I'd say they know we're coming," Idalia said, hefting the strap of her medicine chest higher onto her shoulder.

THE door was opened by an Elf that Idalia could not remember having seen at the House of Leaf and Star before. Taranarya was a textile weaver—some of her designs covered the cushions and pillows in the guesthouse that had been given to Idalia and Kellen when they had first come to Sentarshadeen.

It seemed like a very long time ago.

"I See you, Taranarya," Idalia said.

Taranarya regarded the two of them as if they had just sprouted directly out of the ground.

"We have come to see Andoreniel," Idalia added, when Taranarya did not say anything.

It was, of course, perfectly possible—and within the scope of the complex code of Elven Manners—for Taranarya not to "see" Idalia, and simply close the door in her face. But though technically that was permissible, it very rarely happened in practice.

"I See you, Idalia," Taranarya said at last. "I See you, Jermayan," she added. There was a pause. "Be welcome in this house and find comfort at our hearth." She opened the door wider and stepped back.

It was quite the most grudging welcome Idalia had ever received among the Elves, but Taranarya probably did not wish to admit there was sickness in the House of Leaf and Star—though anyone who could not guess why she was here instead of her cousin Talminonil was thick-witted at best. Talminonil had served in the House of Leaf and Star since before any of Idalia's grandparents had met. She hoped that Talminonil was . . . well, that things weren't as bad with Talminonil as they could possibly be.

Taranarya conducted them to the Room of Fire and Water. By the time they'd reached it, two more servants had arrived to take their heavy outer clothing and Ancaladar's saddle.

The Room of Fire and Water was one of the formal receiving chambers of the House of Leaf and Star, and as such, had been designed to be as much to be a work of art as simply a place where guests were welcomed. As the name implied, the room was designed to be a marriage of fire and water. At one end of the room was an enormous fireplace in the shape of a red-gold dragon, whose enormous tile wings covered the entire wall of the room. At this season, the dragon-hearth naturally contained a well-built fire, and the flames leaped and danced in the dragon's belly.

Of course, the dragon did not bear a great deal of resemblance to an actual dragon. It was much too round and cheerful—something the Elven artisan who had designed the room was undoubtedly aware of. And real dragons certainly didn't breathe fire, or carry furnaces in their bellies. But dragons certainly did radiate heat, just as this dragon-hearth was doing, so in that sense, the symbolism was quite accurate.

At the opposite end of the room there was a fountain, and here the room's colors were deep vivid turquoise and violet, the intense saturated hues a perfect complement to the red-golds and vermilions that surrounded the dragon. Here, a column of water bubbled high into the air, falling back into itself and down into its catchbasin. The glittering motes of color caught within the water were tiny fish-shapes, all made of glass, for living fish would not have been at all happy living in that turbulent water.

The walls between the fountain and the hearth were covered with a mosaic—Elvenware seashells mixed with natural ones at the fountain end, glass tiles at the hearth end—in which the two sets of opposite colors reached out and blended together in perfect harmony, like a vibrant sunset.

"I shall bring tea," Taranarya said. It was obvious that she felt that the room's elaborate beauty would occupy them for some time.

"We have come on the wings of the wind," Jermayan said urgently. "And so our words enter the realms of suitable discourse like summer storms into an orchard, tossing the boughs about and shaking loose the fruit. Yet I believe it is with cause, for I know that which you do not wish to relate. Kellen has told me what he has learned from Rochinuviel, and so you must understand that we already know much of what has happened within these walls. I beg you, do not delay us."

Taranarya regarded him as if he had shouted curses at her. It might not seem so on the battlefield, but to the ears of a gently-bred Elven artisan, this was plain speaking indeed, and it was obvious Taranarya had never heard anything like it in all the years of her long life. She stared at Jermayan for a long moment in shock, then curtseyed deeply and rushed as quickly as she could—without seeming to—from the room.

Jermayan and Idalia looked at each other.

"That certainly went well," Idalia said, after a moment.

"Perhaps we should have brought Kellen with us, to apply his courtly manners," Jermayan said ironically. "But I would truly feel more serene were I to know at once of the health of Andoreniel's Counselors, and have speech of them, and that is a thing neither cups of tea nor sweet cakes can provide."

"I see that Kellen's influence has been pervasive indeed," Idalia said, though she shared his feelings.

If Andoreniel was as ill as Kellen had implied, in Ashaniel's absence the Elven Council was all that was left to govern the Nine Cities. Tyendimarquen, Morusil, Ainalundore, Dargainon, and Sorvare had advised Andoreniel for centuries. Morusil and Ainalundore, at least, had advised Andorieniel's father Arinaldariel before him.

If all of them were sick, or dead . . .

But to Idalia's immense relief, before she and Jermayan actually came to the point of searching the House of Leaf and Star themselves for answers, Taranarya returned, bringing Morusil—and, inevitably, a large wheeled cart covered with savory dishes—with her.

The oldest of Andoreniel's Counselors leaned heavily upon a carved wooden staff as he walked into the room, and his steps were slow and hesitant. He seemed to have aged several centuries since Idalia had seen him last, though it had only been a handful of moonturns, and his ivory-pale skin was now marred with the ugly purple scars of plague.

"You should not be out of bed!" Idalia gasped, rising to her feet to help him to a chair near the fire.

Morusil chuckled faintly. "My dear Idalia, the Shadow's Kiss rested on me very lightly indeed, and that some sennights ago. Indeed, I was considering participating in the Winter Running Dance this year, for the first time in quite some time. But come. I am sure that you have news for me, and I will tell you what I can. Meanwhile, surely there is time to eat and drink." He raised a hand—though he was dressed in Council robes, he wore no rings, for they would have fit him far too loosely now—and Taranarya curtseyed once more and departed, closing the door to the Room of Fire and Water behind her.

They settled beside him around the fire, and Idalia laid out the tea-things upon the table, for despite his protests, Morusil looked far from well. Out of respect for his years, Idalia poured tea while Jermayan prepared them all plates from the—rather hearty—selection of delicacies.

Nevertheless, Morusil came quickly enough to the point.

"You come in a good hour, Idalia, for the Shadow's Kiss lies heavily upon us here. My old comrade Ainalundore has gone to the trees, and Sorvare with her. Only Tyendimarquen, Dargainon, and I remain, and . . . we do not know if Dargainon will recover. As yet, Tyendimarquen has not fallen ill, thanks be to the grace of Leaf and Star. But Andoreniel has not been so fortunate."

"That much Kellen has told us," Jermayan said. "He sent us here from Halacira, where he has destroyed the last of the Enclaves of the Shadowed Elves. Redhelwar follows, to await orders at Ondoladeshiron. Artenel prepares the caverns to become a fortress, for if we are to shelter the women and children of the Wild Lands, we must have shelter to offer them."

Morusil nodded. "It is a plan that contains both good and ill within it, yet I do not see how we can abandon our friends and Allies. Still, I would give much to know how Kellen intends them to reach this shelter. The unicorns tell us that travel will be impossible in the Wildlands until after Kindling, at best; in the High Reaches, it may be late spring, or later. And that is only without considering fear of attack. Yet I know that *Their* creatures already roam the Elven Lands and fill the Lost Lands."

"And Tyendimarquen believes the best course of action is to sit and do nothing," Idalia guessed, "and let everyone who isn't an Elf fend for themself. Well, it's too late for that. Lerkelpoldara has been completely destroyed. Deskethomaynel and Windalorianan have been evacuated, and the survivors have regrouped at Ysterialpoerin. The Shadowed Elves may have brought Coldwarg, Deathwings, and a few other things in through their caves and past the wards, but if the wards in the north haven't already fallen, they're going to fall *soon*, and then you'll have Ice Trolls and Frost Giants here. They move slowly, and they have a mountain range or two to cross, but they'll reach Ysterialpoerin eventually, and then they'll destroy it just as the Coldwarg and serpentmarae did Lerkelpoldara. Only they'll wipe out three cities, not one."

"And should you tell him so, Tyendimarquen will insist the army return to defend Ysterialpoerin to the last Knight," Morusil said, seemingly undaunted by the catalogue of disasters that Idalia related to him. "Yet Redhelwar already knows the threat they face, and he has left them."

"There is plague at Ysterialpoerin, just as there is here," Jermayan said. "So far, by the Grace of Leaf and Star, it has not spread to the army, and Redhelwar wishes to preserve his force. Further, Kindolhinadetil can only feed so many, and the refugees are a great tax upon his reserves. It was thought wise to bring the army to the War City instead."

"It would please me greatly were I to be allowed to know why it was Redhelwar chose to do such a thing," Morusil said mildly.

"Kellen suggested it," Idalia said bluntly.

"Then it is the Wild Magic which guides Redhelwar. I find no fault in that, though no doubt Tyendimarquen will try hard to raise some objection. It troubles me that Ysterialpoerin is left undefended, however."

"Kellen believes—and it has been shown to be the truth—that *They* are attempting to draw our forces in many directions at once, scattering us so that we may be more easily destroyed, while *They* gain the power *They* need to launch *Their* final attack upon us. Though we now know what *They* mean to do, without Andoreniel . . ." Idalia shrugged helplessly.

"The King must live, so that he can rule," Morusil said. "There is no one in Sentarshadeen—indeed, in all the Elven Lands—who would not give up their life for his. All our arts have only held the Shadow's Kiss at bay, for it rests as heavily upon him as it has upon anyone I have seen. Can you, with your powers of healing, do more, Idalia?"

"I can try, Morusil. Fond as I am of Tyendimarquen's optimism and good cheer, I do not think he should speak for the Elves this year," Idalia said.

"Nor do I. In times of peace, his good counsel provides excellent balance. But a balance is composed of many sides."

"I have brought several remedies with me," Idalia said. "We have had some success with them at Ysterialpoerin. And perhaps there will be more that I can do."

For all our sakes, I hope there is.

⮒

ANDORENIEL'S bedchamber was draped in green silk, giving the room the shadowy likeness of a summer forest. A small stove kept the air warm.

If one had survived the plague, Idalia knew, it was still possible to get it—or the other disease—again, though surviving it once seemed to grant a certain resistance to it.

No one who got it a second time survived.

Idalia asked Morusil to wait outside Andoreniel's bedchamber, something the aged Elf seemed ready to do in any event, out of simple common sense. Two Elves in the simple leaf-green robes of Elven Healers sat by Andoreniel's bedside. Idalia recognized both of them from her own stay in the Elven House of Healing. Their names were Volcilintra and Nelirtil, and they were both Master Healers, with centuries of practice at their craft.

"Idalia," Volcilintra said, rising to her feet and coming toward the door. "By the grace of Leaf and Star, you come in a good hour!"

Idalia bowed. The Healers could be nearly as direct as Elven Knights when it suited their purposes. "I wish I did not see you again under such circumstances, Volcilintra."

"Ah, Idalia, we all wish circumstances were other than they were." She glanced at the box Idalia carried beneath her arm. "Perhaps your medicines will have more effect than mine."

"How long has he lain ill?" Idalia asked.

"The fever came ten sennights ago," Volcilintra said. "The Shadow's Kiss had already descended upon Sentarshadeen, though at first we did not see many cases. Now more than half the people are ill, though as yet few have died. We dare not use the House of Healing to treat the cases any longer, for fear of the

Quick Plague that sometimes follows. We have taken a district of the city and made it into our healing place, and keep those who are ill as far apart from one another as we can."

"Yes. We found that to work in Ysterialpoerin," Idalia agreed.

"At first Andoreniel thought nothing of his fever, for there was much to do, and few hands to do it. But a fortnight later the bruising began to appear, and then we knew the nature of his illness. Since then, all we can do has only kept him in life."

They kept their voices low, but Idalia did not worry about wakening Andoreniel. He was far too ill to be awakened, even if she had shouted at the top of her lungs.

Two moonturns since the bruising had appeared. Yet in all the other cases Idalia had seen, the plague ran its course—for good or ill—in less than one. Sometimes much less.

The Healers were very skilled. And Andoreniel was very strong.

Idalia approached the bed and turned back the light coverlet gently.

Andoreniel looked as if he had been severely beaten. His body was wasted; veins and tendons stood out clearly against the bone, and his ribs could be seen plainly. His chest rose and fell with slow, effortful breaths.

Along his neck and arms, spreading along the jaw and extending over his body in the pattern she had come to recognize, the livid purple weals of the plague stood out sharply against his pale skin in winged patterns. No wonder the Elves had named it Shadow's Kiss.

She set down her box beside the bed and opened it.

"Will he drink?" she asked, taking out a vial of brown liquid.

"It is difficult," Volcilintra said. "But we manage," she added simply.

"You must give him this. One vial every six—no, four hours. And there is a salve. Rub it into his skin where you can." The bruised areas were delicate, and the skin there could quickly rupture and bleed at a rough touch. Death followed quickly when that happened. "I will prepare an infusion of herbs. You must wash him with it." She emptied her box. She had brought all of the plague medicine they could spare from Ysterialpoerin, but she wasn't sure it was enough. "I will need a place to prepare more."

"Nelirtil will conduct you," Volcilintra said, drawing the coverlet back up over Andoreniel. "I had thought, perhaps, a spell of the Wild Magic . . ."

"Each of these is infused with the power of the Wild Magic," Idalia told the Elven Healer. "We have tried direct Healing on the plague victims at Ysterialpoerin. It does not work."

THE time had nearly come.

Once again Savilla descended to the Black Chamber.

With each passing day in the World Above, the veil between it and the majesty of He Who Is thinned further. For the first time in uncounted centuries, her creatures, her subject races, walked openly through the Elven Lands, searing the very ground beneath their feet to sterile stone.

The nursery of her creations—that place which the Wildmages had called the Lost Lands—was truly lost once more. Nothing remained but rock and ice and darkness. Zyperis had enjoyed a fine hunt, scouring the land of those fools who had chosen to remain behind, paving the way for her creatures to claim, once again, lands they had lost a thousand years before.

It was good, but it was not enough.

Only a few sacrifices remained, until the bounds were broken, and He Who Is could walk the world once more. This was one of the last.

It would be painful beyond words for her, but it was necessary. Already his power grew, adding strength to the blights and torments she had released upon the Children of the Light, rendering the Wild Magic weak and ineffectual. When He Who Is walked the world once more in truth, the power of the Wild Magic would be gone forever.

Behind her, two of the Lesser Endarkened followed, dragging a unicorn in a sack. Its legs had been broken, and its eyes and tongue had been gouged from its head—these things done by one of the Mage-men that Zyperis had brought her. The Mage-man had acted in exchange for clemency and freedom, but Savilla had no intention of granting either.

The unicorn's whimpers of agony soothed her nerves as she contemplated what lay ahead. This was a delicate time, for after this sacrifice she would be weak. It was good, then, that she had sent Zyperis to the High Reaches to enjoy himself. Her son was young, and—as yet—easily distracted. She did not intend to take him fully into her confidence just yet.

Perhaps not ever.

The Lesser Endarkened gazed curiously about themselves as they entered the Black Chamber. They were the lesser children of He Who Is: wingless, where Savilla and her kind had great ribbed wings; tailless, or with short stubby tails, where those of the Greater Endarkened were long and barbed; hooved where their brethren had long elegant feet with talon-tipped toes. Their skin was often rough or scaled as well, usually ebony instead of the clear pulsing ruby usually found among the Greater Endarkened, and they often had barbed crests and dorsal ridges instead of exquisite curling horns.

Still, they were Savilla's children as well, and had their own place in her dominion.

And today they would serve her to the ultimate of their ability.

The cavern hummed with the power of the many sacrifices she had offered to it in the past hundred cycles of her Rising, and they could sense that.

It would be the last thing either of them ever sensed.

They opened the sack and dumped its contents on the floor. The unicorn writhed weakly upon the stone, blood marring its pale fur.

"Take it and place it upon the spire," Savilla ordered.

The Demons cringed. A living unicorn's horn would kill their kind. To touch one would bring agony. But Savilla knew they would not dare disobey her.

Gasping and whimpering as their flesh bubbled away, the two Lesser Endarkened dragged the screaming, flailing unicorn upright, then lifted it higher. It took all their strength, and the chamber was filled with the burned scent of their flesh by the time they had it poised over the spire.

They let go.

The unicorn screamed as the black glass spire slid through its body. But it was not dead. Not yet.

Waves of its delicious pain washed over Savilla, and the entire chamber vibrated with satisfaction.

The two servants crouched at her feet, mewling with agony.

Savilla reached down and tore their throats out with her hands. Black blood welled over their skin, and they fell to the floor, twitching weakly.

They were not dead, even now. But they would be soon, once she had done what she had come here to do. And their deaths would go to feed the power that would liberate He Who Is.

She bent down and picked up one of the large round stones that littered the floor of the chamber. Dipped it in the blood of one of the writhing Demons.

And struck the spire with all her might.

The spire vibrated, sending forth a high sweet tone that made the entire chamber ring like crystal. The screams of the two Lesser Endarkened and the unicorn blended with the sound, making it richer, fuller.

The Endarkened died first, their bodies turning to liquid in the crystal cry, spreading across the stone and sinking into it.

The unicorn was not so fortunate.

Any creature to die in the vibrations of the Crystal Spire died a death more agonizing than any even the Endarkened themselves, with all their arts, could contrive. The one who struck the spire—and caused the death—shared in every moment of the pain.

That was the price of the spell.

And the death of a unicorn, ultimate embodiment of the Light, whose very body it was agony for one of the Endarkened to touch . . .

Savilla endured as long as she could, but at last the torment drove her to her knees, then upon her face. She groveled in the liquefied bodies of her servants, weeping the thick golden tears of her kind. It was as if she were being unmade. Reduced to humanity. Worse. The agony tore her mind from her, until she no longer understood why she suffered. She did not remember the pain's beginning, and could not believe it would have an end.

But at last—as with all things, save the Endarkened—it was over.

She lay upon the floor of the Black Chamber, too weak to move.

It thrummed with power.

Except for Savilla, the power was the only thing that remained within the walls of living rock. Everything else was gone.

Scoured.

Empty.

Pure.

⤫

A great distance up the narrow path that led to the Black Chamber, Zyperis pressed himself against the wall, shuddering in pain from the echoes of magic. He jerked his head to the side and sunk his fangs into his arm until the blood flowed, but not even that could ease his distress.

He knew what was down here. That was why he had come.

Oh, it was not that he had ever known precisely. But he had known that it was something powerful. Something that his Dearest Mama wished to conceal. Something that required sacrifices, and many of them—he had spies in her household, and even in such a time of plenty as had not been seen in a thousand years, when every Endarkened torture chamber was filled to overflowing and the flesh of slaves graced the tables of even the Lesser Endarkened, the disappearances from Savilla's slave-pens were too great to account for by anything other than the working of great and secret spells.

He had set himself to discover what she was doing.

The capture of a unicorn was a great prize, and he had expected to be invited to witness its torture and destruction. The Mage-men they had taken at Nerendale would be of assistance there—Mama had decreed that they were to be kept alive, and in reasonable health, in case another dragon might be found.

But when the unicorn had not been offered up—and when he had been sent on such a purely *transparent* errand, an entertaining one, but one that any of the nobles of the Court could have as easily accomplished—Zyperis had grown suspicious. What magic could his mother and Queen be working that would involve the death of a unicorn? That her plans neared fruition went without saying, for she could not hope to conceal the creature's disappearance for long.

So he had returned early—disobeying her—and followed her when she slipped away.

He had marked the beginning of the path she took many times, but had never before dared follow her so far along it. Should he be discovered, he would surely be her next sacrifice.

But here the unicorn's magic was his ally, for not only did it mask his own presence, its hateful taint provided a beacon for him to follow.

Never before had he penetrated so deeply into The World Without Sun, and Zyperis had been certain he knew every twist and turn of their vast and beautiful world. Following Savilla, it seemed to him as if he entered another realm entirely—one that promised power, but at a price so high that, even though he did not know what it was, it woke fear in his very bones.

When he heard her speak, he stopped.

And then pain had come. Pain—and terror—and knowledge.

She means to bring He Who Is to walk our world again!

He Who Is would grant them victory over the Children of the Light. His power was unstoppable. The knowledge of Savilla's act should have brought Zyperis great joy.

Except for one thing.

To the one who freed him, He Who Is would grant great favor.

Savilla would be Queen of the Endarkened *forever.*

She would have no successor.

≈

AFTER Jermayan and Idalia had left for Sentarshadeen, Kellen took Vestakia down into the caverns.

This time he took a great many more Knights.

It was not merely that he was concerned about her safety—though Vestakia was an invaluable resource, one they dared not lose—but by now, two days after the battle, the work of refitting Halacira must begin.

Much of the route from the main entrance to the river gallery shimmered with Coldfire now, for the Wildmages had been busy, and they were working quickly to light the lower levels as well. With so many of the side entrances blocked, and soon to be sealed permanently, the cavern air was much more still than it had been when Kellen had first brought his force through here, but Artenel had assured him that there were—or at least had been, before the earth-shaking—many ventilation shafts to the surface, and that he would be able to unblock them within a few sennights.

Of course, each ventilation shaft would present a potential method for the Enemy to gain access to the future Fortress, if not in body, then by poisons, or by small Dark-tainted creatures of their breeding. And Goblins needed no door to enter, being able to pass through solid rock at will.

Artenel would simply have to do the best he could to make the place secure. Perhaps there was something Cilarnen could do to help as well.

⊰⊱

"I am very tired of caves," Vestakia said wistfully, as they descended the wide stairs into the first cavern.

"You will find that these caves are like no others you have ever seen," Isinwen told her proudly. "It is a shame that their beauty must be destroyed, but Artenel will make them a fine home for those who must live beneath the earth."

Kellen ignored both of them. He was concentrating on the caves themselves. And, if truth be told, he was trying not to think of Vestakia at all.

"I don't feel anything yet," she said, her voice bright with relief.

By now the caverns seemed almost as familiar to Kellen as Sentarshadeen or the Wildwoods had become. He and his Knights swept the entry level, carefully checking all the surviving side-galleries. Vestakia exclaimed in wonder at the wall carvings, though much of the finer detail on some of the reliefs was gone now, having simply crumbled away, and in the *xaique* cavern, many of the delicate carved figures lay upon the floor in pieces.

"No . . . nothing," Vestakia said, when they stood upon the edge of the bridge, staring down at the Angarussa. Thanks to Wirance and the other Wildmages, the entire roof of the river-gallery glowed a pale azure now, giving it the odd illusion of being the open sky. For the first time, Kellen could see the details of the ceiling; it had been carefully worked to resemble something crafted of stone blocks and wooden beams, though the whole had been carved out of one piece of cavern rock. If he strained his eyes, he could see the individual blocks of stone, the bolts and plates that held the great rough-hewn beams of "wood" together, and even the subtle grain in the wood, just as if these were beams of ancient oak, worn and shrunken by Time.

Elves did nothing by halves.

"We should go down into the mines themselves, then," Kellen said. "Unless you would rather do that tomorrow?"

"No," Vestakia said with certainty. "I would much rather go to bed tonight knowing I never had to come down here again. It is the most beautiful cave I have ever been in . . . but it is still a cave."

Kellen had only taken a quick tour of the lower levels the previous day, and was grateful he hadn't had to fight down here, for in contrast to the main level, most of the open areas here were about the size of his bedroom back in Sentarshadeen, if that.

Some of them had been carved—apparently with whatever took the fancy of the unknown carver. Others had walls completely smooth, apparently still awaiting the inspiration of unknown hands. In a very few, the wall was rough, and an open vein could be seen within, from which the Coldfire roused faint glitterings, the only proof Kellen had yet come across that Halacira was, indeed, a jewel mine.

Without his Knight-Mage's sense of direction—and the marks he had chalked upon the walls on an earlier visit—he might well have wandered down here forever, for each chamber led into the next with no pattern he could see.

At last they came to an opening in the floor.

Unlike the passage to this level, which had involved a staircase, there was only a wooden ladder leading down through the opening. The ladder was new—Artenel had just built it. The previous one—and Kellen had no doubt one had existed, and perhaps an entire wooden staircase—had been washed away in the flood, as well as whatever machines the Shadowed Elves had assembled.

"This leads to the deep mine," Isinwen said apologetically, indicating the ladder.

"I've been down there," Kellen said. "It's pretty much one big cavern, and as far as I can tell, nothing can get in or out. We don't have Coldlight down there yet, but the ladder's stronger than it looks. Do you think you need to go down, or . . . ?"

Vestakia looked into the pit, and shuddered.

"How large is it?"

"You remember the village cavern at the first Enclave? The one at the bottom of the deep cavern? About that size. Maybe a little bigger."

"Then I should be able to sense anything in it from here."

Nevertheless, she got down on her hands and knees and peered down into the opening, as if she might be able to see something. Kellen shaped a small ball of Coldfire between his hands and sent it drifting past her, down into the cavern below.

Its light gave little illumination. Enough to show that water still lay in pools upon the unfinished rock here, for what Isinwen called the Deep Mine was Halacira as it must have been before the Elves began to improve the caverns. He sent the ball of light swooping and soaring through the darkness as Vestakia concentrated.

"There's nothing," she said at last, sitting back on her heels with a sigh of relief.

※

NOW that the caverns were cleared and guaranteed to be safe, Kellen could turn his mind to other matters. Providing Vestakia with a suitable escort—since she planned to seek out Shalkan—he went to see Cilarnen.

The young High Mage had recovered both from the effects of his first aerial journey, and from Idalia's cordial. Kellen found him in his tent—one of the largest they had brought with them—unpacking his supplies and clucking over each one as if it were a newly-hatched chick.

"Kellen," he said, in obvious pleasure. "Come to seek out the dreaded High Mage in his sanctum?"

"Come to talk," Kellen said. "Providing we can do so privately."

"That, at least, is simply managed," Cilarnen said. "Though I am afraid more complex spells will take another day at least. It is as I feared: My apparatus has been detuned by the flight, and will all have to be reset. But my Wand, at least, is unscathed."

He opened a long bone case—it had, Kellen suspected, originally been crafted as a scroll-case—and removed his wand. He'd done some work on the slender length of ash since Kellen had seen it last: It was now capped at each end with fine silver, and a narrow spiral of silver wrapped its entire length.

He raised it into the air and began to draw, murmuring under his breath. Glowing sigils, each in a dozen colors, appeared in the air and slowly faded. After he had drawn six of them in a circle around them both, he lowered his wand and replaced it in its case.

"There. No one will hear anything we say—or see our shadows, either. Though anyone who walks through the door of the tent will break the spell."

"No one is likely to do that," Kellen said. Anyone coming to the door of Cilarnen's tent, and not receiving an invitation to enter, would simply go away again.

"Then we may speak privately. A useful spell, though a deal more useful, to my mind, in a place with doors that lock. Tea?"

"Since you offer so nicely." Kellen smiled slightly. Apparently Cilarnen had picked up the Elves' habit of accompanying every occasion with tea. "Cilarnen, do you know why you're here?"

Cilarnen shrugged. "You needed me. We left in such a hurry, nobody had time to tell me anything else, and I was too busy packing to ask. But there's something I must tell you, I think.

"You know that Anigrel meddled with my mind before I was Banished and made sure I escaped the Outlaw Hunt. We'd always wondered why. Well, I found out."

Kellen tensed, ever-so-slightly. Cilarnen seemed oblivious.

"He wanted to find you. He knows you are his greatest enemy—or the greatest enemy of that which he serves. He knew that word would reach you, eventually, of a Banished 'High Mage,' alive in the Wild Lands, and we would meet. Perhaps he put a compulsion on me to find you, and the Demon raid just helped things along. Or maybe Kardus helped me because for some reason, your Wild Magic wanted it too. In any event, Anigrel left me my magick because he meant me to kill you with it. I think that's the reason my headaches came back so strongly as soon as I saw you."

"Cilarnen, why are you telling me this?" Kellen asked cautiously. His Knight-Mage powers gave him very little shielding against the sort of magical assault a High Mage could wield. On the other hand, he was physically stronger and faster than Cilarnen.

If it came to a fight.

"Because I looked for his tampering in my mind—and found it. He has no hold over me now," Cilarnen said. "Of that I am certain."

Could Kellen believe this? He wanted to. "Both Shalkan and Vestakia pronounced you free of Taint when you arrived," Kellen pointed out.

"And so I was. And so I am," Cilarnen said. "How do you think Anigrel moved undetected among the City Wards for all those years, yet still conspired with . . . *Them?* Until the very moment the spell saw its best chance of success, and woke into life, I would pass any test you set me. I did not know it myself—but I suspected. How not? Why else would I pass from Anigrel's hands with my Gift intact—unless he foresaw a use for it later?"

Cilarnen's words made sense. And Kellen was inclined to believe him. He would not have mentioned the matter at all—unless he were sure.

"So you are safe from him now?"

"I swear to it by the Light. And that will come as an unwelcome surprise for that upstart carrion-bird very soon, I hope. Kellen, I have scryed within the walls of the City, watched the Council at its deliberations. The Selken grain-ships will not come until spring. There is rationing in the City, and talk of sending the Militia out to seize the farmers' stored provisions. Who knows how many—if any—will survive, if they are sent outside the walls? And Anigrel uses every death to fuel the terror of the Wildmages. I think he hopes to bring Lycaelon to consider . . . an alliance."

"An alliance?" Kellen asked, temporarily diverted from the reason for which he had come. "With whom? He wouldn't let the Elves into the City when Hyandur came; the Armethaliehans think the Centaurs are animals, and—"

"With *Them*," Cilarnen said.

"He can't," Kellen said, aghast. "They can't. They'd never consider it."

"Frighten them enough, and they would," Cilarnen said grimly. "*They* can change *Their* shape to look like anything—I've seen it. If Anigrel tampers with the Wards enough, the High Mages won't have those to warn them. And anybody who disagrees with Anigrel or his Magewardens or Commons Wardens tends to just . . . vanish."

Kellen emitted a low hiss of dismay. This was worse than he'd thought. "You've told Redhelwar all this?"

"Yes, of course, but I'm not sure he completely understands how bad the situation is," Cilarnen said.

Elven emotions were hard for humans to read at the best of times. It was just as likely that Redhelwar understood *exactly* how bad the situation in Armethalieh was getting, and Cilarnen simply didn't realize it.

But it made getting to Armethalieh more imperative than ever.

By now the kettle on the tea-brazier was bubbling violently. Cilarnen busied himself for a moment in preparing the pot, scooping in several measures of Armethaliehan Black and setting out two tall mugs that Kellen recognized as coming from his own supplies.

"It's worse than you think," Kellen said. "The reason you're here is because Andoreniel is gravely ill with plague. Rochinuviel told me he's too sick to give orders, and Ashaniel, who could rule in his place, is at the Fortress of the Crowned Horns and can't return."

"Can't Redhelwar just take over?" Cilarnen asked.

"I don't think so," Kellen said cautiously. "If Andoreniel can't make the decisions that affect the whole of the Elven Lands, his Council must do it—if any of them are still alive. Or, failing that, one of the other Viceroys, maybe. But I'm not sure."

Cilarnen poured the water into the waiting pot, and stared at it as if he would find his answers there. When the tea was ready, he poured it, and spoke.

"So the army cannot—will not—act without orders from the King, or someone who speaks for him. And the King is ill. And you do not think that anyone but Andoreniel will do what needs to be done—which is go to Armethalieh as soon as we can, because from all you have told me, if *They* manage to make *Their* alliance with the City, we are all doomed. But Kellen, what do you want from me?"

"I know that the High Magick can heal. And you said yourself that you removed the *geas* Anigrel had placed upon you."

Cilarnen flung his hands in the air in despair.

"Kellen, I am a half-trained High Mage, not the Eternal Light Itself! An-doreniel has *plague*—he is not—not a wall to blast down! I can do that! I barely undid what Anigrel had done to me without killing myself—I only tried because I was desperate. To Heal properly—that requires study of the body that I have not done, other High Mages working together to balance the spell-energies. I would be as likely to kill Andoreniel as cure him. Idalia is a great Wildmage Healer—Jermayan can do things with his magic that the entire College of High Mages could not imagine—this morning, he built a bridge across the Angarussa that looks now as if it has stood for a hundred years! And you're asking *me?*"

"Yes," Kellen said bluntly. "Because your magick, working with a Wild-mage's, can kill *Them*. And we all know that *They* have sent the plagues."

"You're a fool," Cilarnen said.

"I have no choice," Kellen answered. Though whether to be a fool, or to try anything he could think of, he wasn't sure.

Cilarnen sighed. "I only hope it does not come to that. If it does, I shall try all I can. But I would rather not kill anyone. By accident," he added.

Kellen realized then that Cilarnen had probably never killed anyone at all—unless you counted the Demon at Stonehearth that his spells had helped to destroy. Certainly, in the aftermath of the villages' destruction, and in overseeing what the Demons had done to Nerendale, he had seen death in plenty, but it was not the same.

Even after all the deaths that had followed it, Kellen vividly remembered his reaction to the first death *he* had been personally responsible for. He would cer-tainly be taking Cilarnen into the middle of battle. Would Cilarnen be able to do what was necessary when the time came?

"Cilarnen," he said. "Idalia told me that you are drawing power off the Elven Land-Wards. If we *did* ride to Armethalieh—outside the Elven Lands—would you still be able to cast spells?"

Cilarnen looked thoughtful.

"I suppose I must see. There are . . . people . . . I can ask. Perhaps arrange-ments can be made. Certainly the ancient War Mages did not draw their power from the Elven Land-Wards."

"See what you can find out. And one more thing. When the caverns are fin-ished, there will be ventilation shafts. I need a way to keep . . . things from crawl-ing down them. Things we don't want."

⤜⤛

CILARNEN smiled, relieved that Kellen had finally set him a task within the scope of his abilities. "Now *that* is a simple matter, if you have stonecarvers with you. Simply carve as many cats, or rats, or ferrets as you like, even dogs—anything small enough to fit. I shall enchant them into golems, and they will watch over your airshafts forever."

❧

IDALIA and Jermayan did not return that evening, and Kellen hoped it was a good omen. He was certain that at least Jermayan and Ancaladar would have returned if the worst had happened.

As the camp settled into preparations for the evening meal, Kellen realized he had not seen Vestakia for several hours.

Not that he was looking for her, of course. And certainly, as far as the army had been able to determine, these woods were now safe. And Shalkan would not leave her alone.

Still, he would feel better knowing exactly where she was.

Great wet fluffy flakes of snow were falling as he wrapped his cloak around himself and set out in search of her. And Shalkan, of course. He barely noticed. Compared to the weather near Ysterialpoerin, it was almost warm.

As he'd expected, he found them in the Coldfire-lit grove. At least she wouldn't freeze. Not with Shalkan to warm her.

He cleared his throat.

Both of them looked up.

"It's dinnertime," he said simply. "I've brought yours with me," he added to Shalkan. Some fruit-stuffed buns, made with some of the dried fruit they'd gotten at Ondoladeshiron, and, of course, several bars of the eternal Elven journey-food.

"At least you don't mean me to starve," Shalkan said, switching his tail. "Vestakia has been telling me some very interesting things today. Things you should hear."

"For that matter, I had an interesting conversation with Cilarnen," Kellen said. "But we can leave that for another time. What is your news?"

He unslung the bag from his shoulder and removed the contents, starting with the fruit buns. Shalkan always preferred to eat his dessert first.

"While you were gone, I spent a *very* long time trying to talk to the Crystal Spiders," Vestakia said. "And so I got very good at listening. And I think, now, that I am hearing . . . other things. Things I am not truly meant to hear. I think . . . Kellen, I think I can hear my father's mind."

Kellen nearly dropped the fruit bun he was holding. Vestakia's father was the Prince of Shadow Mountain.

"Oh?" he said, hoping his voice sounded noncommittal. First Cilarnen told him that he had been bespelled to be a magickal assassin, and now this.

"When I was trying to locate the last Enclave of the Shadowed Elves, I kept feeling, very strongly, that it must be far to the south. But the Crystal Spiders could not know that—they have no sense of direction at all!" she added, with a stifled giggle. "I came to realize I felt that because *he* knew where the last Enclave was. If I had only realized it sooner, I'm sure I could have found it faster. You see, now that *They* are so active in the world again, I feel *Them* everywhere now, all the time," she added sadly. She rubbed her arms beneath her cloak, as if her skin crawled. "I can still tell when *They* are coming close, or when I come near to something Tainted, but the other is like a noise that will not stop."

"Vestakia, you must do something about this," Kellen said urgently. "You can't go on like this. Idalia has drugs to shut down the magical senses—"

"Kellen, no. If I really *can* tell what *he's* thinking, even just a little, we can use that! I think, I sense—" She put her hands to her temples and closed her eyes. "There's something we can use, I know there is. He ought to be happy. Shouldn't he? But I don't feel anything like that."

Shalkan cleared his throat meaningfully.

Kellen forced himself not to think. He fed Shalkan another fruit bun, then a journey-bar.

Vestakia was right.

If he was willing to use Cilarnen, knowing what danger he placed the young High Mage in, he must use Vestakia as well.

There could be no difference between them in his mind. In his thoughts.

"What if he finds out what you're doing?" he said at last.

"I don't think he will," Vestakia said slowly. "We have always been . . . linked. That is how he knew I was alive, and why he has searched for me all these years. I think the only difference is that I can hear him now, instead of just him hearing me. It is stronger when I sleep. I think it will keep getting stronger, as *Their* power grows stronger."

Kellen nodded. "I will need to know all you can tell me."

If the Prince of Shadow Mountain was unhappy about something, Vestakia was right. There might be something in that that they could use.

They just needed to find out what it was.

⁓᠊᠊᠊᠊᠊᠊᠊᠊᠊᠊

EVEN after sennights of fighting the plague, the House of Healing was far better equipped for her needs than the Healer's Tents Idalia had left behind, and with the Flower Forest so close at hand—not to mention an entire herd of unicorns— every element of her remedies was easily available.

If only they could stop the plagues and blights at their source!

But that would require defeating Shadow Mountain, and they were already doing their best to do that.

With the help of several of the Elven Healers, she prepared large batches of the cordial, salve, and bath—enough to continue Andoreniel's treatment when the supplies she had brought ran out, and to treat other victims as well. Each was normally used at a different stage of the plague, in hopes of keeping it from progressing further, but Andoreniel's was the worst case she had ever seen, and if he were not Healed quickly, he would surely die.

While she was working—the remedies required careful preparation, but only after they were complete could she use the power of the Wild Magic to charge them—Jermayan entered.

He had gone to see to Ancaladar's comfort, and to see if—perhaps—the power of an Elven Mage might prevail where the power of a Wildmage could not.

But one look at his face told her that he had failed.

"It is as you have said," he told her, taking the long wooden spoon from her hand and slowly stirring the large cauldron of salve that heated over the low fire in the Healers' Stillroom. The mixture required constant stirring if it was not to burn.

"I went to Dargainon's bedside—he is not so ill as Andoreniel, and the Healers think he could recover. But all the Healing spells I know will not heal this plague."

"I don't understand it," Idalia said in frustration. "A Healing spell will heal almost anything. It is almost as if there's something else we need to do first—and I just can't figure out what it is, though every one of us has done every form of divination there is to try to find out."

"It is very much like the time that Petariel was wounded by the Shadowed Elf poison, when we did not yet know what it was," Jermayan said. "The Healers treated the poison, to no effect, not realizing they must Banish the Taint from the wound with a powerful spell before their drugs would work."

"Then there is something here we must figure out how to banish," Idalia said. "But what—and how?"

⤜⤛

THE cordial was ready first—the salve would take the longest, as it must cool and set—and as the Elven Healers began the preparations for the next batch, Idalia prepared to charge the cordial. Once it had been infused with her power, she could transfer it to the bottles from which it could be administered to the plague's victims.

But before she could begin, Volcilintra came rushing into the chamber, so wildly agitated she did not even pause upon the threshold and wait to be noticed as Elven good manners required.

"Idalia! It is the King! Andoreniel wakes!"

❧

AS if they were both children, Idalia raced after Volcilintra until they reached Andoreniel's bedchamber. Nelirtil and another Elven Healer were with him.

But in contrast to the last time she had come here, hours before, Andoreniel lay propped up on several pillows, drinking from a cup that Nelirtil held to his lips. He still looked near death, but now his dark eyes were open and aware.

"Idalia," he whispered, as she entered. "I owe you . . . more than my life."

"Don't talk," Idalia said instantly. "You need all your strength to heal."

She hoped that what she was seeing was healing in truth, and not the last surge of strength that sometimes came before death. But Volcilintra surely had enough experience with plague by now to tell the difference.

"He began to improve almost at once," Volcilintra said, drawing her aside. "He fell into a natural sleep for the first time in days, and now, by the grace of Leaf and Star, he wakes."

"I'm making more medicine as fast as I can," Idalia said. "You will soon be able to treat everyone here. I have given the recipes to the Healers. All three remedies need to be charged with the Wild Magic, but Kellen has Wildmages at Halacira. I am sure he will send some."

"Perhaps it would be better if you remained," Volcilintra said, sounding truly alarmed.

"Be sure that I will remain as long as I can. And that we will not leave you without a way to fight this thing," Idalia answered grimly.

❧

JERMAYAN was waiting for her in the outer chamber, his expression a mixture of hope and wariness.

"It is true," Idalia said, answering his unvoiced question. "It seems that my remedies are Healing Andoreniel—or at least they allow him to rally. But they will do nothing against the Quick Plague, if it comes. And there must be Wildmages here to make and charge the medicines—and we cannot be everywhere at once!" Her shoulders drooped.

"Yet you are here now—and as you told Volcilintra, Kellen will send Wildmages from Halacira to stay with Andoreniel, and to prepare enough of the salve and cordial to treat all of Sentarshadeen. It is little enough, but it is what can be done, and we must not scorn to do a thing simply because it seems inadequate. We are not given to know what action will turn the tide of battle, as Master Belesharon has told me many times. Now let us go and charge the medicines you have already prepared, and then Ancaladar and I will fly back to Halacira and tell Kellen what we now know. It is, you must admit, good news."

Idalia nodded grudgingly. Good news as far as it went, but all Healers knew that so many things could go wrong when a patient was ill.

Thirteen

To Redeem an Ancient Pledge

ERMAYAN RETURNED TO Halacira at dawn, because Ancaladar had simply refused to fly without a good meal and a night's sleep for both of them. And in fact, there was wisdom in the dragon's stubbornness, for Jermayan's news, while grave, was not so urgent that he must wear himself and Ancaladar to the bone delivering it, and it was always possible—in fact, likely—that something would happen soon that would require all of their strength and endurance.

He had made a wide circling pass over the land below as he approached Halacira, at least partly to search for creatures of the Shadow who might have escaped the recent battle. He saw no signs of any such, but he did see Keirasti's troop. They were still four days away from Halacira, but moving in good order. When they came nearer, they would find trail-wands, directing them to the new bridge. They waved and saluted as he passed over them, and Ancaladar flew on.

The camp below him was already awake. He could hear the sound of axes in the forest, and the thin whine of a sawmill. Artenel's artificers had indeed been busy in the scant days since the battle.

He landed in the grove—it, at least, had remained untouched, though elsewhere the forest had been much scarred by the removal of trees—and walked down to the camp. By now there was a wide smooth path cut into the snow from the grove to the camp; the whole area around Halacira was taking on the look of a well-tenanted campsite.

Kellen came up to meet him.

"The news from Sentarshadeen is better than it might be," Jermayan said at once. "Idalia's medicines have had some good effect on Andoreniel's condition. But he remains very weak. She asks that you send Wildmages to Sentarshadeen."

Kellen thought a moment, then nodded. "I can do that. One can go with you and Ancaladar immediately. I can send another two with the wagons—we need supplies, and Sentarshadeen has to supply us, or we're going to starve. I have hunting parties out now, but they're not having a lot of luck. But three is all I can spare."

"The city is well-provisioned," Jermayan said. "And three Wildmages should answer the city's needs."

"I'll ask for volunteers, then," Kellen said. "But come and have breakfast. I've got a lot to tell you. None of it really makes pleasant hearing, but at least it doesn't involve immediate disaster. . . ."

⋙

VESTAKIA stood silently in a thicket to the side of the trail, watching the two Knights pass. She was certain that Kellen and Jermayan had marked her presence, but her hood was pulled down low over her face, and she was turned away. Obviously she did not wish to be Seen, as the Elves thought of it, so Jermayan would not "see" her, and as for Kellen . . .

He did his best to ignore her whenever he possibly could.

She knew the reason for it. No one could know about Mageprice better than a Wildmage's daughter, who owed her very life to the paying of a hard Mageprice. But sometimes it still hurt. Nevertheless, she owed it to Kellen to make the paying of his Mageprice as easy for him as she possibly could.

Because she loved him.

When they were gone, she tucked her cloak up around her and followed the trail back up to Ancaladar's clearing. She had a basket over her shoulder, and a sharp knife on her belt; the reason she was out in the forest, should anyone ask, was to do what she could to gather extra fodder for the horses and oxen; the tender inner bark of trees, the softest shoots of the greenneedle trees, even the buried grasses beneath the snow, if she found a place where she could dig down that far.

But she had really come to talk to Ancaladar.

Last night the dreams that let her see into her father's mind had been more terrible and vivid than ever before. He was not only unhappy, but *afraid*.

What could frighten a Demon?

She needed to talk about it to someone, to try to understand what she'd learned. But Cilarnen knew even less than she did about *Them*—and after what he had seen at Nerendale, she thought it would be cruel to make him think about *Them* any more than he had to.

Ancaladar might know what she needed. He was old, and wise, and he had always been a good friend to her. He hated *Them* as she did, but he was not shocked by *Them*.

She reached the clearing.

Ancaladar was curled up, his head tucked under one wing. His saddle, neatly placed in its blue carrying-bag of waxed silk canvas, was hung from a tree-branch, out of the way of the worst of the snow and damp.

He raised his head at her approach. His great golden eyes flashed with pleasure.

"Ah, Vestakia," he said, in his soft deep voice. "Have you come to keep me company?"

"I have some questions," she said. "And I really don't have anyone else to ask. I hope you don't mind."

"I always enjoy talking to you," Ancaladar answered. "You don't look happy, though."

For a moment Vestakia felt like bursting into tears. She'd never felt less happy in her life, even on the plain facing the Black Cairn.

"I've been having bad dreams," she said, though the words seemed terribly inadequate, compared with the images in her mind.

"Come," Ancaladar said, lifting his wing so she could settle beneath it. "Tell me about them. I, too, have had bad dreams in my time."

Vestakia settled herself against Ancaladar's massive scaled ribs. The dragon's body felt like a sun-warmed cliff, and his calm solidity lent her strength. She wondered if any of them would ever see summer again. She would like to see a summer in the green and pleasant lands of the south. It must be a glorious sight.

In halting sentences she told Ancaladar what she had already told Kellen: that the increased Demonic presence in the world, combined with her sennights of straining to read the minds of the Crystal Spiders, seemed to have allowed her increased access to her father's mind. That she now had glimpses of what he saw and felt—not large ones, fortunately for her sanity—and much of what she could see and understand still baffled her.

"But last night I heard something clearly, because he fears it so. The Queen of Shadow Mountain is calling . . . something from outside the world. Something that can only be called by terrible sacrifices. When it comes, she will have un-stoppable power, and he is afraid that . . . something . . . will happen then. Some-thing he does not like!" She shuddered, and wrapped her arms around herself.

"He is afraid that he will die, for she will not need him anymore," Ancaladar said, after thinking for a moment. "*They* are immortal, and filled with treachery.

If he wishes to become the King of Shadow Mountain, he must kill her in order to rule in her stead, and he cannot do that if she becomes as powerful as he fears. And she, knowing his intent—for it is the intention of any member of *Their* royal house—will certainly kill him, the moment she has no further use for him."

"That," Shalkan said, settling down beside her on the other side, "is typical both of *Their* kind and of a certain nasty sort of human that I hope you will never meet. No wonder the Prince is having nightmares."

He nudged at her shamelessly until she began to rub behind his ears.

"Come to hear the gossip, have you, Shalkan?" Ancaladar asked.

"You can't expect me to spend my time down there in the camp, can you?" the unicorn replied. "Besides, this is far more interesting. And useful. Do go on."

The dragon heaved a gusty sigh, and after a moment, took up his tale again.

"As for what she summons, to give her such power . . . I am afraid I know. Jermayan has told me that the Wildmages' spells seem weakened. I know how they were made strong. Long, very long ago, at the time of the First War, before I was alive, or my grandsire, or his grandsire, before the race of Men was as it is now, there was no Wild Magic as you now know it at all. Then, as now, the Elves fought against *Them*—and *They* nearly won, for in those days, *Their* Creator was able to reach into the World of Form to aid his creation. But Great Queen Vielissar Farcarinon made the ancient pact which brought the Wild Magic into the world and bound it to the use of humans as yet unborn, and sealed He Who Is out of the World of Form."

"And a good thing, too," Shalkan commented, twitching his tail.

"That binding came at a heavy price. The Elves gave up their magic. And we . . . we paid too, for Vielissar Farcarinon had bound us into her Price by our own consent. The magic which had once been the birthright of the Elves passed to humankind, and we waited together through the long centuries for your race to grow old and wise enough to take up the keeping of the Balance."

"But we never did, did we?" Vestakia said softly. Shalkan rubbed his head against her cheek.

"I think you did well enough, when the Dark Times came again," Ancaladar answered. "Little though any of us wished them to come at all. By then you had built cities, befriended the Elves and the Shining Peoples—"

"And the unicorns," Shalkan interrupted.

"And the unicorns," Ancaladar agreed, "and learned the truths of the Wild Magic. And when *They* struck again, *Their* Creator could not reach into this world to aid *Them*."

"But now he can," Vestakia said. Her voice shook slightly.

"Not yet," Shalkan said firmly.

"But soon, if the Queen of Shadow Mountain has her way," Ancaladar answered. "This is what you must tell the others. But I warn you now, they will not wish to hear it."

"Tell them anyway," Shalkan said.

Vestakia reached up and stroked the soft skin of the dragon's jaw-hinge. "Is there anything we can do to stop it?"

"I hope so," Ancaladar answered. "But I do not know."

"They'll think of something," Shalkan said. "Humans always do."

⸎

VESTAKIA only hoped Shalkan was right, but she suspected the unicorn might only have been trying to bolster her spirits. She suspected that Ancaladar was right, and the others would hardly wish to know that they had even more bad news to deal with than they had before.

She supposed it was better to know than not.

She found Jermayan and Kellen in the newly-constructed dining hall. Several pavilions had been taken apart and remade to form a canopy and sides over a frame of raw timber; it was crude by the standards of the Ysterialpoerin camp, but braziers heated it to a temperature several degrees above the air outside and storage chests—lined up in neat rows—provided a place to sit.

And, as always, there was tea.

"I must talk to you both," she said, as soon as she approached them. "And to Cilarnen, too, I think. I have been talking to Ancaladar. He says that I have news for you that you will not like."

Kellen sighed, and ran a hand through his hair.

"Let us go find Cilarnen, then. I have asked him to prepare to look for trouble from *Them*, and he says he must move away from the camp to do it, so I suppose he is packing again."

⸎

CILARNEN was, indeed, packing, and using words over it that Kellen was willing to bet he had never learned at the Mage College of Armethalieh. He had to shake the bell-rope at the door of Cilarnen's tent several times before he was rewarded with an irritable cry from within:

"Oh come in or go away—just leave off that accursed jangling!"

Kellen poked his head through the tent flap. "I assume you mean 'enter and be welcome'?" he asked.

"Oh. It's you. I can't find my Lesser Goetia, and I'm sure I packed it. I have to have it—I haven't memorized all the spells in it yet, and it's important."

"Is it this?" Kellen noticed a book half-buried in Cilarnen's sleeping furs and picked it up.

Cilarnen's face relaxed with relief as he took the book. "Yes. Thanks. It's got the keys for the Ars Tabularum, you see, and—"

Kellen held up a hand. "You'll never make a High Mage of me, Cilarnen, and I beg you not to try. Now. May we come in? Vestakia has something to say, and she says it's important."

"Oh. Yes. Of course. Enter and be welcome."

Jermayan and Vestakia entered the tent, and Cilarnen found them all places to sit.

"We need to be private," Kellen told him.

But instead of the series of elaborate sigils with his wand that Cilarnen had drawn before, he simply sketched one quick gesture in the air, and said a single word. There was a sudden flurry of light and color, spreading out in a ring around them and dissolving into the fabric of the tent itself before fading away. Kellen wasn't quite sure, but he thought they were the same figures Cilarnen had drawn before.

"It's the same spell," Cilarnen said. "No one will see or hear us until the bounds are broken. But I thought you'd want it again, so I turned it into a cantrip. It's faster that way."

"Indeed it is," Jermayan said, sounding impressed.

Cilarnen shrugged. "Nothing to what you can do," he told Jermayan with a crooked smile. "But useful in its own way."

Kellen glanced at Vestakia. She was sitting on one of Cilarnen's chests, twisting her hands together nervously.

"What do you have to tell us, Vestakia?" he asked gently.

"Last night I . . . dreamed. And in that dream, I heard my father's mind. What I heard confused me, so I went to talk to Ancaladar about it, and he explained it to me."

She stopped, and seemed unable to bring herself to go on.

"You must tell us, Vestakia," Cilarnen said gently. "It is better to talk about what you take from *Their* minds, no matter how horrible." He spoke with the bleak voice of experience.

Vestakia took a deep breath.

"The Queen of Shadow Mountain is summoning *Their* Creator, the one the ancient Queen of the Elves banished from the world when the Elves first fought *Them*. Once he has returned, her power will be so great that the Prince of Shadow Mountain fears for his life. She is making sacrifices to allow him to return. That is what I dreamed."

"No . . ." Jermayan whispered. "That *He Who Is* should walk the world again. It must not be!"

Apparently Cilarnen recognized the name as well. He looked at Kellen, and gestured, his hand shaking slightly, toward one of his trunks.

"These books . . . some of them are very old. The oldest ones . . . I don't really understand them. I think they talk about the Black Days. Something you're not supposed to know about, unless you're on the High Council. A time when *They* were still . . . around. The books talk about the ultimate source of *Their* power. It's the opposite of the Eternal Light. Anything you think of as the Light: the Good Goddess, the Herdsman, the Hunter and the Wife. Leaf and Star, I guess, or even the Wild Magic.

"They say that the reason the Light has won its battles is because *He Who Is* was banished from the world. He can only cast shadows here. But if he can come back . . . he won't be casting shadows any longer. He'll be here."

"Well, he isn't here yet," Kellen said briskly. At the moment he had no idea how to fight this new enemy, but he did know that allowing his friends to think of it as unstoppable was putting additional weapons into the Enemy's hands. And that was something they did not need.

"If the Queen of Shadow Mountain is attempting to thin the Veil, and free him," Jermayan said slowly, "perhaps this answers a question that Idalia asked. Our Healing spells should turn back the plague and the blight, but they do not. If *Their* magic grows stronger—"

"Then we can still fight it," Kellen said stubbornly. "If all *They* had to do to gain victory was work this spell, *They* wouldn't have bothered with all the rest. *They'd* simply sit back, do that, then come and wipe us all out once they were invincible. So there has to be something we can do to stop it. If he was locked out of this world once, it can be done again. Jermayan, how did the Elves do it the last time?"

Jermayan shook his head. "Kellen, I do not know."

"Well find out," Kellen said. "Maybe the answer's in Sentarshadeen. You need to go back there anyway. I'll find a Wildmage to fly with you."

❧

WILDMAGE Catreg volunteered to return to Sentarshadeen with Jermayan and Ancaladar. Two other High Reaches Wildmages, Tadolad and Kannert, would follow with the supply sledges that Kellen had dispatched at the same time. The convoy would undoubtedly have to spend the night upon the road, due to the slowness of the oxen and the deep snow, but it was well-guarded, and Ancaladar had seen no dangers in his flight between the city and the camp.

Catreg weathered the new experience of flight with only a few exclamations of dismay. The High Reaches folk were a normally stoic lot, well-schooled by their mountainous homeland, but nothing in Catreg's experience had prepared him to see the world from the back of a dragon. After the first few moments, when Ancaladar settled into high level flight, however, he seemed to enjoy himself, leaving Jermayan to his own thoughts.

Those thoughts were bleak indeed. Kellen seemed to think it would be a small matter to find a way to ban He Who Is from the world once more, yet the spell that Great Queen Vielissar Farcarinon had needed to work to manage it at the dawn of the world had redrawn the map of magic utterly, and such forces were not available to them any longer—at least, not that Jermayan knew of. To defeat the Endarkened was barely possible. How could they manage to defeat a power as great in its Darkness as the power of Leaf and Star was in the Light?

THEY landed, not in the Unicorn Meadow, but at Ancaladar's cave, up beyond the House of Sword and Shield.

"You will wish time to settle your thoughts," the dragon told him firmly. "And Catreg will wish to see something of the city on his way to the House of Leaf and Star."

There was no point in arguing with Ancaladar when he took such a tone; Jermayan had long since given up trying. And in fact, he *did* want time to clear his head before he saw Idalia.

"Pretty place. A bit flat," was Catreg's comment on seeing the horse meadow.

They followed the trails the horses had broken in the snow down past the House of Sword and Shield. There, the snow-paths were well-dug, though the House itself stood empty.

A few minutes' further walk took them into the city itself. Though the streets were swept clear, no snow-sculptures adorned their edges. Some houses were closed up entirely, and many others flew the yellow banners of plague.

"They tell me there is plague in the High Reaches as well," Catreg said, looking around. "If it strikes here, behind your Elven magic, then it must be worse at home."

"I do not know," Jermayan said simply, not bothering to explain to Catreg that there *was* no Elven magic. "But I know that if *They* win, there will be no safety anywhere."

"Everyone knows that," Catreg said simply. "That is why I am here."

AT last they reached the House of Leaf and Star. Jermayan had come to the main entrance, and not to the House of Healing, for he was not certain where Idalia might be found, but to Jermayan's surprise, Idalia herself opened the door.

"Home and hearth," she said briefly, swinging the door wide. "I sent Tara-narya to her bed; if she is not coming down with plague, she is surely exhausted. Catreg; well met. You come in a good hour."

"I come to do what I can, Idalia. Tadolad and Kannert are on the road be-hind me, and will arrive soon."

"Come, then, there is much to do. Have you eaten? There is food and warmth in the Healer's Stillrooms, and from the look of you, you have need of both."

She led them through the hallways of the main house. Jermayan saw very few attendants, for most of the people of Sentarshadeen were either in sickbeds, attending to the sick, or with the army. They walked down a long hallway whose intricately-inlaid wooden floor was designed to mimic the floor of an autumn for-est, down to the drifted leaves, scattered stones, and clumps of colorful mush-rooms. Jermayan heard Catreg snort dismissively.

Truly, Jermayan cared not what the Mountainborn thought of the House of Leaf and Star so long as he would use his magic in aid of the sick.

The House of Healing was filled with familiar smells. There was the scent of simmering medicines, and that of good food: pies and bread kept hot in warming ovens, and soup and stew heating on top of a closed stove. Idalia helped Jer-mayan and Catreg remove the heavy furs and leathers they had worn for their flight, and then hung them to dry.

"Now here is a sorcery I can appreciate," Catreg said, stretching out his hands to the stove's heat.

The stillroom's kitchen was filled with Elven Healers in their green robes, either passing through it to the stillroom itself, or pausing to snatch a quick meal on the way to or from their duties. All, young and old, had the same look of weariness that Jermayan had come to associate with warriors too long in battle.

"Andoreniel continues to improve," Idalia said in a low voice, drawing Jer-mayan aside. "And the others we have been able to treat thus far are also doing well with the medicines. There have been no more deaths. Volcilintra believes Dargainon will recover."

"That makes good hearing," Jermayan said. "Yet I have come to bring you ill news indeed."

"What, more?" Idalia said with a sigh. "Let it wait until we've eaten, at least."

While they were eating, one of the Healers approached their table.

"I See you, Rumonadil," Idalia said.

"I See you, Idalia. I do not wish to disturb you, but you wished to be told at once when the next batch of salve was ready to be charged."

From the tone of Rumonadil's voice, Jermayan surmised, Idalia had insisted upon that *very* firmly.

"And I shall do it," Catreg said, getting to his feet and popping a last morsel of bread into his mouth. "From the look of you, girl, you've been wearing yourself to a wraith at this, and as I recall, the Mageprice for charging healing salves is a light one when it is assessed at all. Go and seek your bed, and leave me to the work I was brought here for. Or if you must make yourself useful, find some way to teach the Elder Brothers to brew a pot of proper tea, and find some butter to put in it, for this maudle would not keep a cat alive."

He bowed to the Elven Healer. "Mistress Rumonadil, my name is Catreg, and I am here to serve you, as the Wild Magic wills."

Rumonadil blinked slowly; the typical Elven gesture of surprise. "Come, then, Wildmage Catreg. Permit me to conduct you to the stillroom, and provide you with all that you may need."

Catreg followed Rumonadil from the kitchen.

"Well, there's plain speaking," Idalia said ruefully.

"I see that our hospitality is not all that it should be," Jermayan said, smiling gently.

"I'm sure that Tadolad and Kannert are bringing what Catreg considers 'proper tea' with them, and there's certainly butter here. High Reaches tea, though they call it Smokeleaf, is not actually made from a leaf, but a kind of bark; I think the tree grows in the Flower Forest. He can certainly go look for some once he's finished with his work. Or I could—"

"You could rest, as he's suggested," Jermayan said firmly. "Though I fear the news from Halacira must come first. Walk with me, if you will, in the gardens."

⤳

BY now Jermayan's heavy winter cloak was dry. As they reached the door, Idalia retrieved her own cloak from a peg. It was one Jermayan had not seen before. The cloak was made of heavy violet velvet, lined with soft deep brown fur. A gift, perhaps, from a grateful patient, for even in the depths of war and disaster, life still went on.

The garden at the House of Leaf and Star was designed to be beautiful at any hour of any season, and even now, at noon, a day or so before Midwinter, it was lovely. Tall hedges of evergreen sculpted the snow into pleasing patterns, and the holly bushes glittered with ice. Here, people had even taken the time to build the ornamental snow-sculptures of gentler times, for the House of Leaf and Star and its gardens were truly the heart of Sentarshadeen, to be tended and defended when nothing else could be. Here the paths were swept clean, and the ornamental benches stood invitingly in their stone bowers. The stone braziers beside the benches were filled and ready, inviting those who wished to sit and linger to kindle them and enjoy a pleasant warmth.

When they had come a good distance from the house, Jermayan kindled two of the braziers, and seated himself upon the bench. Idalia settled herself beside him.

"It must be ill news indeed," she said quietly.

"Kellen asks the impossible, and I do not know how to answer him. Vestakia has had . . . perhaps it is as well to call it a vision."

Quickly Jermayan told Idalia all that he and the others had spoken of at Halacira.

"And I know not what to do. Kellen is certain there is some magic to answer hers. . . ."

"There *has* to have been," Idalia said in frustration. "We're all still here, and you've fought the Endarkened twice before. Only . . . it would be good to know how you could have won."

Jermayan sighed and smiled. "In the First War there were many Elven Mages, and Great Queen Vielissar Farcarinon made her pact with the dragons, so that they added their power to ours. In those days, the world was not as it is now, for Men had not yet come to be, and the Wild Magic was not as it is now. It was then that *He Who Is* was banished from the world. In the Great War, all the races of the Light fought together to defeat the Enemy, and though there were no Elven Mages, there were Wildmages, and Knight-Mages, and dragons, and even, from what Cilarnen tells us, High Mages, all blending their magics together. And so, once again, the Enemy was cast down—that time, so we thought, forever."

"All very nice," Idalia said absently, "but I'm more interested in the First War. If *He Who Is* was banished then, there must have been *something* around that was powerful enough to banish him."

"Idalia," Jermayan said gently, "it was a very long time ago. Before your race had truly taken form. Not even we, with our long memories, truly remember those days."

"Someone must," Idalia said stubbornly. "After all, you remembered *He Who Is*."

"Perhaps, then, we should go talk to Ancaladar," Jermayan said.

ONCE more Jermayan crossed the city, this time with Idalia at his side, and returned to Ancaladar's comfortable refuge beyond the House of Sword and Shield.

The dragon looked as if he had only been waiting for them to arrive.

"Idalia, Jermayan," Ancaladar greeted them in his soft deep voice.

"Hello, Ancaladar," Idalia said. "I've come to ask you a question. How did Vielissar Farcarinon defeat *He Who Is?*"

Ancaladar cocked his head. "She did not defeat him, Idalia. Vielissar Farcarinon riddled with dragons. Every Elven child knows that. If you would gain a prize from a dragon, that is what you must do. Bonding with a dragon to use its magic is quite another matter. And I must warn you, I am already Bonded."

"Oh, can't you just *tell* me?" Idalia demanded irritably. She was instantly contrite. If Ancaladar could tell her what she wanted to know, she was certain he already would have. Sometimes magic was simply . . . inconvenient.

"I'm sorry, Ancaladar."

The dragon lowered his head. When he rested his chin on the ground, Idalia still had to reach up to give him a comforting rub along the soft skin of his jaw. It was odd how a creature so covered with hard scales everywhere else could have parts that were so soft. Quite silky, really. As she rubbed, he half-closed his pupilless golden eyes with pleasure, and she found herself staring into their golden surface.

"If you can't tell us what we need to know, Ancaladar, can you show us?" she said at last.

Ancaladar sighed with relief.

"Here is a riddle, Idalia. If there is will, and desire, and memory, then you can see. What is the answer to that?"

"I really should kick you, Beloved," Jermayan said conversationally.

"No," Idalia said. "It's a riddle—and a simple one. Three people. Desire, that's me, because I need this answer. You're memory, Jermayan, because the Elves are known for having the longest memories of all. And will—who has a stronger will than a Knight-Mage? So that has to be Kellen. The three of us together will be able to see the answer. Right, Ancaladar?"

"Correct, Idalia. You have solved the riddle. If Kellen will come, Jermayan will give you the answer you seek, though he does not know it yet."

Idalia looked at Jermayan, who regarded her with a blank expression. Obviously Ancaladar's words were as incomprehensible to him as they were to her.

"Then it seems I must send for Kellen with all due haste," the Elven Knight said slowly. "And trust he will hold this mysterious task to be as urgent as we do."

≈

KELLEN and Shalkan arrived a few hours after dawn of the next day, having been sent word by unicorn messenger. They rode directly to Ancaladar's paddock, where Jermayan had already erected an ice-pavilion for the spell to come.

"You look awful," he told Idalia as he hugged her. "You should get more rest."

"Pot to kettle," she said simply. "When was the last time *you* slept in a bed?"

Kellen grinned tiredly. "I really can't remember. Before we left for the Gathering Plain, I think—and *don't* ask me when the last time was I was actually warm. Now, why am I here?"

"You said there must be something powerful enough to banish He Who Is from the world," Idalia said. "We know there is, because he was banished once, a very long time ago. Ancaladar and Jermayan are going to help us find it."

"This should be fun," Shalkan said.

"Find it how?" Kellen asked.

Idalia shrugged. "By looking for it."

≈

THE four of them entered the ice-pavilion, while Ancaladar coiled himself around the outside, thrusting his large head into the opening. There were braziers set at the four corners of the pavilion, warming the enclosure considerably, and several thick fur rugs had been placed upon the ice floor for them to sit upon.

"Now what?" Kellen asked, when the three of them were seated in a ring facing each other in the center of the pavilion. Shalkan had taken up a position near the door, beside Ancaladar.

"Idalia must contemplate her desire for this answer," Ancaladar said. "You, Kellen, must will her to succeed. And you, Jermayan, must remember a time before the light of the stars looked upon the face of your father a hundred generations gone."

Kellen barely registered Jermayan's startled sound of protest. He was gazing into Ancaladar's eyes. They had always glowed, but now they seemed to swirl and dance, as though he was looking into the depths of a dancing fire. . . .

A ripple of magic passed from Ancaladar to Jermayan, and slowly the air between them began to . . . condense as Jermayan cast his spell.

The Mountainborn often joked about the temperature being cold enough to freeze fire. This was as if the air were freezing, though the temperature in the pavilion was no colder than it had been a moment before. But slowly, in the space between the three of them, the air itself darkened and solidified, until it had become a perfect egg-shaped piece of ice.

It was so cold that its surface smoked in the pavilion's cool air; so dense that its color was the pale blue of a winter sky; so pure that Kellen could see right through it to the other side.

"Memory," Jermayan said, staring at the ice-egg. "The most ancient memory of all."

"Look," Idalia said.

Kellen looked.

❦

HE was no longer Kellen Tavadon, Knight-Mage.

He was Vielissar Farcarinon, Great Queen, victor of a thousand battles. Since she had been old enough to hold a sword, she had fought—against the Centaurs, against the Minotaurs, against the Bearwards. She had fought the warring Elven tribes who would attempt to take her crown from her, and united them beneath her banner. She had brought her rule to the land from the Forests of Ulayna to the Golden Isles, and united the Hundred Houses. All of them had acknowledged her right to rule, for she was wise, favoring no House over another.

Then, in the moment of her greatest victory, when all the land was at peace, a new enemy had come. Not just an enemy of the Elves, but an enemy of all who walked beneath the Light.

The Endarkened.

❦

HE was no longer Jermayan, son of Malkirinath, Elven Knight, Ancaladar's Bonded.

He was Vielissar Farcarinon, Great Queen, victor of a thousand battles, Elven Mage. Since she had been old enough to enter The Sanctuary of the Star, she had studied the mysteries of the Great Magic that bound the Children of Leaf and Star to the heartbeat of the world, and mastered all its secrets. With that power had come great wisdom, and so she had planned her battles carefully, knowing that the Elves must not forever expend their substance on petty wars between House and House, but must unite together beneath a strong ruler, and end their bickering forever. For there had been omens revealed in the stars at the moment of her birth that foretold that a great enemy was coming, and she knew that she must be there to meet it.

She labored long and bloodily, and at last there was peace. And then, as the prophecy foretold, the enemy came. Winged creatures of Shadow, with sorcerous powers greater than those of the greatest Elven Mage. Once more she rallied her armies beneath her banner, and found, to her horror, that all their power, all their magic was not enough.

But she had been planning for this day for a very long time, and she did not despair. She went into the deep earth, armed only with her wits, her magic, and her love, and found new allies.

The dragons.

There, she made a pact that would change the world forever. She made it willingly, knowingly, gladly, for the enemy they faced was worth any sacrifice.

But it was still not enough to save them.

❧

SHE was no longer Idalia Wildmage, tool of the Wild Magic.

She was Vielissar Farcarinon, Great Queen, victor of a thousand battles, Elven Mage.

With all the limitless power of a dragon to draw upon, she was still not the equal of the enemy she fought. She could destroy them one by one upon the battlefield, but the Power *They* served walked the land beside them, and its power was as much greater than *Theirs* as Leaf and Star was greater than hers.

It was that Power that she must seal away from the world, if all who walked beneath the Light were to survive—and prevail.

There were yet Allies upon whom she might call. Those who loved her people well, who had answered their prayers upon a thousand battlefields, to whom offerings were made at the Nine Shrines in every season. Allies as bright and dangerous as a swordblade, as powerful as the lightning.

As powerful—perhaps—as He Who Is.

❧

IDALIA opened her eyes. She couldn't remember closing them, but obviously she had. The egg-shaped ice crystal was gone. Only a clear pool of water remained, slowly freezing into the ice beneath.

She remembered—as if she had done it herself—what Vielissar Farcarinon had done. It was a spell, but more than that. A Greater Summoning, a magic so old that, like the spells of the High Magick it required precision of place and timing. There were only eight times in the year, and thirteen places in the world where such a spell could be cast, and of those thirteen places, Idalia, even with the help of the spell Jermayan had just cast, knew the location of only six—and two of them were in places where no human could go and survive, no matter how great their magic.

The next time she could attempt the spell was Midwinter, just a day from now.

If she could not cast it then, she did not think they would all survive until Kindling, when she could try again.

Across the circle from her, Kellen and Jermayan were rousing from their trance. Both men looked dazed and only half-aware.

"You've remembered," Ancaladar said with pleasure.

"Yes," Idalia said. "Thank you, my friend."

"I think we've all remembered," Kellen said, still sounding slightly groggy. "I'm just not sure what we've remembered. I remember being a . . . an Elf. And doing a lot of fighting. And then, just when I'd gotten everything sorted out, *They* showed up to ruin everything. So I had to start over again."

"And I," Jermayan said, "I remember making the Great Pact, for I was, then as now, an Elven Mage. Yet even that was not enough to stop *Them*, for *Their* master was on the field of battle as well."

"And I remember what I did to send *He Who Is* back where he came from. But I don't see how I can make it work!" Idalia said.

"*Idalia*," Jermayan said, his voice taut with frustration.

Idalia made a rueful noise, half laughter, half despair. "Tell me, if you can, then, how I am to gain the consent of every living creature in the land to cast a Greater Summoning—in less than a day."

On the face of it, the question was absurd, but Jermayan gave it serious thought.

"We must ask Andoreniel."

"Andoreniel! Jermayan, you *saw* him. He is too weak even to speak!"

"For this, he must find the strength. If anyone knows the answer, it is the King. There are secrets in the House of Leaf and Star held closely against the time of greatest need. And we are in great need now."

There was no way for Idalia to argue with this assessment. All the Wild-mages had felt the Shadow grow in strength over the past several sennights, without understanding how, or why. If there was *anything* she could do to keep He Who Is from granting the Endarkened ultimate power, she must do it at once.

"We'd better go and ask him, then," she said, getting to her feet.

☙

"YOU'LL be careful, right?" Kellen asked. "Whatever you end up doing?"

He was preparing to return to the camp at Halacira. As much as he wanted to stay and see this through to the end, Kellen knew that his place was there, not here. An army needed its commander, no matter how much his heart wanted to stay with his friend and his sister.

"I'll be at least as careful as you would be in my place—and probably more so, little brother," Idalia assured him gravely. "It's a simple spell, really—assuming I can figure out some way to gain the consent of all the land in less than a day, of course. And assuming the Allies that Vielissar Far-carinon summoned up are still around after all this time. But if I can, and they are, I just need to go and call them, and see if they're still willing to help."

"Simple," Kellen said, with a faint smile.

"As simple as anything ever gets," Idalia said. "It worked once."

"Then we'll hope it works again, for all our sakes."

"And if it does—and probably even if it doesn't—I'll see you soon," Idalia said.

She gave him a quick hug. Kellen mounted Shalkan, and the unicorn trotted off across the snow. She watched after him until the two of them, unicorn and rider, had vanished.

"Well, come on then, Jermayan. Let's go do the impossible."

Jermayan bowed and offered her his arm in an exaggerated courtly gesture.

Idalia laughed briefly and strode off ahead of him.

IT was still several hours before Idalia and Jermayan could speak to Andoreniel, for when they reached his bedchamber, he was sleeping, and Nelirtil refused to waken him. Even though her errand was urgent, Idalia had to agree: Andoreniel's life still hung by a thread, and what she had come to ask of him would severely tax what little strength he had regained.

What she needed, nothing short of a miracle could gain her, in any event. The spell of Kindolhinadetil's Mirror, which had merely required the consent of the Allied Army, had taken most of a day to put into place, and the army had been relatively small, and all gathered into one convenient location. For this spell, everyone in the land must be asked, even those who would certainly say "no" such as the Armethaliehans. Even in summer, in peacetime, just the asking would take moonturns. . . .

At last, Nelirtil grudgingly admitted that Andoreniel was awake.

"I trust this is as important as you believe it is, Idalia," the Elven Healer said, with a heavy sigh.

Idalia went in and seated herself beside the Elven King's bedside. She took his hand in hers, very gently. The skin was papery and dry, the once-firm flesh wasted away, until the hand she now held was no more than a claw of bone and sinew. It was the drawn-out fever that had consumed him so; most of the plague victims died long before they reached this state.

It meant that his recovery would be a thing of many long sennights.

She spoke slowly, carefully, in a low even voice. Explaining what she must do, and what she needed. The part of her trained as a Healer rebelled against doing this to a patient under her care—what Andoreniel needed now was rest, and more rest. But the need of the land in his care—of the lands beyond his care—was greater even than that.

His dark eyes watched her face, but he gave no other sign of consciousness.

At last he took a deep breath, obviously summoning all his will in order to speak.

"Tokens . . . Council Chambers . . ."

His eyes closed again.

"Thank you, Andoreniel," Idalia whispered. She could feel in her bones what the effort had cost him. She would ask nothing more.

"The King has answered my need," she said to Nelirtil, as she rose to her feet.

Nelirtil inclined her head. "Do not come to him again, Idalia," she said. The tone of her voice was all-but-pleading.

"I swear to you that I will not, Nelirtil," Idalia answered.

❧

JERMAYAN rose to his feet as Idalia entered the outer chamber.

"More riddles," she sighed. "Maybe you can help solve this one."

"I shall do all that is within my power," Jermayan answered, puzzled.

❧

THE Council Chamber was located at the center of the House of Leaf and Star. It was a high-ceilinged room, paneled and floored in smooth pale wood, completely circular, and unlike nearly every other room of Elven making, had no windows at all. It was illuminated by a large hanging chandelier of mirrored lamps that, when lit, rendered the chamber as bright as day.

As they entered, Jermayan lit the lamps with a wave of his hand. Light flooded the room, illuminating the familiar furnishings.

They closed the door behind them and looked around.

In the center of the room was the frostwood council table, with the Great Seal of Leaf and Star inlaid in its center in purest silver. Set around the table were the Council chairs. Two were draped in white, indicating that two of the

Council were dead. One more was draped in green—Ashaniel's seat—for she was absent. The colored glass mosaics set into the backs of the remaining chairs sparkled brightly in the lamplight.

Hung around the edge of the room were thirteen narrow banners of brightly colored silk, each bearing a single elaborate symbol worked upon it in shining silver. The green one duplicated the design inset into the table. There was a yellow one that oddly resembled the Great Seal of Armethalieh, but none of the rest were at all familiar to Idalia.

"I told Andoreniel what I meant to do, and what I needed. He said something about tokens, and the Council Chamber, but that was all he was able to tell me, and to say that much took all his strength," Idalia said. She looked around again. "There's nothing here but the furniture. And the banners. Is there?" she added unnecessarily.

"The banners are said to be the tokens of the Great Alliance among the Peoples of the Light," Jermayan said slowly. "Perhaps they are . . . something more."

"Only one way to find out," Idalia said.

The next several minutes was spent climbing up on chairs and detaching the banners from the walls, until they lay in a multicolored pile in the center of the Council table. If they were indeed as old as Jermayan suggested, they were in very good condition. And not dusty at all.

She ran the silk through her fingers more carefully, closing her eyes. If she could put a name to what she was doing, it would be *listening,* in much the way she had once listened, using gan stones as markers, to find the source of the drought attacking the Elven Lands.

"There *is* magic here," Idalia said slowly. "Jermayan, I'm pretty sure these are what we need. If they are . . . promises to help against *Them* if *They* come again, then the consent I need for a Greater Summoning has already been asked and given. But I need to test them, to see if that's really what they are . . . and to see if they're still good."

She began rolling the banners up together into a tight bundle.

IT had been many moonturns since Idalia had seen her small house in Sentarshadeen, and so much had happened in the intervening sennights that it seemed as if the place belonged to a stranger. But she had left the dwelling in good order, and everything she needed to cast her spells of Seeking and Knowing was here.

Although the floor would be—perhaps—a bit the worse for her efforts.

She quickly brought a small brazier, a bowl, and a bottle of wine from the kitchen. The herbs she had ready in her beltpouch. With Jermayan's help, Idalia spread the banners out on the living room floor, careful to keep them from touching each other, and settled herself in the midst of them.

Jermayan stood in the doorway of her bedroom, watching.

Quickly she kindled the charcoal. The bowl she would use for her scrying spell was already half-filled with water. Now she added wine to the water, floated fern leaf upon the water—for the scrying spell—and sprinkled other herbs onto the burning charcoal, finishing with three drops of her blood—to Find.

Then she waited.

❧

WHEN I call, will you come?

Suddenly Idalia was . . . elsewhere.

"We will come, son of the House of Caerthalien. Who holds our token holds our pledge, for the aid of all our people, in whatever hour, for whatever purpose. This consent is given freely and without constraint, with our whole hearts and our whole spirits, for the good of all, and against the Shadow. Only the death of all our kind will release us from this pledge."

She was standing in a place she had never seen, an enormous timbered hall. It was not of Elven make, but neither was it of any other design she could recognize. Before her stood a Centaur . . . King.

But the Centaurs had not had a King for uncounted centuries.

The Centaur held out something to her. A bundle of red silk. She felt her hands reach out to take it—only they weren't her hands. They were slender, elegant, yet powerful and masculine, wearing rings she had often seen Andoreniel wear.

"In the name of Leaf and Star, Herdsman Reuden, Caerthalien thanks you for this pledge, and vows to hold it against a day darker than any we have yet seen."

The Centaur inclined his head—equal to equal—and turned away.

"When I call you, will you come?"

"We will come, son of the House of Caerthalien."

Once again the ritual was repeated. This time two stood before her—great shaggy creatures towering eight feet high, looking almost like bears.

No, not bears. *Bearwards*. A race long-vanished from the land. This time, the banner was orange.

Again and again the ritual was repeated.

It was like and unlike the vision she had experienced in the ice-egg. Then, she had *been* Vielissar Farcarinon. Now it was simply as if she were watching through another's eyes, still herself, but seeing and hearing all that the other heard and saw.

The merfolk, clad in a shimmering veil of water and magic, presenting a banner the color of their own ocean.

The folk of the High Reaches—who were also, Idalia somehow knew with the insight of her vision, someday to be the Lostlanders and Wildlanders—with a banner the pale blue of their deepest winter snows.

The firesprites, also veiled in magic to protect the others there from their flame, with a banner of deep rose.

The Shining Folk, in forms too many to count, and a banner of shimmering gray.

The Fauns, and a banner of palest green.

The Minotaurs. A black banner.

The War Mages of Armethalieh, men and women together, in bright armor and gray robes, bringing a banner as golden as the sun.

We will come in whatever hour. Who holds our token holds our pledge. Our consent is freely given.

The vision faded.

As Idalia opened her eyes, she saw most of the banners crumble away to dust. The peoples who had given those pledges were not here to redeem them now. Only the Lostlanders, Wildlanders, and Mountainfolk; the Centaurs, the Fauns, the Shining Folk, the Elves, and the Armethaliehans remained of those who had pledged that day.

But the banner of Armethalieh burst into flame.

She jerked back from the flames with a startled cry, and grabbed the first thing that came to hand—the bowl of water she had used for scrying—to throw upon the flames. But it did no good. The banner continued burn, even in the pool of water, until every scrap of it was utterly consumed.

Armethalieh was Tainted.

Jermayan came forward, hauling her to her feet, pulling her away from the spreading mess of water, dust, and the still-burning banner. He looked as shaken as she felt, even though, she knew, he had not shared her vision. In a normal scrying spell, the vision could be shared, if two were standing over the bowl to-gether. But Jermayan had been standing several feet away, and Idalia had com-bined the spell with another, changing the spell to a certain degree

"It would be good to know what you have seen," Jermayan said, obviously striving to be calm as well.

She shook her head, struggling to clear her thoughts.

"I saw how these banners were created," she said slowly. The Armethaliehan banner—the banner of the War Mages—had consumed itself utterly at last, leaving behind nothing more than scraps of greasy ash floating in the water on the floor. "They were meant to be used just as I intend to use them. They are pledges of aid against the Shadow. The ones that are . . . gone . . . belong to the races that *They* destroyed in the War, so what I saw must have happened a very long time ago."

"Yet one burned," Jermayan said.

"Armethalieh's," Idalia said.

She didn't need to say anything else.

"So," she added, a few moments later, carefully picking up the five banners that were left—Men, Elves, Centaurs, Fauns, and Shining Folk—and rolling them together. She set them aside and went to get a broom to sweep away the dust, ash, and water. "It appears we have what we need. And I know where I need to go. It's a long way from here, and I need to be there by midnight tomorrow."

"Midwinter," Jermayan said. "Ancaladar and I can take you wherever you need to be—but I confess it would be helpful if we knew where it was."

⤜⤛

ONCE, the whole land had been starred with Places of Power where the binding strings that held the world together converged, nine for each of the races who had given the banners to Andoreniel's ancestor.

Most of them were . . . gone. The conflict that had reduced most of the land and waters once inhabited by score of races to lifeless rock had erased them, as it had erased those who had once called upon them.

The ancient Shrines were largely forgotten, even by the Elves and the Wildmages. For a thousand years there had been no need of the great magics and Summonings that could only be done in such places. Even where the information about the locations of the Shrines survived, knowledge of what could be done at them was gone.

Idalia only knew of six that had survived the Great War. Two were inaccessible to humans: One was deep beneath the sea, another was buried in the heart of a volcano deep in the southern desert. Of the remaining four, at the one that had once been the Bearward Shrine, the Mountainfolk now offered to the Huntsman and the Forest Wife. Since it now resonated to their power, it was useless to her. The one in Centaur lands had been incorporated into the middle of a village; to do magic there would do too much damage. The third was in the Delfier Valley.

The fourth was her destination.

Places of Power were tools, as neutral in themselves as the Wild Magic. They could be used for good or ill—they were simply wellsprings of Power; as old as the Earth itself, taking on the characteristics of their surroundings. This was why she could not use the Mountainfolk Shrine; even though the Mountainfolk Wild-mages no longer had any true notion of what it was, their Shrine had been shaped by centuries of intent into a focus for the energies of the Huntsman and the Forest Wife.

But the place to which Idalia and Jermayan flew now was the sole surviving Elven shrine. It had always been a place of power for the Elves, tuned by thousands of years of use to their particular perception of the world, always a force for Good. Essentially, the Elven Shrine, at least, functioned as a supremely powerful land-ward.

And so it would be perfect for what she needed.

She hoped.

It was far to the north of Lerkalpoldara, nearly at the border of the Elven Lands themselves. Beyond those borders lay nothing but a cold barren desert wasteland stretching to the end of the world. Yet this shrine, Idalia knew, had once marked the center of the Elven Lands, not their edge.

Normally they would be in great danger just being here. The north, so Cilarnen had assured them, was long since overrun by the creatures of Shadow. Frost Giants and Ice Trolls, long enemies of the Elves, walked the once-inviolate Elven Lands openly, destroying anything they choose. Fortunately, they were still hundreds of miles away from Ysterialpoerin.

For now.

And even though enemies were everywhere, because of the nature of the Shrine, they would come nowhere near it. They might not even know why they were avoiding it, or that they were. But they would.

And Idalia could use its power to fuel her Greater Summoning.

She had told Jermayan very little about what she intended to do here, in part because she did not know. To call Vielissar Farcarinon's ancient Ally for help against He Who Is, absolutely. But how she would do it, and what form that help would take, Idalia was not entirely certain. She expected the Wild Magic to provide her inspiration when the time came.

As it always did.

And because all her Prices were all now paid, the cost of the spell would be nothing more than her own physical energy—and despite her wish—no, stronger than that, her *need*—to tend to the plague-afflicted of Sentarshadeen, she had forced herself to do little but sleep and eat for the last twenty-four hours. Kellen's supply-wagon had arrived right on schedule, bringing Tadolad and Kannert, the other two Wildmages, and for the moment, Sentarshadeen had as much Charged medicine as it could possibly use, and three Wildmages to tend the sick.

And now she would strike at the root of the problem.

⁂

ANCALADAR landed, and simply *slid*. His great heavy claws made squealing noises against the thick sheet of wind-polished ice. It was scoured to glass-slickness by the unrelenting wind.

At last he managed to stop, fanning his wings wildly, and stood, feet splayed and claws dug in.

They had landed upon the center of a plain at the top of the world. They were so high that there were not even mountains to see, assuming they would even be visible at night. In all directions, the world was . . . flat. Water and cold and the eternal blowing wind had created a surface unnaturally flat from what Idalia guessed might well be a rolling grassy meadow at the height of summer. Now, at Midwinter, it was as flat and even as a stone floor. In places, it gleamed like a mirror, reflecting the veils of multicolored lights that danced through the sky.

"Pelashia's Veils," Jermayan said, looking up. "The unicorn's valley is named for them."

He dismounted with care, though once Idalia had told him where their destination was, he had taken care to wear spiked sabatons over his heavy leather flying boots, and she had done the same, so the icy surface presented little difficulty to them. Ancaladar folded himself, belly-down to the ice, and Idalia lifted down their panniers of supplies before dismounting.

Ancaladar raised himself up again, folding his wings tightly to keep from being blown about like a draconian ice-boat. "I won't be going anywhere," he assured them. "There's nowhere to go."

Idalia laughed briefly.

She looked around. Pelashia's Veils stretched across the sky, a shimmering veil of orange and blue and red, spread across the cloudy scarf of stars that filled the heavens above it, a few brighter stars caught in its folds. The moon was nearing midheaven, marking midnight, when her spell must be cast.

But down below, the gleaming level plain, blue-white with unblemished ice, extended flat and unmarked for a thousand leagues in every direction.

Or nearly so.

A few hundred yards away stood the shrine markers of their destination.

⁂

THEY would be easy enough to miss. Three standing stones, half-buried in ice at this season, set so as to mark the points of a triangle, and between them—completely covered in ice just now—a third flat stone.

That was all. The Shrines merely marked a *place*, after all, and what was done with it and its power by those to whom it belonged, for good or ill, did not seem to matter to the ancient Earth Power that welled forth here. In the echoes of her borrowed memories, Idalia seemed to remember some of the Shrines being enclosed in elaborate temples, their stones painted and ornamented; some venerated in simple woodland glades; some ignored entirely.

This one had simply been . . . forgotten.

She knew that the Elves continued to venerate the powers of Leaf and Star, but wherever they did it, they certainly didn't do it here. And a good thing, too—if *They* had had any idea of the importance of this place, *They* would certainly have done *Their* best to find and desecrate it.

She had never been so cold in her life. The wind was like liquid ice. Every exposed inch of skin—and thank the gods of the Wild Magic there wasn't much of it—seemed to not only freeze solid where it felt the touch of the wind, but to be able to transmit the cold through her blood to the rest of her that was warmly swathed in wool, fleece, leather, and furs. Heavy furs.

She picked up one of the two panniers that Ancaladar had carried, and began walking toward the Shrine. Jermayan lifted the other and followed.

When they reached the shrine, she dumped the contents of both baskets upon the ice and then began building a balefire at the center of the three posts.

Vilya—Alyon—Namarii—Oak—Ash—Blackthorn—Willow—Quince—Larudrall—nine woods of ancient virtue and power. When she was done, the mound nearly filled the space between the pillars, and stood as high as her chest.

So far Jermayan had not asked any questions—even of the indirect Elven sort, though Idalia could tell his curiosity was nearly killing him. Well, all his questions were about to be answered. It was nearly Midwinter Midnight.

"Now I summon the Starry Hunt," she said. "I hope. If I'm right—and they'll come—they should certainly be a match for He Who Is." She turned back to her balefire.

~≈~

JERMAYAN stared at Idalia's back in astonishment not untinged with horror. He would turn her from her course if he could, save for the fact that their situation was too dire.

He understood, now, why she had not named the Ally she intended to summon.

The Starry Hunt! A legend barely remembered among the Elves, something from ancient days indeed, from before the founding of the Nine Cities, from before the Great Pact, when Elven Wars were not bloodless wars of flowers. The Endarkened had not been all the Elves had fought. In the morning of the world, before humans were ever born, the Elves had fought each other: House against House, family against family, sister against brother . . .

Perhaps so that when the Endarkened came, they would be the most perfect warriors the world had ever seen. A match for creatures of blood and pain and death.

In those days, the Powers the Elves cried out to as they lived and died were not powers of joy and harmony and balance.

But it was uncounted thousands of years since the First War.

Those Powers had slept long.

Had—must have—changed with the land and its inhabitants.

Idalia lit the balefire with a wave of her hand. The wood kindled with a great rush of flame. Fire washed over the tall white pillars of the marking stones, its warmth holding the bitterness of the wind at bay.

Then she began to speak.

It was as if she was talking to a friend, though her words were in no language Jermayan understood. It was the most ancient form of the speech of the Elves, the tongue that they had abandoned long ago to speak the speech of men.

Slowly her voice grew louder, more rhythmic. Now she no longer spoke, but chanted. Her voice rose and fell in a cadence as old as the wind and the stars, and as it did, Jermayan felt the first breath of Power wash over him.

He was the most powerful Mage to walk the world in a thousand years. The spells he could summon through his bond with Ancaladar were—nearly— the equal of the Endarkened's. In single combat, spell to spell, he might even be the equal of the Prince of Shadow Mountain.

Yet the Power wakening here was so far beyond his own as to render him the merest child in comparison.

The Starry Hunt had slept. But it was not gone.

He was no coward. Since they had first discovered what it was they fought, Jermayan had expected to lay down his long years upon the battlefield against their monstrous foe, forfeiting all his future for the barest chance at even delaying *Their* victory.

But in the face of the Allies Idalia now summoned, he wanted nothing more than to turn and flee.

Her cries were wilder now, her words whipped away by the wind as soon as she uttered them. The flame of the balefire changed, its flame going from yellows and oranges to a clear blue-white. Idalia flung the bundle of banners into the flame.

Suddenly they were here.

It was as if the sky itself was torn open by their arrival. A host of gigantic Riders stood against it, their star-shod steeds ramping and jostling for position.

He could not look upon them.

Jermayan fell to his knees, bowing his head in utter submission.

～

THEY were crowned with stars.

Stars gleamed from their horses' harnesses. Their horses' bodies were the color of the night sky. Their armor was the gleaming silver of moonlight and midnight and the winter air itself.

There were hundreds of them. Thousands. As many as the stars in the sky.

Too many to count.

Too beautiful to look upon, and too terrible.

"Who summons me?" the Lord of the Starry Hunt demanded. His voice was voice of the stars themselves.

The power of the Shrine poured through her, making her whole body tremble. Idalia no longer felt the cold, nor anything she recognized as fear. It was if she had become nothing more than a voice for the Shrine, a tool to focus and channel its need through her own human desire.

"The Land calls you," Idalia answered steadily. "The People call you. I call you. He Who Is would return to the world, and so we summon you."

"And will you spill your own blood to save the land?"

In answer, Idalia pulled off her glove. She slashed the palm of her hand deeply with her knife and held it out to him. The blood welled up, and dripped to the ice at her feet.

The Lord of the Starry Hunt laughed. His laughter was the roaring of the wind.

He raised his warhorn, and blew a long wailing call. The sound of it shuddered through her body with a terrible sweetness verging upon pain, taking all her strength away with it.

"We ride!" she heard dimly, as consciousness left her. "*We ride!*"

～

WHEN she came to, Idalia was in a different place entirely. The light of earliest dawn streamed through the windows of a small house, and Jermayan was making tea.

The homely reality of such familiar surroundings anchored her to consciousness as nothing else could have. Nothing could have been more different from the last thing she remembered: the night, the frozen plain, the starry spectral riders. Those memories were already fading, as hard to hold on to as a dream. All that remained was the certainty that she had done what she had intended to. But the Power that she had summoned, though of the Light, was as inhuman in its way as the Endarkened were, and thoughts of it were as difficult for mortal minds to retain.

It was not hard to understand, now, why the Elves had let the memory of their Shrine slip away.

Her body was heavy with the weakness of utter exhaustion. Simply casting the spell of Summoning had exacted a high price. She could not imagine any way to have paid Mageprice for such magic, assuming one had been set.

"I was about to wake you. We are in Windalorianan, and I am preparing tea," Jermayan told her, once he saw her move. "It was the nearest place I could think to bring you, but it is not safe to stay here long."

"Not that I would wish to, in any event," Idalia answered.

She sat up. Several hours' sleep had given her the strength for that, at least.

Though Windalorianan had been abandoned in good order by its inhabitants, it had not been possible for the refugees to bring away every possession, and obviously Jermayan had spent some time scavenging the ghost-city as she slept. The stove of the little house—from the look of it, a guest-house, similar to the one she and Kellen shared in Sentarshadeen, if a little smaller—was stoked to warmth with charcoal disks, and she had slept before it wrapped not only in her own cloak, but in an assortment of furs and blankets.

"I am astonished to discover that they left tea behind," Idalia said, stretching.

"Not the tea, but the tea-service," Jermayan said, correcting her. "I always carry tea."

His words were light, but his dark eyes looked haunted. The Elves were a supremely civilized folk—had been so before Idalia's own distant ancestors had learned to clothe themselves. The Powers she had summoned up and set loose last night, the Powers Jermayan's own ancestors had once sworn fealty to, were anything but civilized. No wonder he looked so haggard.

"So my Summoning worked," she said. "And will do—I think, I hope—what I mean it to, and set a shield between the world and He Who Is, so that he cannot enter. But it would be good to know what you saw, as well."

"I saw that which I wish never to see again," Jermayan answered quietly. He poured the boiling water into the teapot, which stood ready. "Idalia, we are no longer a people of magic, nor of the High Gods. Our part in these things we set aside long ago, passing the custodianship of these arts to younger races. To command the Great Magics myself . . . this I accept, for our need is dire. And Ancaladar's company gives me great joy. But to look upon the Starry Hunt . . . to know they once more ride the winds . . . to know that, were I to call out to them, the Star-Crowned might ride to my side on the field of battle . . . Idalia, it makes my heart wonder what place may be left for Men, Elves, and Centaurs upon such a battlefield."

He bowed his head. Several strands of his long black hair had worked their way loose from the warrior's braid coiled at the back of his neck, and fell across his face. Idalia leaned forward and brushed them back gently.

"It is our fight most of all, Jermayan," she said softly. "They'll only fight where we can't. They certainly won't do our work for us. The Wild Magic draws its power from us, and I think—no, I *know*—that strange as they are, the Starry Hunt is still a part of that. If we won't fight—or aren't willing to—they won't, either."

"Then we must each play our part, no matter how large or small," Jermayan said, raising his head. "And not scorn to do the task we are set, even though it seems small and inconsequential in comparison to what others may do."

"Fine talk coming from an Elven Mage," Idalia said.

Jermayan smiled, and poured tea.

⤳

HE was right that they could not afford to stay in Windalorianan long. Although he had sealed the Gatekeeper's Pass between the rest of the Northern Triad and Lerkalpoldara when he had brought Magarabeleniel and her people out, the Shadow creatures that had filled the Bazrahil Valley had long since found other ways over the mountains, and more had since come in over the borders of the Elven Lands. Even as they finished their tea, Jermayan and Idalia could hear Coldwarg howling in the distance.

"Time to go," Idalia said, setting down her cup.

They dressed quickly, and walked outside.

The sky was black with the clouds of an oncoming storm, but no snow had fallen as yet. Ancaladar stood crouched in the street, his vast body filling the entire width of it.

Idalia was still exhausted from the Summoning—that and ravenous—but she was neither so hungry nor tired that she wished to remain in a city that was about to play host to a hunting-pack of Coldwarg, and whatever might be with them. Jermayan helped her to mount. She buckled the straps as tight as she could, only then noticing that the cut she had made in her hand the night before was gone. Not even a scar remained.

Jermayan's magic. Or Theirs. She didn't really care which at the moment.

As soon as they were both safely mounted, Ancaladar took off down the street at a dead run. The city had been deserted for moonturns; drifts of snow sprayed up around him as he galloped. Within moments they were outside the city, in the fields of Vardirvoshanon. Here the wind was nearly as brutal as it had been on the ice-plain, and Ancaladar took expert advantage of it, spreading and lifting his wings and allowing the blast to spin him up into the sky like a storm-tossed leaf.

Once he was airborne, they made a low sweeping pass over the city. In the gray light of dawn they could see how the snow had drifted up over most of the houses, giving Windalorianan a sad haunted aspect. The snow-dunes were crisscrossed by animal tracks, and in the distance, racing over the snow, their dappled white fur making them shimmer in the pale light, were a pack of Coldwarg over a hundred strong.

"It would be interesting to know what they're finding to eat," Idalia commented. Kellen had told her that one of the first things the Coldwarg did when they came into an area was despoil it of game, and they'd certainly been here long enough to eat everything edible.

"That will not be a problem for this pack any longer," Jermayan said grimly.

Ancaladar tilted a wing, and began a low run directly over the Coldwarg.

As he reached them, Jermayan stretched out a hand, and the entire pack burst into flames.

For a moment, the blackening bodies danced in frenzied agony upon the snow before collapsing into ash.

Then Ancaladar turned south again, beating his wings in hard downward strokes to carry them up through the clouds.

⁓

IT was only a short while later before they began their descent once more.

"We can't be at Sentarshadeen already," Idalia said.

"No," Jermayan agreed. "But the army is below us. I wish to speak to Redhelwar. There is an . . . idea I have."

⁓

IT was madness.

Madness equal to the Summoning of the Starry Hunt.

But it would take two moonturns, three, even more, for the army to reach even Ondoladeshiron, and that was too long. Armethalieh would long since have fallen, and *They* would have won.

They needed the army south of the Mystrals *now*.

⸺

THEY were only half a sennight out of Ysterialpoerin, and such an enormous force could not move quickly. At four hours past dawn, the army had barely begun to move, and its line of march, from the Unicorn Knights at the head to the remount herd at the tail, covered two leagues.

Jermayan circled the army once—to warn Redhelwar of his presence—and landed.

"I'm hungry," Ancaladar said plaintively.

"Come to that . . ." Idalia said.

"I believe matters can be arranged," Jermayan said, with a small smile. "Though I fear—for us—the food will be cold."

"I'll settle," Idalia said.

They unbuckled their flying harnesses and dismounted. Both of them sank into the snow to their thighs before it packed hard enough to give them purchase. Even Jermayan found it difficult to move gracefully through that. They began wading through it toward the army, Idalia following in Jermayan's tracks.

Redhelwar met them halfway.

"I See you, Jermayan, Idalia."

"We See you, Redhelwar," Jermayan replied. "We come with fair news."

"Then you come in a good hour indeed."

He turned in his saddle and signaled to Ninolion, who rode up leading two destriers. Jermayan and Idalia mounted quickly, grateful to get out of the snow.

"It would please me were you to inform the army that we will be halting here for a short time," Redhelwar informed Ninolion. The adjutant raised the horn he carried to his lips and blew a complicated series of notes. In moments the horn call echoed up and down the line, as other horn-bearers took up the signal and relayed it.

Redhelwar turned back to Jermayan expectantly.

"My news is long. And Ancaladar informs me he is exceptionally hungry. As, I fear, are we," Jermayan said.

"Then Ancaladar's needs must be met at once," Redhelwar agreed promptly. "And you will take tea and breakfast as you give your news."

⸺

BY the time Jermayan had returned from leading a pair of oxen out to Ancaladar, a shelter had been erected—one of the simple roof-and-sides on poles used to provide quick shelter at the edge of the battlefield. But with a carpet underfoot, and braziers to warm it, it seemed luxury indeed.

As promised, there was tea, and a selection of filled pastries as well. Idalia was sitting on a folding stool already eating when Jermayan stepped inside, having just returned from leading Ancaladar's breakfast out to him.

"To begin," Jermayan said, "in crossing the Mystrals, Kellen destroyed the Shadewalker that laired in the pass. Its presence goes far to explain why there had been no word from Sentarshadeen for so long; no message-riders could pass in either direction while it lived. The caverns at Halacira were indeed the last Enclave of the Shadowed Elves, so that blight upon our lands is ended; they have been cleansed, by Vestakia's word. Kellen's force sustained only minor losses, and Kellen himself is well. Even now Artenel and his Artificers prepare the caverns for their new use. Though the plague has struck heavily at Sentarshadeen, and two of the King's Council, Sorvare and Ainalundore, have gone to the trees, Andoreniel himself recovers, with the help of the same medicines we have used to such good effect at Ysterialpoerin. Kellen has sent three Wildmages to the city, to ensure that there will be no shortage of potent medicine to treat plague-sufferers."

"Leaf and Star," Redhelwar breathed, making a quick gesture over his heart.

"Yet it was that we had wondered why it was that we could not Heal those afflicted with the Shadow's Kiss directly, and why it was that the powers of the Wild Magic seemed to be in eclipse across the land, while *Their* powers grew stronger," Jermayan went on, as calmly as if he were not telling of disastrous horror. "Vestakia had the answer for that as well, and Idalia had the solution. She has called up for us a great ally, one who has not walked our world since before Great Queen Vielissar Farcarinon riddled with dragons. Of this I shall say no more, save that our great Enemy shall be much surprised—and, I think, weakened."

"Then we owe you a debt greater than we shall ever be able to repay, Idalia," Redhelwar said, after a long pause.

⇌

" 'WHAT harms one harms all, beneath the canopy of Leaf and Star,' " Idalia quoted simply. She poured tea for Jermayan, and refilled her own mug and Redhelwar's as well. Several pastries, and a couple of mugs of strong Elven Allheal tea had gone a long way to rebuilding her strength, though a nice long nap wouldn't hurt.

"Now, in the time of *Their* weakness and confusion, would be the time to strike," Redhelwar said, his voice even. "Perhaps even, as Kellen wishes, to deny *Them* Armethalieh. But it cannot be. Kellen's force is too few to stand against what legions *They* might bring into the field. And mine is here. It will be spring by the time I have brought the army to Halacira, and our losses crossing the Mystrals may be . . . not what I would choose."

"Perhaps that need not be," Jermayan said.

Idalia set down her mug and looked at him.

"You know that in ancient days, the Elven Mages could do many things that seem not like simple magic as we know it, but beyond the dreams of the possible," Jermayan said. "I have been speaking to Ancaladar. He tells me that what I imagine can be done. It is not without cost," he added quietly. "But the cost will be ours alone to bear. If it works, you need but take your army through a . . . door . . . we shall make, of four rods' width. You will ride out the other side upon the Gathering Plain, having traveled but a few yards in seeming. You need not cross the Mystrals at all."

"This must be a very great spell indeed," Redhelwar said.

"It will take all the magic we have to cast it," Jermayan said. "You must go as quickly as you can, for to hold the door open will take great effort."

All *the magic?* Idalia thought, with a sudden sharp pang of suspicion. But Ancaladar was a creature of magic. If Jermayan poured all of Ancaladar's magic into this one spell, Ancaladar would die. And if Ancaladar died, Jermayan would die as well. They were Bonded, linked by the strongest of ties.

Suddenly she realized what Jermayan intended, and what it would cost.

"Then we shall do so," Redhelwar said. He was no Mage, but he knew as well as Idalia did what Jermayan intended. "I shall go now and give orders to the army. We must re-form, to take best advantage of your spell." He paused. "You understand, Jermayan, that I can leave no one behind."

"I understand," Jermayan said. "I shall hold the door for as long as you need."

Redhelwar left the shelter. A few moments later Idalia heard the horns begin to sound again, mixed with the babble of voices, as new orders were given.

"Jermayan!" she said.

"You must go with them, of course, Idalia," he said calmly. They will need Healers. And you will not wish to be alone here, when the spell is run."

She nodded.

Somehow she'd always thought they'd have more time, even if not much more. That she'd be the first to die. Something.

She took his hand, imagining the feel of flesh against flesh through the heavy gauntlets they both wore against the cold.

"I would not do this, were it not vital," he said, answering words she could not bring herself to speak. "The army is useless here. Through luck and chance,

They have accomplished what *They* have always wished to do—divided our forces while *They* work *Their* evils elsewhere. I can undo this foul mischance, and I will. Kellen would do as much, had he the power. So would you, or Cilarnen, or any of us."

"I know," she answered steadily.

She had already given up as much. That she had not yet been called to pay her Mageprice was luck, nothing more.

They sat together, quietly, drinking tea, until Redhelwar came to tell them that the army was in position.

<hr />

INSTEAD of a narrow column of march, the army was now assembled into a broad—and much shorter—series of ranks. The Unicorn Knights were at the fore, as always, while behind them was the remount herd and the loose livestock with their handlers. Behind them stood the Centaurs.

But behind the Centaurs were the supply wagons.

Redhelwar was right. Without his supply train—the Healers and their medicines, the tents, the fodder for the animals, the food for the Men, Elves, and Centaurs, the equipment to repair tack and armor, the army was all-but-crippled. There were some things here that could not be replaced at all, and others that could not be replaced quickly. Redhelwar must have them all in order to fight.

But the supply train was the slowest-moving part of the army. For Jermayan to hold the door long enough for it to pass through might be a magic beyond his strength.

Behind the supply train stood the ranks of Elven Knights. Once the huge, slow-moving, ox-drawn sledges were through, the Knights would move fast enough. And if, by some terrible mischance, they were cut off, and marooned upon this side of the Mystrals, they, of all the elements of Redhelwar's army, were best equipped to make their own way across the mountains alone and rejoin it.

"I have brought Cella for you, Idalia," Ninolion said, leading Idalia's cream palfrey up to the shelter. "I know you will wish to ride her."

He had also brought Valdien, Jermayan's warhorse, for Jermayan would need a mount that he could ride back to Ancaladar's side—and one that he could command to return to the army without him.

"My thanks," Idalia said briefly. She took the mare's reins.

The shelter had not been packed. Redhelwar had done all that he could to make Jermayan's task easier. He had lightened the sledges of everything that could possibly be left behind. It was not much, but the snow around the army's stopping-place was starred with neat cairns of discarded material.

"Be well, Idalia," Jermayan said.

Idalia took a deep breath. "Be sure I shall tell Kellen all you have done," she said.

"Then I hold myself satisfied," Jermayan answered simply.

He turned away, and mounted Valdien, and rode out to Ancaladar. Idalia mounted Cella, and rode to take her place in the line. The Healers and the Mountainfolk rode just ahead of the wagons, for they must be certain to reach the other side, of all the elements of the army.

A few moments later Valdien, riderless now, came galloping back.

That was the signal.

The army began to move forward.

Several hundred yards in advance of the army's line, Idalia saw a faint sparkle on the snow. No, in the air above the snow. It danced and shimmered on the air like Pelashia's Veils, until a curtain of light formed, strengthened.

The air was filled with magic. It prickled on her skin, lifted the loose tendrils of her hair. It was as if she could swim in it.

In the distance, she could see Jermayan, sitting on Ancaladar's back.

The unicorns went from a trot, to a gallop, to a leaping, bounding run.

Passed through the veil of light.

Vanished.

Behind her she could hear the cries and the whip-cracks of the drovers, as they goaded their stolid charges into something faster than their normal ground-eating plod.

The ground shook as the remount herd thundered forward at a dead run, kicking up waves of snow that sparkled in the sun, clearing a path for those who followed after. Some of the animals tried to dodge aside at the last moment, and were expertly forced back into the herd by their mounted handlers. Behind the herd of horses came the slower-moving ox-herd, goaded to frenzy by a mob of howling Centaurs, waving hats and blankets. The oxen did not try to dodge the doorway. They simply put their heads down and ran, and woe betide anything that got in their way.

They, too, passed through the shimmering doorway of light and vanished.

The Centaurs that had not been with the ox-herd were the next to reach the door, their long ranks galloping in close formation. Sunlight sparkled off their armored flanks, and their long tails floated behind them as they galloped forward, arms pumping, heads down. As if they passed into a waterfall they vanished, rank by rank.

Behind them the Healers and the Mountainfolk galloped, too—the Elven Healers and Idalia on their palfreys, the Mountainfolk on their sturdy shaggy ponies. How long now had Jermayan held the spell? Less than half the army had passed through, and the fastest half had already gone.

With all her heart, she wanted to stop, to turn aside, and knew she could not. She passed through the door.

There was a sudden sensation of darkness and falling. Not cold, but a shocking and entire absence of warmth. The transition seemed to take forever, and no time at all.

Then there was light again, and instead of brightness, the day was dark and gray, the air chill with a denseness that spoke of heavy snow to come—soon.

"Keep moving!" she heard. "Keep moving! There are others right behind you!"

Cella was normally the mildest and most easygoing of mounts, but the gentle mare had never in all her days experienced anything like the passage through the door. Idalia had no difficulty in obeying the unknown person's orders, because Cella laid her ears flat back and bolted forward at a dead run.

When Idalia finally regained control of her mount several minutes later and was able to pay attention to something other than Cella, the scene that met her eyes was barely-controlled chaos.

In the distance—at least a mile behind her—she could see the shimmer of Jermayan's door. Leading away from it, there was a wide swath of trampled snow. The herds had simply . . . fled. Their handlers had not tried to stop them, for the most vital thing at the moment was to clear the area around the door itself. And many of the handlers had been thrown from wildly shying mounts as they came through. The Centaurs had carried them to safety, but Idalia could see blood on the snow. There were injured.

The Centaur army was scattered in clumps over a great distance, in two wide arcs to each side of the doorway, a ragged line of warriors almost a mile in length. Some of the Centaurs were sprawled in the snow, others had Elves mounted on their backs—the injured horse-handlers, Idalia guessed.

Riderless horses—those that had not simply followed the herd—were running everywhere.

It looked like the aftermath of a battle.

Few of the other riders that had come through the door at the same time she had fared much better than she and Cella, though most of the Mountainborn had at least stayed in the saddle. The important thing, now, was to keep the doorway clear.

She rode up to the nearest Centaur she saw.

"That stand of trees! It should be far enough from the door! We must move the injured there and reorganize!"

He nodded. The Unicorn Knights were already regrouped in good order, but they could not approach the main army. The Centaurs were scattered.

The Centaur Captain raised his horn to his lips. Compared to the sound of the Elven horns, it was harsh and strident, but it performed its task just as well.

The Centaurs began re-forming into units, converging on the thicket of trees in the distance, and the Mountainfolk and the Healers followed.

In the distance, three sledges came through the door, side-by-side.

The oxen bawled in terror. They had been moving at what passed for a swift trot among their kind before, but now they shifted into an all-out panicked gallop, lunging forward across the well-beaten snow as fast as they could go.

If they run into each other—if the traces break—if one of them breaks a leg—

Then there would be a barrier in front of the door that no one could shift.

And the rest of the Elven Army would ride right into it, with no way of knowing what they were about to encounter.

But the others had seen the danger as well as she had. The Mountainborn Wildmages turned and rode back.

"I will Speak to them as they come," a Wildmage named Ardir said, as the first three sledges thundered past, miraculously unscathed. "You all must help me."

"Consent freely given, as is our aid," Hudirg answered.

"Of course," Idalia said. Behind her, she heard murmurs as the other Mountainborn each offered up his or her own consent.

The next team was already coming through. Behind the Wildmages, some Centaurs rushed to the heads of the lead yokes of the other ox-teams, grabbing their headstalls and turning them away from each other and slowing their headlong flight.

She had no time to think of Jermayan now, only to offer up a quick prayer to the Gods of the Wild Magic that Ardir's spell—and Jermayan's—would hold for as long as they needed it to.

Ardir took a handful of herbs from a pouch on his belt, quickly pulling off his glove and slashing his hand, moistening them with his blood.

He raised both hands, bare and gloved together, stretching them out toward the oxen coming through the doorway. Idalia could see his lips move, but heard no words.

Suddenly her senses seemed both sharpened and dimmed—sight was nearly gone; the world was a dim place of dull confusing shadows, but scent was now keen: she could smell snow, and wind, and an oncoming storm; the bright verdant scent of distant trees, withered grass beneath the snow, the possibility of a buried stream, horses, Centaurs, Men, other things for which she had no name.

And there was more.

It seemed as if she could suddenly feel the blind animal terror of the beasts at having been wrenched so suddenly out of the familiar world they knew—and then felt, as well, waves of soothing calm and love wash over her, stilling that terror and replacing it with the assurance that all was still well.

Though they had begun by bolting forward at the same dead run as the first three teams, this set finished by trotting forward gently, and allowing themselves to be led off by the next set of waiting Centaurs.

Over and over the same performance was repeated. The ox-teams would appear through the veil of light, panic-stricken and frenzied, and Ardir would speak to them with his magic, causing them to trot calmly away.

But such magic came at a price. Though only Ardir would pay the Mageprice for this spell, they were all giving Power to it, and Idalia had been exhausted to begin with. She had not hesitated, for the very survival of the army depended on keeping the doorway clear, but as team after team of oxen came through and was lulled, she felt as if her own life's blood was being poured out with the spell.

She hardly believed her eyes when ox-carts were at last replaced by horses. The Elven Knights were riding through, moving over the beaten snow in a swift glitter of lances and armor. Though the destriers danced and shied at their passage through the door, they did not break ranks, nor once slow their headlong pace. The wall of Elven Knights swept across the snow like a sword-stroke, following the beaten path in the snow, clearing the way for those who came behind as fast as they could.

Redhelwar rode in their midst.

And as the last of them rode through the doorway, the shimmering dance of light . . . vanished.

It is done, Idalia thought.

It was the last thing she remembered.

Fourteen

In the Room of Autumn Birches

THE WORLD WITHOUT Sun was the true center of the universe, and all knowledge, whether good or bad, resonated there. When the ancient Power came back into the world, Savilla knew it. It summoned her out of her deepest contemplation, that state which a mere human might mistake for death, as she felt the painful tides of Light dispelled some of the web of glorious Darkness she had so painstakingly wrapped around the World Above.

And thicken the Veils she had worked so hard and so long to thin.

She rose from her bed, veiling herself in magic to keep from summoning all her Court into consciousness, for in the World Without Sun, all time was measured by the Queen, and when she Rose, so did all the Endarkened. And it was not her wish, just now, that this should happen. Alone and unadorned, she padded through a dark and silent world, her only companions the breath of the Deep Earth, and the cries—faintly heard—of the mortal captives in their slave pens, whose bodies still measured time by the lights in a sky they would never see again.

Her senses were keen, honed by the spells she had cast Rising after Rising.

She knew what had summoned her out of contemplation.

The Starry Hunt rode the world once more.

The doorway by which she had meant to bring *He Who Is* into the world once more was . . . closed.

But not locked.

Great as their power was, it was not great enough for that.

She was old in power and pride. A lesser Endarkened would have raged against this setback, this unspeakable defeat when victory was so near she could nearly sink her fangs into it.

But Savilla had stood upon the battlefield and watched Uralesse utterly humbled, his power broken by creatures who were less than vermin, the glorious power of the Endarkened at the time of their greatest strength cast down. With the ragged remains of her father's Court, she had retreated to the World Without Sun, to spend centuries in furious contemplation of their losses. She had not spent them in anguished yearning for what might have been, but in scheming to destroy her father, so that she might take his place and lead her people to a greater glory.

She had patience. She had vision.

She had eaten Uralesse's flesh and ascended to the Throne of Night.

She would not allow another defeat, no matter how maddening, to turn her mind from the victory that must belong to the Endarkened.

The door she had made, in blood and pain and endless sacrifice, was still there.

She could open it.

But to do so now would take a sacrifice greater than any she had offered up yet. A sacrifice made not in a place of Darkness, but of Light.

With a more powerful offering than even a unicorn's death.

Or the death of a hundred unicorns.

But when she had accomplished this, she would rip the door between the worlds open so wide that that no power the Light could invoke could seal it again. *He Who Is* would be free to aid His creation once more, just as it had been in the glorious days of their beginning.

Savilla dispelled the veil of magic that surrounded her, and felt her Court begin to rouse.

There were plans to make.

The time of the final battle was nearly at hand.

And she meant to win it.

Once and for all time.

"YOU should have told us you were already paying Mageprice," Marocht said reprovingly.

Idalia opened her eyes. The familiar roof of the Healer's tent lay above her.

"You had cast a great spell recently, had you not?" the Wildmage Healer repeated, her weather-seamed face crinkled in disapproval as she gazed down at Idalia.

"I . . . yes," Idalia admitted sheepishly. "But your need was great."

"That's as may be," Marocht answered. "Perhaps not so great that we needed to lose you, Idalia."

"Which, as it turns out, you have not," Idalia pointed out reasonably. She struggled to sit up, and was rewarded with a blinding headache.

"Ah, but for a few days yet, you may wish you *had* been lost," Marocht said with satisfaction. Marocht always took great satisfaction from seeing the worst possible side of anything. "Now I shall bring you a nice bowl of broth. After fasting so long, you will not be able to keep aught else down."

"So long?" Idalia said, puzzled. "How long have I slept?"

"Three days. We have had time to reach the Gathering Plain, and make our camp here, carrying you with us like a bundle of hides for market. And shall be here a sennight more, I fear, while we seek out the horses and the rest of the cattle—though no doubt the silly nags will all come drifting back when they're hungry enough. If they haven't run all the way to Sentarshadeen by now. At least the unicorns can earn their keep by looking for them."

Idalia did have to smile at that. Trust Marocht to come up with the notion of the Unicorn Knights earning their keep by becoming horse wranglers.

She lay back against the pillows. Even so short a conversation had exhausted her.

A few minutes later, Marocht came back with a large bowl of broth. To her surprise—though it should not really have come as one—Idalia was too weak to feed herself.

"Told you," Marocht said with satisfaction.

"Was anyone else injured coming through?" Idalia asked, between spoonfuls of broth.

"Eh," Marocht said dismissively. "Sprained ankles, cracked skulls, a broken wrist or two. Easily mended. Our spells have not worked so well or so fast since last spring. There must be luck in that door of Jermayan's."

"I suppose so," Idalia said. For a moment she had actually managed to forget the price of being here, but now the grief of her loss rose up in her like weariness.

"You're tired," Marocht said firmly. "And the soup is gone. Sleep again. We will talk more later."

FOR the next several days, Idalia did little more than eat and sleep. News slowly trickled in to her—courtesy of Marocht, who was wise enough to know that her patient would recover more swiftly if her inquisitiveness were kept satisfied.

Redhelwar had sent messengers to Halacira to let Kellen know that the army was now at Ondoladeshiron, and would be moving south as soon as possible.

Messengers coming north from Sentarshadeen had brought their news in turn: Andoreniel continued to recover.

Most of the horses and oxen had been recovered, though a few had fallen afoul of predators, or had broken legs or necks in their headlong flights.

The army was ready to march.

One full sennight after Jermayan had cast his spell, the army stood in marching order upon the Gathering Plain, perhaps four moonturns before they would otherwise have reached it. Another fortnight, at most, would see them at Halacira.

A heavy wet snow was falling, and visibility was poor, but if they waited for good weather, they would wait here until spring. The Wildmages were still recovering from the spells they had cast to ease the passage of the oxen through the doorway, and would not wish to shift the weather in any event, lest they make it worse elsewhere. They would all simply have to endure. They should be able to ride out of the worst of the storm in a day or so, once they passed off of the Plains of Ondoladeshiron and into the forests of the lowlands surrounding Sentarshadeen. That terrain would have its own hardships—most of all the thick forests, which would make the passage of the ox-drawn sledges difficult—but at least they would be different ones.

Idalia sat in Cella's saddle, in her place beside the Healers' wagons. The loss of Jermayan was a dull ache in her chest. No one had spoken of it to her, and for that much she was grateful. Everyone here had suffered losses in the moonturns past; hers was no different for having come quietly, in a moment freely chosen, rather than in the wild melee of a battlefield, at the edge of an enemy's blade.

The column had just started to move when there was a clamor of horns. After so long, she could decode the signals without effort. *Enemy sighted. In the sky.*

The column halted again. The skirmishing units deployed. She couldn't see them from where she sat, but she could imagine their movements, nearly as clearly as if she possessed Kellen's battle-sight: the groups of twelve under their sub-commanders fanning out from the column on each side, forging through the heavy snow and turning to face the enemy coming from above.

She wondered what it was. She knew that the Deathwings hated to fly in snowstorms, and they hadn't been sighted south of the Mystrals, but the chance to strike at a prize as tempting as the full Elven Army would surely lure them out of hiding. . . .

Suddenly the horns sounded again.

A friend! A friend!

Idalia stood in her stirrups, scanning the sky.

A great black winged shape was sweeping toward the Elven Army, flying just below the clouds.

She knew that form.

Ancaladar.

Jermayan was alive.

She forced Cella through the press of riders around her, working her way to the edge of the column. The dragon was circling now, coming in for a landing.

It was not one of Ancaladar's better landings.

The dragon did what could only be described as a belly-flop into the snow. Instead of back-pedaling with his wings, as he usually did, he simply folded them in and allowed himself to slide, until the snow heaped up enough in front of him to bring him to a stop.

Idalia urged Cella onward through the snow. Ahead of her trotted two of the skirmishing units, Redhelwar, Adaerion, and their adjutants.

They reached Jermayan and Ancaladar.

Even though she could see little of Jermayan beneath his furs and armor, it was not hard to see that both he and Ancaladar looked exhausted. Dazed. Even the dragon's scales had lost their iridescence, and were the dull black of soot.

But they were here.

"I See you, Jermayan," Redhelwar said calmly, looking up at Jermayan. "It is a thing I confess I had not expected to do again. But you come in a good hour. We were about to embark for Halacira, to rejoin the rest of the army. We were delayed here longer than we expected. The passage through your door was not without its moments of interest, and it has taken us nearly a sennight to gather up the herds and put the army into marching order again. While your door is a useful tool, I do not think it is one I shall employ again."

"I See you, Redhelwar. And I say to you that it is welcome news that you do not wish me to open that door once more, for that is something I shall never be able to do again. But that is a tale that can be told another time. I would not wish to delay the army's march. Ancaladar and I will scout ahead for you, as always, but do not, I pray you, look to us for more than warning of any danger, for we can give you no more than that."

"That is all we will need," Redhelwar answered firmly.

"It would gladden my heart were you to ride with us, Idalia," Jermayan said, looking to her at last.

"Ancaladar?" Idalia asked. The dragon didn't look as if he could take off at all, let alone with two passengers.

The black dragon swiveled his head to look at her. The golden eyes glowed with faint mirth.

"Idalia, you weigh nothing at all. You will not tire me, I promise you."

She scrambled from her saddle to the dragon's back, and quickly cinched the flying straps tight.

⟨≋⟩

ANCALADAR was as good as his word. Though his landing had been a cause for concern, the dragon's leap into the sky had something of his usual verve, though his takeoff run was far longer than any Idalia could ever remember. But at last he spread his great wings with their familiar snap, and rose swiftly into the air.

In moments they were above the clouds, into the brilliant—and much colder—upper air.

"You're still alive," she said unnecessarily. She leaned her head against Jermayan's fur-covered back, reassuring herself that it was true.

"Alive," he agreed.

There was a long pause.

"Idalia. I do not know how to explain what I do not understand. To make and hold such a portal as Ancaladar and I made to send the army through to On-doladeshiron . . . it is the Great Spell that was given, long ago, to any who are Bonded to a dragon to cast. Not to open a door, perhaps, but one single spell of such power for each such Mage to cast once in his life, and it should have consumed us utterly. But as the door closed . . . the Starry Hunt . . . *came* for us," Jermayan said.

Idalia could not imagine it, though she tried very hard. She could barely retain the memory of Summoning them, so ancient and wild was their power. To see them, in the calm and normal light of day, was something so far beyond the realm of normal experience, even for a Wildmage who had once been a Silver Eagle, that even her imagination failed.

It was simply too much.

"And then what happened?" she asked.

"They came. They . . . went. After a little time, we flew back to Ysterialpo-erin. Ancaladar had just enough strength for that. And fortunately for us, it was not far."

There was another long pause, and Idalia knew that Jermayan was gathering himself to say something he did not wish to say.

"We . . . live. But we will cast no more spells."

She had been prepared to hear far worse.

"You idiot! Do you think I care about that?" Idalia demanded. She hugged him fiercely. "I loved you when you were a simple Elven Knight, and I shall love you now that you are a simple Elven Knight once more."

"With a dragon," Ancaladar said.

"With a dragon," Idalia agreed.

Had the Starry Hunt turned Ancaladar from a creature of magic to a creature of flesh-and-blood? Ancaladar himself might not know. It might simply be that his magic had been drained so far by the spell that only enough remained to keep himself and the Bond alive, thanks to the Hunt's intervention.

In the end, it really didn't matter.

He was back.

⨠

KELLEN had become used to riding out to what he had gotten used to calling "Ancaladar's Grove" every morning at dawn to see if there was news from Sentarshadeen. Without a detachment of Unicorn Knights in the camp, it was simplest for him to check the grove for messages personally, since Unicorn Scouts were the fastest form of communication between the city and the camp.

And besides, it gave him private time with Shalkan.

The Halacira camp was quickly taking on the aspect of a small city. Tents were being replaced by buildings of wood and stone—the surrounding forest would never be the same, but that was a small price to pay, in Kellen's opinion. They had kitchens and a sawmill, thanks to Artenel's tireless labors, as well as a bathhouse.

And the news from Sentarshadeen was good.

The plague victims there continued to recover, and no new cases had been reported. Though Andoreniel's name was not mentioned, Kellen knew that the King's health must be continuing to improve as well.

He was puzzled at the continuing silence from Idalia and Jermayan. Midwinter had passed. She would have done her spell, if she had been able to, and he had heard nothing.

Obviously, that meant that she had done *something,* for if she had been able to do nothing at all, she would still have been in Sentarshadeen and would have written to him herself.

He wondered what it was that she *had* done.

Her continued silence worried him.

But he'd had little time to brood over it, because first the supply wagons had returned from Sentarshadeen—to everyone's great relief, since with even the Wildmages to Call the sparse game out of the forest into hunting range, supplies were running short, and even the best-trained Elven destrier would not eat meat.

Next had come the matter of providing Cilarnen a place to work.

A tent would not do—the largest they had was too small for his needs, Cilarnen informed Kellen, and the spells of the High Magick used too much fire. Half his energy would be spent in keeping his workplace from burning down around him. And Cilarnen's work was vital.

Even with the power he had to draw upon, Cilarnen lacked the ability to create an ice-pavilion such has he had used in the north. Besides, here, in the Avribalzar Forest, his surroundings lacked the same dry cold that was to be found west of Ysterialpoerin. The ice of such a structure would surely have rotted within a sennight.

Cilarnen's workspace must be wood. Or stone.

And the sooner it was in place, the sooner he could start working the spells they needed.

At least it turned out that they hadn't had to *build* it. All that had been required was providing Cilarnen with enough cut lumber deposited at a place Cilarnen selected, a suitable distance from the main camp. Cilarnen's magick had done the rest, creating a finished building the size of Redhelwar's pavilion from a pile of lumber between sunset and dawn.

There had not been enough to finish the entire structure, so the roof was made of saplings that Artenel and his sawyers had not provided. They were of an eerily uniform thickness and length, and every single one of them had been stripped of their branches and bark by the same unknown forces that Cilarnen had called up to build his sanctum.

He'd looked very smug when Kellen had come out to see him the following morning, a little worried about Cilarnen having spent the night alone in the cold and the snow. There were certainly no Tainted creatures making their home in the Avribalzar Forest, but if there were Demons raiding in the Delfier Valley, and Ice Trolls and Frost Giants north of the Mystrals, anything at all might show up here without warning.

"Like it?" Cilarnen had called.

Kellen had stared in resigned envy at the snug-looking round structure where none had stood the day before. Resigned, because after such a spectacular success Cilarnen was going to be even more difficult to live with than before—oh, he did his best to be polite and to fit in, but when he became obsessed with working out the details of creating or adapting one of the spells of the High Magick to serve Kellen's needs, nothing else but his work existed for him.

One of the reasons Cilarnen drove himself so hard and so dangerously, Kellen knew, was guilt. Guilt that he had not been able to save the folk at Nerendale. Guilt that Anigrel had attempted to use him as a weapon.

Guilt that when every possible warrior was needed to battle on the side of Light, the High Mages had not only refused to fight, but had done everything they could to give aid to an Enemy that nothing living should help.

And envious, because the wooden building looked as if it would be much warmer and drier than Kellen's own tent. And Cilarnen wasn't even going to use it for sleeping. His tent—where he would sleep and take his meals—was pitched a few feet away from his new sanctum.

Last of all, in the middle of everything else, there was Vestakia to worry about, at least as much as Kellen dared. Her understanding of the images she received from her father's mind seemed to grow clearer by the day, but such clarity did not come without a price. She looked as unwell as Cilarnen did, as if she, too, were yoked to energies nothing mortal should be allowed to bear.

And then, six days ago, when Kellen had gone to Ancaladar's Grove to see what dispatches—or messengers—might be awaiting him from Sentarshadeen, and to drink his morning tea in peace, he saw something that had stunned him completely.

Riasen, Captain of the Unicorn Knights, and Elariagor were standing in the clearing. The pale golden unicorn stood regarding Kellen with faint amusement sparkling from her turquoise eyes.

"Did you miss us?" she asked, switching her long tufted tail.

"I— What— Who—" Kellen sputtered.

He neither spilled a drop of his tea, nor was in any way incapable of dealing with an enemy attack—should one happen to appear in that moment—but for just an instant, his mind was incapable of understanding what he saw. Riasen could not be here. Riasen was with the army, on the other side of the Mystrals, marching toward Ondoladeshiron, and Kellen would see him and the others sometime in late spring. Not now, three days after Midwinter.

"The army rests at Ondoladeshiron, Kellen," Riasen said. "All of it. Now. Redhelwar directs me to inform you that we shall be with you as soon as we can—there is the small matter of the herds to gather back together and a few other insignificant trifles to take care of before we march. Yet it grieves me to tell you that our passage was bought with a life. Two lives. Jermayan and Ancaladar have given their lives for the spell that brought us here so quickly."

The army was at Ondoladeshiron. If Riasen said it, Kellen had no doubt that it was true. And that Jermayan and Ancaladar were dead . . . that must be true also.

"What spell?" Kellen asked bluntly.

"Two days ago, Ancaladar joined us upon the march. It was a surprise to us, as last we had seen of him, Jermayan, or Idalia, they had gone to bear Cilarnen and Vestakia to you at Halacira. Idalia brought us the joyous news that Andoreniel gains in strength, and that *They* had been struck a grievous blow by a spell she had but lately done, and would now be cast down in disorder and confusion."

So the Greater Summoning had worked. But . . .

"Redhelwar said that the time to strike was now, in *Their* hour of greatest weakness, but that by the time he had reached Ondoladeshiron, it would be too late, for *They* would have regained *Their* equilibrium. And Jermayan said that it was possible to make a door through which Redhelwar's whole army could pass, stepping from the outskirts of Ysterialpoerin to the Gathering Plain in but an instant, but that the spell would require all of the magic that he and Ancaladar possessed."

And that, Kellen knew, meant their deaths.

"And so they cast it, but passing through the veils was a great shock, and the animals did not like it overmuch. The herdsmen say we shall be collecting them for some days yet."

"It is not a door that I want to go through twice," Elariagor said feelingly. "Blackness and falling and cold—no wonder the oxen and the horses ran as if *They Themselves* were chasing them. If Ardir had not been there to cast his spell of Animal Speaking, the ox-teams would have done just the same thing, and they were hitched together in teams of twelve and had sledges attached to them besides. It would have been a great mess, with three thousand Elven Knights who could not see what they were riding into set to come just behind. Do imagine it, Kellen."

Kellen could: the oxen crashing into each other in panic, creating a huge barrier of tangled traces and wounded animals to block this mysterious door. And then, crashing into it, the Elven Knights, who would be coming through at a dead run, because Jermayan could surely not have held the door open forever.

"It will be good to hear what you may say to me of my sister, Idalia," Kellen said carefully.

"She is well," Riasen said, sounding a little surprised that Kellen had asked. "She shared in the spellprice for Ardir's spell, and of course, since it came so soon after the previous work she had done, she was greatly weakened. But she rests now in the Healers' care. You will see her, once the army comes."

"That makes good hearing," Kellen answered automatically.

He doubted Idalia was doing much resting, knowing that Jermayan was dead.

⁓

BUT he did not have much time to dwell on this new loss. With the army south of the Mystrals, Andoreniel on the road to recovery, and He Who Is having been blocked from aiding the Endarkened—somehow—first thing Kellen wanted was more information about exactly what it was that Idalia had *done*.

For that there was only one place to go.

He provided Riasen and Elariagor with the camp's hospitality—fortunately, tea had come with the supply wagons, and there was someone else to brew it—before they continued on to Sentarshadeen, to give a report to Morusil as well. Kellen had added his own reports—brief, as there was nothing *to* report—and sent them on their way.

"Well, that was entertaining in a quiet way," Shalkan said, as they headed along a well-cleared snow path toward Cilarnen's clearing. The path was well-cleared because Cilarnen had several ice-golems whose sole job, day and night, was to clear and maintain paths through the forest, which they did until they melted or fell to pieces. When he lost enough of them, Cilarnen simply made more and set the new ones to work.

Kellen found it more than a little unsettling, though it was nice to have the nice wide paths through the forest shoveled and swept down to scraped and textured ice.

"No," Kellen said, after a moment's thought. "Not really. It's good to have the army here now, and not four months from now, though. I wish I knew what Idalia's Greater Summoning actually . . . summoned. And . . . Jermayan was my first real friend. You're my friend, too, Shalkan, but in some ways that's different. We're bound together by magic. Jermayan didn't have to be my friend, didn't have to have anything to do with me. He could have let someone else go with me to the Keystone. He was the first person—well, aside from you—to think that I might be something more than just a really bad Wildmage."

"I know," Shalkan said simply, leaning against him for a moment.

As they reached the clearing where Cilarnen now lived, they heard a sudden shout of anguish. The door to the wooden hut burst open, and something small and gray streaked out across the snow.

"Catch it! Catch it! I'm not finished with it yet!"

Kellen grabbed for it and missed. Shalkan stamped down with one cloven hoof, pinning it to the snow.

Kellen picked it up as Cilarnen—barefoot, in a long gray robe—came running over the snow toward him.

The thing Kellen had in his hands resembled a ferret—Kellen had seen pictures of the creatures by now—except for the fact that it was made of stone, its body a uniform gray color. It writhed and twisted in his grasp, striking and biting at his hands, but though its small stone teeth could penetrate his heavy gloves, they had no chance against the armored gauntlets beneath.

Cilarnen slipped a noose woven of thin strands of red silk around the creature's neck and it instantly became what it had been in the beginning: a lifeless marble carving.

He took it back, and only then seemed to notice that he was standing barefoot on snow.

"Yah!" he announced inelegantly, and ran back the way he'd come, holding the stone ferret in one hand and holding up his robes with the other, hissing to himself at the cold.

Despite the sadness of the news he'd received this morning, Kellen *did* have to smile to himself. This was hardly the image of serene and perfect all-knowingness that the High Mages of Armethalieh would like to project, but it was a much more human one. When he thought of the High Magick, which had managed to free itself from Balances and Mageprices to become a weapon with nothing to hold it in check, Kellen would much rather think of Cilarnen hopping barefoot over the snow because he'd forgotten his boots in the excitement of working out a spell than of his last sight of the High Council on the day they had Banished him—bloated with smug arrogance, drunk with power, and certain that killing a seventeen-year-old boy would have absolutely no consequences.

There were always consequences.

A few moments later, Cilarnen came back, having added boots and a cloak to his robe.

"Thanks for catching that," he said to Shalkan and Kellen. "I think I need to put the spells on in a different order, really, and that one got out of the box. I really think it's better if they know who they're supposed to serve, and how, before I wake them up."

"Why are you having a problem?" Kellen asked. "You've made dozens of golems before."

Cilarnen shrugged. "According to theory, the Enlivening Spell makes the statue take on the essential nature of its form. So hounds act like hounds; birds, birds; and so on. I was making servants. Maybe that made a difference. But a ferret's essential nature is to . . . ferret. Which means I had better put any compulsions on its nature in place first, I think."

"That sounds like a good idea," Kellen agreed.

"But you didn't come to talk to me about the ferrets. I told Artenel he couldn't have any of them—or the snakes either—until the end of the sennight."

"No," said Kellen. "I need something else. And I have bad news."

"It's about that thing that came a few days ago, isn't it?" Cilarnen said.

"Tea," he said next, regarding Kellen's blank expression.

~⁂~

"YOU were raised in the City. You know we work at night," Cilarnen said, handing Kellen a mug. He knew Shalkan's tastes by now, and tipped several honeydisks onto a plate and held them out to the unicorn. Shalkan took them delicately, one by one.

"In fact, I was just finishing up with the latest batch of stone ferrets before going to bed now, as it's simple work and doesn't require much concentration, really. But Midwinter was a time of—oh, say it was as if everything was very clear and quiet, so that I could see a long way. So I wasn't going to waste it on stone ferrets. I wanted to check as much of the Borders as I could, then see what was going on in Armethalieh.

"Well, as I've told you before, those big cities the Elves have up there are pretty well gone. I've only been as far north as Ysterialpoerin, and I've only been there once, but I tried looking for other things in the north that looked like that big house I was in—and felt like it, too—and I found two that were empty, and one looked like it had been burned. Since it had been looted, I could follow objects that had been taken from it, and a lot of them kept leading me back to Ysterialpo-erin, but enough of them didn't that I could start to trace the Frost Giants; figure out where they are, and where they're going. I was in the middle of doing that—it's very boring, so I don't bother you with it unless there's actually something in-teresting going on—when all of a sudden there was this . . . it was as if there were a fire, and somebody had thrown an enormous load of coals and oil onto it."

"I don't get it," Kellen said, shaking his head.

"You really weren't paying attention at College, were you?" Cilarnen said. "Well, they didn't really want to teach us this stuff. We might have learned to think. Okay. Think of the world—everything you know—as a pond of fish. All the fish in the pond are Powers—what the College teaches us are Illusory Crea-tures and Imaginary Constructs, but are actually real, just like Shalkan."

"Okay," Kellen said. Shalkan snorted in amusement.

Cilarnen seemed so surprised by things that Kellen took for granted—that the Shining Folk were real, for example—but then, Kellen and Cilarnen had learned about magic and the world in two entirely different ways.

He supposed that meant that they saw the world in two entirely different ways, too.

"Now imagine I'm looking into that pond on Midwinter night, talking to some of the Powers—fish—and doing my best not to be seen by others, when suddenly, from nowhere I can see, a giant fish, bigger than all the other fish, ap-pears in the pond."

"Is it a good fish?" Kellen asked dubiously.

Cilarnen snorted. "A very good fish, I think, as it immediately started eating some of the fish I'd been trying to hide from. But still a very scary fish."

Midwinter would have been when Idalia had done her spell.

"So where did this, er, 'fish' come from?" Kellen asked.

"*I* don't know!" Cilarnen said in exasperation. "Somewhere that isn't here. Where that is, and why it's showed up just now, the Light only knows."

"What else can you tell me about it?" Kellen asked.

"Is that what you came to ask me?" Cilarnen asked, sounding incredulous. "Do you want me to summon it up and *ask* it? Kellen, I'd rather summon up one of *Them*, believe me! It's destroying our enemies, but that doesn't mean . . . look. A candle is a good thing to have inside your house, right? A forest fire isn't. But they're both flame."

"I guess," Kellen said doubtfully. Any time Cilarnen tried to explain some-thing to him about magic—or *magick*—he only confused Kellen further.

"You're saying it's one of the Old Powers," Shalkan said helpfully.

"I have *no* idea," Cilarnen answered fervently. "I don't even know what an 'Old Power' is."

"You know I went to Sentarshadeen a few days ago," Kellen said. "Jermayan, well, needed help with a spell. We needed to figure out a way to keep He Who Is out of the world."

"Oh, is *that* all?" Cilarnen said sarcastically.

"Well, Idalia—and Jermayan, and Ancaladar—figured out among them that Great Queen Vielassar Farcarinon had done it once before, so it ought to be possible to do it again. And apparently it involved something called a Greater Summoning."

Cilarnen went very still.

"And she . . . did this . . . Greater Summoning. At Midwinter."

It was not a question.

"She was supposed to. If she could gain the consent of all the land. I haven't heard from her since I left Sentarshadeen, but since you say this 'Big Fish' has appeared, I suppose she managed to gain what she needed and did the spell. Redhelwar says it was something that threw *Them* into confusion."

Cilarnen laughed shakily. "A Greater Power of the Light! Kellen, there are times when it's a *good* thing that you have no idea of what you're talking about! And to think I worried about calling up a mere Elemental! Yes, I would say that Idalia's Summoning worked. But as for telling you precisely what it was she called . . . that I cannot do, save that it is old, and powerful, and on our side. But how could you have heard from Redhelwar so quickly?" Cilarnen asked. "Some new spell?"

Cilarnen's innocent question reminded Kellen that despite their cause for rejoicing, there was also new cause for grief.

"Riasen was at Ancaladar's Grove this morning. The army is at Ondoladeshiron. Jermayan . . . brought them south through some kind of portal. He and Ancaladar died doing it."

"Dear Light," Cilarnen said quietly. "Kellen, I am so sorry. I know he was your friend. And Idalia's."

"We needed the army here," Kellen said simply.

They sat in silence for a moment.

"Kellen," Cilarnen said. "Your Wild Magic—it's all about balancing things, isn't it? So everything has an opposite?"

"I suppose so," Kellen said. He'd never really thought about it. The Wild Magic was about doing, not about thinking about doing.

"So He Who Is has an opposite too?"

"I guess so."

"So this Greater Power that Idalia has summoned must be that opposite. Or at least a part of it. Because if everything were really back in balance, we'd already have won."

Kellen thought about it. It seemed right. If there was one thing he knew for sure about the Wild Magic, it was that it didn't solve your problems for you. It helped, but you had to help yourself as well.

"Then Redhelwar's right," Kellen said at last. "*They're* as weak now as *They're* going to be. And if the Greater Power can keep *He Who Is* from getting through for at least a while, this is our best chance."

"To do what?" Cilarnen asked.

"To deny *Them* Armethalieh," Kellen said. "And—if possible—to convince the High Mages to fight on our side."

Cilarnen laughed bitterly.

"Well, so long as you're not planning to do that today, I'm going to bed. Unless there's something else you need right now?"

"Not today," Kellen assured him.

❧

THAT had been almost a sennight ago.

Today . . .

Today he'd discovered that Jermayan was alive after all.

"I just thought you'd like to know," Shalkan said casually, when Kellen came to the Grove that morning, "that when I was out for my morning canter, I saw a dragon in the sky."

Kellen simply stared at him.

"A dragon," Shalkan repeated patiently. "A *black* dragon. In the sky. Flying."

"An-Ancaladar?" Kellen stammered.

"Do you know of any other dragons?" the unicorn answered. "They're flying with the army. It should be here in a sennight or so."

"I— But— How—? I mean . . . Jermayan *couldn't* have been wrong about his spell. *Could* he?"

"No," Shalkan said. "I think, when you talk to him, you may find him just as surprised by this turn of events as you are. But it's just possible—with one of the Great Powers afoot in the world again after so long—that we should not expect everything to go as we have been used to. Just a thought."

"Huh," Kellen said. "Well, if they aren't going to, we could use a few more of them going this way. I'm going to go find Keirasti. We'll tell Vestakia."

"And I suppose you'll want me to tell Cilarnen," Shalkan said, trying to sound cross, and failing.

"You know he'll feed you honey-disks."

"Honey-*cakes*," Shalkan corrected eagerly, turning and trotting off.

❧

KEIRASTI'S troop had made their way to the encampment a few days before. Kellen walked back down into the camp to share the good news with her.

She did not answer at her tent, and the flap was pinned back, indicating that she was not there. Maredhiel told him that Keirasti had gone down to the Angarussa, as she frequently did on her early morning rides. He saddled Firareth and found the Elven Knight, as he so often did, standing in the snow gazing out at the new bridge, Orata's reins in her hand.

"I See you, Keirasti," he said.

"I See you, Kellen," she said, without turning around. "I promise you, if I see another four centuries, and spend all of them standing here, I shall never get used to this bridge, useful though it is."

Was that how old she was? He'd never asked, of course. He didn't know whether it was rude or not to ask Elves their ages. It had simply never come up.

Well, Idalia *had* once said that Keirasti was old enough to be his grandmother. . . .

And apparently more, by several hundred years.

"I have good news," he said. "I've just spoken to Shalkan. He tells me that Jermayan is alive."

"Alive!" She turned around. "Leaf and Star! This news comes in a good hour! It . . . would be good to know how such a thing can be, of course."

"I'm not really sure, and neither is Shalkan. But he and Ancaladar are with the army, and they'll be here soon. We can ask them then. I was hoping that you'd accompany me to let Vestakia know."

"Now this is a duty I shall be happy to discharge," Keirasti said, grinning broadly. She swung up into Orata's saddle and the two of them turned back toward the camp.

꩜

VESTAKIA simply burst into tears when she heard, flinging herself into Keirasti's arms.

It was one of the reasons Kellen hadn't wanted to be alone with her when he gave her the news.

He knew that every night now, when she slept, Vestakia's dreams took her to Shadow Mountain, into the mind of the Prince of Shadow Mountain. Closer, each night, to his innermost thoughts and plans.

It was a place nothing of the Light should have to go.

But the images—the impressions—Vestakia was able to relay to him were important than even Vestakia's life.

They were changing *Their* tactics.

Vestakia wasn't completely sure, but she had the idea that Shadow Mountain was calling its Allies back to it, out of the Elven Lands and the High

Reaches. The Ice Trolls and the Frost Giants. Something *They* called Dwerro. Others she wasn't quite sure of.

Every creature that owed fealty to *Them,* and could withstand sunlight, was being massed together.

I think They're *finally going to meet us on the battlefield,* Kellen thought.

But by now Kellen was wise enough to know that the traditional battle the Elves had always hoped for could only end in disaster for the Allies. Even if their numbers were evenly matched—something he had no way of knowing—the Endarkened would have more powerful Mages at their beck, and far more of them, than the Allies could possibly hope to put into the field. Even with this new Ally that Idalia had summoned.

Unless they could take Armethalieh before the battle and turn it to their side.

He made up his mind.

When he left Vestakia in her tent, he sought out Isinwen.

⟞⟝

EVEN in a camp with no prospect of imminent battle, there was much to do. Those who were not on patrol were hunting, or felling trees to feed Artenel's seemingly-endless need of lumber. And anyone who was not doing that had armor and tack and weapons to care for, sword-drill to perform—for the army could not be allowed to grow slack in its temporary leisure—or the thousand small housekeeping tasks of an army in the field. In addition to all this, everything must be kept organized and running smoothly, and as Kellen's Second, much of the work of seeing that everyone knew where they should be and what tasks fell to them in the particular hours of each particular day fell to Isinwen.

He rose to his feet as Kellen stepped into the large tent—made from three others—that had been designated the command center. It would be nice to have a more permanent structure, Kellen supposed—even six braziers were not enough to truly warm it—but it was only temporary. Most of the army would be moving onward soon, and with it the need for such a place would end. Only Artenel's artificers, and a few hundred Knights left to guard them, would remain to continue the work on Fortress Halacira. It was one of the reasons Artenel was doing his best to get so much of the work done now, while he still had so many hands to aid him.

"I See you, Kellen. There is fresh tea made."

"I See you, Isinwen. I come to begin the day with good news, lately received. The army marches south from Ondoladeshiron, and should join us in a sennight or so. And better: Jermayan and Ancaladar march—or rather, fly—with them."

"I do not ask how such a miracle occurred," Isinwen said firmly. "It is magic, and this is something I have never understood. But I am grateful for it."

"So am I," Kellen said. "And since this is so, I find I must go to Sentarshadeen after all, and that immediately. I shall leave Halacira in your charge, unless you counsel me against it."

Isinwen paused to consider.

"I believe we are secure here. Vestakia can warn us of *Their* approach, and
the caverns make a more secure fortress by the day. The forest—what there is left
of it—is free both of any Tainted enemy and any merely mortal foe. The camp
runs smoothly, and riding Shalkan, your journey will be a swift one. Besides,
should there be grave need, I believe Cilarnen will be able to send word to
Shalkan over a distance, if not to you."

"You're probably right." While it was true that the Wild Magic seemed to be
incompatible with the High Magick in some mysterious way—and so Cilarnen
could not reach Kellen directly—no such difficulty existed between Cilarnen
and Shalkan. Not only would Cilarnen be able to locate Shalkan by magick, he
should also be able to talk to him.

"I'll be back in a day, then. Two, perhaps."

"And all will be just as you have left it. Leaf and Star go with you, Kellen."

"And abide with you, Isinwen."

SOON Kellen was riding over the snow on Shalkan's back. Except for the snow,
and the fact that he was riding *to* Sentarshadeen instead of away from it, the previous several moonturns could almost not have happened. He and Shalkan were
off on their own, upon an adventure.

And what would happen when he reached his goal was as much a mystery as
it had been on that other occasion.

Very soon they reached the edge of the area where his army had been log-
ging, and the forest once more resumed its serene beauty. There had been several
snows since the last time the supply sledges had traversed the road between Halacira and Sentarshadeen, and the road was only discernible as a wide space
where the trees were not. But that didn't matter to Shalkan. The unicorn ran
across the top of the snow, not even leaving footprints behind.

"And may your humble steed ask what you're going to do in Sentarshadeen?" Shalkan asked, as he covered the distance to the city in a ground-
eating lope.

"If Firareth were here, I'm sure he wouldn't be interested," Kellen answered.

Shalkan bucked warningly.

"All right! I'm going to ask Morusil for the army. He's the one who's been
signing the dispatches in Andoreniel's name," Kellen said quickly. He had no de-

sire to end up on his back in the snow, and no doubt of Shalkan's ability to put him there, Knight-Mage or not.

"So you're going to take command?" Shalkan asked.

"I don't want to. Maybe there's another way. But we have to take Armethalieh *now*. Before *They* figure out just what's going on with that 'Big Fish' Cilarnen told me about. And that means taking the army over the Border. Into the Wild Lands. All the way to Armethalieh."

"It's a long way," Shalkan said.

"You did it in—what? A day and a half?"

"I took us from Armethalieh to Idalia's cabin," Shalkan corrected. "And I'm a unicorn, if you'll kindly remember. It's at least a moonturn from Idalia's cabin to Sentarshadeen—in summer. So perhaps two, in winter, from Sentarshadeen to Armethalieh, if nothing goes wrong, and your army makes *very* good time."

"At least most of it will be downhill," Kellen said, remembering the terrain he and Shalkan—and, later, he and Shalkan and Idalia—had crossed.

"So you can slide all the way there," the unicorn agreed, picking up his pace.

⟡

SENTARSHADEEN looked peaceful and untouched, though Kellen knew from the dispatches that the Shadow's Kiss had struck here at least as hard as in any of the surviving Nine Cities. But plague was a quiet assault, and at least he had seen nothing of the forest blight that was ravaging the Wild Lands on his ride here. So far this part of the Elven Lands had been spared that, at least.

When Kellen reached the Unicorn Meadow, he unsaddled Shalkan—he knew that Shalkan would be eager to exchange gossip with the unicorn herd here, and he'd be sure to hear the choice bits of it later—and carried Shalkan's saddle down to the House of Leaf and Star.

The door opened as he reached it.

"I See you, Kellen Knight-Mage."

Kellen regarded the woman standing there. "I See you," he said politely. "I greet you in the name of Leaf and Star."

"My name is Taranarya. Be welcome at our home and at our hearth."

⟡

SHE conducted him to a room he'd never seen before—though Kellen suspected he'd have to be a great deal older than he was now before he saw *all* the rooms of the House of Leaf and Star—and asked that he accept the hospitality of the house. Kellen was resigned to a certain amount of formality; if someone didn't come along in a reasonable time to ask him his business, well, he'd just go looking for them.

Meanwhile, there was plenty to look at here.

The waiting room Taranarya had conducted him to was designed to resemble a birch forest in autumn—without, however, slavishly copying it. Kellen wasn't quite sure how the Elves managed to convey such a powerful suggestion of autumn forest, because whenever he looked directly *at* something—the pale cream wood paneling of the walls, the intricate geometric pattern of the black and yellow carpet, the four cylindrical stoves at the corners of the room—it didn't look particularly sylvan. But when he looked at the room out of the corner of his eye, the forest was there: the tumble of yellow leaves underfoot; the tall slender birch trunks against a backdrop of more yellow leaves; it almost seemed as if he could hear the wind through the branches.

He was always amazed by what you could do without magic.

∾

HE hadn't been there very long before two more Elves appeared, bringing tea and a selection of pastries. He recognized one of them from one of his first visits to the House of Leaf and Star.

"I See you, Lamarethiel," he said.

"I See you, Kellen," Lamarethiel replied.

"It would please me greatly should you and your companion desire to stay and drink tea with me," Kellen said cannily. "I have been long away from Sentarshadeen, and would know how the city fares."

He had counted on the fact that Elves were constantly curious, and always willing to gossip—and that someone who served in the House of Leaf and Star would probably know almost as much about what was going on as, well, a unicorn.

Lamarethiel and his companion, Javondir, did not disappoint him. Kellen heard—after a discussion of the weather, which, since he was going to be taking an army through here soon, was actually something that interested him for a change—all the details of the arrival of the Wildmages Catreg, Tadolad, and Kannert and their strange ways—butter in their tea!—of the wonderful recovery of the Shadow-kissed over the last sennight—and particularly since Midwinter—of the fact that Dargainon was expected to recover fully, that Tyendimarquen still showed no signs of plague—by the grace of Leaf and Star, and that Morusil was still well. In fact, since Midwinter, there had been no new cases at all.

In turn, of course, Kellen was expected to provide news of his own, and so he did. He spoke of the final battle against the Shadowed Elves at Halacira, and their complete defeat. Of the building there of a new fortress where the families of the Allies could take refuge within the Elven Lands. Of the fact that Redhelwar's army, even now, marched south from Ondoladeshiron to join him at Halacira.

"There is more, of course, but it is news best shared first with the King's Counselors. I had hoped, of course, to speak to Morusil. . . ."

"I shall see if he is here," Lamarethiel said, rising to his feet gracefully. "And I thank you for the news you have brought, Kellen. It has made . . . interesting hearing."

"I have enjoyed the chance to tell it," Kellen answered politely.

He was definitely getting better at dealing with Elves.

After Lamarethiel departed, Javondir excused himself, saying that he would bring fresh tea.

Kellen went back to admiring the room, trying to decide just *how* the illusion of a forest was created.

When Javondir returned, bringing fresh tea, Morusil was with him.

Idalia had said that Morusil had survived the plague, but Kellen had left Ysterialpoerin before the first cases had appeared there, and he had never seen what the plague left behind in its aftermath. The livid bars of purple that marred Morusil's face and neck came as a wrenching shock to him. He sprang to his feet as the aged Elven Counselor entered the room, leaning heavily on an ornate wooden staff.

"Morusil! I— That is, I hope I find you well."

Morusil chuckled. "Extremely well, my brash young Knight-Mage. I shall tend my gardens for some years yet." He lowered himself into a chair.

Thus rebuked, Kellen sat again as well. Javondir replaced the empty pot with a fresh one, and withdrew, this time closing the doors to the room behind him.

"And—so I hear—things have gone well for you at Halacira as well, and we shall be welcoming guests within our borders soon."

"In spring, I think," Kellen answered. "Travel simply isn't possible in the winter."

"Yes, the winter has been unusually hard. But it promises an excellent—if wet—spring. The fruit trees should flourish, if the orchards receive proper drainage."

And they were back onto the topic of the weather.

After several more cups of tea—at least Kellen was able to turn the topic of the weather to conditions south of Sentarshadeen, which actually interested him—Morusil allowed Kellen to turn the conversation to more practical matters.

"But you will not have come to talk about the weather."

"Actually, it is a matter of interest to me, for the reason that the weather always affects the army, especially when it must travel. And I—hope—that the army will soon be traveling a very great distance."

"I am told that the army has already traveled a great distance. From Ysteri-alpoerin to Ondoladeshiron in one footstep is a great journey."

"The Enemy is not at Ondoladeshiron, Morusil. And it isn't *Their* goal. For moonturns we've known *They* mean to take Armethalieh. Now we know that Idalia has called up, well, Cilarnen isn't really sure what. Shalkan calls it a 'Great Power.' But whatever it is, *They* don't like it. And it seems to be interfering with *Their* plans to call up *Their* own Great Power: He Who Is. While *They're* figuring out just what to do about it, *They're* going to be about as disorganized as *They're* going to get."

He took a deep breath.

"But there's bad news to go with the good. Vestakia can see into her father's mind a little. What she's seeing seems to say that *They* are finally massing an army for an all-out battle. If *They* do that—and have Armethalieh to draw on—we don't stand a chance."

"You would not have come here solely to tell me that we are doomed, Kellen. That is not in your nature," Morusil observed.

"No. I have come here to tell you that we need to take the army to Armethalieh *now*. Get there before *They* do, and convince the Armethaliehans to fight on our side."

"It would please me to know how you intend to do this, as they will listen to none of us."

"They'll listen to Cilarnen," Kellen said grimly. "He's one of them. It's true he was Banished, but he was supposed to have been stripped of his Magegift before they turned him out, and he still has it. That will make them listen. He can tell them about Anigrel, and everything he's done to betray them to the Enemy. The High Mages are powerful. I don't think Anigrel can fight them openly and win—and if he tries, he'll just be proving that Cilar-nen's right. Morusil, it's the only chance I see for us. We can't let *Them* take Armethalieh."

"But to take the army out of the Elven Lands," Morusil said slowly. "Under whose command?"

"Redhelwar is the commander of the army," Kellen said, feeling his way. "If he is ordered to go west and prevent *Them* from taking Armethalieh, he will do that."

"Taking the advice of his Knight-Mage as to the best way to proceed," Morusil said.

"I hope Redhelwar will always listen to the counsel of the Wild Magic," Kellen said honestly. "Mine, and Idalia's, and Jermayan's, and that of all the other Wildmages who ride with the army."

"A good answer," Morusil said. "Yet I can still not give you the answer you hope for. That answer must come from the King, and Andoreniel is yet too weak to give counsel."

"Morusil, I *must* have an answer. Redhelwar will be at Halacira within a sennight," Kellen said desperately.

"And Halacira lies two days' ride from here. Yet I believe an army travels more slowly than a single rider, especially in winter. So it will be perhaps ten days before I see you again. Leaf and Star grant you can obtain an answer at that time."

And Gods of the Wild Magic grant that it's the one I need.

But there was nothing more he could do here, and Kellen knew it. If any of the surviving members of Andoreniel's Council was willing to grant Kellen's request, it was Morusil. Tyendimarquen would have refused out of hand, and Dargainon would simply have debated both sides of the matter until the Demons arrived in Sentarshadeen itself.

"I thank you for all your help—both that you have already given me, and that you have yet to give. And may Leaf and Star watch over us both."

"That is a prayer I make daily, Kellen Knight-Mage."

⟨≈⟩

WALKING back out to the Unicorn Meadow through the snow, Kellen did his best to believe that his visit to Sentarshadeen had not been useless.

He knew he'd needed to go, to put his request before Morusil.

At least he'd gotten orders to bring the army as far as Sentarshadeen. What they were going to do with it here if they *didn't* take it to Armethalieh, he didn't know.

"I take it you didn't get what you wanted?" Shalkan asked, apparently materializing out of a snowdrift.

Kellen produced a couple of iced cakes out of his tunic—when confronted with a plate full of pastry, he'd automatically tucked several away for the unicorn. Lamarethiel and Javondir might have thought his behavior a little odd, but they'd never been confronted with a greedy unicorn with a sweet tooth demanding to know why they hadn't brought him back anything from an Elven tea.

"Yes and no. In other words, Morusil heard me out, and told me to come back with the whole army, when he'd let me know."

"A little ambiguous," Shalkan remarked, around a mouthful of cake.

"I suppose he can't say much else," Kellen said reluctantly. "He can't give me—or Redhelwar, really—the army without Andoreniel's permission, and Andoreniel is still too weak to be consulted. Morusil's hoping he'll be stronger ten days from now."

"Let's hope so," Shalkan said.

KELLEN did not spend the time waiting for Redhelwar to arrive in leisure, how-ever. Even though he only had a few thousand horses, there were preparations to make to leave Halacira, especially since he must provide for a permanent force to be left behind. As he was doing that, he also sent a dispatch to Redhelwar, so the General would know he was now to proceed directly to Sentarshadeen.

Kellen did not think at all about what he would do, or need to do, if he did not receive the answer he needed when he returned to Sentarshadeen. None of this, as Kellen had realized long ago, was about him and what he needed. It was all about the Wild Magic and its balance, and whatever was best for that was what was going to happen.

He only hoped his nerves could stand it.

Meanwhile, there was the far more mundane (but still important) matter of telling Cilarnen it was time to pack and move again—and this time, if Fortune favored them, Cilarnen would have no fixed workspace ever again.

But here Cilarnen had anticipated him.

"I shall need two oxen," he said, when Kellen came to tell him the news. "Six draft horses would be better—faster—but I suppose they can't be found. And at any rate, I shan't need to travel any faster than the army does."

"Would it be a great deal of trouble, o' Exalted High Mage, if you told me just what you're talking about?" Kellen asked.

In answer, Cilarnen pulled out one of his books and opened it. There was a drawing of a cart unlike anything Kellen had ever seen, though it looked a little like the wagons in which the Elven children had first been sent to the Fortress of the Crowned Horns: a little house on wheels, with a door, windows, and roof. Kellen even saw what looked like a hearth built into one side. The conveyance was drawn by four large horses.

"The drawing doesn't show much, so I cast Knowing on the chapter. This is how the War Mages carried their equipment to war. I can store everything I re-ally need here. I could even sleep in it, if I had to, but I'd really rather not."

"Cilarnen," Kellen said doubtfully, "I don't think we have time to build something like that."

"Did you have to build my last work area?" Cilarnen demanded scornfully. "I admit I'd need help if it were going to have wheels, and axles, but it's going to be on sledges, like the heavy wagons—which is why I'd need six horses instead of four, if I were going to use horses at all. I'll be fine. Artenel won't even have to cut any more planks; I can just take apart my sanctum and re-use the wood from that."

"Well, I'll look forward to seeing it," Kellen had answered.

"Don't forget the oxen."

Making the war-wagon had taken Cilarnen a little longer than constructing his round house, but three days later, after Kardus had led a yoke of oxen up to him, Cilarnen had driven it down into camp. It looked, Kellen had to admit, very much like the picture Cilarnen had shown him.

And by then it was time to leave.

※

JOINING up with an army on the march—especially such a comparatively large army—was a complex logistical problem, especially in an area like the Avribalzar Forest, where both forces must move along the War Road in long narrow columns, hemmed in by the trees.

In the end, Kellen simply distributed his forces along the line of march re-formed into their traditional units—or what was left of them after Halacira. His own command was one of the hardest hit: Only six of his Twelve survived, and almost half of them had been new after the Second Battle of the Caverns.

Then, as their places appeared in the line of march—Healers, Knights, supply-wagons—each element of the army moved fluidly into the gaps Redhelwar left for them. Cilarnen and Vestakia rode with the Healers.

And once more Kellen and his command became a part of the main army.

Unfortunately—from Kellen's point of view—this maneuver was all-too-easy to accomplish, even after all his warnings to Redhelwar. Even after a thousand years—and, for all he knew, after five thousand years—the elements of the Elven Army marched and fought in exactly the same position and order.

And that meant that when the Allies finally met the Enemy on the battle-field for the first time in a thousand years, the Enemy would know exactly where to strike for greatest effect.

Fifteen

The Road to Armethalieh

AT THE END of the day, when the army made camp, Kellen was at last reunited with Idalia and Jermayan.

He had seen Ancaladar flying back and forth above the trees several times that day, of course, but though the sight did much to reassure him that Jermayan was indeed alive, it did nothing to answer Kellen's many questions.

But that night, after camp had been pitched and the simple housekeeping chores of life upon the road attended to, the five of them gathered together in Idalia's tent.

Kellen was instantly struck by how *changed* Jermayan seemed. While both Cilarnen and Vestakia looked as if they were being consumed from within—by different but equally catastrophic fires—and so glowed far too brightly, Jermayan looked as if some natural illumination that he should properly possess had been extinguished.

The explanations—both Jermayan's and Idalia's—took several hours, starting with Idalia's realization that the imminent arrival of *He Who Is* back in the world from which he had been banished uncounted millennia before was keeping the Wildmage magic from working properly, to the discovery of the ancient Tokens hanging in the Council Chamber of Sentarshadeen, to the summoning of the Starry Hunt.

At least now Kellen had a name for their new ally, though from the explanation he received, it was actually a very old one.

From there it became Jermayan's story: his realization that the appearance of the Hunt in this world meant a period of unsureness and confusion for *Them*; his realization that by expending all of his and Ancaladar's magic to open a door to Ondoladeshiron he could gain the army precious time so that they might meet the Enemy while it was still disorganized; their rescue by the Starry Hunt as they lay dying.

But at a price.

Happy and grateful as he was to have his friends restored to them—especially for Idalia's sake—Kellen privately lamented the loss of Jermayan's powers as an Elven Mage. Cilarnen's abilities were not nearly as great, and the sort of things that Kellen, or Idalia—or any of the other Wildmages, for that matter—could do were entirely different than what he had seen Jermayan accomplish.

The loss of Jermayan's magic might cost them dearly.

For one thing, Kellen had been counting on Jermayan to break the wards around Armethalieh—or at least bend them a little—so that they could get Cilarnen into the City to talk to the High Council. Assuming, of course, that they could get to Armethalieh in the first place.

He said as much to Cilarnen, much later that night.

They were alone. He had walked Cilarnen back to his fancy cart—Cilarnen didn't actually sleep in it, but he pitched his tent beside it. In a camp on the move, there was no possibility of the privacy Cilarnen preferred, but the young High Mage had placed his tent and wagon at the edge of the camp, near the horse-lines.

Cilarnen made a small sound of amused surprise.

"I know Jermayan's power is—was—vast, but I do not know if he could have broken the wards, Kellen, without destroying the City down to its foundation stones. Remember what they were designed to keep out in the first place. I've been thinking about the problem, though, and I think I have another solution to it. One *They* would never think of, because *They* couldn't use it without destroying *Themselves.* But we can—if Redhelwar will give me the proper tools to work with."

"I'm sure he will, if he can," Kellen said cautiously. He already knew from experience that Cilarnen's idea of "the proper tools" could be eccentric, to put it charitably.

"If he gives me the Unicorn Knights, I can breech the walls of Armethalieh," Cilarnen said, with absolute certainty.

But would they reach the walls of Armethalieh?

⟨⟩

FOUR days after Kellen's force had rejoined the main army, the Allied Army—Men, Centaurs, Elves—gathered in the fields and orchards beyond the Unicorn Meadow at Sentarshadeen.

It had snowed every day since Kellen had returned from his last visit to Sentarshadeen, but Jermayan assured him that there was usually a break in the weather just after Midwinter, and it had finally come. The day of their arrival had dawned bright and clear and cold, and the Wildmages had assured Redhelwar that the clear weather should hold for at least the next fortnight.

Kellen had spoken extensively to Redhelwar, both about Vestakia's "visions"—there was really no other good word to describe the information she relayed to him and Idalia—and also of what Cilarnen saw when he looked into Armethalieh. Though Redhelwar was just as dismayed as Morusil had been by the prospect of taking the Allied Army outside the Elven Lands, he agreed that there might be no better chance to deny *Them* something *They* seemed to want very much.

And it was not simply the fact that Armethalieh might be the key to defeating *Them*. By taking the army outside the borders of the Elven Lands, they would draw the Enemy's attention to themselves and away from everything else.

And at the moment, that was vital, too.

Not all the Wildmages were with the army. Some of them had remained with their families in the High Reaches, and were in frequent communication with their partners who had joined the army. They passed news of Demonic raids of increasing ferocity, of spreading plague and blight, of the encroachment of monstrous creatures beyond the experience of any but the Lostlanders.

If the army could occupy the Enemy's full attention, perhaps it could gain the non-combatants a breathing space.

THE army reached the edge of the Unicorn Meadow at noon.

Kellen and his troop were escorting Redhelwar, riding at the front of the column. Cilarnen, Idalia, and Vestakia rode with Redhelwar as well; Cilarnen had pointed out cheerfully that there was no point in having a destrier if you weren't going to ride him, and it was perfectly true that Anganil sulked if he didn't get what the black stallion believed was his proper due.

Behind them, the army was spread in a wide column. They'd left the forest that morning and changed formation to one more suited to open country; the unicorns moving off to the left and ahead; the Knights organizing in ranks behind their Commanders and Sub-Commanders; the Centaurs and Mountainfolk behind them behind their own commanders; then the Healers and Wildmages, the supply wagons, the herds, and the rear guard.

All very impressive.

When they reached the edge of the Unicorn Meadow—it still managed to look manicured, even covered in well-trampled snow—Kellen could see there was a pavilion set up in the middle of the meadow.

It looked very much like the one he'd been greeted by when he'd returned from the Black Cairn, except for the fact that this one was green and silver instead of yellow and red.

Redhelwar gave the order for the army to halt.

Dionan raised his horn to his lips and blew the signal. In seconds it passed back down the line, echoing and doubling through the crisp winter air.

"It would please me if you accompanied me, Kellen," Redhelwar said.

"It would give me great joy," Kellen answered politely.

Side by side, they rode forward toward the pavilion.

⁓

THE interior of the pavilion was set up in what Kellen considered to be pretty much traditional style by now for this sort of thing—a wooden floor laid down on the snow, with carpets over that. Braziers to heat the tent almost to the temperature of an indoor room. A table laid out with a tea-brazier and service, as well as several plates of delicacies.

Both Morusil and Tyendimarquen were there, as well as several other Elves whose names Kellen did not know. Several of the Elves bore the same livid purple scars that Morusil did, indicating that they had caught—and survived—the plague.

Andoreniel was not there. Kellen had not really expected that he would be.

"Enter and be welcome," Morusil said. "I know that your stay must be brief, for you will not wish to leave your army standing in the cold without direction."

"That is so," Redhelwar agreed, "and we are all grateful for your kindness."

He seated himself at the table, and Kellen, without much choice in the matter, seated himself beside him. Redhelwar removed his fur mitts, gloves, and armored gauntlets, setting them on the table beside him, and accepted the cup of tea that one of the courtiers poured. Kellen was glad to see that it was one of the small cups, indicating that this was just going to be a brief tea-drinking before they got down to business.

He did the same with his own gloves and gauntlets, and accepted his own cup. He settled his mind, breathing in the fragrance of the tea. Whatever was to come, the decision had already been made. There was nothing to do about that.

The tea smelled of cherries and mint. A kind he had not tasted before. He savored it, letting go of worry.

The Wild Magic might want him to die—well actually, the Wild Magic probably didn't care whether he, as a person, died or not. As far as he could tell, the Wild Magic didn't care a lot about *Kellen Tavadon*. But the Wild Magic didn't want the *world* to die. The Wild Magic wanted the Balance to be kept. The Wild

Magic was all about Balance, and he was an instrument of the Wild Magic. It was his job to be the best instrument of its balance that he could be. And so far, as far as he knew, he'd done everything he could to be a good instrument, and act in accordance with what it wanted him to do.

So whatever happened here today would be—would have to be—another part of the Wild Magic's mysterious balancing.

So he should stop worrying.

They drank tea.

Redhelwar and Morusil—and even Tyendimarquen—talked of the weather. It was going much as it had in other years. The Winter Running Dance, alas, would not be held this year, though the weather would have been exceptionally fine for it. But perhaps the snow would have been too heavy. The orchards looked to bear well in spring. It was possible they could look to see the *vilya* fruit next year.

At last the tea was finished, and they set aside their cups.

"Andoreniel continues to grow in strength, as I have promised you," Morusil said, "and I have laid your problem before him. He has bade me give this to Redhelwar."

There was a box upon the table, made of the same pale wood as the conference table in the Council Chamber. Morusil opened it.

Inside it was a ring.

It was large—it would cover the wearer's finger from knuckle to knuckle. The stone was a huge green oval, of the deep yellow-green of forest moss. Kellen had seen Ashaniel wearing gems of the same color.

He'd seen Kindolhinadetil wearing a ring like it. And Rochinuviel.

Morusil took the ring from the box and handed it to Redhelwar.

"Who wears this ring acts in Andoreniel's name," Morusil said. "He bids you go and do as you think best, even to the walls of Armethalieh, for the good of all who walk in the Light. And may Leaf and Star go with you."

Redhelwar slipped the ring onto his finger.

Paired with the scarlet of Redhelwar's chosen color, the green of the gem glowed even more brightly, as if it were lit from within.

The meeting seemed to be over.

Redhelwar rose to his feet. "I thank Andoreniel for his trust. I vow to you all that I shall not fail it, so long as the trees grow and the stars burn. Leaf and Star abide with you all."

≈

"IT is perhaps more freedom than I would have wished," Redhelwar said quietly, as they rode back to the army.

The ring was tucked down inside his glove now, since he could not wear it beneath his gauntlet.

"I am not entirely sure what just happened," Kellen confessed. "The ring Morusil gave you from Andoreniel . . . it looks like the rings I have seen the Viceroys wear."

"Yes," Redhelwar said. "The army has become . . . a city. The Tenth City. And so, now, Andoreniel can command. But I can also . . . refuse."

Kellen's eyes went wide with surprise. He hadn't known the Viceroys had that kind of power.

And now Redhelwar was—in all the ways that mattered—a Viceroy.

"We need this," he said.

"Yes," Redhelwar said. "But I look forward to the day when I can surrender this power again."

⁓

WHEN they returned to the army, Redhelwar gave the order for the army to advance once more. They swung to the right, their path leading them in a broad arc around the city, to a place where they could cross the river that was Sentarshadeen's western border easily.

"So?" Idalia asked, riding up beside Kellen. "I assume we're going to Armethalieh."

"Yes," Kellen agreed. "Andoreniel has given Redhelwar a Viceroy's ring. Redhelwar says we're a city now."

"Convenient," Idalia said. "He won't have to wait for Andoreniel's orders, and can do pretty much whatever he deems right for the safety of the Elven Lands. It's been done before, but . . ."

"Not in a thousand years or so?" Kellen said, guessing.

Idalia grinned at him, silently confirming his guess.

⁓

THAT night they made camp at the edge of the Elven Lands. Tomorrow morning they would cross the Border into the Wild Lands, leaving the protection of the Elven land-wards behind.

Both Kellen and Cilarnen had spoken to Redhelwar of Cilarnen's plan for breeching the walls of Armethalieh using the Unicorn Knights, and Cilarnen had obtained both Redhelwar's approval and the Unicorn Knights' agreement. Kellen still wasn't entirely sure what the plan consisted of, though Cilarnen had explained it: It wasn't that Cilarnen was ever *intentionally* mysterious, it was simply that when he was speaking about the High Magick, he might as well be speaking in some utterly foreign language. All of the words seemed simple and commonplace, but all put together they didn't make any sense that Kellen could see. All he got out of the explanation was something about dancing.

But the unicorns themselves seemed to approve of the plan, and Cilarnen thought it had a good chance of working.

So from now on, Cilarnen camped with the Unicorn Knights, and drilled them in the part they were to play in the few hours they could spare from other duties. Fortunately, unicorns could see in the dark, and there was always Magelight.

⤚⤙

"DO you think this will work?" Kellen asked Shalkan.

The two of them were standing at the edge of the field, watching Cilarnen with the unicorns. He rode ahead of them on Anganil, the black stallion's body invisible in the winter darkness. Only the crown of Magelight he wore made him visible.

Behind him the unicorns followed, their horns and bodies glowing faintly. They looked like living Elven lanterns: gold, silver, russet, and the deep midnight blue that the coat of the black unicorns gave off at night.

"Maybe," Shalkan said consideringly.

"No, no, *no!* Menerchel, you and Hindulo need to go *left*, not right! Nelarussa, that's too slow: you and Rochovoth must keep the space between you and Orchel *precisely*. And Araveth, you're going too fast. It's a pattern, not a race. Back to the beginning."

The ball of Magelight trotted off. The unicorns followed.

"And whatever it is they're going to be doing," Kellen said, "they won't be doing it in an open field in peace and quiet. Well, relative peace and quiet anyway. They'll be doing it in the middle of a battle. With Leaf and Star alone knows what trying to stop them."

"Then we'd just better hope that Cilarnen's a good teacher," Shalkan said. "And that he has enough time before we get there."

⤚⤙

THE following day they crossed over into the Wild Lands.

Almost instantly Kellen could sense a change in the landscape.

Everything seemed . . . diminished . . . as if the life had been sucked out of it. Though the countryside was winter-barren, it managed to look as if nothing ever *had* grown there, not only since the Great Drought, but in living memory.

Around midday, they saw the first refugees.

From his previous trip to the Elven Lands, Kellen knew that there were no villages, Centaur or human, within a fortnight's travel of the Border. They were traveling through open country now, and would be for some time; Redhelwar's maps weren't as detailed here, but they showed only one range of high hills (Kellen recalled them vividly; it was where he and Shalkan had fought off the Outlaw Hunt) and a forest beyond it which marked the far edge of the Delfier Valley. Those should be the only real impediments to the army's march.

Aside from whatever the Enemy chose to do.

The unicorns, as always, were the far-forward scouts. Riding between them and the rest of the army was another troop of knights led by Nithariel. She and her Knights could receive their reports and bring them back to Redhelwar without causing distress to the unicorns.

The army forged forward steadily, covering the leagues that separated them from Armethalieh at a steady, ground-eating pace. Overhead, Ancaladar soared and wheeled through the clear empty sky. Since Jermayan could no longer communicate with the forces on the ground by magic, he now carried one of the Elven war-horns. The various calls would provide nearly as much advance information as magical speech.

Kellen's troop had been made up to full strength once again, and as a skirmishing unit, his Twelve was riding on the flank of the army, ready to break away immediately to deal with any danger that might present itself. The position gave him a good view of the road ahead, and so he was able to see when Riasen rode back to Nithariel, and Nithariel in turn rode back to Redhelwar.

"Something's up," he said to Isinwen.

"I do not doubt we shall soon discover what it is," Isinwen said placidly. "As always, I await any order you choose to give."

"If I ordered you to go and ask Redhelwar what was going on, he'd have both our heads, and send us off to horse-duty for the rest of the campaign," Kellen said.

"Why so I had believed. But I did not like to put my own opinions before those of so worthy a Knight-Mage and battle-commander," Isinwen said blandly.

"You know, I really think you're wasted here," Kellen said. "You should be off amusing the unicorns."

"Alas," Isinwen said. "My wife would hardly approve. Nor, I think, would the unicorns take pleasure in my company. Ah, here is news."

Dionan rode back down the line.

"Nithariel and Riasen report a band of travelers on the road ahead. Refugees from Greenpoint, Riasen believes, and without Taint, Elariagor says. Ride up to them and discover their condition. They may take sanctuary beyond the Border."

Kellen raised a hand in salute and pulled his troop out of line. In moments they were cantering up past the head of the column.

~≈~

THE band of travelers were a ragged collection. Kellen counted a dozen humans and six Centaurs. Four of the humans were women. One was carrying a baby, well muffled-up against the cold. All of the Centaurs were carrying heavy packs, and one of the men was leading a shaggy pack-pony as well. The beast looked exhausted, as did the people.

"We mean you no harm," Kellen said, dismounting from Firareth's saddle. "I'm Kellen. We've come to offer the sanctuary of the Elven Lands. The Border is just a few miles up the road, and the Elven city of Sentarshadeen is just beyond it. They'll take care of you there."

"Huntsman be praised!" one of the Centaurs said. "Is it true . . . the Elves will open their borders to any who come?"

"Any who are of the Light," Kellen said firmly. "But what are you doing here? Riasen—the unicorn rider—said you were from Greenpoint."

"Greenpoint isn't there anymore." It was one of the men who spoke. "My name is Jasson. I was a blacksmith at Greenpoint. We have heard that the Shadowkin rise again, but thought they would not come to us here in the west. When the hunting began to fail just after Second Harvest, we thought it was simple misfortune, but . . ."

To Kellen's dismay and horror, Jasson began to weep, covering his face with his hands.

"We were in the woods, searching for wildgather," one of the women said. "Something . . . came."

"We are all that is left," another of the Centaurs said. "We have been on the road this past moonturn. My brother Sarick and I fish for Greenpoint. We were out on the ice when we saw the smoke. By the time we returned, the village was gone. No one was left. Only those who were away, like Sietta, or whose shops are far from the village, like Jasson. The village had burned. Even the stone had burned. There were not even bodies."

Demons. It must be Demons.

Demons had raided Greenpoint a moonturn ago, and taken everyone there as slaves . . . or food.

"I am sorry for your loss," Kellen said quietly. "But the Shadowkin have not yet crossed the Borders of the Elven Lands. Beyond Sentarshadeen we are building a place for you to live, where you can be safe. In Sentarshadeen they will show you how to get there."

"But what of you?" Sietta asked. "Can you not take us there yourselves? Won't you protect us?"

"I'm sorry," Kellen said. "We're going the other way. We have to go to fight the ones who destroyed your village."

Quickly he emptied his saddlebags of all the food he was carrying, and the rest of his troop did the same. A few trail-bars, some dried fruit—it wasn't much, but it would be enough to get them over the Border, and Halacira was being provisioned from Sentarshadeen. They'd be safe at Halacira.

But how many more victims of *Their* cruelty would the army encounter on the road to Armethalieh?

The refugees moved wearily up the road. Kellen rode back to make his report to Redhelwar.

⤝⤞

"WE will not be able to feed them all, Kellen," the Army's General said. "If we encounter more, you must think of the army first."

"I know," Kellen said.

It was a bitter truth. But there would be no chance to reprovision the army between here and Armethalieh—and probably not even then, unless they raided some of the Delfier Valley farms and took what they needed by force. The army would need everything it had to feed itself.

⤝⤞

LATER that day, they fought off their first Demon attack.

They saw no more refugees, but the unicorns ranged farther from the column now, and brought back reports of the tracks of both Coldwarg and serpent-marae. The monsters that were *Their* most efficient tools ranged freely here in the Wild Lands, and Redhelwar ordered the army to be especially alert.

Suddenly he heard an outcry from farther back in the column. Vestakia.

There was an urgent cascade of hornsong from the sky.

Something coming from the sky.

The column stopped. The skirmishers deployed. The Unicorn Knights came riding back toward the main body of the army, stopping less than half a mile away. Shalkan was with them. Nithariel's troop passed Kellen's as she rode down the line toward her place in the formation, her Knights galloping all-out through the snow.

Kellen heard Ancaladar shriek with anger—a sound he could not ever remember hearing the dragon make before.

There were Demons in the sky.

Only two, but from all Cilarnen had told them, one could destroy a village. Two might well be able to slay half the army.

For a moment, the two-bat-winged forms swooped and danced around Ancaladar as the dragon lashed out at *Them* with claws and tail. But without Jermayan's magic, he and Ancaladar were powerless to affect the creatures, and the Demons knew it. With one powerful blow—not even a spell—one of the Demons knocked Ancaladar out of the sky, but the dragon and his rider were not their main target.

The army was.

Suddenly Cilarnen and Anganil came bolting out of the column past Kellen. The destrier's reins were looped around the saddlehorn; Cilarnen had both hands raised to the sky.

Lightning.

By now Kellen had seen more wild weather than he actually cared to. He'd seen storms, and he'd seen lightning. But only lightning up in the sky—great flashes of light that turned the night to day, or jagged bolts of light crossing the sky, as if the night were cracking to let the morning in.

Not like this.

This was lightning coming out of a clear blue sky. Coming without warning. A jagged column of blinding white fire lanced down out of the sky with an ear-numbing crack—once, twice—and when it was done, the Demons in the sky had been slammed to earth in the center of a huge lake of charred grass and mud, their bodies nothing more than twisted, still-smoking embers. Though the bolts had struck almost half a mile away, a ripple of unease moved through the army, as startled animals reacted to the sudden blast of light and noise.

And, horribly, the Demons were still moving.

"*They* aren't dead!" Cilarnen cried.

Shalkan was the first to reach them, slipping and skidding in the ice and mud, followed by the rest of the Unicorn Knights. By the time he had, the Demons were already beginning to heal. But they were still weak enough that the unicorns, trampling and goring, reduced them quickly to inanimate ash.

It was all over very quickly.

Kellen rode up to Cilarnen as the Unicorn Knights retreated. Cilarnen swung down awkwardly from Anganil's back, dropped to his knees, and plunged his hands into the snow.

"Aaah—! By the Light, that hurts," Cilarnen gasped. He raised his hands out of the snow after a moment, and Kellen could see that they were red. Burned. Blisters had formed and already broken, and thin trickles of blood, mixed with melted snow, were running down his wrists. Cilarnen inspected the damage and plunged his hands back into the snow again.

"What did you *do?*" Kellen demanded, swinging down out of his saddle.

"Lightning," Cilarnen said succinctly. "It's a complicated spell, but I have it as a cantrip. I've only prepared a few more, though, so I hope there won't be many more visitors. It won't kill *Them*, of course. But it slows *Them* down."

Despite the cold—Kellen felt it even through layers of armor and padding, and Cilarnen was only wearing a robe—Cilarnen was sweating heavily. Drops of perspiration fell from his forehead to the snow, melting small pockmarks in it.

"I'm going to need leather armor," Cilarnen said meditatively. "Something made without any metal at all. I think I would have fried myself if I'd been wearing my chain shirt."

"Cilarnen," Kellen said again. "What did you *do?* You burned your hands. And you're outside the Elven Lands. You can't be drawing on the Land-wards now."

"Always asking useless questions," Cilarnen said with a shaky laugh. He scooped up a handful of snow and held it to his face. "You might actually have made a decent High Mage, Kellen, if you'd had decent teachers. Not that—I suspect—there are many left in Armethalieh. Or maybe the High Magick and the Wild Magic really have more in common than I think, if you go back to their roots. Yes, we're outside the Elven Lands. That's blindingly obvious. I'm using wild elemental energy now. The same thing my ancestors used. It's . . . stronger. I didn't compensate for that. But I talked to the Fair Ones while I was still back in Halacira, and they agreed to lend me their strength. Because if *They* win, the Fair Ones will all be gone, too. It just hurts, a little. You're supposed to start when you're a child, with the simplest Forces, and I can't."

Cilarnen's teeth were chattering with cold now.

"Well, you've done enough for one day," Kellen said. He heard no further horn-calls. The two Demons must have been acting alone.

He bent down and scooped Cilarnen up into his arms. Cilarnen was heavy, but proper Mageborn were slightly-built, and Kellen had the muscles that came from wearing armor day in and day out, and swinging a heavy sword on top of it. He wouldn't want to do this as a regular thing, but it was certainly possible for him to lift the smaller man. With Cilarnen in his arms, he stepped up into Firareth's stirrup, swinging his leg over into the saddle. The buckskin destrier stood rock-steady as he mounted.

"Hey!" Cilarnen protested.

"*You* are going off to see Idalia," Kellen told him, turning Firareth back toward the column. "Burned hands are no joke, and you'll need to change into something warm and dry. We can't afford to lose you."

⤳

THE Golden City of Armethalieh, City of a Thousand Bells, had once held spell-bound beneath its rule all the land from the edge of the Western Sea to the farthest reaches of the Delfier Hills.

Now it did not even rule itself.

Fear ruled Armethalieh.

High Mage Astranis of House Nerawell was the son and grandson of Mages, and could trace his exalted and unblemished Mageborn lineage all the way back to the ancient days of the City, in a peaceful and unbroken record of privilege and service. The sons of House Nerawell had all led lives of duty to the City and service to the Light. The daughters had all married well, and presented their husbands, in due time, with proper Mageborn sons and daughters to continue the great name of Armethalieh, unchanged and unchanging.

But now there was change.

Nerawell was one of the High Houses—the Nerawell lineage was closely connected with the High Council itself, by marriage if not by the felicity of actually possessing a seat on the Council. Astranis knew nearly as much about what went on in Armethalieh as Lycaelon Tavadon himself.

And none of it was good.

In the last half year had come, first, the Banishment of the Arch-Mage's own mongrel son. Of course there was bad blood there, and the matter should have been dealt with—quietly—long before. But now both children were gone, and Light knew it was for the best. Perhaps Lycaelon might marry again; a suitable girl this time.

But then—so it appeared—the Wildmage taint that had surfaced with the boy had not been entirely rooted out of the City. The Council had acted rashly, restricting the Bounds back to the City walls, leading to, of all ridiculous things, a revolt among the farmers. The famine that had bred among the Commons had at least had one useful result: it had forced the rest of the Wildmages hiding in the City out into the open, leading to a purge of the Council, and the Banishment of several of the ringleaders, the young sons of several of the Council members and their families.

That Lord Volpiril had been involved in any way had been a surprise, though. Astranis had always thought the man had been sound.

Astranis had looked for things to return to normal, then. The Bounds were being expanded once more. Lycaelon had adopted a new Heir—still Commons blood there, of course, but Mageborn on his mother's side, and raised in a good home. And at least both parents were Citizens.

But then Lycaelon had put the boy on the Council. And now the Council was seven, not thirteen. It had been eight until a moonturn ago, but Lord Meron had resigned unexpectedly, giving reasons of ill-health and a desire to put his personal affairs in order.

Astranis was unconvinced. He suspected a visit from the Magewardens, rather than ill-health, was behind Lord Meron's decision.

The Magewardens! There was something that should be a bitter tea in every Mageborn's cup. The Mageborn *ruled* Armethalieh. They always had. Now, suddenly, there was a ruling council set *over* the Mageborn—a gaggle of low-rank, Low House, social-climbers whom no one knew, and no one could control.

Save Lycaelon's whelp, Anigrel Tavadon.

It was he who was the true power in the City now, not the Arch-Mage. Anigrel said that the Wildmages were still among them, seducing their sons and daughters just as they had Lycaelon's and Volpiril's and so many others. Anigrel said that only the Magewardens could be trusted to seek out the Wildmage corruption among the ranks of the Mageborn and keep it from spreading so disastrously again.

Oh, Astranis had to admit that the boy did have a few good ideas. The extra taxes on magick, for example. That had been an excellent notion. And the formation of the Commons Wardens. That kept the people out of trouble. The passes that kept them in their homes at night were a good notion as well. He did admit that.

But being spied upon, as if he were one of them, his own actions called into account . . . ?

Intolerable!

But there was nothing to be done about it.

He already knew that.

He had learned from the lesson of Master Undermage Hendassar.

He had known Ulfeson Hendassar for nearly forty years. He lectured at the College—on History of the City—and they had played *shamat* at the Teahouse of the Thousand Towers each Light-Day, over many cups of the Thousand Towers' finest brewings.

When the Magewardens had first been formed, Master Hendassar had spoken out, strongly and publicly, against them. He had said there was no precedent for such a body. That it infringed upon the inviolate sovereignty that was every Mageborn's right, as embodied in the City Charter itself.

All these things were, as Astranis knew himself, perfectly true. But he also knew that when the Magewardens had the backing of the Arch-Mage and the Arch-Mage's new son and heir, it was perhaps more prudent not to say them aloud. He had said as much to Ulfeson. But Ulfeson would not take the hint.

And then, one Light-day, Astranis's *shamat*-partner was not there.

No one knew where he'd gone. No one wished to know. Astranis had stopped by his rooms at the College—Ulfeson had never married, and did not keep a house—only to find them gone as if they had never existed at all.

No one ever explained why Ulfeson Hendassar had vanished, or what it was he was supposed to have done. Everyone assumed he was part of the Wildmage conspiracy that later tragically claimed the lives of two of the members of the High Council itself.

Astranis knew better.

He kept that knowledge to himself.

For his sons' sake, and their sons' sake. For the good name of House Nerawell. Even for the sake of his wife and daughters.

Anyone in Armethalieh who disagreed with the Magewardens—with Lord Anigrel—simply vanished.

He didn't know why.

It wasn't good to wonder why.

⤜⤚

"I fear the Wildmages are becoming more powerful, Father," Anigrel said quietly.

The Nocturne Bells—the first ring after Midnight Bells—had just rung, heralding the deepest part of the night.

The two High Mages stood in Lycaelon's study in the Council House at Armethalieh. The air thrummed with Power, for each night the Council Chamber which was the true heart of Armethalieh became the workplace for the High Mages to cast the spells that kept the City running so efficiently.

Tonight was not one of Anigrel's nights to stand in the Circle, though as always these days, his Magewardens were present. Tonight, the spell being cast was merely one to strengthen the timing-spells on the bell-towers, so that all of the carillons of the City struck when and as they were supposed to, and the weight and vibration of the great bells they held did not weaken the fragile and beautiful bell-towers.

Anigrel's personal attention was reserved for other matters, such as the City Wards.

The work was going far more slowly than he had hoped, and often over the past several sennights he had felt the lash of his Dark Lady's impatience. But he dared move no faster. Armethalieh was a city of law and custom—oh, the ancient immemorial custom!—and to work the spells that checked and cleansed and strengthened the Wards of the City Walls outside their proper time would draw attention he could not afford.

He had gained access to nearly all of the secret—and largely proscribed—Council archives during his tenure as Lycaelon's confidential secretary, and so he knew that the highest levels of the Mageborn remembered his Dark Lady and her kindred very well. Had not Lycaelon attempted to turn young Kellen Tavadon from his ill-advised dabbling in the Wild Magic by warning him it would lead him into the Dark Lady's embrace?

As if such a thing were likely.

Still, it was more than enough warning for Anigrel. The High Mages—or enough of them—remembered the days of the Shadow War and the enemy they had fought. If they truly understood what it was that he did here on those nights when he tampered—oh, so carefully!—with the City Wards, they would rise up in a body and destroy him.

Meanwhile, he must content himself with the small victories he had gained. No longer did he need to fear that his own Darkmage spells could be detected by the City Wards. Their ability to detect his work had been the first thing he destroyed, in accordance with a plan set down long ago.

Next, he had opened a thousand tiny cracks in the City's magical defenses. It was not enough to allow the Dark Ones to enter, or even to work their greater spells, but they could . . . influence . . . events in the City now, albeit subtly.

So long as he continued to work upon the Wards.

For Anigrel had quickly discovered, to his and his Dark Lady's great dismay, that somehow the complex, centuries-old spell had a life of its own, almost as if it were a living thing. Time and again he would return to the Circle to continue his work, only to discover that work he had done before must be redone, for damage he had done to the City Wards, changes he had made to suit them to his own purposes, had somehow been undone.

He had set his Magewardens the task of seeing who might be tampering with the Great Seals upon the City against his will, but they had found nothing.

And if his Magewardens could find nothing, well, then, there was nothing to find.

He could only conclude that the spell was repairing itself. But he dared not make more and greater changes each time. He was already working upon the Wards as quickly as he dared—unless, of course, he could gain absolute control of the Council.

Meron's departure had helped. High Mage Meron had always been a strong voice for caution and moderation, even now. With Meron gone, it would be far easier to convince the remaining Council members of the necessity of accepting the new proposal he was about to put before them.

Armethalieh must have allies.

The continuing raids in the Delfier Valley had helped. The force Lycaelon had sent to Nerendale several moonturns ago had simply vanished, along with—so the Council presumed, since no one had ever been sent to check—the entire village. Other troops of Militia, other villages, had followed in Nerendale's wake, until the Council had simply stopped answering the increasingly desperate pleas for help from the villagers.

The petitions, of course, continued to arrive. Proof, so Anigrel assured the High Council, that a vast and terrible army of Wildmages even now infested the Delfier Valley, and had set its sights on nothing less than the destruction of Armethalieh herself.

"We must defeat them," Lycaelon answered somberly. "We cannot allow this hallowed citadel of the Light to be defiled by their kind. We are all that remains of those that the Light created in Its Own Image."

"Your words are wise, Father," Anigrel said. "And I am certain the Council will heed them, when you present your plan. But I wonder if we must truly fight alone? You know that long ago, there were others who stood against the Wildmages. Others who thought, as we do, that the chaos and misrule of the Wild Magic must not be allowed to spread."

Once, before he had weakened the Wards and allowed his Dark Lady's influence to enter the City, Lycaelon would have instantly greeted Anigrel's words with horror. Now the Arch-Mage merely looked hopeful. And interested.

The sennights since Anigrel's accession to the High Council had taken a fearful toll on Lycaelon Tavadon. Only last spring he had seemed to be a man in the vigor of his late middle years; incorruptible, indestructible, a mighty pillar of magick who would endure forever.

Now it was as if everything Anigrel did to weaken the City Wards weakened Lycaelon as well. The Arch-Mage's skin had the translucence of age, and his hair, once raven-black with distinguished wings of gray, was now entirely white. The staff of office he bore was no longer merely an ornament of rank, but needed for support as well.

He had grown old.

Soon there would be a new head of House Tavadon, and another vacancy on the High Council.

The Arch-Mageship itself.

And then, at last, Anigrel could claim outright what he had sought for so long: absolute dominion over Armethalieh. As its new Arch-Mage.

"What are you saying, my son?"

"Since I became a member of the High Council, I have delved deep into our ancient archives, searching for any knowledge that might help us in this, our time of greatest peril. I have read much of the days of the Founding of our City, when—rightfully!—we sequestered ourselves from the Taint of the Wild Magic and the blandishments of the Other Races. But we were not the only ones who did. There were . . . others. Others who suffered just as terribly at the hands of the Wildmages, the Elves, and the Beast-creatures. They withdrew to a secret citadel far to the north, hiding themselves from the sight of all. They, too, believe in Purity above all things, and understand the need to destroy our enemies, for those enemies threaten them as well. Long have they hidden from their ancient foes, fearing to be destroyed completely. But now . . . I think they might aid us."

Lycaelon hesitated. "You say they believe as we do?"

Anigrel smiled. "Their enemies are ours, and have been since before the first stones of these walls were laid. What more proof can we ask?"

Lycaelon sighed deeply. "And yet . . . an alliance."

"Of two peoples with a common enemy, and a common goal," Anigrel said subserviently. "But of course, it is only a thought. You are so much wiser than I, and will know what is best for the City. But I think they would aid us, if we asked. You know that there have been . . . rumors . . . of great battles far to the east. I think they already stand against our enemies there."

"You have given me much to think about, my son," Lycaelon said. "Perhaps we must consider this matter further. For the good of the City."

Oh yes, "Father," Anigrel thought. *For the good of the City.* Lycaelon might dismiss the idea of an alliance the first time he heard it, but word of more atrocities would soon reach his ears. He would not forget that his beloved son and heir had told him that there were others who might fight Armethalieh's battles for her.

Soon he would tell Anigrel to invite them in.

⤳

THOUGH they saw no more Demons as they headed west and south, by the end of the first sennight of march, the Allied Army had seen just about everything else that the Enemy could field, and the constant clashes were beginning to take their toll.

They never saw the creatures in any great numbers. Vestakia's dream-visions continued to send the same chilling message—the Enemy was calling all its creatures to itself, now, preparing for one final strike at Armethalieh. And it intended to arrive there in force.

Vestakia could even tell them where the Demon army was. Its course paralleled their own, several hundred miles to the south, since *They* had been forced to detour around the Elven Lands instead of fighting *Their* way through the re-born Land-wards after the arrival of the Starry Hunt. Its presence was a constant source of misery for her, and at first Kellen had feared that the Demons would at-tempt to raid the army to kidnap her, since they had been hunting her to return her to her father all her life.

But when days passed without an attack, he realized *They* were holding off from a combination of cowardice and arrogance. Cowardice, because the army had so swiftly killed the last two of *Their* kind that had come. Arrogance, because *They* knew they would face the Allied Army at Armethalieh, and *They* were cer-tain of victory then.

Still, what the army did encounter was daunting enough.

Coldwarg—not the gigantic packs that Jermayan had reported seeing in the northern Elven Lands, but small groups of a dozen or so. Dangerous enough, but they could be killed, especially with enough defenders.

The serpentmarae were easier to destroy than the Coldwarg. Not nearly as hardy as the Coldwarg, they could often be run down by the Centaurs and speared to death.

The army had also been attacked one night as it was making camp by a band of what Isinwen had later told Kellen were Ice Trolls—squat blue-skinned crea-tures that went naked even in the cold. They used a kind of throwing-stick to launch arrows. They were fast as a running horse, and deadly foes, far stronger than Elves, their skin as tough as boiled leather. They had accounted for more than a few casualties in the camp, but again, they were only a few dozen against a force of thousands, and it was impossible for their small band to defeat Redhel-war's army.

But each pinprick attack, each delay, sapped the army's spirit.

Far more disheartening was the growing stream of refugees—more each day—that the army on its march encountered heading in the opposite direction. Winter—especially this winter—was no time for travel—yet with the Demon Army on the move, every village and smallholding within miles of its path had but one thought: *Get away.* They had packed everything they could—sometimes it was no more than the clothes on their backs—and were heading eastward to-ward the Elven Lands, hoping for refuge there.

Many of them did not make it. Riasen and Nithariel and the other scouting parties reported the discovery of body after frozen body in the snow.

Fear is doing the Demons' work for Them, Kellen thought in anger. *If this goes on much longer, there will be no one left alive to save.*

But it was the living who truly tore his heart out, for there was nothing the army could do for them. They had no supplies to spare—not food, nor blankets, nor medicine, nor even heating charcoal. These were not fighters who could be absorbed into the Army's ranks—even if there were weapons and armor to be found for them, not to mention supplies to feed them. These were cowed terrified farmers and laborers. There was nothing at all the Army could do but promise them that there was refuge farther east. They could have stripped their supplies train bare and not made a dent in the needs of the ragged, starving people they encountered, only destroyed themselves before they met the Enemy they were going to fight.

And They *know it*, Kellen brooded.

It was one more aspect of the War of the Spirit that was the real battlefield upon which this conflict was being fought. The Enemy wanted them to give up—to *despair*—long before the time came to raise their swords upon the battle-field. Each bloody meaningless death in a minor pointless skirmish, each child left to freeze in a snowbank, fueled the Demons' power and sapped the Allies' will to fight, and both sides knew it.

And there was nothing the Allied Army could do about it.

They could not split the army to go to the aid of the refugees, giving them safe escort back to the Elven Borders.

They could not give up their supplies to feed them.

From the very beginning *Their* strategy had been to fragment the Allies and the army, to reduce the Forces of the Light to a scattered handful of tiny, easily-disposed-of groups. No matter how subtle the trap, the Allies could not afford to let that happen. Not now, when their greatest—perhaps their last—battle lay just ahead.

But it was the hardest thing Kellen had ever done, or helped to do. Not only to ride past people in need, day by day, but to watch his friends wasting away before his eyes.

Cilarnen was the worst, because Kellen dared not think about Vestakia at all. She spent much of her time with Shalkan, guarded by the Unicorn Knights, drawing strength from Shalkan's presence and steadfast love.

He hoped Shalkan was telling her how wise and brave and beautiful she was.

Cilarnen . . .

He only hoped that Cilarnen would die.

Not because he hated Cilarnen. In the past weeks, he had come to like him very much—admire him, in fact. Cilarnen had given up far more than Kellen had in Armethalieh to fight for what he believed was right. And Cilarnen still loved Armethalieh and the High Magick—so much that he was willing to fight them, *for* them.

If Cilarnen—one of the most privileged of Armethalieh's citizens, with the most to lose by thinking for himself—could throw off the City's brainwashing, that meant there was hope for everyone who still lived there.

But what Cilarnen was doing to work the High Magick now was horribly dangerous. He was the first to admit that he didn't entirely understand it, and that what he did understand of it he was doing entirely wrong, without the years of training and preparation he should have had. The High Magick was not a toy to be played with, and in the end, what Cilarnen was doing could do worse than kill him.

It could burn out his Magegift forever, beyond any hope of repair.

For someone like Cilarnen, to live without magick would be worse than death.

And so they rode onward, each day bringing them closer to the City.

⋙

SHE could hardly tell the difference between waking and sleeping any longer.

The only time she was truly certain she was in the world any longer was in the early evening and morning, when she watched Cilarnen and the Unicorn Knights dancing over the snow.

They were beautiful, floating like stars.

She could feel their love.

"*Tell him that I love him,*" she had begged Shalkan, crying because she was so very tired.

"*You know that I can't,*" the unicorn had answered, gently nuzzling his soft muzzle against her cheek. "*Dry your tears, Vestakia. He mustn't see you like this.*"

She knew that. She was the daughter of a Wildmage. Her mother had paid the ultimate price so that Vestakia could live. So that the Prince of Shadow Mountain could not claim his prize.

He would not have her now.

She would not destroy the weapon the Wild Magic had forged against him.

And so, each day, she soothed her burning eyes with snow compresses, and went with Idalia to Redhelwar's tent before the army began to move for the day. And there she told them what she had dreamed in the night.

Troop strengths. Dispositions. The details of raids on the surrounding countryside, if she knew them. Where *They* were, what *They* were doing, what *They* planned.

Always now, when she moved, she seemed to feel the rustle of great wings at her back.

⋙

"WE shall dispense with the regular order of business today," Lycaelon Tavadon said. He glanced around the Council Chamber, at the six High Mages seated with him.

Lorins, Ganaret, Nagid, Dagan, Harith. All that remained of the old Council.

And Anigrel. His beloved son. The man who would save them all.

Harith, as always, his ally. Ganaret, always willing to endorse any project that involved exalting the Mageborn. Nagid, only interested in his own comfort at any expense. Lorins, a clever and ambitious man, had become one of Anigrel's strongest supporters. Dagan . . . well, Dagan was on the verge of becoming Unsound. Anigrel had said so.

It might well be time for Dagan to retire into private life. The Council had never functioned so effectively as it had these past few moonturns. It would function even more efficiently with six than with seven.

"Lord High Mage?" Anigrel said. "What is your will?"

Lycaelon liked that. No argument about the proper forms. Perizel had always argued.

"You will all have seen the latest report from Barrowmede. Another of our villages lost to the work of the Wildmage menace. We dare not allow them to continue their destruction of our lands."

Ganaret raised his hand for permission to speak.

"Lord Ganaret?" Lycaelon said graciously.

"With respect, Lord Arch-Mage, what spells are we to set to stop them? No Mage who has gone forth from the walls has ever returned."

Lycaelon smiled. "An excellent point, Lord Ganaret. I do not propose to send our Mages against this devious foe. I propose an alliance, between Armethalieh and another ancient foe of the Wildmages. Even now this enemy fights them on their own ground. With the Council's gracious approval, I shall invite them to come here, so that a formal treaty can be sealed between us, and together we can destroy our mutual foe."

"But who are these people?" Lord Harith asked. "Why have we not heard of them before now?"

"With your permission, Lord Harith, I will tell you all I have learned," Anigrel said modestly. For the next several minutes he told the High Council very much the same things he had told Lord Lycaelon—of a hidden race, strong in Magery, who, seeing Armethalieh about to go down to defeat at the hands of their ancient, hated enemy, had ended their millennia of cloistered isolation to attack their mutual foe.

"And now they will come here, to join their power to ours, if we will only ask them. Together we will have the strength to defeat the Wildmages for all time. I ask you, Mages of the High Council. Will you do it—for Armethalieh, and the Light?"

"I call the vote," Lycaelon said.

It was unanimous, of course.

It always was, these days.

Their new allies were to be asked to come.

Lord Anigrel said that they called themselves The Enlightened.

Sixteen

The Battle for Armethalieh

THEY MOVED OVER the land like a plague of darkness, and in their wake, nothing lived, and nothing grew.

They moved slowly, but Savilla did not mind. After the recent setback in the Room of the Obsidian Spire, the destruction around her was balm to her senses. Soon every slight, every humiliation of the last thousand—ten thousand—years would be repaid a hundredfold.

From every corner of her shadowy empire, she had recalled her ancient servants—the Ice Trolls, the Frost Giants, the bestial dwerro. They marched now beneath her banners, just as it had been in the days of old, protected by the shimmering veils of Darkmagery through which the army moved. Far above the army, the giant white forms of Deathwings soared. Around them, Coldwarg darted in and out, searching for anything they might devour, and the towering Shadewalkers ranged farther still, herding terrified victims into the army's path.

It was a glorious sight.

Far afield, the Elves, too, marched toward Armethalieh, thinking they would save it.

They did not know that even now, their pathetic attempts at succor were a part of her plan.

Let them reach Armethalieh.

Let them show themselves to the Mage-men of the Golden City.

Her pet had already sent word that the Mage-men intended to offer an alliance, but an alliance was no part of her plan. She wanted an utter capitulation. The sight of an army of their most hated foes ringing their treasured city should provide that. They would rush to open their gates to her then, doing whatever they had to, to make it possible for her to enter.

Or . . . better yet.

Let them come out to her.

Since the Starry Hunt had come back into the world, her darkest enchantments had lost much of their potency. It was only temporary, but it was one more insult that she intended to repay in full measure as soon as she had brought *He Who Is* into the world.

As soon as she had obtained a suitable sacrifice. A sacrifice of ultimate purity and power, offered up at a time and place that would not simply open a door between the worlds.

But would rend the veil between them asunder forever.

And then . . .

She could devote herself entirely to pleasure.

Her gaze fell upon the form of Prince Zyperis, where he soared over the marching column of subject races and Lesser Endarkened that marched beneath her banners.

Yes.

One of her greatest pleasures—soon, and for thousands of years to come—would be in schooling her son and lover to ultimate obedience. She had been forced to allow him far too much freedom while she was occupied with other, far more pressing matters.

Soon it would be time to call him to heel.

⧽

"*THEY* intend to make a Great Sacrifice at Kindling."

Vestakia's words were no more than a whisper.

It was the morning strategy meeting in Redhelwar's tent.

Redhelwar's tent was always the last thing to be packed, being bundled onto its wagon when the rest of the army was already starting to move. The meeting was the last thing held each morning—after Cilarnen had gotten in his hour or so of practice with the Unicorn Knights.

Cilarnen no longer spent his nights in spellcraft and meditation; in an army on the move, it was simply impossible, and he was devoting every minute he had to perfecting the spell that he and the Unicorn Knights would cast at Armethalieh. The only one who was not a part of that spell was Shalkan; once again, Shalkan's own Mageprice set him apart.

In the moments Cilarnen could spare from working with the Unicorn Knights, he assembled the cantrips that would serve him best in the field, and—

Kellen supposed—snatched an hour or two of sleep here and there, in Anganil's saddle as often as not.

He looked as if he were dying of fever.

⋙

TODAY they had reached the edge of the Delfier Valley.

Armethalieh itself was only a few days away. Less, really, for the edge of the High Mage's weather-spells was just ahead. They would cross them in a mile or so.

Behind them, the landscape still labored under deep winter and heavy snow. Ahead, at the valley's westernmost entrance, there was less than a foot of snow upon the ground. Ancaladar had flown over the Delfier Valley yesterday—the Bounds did not keep anyone out as the Elven Landwards or the City-Wards did; they simply marked the edge of where spells of the High Magick could be cast— and said that everywhere he flew it was the same. Only the lightest dusting of snow covered the ground.

Here, the course of the Demons' raids could be plainly seen. Ancaladar and Jermayan had reported seeing the burnt-out remains of several villages on their overflight. They could not name the villages that had been destroyed. Even Cilarnen could not do that. A proper young High Mage's knowledge of geography stopped at the City Walls, and Cilarnen knew more of the geography of the Elven Lands than he did of the Delfier Valley just a few miles from the city where he had been born and raised.

Without Jermayan's magic to shield them, he and Ancaladar had not dared approach Armethalieh closely, though Ancaladar was willing to risk such a flight tonight. The High Mages would be awake, and active, but their attention would be elsewhere. A black dragon against a black sky, flying quickly, would not be seen. And Ancaladar was still capable of seeing far more things than a human could.

"'A Great Sacrifice,'" Idalia echoed, puzzled.

"*He* has just learned of it," Vestakia said. "*He* is very . . . I am not sure what. *She* means to make it at a Place of Power somewhere near Armethalieh. *He* spies on *Her*. When *She* has made this Sacrifice *She* has spoken of, not even the Starry Hunt can keep *He Who Is* out of the world."

Kellen looked at the others—Idalia, Jermayan, Cilarnen—inquiringly. Among them they represented—or had represented, in Jermayan's case—all the forms of magic that existed in the world, and so represented a sort of informal Council-Within-a-Council in Redhelwar's army. Everyone knew that the battle that would be joined—in only a few days, now at most—would be fought more with magic than with swords and lances, and High Mages and Wildmages had the best idea of the form a battle of magic would take.

"Well," Idalia said slowly, "I suppose it isn't hard to guess *where* She means to do it. There's one of the old Places of Power in the Delfier Valley—a Shrine, like the one in the north where I summoned the Starry Hunt. The one in the Delfier Valley belongs to Men, but unfortunately for us, all the Shrines are completely neutral. Anyone can use them, and for any purpose, even a bad one. I'm not entirely certain where it is exactly, though I could find it if I had to; it's been forgotten for longer than the walls of the City have stood."

"Kindling is only a day or two away," Kellen said slowly. "That doesn't give us much time. But what's a 'Great Sacrifice'? Is it something you do? Or something you have?"

"It's—I'm not sure," Cilarnen said. "But if I had to guess from what's in my old books—and from the look on your face, I'd better—it would be a person. Someone who symbolizes the Land Itself. And considering what we know about *Them* and how *Their* magic works, I'd say it would be a blood sacrifice."

"A King would be the only one who could symbolize the Land," Kellen said. "But Andoreniel is safe in the Elven Lands. And Sandalon is safe in the Fortress of the Crowned Horns. So is Ashaniel, for that matter. And there aren't any other kings."

Idalia frowned. "The Centaurs don't have Kings. Not any more. No Centaur *She* could sacrifice at the Delfier Shrine would symbolize the Land. The same holds for the Mountainfolk, because whoever *She* tried to sacrifice at the Delfier Shrine at Kindling, *She'd* have to find someone the Shrine itself would recognize as a King of Men—isn't that right, Cilarnen?"

"Magic has rules," Cilarnen said firmly. "Well, the High Magick does. And what I read about the Great Sacrifice was in a book about the High Magick—or its ancestor, anyway. So I'd say that this old form follows a lot of the same rules as what I do. The Sacrifice can't be just anybody. It has to be a specific somebody. At a specific time. The best and most powerful sacrifices—the only kind my book talks about, actually—went willingly, joining their personal power to the Land's power for the good of all, but I really don't think *that's* going to happen. And I think . . . She doesn't have *Her* sacrifice yet. Or *She'd* already have taken the shrine and just be waiting on top of it for the right time."

"*She* doesn't want *Him* to know," Vestakia said softly. Her voice was dreamlike, as if she were still asleep. "And . . . I don't know who the sacrifice is, but . . . I know that what *She* does will give *Her* a lot of power. And I think it frightens *Him*."

"It would frighten anyone," Kellen said quietly. "We'll stop it." He spoke with more certainty than he felt, but he could not bear the sight of her pinched, haunted, face.

Suddenly she gasped and doubled over.

"*They're* coming!" she said. "*They're* approaching from the south."

"To horse," Redhelwar said quietly. "We must reach Armethalieh before *Them*."

~⦈~

LESS than an hour later they crossed over into the Delfier Valley, and the army's speed increased.

Their army was still too far away too see—at the far end of the valley, coming up the southern road, the one Cilarnen had taken toward Stonehearth many moonturns ago—but everyone in the army, whether they had magic or not, now could sense *Their* approach. It was as if the air were filled with a constant irritating whine, and there were a shadow over the face of the sun. Half the outriders had dropped back simply to keep the horse herds from bolting, and even the normally stolid oxen, the last creatures to be affected by anything, were on the verge of panic.

But Idalia and the other Wildmage Healers had been preparing for this all the way here. At the first stop of the day, they moved through the army and the herds, distributing doses of the same bright green cordial Kellen had been dosed with by Shalkan when he began his climb to the Black Cairn. It shut down the magical senses—even in the non-magical—and made the presence of the Demons easier to bear.

"How much is there?" Kellen asked.

Idalia had brought a large bucket of faintly green-tinged water to where he and his troop were resting. After all of the Elves had drunk a cup—Kellen, of course, did not—the destriers were each encouraged to drink a bowlful. As Kellen recalled from Shalkan's explanation, it would taste good to them, and calm their nerves.

"Enough to dose the worst cases at full strength for three days, and to take the edge off the entire army for the same time. We've put it in the drinking water, by Redhelwar's command. Don't worry. There are a few barrels of pure water left for the Wildmages. Or you can melt snow."

"If I can find any," Kellen said, looking around. After the landscape he'd been riding through most of the winter, this looked like high summer. "Did you give some to Vestakia?"

"She refused."

"Make her take it. Or I'll come and pour it down her throat myself."

Idalia opened her mouth to protest. Kellen cut her off.

"We need what she can still tell us. And she needs rest. We already know that *They're* there, and where *They're* going. If *They* attack us in the next few hours, I'm sure we'll notice without any extra warning."

Idalia smiled. "I'll tell her you said so."

"Just tell her she has to take it."

"I will." Idalia picked up the empty bucket and moved on.

⇜⇝

AS they rode deeper into the Delfier Valley, it became apparent to the Allies that the Demons did not mean to engage. Everyone knew how fast *They* could move—especially the Endarkened themselves, covering miles in seconds. Yet *They* held back, allowing the Allies to push on down the Western Road toward Armethalieh without opposition.

"What are *They* planning?" Kellen demanded.

He was riding beside Redhelwar, at the front of the Allied Army. Soon they would have to stop to make camp. It was possible the attack would come then. Though the Demons marched—and flew—in the day, many of those who marched beneath *Their* banner were creatures of the night.

And tomorrow—if they survived the night—the army would reach Armethalieh.

"Perhaps to have all of *Their* enemies in one place before *They* destroy them," Redhelwar answered, falling easily into the informality of War Manners.

"But *They* don't want to destroy Armethalieh. *They* want to devour it. It's us *They* want to destroy," Kellen said.

"Does the Wild Magic not counsel you?" Redhelwar asked. There was an undertone of worry in his voice.

"It doesn't suggest I'm doing anything I shouldn't be doing—or that you aren't," Kellen said. "So I suppose we're both doing what we ought to be right now by going straight ahead. If Ancaladar can make a flight over the City tonight, we'll have fresher news. And Cilarnen intends to scry, to see what's going on with the Council. They have to know that there are two armies out here. They'll be meeting in an Emergency Session tonight, more than likely. He'll be able to find out what they're talking about."

"And perhaps tomorrow he can speak to them in person, and bring them to their senses," Redhelwar said.

"I hope so," Kellen said grimly.

⇜⇝

THEY set up camp in expectation of being attacked at any moment, with a third of the camp on watch at all times. It was all they could do; they dared not march through the night. The Demon army was more than human. They were only flesh and bone. Even if Coldfire would allow them to see in the night, they dared not arrive at the sight of the battle unfed and exhausted.

Kellen was up at the Unicorn Camp. Not only did being there allow him to spend time with Shalkan, he would be nearby when Cilarnen finished doing . . . whatever it was that Cilarnen did. He wasn't really in the mood to sleep, anyway. And his troop had the second watch, the hardest of the night. He'd sleep for a few hours after that, he promised himself.

Every now and again he glanced over at Cilarnen's wagon. It seemed to glow faintly, though there was no actual light showing.

"You'll wear yourself out with all that staring," Shalkan told him.

The closeness of the Demons affected everyone. It was as if *Their* mere presence was a beacon, radiating despair. But the unicorns, of course, were the hardest hit by *Their* nearness. Shalkan's fur twitched constantly, as if invisible flies were stinging him, and his tufted tail was in constant motion, though he made no reference to the cause.

"I know," Kellen said, sighing. "I just wonder what he's doing."

"If you'd stayed in the City, you'd know, of course," the unicorn reminded him.

Kellen shuddered faintly, and not from the cold. Shalkan snickered, but his ears twitched, raising and flattening, as if he were trying to find relief from an itch he couldn't reach.

Cilarnen obviously adored the High Magick, every single finicking rule and regulation of it.

Kellen would rather be wrapped in chains and drowned.

"I can tell exactly what you're thinking, you know," Shalkan said.

"Is it that obvious?" Kellen asked ruefully. He was willing to endure more than usual of his friend's teasing tonight, if it could distract Shalkan from his own discomfort.

"Be glad that the requirements of Knight-Magery do not include concealing your feelings, or you'd never manage it."

"If it was something Master Belesharon wanted me to learn, believe me, I'd learn it," Kellen said feelingly. "I can *still* feel the bruises I got in the House of Sword and Shield."

He sighed again, and looked upward. The night was clear—the High Mage's weather-spells saw to that—and it almost seemed as if he could see the Starry Hunt riding across the sky. The air here swirled with Power, and not all of it was Dark. When they did face the Demon Army, they would have powerful allies.

But . . . powerful enough?

"Light blast and curse them all!"

Cilarnen came stamping down out of his Mage-wagon, wearing nothing but a thin woolen shift.

He regarded Kellen sourly—looking like the oldest and crankiest High Mage in all of Armethalieh—and continued across the camp—barefoot—to his tent.

When he emerged, several minutes later, he was dressed, but in no better humor. He accepted a mug of tea from Menerchel, and came over to Kellen.

"Nothing," he said succinctly.

"They weren't meeting?" Kellen asked.

"I mean I could see nothing," Cilarnen said. "Not even the surrounding countryside!" He drank tea, obviously extremely frustrated. "I don't think it's because *They* are doing anything to Shield *Themselves*. And I really hope *They* can't be shielding the City. I just think there's too much Power around. It makes it impossible to see. You'll have to hope Ancaladar can give you better information."

"You did all you could," Kellen said.

"What good is that if I couldn't do what you need?" Cilarnen demanded. He took a deep breath and drained his mug. "I need to go check my spellbooks. There are some other things I need to prepare for the morning."

"Charming company, High Mages," Shalkan said, when Cilarnen had gone.

"He's working too hard," Kellen said, as if that were something they didn't both already know. "He's trying to do the impossible. And he thinks it's his fault that the High Mages are all idiots. *I* don't think it's his fault."

"So you forgive him?" Shalkan asked. He raised a hind hoof, and set it down again, carefully.

"I never blamed him," Kellen said.

He was surprised to discover, when he said it, that it was the truth.

And always had been.

⌦

ANCALADAR returned from his overflight of Armethalieh just before Kellen was about to go on watch. He and Jermayan had even more bad news.

The only good news Ancaladar brought was that he could—even now—see the Wards around the City.

They had been changed. Even if the army reached the City walls unopposed, it could never enter, even if the gates were opened to them.

The Wards now blocked the entry of Elves, Wildmages, Centaurs, Otherfolk . . . of all who rode with the Allied Army, only a few of the Mountainfolk and Wildlanders would be able to enter, and they would probably be killed by the City Guard and the Militia.

If the Allied Army actually reached the City, it would be trapped against its walls as if they were a high cliff.

And beyond Armethalieh was the sea.

◆

THE army marched before first light. There was no time this morning for Cilar-nen's practice—if the unicorns weren't ready now to do what he was going to ask of them, they never would be. Kellen only hoped they would be able to do what Cilarnen asked of them even with the Demon Army right in front of them. None of them had considered the effect the Demons would have on the unicorns.

Because no one has faced a Demon army in a thousand years. And no matter how good the records are that the Elves have kept of the Last War, information—vital information—has been lost.

Perhaps War Mages could have Shielded the unicorns.

If they'd had enough of them.

It was too late to worry about that now.

The only encouraging news—though it was more than a bit puzzling, and right now none of them was in a mood for mysteries—was that the Demon Army had not attacked in the night. Every mile they rode today would bring them closer to Armethalieh, and after a certain point, there would be no way the sounds and sight of a battle could fail to reach the attention of the High Mages—and, probably, everyone else inside the City, considering the tactics the Demons would undoubtedly use on the battlefield.

If it was still the Demons' intention to take Armethalieh through trickery and misdirection, *They* would not dare attack the Allied Army where the Armethaliehans had any chance of seeing the battle while the City Wards were even partially in place. If the High Mages, even cowed and befuddled as Cilar-nen had reported them to be, figured out that there were *Demons* outside their walls, they would probably join forces even with Elves to fight *Them,* and that would put an end to the Demons' plans to subvert the City through deception.

◆

"THEY'RE *gone!*"

Vestakia's scream was a wail of pure terror, rousing Idalia from an uneasy sleep inside the Healer's wagon. She'd been awake all night, ministering to the army with the senses-dampening cordial. She'd persuaded Vestakia to take an initial dose of the pure cordial—in the name of getting a few hours' sleep; Kellen was right about that—but after that Vestakia had refused to take any more. She was right about that, too.

"Vestakia? Who's gone?"

"*Them. Their* army. Idalia, *I can't sense* Them *anywhere.*"

Idalia was suddenly completely awake. "I'll go tell Redhelwar."

◆

THEY had moved through the night, her pets, her children, her slaves. All of those who could not disguise their true nature she had sent to wait at the Place of Sacrifice, under the command of her son and lover. Tomorrow night she would make the Great Sacrifice that would rend the Veil forever.

In company of the rest of her Court—some in the form of humans, some in the form of horses—Savilla had ridden at last to the walls of her greatest prize. It was nearly within her grasp at last.

And before she had gone, she had done one last thing.

It was a powerful spell. It had required the sacrifice of all of the captives they had collected along their march. But for a few brief hours—as the Brightworlders reckoned time—their very essence would be masked from any who might sense them for what they truly were.

Time enough and more to take into her hands the last of her pawns and playing pieces.

⇌

"MY Lord Arch-Mage."

Lycaelon smiled. "You are very formal with me this morning, Anigrel."

"It is a day for the greatest of formality, Lord Arch-Mage, for it is a day that will change the future of Armethalieh forever. The delegation of the Enlightened has arrived. They await us outside the walls. Let us ride forth and escort them into the City."

He had spent last night in communion with his Dark Lady, preparing for this moment. She was very near now. Soon he would behold her face, flesh to flesh, for the first time in his life.

He would give her Lycaelon.

Then he would return to the City, alone, to tell the High Council that the Wildmages had captured and killed the Arch-Mage. He would tell them that an emergency Working must be done to strengthen the Wards upon the walls.

But he would not strengthen them. He would destroy them completely.

The time for subtlety was nearly past.

But just now, a little subtlety was still needed. Enough to overshadow Lycaelon's will, to convince the Arch-Mage that it was, indeed, a very good idea to ride out with Anigrel to meet these new allies . . .

⇌

IDALIA rode up to Redhelwar and Kellen. It was two hours before noon. The walls of Armethalieh were already visible in the distance.

"*They're* not going to attack," she heard Kellen saying, as she approached.

"In fact, Vestakia can't sense *Them* at all any longer all of a sudden," Idalia said. "Though somehow I doubt that *They've* left. And the dose of potion I gave her wore off hours ago."

"*They* haven't," Kellen said concisely. "Jermayan may not be able to speak from Ancaladar's back any longer, but he can still talk." He pointed up toward the sky where, high above, Ancaladar's black form circled. Intermittently, flashes of light appeared, as if Jermayan were holding . . . a mirror?

"Jermayan knows the mirror code," Kellen explained, "and here, where the skies are clear all day and the air is always calm, he can use it. I can't read it, but Dionan and Redhelwar can. Jermayan says that *They* have split the army. Most of *Them* are about twenty miles off in that direction—" He pointed.

Idalia groaned faintly. "That's about where I think the Delfier Shrine is. Too bad we couldn't afford to put part of the army on top of it to defend it."

"They'd have been slaughtered where they stood," Kellen said simply. "It's more important to take the City, and keep *Them* from getting *Their* hands on the Great Sacrifice—whatever it is—and taking it to the Shrine, than to try to hold the Shrine. Especially since that's something we couldn't do anyway."

"Kellen," Redhelwar said suddenly. "They're opening the City Gates."

In the distance, Kellen could just make out the Delfier Gates beginning to move. Not the Lesser Gates, the ones that were opened for the Farm Caravans—and to cast out Outlaws—but the Great Gates themselves, the ones that stood as high as the City Walls.

"They're going to ride outside the walls?" Kellen demanded in disbelief. "Somebody get Cilarnen."

⤚⤙

BY the time Cilarnen had ridden to the top of the column, the gates were almost completely open. Cilarnen stared, as disbelieving of the sight as Kellen.

"The Great Gate hasn't been opened in . . . even Master Hendassar wasn't sure of the last time it had been opened," Cilarnen said in awe. "They must have seen us, and be planning to attack us. I think—I hope—I can Shield well enough to stop the first attack; once they recognize they're facing High Magick, they might break off," he added. But he didn't sound certain.

"And if Ancaladar makes a pass over them, their horses certainly won't stand."

"That's true enough," Kellen agreed. Fortunately, they didn't have to try to figure out a way to tell Jermayan to try that. Jermayan had been trained in the House of Sword and Shield for far longer than Kellen had; if Cilarnen could think of something like that, certainly Jermayan would, too.

"Line halt. Skirimishers to the fore," Redhelwar said.

The horns echoed back down the column.

"Here they come," Cilarnen said nervously, as the first horses came through the gates—still miles away—at a slow walk. "City Militia. Wait. They're carrying the Arch-Mage's banner. I recognize House Tavadon's colors. And Lord Anigrel is with him—see the cadet pennon? They shouldn't be here."

"Oh, Gods of the Wild Magic," Idalia groaned. "Who symbolizes the Land in Armethalieh but the Arch-Mage of the City? *Lycaelon* is to be the Great Sacrifice! Anigrel must have told him some tale to convince him to come outside the walls where *They* could get at him!"

"Look," Kellen said, pointing. "There *They* are."

Another group of riders had just come out of the forest, directly opposite the City gates and the emerging High Mages.

There were perhaps twenty of *Them*. Once *They* had taken *Their* position, *They* stopped and sat perfectly still. *Their* horses were whiter than snow, as were *Their* flowing garments. Even *Their* hair was white. *They* wore no armor, carried no weapons. *They* radiated beauty and calm purity.

"Stop the Armethaliehans before they reach *Them*," Redhelwar said.

Dionan blew the order. *Skirmishers to the charge.*

⸎

KELLEN and the other skirmishing units galloped across the snow at a dead run, the only thought on anyone's mind to reach the Armethaliehan party before it could reach the White Riders.

Kellen knew what this must look like to those watching from the walls: an attack—by the Elves—on the Arch-Mage and his escort.

He couldn't allow that to matter to him. There would be time later to explain. Right now, they had to stop the Demons from getting *Their* hands on the one thing *They* needed to win.

⸎

EVEN though the skirmishing units were farther from the Armethaliehans than the Armethaliehans were from the White Riders, for a few moments it actually looked as if they would reach them first. The Armethaliehan party was moving forward at a slow ceremonial walk, and the White Riders were not moving at all.

Kellen's first hope was that the sight of sixty Elven Knights bearing down on them at a thundering gallop would simply cause the Armethaliehans to turn and dash back inside their walls. It would have been the smartest thing to do.

But the City Militia that formed Lycaelon's honor guard had no concept of warfare or proper tactics. When they saw the enemy approaching they stopped, milled uncertainly for a moment, then formed a protective barricade around Lycaelon and Anigrel, stopping dead where they were. He saw Lycaelon raise his staff of office.

"Scatter!" Kellen shouted. He urged Firareth to an even faster pace as the riders around him broke ranks in every direction.

The lightning bolt struck just where he'd been a moment before. He saw Lycaelon reel back with the effort of casting so powerful a spell, and consoled himself with the knowledge that Lycaelon—unlike Cilarnen—probably did not have more lightning bolts in reserve.

Now the White Riders spurred *Their* mounts forward.

IF *They* had dared to take on *Their* true forms, it would have been a slaughter instead of merely a battle, but here, so close to the walls, *They* must continue to seem to be human.

Kellen dropped instantly into Battle-mind.

It was unlike any of his previous experiences. This time the double-sight did not come, overlaying his vision of the enemy with a map of their potential attacks and his. This time, it was as if he simply surrendered himself completely to the Wild Magic, becoming a tool for it to move as it willed. He felt fully alive, fully aware, fully present—but his volition had become a part of a force far greater than himself.

He could see—could *feel*—every one of his own people around him, as much a part of himself as his sword, or the fingers of his own hand. He shouted orders, moving them into position for the attack. Far behind him, he sensed that Redhelwar, seeing that the first assault had failed, was sending reinforcements. Kellen noted their kind and number, and when they would arrive, and returned to solving the puzzle of the battle. The proper solution would lead to victory.

This enemy could not be killed.

But it must *pretend* to be killed, hurt, driven back.

Because the Armethaliehans were watching from the walls of the City, and there was still a need for deception.

The Elven Knights drove into the middle of the White Riders, slashing at them frantically. If they could only reach Lycaelon's Militia . . .

But even now, beyond the press of the shining white horses, Kellen could see that a few of the White Riders had refrained from joining battle with the Elves. They were urging Lycaelon and his guard onward, into the forest.

Fifteen against sixty. And despite those odds, the Elven Knights were taking the worst of it. The white horses fought as viciously as their riders, kicking and snapping and rearing. It was only the fact that the two forces were so thoroughly intermingled by now that kept any of the High Mages watching the battle from the walls from using spells of their own, Kellen was sure. And cantrips such as Cilarnen possessed took time to prepare. The one that Lycaelon had used must be the only one he had. Anigrel might not have any at all.

All around him he could hear the shouts of battle and the screams of the dying.

He closed with a White Rider. Light At The Heart Of The Mountain rang as it slid up the enemy's blade. The two stallions jockeyed for position, their bodies slamming bruisingly against each other as they circled and snapped.

Suddenly there was an earth-shattering roar as the air split; a blinding flash of light. Lightning struck the ground—once, twice—between the retreating Militia and the forest.

Kellen did not need to turn his head to see. He already knew—had known from the moment he had given his first orders—that help was coming. Cilarnen and the Wildmages had arrived.

The Militia turned and broke, then—not even the White Riders accompanying them could prevent it. Their horses—Anigrel and Lycaelon were still with them—turned and bolted for the still-open City gates.

But by now the tide of battle had swept through that area, and the panicked animals were running directly into a tangle of Elven cavalry that was being cut to pieces by a cluster of White Riders. They had been forced so close to the City walls by their foes that they were under attack from the guards on the walls as well, and their losses were heavy.

Suddenly there was another flash—not of lightning this time.

And now Kellen faced, not a White Rider and his moon-pale stallion, but two Demons with glowing yellow eyes and great scarlet wings.

Firareth gathered himself on his haunches and sprang backward. Kellen slashed downward with his sword. The Demon lashed out—

And Shalkan was suddenly between him and the blow.

Every hair on the unicorn's body was fluffed out like a cat's. A sound Kellen had never heard the unicorn make came from Shalkan's throat. He *hissed*.

The Demons—both of them—leaped back.

The Unicorn Knights had arrived.

Now they had a chance, because the Demons dared not allow the Unicorn Knights anywhere near them.

The Elven Knights were desperately trying to disengage, attempting to clear the way for the Armethaliehans to get back into the City. But now that they had seen the true face of the enemy, the Militia was attempting—in a gesture as gallant as it was hopeless—to stand and fight.

The Demons cut them down in seconds. Kellen saw two of the towering winged creatures grab Anigrel and Lycaelon and launch *Themselves* into the air.

There was another flicker as the spell the Wildmages had cast ebbed and died, and the Demons were gone. The White Riders appeared in their place once more. Kellen looked for the two in the sky, and could not find them—then saw, far in the distance, two white horses running at top speed into the trees, each bearing on its back a rider in the robes of an Armethaliehan High Mage.

The Allies had lost.

The Demons had gained *Their* sacrifice.

The remaining White Riders weren't attacking any longer, but now allowing the Unicorn Knights to drive them off. In fact, they were fleeing the battlefield.

He realized he was still shouting orders as the Battle-mind ebbed and left him. Retreat—regroup—rescue the wounded. Shalkan and the Unicorn Knights had already retreated from the battlefield. Now it was up to the survivors of the rescue attempt to escape the killing ground before they were attacked by the High Mages.

Of those who had ridden out against the White Riders, two-thirds were dead.

❧

"WE have to get into the City and talk sense into these people," Idalia said grimly, when Kellen had returned with the remains of his force. "The Sacrifice will be tonight—at midnight; Kindling Eve—but we can stop it if we can get enough of the High Mages to help. And for that, we have to get into the City."

"Then it's up to the Unicorn Knights and me," Cilarnen said. "We'll take the Wards down, and then Ancaladar can open the Gates."

"They'll shoot at you from the walls," Kellen said. "They can't be sure of what they saw, but they're sure of one thing. We're the enemy. And the Arch-Mage has just been kidnapped—and as far as they know, killed."

"Then we'll have to dodge," Cilarnen said simply.

"How will we know when your spell has run its course?" Redhelwar asked.

"Oh, you'll know," Cilarnen said. "Believe me, you'll know."

"We had best move the rest of the army up into position outside the City," Redhelwar said. "Perhaps it will dismay them."

Cilarnen went to prepare the Unicorn Knights.

Redhelwar gave the Elven Army the order to deploy itself for battle.

❧

THIS is it, Kellen thought. Not the final battle itself, but surely the beginning of it. The army made its dispositions: infantry, light cavalry, heavy cavalry, the remains of its skirmishing units. All deployed around Armethalieh, a city they must both protect, and defend themselves from, in the event the High Mages chose to attack.

Redhelwar did not plan a line of retreat. There would be no retreat from this battle.

There was nowhere to go.

❧

"LEAF and Star—and the Light—go with you," Redhelwar said to Cilarnen.

The young High Mage sat on Anganil's back. The black stallion danced in place, eager to be gone. A few hundred yards away the Unicorn Knights stood, waiting.

"Good luck," Kellen said quietly.

Cilarnen nodded, saying nothing.

Then he turned, spurring Anganil forward.

Kellen rode out to stand with Shalkan. And to wait.

❧

THE unicorns spread out behind Cilarnen, running single-file at first. Any of them could easily have outpaced Anganil, but they didn't.

"It's a dance, not a race."

Kellen remembered Cilarnen saying that. Now he was dancing for the lives of everyone in the land.

They ran down toward the walls of Armethalieh. Suddenly Anganil turned and pivoted in his tracks, turning back the other way. The twenty unicorns gave way before him, and in moments he was followed by a double column of ten.

Turned again.

Circled.

Turned back toward the walls, the unicorns following in single file once more. And now their coats seemed to be glowing more brightly than they had been a moment before.

Pivot, stop, circle, turn . . . it was like watching a flock of birds in flight, and with each figure, the unicorns glowed brighter. Soon Anganil was glowing, too, and finally Kellen began to have an idea of what it was he was seeing.

They were a wand. Cilarnen and the unicorns were a wand. He was using them all to draw an enormous glyph—on the land, instead of in the air. They were *dancing* it.

And when it was complete, the spell would be cast.

They reached the walls of the City, but they still didn't run in a straight line. Backward, forward, spinning and turning; if Anganil had not been an Elven-bred destrier trained for war, he would already have foundered.

How long could they keep that up?

How long did they *have* to keep that up?

The line of unicorns—and one destrier—disappeared around the curve of the wall.

"Wait. Where are they going?" Kellen asked.

"To ride three times around the City walls," Shalkan replied quietly.

"But . . . the *docks* are on the seaside of the City," Kellen said. He knew the docks well. They'd been his favorite place in the City. A unicorn could navigate them easily; he'd never yet seen the terrain a unicorn couldn't get over. But he couldn't imagine riding even an Elven destrier over the docks.

"Cilarnen will manage," Shalkan said. "He has to."

Even with them out of sight, Kellen could feel the spell build. It was an odd sensation. He knew what he was feeling had to be High Magick, since the spell was Cilarnen's, and Cilarnen was a High Mage. Normally—at least since he'd become a Wildmage—Kellen couldn't sense the workings of the High Magick any more than Cilarnen could sense the Wild Magic. The one time he'd been in contact with High Magick and *had* sensed it—in the spell of Kindolhinadetil's Mirror—it had just *hurt*.

This was different.

It was as if there were something important, and maybe interesting, and not all that bad, just out of reach.

If Cilarnen was right, a long time ago—a very long time ago—High Mages and Wildmages had worked closely together. Hard as it was to believe, Idalia said that their magic had all once come from the same place.

"Where are they?" Kellen muttered.

"It's a big place, your City. Give them time," Shalkan said.

Suddenly Cilarnen and his dancers burst out on the other side of the City, all of them running side-by-side.

Kellen saw archers run to the walls. The High Mages who had been there during the battle with the White Riders had long since departed—probably to discuss what it could possibly mean in great detail somewhere much safer.

And then Ancaladar plummeted down out of the sky.

The City Wards would keep him from descending to the walls themselves, but the City Guard didn't know that. The great black dragon made a pass over the City, as low as he could.

Kellen heard screaming. The archers fled from the walls.

"Won't do a lot for our position as their saviors, but it will keep Cilarnen from getting shot," Shalkan commented.

"Right now that's all I'm worried about," Kellen said fervently. "Let's just hope they don't figure out there's nothing Ancaladar can actually *do*."

"Hard to figure out anything when you're hiding under a bed," Shalkan replied.

SECOND circuit. Now trails of colored light followed the unicorns, hanging in the air behind them as they ran. Somehow Kellen had expected them to make the same moves this time as before, but they didn't. The passages were more elaborate, different, conducted at a faster pace. They moved as if they were sets of human dancers, tracing elaborate figures across the trampled ground.

And once more they vanished around the curve of the wall.

Ancaladar was still wheeling and swooping over the City, like an enormous and terrifying bird of prey. It would be someone very brave—or very foolish—who dared to go up on the walls to shoot at the unicorns.

Or a High Mage.

Why don't the High Mages attack? Kellen wondered. In their place, he would have given such an order long ago.

But without the Arch-Mage—or Anigrel—he suspected there was no one left in the City willing to take the risk of doing so. From everything Cilarnen had told him about what had happened in Armethalieh in recent moonturns, the place was even more hidebound than it had been when he left. Now nobody dared to do *anything* without the High Council's express permission. And the High Council didn't dare to do anything without the Arch-Mage and the Mage-wardens' approval. And Anigrel controlled the Magewardens.

So at the moment, nobody in Armethalieh probably dared to do anything at all.

Again Cilarnen and the unicorns appeared, this time enmeshed in a web of colored light. It trailed behind them, the streamers taking longer now to fade away, and the unicorns' bodies glowed so brightly that they cast shadows against the pale stone walls of Armethalieh, even in the winter sunlight. Anganil was covered in foam—Kellen could see that much from where he stood, and he could imagine the rest; how the black stallion's lungs labored for air, his sides heaving with exertion as he fought for breath.

"This is the last circuit," Shalkan said.

"If Anganil should fall . . ." Kellen said.

"It will all have been for nothing," Shalkan said, "if they cannot complete the last circuit of the spell."

Now the unicorns turned and spun in the most elaborate set of figures yet, with Cilarnen and Anganil at their center. The black stallion ran in a straight line now, parallel to the walls, just far enough from them that the Unicorn Knights could weave back and forth around him.

"Someone's going up on the walls," Kellen said.

In the distance, he saw three figures ascend the walls, their upper bodies just visible over the top. Robed Mages. Over their gray robes, they wore the black tabards of Magewardens.

He heard Redhelwar call out to the archers to prepare to loose, but at this distance, the shot was an almost impossible one, and any arrow that fell short might hit one of the unicorns.

Suddenly one of the standing figures fell, an arrow through his shoulder. The others looked skyward, pointing.

Jermayan.

Ancaladar could not penetrate the City Wards, but an Elven arrow could.

And Jermayan was an expert marksman.

The two remaining Magewardens hesitated. Jermayan fired again— apparently a warning shot, as neither fell. Ancaladar swooped as low as he could.

They fled, carrying their wounded comrade.

Cilarnen and the unicorns passed around the curve of the City walls for the last time.

"They will try to stop him at the docks," Kellen guessed.

"If they dare," Shalkan said. "Ancaladar can be . . . very persuasive when he tries."

"Then we've got to assume he'll succeed. And we must prepare to enter the City."

"Good luck," Shalkan said. "I'll see you when the battle is over."

Kellen hugged his friend—it might be for the last time, but he had to believe that it wouldn't be—burying his face for a moment in the soft fur of Shalkan's neck. Just for a moment, he inhaled the spicy cinnamon scent of unicorn. Then he took his helmet from Firareth's saddle and settled it into place, mounted Firareth, and rode back to take his position with the Elven Army.

Shalkan trotted away.

AS he rode back toward the army, it felt as if he rode through water. All around him he could feel Cilarnen's spell building to its climax. It made his skin itch, made the air he drew into his lungs feel thicker than fog. He wondered if the other Wildmages could sense it as well.

Idalia and Vestakia were waiting with Redhelwar. Vestakia was barely able to stay in her saddle. She was nearly doubled-over in pain and weakness, though Kellen doubted that she sensed the High Magick at all. Kellen did his best to ignore her distress, knowing that his indifference was the only help he could give her now.

"You'll need to see me to the gates, brother dear. Then, I expect, your place is here." Idalia shook her head, as if flies buzzed around her. "Not long," she said, sounding hopeful.

Kellen nodded. Soon Cilarnen's spell would work or it wouldn't—and either way, this wave of High Magick that surrounded them would crest and break.

They'd talked about having him accompany Idalia into the City to talk to the High Mages, but his battle skills were too vital to the army. Jermayan would go with her, and Cilarnen. If Cilarnen of House Volpiril could not convince the Mages of Armethalieh to ally themselves with the Allied Army against the Demons after what they'd seen today, then no one could.

"Vestakia?"

The fact that she was here—rather than back with the Healers—must mean that she had something that needed to be said. She was stubborn—it was what had kept her alive all these years—but she wasn't foolish. She wouldn't take risks that didn't need to be taken.

"*He* will attack soon. *She* is keeping most of *Them* with *Her*. At the Shrine. But there are others *He* can call upon. I cannot sense *Them*, but . . . *She* does not want *Him* to attack, but *He* will, I think." Vestakia forced the words out in effortful gasps, as beads of sweat ran down her face.

"Then it is time for me to give you this," Redhelwar said, holding out his hand to Kellen.

On Redhelwar's palm rested the green-stoned ring he had gotten from Andoreniel.

"This is your time, Kellen," Redhelwar said. "Use us all well, in the name of Leaf and Star."

He had never meant for this to happen, but as Kellen stared at the ring, a sense of rightness, of inevitability, settled over him.

This was the moment he had been training for, had been shaped for, from the moment he had been born. Every person he had ever known, everything he had ever done, had led him to this day, this hour.

He took the ring, and with it the command of the entire Elven Army.

"The gods of the Wild Magic guide us all, Redhelwar," he said softly. He slipped the ring into his belt pouch.

"Vestakia, go and wait with the Healers. Redhelwar, you must see Idalia to the City gates. Isinwen, my compliments to Nithariel, and it would please me greatly if she would see if the Enemy is indeed moving up to prepare for battle. Dionan and Ninolion, I wish to change the dispositions of the troops; you will oblige me by telling the Centaurs they are to take the center, Wildmages in *their* center. The Knights will flank; split them evenly by commands. I will send further orders once you have begun. Adaerion, please bring me Belepheriel at once."

"I see them," Idalia said, looking behind him. "Cilarnen's riders."

Kellen barely glanced up; he was still giving orders. If they were about to be hit, they were *not*, by Leaf and Star, going to be in the same positions they'd been in a thousand years ago. With the heavy cavalry-infantry—the Centaurs—as their center, they could absorb the first assault of the Enemy and hammer it with the fast-moving flanking wings of Elven cavalry, rather than having the cavalry hemmed in by the slower-moving Centaurs.

But suddenly the wave of magick . . . broke.

Kellen reined Firareth around.

The Unicorn Knights had swirled to a stop in front of the Gates of Armethalieh. And for a moment, the City Walls themselves glowed brighter than the sun in the sky.

Then the light faded.

The Unicorn Knights turned away. Anganil began to walk, very slowly, back toward the Allied lines. His head was hanging and his sides heaved. Cilarnen dismounted and led him as the Unicorn Knights formed a protective honor guard. The stallion had truly given his all for the spell.

And there was a creaking, crackling, crashing sound from within the walls of the City itself.

"The towers are falling," Idalia said, very quietly.

Armethalieh was known as the City of a Thousand Bells, and most of those bells were suspended high in lacy decorative spires.

Set by magick. Worked by magick. Held in place by magick.

Cilarnen hadn't just taken down the Wards of the City Gates.

His spell had removed the Mage-spells from the entire City.

And now the towers that were sustained by magick were crumbling to earth.

With the Wards gone at last, Ancaladar settled on the wall and leaned over the edge of the Gate.

"Time to go," Idalia said.

"You'd better take Cilarnen another horse," Kellen said.

"We'll ride double," Idalia said. "Not much use for horses in the City, as I recall."

"Good luck," Kellen said.

"Leaf and Star," Idalia answered.

She and Redhelwar rode out to meet Cilarnen.

"Go and take Anganil," Kellen said to Reyezeyt. "The unicorns won't be able to approach the army."

He returned to giving orders.

❧

PRINCE Zyperis stood in the midst of his army. His beloved Queen and Mama had given him command of all but the Dark Guard itself. Them she had taken with her to winnow the remaining villages in the Delfier Valley, for the sacrifice to come must be prepared in blood, and the last of their previous captives had gone to fuel the Concealment Spell that had allowed her to approach the City walls and steal away the Great Sacrifice.

When the hateful sun had left the sky, it would not rise again, for tonight, Time would stop forever. The blood of the Great Sacrifice would be spilled upon the Standing Stones, and *He Who Is* would enter the world once more.

And grant to she who had given him his return, power and favor above all the rest of his creation. She would see all, know all.

Know how her son had plotted against her.

And would punish him.

Forever.

There must—there must!—be a way out of the trap that Zyperis saw closing

so inexorably around him. But he could not see it. If he destroyed the Great Sacrifice now, sabotaging Savilla's spell, he doomed himself, for her wrath would be
inventive and lingering.

If her spell succeeded . . .

He was doomed as well.

He could feel some sort of Magery building in the distance, at Armethalieh,
but his Queen had told him that Armethalieh was no longer a matter for their
concern, now that the Sacrifice was theirs. Once *He Who Is* walked the world
again, the Endarkened would have more than enough power to smash them all:
Elves, Wildmages, High Mages: all. All he need do was remain here in case the
Elven Army attempted a futile rescue attempt of the Sacrifice. Then he could
amuse himself by destroying them.

Amuse himself. As if he were still a child, to be distracted with toys. She
still underestimated him.

As he had underestimated her.

The time that he could safely have slain her had passed.

The Magery he felt was a creation of great power, disturbingly so. Yet it was
not directed at them—the Enemy—but at Armethalieh. Foolish Lightborn! Was
it possible that—even now—they did not know who their true enemy was?

Then the spell reached its peak.

Zyperis felt the wave of magic crest over him. It was painful, as all spells of
the High Magick were to his kind, but it could not truly harm him. Only a blending of High Magick and the Wild Magic could do that, as they had learned to
their cost. But the pain brought with it knowledge, as the dying ebb of the spell
told Zyperis everything about its construction and its purpose.

The Wards were down. The City was open.

Cloaking himself in invisibility, he flew to the edge of the forest to see what
had transpired. But he did not see what he expected to see.

There was a dragon—a dragon!—crouched upon the City walls. Instead of
the radiant wellspring of Power that he had expected to see, that he had yearned
to capture for himself, its magic was dim and flickering, nearly extinguished.

Beneath its watchful gaze, the gates stood open. A troop of Elves rode forward, into the City.

But the attack that Zyperis expected did not come.

No gray-robed High Mages strode forward to cast them out with savage
spells.

If the Wildmages and the High Mages make an alliance . . .

Even now—oh, surely, they could not win! But it might cost more of the
precious lives of the children of *He Who Is.*

If he could prevent that, his Mama might be pleased.

He might save his own life.

She had told him not to attack the City for any reason.

But she did not know about this. Surely she would wish him to prevent this if she *did* know.

It would be far simpler for him to ask her for forgiveness later.

He could certainly fly down into the City by himself. He was the Prince of the Endarkened, and the City lay helpless and unWarded before him.

But . . . he had just seen a Wildmage enter. And he knew there were High Mages there. He had no intention of being killed when there were easier, safer ways of accomplishing his goal.

Zyperis flew back to his army and gave the order to attack.

Seventeen

Sealed to the Light

"YOU HAVE DONE well, my sweet slave."

Lycaelon Tavadon heard the words only dimly. His mind was filled with horror. So much, so many impossibilities, had happened in so short a time, that he could not think.

He felt ill, feverish, as if he had drunk poison.

Every time he opened his eyes, all he saw was the monsters that had walked the land in the Black Days of ancient memory, the legend of their existence preserved in texts permitted to the study of only the highest ranks of the Mageborn—and then, only when they had proven themselves both sincere in devotion to the City and truly possessed of a need to know.

And his son, his beautiful son, was laughing.

"My Dark Lady, my glorious Queen," Anigrel said. "You are more beautiful than I could have dreamed. But . . . why am I here? I must return to the City, to take down the Wards so you can enter."

"No. The time for that has passed."

"Anigrel . . ." Lycaelon moaned.

He realized he was lying on the forest floor. Dim memories of a nightmare ride through trees came back to him. They had been riding out of the City to greet their new allies, and then . . . and then . . .

He struggled to his knees, forced himself to open his eyes.

Anigrel stood beside one of those . . . creatures. Her wings were spread, mantling his body. His face wore a look of radiant triumph.

"The Arch-Mage looks confused," she said.

A thrill of sick horror coursed through Lycaelon to hear human speech coming from such a creature. Bile rose in his throat.

"Perhaps you should explain yourself to him. It would please me very much."

"Dear Father," Anigrel said fondly. "Here is my true and only mistress. I have served her all my life, from the time I was a child. Everything I have ever done has been to her glory. There have never been any plots among the Mageborn, nor was House Volpiril guilty of anything, save, perhaps, ambition. I created young Cilarnen's cabal myself. I murdered Lords Vilmos, Arance, and Perizel. The information brought to the Council through the Magewardens is all lies. For moonturns we have tampered with the City Wards, allowing the influence of the Endarkened to spread throughout the City, and now they will claim their ultimate victory. Today."

The Demon standing behind Anigrel gasped, as if in ecstasy.

"Lies . . . ?" Lycaelon said. "You . . . lied to me?"

"I did not lie. I told you I acted for the good of the City, and so I have. It is good that Men serve their proper masters. The Endarkened. We have been a blight upon the land for too long. No longer."

"You have learned all your lessons well," the Demon told Anigrel. "Now you will serve me in the best way you can, and have the reward I promised you so long ago."

"Yes, Mistress," Anigrel whispered.

She put her arms around him from behind, running her hands over the heavy silk of his Magerobes. The rank-tabbard he wore, embroidered both with House Tavadon's colors of black and white and with Anigrel's own chosen colors of gold and red, covered with the elaborate heraldry of his rank and honors, slipped from his shoulders and fell to the muck of the forest floor.

Anigrel tilted his head back, exposing his throat, as he sighed in ecstacy and utter submission.

Delicately the Demon Queen parted the gray robes and the fine linen tunic beneath, until Anigrel's bare chest was exposed. The Talisman of the Light that he wore glinted against his pale skin on its fine golden chain.

And then, before Anigrel could move or protest, she tore open his ribs and plucked out his heart.

Blood sprayed over Lycaelon as Anigrel's body dropped to the ground. The Arch-Mage scrabbled backward through the cold wet leaves with a despairing cry.

The Demon bit into the still-pulsing heart as if it were a choice piece of fruit. Chewed. Swallowed.

"Perhaps too quick," she commented. "But he has annoyed me for a very long time with his protestations of soft human love. Do not hope that you may join him, Mage-man. I have something special planned for you. Something rich and rare. I shall enjoy it very much. Perhaps you can bring yourself to enjoy it, too."

❧

"I do not wish to leave you here," Redhelwar said uneasily, as Idalia and Cilarnen dismounted at the City gates.

"You are needed with the army," Idalia said. "You must go. Besides, we have Jermayan and Ancaladar."

"Be sure that I will defend both Idalia and Cilarnen with my life," Jermayan said, stepping out through the open gates.

"And I," said Ancaladar, craning his long neck down so that his head was on a level with them. "I think they might not wish to upset me, you know."

Behind Jermayan, the Delfier Plaza stood as empty as if Cilarnen had obliterated all of the inhabitants of Armethalieh along with its magick.

"Come on," Cilarnen said. "We have to get to the Council House. The first thing that has to be done is to re-cast the Wards. Properly, this time. The way they should be."

"And I will close the gates," Ancaladar said, as they stepped inside.

❧

SHE had been gone from this city almost half her life, and certainly for the best part. As she heard the bronze panels of the Great Gate bang closed behind her with Ancaladar's enthusiastic help, all she could think of was that this city that the High Mages were so proud of was much cruder and shabbier than she remembered it being.

Not smaller, of course. It was larger than all of the Elven Cities—probably put together. But then, no Elf would consider, even for an instant, living in the ugliness and squalor of the poorer quarters of Armethalieh. Nor would they be willing to live so closely packed together. It would not even be possible, without magic. A lot of magic.

"Cilarnen, did you take *all* the magick off of the City?"

He chuckled, shaking his head. "No. I haven't got that much power, even with the help of the Shining Ones. But the Wards seem to be linked to a lot more spells than I thought. It isn't as if I ever really had a chance to study the spell, or I could have done a much more elegant job. The bell-towers, though . . . I think they must have been linked to the Wards, somehow. I hope no one was hurt when the towers collapsed, but it was only the tallest spires that fell, and all of those would have been in the Mage-quarter, or near it—the Temple of the Light, the Mage College, the Great Library, the Garden Park. The Council House itself will be safe. It does not have a tower. The other carillons—in the Merchants' Quarter and the Garden Market—are all fairly sturdy. They will be dis-timed, and will no longer ring, but I do not think they will have fallen. The carillons in the Nobles Quarter will all have shattered, but they are not heavy ones, and the Nobles will complain, but they are always complaining, and here we are."

Before them stood the bronze doors of the Council House. They were flanked on each side by a row of Stone Golems. Cilarnen reached out, cautiously, and tapped the nearest one. It did not move.

"Perhaps they, too, have been disenchanted," Jermayan said musingly.

"I think so," Cilarnen said cautiously. "I've been Banished, Idalia's a Wild-mage, and you, well, you're an Elf. They shouldn't let any of the three of us within a hundred yards of these doors without trying to tear us into pieces."

"That's comforting, I don't think," Idalia said.

"Well it is," Cilarnen insisted. "If they aren't attacking, it means my spell took down not only the City Wards, but every piece of defensive magick Armethalieh has, at least in the Mage Quarter, where most of the spells would be. Not so good when you consider that there's a whole Enemy army outside right now trying to get in, but since we're trying to get in, too—without being killed—it's a good thing for us."

"Lead on, then," Idalia said.

Cilarnen mounted the steps and pushed at one of the great bronze doors. Since the doors normally opened and closed by magick, it took the three of them to move it, but at last they got it open.

~

"NO—no—no!" A gray-robed Council Page stood in the center of the hallway, eyes wide with terror at the sight of the three strangely-garbed intruders. "Get back!"

The boy was a few years younger than Cilarnen was, and obviously half-mad with fear. Cilarnen had never served as a Council House Page because of his rank, but he knew the duties that the Pages performed. This young man would have been supposed to wait in the hall and watch over the doors, but—especially today—he would never have expected them to open.

And Cilarnen well knew what a horrifying sight he and his two companions presented in their furs and armor.

"I am Lord Cilarnen of House Volpiril, and I must see the High Council at once," Cilarnen said. "You must conduct us to them immediately."

"I— I— I— Wait here." The Page turned and fled, his soft boots scuffling across the black and white marble floor.

"Do we wait?" Idalia asked.

"No," Cilarnen said. "I think I know the way."

⁂

BUT they had not gone more than a few steps toward the Council Chamber be-fore their path was blocked by six Magewardens.

"I am here to see the High Council," Cilarnen repeated.

There was a sudden flare as the Magewardens' Spells raged and died against the violet glow of Cilarnen's Mage-Shield. One moment Cilarnen had been standing, apparently defenseless. The next, the air between him and the Mage-wardens was filled with the shimmering light of his spell.

"Do you think I am an idiot?" Cilarnen demanded angrily. "The Arch-Mage has been kidnapped by Demons—Demons whom *you* serve, because Lord Ani-grel is your master! You all saw *Them* today, if you aren't blind. Now get out of my way, before I do to you what my friends are going to do to *Them*."

"Cilarnen?" one of the Magewardens said, stepping forward. "Cilarnen Volpiril?"

"Geont?"

Geont Pentres had been one of his fellow conspirators—in a conspiracy, Cilarnen knew now, that had been created entirely by Anigrel to gain himself a Council seat and remove those members of the High Council—like Lord Volpiril—who could interfere in his plans to hand Armethalieh over to the Demons.

"You were Banished. Stripped of your Gift. What are you doing here? How do you know me?" The young Magewarden stared at Cilarnen, frowning in con-fusion.

"Once we were close friends, Geont. Anigrel lied to us both. I was Banished—but *not* stripped of my Magegift. Your memories were changed, if you do not know me. I am sorry to see you have become Anigrel's hound. Once you would have given anything to save Armethalieh from the same enemy you now serve."

"I still will. Do you swear by the Light that you come here in peace?"

"I swear it, Geont. And these who are with me come in peace as well. They're my friends."

Geont Pentres stared past Cilarnen, now looking not only confused, but appalled.

"An Elf. And . . . a woman."

Cilarnen smiled. "She's Lord Lycaelon's daughter, Geont, so I'd take that look off my face if I were you. Don't bother saying that you don't remember her, either. You don't remember me, after all. Yes, they are my friends and comrades. And there is a Demon Army outside the City. And we need to see whatever is left of the High Council. Right now."

"Dyvel, go and tell the High Council that Lord Cilarnen Volpiril . . . Lady Idalia of House Tavadon, and . . ."

"Jermayan of Sentarshadeen," Idalia supplied helpfully.

"—Jermayan of Sentarshadeen, Elf, wish to see the High Council," Geont said.

"You can't do that!" Dyvel gasped in shock.

"Is Lord Anigrel here to stop me? Is the Arch-Mage?" Geont demanded. "No. They were both carried off this morning by monsters. And even if House Volpiril is a forcing-house of treason, I for one would like to know what Lord Cilarnen is doing here with his Magegift intact, and strong enough to hold off the six of us. He was only an Entered Apprentice when he was Banished."

Dyvel bowed and retreated.

"And the rest of you," Geont said. "I am certain you have somewhere else to be. Go there. Lord Cilarnen has given me his word that he comes in peace."

The other four Magewardens didn't look very much as if they liked being dismissed, but they went.

"Now, Lord Cilarnen, if you would dismiss your Mage-Shield, it would ease my mind very much," Geont said. "I swear by the Light I will attempt no spells against you. I do not think I could prevail, in any event."

The purple glow of Mage-Shield shimmered and died.

"And now?" Idalia asked.

Geont ignored her. Cilarnen sighed. "Do, please, Geont, answer the Lady Idalia's question, in the name of the Light and the peace between us."

"We must await Dyvel's return. The High Council is in sealed conference. There is much to do. If you wish a fair hearing, you must wait to be summoned."

"There certainly is much to do, since the City Wards have been brought down," Idalia said tartly.

Geont opened his mouth to deliver a stinging rebuke.

"Geont," Cilarnen said quickly. "Our other friends—what happened to them? Jorade Isas? Kermis Lalkmair? Margon Ogregance? Tiedor Rolfort? Do you know?"

Geont looked at him. "They are not my friends. I do not know them. One hears gossip, of course. Rolfort is a Commons name. Of him I know nothing. But there was some scandal with the Lalkmair heir some moonturns ago. His father stripped him of his Gift, and he killed himself soon after. Young Ogregance is apprenticed to his father; he was supposed to test for advancement in the fall, but did not. I see Jorade Isas at the Golden Bells now and then, but I swear to you, we do not know each other."

Cilarnen bowed his head. "Thank you, Geont. You have told me what I wished to know. If not what I wished to hear."

Dyvel returned a moment later, almost running. "They will see them!"

"Come with me," Geont said.

※

THE three of them stood in the center of the black and white marble floor of the Council Chamber, staring up at the black marble bench at the High Council.

Only five seats were filled now: Lorins, Ganaret, Nagid, Dagan, and Harith.

The High Mages had suffered a series of nasty shocks today, starting with the kidnapping of their Arch-Mage, and continuing with the "attack" on their city by a large black dragon and Cilarnen's unicorn-cast spell. Yet they merely looked cross and bored.

"Well?" Ganaret demanded.

"We have come to tell you how to save yourselves," Cilarnen said. "And to save Lord Lycaelon, too. And to tell you of a plot that has been brewing here in the City for many moonturns, though it is not the one you believe."

"Will you speak of this under Truthspell, boy?" Nagid demanded.

"You will address me properly, by my rank and House," Cilarnen said evenly. "I was Banished unjustly, for crimes I did not commit, and so I claim all that was taken from me."

"You committed treason, as I recall," Harith said.

"At Anigrel's instigation," Cilarnen said. "Yet—I believe—the charge for which I was Banished was Wildmagery, and I am no Wildmage. Now and always, my devotion is to the High Magick, and my loyalty is to the Golden City."

※

IDALIA ground her teeth in frustration, listening to Cilarnen's calm demand for an empty title. Yet she knew it was necessary. If he could not get the High Council to treat him—all of them—with respect, they would not listen. And if they would not listen to them . . .

None of this would work.

She needed their help.

The time was drawing near to pay her final Price.

All the time they had been riding toward Armethalieh, she had felt it, without understanding quite what it was she was feeling. And then—when the Demons had taken Lycaelon—everything had become completely clear in her mind, just as it always did for a Wildmage at the moment when Mageprice came due.

Paying this one was just going to be a little more complicated than most. And require a lot more outside help.

‌

✎

‌

"IT is true," Ganaret said. "Lord Cilarnen is no Wildmage. Nor, apparently, is he without the Magegift that should have been Burned from his mind at his Banishing. How can this be?"

"Cast your Truthspell and ask me," Cilarnen said, smiling calmly.

‌

✎

‌

A Journeyman Mage was summoned to the Council Chamber, and the spell was cast.

Cilarnen spoke then, carefully, persuasively. Of the days of famine in Armethalieh. Of the cabal he had formed. Of "Master Raellan"—Anigrel in disguise—who had brought them all together and set their feet on the path to treason, carefully shaping their plans and causing them to do things they would not otherwise have done.

Anigrel, who had been supposed to Burn the Magegift from his mind on the eve of his Banishment, and who had not.

He spoke at length of Anigrel, whom the Allies knew to be a pawn of the Demons. How Anigrel had lied to the High Council, telling them that the Elves and the Wildmages were attempting to destroy them, when it had been Anigrel and the Demons all along. Of how the Demons had raided the villages in the Delfier Valley, slaughtering both the farmers and the Militia and Mages sent to save them. He had seen *Their* attack on Nerendale himself: As a witness, under Truthspell, his testimony constituted proof under the Law of the City.

He spoke of how the Elves and their ancient Allies had been fighting against *Them* to save them all.

"And now—tonight—the Demon Queen will sacrifice the Arch-Mage to bring *He Who Is* back into the world, if we cannot stop him," Cilarnen said, finishing his explanation at last. "To do this, you must help them—the Elves, the Wildmages—just as your ancestors did a thousand years ago. You must do this in the name of the Eternal Light."

"This cannot be true," Harith said in a shaking voice.

"My son does not lie."

"*Father!*"

Setarion Volpiril stood in the doorway of the Council Chamber, wearing the gray robes and rank tabard of a High Mage of the Golden City.

"Lord Volpiril, you should not be here," Lord Ganaret said quietly. "You have given your oath."

"'I shall work no treason—against the High Council, against the City . . . or against the Arch-Mage,'" Volpiril agreed, quoting the oath he had been forced to swear, his deep voice resonant and steady. "Yet tell me, Lord Ganaret, how is it treason to come here and tell you what you all know: that my son speaks the truth?"

He stepped further into the chamber.

"We have all seen our friends and colleagues . . . vanish. In the past moon-turns we have been told that they conspire with Wildmages, or Commons, or Selken Traders, or we have been told nothing at all. This day we have seen with our own eyes the creatures from the Black Days seize Lord Lycaelon. Lord Cilarnen tells you that they mean to use him to end our world. Do you wish to do their work for them? Today I have seen unicorns, and dragons, and creatures my masters in the Art Magickal have told me were only illusion, as real as my own flesh. If we do not believe this truth, we will not live to see another sunrise. And by the spells that bind me still, if this were treason I would be dead before you now."

"We must vote," Lorins said, a whimper in his voice.

"*Vote?*" Idalia demanded. "What in the name of Leaf and Star can you possibly have to vote on?"

"Nevertheless," Lord Ganaret said, "everything must be done in the proper form. If you wish our help, madame, all must be done by the will of the Council as a whole. Now, I pray you, withdraw and leave us to our deliberations."

Ganaret waved a hand dismissively, indicating that the three of them should step back to the center of the room.

RELUCTANTLY, Idalia and Jermayan did as they were bid. Rather than join them, Cilarnen crossed the room to where his father stood.

"My Lord Father," he said, bowing his head.

"You dress the part of a mountebank," Volpiril said, smiling faintly.

"It is cold outside the City walls," Cilarnen said.

"I have misjudged you," Volpiril said.

"No, Father, I think you judged me well enough. Let me remove the spells that bind you. We will need all your gifts."

"You will need me, you think, to bring the Council to heel," Lord Volpiril said.

"If you can," Cilarnen answered steadily.

He knew, from the brief viewings he had done of the Council and the City—and what Idalia had told him of her own scrying while it had still been possible for Wildmages to see into City lands and the City itself—that things had been very strange and difficult here since he had left. His father had always been an ambitious man, placing his ambition before everything, even his own son. But among the High Mages, ambition and the good of the City were one, at least among the best of them.

In this moment of greatest danger, after seeing the City suffer around him for so long, having seen their ancient Enemy in the flesh at last, Volpiril would do what needed to be done so that Armethalieh might live.

"Lycaelon's whelp is a Wildmage," Volpiril pointed out, nodding toward Idalia.

Cilarnen smiled. "Both of them are, Father. And Kellen is my closest friend."

Volpiril raised his eyebrows. "Ah. Well. House Volpiril has always had a talent for advantageous alliances. If you can unbind the spells of the Arch-Mage of Armethalieh, I suppose I must learn to trust your judgment."

Cilarnen withdrew his wand from inside his robe. The spells binding his father were not so much complex as powerful. They fed into the very structure of the City itself. But his power was greater, fed by the Land.

Cilarnen traced a glyph in the air, and whispered a quiet word.

Green fire raced over Volpiril's body, and the High Mage gasped.

"I am free," he said.

⁂

"I am afraid the Council can come to no determination regarding your petition," Lord Harith said. "We must, therefore, request that you leave us to deliberate further before we may call the vote. Be certain that we will—"

Before Harith could finish speaking, Volpiril strode up the steps and seated himself in Lycaelon's seat.

"I take, once again, my seat on the Council," he announced. "As my son is no traitor, I see no reason to forgo my place. Harith, stop making those unpleasant faces. As you know perfectly well, the Lady Idalia is Lord Lycaelon's daughter, and irregular as it is for a woman to speak in Council, this is a day of many irregularities. Next, I believe that having heard Cilarnen Volpiril's Truthspelled testimony, no further deliberation is necessary: What he has said beneath the compulsion of the High Magick and the Eternal Light is certainly truth beyond all disputation. Is there any among you that wishes to argue this point?"

None of the members of the High Council said a single word. A look of satisfaction settled over Lord Volpiril's features.

"Excellent. I am pleased to see that none of you would wish to shame your tutors by forgetting your first lessons in the Art Magickal. Having settled to all of our satisfactions that Cilarnen Volpiril has spoken truth, it is equally undeniable that it is a truth that requires immediate action—not further debate. Is there anyone here who feels that the fact that the world will end at Midnight Bells is *not* an urgent matter?"

Again, there was silence.

"I shall take your continued silence for agreement, my Lord Mages. Therefore, I call the vote now, and not at what future time it would best please you to delay it to, my Lords Ganaret and Harith. The matter upon which we will vote, first, is whether to render all aid to Cilarnen Volpiril and Idalia Tavadon as they ask for it, against our ancient enemy. I remind you all that to vote against this is to doom the world to the rule of *He Who Is*. I now call the vote."

The vote, needless to say, was unanimously in favor.

"Now," Volpiril said, looking down at his son. "I presume the . . . three . . . of you came here with some plan?"

⁌

KELLEN heard the bronze gates of the City close with a resounding crash, and banished Idalia, Jermayan, and Cilarnen from his mind. He could not afford to think about them.

He rode among the elements of the army, speaking to the commanders, giving encouragement where it was needed, explaining his plan. They were to hold the plain before the City, keeping the Demons from reaching Armethalieh. They must give the High Mages time to re-cast the City Wards that would keep the Demons out of the City, and discover a way to rescue Lycaelon, if they could. The rest—perhaps even Lycaelon's rescue—was up to the others.

He'd thought there might be some uncertainty, even some resentment, at the abrupt change of command. Even though the Elven Army had never actually been in battle before this season, most of the Elven Knights on the field today had served with Redhelwar for centuries, and they and the Centaurs had been under his leadership in all of the battles they'd fought together.

But Kellen sensed no resentment among them. Only approval and acceptance. He had earned it, he realized. Everything he had done, fighting beside them, leading ever-larger commands into battle, had gone to building their trust in him. Kellen Knight-Mage.

Nithariel reported movement in the distance, and Kellen sent the unicorns on an extended sortie for detailed information. Their speed—and the fact that most of the Enemy couldn't approach them closely—would protect them.

He had his army positioned as well as possible now, considering the fact that their backs were to the Golden City and they could not retreat into it—or into the sea.

He held Belepheriel's troop back as a reserve. They would be needed in order to relieve the cavalry wings, give them time to disengage and—if they were incredibly lucky—get to their remounts.

The Centaurs would simply have to stand. But Kellen did not mean them to stand for long. Hold against the first charge, then collapse and fall back, drawing the Enemy in with them to where the two cavalry wings could swing in on *Them* and hack them to pieces.

If the battle went the way he hoped.

And no battle ever did. He already knew that.

In the distance, he heard the silvery sound of the Unicorn Knights' war horn. *Enemy sighted.*

"Sound the horns," Kellen said to Dionan. *One thing, at least, can go just the way it has gone for the last thousand years.*

All around him, from every part of the army, the war horns sounded the call to battle.

In moments they saw the first outliers of the Demon Army: Deathwings and Coldwarg. But the Elves knew how to fight the Deathwings now. They launched flaming arrows into the sky, and for each one that found its target, a Deathwing burned.

Behind them ran an undulating wave of Coldwarg, and among them, ten times their size, enormous black creatures similar to the one Kellen had killed in the mountain pass. Shadewalkers.

They could be killed.

He felt as if he stood above the battlefield now. He could see the enemy moving through the trees. Goblins and Frost Giants. Ice Trolls. Dwerro mounted on the backs of serpentmarae. And behind them all, their leader. Kellen could not see him clearly, even with the battle-sight, only a shining blackness where he was.

But he was the one Kellen needed to kill.

Somehow.

He called out orders, making final dispositions of his troops now that he could see the enemy they faced. The first of the Frost Giants broke through the trees. They hesitated, confused; they had expected to face a line of Elven Cavalry and saw only Centaurs.

The Centaurs roared a battle cry and charged forward.

The battle was joined.

≌

"A proclamation?" Lorins said.

"It must be done," Cilarnen said. "You must tell the people of the City—at once—where the power of your spells comes from, and what part they play in aiding you. Their aid must be freely given."

"This is *heresy*," Ganaret said.

"Do it," Volpiril said. "It seems nonsense to me, and I am certain it will cause riots. But there is rioting already, Ganaret, or have your servants not informed you? It will be done within the hour. Now come. This chamber is needed for other matters."

The six members of the High Council—and the three envoys from the Allied Army—walked from the Council Chamber. Standing outside in the hallway were a hastily-summoned Circle of High Mages. Not one Magewarden stood among them.

"My lords of the Council. For what purpose have we been summoned here at such an unreasonable hour?" the eldest of them demanded.

"The Wards have been breeched," Ganaret said. "You must rebuild them. At once."

"But— But— But— It is not the proper Hour for such a Working! Our preparations . . . it will take Bells . . ."

"Then begin at once," Ganaret snapped. "Or do you wish this City to be undefended?"

"I can help them," Cilarnen said. "I think it can be done more quickly. But there is much to do. If I am to work here, you must do as Idalia and Jermayan ask you to do. For the good of the City."

"I will not work in a Circle with this . . . barbarian!" the elderly High Mage said.

"You will stand in the Great Circle with my son, Lord Kerwin, or none of us will stand anywhere at all," Volpiril said. "Have both your wits and your knowledge of the Art both deserted you, that you do not recognize what he is? See that he has what he requires. Come, Lord Ganaret. You have a proclamation to write."

Suddenly there was a sound of horns, audible even within the halls of the Council House itself. A moment later, the roar of a dragon—Ancaladar—shook the walls themselves.

Lord Kerwin flinched. "What— What— What was that?"

Volpiril smiled. "Our Allies. And if you do not wish to meet them, I suggest you work well and quickly."

He turned away.

IDALIA and Jermayan followed the others to another room. Like the Council Chamber, it was crafted all in black and white marble, but this room had a large round ebonywood table in its center. Thirteen chairs ringed it. One, of course, was more elaborate than the rest, and Volpiril seated himself in this one. Apparently he had decided to declare himself Arch-Mage in Lycaelon's absence.

Idalia disliked him completely—he was a High Mage, after all, and had done much to ruin Cilarnen's life—but she certainly admired—if that was the right word—his ruthless single-mindedness. A lesser man—such as any of the rest of the High Mages—would still be sitting in the Council Chamber, arguing about whether or not Cilarnen was telling the truth under a spell that not only compelled him to tell the truth, but enabled all of them to tell whether he was telling the truth or not.

A Page entered at Volpiril's summons.

"Bring tea and food. Send for Lord Lycaelon's secretary. A proclamation must be drafted, and we will require the Arch-Mage's seal. If there are any who have urgent business with the Council, send them here."

"I . . ." the Page was about to protest, and obviously thought better of it. A lifetime in the Golden City taught nothing, if not obedience to those who wore the gray robes of Magehood.

"Yes, Lord Volpiril. At once, Lord Volpiril."

"SO you now think you have all you would once have reached for, eh, Volpiril?" Lorins said.

"I have the distinction of not having served under a Darkmage these past moonturns, if that's what you mean, Lord Lorins," Volpiril said silkily. "Unlike all the rest I see here at this table."

"We have work to do, and not much time—in case none of you have noticed," Idalia said tightly.

Volpiril inclined his head condescendingly.

"I beg your pardon, my lady Wildmage," he answered smoothly.

"*Wildmage?*" Harith said in horror. He began to rise from the table.

"Sit down!" Volpiril thundered. "If we must ally ourselves with Wildmages to save ourselves from Demons, then that is what we shall do. Lord Anigrel has told us time and again that the Wildmages are evil—I believe that is reason enough to think kindly of them. It need not leave this room."

"But . . . but . . . the Wild Magic is Tainted. It leads to Congress with the Dark," Lord Dagan sputtered.

Volpiril regarded him balefully. "Perhaps in time. None of us will argue that it is *not* a sorcery of anarchy and disorder. But if it *does* lead to Congress with the Dark, it will not do so today. And it is today that is my concern. Were Lady Idalia a cesspit of foulness, Lord Cilarnen would not ally himself with her. Nor would our ancient Enemy be working so hard to destroy the Wildmages. Now, if we may continue?"

"Thank you—I think," Idalia said sourly. "In fact, if you kept accurate records, you would know that the Wild Magic is the older form of magic. Cilarnen believes that what you call High Magick was created during the Last War specifically to fight against *Them*. We have found that the spells of the Wild Magic, and the High Magick, working together, can kill *Them*. And nothing else can. This may be why it was invented in the first place."

Volpiril, Leaf and Star blight him, actually looked interested. He summoned a Page.

"Send for Dyren Lalkmair," he told the boy. "If we are to speak of ancient magicks, he must be present. And by the Light, Lord Ganaret, if you tell me one more time that this is either irregular or unseemly, I shall take you to the walls and feed you to that Light-blasted dragon that sits there myself."

Idalia glanced sideways. Jermayan looked amused—not that anyone at the table but she would be able to tell.

~⁂~

THE Frost Giants, just as Kellen had hoped, charged. The Centaurs fell back. The wings of the Elven Cavalry swept sideways to give them room—and to deal with their own enemies. Kellen's reorganization of the army bore useful results almost at once: the Frost Giants were not used to dealing with an enemy who used tactics so similar to their own, yet were so much smaller than a mounted Elven Knight. Their comparative slowness was costing them as they faced the Centaurs.

On the wings, the cavalry formed squares, protecting the archers, both mounted and foot, who fired on the Deathwings and Coldwarg. Square was the safest and most effective method of repulsing the attacks of the giant white wolflike creatures; though there were casualties, the Elves were not losing as many as they could be. And the Coldwargs were dying.

The Shadewalkers presented a more difficult problem with their ability to heal their wounds so rapidly, one that cost all who faced them dearly. But arrows and cast lances could weaken them, and they, too, could be killed.

Suddenly the wind rose. There was always a steady wind coming in off the ocean, but now that wind increased tenfold. Kellen felt a ripple of Wild Magic over his skin. The Wildmages were working the weather, and he wondered why.

Suddenly he smelled smoke, and understood.

One of the burning Deathwings must have set the forest on fire.

It would have been winter-dry to begin with—not much snow here—and he suspected that Demon magic had simply killed all the trees where they stood. If there were fire, the Delfier forest was going to go up like a torch, and if they didn't want to be caught in a firestorm, somebody was going to have to do something about it.

The fire spread.

It began to rain.

He saw—sensed—a break in the line, and spurred Firareth forward, shouting orders.

⤜⤐

BY the time Lord Lalkmair had arrived, tea and food had also arrived, and Cilarnen's proclamation had been drafted and sent to be copied and distributed over the Arch-Mage's seal, though Lycaelon's secretary, Journeyman Nircan, had bleated and whimpered and had to be threatened severely before he would comply. The proclamation was simple and blunt, stating simply that the spells of the Mages of Armethalieh were fueled by the energy granted them by the people of Armethalieh, drawn from their bodies by the Tokens of Citizenship which every Citizen of Armethalieh wore.

"And henceforward they may choose to wear them—or not," Idalia said firmly.

She knew this was what Cilarnen would have wanted. What the basis of the High Magick had to be in Armethalieh, from now on. Power—participation in any spell of the High Magick—must be a gift freely given, just as it was for the Wild Magic.

"Preposterous!" Nagid said, pounding his fist on the table.

"If they don't choose to wear them, they can leave," she said.

"Leave?" Ganaret said. "Where in the name of the Light will they go?"

"Anywhere they wish," Idalia said. "There is more to the world than just one city."

"Write it down as she wishes," Volpiril said, interrupting what promised to be another long drawn-out argument. The High Mages might despise women, but they seemed to be more than willing to argue with her. "There is reservoir enough at the Temple of the Light for a sennight at least. We must survive today before we worry about the future. Light knows, half of them won't see it and the other half won't believe it." He smiled wolfishly at Idalia. "And any who do will blame Lord Lycaelon for this decree, not me."

She smiled back. "And all of you will have a lot of explaining to do, when we win."

❦

DYREN Lalkmair was the very image of a befuddled scholar-Mage, but even Idalia had heard of him, for he had been famous—or infamous—among the Mageborn in the City since long before she had been born. There was nothing he did not know about the history of the High Magick. Which meant, of course, that his studies had veered very close to the edges of the Proscribed Arts even at the best of times.

Frankly, considering the way things had been going in the City lately, she was surprised he was still alive.

He entered the room and stopped, staring at Jermayan.

"One of the Elvenborn," he said in disbelief. "Here?"

He looked at Idalia. "And Lord Lycaelon's Wildmage daughter?"

He regarded Lord Ganaret sternly. "And Lord Volpiril, sitting in conclave among you once more? You have much to explain, Lord Ganaret. For years you have forbidden me the slightest freedom in my studies, saying that such license would lead to unsoundness, chaos, and anarchy. And yet, I find that you have taken far more liberties than I would ever have considered."

"Perhaps you have noticed that the City is on the verge of being overwhelmed by Demons, and that there is a dragon sitting on the walls?" Lord Volpiril asked.

"No, no, I have no time for such things," Lord Lalkmair said. He stopped, seeming to suddenly take notice of what Volpiril had said. "Demons? A dragon? No, not possible. The Great Dragons were all killed in the Darkmage Wars. And the Demons were destroyed at that time as well."

"*They're* sitting right outside the walls," Idalia said. "Do you want to go look?"

"Certainly not, Lady Idalia," Lord Lalkmair told her acerbically. "It would undoubtedly all be Wildmage illusion."

"It is not Wildmage illusion," Jermayan said firmly. "Nor were *They* all destroyed. *They* have returned. *They* have kidnapped the Arch-Mage Lycaelon Tavadon to use as a sacrifice to summon *He Who Is* back into the world, and we must stop him."

"Well, that's very interesting. There must be an ancient Land-Shrine around here somewhere. I always thought there might be. But the Council would never approve my petition to go outside the walls to look for it." Lord Lalkmair didn't sound in the least worried by the possibility of the imminent destruction of the entire world.

At least Idalia now knew why Dyren Lalkmair was still alive. Anigrel hadn't bothered to kill him because the man never took his nose out of a book long enough to notice what was going on around him.

"Sit down, Lord Lalkmair," Volpiril said. "We must know all you know of Wildmagery, and how our Art began."

Lord Lalkmair seated himself, with some hesitation, at the ebony table. "If you wish to know such things, Lord Volpiril, why not ask the Elf? Or the Wildmage? By the Light, either of them know more than I—and do not risk Banishment for speaking of them!"

There was a faint chuckle from a few of the High Mages seated around the table.

"We don't really have time for this," Idalia said. "Though we do need Lord Lalkmair's help. As Jermayan has said, *They* intend to sacrifice Lord Lycaelon at the Delfier Land-Shrine tonight at midnight. We must stop *Them*—by taking *Their* sacrifice from *Them* before *They* can use it."

Volpiril frowned. "You cannot mean us to *fight* our way to the Shrine?"

Idalia shook her head. "If the entire Allied Army can't do it, Lord Volpiril, you certainly can't. I'm talking about magick. Pure High Magick. With some Wild Magic mixed in."

Lalkmair looked interested at last. "Certainly we have enough of Lord Lycaelon's personal items to create a Bond of Sympathy. The difficulty would be in raising enough Power to penetrate the Darkmage spells that will already have been cast. But adding the Forbidden Magic as well . . . that might very well disrupt the Etheric Currents to such an extent to allow a spell of lesser force to slip through the interstices in the Darkmage Working. It will still require an enormous amount of Power, but I believe it can be done. An adaptation, in a way, of an Apportation Spell—oh, I know, Lord Volpiril, that such an adaptation requires months of review by the appropriate committee, but . . ."

"Just this once, Lord Lalkmair, we will bypass the review," Lord Volpiril said, with a long-suffering sigh. "Please determine precisely what items you will need for this spell, and what Mages you will require for the Circle, and assemble them here."

"I'll help him," Idalia said firmly. She was very much afraid that if Lord Lalkmair went wandering off, he'd become caught up in some obscure byway of research and forget to come back at all.

"Oh, please," said Lord Lorins ironically. "Do feel free to treat this City as your own."

"We shall," Jermayan said, getting to his feet and placing a hand on his sword. "Since we are saving it for you."

"And while we're gone," Idalia said, "it might be a nice idea to see if you can round up any of your precious Mages who might actually be willing to poke their noses outside the walls and *fight* for it, instead of leaving Kellen and your so-called 'Lesser Races' to do all the work."

⤝

CILARNEN had never thought—even before his Banishment—that he would ever be standing here, in the Grand Circle of the Council House, preparing to cast the most important and most sacred spell of the City.

Seventeen others stood with him, all men far older and—he would once have thought—wiser than he. All of them were of the highest rank of Mage-hood, High Mages all.

The last rank Cilarnen had formally attained was that of Entered Apprentice.

Yet he would be leading the ritual. He had claimed that right, and no one had argued.

It should have been Lord Kerwin's position—of all the Mages gathered here, Lord Kerwin of House Festalen was the most senior Mage. Yet when Cilarnen had claimed the position of Keystone, Lord Kerwin had not said a word.

If Lord Kerwin had not been thoroughly cowed by Cilarnen's father, he was doing a good imitation.

Of course, the fact that the Council House was only a few yards from the Delfier Gate, and that—in the absence of the wards—the sounds of the battle outside the walls were clearly audible inside the Council House might well have had something to do with it. Cilarnen had been in a few skirmishes, though not in a battle on this scale. And he'd seen more death and destruction than he really wanted to, through the Glyph of Far-Seeing. But for people like Lord Kerwin, the sounds he was hearing now were entirely new, and it was obvious that the venerable High Mage didn't care for what he was hearing at all.

Proper Mage-robes had been brought for Cilarnen to dress himself in—they lacked the tabard that showed his house colors, rank, and magickal honors, but they would do—and the Master Spellbook had been brought from the Council Archives, so he could read over a spell he had never expected to see, let alone cast.

It was long and complicated.

But he was a quick study. He'd had to learn to be.

And it wasn't as if he was going to be the only one casting this spell for the first time. Of the seventeen of them gathered here in the Council Chamber, only Lord Kerwin had ever participated in the Casting of the Wards before, and that only as a Journeyman, assisting the Mages. Until Anigrel had come to the Council, the High Council itself had re-cast the Wards each moonturn. Now, they dared not trust the work to any of those whom Anigrel had chosen to take their places.

There would be thirteen of them doing the actual Casting. The other five—High Mages all—would prompt them through the ritual, doing the work of Journeymen to keep the braziers stoked, and, if disaster struck and someone could not go on, hope to take his place in the Casting before the ritual unwound itself.

"You wear no City Talisman, Lord Cilarnen," Lord Kerwin said.

"No. I do not need one."

It was why he was taking the key position in the ritual, bearing the Great Sword of the City. With the Elemental Energy at his command—he hoped—the Casting would go faster. The wards would be stronger than before.

They needed to be.

"How is that possible?" Lord Kerwin asked. He did not seem angry, only puzzled.

And more than a little terrified by the sounds coming from outside.

Cilarnen only wished he could be there as well as here. He was needed in the battle. His spells could make a difference. But there were many battles to fight. This was another. Perhaps, when the City Wards were up again, he could go out and join them.

"Once, long ago, the High Mages drew their power, not from the people, but from an alliance with those whom you now call Illusory Creatures: the Great Elementals. I have made this pact again—one that I look forward to ending. But not yet. Come. We have much to do."

⊗

IT had been hard enough to persuade them to work in daylight. Harder still to convince them that the spell could be done outside of the proper ritual Hour. But Cilarnen's studies had convinced him that it could. It was easier to do it at the proper time, of course. And of course the most subtle and delicate spells were impossible to do outside of the proper ritual Hours. But the spell for the City Wards had been cast and overlaid so many times over the centuries that it must be burned into the stones of the City by now. It would be harder to do during the day, in the middle of a battle, at the wrong Hour, but it *could* be done.

All it would require was more Power.

He could provide that.

If it doesn't kill me.

When he had been Student-Apprentice, in his first years at the College, Cilarnen and the other boys had terrorized themselves deliciously with tales of spells that required a life to feed the casting. Such things were unknown in the High Magick, of course, though occasionally, as he had found out later, accidents did occur in ritual, when a spell went awry.

It was a different thing than the Wild Magic, when a Wildmage might be asked to offer up his or her life as the Price of the spell.

But the two forms of magic had, so Cilarnen now believed, once been one.

And if that Old Magic now asked for his life in exchange for the restoration of the true and proper wards to Armethalieh's walls, well, he was willing to give it. It didn't matter if the people were ungrateful, or had no idea what he was doing. You didn't do the right thing because people thanked you for it. You did it because it was right.

He stepped to his place in the Great Circle. Kerwin handed him the Sword of the City.

The other twelve High Mages took their places on the working keys.

"We will need Mage-Shield cast around the Council Chamber before we begin, because the Wards are down," he said. "Lords Henius, Vacion, if you would?"

A violet shimmer wrapped itself around the walls and ceiling, dimming the light.

Chadure and Segnant placed the first measures of incense upon the braziers, working their way sunwise around the room, until all eight braziers were wreathed in smoke. They stepped back to the walls.

Cilarnen raised his sword and drew the first Sign upon the air.

The twelve Mages surrounding him mirrored his actions with their wands.

It was begun.

❧

KELLEN thinks I cannot handle a sword.

The thought came to him briefly, randomly, as he paused for a moment, panting for breath.

The room was so filled with smoke he could barely see.

The Sword of the City . . . glowed.

His robe was plastered to his body with sweat. The room was like a furnace. There was nothing to be done about it. The High Magick was an art of self-control and privation. Mages were trained to endure hardships that would destroy lesser men.

He moved quickly to the next figure.

Astrelus had collapsed. Chadure had taken his place.

They had been working for—he estimated—a Bell. The full ritual took three Bells as the High Mages worked it. Time for the Power to rise and settle. But with the Elemental Energy at his command, Cilarnen did not need to wait, nor would he. The army outside their gates did not have Bells—or hours, as the Elves reckoned time. The Wards must be restored as quickly as possible.

And somehow, the Wards themselves were *helping*.

The High Magick was an inert machine, a *thing*. He had always been taught that. It had no life beyond what a High Mage gave to it—certainly no consciousness, no *will*. Yet when Cilarnen had begun the ritual, drawn the first Glyph, he had sensed . . . something . . . rousing itself to meet his own intent. Something of the Light.

No High Mage would have accepted that touch. But Cilarnen had learned much in his travels outside the City. He had bonded with Elementals, wild and tame. And so he had reached out eagerly to that slumbering life he sensed, trying to draw it toward consciousness, feeding it not only the scripted power of the spell, but the raw Elemental force that he carried within his own body.

Slowly, it began to wake.

The Wards of the City were complex, formed of layers of intention. To protect, to guard, to make of the walls and the very air above Armethalieh a defense against anything that was not, ultimately, of the Light. To do this they must be filled with an ultimate understanding of the Light, its nature and its purpose, laid down from the very beginning of the City. An ability to see into the very souls of any creature who might presume to pass through the Gates, to breech the City's walls by any means.

To know . . .

To see . . .

To understand . . .

The air was thick, as if he moved so fast it could not part before him. The sword flashed each time he moved it, so brightly that he could not see the shapes of the glyphs he drew in the air. When he had begun, it had been heavy. Now it seemed to move of itself, drawing him with it.

His heart pounded in his chest.

His hair was plastered to his scalp. Sweat rolled down his face, into his eyes, blinding him. But he no longer needed to see.

Five glyphs left. The most important ones.

The Seals of the Four Quarters. And the Binding Seal.

First, to the north. He stumbled as the sword seemed to haul him in that direction, but righted himself in time. He could not fail now. No one else could take his part.

Down. The tip of the sword rang from the floor. Up. Around. The complicated tracery of the North Gate, glowing in every shade of blue that there was.

Finished. Sealed.

He swept the blade sideways.

East. The blade rang against marble.

The Seal glowed in every shade of gold, from deep amber to palest yellow. Sealed.

South. Down. Up. Heartsblood scarlet, violet, palest pink, ruby. The sword shook in his hands. He clutched the hilt tighter.

All my will, all my strength, everything I am, I give to this Working . . .

Done. Finished. Sealed.

West. A green so dark it was nearly black, the pale green of new leaves, the dusty green of the ocean, the bright green of new grass. All the shades of green that the Demons would take from the world if *They* won.

Finished. Sealed.

He swept the sword back through the North Gate, linking them all.

The four Seals burned in the air.

Now the Great Seal to link them all and set the spell. Without it, all that had come before was useless. He stepped back to his first position.

He was cold.

He raised the sword in salute. Suddenly it was a dragging weight in his hands, where moments before it had been light. He could barely lift it.

He gritted his teeth, and flung it up into the first line of the Great Seal.

Blinding white light followed the tip of the sword, cascaded back down the length of the blade, over his hands. It should have been hot, but it was cold, cold, it seemed to be draining all his strength.

He would finish this. He must.

The Great Seal was the most complicated of all. He worked quickly, desperately, forcing the sword through the complicated arcs. Smaller and smaller, and each loop and whorl must be exact, just as Master Tocsel had taught him.

He was hot. He was cold. He could not tell which. The smooth marble floor beneath his feet had become a thousand knives, and his sweat had turned to blood. He could taste it. Each beat of his heart was slower.

One . . . more . . .

He raised the Sword of the City in the final salute.

All five Seals vanished.

The spell was cast.

He . . . *felt* . . . the Wards reform. He felt the City awaken, the spell that rendered it, in some sense, a living thing remade at last. Felt it reach out, eagerly, for the power he had promised it, the power it needed to do its work.

And then Cilarnen Volpiril knew nothing more.

❧

THE fighting had been going on for hours. The sun was setting. The Allies were holding their own, though their losses had been heavy. It was a consolation that the Enemy's losses seemed to match theirs.

No more Deathwings prowled the sky, and they hadn't seen either a Cold-warg or a Shadewalker in hours. The Frost Giants had tried a flanking attack, but had been stopped by Belepheriel's Knights. The Elven Commander had fought them all the way to the water's edge; many of Belepherial's command would have their names entered in the Great Book at the House of Sword and Shield for their work this day. But Belepheriel still lived, and the Frost Giants had been stopped.

And the High Mages of Armethalieh had joined the fight.

Not many. Kellen didn't think the City had many to spare. But the Lesser Gate had opened, and ten young men in gray robes with ill-fitting breastplates over them had come riding out toward the army.

They'd looked terrified.

Dionan had brought them to Kellen.

"I— You— You're Kellen Tavadon," their leader said.

"Yes. You?"

"Geont Pentres. Of House Pentres. I—"

"Do you know any spells?"

Pentres looked affronted. "Of course I do! I am a Journeyman Mage!"

"Will you work with Wildmages?"

From the look on his face, Kellen might have been asking him if he'd work with Demons, but he nodded, swallowing hard. "Yes. We all will. That's why we came."

"Good. Dionan. Find the Wildmages and take these to them. Tell them we have High Mages now and have them tell them what to do."

❧

VOLPIRIL had said there were riots going on in the City, but Idalia saw no sign of them as she and Jermayan followed Lord Lalkmair back to his house. The

Mage Quarter looked very much as she remembered it from her girlhood; a series of nearly-identical imposing (pretentious) mansions set widely apart. Except for a few servants here and there, the streets were deserted.

It might have been any ordinary day in Armethalieh.

"They seem to be exceptionally calm," Jermayan commented.

"Exceptionally stupid," Idalia said waspishly. "Until one of *Them* is actually here in person, I doubt most of them will either know—or care—what is going on outside the walls." She sighed bitterly.

"Yet Lord Volpiril seems to be . . . helpful," Jermayan said cautiously.

"That's a little odd, I'll admit. I think partly he's out for revenge on the rest of the Council—and Lycaelon—for what they did to him. Not that I'm complaining, since it works to our advantage right now. But the moment we don't have a common enemy, we'd better watch our backs."

"May that day come swiftly," Jermayan said.

"Yes," Idalia agreed, realizing what she'd said. "I hope, for all our sakes, that it does."

It was about half an hour's walk—two chimes, by City reckoning—to Lord Lalkmair's mansion, and Idalia supposed they were being watched from every house they passed. But the City Watch didn't come into the Mage Quarter unless it was specifically summoned, nor did the Militia, and today both bodies had plenty to occupy them elsewhere.

The Magewardens might have been a problem: From what Idalia knew of them, they went everywhere and did pretty much as they pleased. But they were unlikely to ignore a summons from the Arch-Mage himself, and Volpiril had taken the precaution of ordering all the Magewardens brought to the Council House, by a decree sent out over Lycaelon's personal seal. She didn't know how many of them there were, but six High Mages ought to be able to keep them in line, and she knew from her own youthful experience that there were prison cells beneath the Council House. They might all be there already.

If so, good.

They stopped on the paving in front of Lord Lalkmair's mansion. Like most of the High Mage's houses, the front doors were flanked by a pair of stone statues; in this case, a pair of large marble eagles, each holding a torch in one uplifted claw.

"Perhaps I should go first," Lord Lalkmair said, nodding toward the eagles. "They are bespelled, you know, to attack strangers. I am not sure they would harm the Elf—Jermayan, did you say? Such a *foreign* name—but they would not like a Wildmage at all. No, indeed. However did you come to find the Forbidden Books, Lady Idalia? You must tell me."

Idalia sighed. "There will be time for study later, Lord Lalkmair—*after* we have the spell and have cast it. And I do not believe your guardians will be bothering anyone today."

She strode up the walkway and tapped one of the eagles on the chest.

It didn't stir.

"How odd," Lord Lalkmair said, following her and peering over her shoulder. "Yes, indeed, you are quite right. The spell has been completely distempered. Most peculiar. I should have noticed myself. Thank you, dear child. Pray, come inside."

The three of them entered the house.

Eighteen

The Light at the Heart of the Mountain

A BUTLER STOOD at the door, ready to receive guests, of course: No matter how eccentric Lord Lalkmair might be, he was still a High Mage of Armethalieh. The man was dressed in the House Lalkmair livery; Lord Lalkmair's colors were rust and ochre. His eyes widened when he saw Jermayan and Idalia.

"Well, Parland, don't just stand there like an Imaginary Creature! My cloak, and those of our guests. Tell Cook to have tea and cakes sent to the library. And be quick; I do not like to leave the door open. And I do not wish to discover any of you skulking in doorways, either."

Parland bowed. "Yes, Lord Lalkmair. Ah, my lord is aware that one of his guests is . . . an Elf?"

Lord Lalkmair turned to regard Jermayan. Jermayan had removed his helmet—he had not worn it in the Council Chamber, but he had replaced it for the walk to the house, in case there was any need to defend them—and his Elven features were plainly visible. Lord Lalkmair sighed.

"Indeed, Parland, your acuity has not diminished with the passing of years. My guest is indeed an Elf. His name is, is . . ." Lord Lalkmair seemed to have forgotten it again.

"Jermayan," Jermayan supplied.

"And were his presence not known and welcomed by the High Council, he would not be here. Now, have I satisfied your curiosity thoroughly?"

Parland bowed, saying nothing.

"Indeed," Lord Lalkmair grumbled. "My servants are a great trial to me.

Kermis could keep them in line, but . . . but . . ." His face clouded and he fell
silent.

Kermis Lalkmair. That was one of the names Cilarnen had mentioned.
Dyren Lalkmair's son. When Anigrel had framed him for treason, the man before
her had stripped his son of his Magegift, and Kermis Lalkmair had killed himself.

In the Council Chamber, Idalia had thought of him as a kindly, befuddled, bum-
bling old eccentric, but suddenly Dyren Lalkmair didn't seem so much like that after
all. He was a man who could destroy his own son's life for the sake of his own pride.

Like Lycaelon. Like Volpiril.

"Come," Lord Lalkmair said. "Let us go to my library, Lady Idalia. We shall
search for what you need."

⁓

AS a child, Idalia had spent many illicit hours in her father's library—as, she had
later learned, her brother had also done.

Lord Lalkmair's library was nothing like it.

Just to begin with, it was much larger. And messier.

Bookshelves filled every wall. Books were crammed in on top of books, and
when that space was filled, they were stacked upon the floor. The center of the
enormous room was filled with the longest table she had ever seen, and it, too,
was stacked with books, scrolls, and various small objects. The entire ceiling was
lit with Magelight, which was fortunate, as shelves obscured the room's large
windows, blocking off all natural light.

The room was entered, of course, through a Mage-door, which opened at a
touch from Lord Lalkmair. Since the servants were to follow, he left it open,
but when he closed it again, there would be no way out until he opened it
again.

Of course, Idalia thought with mordant humor, all the sealed doors in a
High Mages' house were said to open upon the Mage's death, so they did still
have one way out.

Lord Lalkmair scooped books onto books and moved armfuls of scrolls out of
the way, clearing himself a place to work. He opened one of the boxes on the table
and drew out a sheaf of blank parchment and a thin silver rod: writing implements.

"Now, Lady Idalia. Let us speak of this spell."

⁓

"WHERE is my son?"

In the makeshift Council Chamber, the High Mages had been in the midst of dealing with a report from the City Watch when they felt the Wards rebuild themselves.

Every Mageborn in the City, down to the lowliest Student Apprentice, must have felt it. The very stones rang with a power Volpiril had never felt before in his life, as if the Pure Light itself had burst forth from the Sanctuary of the Temple. Not since the days of Camorin Andralan, First Arch-Mage, had a power so pure and strong been unleashed in the Great Circle.

Such power could not be summoned forth without . . . sacrifice.

Interrupting the report of Guard-Captain Madus in midsentence—fires were burning in Bending Square and all across the Low Market, and due to the disruptions caused by the fall of the bell-towers, many of the wells were dry, and there were not enough Journeymen available to combat every fire in the City by magick—Volpiril leaped to his feet and ran for the Council Chamber, his gray robes belling out behind him.

The spell had run its course. The golden doors, sealed by magick for the duration of the Working, opened at a touch. Clouds of incense rolled out into the hall. The Mages who had performed the Working stood—or sat, or lay—upon the marble floor, dazed. Volpiril had eyes for none of them.

In the center of the pattern, the Great Sword of the City still clutched in his outflung hand, lay Cilarnen.

His son. The jewel, the crowning pride of House Volpiril.

No Mage lived forever. What any man built, he built for the future, for his sons. All that Lord Volpiril had done, he had done for two things: for Armethalieh, and so that Cilarnen might rise to greater heights than he himself would ever reach.

He had seen all that snatched away when Lycaelon—Light curse and blast his name!—had told him that Cilarnen was a traitor. Had gloated over him, as though Lycaelon's two mongrel whelps had not both been Banished as Wildmages.

Volpiril had cared about nothing after that.

When Cilarnen had returned, he had not cared that the boy had obviously been driven to the verge of madness by his unjust Banishment. Madness itself stalked the land, in the form of Demons. Destroy them, and there would be time to repair every harm the world had done to Volpiril's only heir. His Gift was intact, and he was still loyal to the City. Nothing else mattered, save surviving the day. To that end, Volpiril would conspire with Elves and even Wildmages, to save Armethalieh and his son.

But now . . .

He was so still.

He knelt beside Cilarnen. Stiffly. Old bones. Mageborn did not marry early, and Cilarnen was his youngest child.

The only one who truly mattered.

Then the boy's lips parted in a sigh, and Volpiril knew that he still lived. He straightened.

"Send for the Healers!"

⟨⟩

A few hours before sunset, the City opened her gates to their wounded.

During a lull in the fighting the City Militia rode out.

The battle ebbed and flowed like the tide of a great ocean. Not every unit was engaged at once. The line stretched for miles; the thousands of Elves, Centaurs, and Men of the Allied Army slowly being winnowed by the onslaught of the Enemy. At least the forces in the field against them could be killed, and Kellen's troops killed them. But each death came at a high price.

The Allies gained ground, forcing the line forward, into the forest. Yet they dared not advance as far as the Demons might allow them to. Their purpose was to protect Armethalieh, not to follow the retreating Demon army. And so Kellen held his forces back, kept them on the killing ground hour after hour, as monsters for which he had no name threw themselves against his lines.

The Militia who rode out through the Lesser Gate were only a few hundred men. Toy soldiers in toy armor, on horses that looked like scrubs next to the Elven-bred beasts. But their captain, Amrun, had brought fresh news from the City.

The Wards were back in place, and the High Council was working closely with Cilarnen, Jermayan, and Idalia. Amrun knew nothing more, save that Lord Volpiril had ordered them to aid the army—and he had brought a message from Idalia.

Somehow, she had convinced the High Council to open the City to the Allied Army's wounded.

When had Lord Volpiril been returned to the Council?

Kellen didn't care. All that mattered was that he could shelter the injured in a place where the Enemy couldn't reach them. What the City would make of the influx of Centaurs, Elves, and Mountainborn he neither knew nor—at the moment—cared.

But Vestakia could not join them. The Wards would permit it, but the people within . . .

He sent word to the Healers, sent what was left of Belepherial's command to escort them and the wagons into the City.

Sent Amrun and his men to fight beside the Mountainborn. Safer than putting them where they would be distracted by fighting beside people no one born in the City had ever expected to see in the flesh. But they would see enough on the battlefield to distract them, perhaps fatally.

Kellen knew he was sending them to die, and tried to shut the thought from his mind.

There was a break in the line.

He rode toward it.

⁓

IF Armethalieh had not sent High Mages, they would all be dead now.

Scattered pockets of Magelight and Coldfire—two names for what must be an identical spell—illuminated portions of the army, and turned the roiling black pall that hung above the battlefield to a deep indigo. Fortunately, the Elves' night vision was good.

Not that anybody could see much of anything in the smoke.

And Kellen needed no sight to see at all.

Firareth had exhausted the last of even his great resources at sundown; Kellen was riding Valdien now. The Elven destrier seemed to know Kellen's need was great; Jermayan's mount had accepted him unquestioningly.

There was a flash of light as a column of fire arced down from the heavens, followed by the red-gold flare of Fire. Kellen smiled grimly.

The Allied Army was—impossibly—holding its own upon the field, and—because of that—the Demons *Themselves* had come at last to the battlefield, only to find that *They* had waited too long.

The Allies were ready for *Them*.

High Magick and Wild Magic—together—could slay Demons. And every single one of the Mages Armethalieh had sent was acceptable to the unicorns.

There were, in fact, more unicorns on the field now than when the battle had started. Kellen didn't know where the rest of them had come from, but he was glad they were here. They protected the High Mages far better than anything else could; the Demons dared not approach them.

Some of the High Mages were even mounted by now, taking the places of fallen Unicorn Knights.

Another flash—more lightning. A spell the Wildmages could not cast, but—apparently—a simple spell of the High Magick. He saw, with eyes that saw everything, the Demon pinned to earth by the column of white fire. Saw the swarm of dwerro move up to protect their fallen lord, trying to buy *It* time to Heal *Itself*. Saw the Elven cavalry slam forward, clashing with the misshapen creatures on their hideous mounts, trying to force them back so that the Wildmages behind them could make the final kill. Both sides slipped and slid in the slurry of mud and blood beneath their animals' hooves.

In the sky above, the Starry Hunt's forces mirrored the actions of the troops on the ground below. A thousand times, since the Demons *Themselves* had taken to the field, the Allied forces would have been annihilated in a heartbeat, save for the ghostly star-crowned cavalry that rode above them, hunting down the Demons' spells as if they were living foes.

Kellen's sword was slicked with blood, his surcoat and armor was sodden with it, but Kellen's own true battle was yet to come. At the rear of the Dark Army stood the Demon General, waiting. It was *He* whom Kellen had to destroy.

But it was not yet time.

They were fighting in the forest itself now.

Each lightning strike—each Fire spell—rekindled the trees around them, though they were hardly more than columns of charcoal now. But even charcoal could burn.

And so, despite all other calls upon their energy, the Wildmages continued to duel with the Demons over the weather, forcing it to rain, and rain hard. Steam and smoke boiled up out of the trees and the ground, veiling the whole landscape in a choking fog. If Kellen had not been able to see with his battle-sight, to give orders constantly and clearly, the Allied Army would have been lost in confusion long ago.

The City Wards might be in place, but the walls of Armethalieh were only stone, and stone could be destroyed . . . if it could be reached.

They didn't need the City if *They* could perform *Their* Great Sacrifice.

But *They* would certainly want to destroy anyone who could possibly stop *Them*.

The hours passed.

The battle continued.

❧

ZYPERIS had expected a quick and definitive victory to lay at his Queen and mother's perfumed and gilded feet.

But it did not happen.

Every attack he made was countered. The beautiful children his glorious Mama had bred and nurtured were slaughtered, brushed aside, as if they were not terrifying. The Deathwings fell from the sky in flames.

True, the ground ran red with blood. Coldwarg tore unicorns limb from limb. Frost Giants battered Elven Knights to death with their iron clubs. Shade-walkers ripped Centaurs apart as if they were gutting rabbits.

But it was not enough. Never enough.

They could not reach the City.

Time passed. The hateful glowing orb by which the Lightborn reckoned time moved across the sky. The mortals died by the thousands, but the creatures Prince Zyperis commanded died, too. And he was no closer to entering the City than he had been when he had begun. Somehow, no matter what he did, no matter what orders he gave, the troops of the hated Lightborn were there before him, spending their foolish lives recklessly to keep him from his rightful prize.

Then—suddenly—he felt a sudden upwelling of the High Magick and knew that he had miscalculated. Disastrously.

The City was Sealed against him once more.

Properly sealed, in a way it had not been since Queen Savilla's Mage-man had begun his tampering. No breath of Dark Magic could cross its walls now to touch the minds inside.

And as the human city was sealed, so he, too, had sealed his fate.

But . . . there was yet one thing he might do to redeem himself in the eyes of his mother, his love, his glorious Crown of Pain. He understood, now, why the Lightborn enemy had reacted as if it were the fingers of one fist. Why, even though individually they were so weak and powerless, they were such a formidable enemy.

A Knight-Mage was their commander.

Zyperis had not yet been born in the time of the Last War, but his mother had spoken to him of Knight-Mages, and he knew that this one had resisted her at the Black Cairn. Better that she had killed Kellen Tavadon then, instead of trying to make him her pawn.

If Zyperis killed him now, his mother would forgive him everything. With Kellen dead, he would destroy the army, obliterate the city, leave nothing behind but a wasteland in celebration of Queen Savilla's glorious victory.

And so he had waited for a lull in the fighting, and gone to summon his own personal guard to join him upon the battlefield. The preliminary sacrifices at the Place of Power were nearly done; his Mama would not miss them. It was only a few dozen of the Endarkened—and Lesser Endarkened at that—out of the hundreds gathered there. The Lightborn would be defenseless against their strength and magic.

But they weren't.

They, too, died.

He called the rest of them back. He must save them, now, for the moment when he took the battlefield himself.

And destroyed Kellen Tavadon.

Personally.

EVERY chamber within the Council House that could be used for the casting of spells was occupied by Mages.

Now, at last, Armethalieh had entered the fight.

Rain lashed and battered the City itself, a storm such as had not been seen within the City walls since the first stones were laid.

The Apprentices watched the battle from the walls, and brought back word of the battle's progress, though they barely understood what they saw. When they had reported that the forest was burning, Idalia had demanded that the Mages re-move the weather-shields from the valley, and bring rain to quench the fires. The Council had had to go to the walls themselves and gaze out at the carnage below before they would agree, but after they had seen it, they made no more trouble.

As far as the eye could see—for mile upon mile—there was nothing but fire and burnt and dismembered bodies. The forest was in flames, all the way to the horizon.

The Mage College had become a hospital for the army's wounded. The stu-dents had all been sent to their homes, the Mages who normally occupied its grounds had been called away to Workings. Binding spells wreathed the Mages own defenses, so they would not attack the Allies, and the tents and wagons of the Healers now filled every open space.

There were few wounded.

⚬

NO bells rang in Armethalieh tonight. The City of a Thousand Bells lay mute beneath the fury of the magic-and-magick-called storm. But the High Mages did not need the City's bells to reckon time.

It was nearly midnight. Their spell would be timed to match that of the De-mon Queen. They had spent precious hours as the day drew on preparing and adapting it from the old records in Lord Lalkmair's archives, and then rehearsing it, because they could afford no mistakes. It would work precisely as the Wild Magic had promised Idalia that it would.

In the Council Chamber, Idalia prepared to begin.

She wore nothing but a light gray Mage-robe, her hair loose and unbraided down her back, and of all the things that had happened in the City today—dragons, Elves, Wildmages, spells, an entire Demon army right outside their walls—it was this that had stunned the Mages of Armethalieh nearly to the point of frothing catatonia.

A woman dressed as a High Mage.

A woman in a Mage Circle.

At least she knew now where Cilarnen got his stubbornness from. Lord Volpiril had done everything up to and including threatening the High Mages with death and immediate Banishment to get them to work with her, and it was as much an acknowledgment of their desperate situation as it was a tribute to the force of his personality that he had succeeded.

Thirty-six Mages stood with her, Setarion Volpiril and Dyren Lalkmair among them. In a moment, she would step into the center of the Circle, and they would begin.

She had not told Jermayan the truth.

He believed—everyone here believed—that the spell they were about to cast would bring Lycaelon Tavadon here from the Spellstones, whisking him out from beneath the Demon Queen's hand to join her at the moment her spell was cast.

It wouldn't. No human magic—not even a Triple Circle—was that powerful. But the spell surrounding the Demon Queen's altar would permit a substitution, so long as what was substituted was closely enough related in blood and magic.

A daughter for a father.

A Wildmage for a High Mage.

Tonight she would die.

But this was the Mageprice asked of her—and that she had consented to—long ago. To give her life. And because she was a willing sacrifice—not one ripped unconsenting from life in blood and fear, but a death hallowed by the Wild Magic—her death could not be used to break the bonds that would allow *He Who Is* to return to the world.

"It is nearly time," Jermayan said to her.

"Yes," Idalia said. She reached into the pocket of her robe, and drew out her Three Books. She took Jermayan's hand, and placed them into it. "I want you to keep these for me. I do not think they would . . . do well within a Mage Circle."

"Perhaps not." Jermayan smiled, but his dark eyes were worried.

"Perhaps there is something you would wish to give me in return?" she asked.

It would not matter now.

He smiled, and reached up to unclasp the chain from about his neck. "I have waited long to give this to you, Idalia. I had thought this day would not come."

He clasped the silver eight-pointed star around her neck. An Elven Betrothal Pendant. It settled in the hollow of her throat, still warm from his skin. She reached up and touched it with the tips of her fingers.

She could not say goodbye. If she did, he would know what she meant to do. It was possible he might even try to stop her, offer himself up in her stead, and there was no time to explain why that could not be. He would know soon enough. She had kept the truth from him—selfishly—because every moment in these days that could be spent without pain was a gift from the Gods, and she would give up none of them. Instead she smiled, saying nothing at all.

"Come, Lady Idalia," Lord Volpiril said.

She turned away and stepped into the Circle.

~

JERMAYAN watched from the edge of the room as Idalia stepped away and took her place at the center of the gray-robed High Mages. The room began to fill with smoke, making him wish to cough, but he schooled himself against it sternly. Only a few moments. Midnight would come, and Lycaelon Tavadon would join her in the Circle.

And they could leave.

He did not like the human city.

It was too crowded, too filled with ugliness and hate. There was nothing here of appropriateness and harmony; no respect for the natural world that was the gift of Leaf and Star. No wonder they had fallen so easily to Anigrel's plots; these humans were already half in love with Darkness. It made him sad. Far better to face that Darkness openly upon a battlefield than to pretend it did not exist, dulling your own senses until you saw nothing at all, not beauty or ugliness, truth or lies.

Perhaps they could take Cilarnen with them when they went.

He knew the boy rested now in the care of the High Mage Healers. The spell that had raised the Wards of the City had cost him dearly, though his father swore that he would live and heal. Cilarnen had spoken of the High Mages as great Healers, and even Idalia did not have many ill things to say of them, save that they were reckless and arrogant. In Jermayan's opinion, those were bad enough things to say of any Healer, save that she said one thing more.

That they took away inconvenient memories.

The Elves lived long, longer than any of the other Children of the Light. More than any, they were the sum of their memories. To destroy—to remove—a person's memories, yet leave them alive, not knowing what they had lost, was a transgression so black that Jermayan could barely imagine it. Yet it was an act the Mageborn of Armethalieh performed as a matter of course. Both Kellen and Cilarnen had lost memories—their past—beyond recovery, changing the people they might have been.

Jermayan only prayed that the High Mages would not meddle so again with Cilarnen while he lay helpless in their hands.

Idalia stood quietly in the center of the High Mages as they moved about her, casting their spell. Jermayan felt nothing. He did not expect to. Perhaps he was still an Elven Mage, though he lacked all ability to work any magic, but it did not matter: Elven Magery would be as blind to the High Magick as any High Mage was to the workings of the Wild Magic. The spell being raised before him, no matter how powerful it was, was something he could neither sense nor feel. All he could sense was the passage of time, moving inexorably toward midnight, and the sound of the storm that battered the City. Even the sound of the battle he knew to be raging outside the City walls was muted, hushed to silence by the restored City Wards.

Suddenly there was a flare of light, startling him.

The Mages reeled back, staggering and falling.

He pushed through them.

Idalia was gone. In her place, crouched upon the floor, lay the naked form of a haggard old man. He was filthy and disheveled, his mad eyes staring about him in terror. He drooled in fear.

Suddenly Jermayan realized what she had done.

She had not called her father to her.

She had substituted herself for him.

He ran from the chamber, shouting for Ancaladar.

≈

IT was nearly midnight.

He was tired.

He could not afford to be tired.

Lightning crackled across the sky in a nearly-constant display now, more of it natural than belonging to any High Mage spell.

He had sensed the High Mages die, one by one.

Less than a third of the Allied Army remained alive.

Above the battlefield, the Starry Hunt rode, lending their strength to the battle. The eldritch Riders struck down as many of the foe as did their mortal comrades in arms, and still it was not enough.

The Endarkened were coming in force.

But now it was time.

The Demon Prince himself was taking the field at last.

"Shalkan!" Kellen shouted. He vaulted from Valdien's back, slipped as he found himself thigh-deep in mud. Staggered.

Saw radiance come galloping toward him across the battlefield.

His first friend. His comrade.

With him now, at the end.

He threw himself into Shalkan's saddle—sometime, during the past hours, someone had helped Shalkan into his gear.

He drew Light At The Heart of the Mountain and Shalkan leaped forward. There was no need for words.

⚬⚬

ZYPERIS saw the Knight-Mage come riding toward him on the white unicorn. He snarled in anger and lust. A unicorn! But the pain would be worth it. He would kill them both, do what his Queen, mother, and lover had been too short-sighted to do.

Then he would destroy the City.

He spread his wings and launched himself forward.

⚬⚬

THE Demon towered above them, nearly eight feet tall in its glittering black armor. *Its* scarlet wings were spread wide, and *Its* sword flared with black light.

It threw back its head and howled.

Water Mind.

The most dangerous gift of a Knight-Mage. To move through the currents of a battle like a fish through water, to be able to fight beyond exhaustion.

To fight at the top of his strength until he died.

Kellen leaped from Shalkan's saddle. The unicorn spun away, moving as if he were Kellen's reflection. The Demon hesitated, seeing two targets where there had been only one a moment before.

Kellen feinted, drawing the Demon's attention. *It* attacked him. Kellen slipped away.

The utter calm of Water Mind enfolded him. He was no longer Kellen. Shalkan was no longer Shalkan. The Demon was no longer a Demon. The three of them were partners in a dance, all moving as the Wild Magic willed.

Kellen was at peace. Utter peace.

All was as it was meant to be.

This was the moment he had been reaching toward from the moment he first drew breath.

Shalkan struck. The Demon howled in fury and in pain.

Kellen did not know why he was here. His sword could not slay the Demon. Any cuts his blade made would instantly heal.

He only knew that this was where he must be. Here. Now.

The Demon Prince turned on Shalkan. Kellen struck. His blade sliced deep.

He could not kill, but he could wound, and the wounds were painful ones, angering the Demon Prince.

Turn and cut.

There were only seconds before *It* chose to ignore one of them and kill the other.

It did not matter.

⋙

IDALIA opened her eyes.

The blade flashed down.

Struck.

Savilla's mouth opened in a scream of horror and despair.

⋙

SUDDENLY the sky was filled with light. Light everywhere, and Kellen was filled with an uprush of Power so great it made him scream, ripping him from Water Mind with the force of a sudden drench of ice water. It was the power he had felt at the Black Cairn, but a hundred, a thousand, times stronger, and this power held nothing of the Dark. Only Light. It filled him, filled the blade in his hands, filled Shalkan, filled everything he could sense save the black Void before him.

He struck, plunging the radiance in his hands into the Darkness before him. He felt the Light fountain through him, filling the Darkness, filling the Void, obliterating it as utterly as sunlight destroys shadow.

Blinding him.

There was a scream. He heard it with more than his ears. He seemed to hear it with every sinew of his body. It stopped his breath; it seemed to stop his heart, just for a moment.

And in the midst of that light, he heard the echoing thunder of celestial hooves, as the Starry Hunt, the work for which it had been summoned complete, swept across the battlefield one last time . . .

And was gone.

When he could see again, when he could breathe . . .

The Demon Prince was gone as well.

Gone.

"Dead," Shalkan said. "Get up. We have a chance now."

Kellen dragged himself to his feet, using Shalkan's saddle as a brace. He'd been on his hands and knees in the mud; by the time he was on his feet, the unicorn was coated liberally—even more liberally—with mud as well.

But he hadn't dropped his sword.

Kellen flung his leg over Shalkan's back.

"Come on," Kellen said. "I need to find a horse."

"You're welcome," Shalkan said.

~

JERMAYAN flung himself onto Ancaladar's back and the great dragon leaped from the walls into the storm.

"The stones!" Jermayan shouted. "We must get to the stones!"

He clung tightly to the saddle. He had not used the straps. There was no time.

Idalia had substituted herself for the sacrifice.

In midair Jermayan felt the tide of magic reach him, as vast and overwhelming as a crashing ocean wave. It filled him, filled Ancaladar, restoring all that had been taken from them, and more.

He had the power to destroy those who had taken his love, his life, from him, and he used it.

~

VESTAKIA had been beneath the walls of the City, among the supply wagons. The proximity of so many Demons was constant agony, but like everyone else among the Allies, she had a job to do.

She and several others—cooks and wagon drivers, laundresses and carpenters—those who could neither fight nor heal—took charge of getting the Allied wounded into the City. If they could make it to the rear of their own lines, Vestakia and the others would bring them the rest of the way. Carrying them if they had to. Guiding them through the rain-lashed night to the safety of Armethalieh's walls if they could still walk.

Often someone went inside with one of the injured.

Vestakia never did. She did not dare. Just as she had not dared to take her rightful place among the Healers within the City walls.

The Armethaliehans would only see her appearance, not who she was.

But this, too, was vital work, for many wounded would have died at the edge of the battlefield without the help of Vestakia and the others to get them to safe haven.

She was certain that this wasn't what Kellen had intended for her to be doing. Kellen had expected her to find someplace safe to hide until the battle was over, Vestakia suspected. She knew he thought she had already done more than enough.

Well, so had everyone here. Jermayan. Idalia. Cilarnen. Kellen himself. Not to mention hundreds of people whose names she didn't even know. She would not ask for special treatment, though right now all she wanted to do was lie right down in the cold mud and sleep until everything was decided, one way or the other.

In her mind Vestakia could feel her father—so close now!—and feel his certainty of victory. The fear he had felt before was gone, replaced by lust. Not even to kill, but to destroy, to obliterate.

To *taint*.

Suddenly there was a rush of air above her head.

She looked up.

Ancaladar leaped from the walls of the City in a rush of wings.

She was staring after him in confusion when the world dissolved in light.

It was as if in that one brief moment Vestakia was a child again, warm and safe and loved. Held in her mother's arms, too young to understand the curse of her Demon appearance, too young to understand the tragic price Virgivet had paid to win Vestakia her human soul. All her pain and weariness was gone, washed away by the light.

And when it faded, the touch of her father's mind was gone as well.

Gone.

Vestakia stood in the cold mud, gasping in surprise and wonder. She touched her own face with trembling fingers, as if to assure herself she was still real.

He was gone.

She was certain of it.

It was as if a poison-filled wound had suddenly been healed. Even the memories of what she had gained from the Demon Prince's thoughts were dim and fading quickly, as if it had suddenly become impossible even to think of him.

Then a sudden gust of cold wind sprayed her face with rain, and a shout from the battlefield recalled her to herself.

There was still work to do.

There would be time later for joy.

~⌘~

SAVILLA stood over the Stone of Sacrifice, the broken blade in her hands. She looked down at the body of the small mortal female.

All her plans, ruined.

All around her the proud Endarkened groveled upon the ground, writhing and whimpering in pain. The bolt of pure *Light* that had been released when she had plunged the knife down had killed half of them where they stood, and weakened the rest nearly to the point of death, draining them of power and magic. They moaned and cried like lost children, their howls of agony rising above the howling of the storm.

Only she stood unscathed.

He Who Is had been sealed away from the world more thoroughly than ever before. Any who dared attempt to call him across the Veil again would be met with the fury of a cheated god.

Even his beloved perfect children.

She shrieked her anger and despair to the sky, her body vibrating with the agony of the backlash of the spell. But she would not yield. How could this have happened? *How?*

"Kill them all!" she howled.

Her Court, not understanding—yet—what had happened, cowered back from her wrath. She reached for the nearest body, dragging the Endarkened to his feet. His yellow eyes were clouded with pain; his wings drooped limply. She dug her talons into his throat, wishing it was Zyperis's. Black blood oozed around her fingers, and the Endarkened whined.

"*Go*," she growled, her yellow eyes burning into his with the force of her rage. "Kill the Lightborn."

A few of them moved—too slowly!—to obey.

"Queen Savilla!"

She looked up.

There was a dragon in the sky.

Something to kill.

She spread her wings.

⤛

JERMAYAN saw the Demon Queen below him, saw Idalia's lifeless body spread upon the flat stone.

A bolt of golden fire leaped from his hand toward the Demon Queen.

Shields flared around her as she countered his attack, and he saw her smile, anticipating victory.

But he did not falter.

Change and change, as the Demon Queen's shield passed up and down the harmonics of magic, attempting to turn itself from a defense to an attack. But each time she changed her shield, Jermayan changed his attack, occupying all her energy with countering him. She had to devote all of her power to her defense; there was nothing left over for her to mount an attack in turn. She spread her wings and vaulted into the sky; to attack, to evade; it did not matter. Ancaladar danced upon the storm like a hawk. Wherever she went, he followed.

And at last—very quickly, in the end—her defenses fell.

The Demon Queen, Leader of the Endarkened, ignited in a flare of light. She was consumed utterly, beyond any possibility of rebirth.

When her acolytes upon the ground saw that, they began to run.

Jermayan and Ancaladar followed.

⁓

HE didn't even know the name of his horse. He'd found it running loose on the battlefield, and he'd needed a horse.

But the tide of battle was turning.

His Command Staff was dead or scattered. Redhelwar was on his left flank, pulling the remains of the Centaurs together, trying to get them into some kind of order. He'd ordered Belepherial to look for the unicorns. Some of the Enemy was running, and he wanted the unicorns to follow.

If any of them were left.

A Coldwarg—alone, wounded, but still dangerous—staggered toward him. Its back was stickered with Elven arrows, and foam drooled from its jaws, but it gathered itself to leap. His mare swung sideways, staggering a little with exhaustion, and Kellen struck, ending the beast's life.

They'd held.

It was after midnight. The world was still here.

The Wards were back in place around Armethalieh.

It was time now to take the Delfier Shrine.

⁓

IT was dawn by the time Kellen and his force reached the Standing Stones.

The storm had passed. The sun had risen. The sky was bright and clear.

He'd left two-thirds of the surviving army under Redhelwar to guard the City and gone on toward the Place of Sacrifice. All they were doing now was hunting down what remained of the Demon Prince's army. They'd seen very few of the Enemy, and only in small groups; easy to kill. They took no prisoners, left no one alive.

Vestakia was still alive, safe among the supply wagons. He'd had a report.

The Elven Knights moved at a slow walk. They had been fighting since noon of the previous day, and both Elves and horses were exhausted.

The long heavy rain had washed away all trace of snow. There'd been a ground fog earlier, but as the sun had risen it had lifted, and now only a thin mist remained. Visibility was limited, but not too bad. The mist leeched color from the world—not that there had been much to begin with. The ground was black with mud and ash. The trees were black with char. The air was white. Only the sky was blue.

But it was a blue sky Kellen had not been certain he would live to see yesterday.

They had met the Demon Army and broken it completely.

Their own force had been nearly destroyed. Less than a quarter of those who had begun the fight still lived. But they had faced an army twice their size—Demons, Coldwarg, Deathwings, creatures out of Kellen's darkest nightmares—and held. Had killed everything that came at them until the few—the very few—survivors had run.

They had kept *He Who Is* from entering the world.

Armethalieh was safe.

He hoped they'd be grateful, and wondered if they would be. Or if they'd still think this was some sort of complicated Wildmage plot. *Probably,* Kellen thought tiredly, since everyone Armethalieh had sent to the battle was dead.

Well, my friends are dead, too.

Riasen. Menecherel. None of the Unicorn Knights had survived the night's battle.

He'd finally gotten a report.

Keirasti. He would miss her calm wisdom, her rough humor.

Isinwen. Reyezeyt. None of his own troop had survived the battle. He had been in command of all, and had made the Enemy pay as high a price for every life he had been forced to spend as he could, but they had still died.

Wirance. Catreg. The Demons had known that the Wildmages posed the greatest threat to them. They had fought savagely to reach them across the battlefield. And for their part, the Wildmages had spent their lives—not recklessly, but with full intention and a kind of joy, knowing that their lives were a gift they gave to their comrades in arms, a gift to the future, a gift to hope.

But they were still dead, and he would miss them.

He would miss them all. No victory could sweeten the bitterness of that loss, only soften its horror.

As they came closer to the Standing Stones, Kellen smelled . . . flowers?

The ground was covered in flowers.

He dismounted.

"Wait here," he said.

He walked forward.

Before the battle, this had been the heart of the Delfier Forest, and like the rest of the forest, it had been reduced to burnt trees and ash.

But here, new life was beginning. He could see the shoots of new growth springing up out of the forest floor, among the flowers. Vines twined around the dead husks of trees, unfolding even as he watched. There were flowers everywhere.

When he got closer, he saw Ancaladar.

The black dragon's scales glittered in the morning light, as radiant as they had been the first time Kellen had seen him.

Ancaladar lifted his head.

Kellen stopped.

Jermayan was kneeling at the center of the Standing Stones. They were wreathed in flowers, overgrown with them.

He held Idalia in his arms.

She was dead.

"No," Kellen whispered.

This wasn't the way it was supposed to happen. Idalia had been going to do a spell in the City. That was what she'd told him. She hadn't been supposed to be here.

At the sound of his voice, Jermayan looked up at him. For a moment their eyes met. Then Jermayan set Idalia down among the flowers, very gently, and got to his feet.

"Jermayan," Kellen said.

But Jermayan turned away, toward Ancaladar, setting his foot into the stir-rup and mounting Ancaladar's saddle.

"Jermayan!"

But the dragon had spread his great wings and leaped into the sky.

The last sound Kellen heard was the howl of grief, two voices mingled together.

⌘

KELLEN'S Knights returned slowly to the City walls, passing across the battle-field once more. Idalia's body, wrapped in Kellen's cloak, lay across his saddle. He led his horse.

All around them, the forest was filling with flowers. They spread at a more-than-natural rate, a living carpet growing outward from the Delfier Shrine, cover-ing the burnt ugliness of the long night's battle with a victory carpet of living green. Everywhere Kellen looked, new life was beginning; tiny white flowers raised their heads through the ash of the forest floor, tendrils of palest green appeared from seeming nowhere to twine themselves around the burnt husks of the trees.

He tried to care. Surely such a powerful sign meant that their victory was a true one, and that the power of the Endarkened had been broken once again.

Perhaps, this time, forever.

But as they walked across the battlefield, picking their way with care among the shattered dead, their feet and the horses' hooves splashing through the pools of water and blood, what Kellen saw was the cost.

No cost would have been too high to save the world—the Light—from the Demons. He had been prepared to spend himself, his friends, everything he held dear to gain that victory. But the one price he had never thought to pay was to stand alive in the aftermath and count his dead.

It was hard. It was very hard.

But it was his Price, Kellen realized. The price of all the Wild Magic he had taken up and used, not counting the cost at the time, knowing that payment would someday come due but knowing he must have the spells at the time.

Well, now payment was due.

He must forgive. Himself most of all.

For being alive.

As they approached the City walls, he saw that Redhelwar had been busy in his absence. The Enemy had never managed to reach the rear guard, so they'd successfully held on to some of their supply wagons, sheltering them beneath the City walls when they'd moved the wounded inside the City. In the mile or so of clear bare untouched ground between the edge of the battlefield and the City walls, Redhelwar had put up the pavilions. Against the austere pale stone of the City walls, the colorful silk canvas of the Elven pavilions looked strange and alien; the two halves of Kellen's heritage, brought together at last.

Redhelwar rode out to meet him. He looked, questioningly, toward the shrouded bundle on Kellen's saddle.

Kellen took a deep breath. "Idalia was at the stones," he said. "I don't . . . I don't understand what happened. Jermayan and Ancaladar were there with her. But they . . . left. I couldn't stop them."

Redhelwar bowed his head. "We have won a great victory, by her sacrifice, and the sacrifice of many others. It would be good to hear what orders you give now, Kellen."

Kellen considered for a moment. He pulled off his gloves, then his gauntlets, and dropped them into the mud. He reached for the pouch on his belt, and fumbled at it until he got it open. The ring was still there. He pulled it out, and held it out to Redhelwar.

"I have no orders, Redhelwar, Army's General. I return to you Andoreniel's ring, and with it, his army. The task set me by the Wild Magic is done."

Redhelwar took the ring, closing his fingers over it.

"Then see to your horse, Kellen, then find a bed, and sleep. By the grace of Leaf and Star, we have won the battle. And perhaps, some day, we shall rejoice in it."

Nineteen

In the Temple of the Light

CILARNEN AWOKE WITH a shudder.

He'd had the most amazing dream. He'd been . . .

He looked around.

He was in his rooms. His *old* rooms. In House Volpiril.

He flung himself out of bed, his mind reeling. It *couldn't* all have been a dream! He remembered . . .

He ran to his windows and looked out. The garden looked just the same as he remembered. It was daylight.

They were all still alive.

Idalia's spell must have worked.

There was an unfamiliar weight around his neck. He reached beneath his nightrobe and touched it. A City-Talisman, on a gold and sapphire chain, the same sort he'd always worn it on. He drew upon its stored power, feeling, beneath it, the link to a greater wellspring of stored power, and touched the City Wards beyond.

They were intact. Everything was as it should be.

He remembered now. Standing in the Circle, the Great Sword of the City in his hands, Elemental Energy surging through him as he fought to complete the spell, feeling a link with a dreaming half-conscious force much greater than himself that had taken and taken and *taken*, using everything he had to rebuild the Wards. Purging him of his link to the wild Elemental energies he had wielded for so long, draining him utterly.

He remembered the harsh caress of the Elemental as they released each other, their bond—and the need for it—ended.

Felt the spell continue to drain him for an instant more, sucking forth the tiny reservoir of personal Power he possessed.

And then . . . ?

And then his father had brought him back . . . here?

How long had he slept? What had they done to him as he slept?

Nothing, Cilarnen realized with a pang of relief. His mind, his memories, were his own; he knew that with a bone-deep certainty. If they weren't, how could he remember Kellen, Idalia, Jermayan, Kardus, every day of his Banishment? If they *had* tampered with his mind, surely he would not think of them—Elves, Wildmages, Centaurs—as his friends?

He must have news.

He went to his closet and dressed quickly, and went downstairs.

HIS father was sitting in the Morning Room, a pile of papers at his elbow.

"Cilarnen," he said. "I confess I had not expected to see you rise from your bed so soon."

"My Lord Father," Cilarnen said, making a formal bow. His City-manners returned to him easily, as if he had never left. He had the odd feeling he *hadn't* left, even though his memory told him otherwise.

"Sit. I shall ring for breakfast. You will, I am certain, wish to know all that has transpired in recent hours."

"I . . . of course." Cilarnen seated himself in his accustomed place. It was hard to imagine doing otherwise.

Lord Volpiril raised a hand and sketched a sign in the air. There was a distant sound of ringing. In a moment, a servant appeared and was given his orders, and disappeared again. Out of long custom, father and son sat silently until the food was brought and served, and the servants had departed once more.

"I suppose they did not feed you so well outside the walls?" Lord Volpiril said, once Cilarnen had begin to eat.

"The food was well enough, my Lord Father," Cilarnen answered. "I did miss the tea. But tell me, my friends—are they well?"

Lord Volpiril sighed. "The Lady Idalia's spell went, perhaps, differently than we had expected. She is gone."

"Gone? Gone *where*?"

Lord Volpiril frowned, reminding Cilarnen that no matter how much things had changed, this was not a tone he might take with his father.

"She vanished from the Circle just as Lord Lycaelon appeared. The Elf who was with her seemed to take it somewhat amiss. Beyond that, I know nothing, for he took his dragon and left the City. Soon after that, there was a great flux of the Light. It refilled the reservoir in the Temple of the Light to overflowing and recharged every Talisman in the City. Though the battle outside the walls continued, it moved into the forest. Now it is over, and the Elves have made themselves a tent city outside our gates."

Lord Volpiril's tone was faintly disapproving.

"I must go and see if they're all right," Cilarnen said.

"You must eat your breakfast," Lord Volpiril answered firmly. "After that, there is much to do."

"Yes," Cilarnen said levelly. "We must welcome our allies into the City and see to their needs."

Father and son gazed at each other for a moment in silence.

"Things must change in Armethalieh, Father," Cilarnen added. "What happened here cannot be allowed to happen again. Ever."

"You cannot understand what you ask," Lord Volpiril said. "Yesterday—last night—we did what we had to in order to save ourselves from immediate annihilation. But now the threat is over. We can return to our own ways, as the Elves can return to theirs."

"No we can't," Cilarnen said stubbornly. "It was just those 'own ways' that got us into all this trouble in the first place. You—me—everyone here—cutting ourselves off from the world. The High Mages *taking* from the people without telling them. All magic has a price that must be freely paid, and all help freely given. It is the first and highest rule, the one the Wildmages live by. We have to live by it, too, we High Mages. And if the people don't want to give up their power for what we have to offer them, we have to let them go—not tell them there's nothing outside of Armethalieh's walls that anyone could want."

"So that Light-blasted woman said," Volpiril growled.

"Well, she was right."

"She had the unmitigated gall to force the High Council to issue a proclamation to that effect."

Cilarnen laughed. "And I suppose you did it because you were sure that nobody would see it?"

Volpiril smiled unwillingly. "And I am quite certain that no one did."

"Well, you shall have to issue it again," Cilarnen said simply.

"That will hardly be possible," Volpiril answered.

Cilarnen gazed at him levelly, and Volpiril went on.

"Only the Arch-Mage could issue such a proclamation. Lord Lycaelon . . . he will never be well enough again to resume his duties. Though I am certain you well know I bear no love for him, believe that I am telling you the truth. He is broken in body and spirit—if not in mind—by his ordeal among the Demons.

Worse, to know that Lord Anigrel, his heir, had been—so Lord Lycaelon has told us—the catspaw of the Demon Queen since earliest childhood, and conspired from the very beginning to give Armethalieh over to her completely . . . it has nearly destroyed him. He has resigned from the Council. At the moment, the High Council acts in a body to handle what business it may. But there are eight vacant seats, and it will be a year, at least, before they can all be filled, as no one will wish to come to another hasty decision about who may be added to its ranks. One of the five who are now on the Council must, inevitably, be the new Arch-Mage. But I like none of them. All of them truckled to Anigrel—as I have told them. And none of them will approve of . . . change."

"You must retake your seat, Father. The oath you swore to Lycaelon no longer binds you."

"It does not, of course. But it forced me to resign. And I while I could constrain them to accept me among them once more while there were Demons at the gates and they were mad with panic, they will not do so now that the threat has passed. Perhaps I shall regain my seat on the Council in time. But I shall never rule Armethalieh as I once hoped to do." Volpiril sounded faintly regretful.

"There has to be a way to save them from themselves," Cilarnen said fervently. "There *must*."

"Perhaps there is," Lord Volpiril answered thoughtfully.

❧

THE aftermath of any battle was neither quick nor clean, even if the victory was decisive.

When Kellen awoke a few hours later, he joined the work-parties who were clearing the battlefield.

At home, the Centaurs took their dead to special fields miles from their home villages and left them on the surface of the earth, there to become one with the earth once more over the course of seasons. The human farmers who lived in the Wildlands buried their dead in the same fields. The Elves hung their dead in the trees. The Mountainborn and the Wildlanders built stone houses for theirs, where their bodies could rest undisturbed.

None of these things could be done here, for the thousands of fallen upon the battlefield. And there were horses, and the enemy dead as well. All must be disposed of—or at least moved far from the City walls before they attracted predators.

All across what had once been the battlefield, there were pyres of burning bodies. They had separated the Enemy dead from their own, burning them first. Some of the Tainted bodies were already turning to a sort of stinking jelly where they lay—those, the Allies had found, ignited swiftly and burned as if they were soaked in oil.

Those that had fallen in the forest, Ally and Enemy alike, were already cov-ered by the carpet of living green. They left those alone.

But that left many more.

The Elves had simply refused to burn their dead. They were carried deep into the forest and laid, naked, upon the carpet of thick green life that had grown up there. Wagon upon wagon, piled high with bodies, made their slow journey into the woodland—by now nearly every tree was wreathed in green, and some were even sprouting new leaves—to return, empty, and be filled again. Even the Healers had returned from within the City to lend their aid.

The Great Gates stood open now.

Kellen stood at the head of one of the oxen, dragging a dead horse from the field. It was heavy work; the churned ground was still muddy, and the beast might be sure-footed, but he tended to slip. Still, the work had to be done.

And it kept him from thinking.

Armethaliehans moved across the battlefield as well, performing the lighter, simpler tasks of retrieving swords, weapons, and gear and bringing it to the camp. It, too, must be sorted, so that nothing Tainted would be saved to cause further potential harm.

Redhelwar had said, when Kellen had seen him earlier, that the Armethaliehans were helping as much as they could. They had sent food to the army, and were allow-ing them to enter the City—though not to go outside the area close to Delfier Square, the Council House, and the Mage College, where their wounded still recu-perated. It was honestly more than Kellen had expected of them. One did not over-throw a thousand years of indoctrination and prejudice in a single night, even if it were a night unlike any that had come to Armethalieh in a thousand years.

Still, the sooner the army could leave here, the better Kellen would like it. It wasn't so much that he didn't *trust* the High Mages . . . well, to be fair, he didn't. He was just wondering when—or if—they were going to realize that all they had to do to create that perfect world they'd dreamed of, without "Lesser Races" in it, was to turn on the remains of the Allied Army as it sat beneath their walls. Be-cause right now, there was very little the Allies could do about the High Mages, if the High Mages chose to attack.

He only hoped they'd remember that those so-called "Lesser Races" had just saved all of their lives.

Kellen patted the ox on the shoulder, urging it to move on.

The air was filled with the scent of green growing things, overlaying the smell of blood and death. Amid the shouts and cries of the workers, Kellen caught a snatch of birdsong.

He wondered just how long it was going to take to wipe away all trace of the battle.

WHEN he got back to his tent—not his own pavilion, but the one he was using now—Cilarnen was waiting for him.

It was a shock to see him. Cilarnen looked every inch a Mageborn. He was dressed head to foot in Armethaliehan garb, wearing what Kellen supposed must be House Volpiril's colors, copper and green. Only his heavy fur-lined cloak and sturdy—though elegant—calf-high boots made any concession to his present surroundings.

But he looked far better than he had when Kellen had seen him last. The drawn, pinched, feverish look was gone from his face, and color had returned to his cheeks.

"You're alive!" Cilarnen said, grinning with relief.

"Redhelwar told me you were, but it's good to see it for myself."

"Idalia isn't."

Kellen hadn't meant to blurt it out like that. She'd been Cilarnen's friend as well. And it was unfair for that single death to hurt so much more than all the rest, but there were moments when it seemed to Kellen that Idalia's death summed up for him every loss he had suffered in this war.

Cilarnen looked away. "I'd hoped . . . Lord Volpiril told me she vanished from the Circle, and Lord Lycaelon took her place."

"We found her body at the Stones."

Cilarnen reached out and put a hand on Kellen's arm. "I am so very sorry for your loss, Kellen. I know—if you could you would have died in her place."

"Any of us would," Kellen said quietly.

"Jermayan?" Cilarnen asked.

"He was with her when we . . . found her. Alive, but I do not know where he and Ancaladar are now."

Cilarnen sighed. He looked around. "So many dead. In the City . . . our losses were light by comparison, but much was destroyed. And as soon as we can, we must send to see what is left of the Delfier villages and the Home Farms. If anything. We shall need those Selken grain-ships that are coming, and more besides. I do not think that anyone will be planting anything this spring."

Kellen shook his head. "The fields may come up by themselves, though. Look at the forest. It is green already."

"Thank the Light for that."

"Leaf and Star."

"The Wild Magic," Cilarnen said.

The two of them smiled at each other, and Kellen felt some of his heartsickness ease.

"What will you do now?" Cilarnen asked.

Kellen hadn't really thought about it. "I suppose, eventually, I'll go home. Back to Sentarshadeen."

"But Kellen, *this* is your home. Armethalieh."

Kellen shook his head, as certain of that as he'd ever been of anything in his life. "Cilarnen, whatever has happened, I'm still a Knight-Mage. There's no place for me in Armethalieh, and there never will be."

"Don't be so certain of that," Cilarnen said, smiling faintly.

"Oh?" Kellen said. "I suppose you're going to change things around here?"

"I might," Cilarnen answered. "They're going to make me Arch-Mage."

≈

IT was an ancient Law of the City, and one that had only been invoked once before in all Armethalieh's thousand-year history. Yet it *was* a Law of the City—and as such, it could be brought before the Council as a petition.

Volpiril had done so, early that very morning.

"My lords, I come before you today not as a member of this so-august and so-worthy body, but as a humble petitioner," Volpiril said.

If the towers had been functioning, it would barely have been halfway through Morning Bells, but the High Council had been sitting since Second Dawn Bells. Between Cilarnen's spell of the day before, and the storm the Mages themselves had allowed to lash the City, Armethalieh was in ruin and chaos. Work-parties must be assigned, Mages must be set to the task of repairs and spellcasting, the Commons must be advised and soothed.

Normally, none of these tasks and decisions ever reached as high as the High Council, for Armethalieh was run by a complicated—and very efficient—bureaucracy of many interlocking Councils. But after the events of the previous night, too many of the Mageborn who formed the links in that chain were absent—or dead on the Allied battlefield. The entire Militia, who should have been able to support the City Watch in keeping the Commons in their place, was dead. Much of the Watch's functions had been taken over moonturns ago by the Commons Wardens, and the Commons Wardens were not to be trusted. They were being held under guard in one of the warehouses until their memories could be thoroughly gone over and edited. The Magewardens filled the cells below the Council House, and were being similarly—though more immediately—dealt with.

Meanwhile, the High Council floundered, bogged down in petty details it had never been meant to deal with.

"Oh, make your petition and have done, Lord Volpiril," Ganaret said irritably. "What is one more petition on a day like today?"

"My lords, it has not escaped my notice—as I am certain it has not escaped your own—that Armethalieh is at present without an Arch-Mage to rule her."

"This is no news," Lord Dagan said. "I suppose you wish to put yourself forward for the position, Lord Volpiril? You have always wished to take Lycaelon's place."

Lord Volpiril bowed. "Acute as always, Lord Dagan, but no. Perhaps it has escaped your notice that I am not a member of the High Council at this present. No, I have another candidate in mind. But first, I would pose a question to you all: If you were to vote at this moment, for whom would you vote as Arch-Mage? The vote, as you know, must be unanimous—among so small a Council as this."

There was silence from the five men above him upon the black stone bench. Lord Volpiril smiled.

"I see what you have already seen yourselves: None of you will support the accession of the others. Yet there must be an Arch-Mage. And in these times, more than ever before, he must be one with a wider knowledge of the world than any of us has. One who is not mired in the past, in the empty traditions that have already nearly doomed us all. One who can make Armethalieh truly a golden city, a city of the Light, once more.

"Consider, my lords. The harbor has been swept free of ships, many of them destroyed. The Delfier Valley has been scoured. We shall have to rely upon the Selkens—foreign trade—to feed us in the coming seasons. We dare not alienate them. We must resettle the Delfier Valley, and the folk to farm it must come from somewhere. We must—somehow—explain to our people not only what has happened this night past, but what has happened in all the moonturns of Lord Anigrel's poisonous influence that preceded it. Who shall do these things? You, Harith? You, Lorins? Ganaret? Nagid? Dagan? Which of you shall embrace this troublesome future with an open mind and willing heart?"

There was silence from the High Mages.

"Oh, do tell us your amazing plan, Lord Volpiril—since you so obviously have one," Harith said pettishly.

Lord Volpiril bowed mockingly. "Lord Cilarnen has the necessary qualities to do all these things. He is a friend to the Elves and the Wildmages. He has saved the City. Elect him Arch-Mage—let him rule with your guidance, and the guidance of those others who will join the High Council in the moonturns to come. That is my petition."

"Impossible!" Ganaret roared. "He is but an Entered Apprentice! A child!"

"He has cast a spell at Master level," Volpiril said. "You know that perfectly well. Waive the tests."

"It can't be done," Nagid said. "He was Banished."

"Unjustly. By a Creature of the Dark," Volpiril said inexorably. "And by his actions, both in the world beyond our gates and here, he has proven himself not a child, but a man."

"It is . . . irregular," Lorins said. "People will say he is Anigrel come again."

"That is a valid consideration," Volpiril said. "And so, to avoid it, I suggest that he be appointed by not this Council alone, but by all Mages of Magister rank within the City. There is precedent, my lords. It was done once before. Thus did Camorin Andralan become Arch-Mage over Armethalieh, by the proclamation of all his peers."

"And if they fail to acclaim him?" Ganaret asked suspiciously.

"Then you may return to your wrangling as the City falls to dust around you," Volpiril said. "If you are so foolish and so blind as to wish that for Armethalieh, then I do not think she deserves to survive."

For long moments the five Council members conferred among themselves, behind a spell-barrier that made their words inaudible to Lord Volpiril. At last Ganaret leaned forward again.

"Very well, Lord Volpiril. Your petition is granted. The High Mages of the City will be summoned together to vote as to whether to accept Cilarnen Volpiril as the new Arch-Mage of Armethalieh—if you, yourself, agree never to seek a seat upon this Council again."

Lord Volpiril smiled sadly, bowing his head in submission. "My lords, you are all as aware of my ambition as you are of your own. But Cilarnen tells me there is a price and a cost for all things of worth, my Lord Mages. If that is to be mine, then I hold it a light one."

❧

THE conclave took place at the Great Temple of the Light at the center of the City. Every place was filled.

Cilarnen stood before the Altar of the Light, flanked by Lord Volpiril and the Chief Priest of the Light.

When his father had come to him a few hours before, after leaving the Council House, and told him that the Mages of Armethalieh were to vote on whether or not to appoint him Arch-Mage, he'd thought his father was joking—except for the fact that Volpiril never joked.

"You wanted to save them from themselves," Volpiril said. "This is the only way."

"But . . . *Arch-Mage?*" Cilarnen said. "I know nothing of being Arch-Mage."

"Nor is your election certain. And if you are elected, I promise you a life of frustration and heartache, dealing with fools and greedy imbeciles—and those are only the ones I know. You will have seven new self-seeking idiots to block your every act, once the Council returns to full strength. You will have to lie, flatter, bribe, and threaten them to get them to do what you want, and if it goes on for long enough, you may not remember what, in fact, you originally wanted of them."

"Oh, I shall remember," Cilarnen said. He thought of what he had seen at Nerendale; the Demons slaughtering the farmers, the Militia, Thekinalo and Juvalira. Those days must never come again. "I will always remember. And perhaps good people can be found for the Council posts. That is always a possibility, my Lord Father."

"First, you must achieve the appointment. Now come. We must be at the Temple of the Light at noon."

"Noon? Today? But . . . we will hardly have time to speak to everyone. How will they . . . ?"

"Armethalieh is still the City of Mages. There is a spell."

AND so here Cilarnen stood before the High Altar, awaiting the spell that would be cast over him, allowing everyone in the room to see, not his mind, but his heart.

If such a spell had been cast over Anigrel, he wondered, would things have worked out differently? Or would Anigrel's Darkmagery have allowed him to twist the spell, and allow him to show them only what he wanted them to see?

His father spoke first, briefly, telling the assembled Mages what most of them already knew: that Lord Lycaelon had resigned, that the Council could come to no agreement upon who should be the next Arch-Mage from among their numbers. He reminded them all that an Arch-Mage could be chosen from any of sufficient rank by the vote of all the Masters in the City, as it had been done in Camorin Andralan's time—a precedent that was still Law, though it had never since been invoked. He told those who did not know it that Cilarnen, having cast the spell to restore the Wards around the City, was indeed of Master rank, having cast, not only a Master Spell, but the most complex Master Spell of all.

A simple spell of *Knowing* placed all of Volpiril's complex arguments in favor of Cilarnen's candidacy into all of their minds at once, and Cilarnen blinked, stunned at the depth and breadth of his father's trust in him. He only prayed he could do half the things Lord Volpiril hoped he could—not only for the good of the City, but for the good of everyone in the Land.

Now the time came when he must, himself, be judged.

Together, Volpiril and the Priest of the Light lifted their wands and began to draw glyphs about him. As each one settled over him, Cilarnen felt a tingling sensation as the spell began to settle, and he began to hear a whispering sound, as if he stood beside the ocean, instead of in the Temple of the Light. The room blurred, becoming brighter.

He wasn't good enough. They'd reject him.

He was vain. He had a terrible temper. He liked to show off. He was . . . arrogant. Much too proud of being a High Mage—he knew it. He'd never understand the Wild Magic, and deep down, he really didn't want to try. Though, actually, it was fascinating, because he knew that it and the High Magick had been one magic once, long ago. Maybe Dyren Lalkmair could teach him more.

He really saw no reason why Lord Lalkmair should not be allowed to conduct his researches as he pleased.

He thought Elven tea tasted terrible. He'd missed the food from home, although he'd tried to be polite. His feelings got hurt much too easily, and when they did, all he thought about was getting back at the person who hurt him. Of course, that passed very quickly, and he was ashamed afterward, but . . .

He liked fashionable clothes. And being comfortable. He liked jewelry, and scent. He'd missed the rings and jeweled chains he now wore. He didn't like living in a tent in the cold. But he loved Anganil, and riding at a gallop through the snow. And Shalkan . . . oh, it had been worth everything, even Banishment, to see Shalkan and the other unicorns!

But to be home, home, *home* again. Armethalieh was where he belonged. He had been homesick every minute he was gone, and when he'd discovered how much danger his beloved City was in, he'd been terrified. When he'd first met Kellen—and been afraid that Kellen wouldn't help—he'd been so afraid and angry that he would have done anything to force Kellen to help them, because Armethalieh was in danger and the thought that she might be destroyed terrified him more than the thought of his own death.

He thought of Stonehearth. Grandur and Sarlin and all his Centaur friends there. They'd been so kind to him when he had not deserved it.

They'd taught him, he realized now, to be human. To see past surfaces. To see *people*, no matter how they were shaped.

It was a lesson Armethalieh desperately needed to learn.

Finding out back in Stonehearth that his Gift wasn't gone—that he could do something to help, to *fight*—was a moment of both terror and joy. Because he could do so little by himself. And because his Gift was supposed to be gone— Anigrel had been supposed to destroy it—and that meant that things were even worse in the City than he thought.

But he was here now, home now, and no matter what happened here today there would be *something* he could do to help Armethalieh.

The spell faded. The chamber darkened, and he could see properly again. Cilarnen swayed a little, blinking in confusion. Lord Volpiril put a hand on his arm, steadying him.

"My lord Mages," Volpiril said. "It is time to vote. Do you accept Cilarnen Volpiril of House Volpiril as Arch-Mage of Armethalieh . . . or no?"

His father had told him in advance how the votes would be signified. Blue Magelight for "yes." Red for "no." Unlike a vote of the High Council alone, only a simple majority would be needed here.

But when the lights began to rise up in the Temple of the Light, every one of them was blue.

⟋

THE ceremony itself—the formal investiture—would not occur for a sennight, as—this time—the High Council was determined to do everything in the traditional fashion. Though Cilarnen was technically a member of the Mage Council, he would not join it until then.

He did not mind. Let them have their small victory. He had won the greater war.

At last, released, he had gone outside the walls to find Kellen and seek news of his friends.

And to tell them his.

⟋

"ARCH-MAGE?" Kellen's jaw dropped gratifyingly. That gawky farmboy look was back.

Cilarnen found it rather endearing, actually. If—after all Kellen had seen and done—he could stand there and gawp at Cilarnen like a rustic fresh from the villages, well, perhaps Cilarnen need not worry *too* much about becoming cold and distant and proud once he was given the ring and staff of the Arch-Mage's office.

"Apparently nobody else wanted the job," Cilarnen said, though that wasn't exactly true. "Do you want to come to my investiture? Kardus will be there."

"Kardus is a *Centaur*," Kellen said, nearly sputtering.

"I know Kardus is a Centaur," Cilarnen said patiently. "But he's my friend. And since I'm going to be making a lot of changes in Armethalieh, I thought I'd give everyone fair warning of what to expect. I've asked him to stay and help me settle in. And he's agreed."

Kellen shook his head. "'Know what to expect.' They'll never expect you."

"I know. But they're stuck with me now. The appointment of an Arch-Mage is for life—or until I resign. And I intend to live a very long life, and make a lot of changes. You'll see."

"I suppose we all will," Kellen said.

⁓

THAT evening Kellen dined in Redhelwar's tent. It was a melancholy occasion, with so many familiar faces absent, but Vestakia was there.

With the death of the Prince of Shadow Mountain—her father—and the routing of the Demon Army, Vestakia, too, had recovered much of her health and former vitality, though she was still too thin. But the wellspring of life that surged outward from the Standing Stones had affected her as much as anyone else.

"The Healers say that the wounded are recovering much faster than normal," she said. "And the Wildmages—" *those who are left*, Kellen mentally supplied, "well, they say their Healing Spells are working far better than even *they* expect. So it is a very good thing for everyone!"

"A very good thing indeed," Redhelwar agreed. "The army should be ready to return to Sentarshadeen within a sennight. The Centaurs, the Wildlanders, and the Mountainborn wish to go directly home, of course, and I see no reason why they should not. Which is why I have another task for you, Kellen."

"As always, I am at your disposal," Kellen said automatically.

"Good," Redhelwar said. "I wish you to take a strong force, five thousand horse, and follow the trail of those creatures who fled the battle. I do not think—now that *Their* power has been broken—that they will be able to enter the Elven Lands, but I will not have them settle in anywhere to cause trouble. Take any who will volunteer to go with you—by now you know the quality of this army as well as I. It would please me greatly did you report upon your progress when you can."

"I will leave at once," Kellen said. He'd be just as glad to be gone from Armethalieh, all things considered.

Redhelwar hesitated. "Do all that you can, but join us in Sentarshadeen in three moonturns. We shall . . . say goodbye to Idalia then. You will wish to be there. Andoreniel will wish it also."

Kellen bowed his head. "I'll be there."

⨫

HE spent the next day assembling his force and getting together his supplies—all from Armethalieh, this time. Early the next morning, they rode out. No trace of fire damage was visible in the forest now.

Though Vestakia would have been useful in tracking the Tainted creatures, Kellen left her behind with Redhelwar's force. Her presence was not absolutely vital to the success of his mission, and she was still recovering from the effects of her long linkage to the Demon Prince's mind. It was better that she travel with the slower-moving army, in relative safety.

After so much death, so many losses, he could no longer bear to risk her life.

Scouts ranged ahead of the column of Elven Knights and light mule-drawn wagons, searching for signs of the Enemy, whether its monsters, or the vassal-races that had fought beneath the Endarkened banner. Kellen doubted they'd find many of either here in the Delfier Valley; it was far too warm, and the creatures of the Endarkened were creatures of darkness and cold. Without the magic of their masters to protect them, this would not be a comfortable place for them. Still, it didn't hurt to be careful.

And vigilance took his mind off other things.

Idalia had not been laid to rest here in the forest. Redhelwar had told him that she was being taken back to Sentarshadeen. The Wildmages had bespelled her body until it could be hung in the Flower Forest itself. It was, Kellen knew, a very great honor.

He'd rather have had his sister back.

They spent three days in the Delfier Valley, crisscrossing it, looking for signs of the Enemy. They found none. But they did find a number of villages that had been hastily destroyed by Demon magic, their inhabitants taken to fuel the Demon Queen's spell, and a few terrified surviving refugees who told grief-stricken tales of Demon raids. They fed them, did what they could for them, promised them that the Demons were gone, and sent them to Armethalieh, promising them that more help would be provided to them there.

Now, at last, it was true.

On the morning of the fourth day, they reached the edge of the bounds.

Here they stopped to convert their wagons to sledges, though even beyond the edge of the Mages' weather-workings, the snow was beginning to melt and soften. Despite that—and though the Wildmages who still traveled with them said that the time of heavy storms were past—True Spring was sennights away.

Kellen held himself fortunate that he *did* have Wildmages. Though the Mountainborn were returning home, several of the surviving Lostlander Wildmages had agreed to accompany Kellen's army—at least as far as their own settlements at the western edge of the Elven Lands.

They journeyed onward.

~❧~

THEIR first destination was Stonehearth.

The Centaur village was the closest settlement outside the Delfier Valley, south and east of Armethalieh. It was where Hyandur had taken Cilarnen, and Sumaraldiel, one of Kellen's trackers, reported that *something* had passed this way ahead of them, a day or so before, though the wind had blurred the tracks in the snow so much that he could not tell what it might be.

Whatever it was, Kellen was sure it must be something bad. The Delfier Valley refugees would have headed for the City, and Wildlanders in this area would not have dared to move at all—at least not in the last few days.

He was right.

They caught up to them just outside Stonehearth; a mixed force of Frost Giants and dwerro traveling together. Less than fifty of them, but certainly enough to destroy Stonehearth, if they managed to reach it. They were quickly and efficiently overwhelmed by a tiny portion of Kellen's force, without injury to the Elven Knights.

But the battle made Kellen think, and think hard.

The remains of the Enemy forces would be straggling across the Wild Lands in small clumps such as these—all across the Wild Lands. If he kept his own force together—large, comparatively slow-moving—he would never be able to search out all their hiding places before they dug in. Or raided and moved on. He wasn't sure where the Enemy stragglers were going—probably they didn't know themselves, but it was a good bet they were trying to either get back to the Demon stronghold—wherever it was—or at least back to the mountains beyond the Elven Lands before summer.

That evening he called all his Commanders together.

"I have a proposal to make to you," he said. "You saw the battle we fought today—not much of one, compared to the Battle of Armethalieh. You know the orders Redhelwar has given us. Given me. I believe that the enemy that we follow will be scattered and disorganized, fleeing—as this one did—in small groups. Easy to kill. I propose, therefore, that we seek him out in the same fashion. In small groups, no more than fifty horse each. In that fashion, we can cover much more territory, find the places they are most likely to seek out. I believe they will attempt to raid the villages and farms of the Wildlands first, and then head around the edge of the Elven Lands into the High Reaches if they can. Just as we do, they will need food and supplies. They may have other needs as well. But whatever they want, we can't let them have it."

"You propose, yet you do not order," Calundil observed quietly.

"Today we won our battle without injury," Kellen said. "If we do what I propose, we will face our Enemy perhaps on equal terms, perhaps at a disadvantage. Thus, I would hear your words—all of you—before I considered giving orders."

"It would be good to know how we will provision such smaller commands," Laurindiel said. "We do not have the capacity to send provision trains with as many forces as you propose to create. I speak without disrespect; even had you decided upon this course before we left, neither we nor the human city could have provided the wagons and the draft animals that would be needed."

"I have considered that," Kellen said. "We have enough wagons to equip perhaps half our force. For the rest—the Wild Lands are well-settled. I believe the villages will provision us. I do not expect you to go so far as to be completely out-of-touch with one another, and . . . the power that began at the Standing Stones in the Delfier Valley is spreading, I think. Meriec, we would welcome your counsel."

Meriec was one of the Lostlander Wildmages who traveled with the army. Even now he wore the traditional Lostlander garb of high sheepskin boots over thick full breeches, heavy knee-length tunic, and long goatskin coat, though, as many had, he had taken the opportunity on the journey south from Sentarshadeen to add a heavy cloak of Coldwarg fur to his outfit. There was one thing good about the hellbeasts, Kellen thought. If you could manage to kill and skin them, they did provide nice warm fur.

Meriec stood and bowed.

"I and my brothers and sisters agree, Kellen Knight-Mage. The power that Idalia Wildmage called forth at the Standing Stones continues to pour forth over the land, healing all that was blighted. We all feel it, as must you. The Springtide will be more than fruitful—and there is more. Those beasts not slain by the Tainted creatures will be returning to their old places, and the creatures of byre and pasture will bring forth young in great numbers, come the day."

"Still," Kellen said, "I suppose that still means 'no hunting.' So many animals have been killed off that we'd better not touch the rest. So we'll have to rely on our supplies, and on what the villages can give us. If you all agree to my plan."

"Indeed, Kellen, it would be foolish of us to doubt this plan. It seems a sound one. And you have led us to one great victory already," Vorendel said chidingly. "So I believe I speak for all here when I say that we will do as you ask."

Kellen looked around the tent. The Elves all nodded.

"Then we take a day here to make our dispositions. Tametormo, bring your Twelves and ride with me on to Stonehearth. From there I shall head south and east into the High Reaches. Any of you may find me along that route."

⤚✦⤙

DID I do the right thing? Kellen wondered.

He rode Firareth a little away from the camp, out beyond the pickets. It was already dark, and he conjured a ball of Coldfire. The ball of azure light turned the snow around him a brilliant blue.

Above him the sky was bright with stars. Meriec was probably right. Winter must be almost over.

It was going to be a glorious spring.

He was actually surprised when Shalkan came trotting up to him. He hadn't seen Shalkan for several days—since the two of them had slain the Prince of Shadow Mountain, in fact—and he certainly hadn't seen him lurking around the edges of Kellen's makeshift army as they'd ridden through the Delfier Valley. But still, here he was. The unicorn looked, as always, composed and imperturbable.

"I didn't expect to see you here," Kellen said.

"We aren't finished with each other yet," Shalkan replied.

"I guess we aren't," Kellen said. "So . . . Cilarnen is going to be Arch-Mage of Armethalieh."

"So I heard," Shalkan said. "Nice of you to tell me."

"I haven't seen much of you lately."

Shalkan snorted rudely. Kellen sighed. The unicorn wasn't going to let him off the hook that easily. But it wasn't his fault. He hadn't really been that accessible. Not to a unicorn, anyway.

"I'm sorry," he said penitently. "I'll try harder to make myself available."

"You'd better," Shalkan said meaningfully. "I still have to keep an eye on you, you know."

"It's not like I can get into that much trouble out here," Kellen pointed out. How was it that Shalkan could manage in only a couple of words to make him feel as if he'd never been anywhere or done anything—and still needed looking out for?

"You're going to Stonehearth tomorrow. And trust me, Sarlin will bear watching."

Sarlin? Oh. "The Lady of Stonehearth. Cilarnen mentioned her. Don't worry. I won't get into trouble." No point in wondering how Shalkan knew something he'd only decided a few minutes ago. Kellen had long since realized that unicorns had their own sources of information.

"See that you don't."

"So . . . do you want all the details?"

"It would be a nice gesture on your part," Shalkan said grumpily.

Quickly Kellen told the unicorn all that he'd discussed with the Elves under his command, about splitting the army up into a number of small mobile units, in order to cover the whole of the Wild Lands more swiftly and efficiently.

"Thought that up all by yourself, did you?" Shalkan said, when he'd finished. Kellen sighed. Shalkan snickered.

"It needs to be done," Kellen said.

"It does," the unicorn agreed. "And afterward. What then?"

After Sentarshadeen. After the funeral.

"I don't suppose I've thought that far ahead," Kellen said.

"You'll have to eventually," Shalkan said.

"I know," Kellen said.

"Go to bed," Shalkan said. "You'll have a busy day tomorrow."

⁓

TWO days later, Kellen and his troop rode up to the gates of Stonehearth.

He was relieved to see that the village appeared to be in good shape. Cilarnen had told them of the devastation the Demons had caused here several moonturns before, and the southern route had been the main line of march for the Demon Army on its path to Armethalieh. But Stonehearth seemed to have escaped.

The gates were already open as he and his Knights approached. Several Centaurs trotted out through the snow toward them, a young blonde Centauress in the lead. She must be Sarlin, the Lady of Stonehearth.

Kellen reined in Firareth and waited for them to approach.

"I greet you in the name of Andoreniel, King of the Elves," he said, when she reached them. "And I bring you good news: *They* have been defeated."

"'They'?" Sarlin only looked puzzled. And worried.

Despite himself, Kellen smiled. No need not to speak *Their* name anymore, lest it draw *Their* attention.

"The Demons. They have been defeated. You are safe now."

Now a look of joy suffused Sarlin's features.

"Herdsman be praised! Then . . . you are Elves?"

Kellen reached up and pulled off his helmet. "My Knights are Elves. My name is Kellen Tavadon. I—"

"You are from the human city! You're the one Cilarnen went to look for! Did he find you? Is he—"

"Cilarnen is safe and well," Kellen said. "And he is a great hero. And a friend of mine."

"Oh, I knew he would be!" Sarlin gasped, rearing up on her hind legs in her excitement. "Can you— Will you come in? All of you? Will you tell me about him?"

"Gladly," Kellen said. "We need your help, as well."

"We will do anything," Sarlin said fervently.

�⚭

THEY stayed three days at Stonehearth, using it as a base as they swept the surrounding area, looking for signs of the Enemy.

They found one or two, wounded stragglers from the party they had slain. They also found a pack of Ice Trolls, dead of sunlight when their magic failed them. They burned all the bodies.

Kellen found himself glad of Shalkan's warning. Sarlin—whether because Kellen was Cilarnen's friend, or because she was simply relieved that the Demons were gone—was just a bit . . . fervent. Kellen found himself rather uncomfortable in her presence. But there was little to be done about it, save make certain that he was never alone with her, and that was easy to arrange, as the addition of fifty Elven Knights—and their mounts—crowded the Centaur Village almost to bursting.

One thing Kellen did find very useful in his time at Stonehearth was that Sarlin—and the rest of the village elders—were able to provide him with detailed information about other villages in the area, something the Elven maps he had brought with him sorely lacked. As Kellen had hoped and expected, they were little more than a day's ride apart—at least for Elven destriers—and Sarlin assured him that every village and farming community in the area would be as happy as Stonehearth had been to host them, out of gratitude for the news they brought.

On the third day, Kellen and his Knights moved on.

⚭⚭

FOR sennight after sennight, the Elven Knights rode across the Wild Lands. After the first few villages, Kellen left the others to their work and rode out with Mirsil and his Twelve to find one of the other bands of riders. His plan had evolved; now fast-riding skirmishing units criss-crossed the Wild Lands, rarely more than half a day's ride from one or another of Kellen's bands of searchers.

It was a method of solving the problem of cleansing the Wild Lands that the Elves would never have considered for themselves. Kellen had come up with it almost without thought; another gift of his Knight-Mage skills.

And everywhere they went, they brought with them the news that the Demon Army had been utterly routed.

Sometimes it seemed that they did not need to bring the news at all. As the sennights passed, even though they moved farther east and north, spring was rapidly approaching. Even the enormous blanket of snow that had fallen over the past hard winter was melting away—now the ground was visible in places, with the first shoots of spring grass pushing up through the dead growth of the year before—and the trees were setting their first leaves.

They encountered stragglers from the Demon Army constantly, of course. Hundreds of them, overall. But their enemies had only had a few days' head start, and had wandered, disoriented, with no clear plan. Kellen's strike forces dealt with them quickly and efficiently, and while there were a few casualties—both in villages, and to the Elven Knights—not one of the Enemy that they faced survived, nor got as far east as the High Reaches.

And at last, Kellen and his Knights reached the Border of the Elven Lands.

Twenty

To Honor the Fallen

I

T WAS THREE moonturns, almost to the day, since they had left Armethalieh, and winter was over. It was hard, now, to believe that the ground had ever been covered in snow, and that Kellen had ever spent his days and nights worrying about freezing to death.

There was no longer any need to worry about fodder for the horses and mules. Grain would have been better, of course, but the ground was covered with lush thick grass, and after an entire winter of dry fodder, the animals took to it greedily. With the little grain they had left—and the fact that they took the last part of the journey east by easy stages, having, so far as the Wildmages could tell them before they left, scoured the Wild Lands of the Enemy—they did well enough.

As Redhelwar had asked, Kellen had sent him regular reports. And in fact, he had much to report.

Every sign of the blight the Demons had spread—both to the land and the people—was gone. As Meriec had prophesied back at Stonehearth, the wild creatures had indeed returned to their old ranges—Kellen had seen several herds of deer already, as well as birds of every description—and the farmers reported that the flocks and herds were all being, well, *fruitful*. The births of twin lambs and calves had become the rule instead of the exception. And apparently the crops were going to do well, too—though Kellen wasn't sure how anyone could tell this early in the season. But that was what everyone told him, so he dutifully wrote it all down and sent the information along to Redhelwar.

Idalia would have been so happy to know all these things.

꙳

"YOU should dismiss us, you know," Tametormo said, as they reached the boundary of the Elven Lands.

"I . . . er, it would be good to know your thoughts, of your courtesy," Kellen said.

In the days and nights of their journey north, he had come to rely upon Tametormo as his Second. Their relationship lacked the easy familiarity of the one he had had with Isinwen, or the close rapport he had shared with Ciltesse, but he trusted Tametormo to advise him on the things a commander needed to know.

He'd been lost in thought—not thinking of very much, aside from being alert (as he always was) for possible danger on the road ahead, and wondering what he would *do* with himself once he got to Sentarshadeen. He rode at the head of the column of Knights; in less than an hour they would cross the Border, and be back in Elven Lands again.

At last.

"We will enter the Elven Lands, and go beyond Sentarshadeen, to the place where Redhelwar gathered us together to await Andoreniel's word. There, I am certain, he awaits us now. But the time for the army is past. I do not believe that any of us here calls Sentarshadeen home. For my part, I long to see the plains of Ondoladeshiron again. So, when we arrive there, Commander, dismiss us, that we may go home," Tametormo said.

"I . . . yes. Of course. I thank you for your courtesy in telling me that which I did not know," Kellen said.

"You are a great leader, Kellen Knight-Mage," Tametormo answered. "And I and my House shall honor you for that until the end of our days. Your name will never be forgotten, so long as the trees grow and the stars burn. But you will never be an Elf."

And I will never understand Elves, either.

꙳

IT took them another half day to reach the place that Tametormo had spoken of, and just as he had said, there was a camp waiting there for them.

It was small. There were no Healers' pavilions, no row of tents for the Engineers, Armorers, and Artificers. No separate camp for the Centaurs and the Mountainfolk. There were only a few animals waiting in the horselines, though Kellen saw wagons of fodder and a proper herd of remounts grazing out in the meadow.

Most of the Elven Army, it was obvious, was already gone.

Kellen led his troops around the edge of the camp, to the flat plain beyond. Redhelwar rode out to meet them.

He looked at Kellen expectantly, and Kellen was suddenly very grateful for Tametormo's words of advice. He turned Firareth about to face his command. There was a momentary flurry as the Elven Knights elegantly re-ordered their ranks, regarding him expectantly.

What should he say?

"It has been my honor to command you," Kellen told them, standing in his stirrups and pitching his voice so that his words could be heard clearly. "You have done all I have asked of you, and done it well. I dismiss you now. Leaf and Star go with you."

There was a moment of stillness. And then, as simply as that, they were no longer an army. The Elves broke ranks, heading quietly for the horselines to un-saddle their mounts.

Kellen turned to Redhelwar.

"And I dismiss you, Kellen Knight-Mage. Our work here is over. In a day or two, those you have commanded will go to their homes, when they and their horses have rested. These tents will be struck, and in time, there will be no sign that there was ever an encampment here. Which is as it should be.

"But you have a home to go to now. And you should seek it."

Kellen sighed. "I will. But . . . It would please me greatly to hear whether you have had any news that I have not heard."

Redhelwar met his gaze steadily. "Vestakia has returned to her home in Sen-tarshadeen. She is well, and spends much time assisting the Healers. We know not where Jermayan may be. I am sorry."

Kellen bowed his head, turned Firareth, and rode away.

＊

HIS destination was the stables at the House of Sword and Shield.

It seemed like an eternity ago that Jermayan had first brought him here to study with Master Belesharon. He had destroyed the Black Cairn, discovered his own Gift, battled Master Belesharon's Knights in the Teaching Circle and won. He had thought himself well-versed in the ways of the world, a seasoned warrior already.

He'd had no idea.

Kellen found an empty stall and untacked Firareth, brought him a bucket of oats and then brushed him while the destrier ate. Firareth had shed much of his winter coat in the past sennights, but the floor of the stall was still covered with fluffy puffs of tawny horsehair by the time Kellen was finished with his work. When they were both done, he put a hand on Firareth's shoulder and urged the old warrior out into the sunlight. Time for Firareth to take a well-deserved rest, and idle in the sunlight and green grass, turned out to pasture among the other warhorses.

Firareth regarded him curiously.

"Well, go on," Kellen said. "I'll call you if I need you."

Firareth tossed his head and trotted off toward a group of other destriers standing nearby. Kellen wasn't at all surprised to see Valdien among them.

"Well, here we are," Shalkan said.

"Here we are," Kellen echoed.

"You really ought to go home and have a bath," the unicorn observed. "That armor's much too hot for the season. When's the last time you had it off, anyway?"

"I can't remember," Kellen said. Probably at the last village they'd visited, and that had been over a moonturn ago. Well, he took it off at night. Most of it, anyway.

And it *was* hot.

He reached out a hand—he'd taken off his gauntlets in order to groom Firareth. Shalkan slipped his neck beneath Kellen's palm, and Kellen stroked his fingers through the unicorn's downy coat.

"Do unicorns ever shed?"

Shalkan just snorted, not answering. "Go home," he repeated. "Assuming, of course, that you still know the way. And try not to be surprised if you see unfamiliar faces in the streets. Armethalieh—among others—has sent a delegation of honor to the ceremony."

"*Armethalieh?*"

Kellen could not have been more stunned if Shalkan had told him that the *Demons* had sent a delegation.

"The look on your face is priceless."

Kellen had to smile. "Well, Cilarnen did say he was going to change things."

"And he is. And for the better."

"When is . . . ?"

"The day after tomorrow. If you hadn't gotten back when you did, they were going to send someone out to look for you."

Kellen sighed. "I suppose I'll see you around?"

"I certainly won't leave without telling you, after all we've been through together."

"Thanks."

Kellen turned and started walking up toward the city.

⤜≈⤛

BY the time he reached his house, it was dusk. He saw a few people along the way—only Elves—and he'd never been more grateful for Elven politeness, for nobody stopped him or tried to speak to him. He had, he realized, absolutely no idea of what to do with himself. Oh, there was the ceremony to honor Idalia. He hated the idea of it, but he knew he had to attend, because it was important. But after that?

His Naming Day anniversary would be in a few months, he realized—not that the Elves celebrated such events, he suspected.

He'd be eighteen.

It was the beginning of most people's lives, and . . . not that his was over, but . . .

He just felt as if he'd already done everything he was supposed to do with his life, and that there was nothing left to do.

He reached the door of his house. To his surprise, there were lanterns outside, and they were lit. He stopped, frowning in confusion.

This *was* his house. He was certain of it. The Elves certainly wouldn't have given it to someone else.

As he paused on the doorstep, hesitating, the door opened.

A slender elegant Elven man stood there. He looked familiar. As he saw Kellen, his face took on a pleased expression.

"I See you, Kellen. I had expected you long ago. Come, enter. You will be hungry, and weary from the road. All awaits you, just as you would wish it."

Suddenly Kellen realized who this was.

Vertai.

Many moonturns ago, when Idalia had left their house to go and live with Jermayan, Kellen had somehow, suddenly and mysteriously, acquired a sort of servant—or assistant, he had never quite been able to figure out Vertai's relationship to him, and Vertai had been expert at not answering that question. But since—at that time, and probably still—Kellen had possessed no ability to keep his wardrobe in order, his larder stocked, or even cook and clean, Vertai had taken on all of those tasks, generally performing them while Kellen was away receiving his lessons at the House of Sword and Shield.

"I See you, Vertai. And thank you," he added, bowing. "I am grateful for your aid."

He walked inside.

"Your robe is laid out, and I shall prepare tea. Perhaps you would care to suggest a suitable blend."

"I am sure that you will know a tea appropriate to the season."

He walked into his room, surprised at how small it seemed. And not surprised to find several things from his packs already neatly laid out in the appropriate places. Apparently his luggage had preceded him and already been un-packed.

He removed his armor and set it aside. Cleaning it could wait until he bathed. He unbraided his hair—it had gotten very long over the past moonturns—and combed it out. Then he put on the robe that was laid out for him on the bed—relieved to see that for once it wasn't green, but a pleasing fawn color—and matching house-boots and went out into the main room.

The tea—thanks to the Elven "small magics"—was already waiting for him. Kellen picked up the cup and sipped gratefully. The taste was unfamiliar, yet soothing. He remembered a conversation he had once had—it seemed so long ago!—with Dionan and Redhelwar about brewing and blending tea. They'd said the teas of springtime were subtle. This must be one of them.

"I thank you for this, Vertai," he said.

"I shall prepare your evening meal, and then I shall depart to my own home. Tomorrow, you must expect a visit from Tengitir. Your robes for the ceremony are prepared, but they will need a final fitting."

Kellen tried not to sigh. If he'd needed anything to convince him that the war was over and everything was swiftly returning to normal, a visit from the Elven seamstress who specialized in clothing for the non-Elven was defi-nitely it.

"I shall attempt to conduct myself properly," he said.

"You will rejoice to know, as we all do, that Andoreniel is in the fullness of health—indeed, that all who suffered the Shadow's Kiss have recovered com-pletely. He has asked after you, and hopes you will come to see him when you may."

That was certainly good news. Kellen had to think a moment before he could frame his next question politely—which was to say, in a form that was not a question. After so many moonturns of free-and-easy War Manners, it would take some time to settle fully back into formal Elven politeness again.

"There are many people living at the Fortress of the Crowned Horns," he said at last.

"The snow is still deep in the mountains, so I have heard. Andoreniel in-tends to send a convoy to them within the sennight, bringing news of our vic-tory, and conveying all within back to their own homes."

And undoubtedly, Kellen thought, they would all be very grateful to go there.

⌐⇌¬

TWO days later, the nobility and the aristocracy of every race in the land gath-ered together to bid their last farewell to Idalia.

Andoreniel and the Viceroys of the Nine Cities were there: Vanantiriel, Viceroy of Windalorianan; Kindolhinadetil, Viceroy of Ysterialpoerin; Magarabeleniel, Vicereign of Lerkalpoldara; Rochinuviel, Vicereign of Ondoladeshiron; Arelin, Viceroy of Deskethomaynel; Attindorande, Viceroy of Valwendigorean; Falmielandiel, Vicereign of Realthataladon; and Sildonaure, Viceroy of Thultafoniseen.

Though several of their cities lay now in Dark-blasted ruins that would take years to rebuild, and too many Elves to count lay dead, the Elves showed no sign that this was anything but a great victory, in their manner or their bearing. For the third time in their long history, they had faced the power of Shadow Mountain and broken it—perhaps, this time, forever.

Several High Chiefs of the Mountainborn were also here to pay their respects. The Mountainborn had no King, but in his time with the army, Kellen had learned a little of their ways. The families were organized into clans, and the clans gave their allegiance to chiefs, whose ultimate purpose was to settle those disputes which could not be settled by any other means. Six Chiefs of the Mountainborn stood here today—all who could be spared from the work of rebuilding their land that the Mountainborn had before them. They were dressed in their finest garments, soft embroidered woolen tunics and trousers, long coats, wide-brimmed hats trimmed with bright feathers.

Kellen remembered wearing Mountainborn clothing. Shalkan had particularly hated the hat.

The Lostlanders did not organize into clans as the Mountainborn did; in the harsh northern land where they had lived until Atroist had brought them south, the Wildmages had been, not only their sole defense against the nearly-constant Demon raids, but the final authority in all matters. To this final ceremony they had sent Feyrt, their Belrix—War King—with his surviving council of Wildmages.

The Lostlanders stood with the Centaurs—which made sense, since the Lostlanders intended to remain in the Wildlands and live among the Centaurs and the human farmers. Kellen recognized Kreylmedd, who had been warchief of all the centaurs in Redhelwar's camp. The grizzled old veteran had lost an arm in the fighting, and many new scars made white streaks across his chestnut hide, but he had survived. There were about a dozen Centaurs present, men and women both: some who had served in the army, some who were leaders of their home villages.

And, as Shalkan had warned him, there was a delegation of High Mages from Armethalieh, including not only the current Arch-Mage . . .

But the former Arch-Mage.

Lycaelon Tavadon.

His father.

Kellen did not know what he expected to feel when he gazed on his father's face again. Shock? Anger? Triumph? In fact, he felt nothing, not even relief that he felt nothing. Lycaelon looked terribly ravaged; his hair had gone quite white, and a young man in gray Mage-robes stayed beside him at all times to offer support.

The ceremony itself took place at the edge of the Flower Forest. It looked more vibrant than Kellen could remember ever having seen it.

In fact, it looked . . . larger.

Yes, there was definitely new growth there at the edges.

The Flower Forest was expanding. Another good sign that their victory had been decisive.

He had not yet spoken to Andoreniel, a lapse in manners he knew he'd have to take care of as soon as the ceremony was over. He had sent a message to the House of Leaf and Star yesterday, requesting to be excused from any active participation in the ceremony today.

He couldn't think of anything he wanted to say.

He was glad they were all alive. He was glad the Demons were gone. He knew—he *knew*—that Idalia's death was not too high a price to pay for that.

He just couldn't bring himself to say it out loud.

⁓

ANDORENIEL had given his permission, of course, though naturally Kellen still had to attend. So now here Kellen stood, among all the other dignitaries, wearing elaborate robes of green and silver—fortunately, Vertai had been there at his house this morning to help him dress, or he'd still be trying to figure out how to get into them—standing beside Redhelwar, who was equally magnificent in red and gold.

One good thing about all this was that Lycaelon probably wouldn't even recognize him.

Beyond the ranks of those who had a formal place in the ceremony stood those who had come just to be there. Most of them were the citizens of Sentarshadeen—all dressed in white—but at the edges of the crowd, Kellen saw some distinctly human faces, and a few Centaurs as well. Probably there were even some Otherfolk here, if he took the care to look closely.

Everyone had loved Idalia.

He turned his attention to the table set just outside the Flower Forest. It stood upon a pure white carpet—the first he had seen anywhere in the Elven Lands—and the table was covered in a white drape. Upon the table stood a green glass lantern, similar to the ones the Elves hung outside their homes at night.

Andoreniel came and stood behind the table. He placed his hands upon the lantern, and suddenly it was lit—somehow without magic, Kellen knew.

The people gathered in witness, already quiet, stilled even further.

"We have come to say our last farewell to Idalia Wildmage, Beloved of the Elves and of all, who stood between us and the Shadow, and through her will, her courage, and her grace, allowed the Light to prevail once more," Andoreniel said.

❦

THERE was a brief ceremony, silently conducted by Andoreniel and Rochinuviel. It almost seemed like a dance. It reminded Kellen, just a little, of what Cilarnen had done with the unicorns outside the walls of Armethalieh, though he felt no magic in it, only a faint sense of peace. At the end of it, the two of them carried the lantern into the Flower Forest.

Is that it? Kellen wondered. But nobody seemed to be moving.

When they returned, a new air of expectancy suffused the gathering.

"Now let us recall her life," Andoreniel said.

❦

KELLEN realized he had subconsciously been expecting something like this— and dreading it. One by one, representatives from the gathered dignitaries advanced to the now-empty table to speak of Idalia, and what she had meant to them. Kearn was there—he spoke of his long friendship with Idalia, of how she had always traded with him sharply but fairly.

An ancient Lostlander Wildmage—a white-haired woman, quite blind— spoke on behalf of Atroist, sharing his memories of Idalia. Atroist, Kellen discovered, had been her grandson.

Vestakia spoke, telling them all of the first time she had met Idalia, how Idalia had taken her into this very Flower Forest to discover whether her half-Demon heritage would be a threat to them. She spoke of Idalia's unfailing—and unflinching— kindness and friendship to her, from the first moment she had seen her.

Though Vestakia's appearance caused some consternation among those who had never seen her before, there was no fear. Everyone knew that the Demons were defeated and gone.

Others spoke, though briefly.

Cilarnen spoke, telling not only of the kindness he had received from Idalia, but of how much he had learned from her.

"—for she was the first true Wildmage I had ever known. I am a High Mage of Armethalieh, a Master of the Art of High Magick. All my life I had been raised to think of the Wild Magic as something little different than the Dark-magery itself, and Wildmages as little better than Demonspawn. Idalia did not even bother to tell me it wasn't so. She simply *showed* me it wasn't, by everything she was and did."

And then, to Kellen's vast and unsettled surprise, Lycaelon Tavadon came forward to speak. The young gray-robed Mage by his side assisted him to the table; when he stepped away, Lycaelon leaned upon it heavily.

"Idalia was my daughter. But I do not come today to praise her as a daughter. I never valued her as a daughter, and never knew her. For her entire life—every hour and day of it—I was her unswerving enemy, and when I discovered that she still lived, I sought her death with all the power at my command. But she . . . transcended all that she had been as a child of the City. All that she might have been as my daughter. She died, not as an Armethaliehan, but as a hero to all the land. And it is for that which I praise her to you here today."

He bowed his head, and the young Mage came to help him away.

No more speakers came forward. The ceremony was finally over.

It had been a moving and honest speech, and Kellen was mildly surprised that Lycaelon had made it—though he was actually more surprised that Lycaelon had made the journey all the way here to the Elven Lands at all.

Did it make a difference to his feelings about his father?

Kellen wondered.

No. It had been something of a shock to see his father here today, but, seeing him again, Kellen realized that all feelings for the man who had given him life—whether they were feelings of hatred or love—were simply gone. Lycaelon had never given him a chance to love him, and all hatred had been burned away by the intense self-knowledge required of a Knight-Mage.

If Lycaelon had not been who he was, Kellen would not have become who *he* was.

And if Kellen had not been who he was, the Demons would have won.

All went as the Wild Magic willed—and as Idalia had told him once, the Wild Magic wasn't a tame magic, and its workings weren't always comfortable. In a way, it had needed Kellen and Idalia, so it had created them, by sending their mother Alance to Armethalieh in the first place.

He could live with that.

They truly had sent Idalia to rest, Kellen realized suddenly. For the first time since he had seen her body at the Standing Stones, he felt at peace. The ache of her loss was still there—and would be with him for a long time to come, he knew—but it no longer felt like a wound that would never heal.

Suddenly he felt a sense of Presence.

"When the time comes, you must . . . let go."

In the Caverns at Halacira, a Price had been asked and granted. He had thought it would be a heavy one, as so many of the Prices of the Wild Magic were.

Now, here, today, he realized that paying it would free him, not burden him.

And that he had been paying it ever since the end of the Battle of Armethalieh.

Let go.

It was time to let go of all that the Wild Magic had made of him.

Not to let go of being a Knight-Mage . . . that was something he would be until the day he died. But to let go of being a Commander of Armies. A General. Someone who had learned to see other people as tools and weapons.

He must let go of war, and battles, and death.

Let go of the deaths of his friends and loved ones, and keep their lives instead. Let go.

Yes, Kellen thought, with a sigh. *I can do that.*

The sense of Presence lifted.

He looked around, feeling, as he always did afterward, as if he'd just awakened from sleep. The world seemed somehow fresh-washed and new, as if it were a place he'd just now come back to.

He sought out Andoreniel.

"I See you, Andoreniel," he said politely, when Andoreniel noticed him.

All around them, the people were returning to their homes, in the quiet graceful way that Elven ceremonies ended.

"I See you, Kellen," Andoreniel said. "It pleases me to speak with you once more."

"And I with you," Kellen said. "It occurs to me that I have been . . . too long away from civilized things."

"That is often the case, when one must do battle to keep those things safe," Andoreniel said. "It would please me greatly were you to consent to dine with me tonight. It will be a quiet meal, and there are matters I would speak of with you afterward."

A quiet dinner sounded just about right to Kellen. "It will be my pleasure," he said, bowing.

HE moved out around the edges of the crowd that was still assembled there, thinking of nothing so much as going home and brewing up a nice pot of tea. He didn't trust himself to make a drinkable pot of Elven Tea—well, not one he'd offer to one of the Elves, anyway—but Vertai had somehow seen to it that the larder was stocked with a fine assortment of Armethaliehan teas as well, and a large pot of Armethaliehan Black would be just the thing. Along with a good slice of the breakfast pie he hadn't had any appetite for this morning.

"Kellen! Hey!"

There was just about only one person in the entire Elven Lands who would hail him in that fashion. He stopped and turned.

Cilarnen was running after him, clutching his Staff of Office in one hand and attempting to hold onto his high-crowned Arch-Mage hat with the other. His long gray robes and ornately-embroidered tabard flapped wildly about his ankles as he ran.

Kellen grinned despite himself. That was a sight he'd never expected to see—a High Mage of Armethalieh—and not just any High Mage, but the Arch-Mage—running like a common servant.

Things had indeed changed.

"Kellen," Cilarnen said, catching up to him. "Were you just going to leave without saying goodbye?"

"You looked busy," Kellen said. Actually, Cilarnen had looked surrounded by High Mages, and that was somewhere Kellen didn't really want to be. "I thought I might see you later." Certainly Vertai would know where to find Cilarnen. The Elven penchant for gossip was one thing that the war hadn't changed.

"See me now," Cilarnen suggested. "We'll be leaving in the morning. I can't stay away from Armethalieh very long. Light alone knows what the Council will have done while I'm gone, even with Kardus there to tell them not to. I left him my seal."

"In that case," Kellen said, "they're probably still paralyzed with shock. Come and drink tea with me."

The two friends walked in silence for a while.

"I've never seen you dressed like this," Cilarnen said doubtfully, regarding Kellen's formal Elven finery.

"And I've never seen you dressed like that," Kellen said.

"You just look—"

"Appropriate," they finished together.

"It isn't exactly the way I thought it would be," Cilarnen said. "Being, well, Arch-Mage."

"Worse?" Kellen asked.

"And better," Cilarnen said. "Now that the people know that they're a part of the High Magick—really a part, because we couldn't cast our spells without what they give us—things are different in the City. They can choose to wear the Talisman and stay . . . or leave. Nearly everyone has decided to stay. Those who haven't, well, they can go anywhere they want. Or that will have them. There's an amnesty—they have until the end of the sailing season to make their arrangements to leave; I'm not just going to throw anyone out, no matter what the Council is urging. Next year . . . well, I'm going to start trying to get the Council to ease the restrictions on new goods. We'll have to, because of the trade we need to do. But Father was right. I can't do everything at once. I only wish I could."

"You've made more changes in the last few moonturns than the City has seen in the last thousand years," Kellen reminded him. "The rest will come in time."

"It would come faster if you were there to help. Won't you come back to Armethalieh, Kellen? We could use you there. And . . . you heard what Lord Lycaelon said today. Can't you forgive him? He's suffered greatly, you know."

Kellen stopped walking, honestly stunned that Cilarnen couldn't see what he himself saw so clearly.

"Truly, Cilarnen, there is nothing to forgive. You know Lycaelon's wife—my mother, and Idalia's—was Mountainborn. I think, you know, that she may have been a Wildmage as well. And the Wild Magic moves as it wills. I think that everything that happened between us was all part of that, to make me what I needed to be."

Cilarnen stared at him, obviously accepting Kellen's truth but not understanding it. He shook his head ruefully. "I will never understand Wildmages. The Wild Magic is just too . . . messy."

"But effective."

"Oh yes. I do grant you that. But . . . will you come back?"

"No. I told you that already. Wherever I belong—and I don't know where that is yet—it isn't Armethalieh."

They reached Kellen's house, and went inside, and spoke of other things.

⁓

THAT night Kellen ate dinner at the House of Leaf and Star. As Andoreniel had promised, the evening was quiet and intimate. Besides Kellen and Andoreniel, the only others present were Morusil and Redhelwar.

The plague-scars on Morusil's and Andoreniel's faces had faded nearly to invisibility, though both Elves would carry the mark of the Shadow's Kiss to the end of their lives, as would so many others throughout the land. But from the moment the power of Shadow Mountain had been broken, there had been no more deaths, and all who had been afflicted had recovered rapidly and well.

Talk during the meal was idle, and mostly of inconsequential matters— crops to be planted, festivals to be held, new artworks planned by this Elven master or that. Redhelwar spoke of his desire to return to Windalorianan, to help with the rebuilding of the city, and to return to the care and breeding of his beloved horses. Morusil spoke of his garden, and how very well it was doing already. He confirmed what Kellen had suspected—that the Flower Forest was, indeed, expanding.

After the meal, they retired to Andoreniel's private study, a place Kellen had never been. Like Ashaniel's solar, the walls were made of many tiny panes of glass, and through them, Kellen could see the garden that surrounded the House of Leaf and Star filled, at this hour, with its hundreds of multicolored lanterns.

The study was filled with lanterns as well, tiny copies of the ones outside. It gave the effect of bringing the garden inside in an unbroken sweep of flickering rainbow light. The effect was deliberate, Kellen knew. The Elves rarely did anything by accident.

"There is only one last thing to be done to set all to rights," Andoreniel said, once all of them were seated. "And it would ease my heart greatly to know that I might set this task into the hands of a friend."

There was a moment of silence before Kellen realized that they were waiting for him to speak.

"It would please me greatly to know what this task might be," he said.

"A convoy goes to the Fortress of the Crowned Horns to bear the glad tidings of their liberation to the Crowned Horns' defenders, to tell Master Tyrvin his long task is at an end, and to begin to bear the inhabitants away to their homes. It has been much delayed by weather—something of which you and Redhelwar know as much as any, Kellen, for you have fought many battles through those mountains. And I know that you are weary and long for rest. Yet I would be grateful could you bring yourself to go into the north once more and bring my Queen and my son home to me."

"Yes, I . . . of course. I would be honored to lead such a convoy," Kellen said, after a short pause.

When Andoreniel had begun speaking, he'd thought it would be something difficult.

"I hope that Vestakia will accompany you on your journey. I know that the Enemy has been defeated, but . . ."

"It is still good to be sure," Kellen finished. "I cannot speak for Vestakia, but I'll ask her." *I'm sure that she's really looking forward to spending another moonturn camping in the snow.*

But to his surprise, she agreed.

⸎

THE preparations for the convoy had all been made while Kellen had still been leading his troops toward Sentarshadeen. Kellen suspected that Andoreniel had hoped all along that Kellen would be the one to lead it north.

He really didn't mind. It was a simple easy task, after all that had gone before it. The land was at peace, and in the full bloom of Springtide. Though he rode armed and armored—but in a much lighter cloak and surcoat than he had worn for the winter fighting—he really didn't expect trouble.

Though, as always, he rode prepared for it.

THE journey took them a fortnight. At the end of the first sennight, they reached the village of Girizethiel and reprovisioned. Girizethiel marked the point at which the convoy left the rolling open country and began to ascend into the mountains themselves. Another sennight would see them at the Fortress.

Though the Unicorn Knights themselves were gone, the party was not without unicorn companions, for a small band of unicorns had apparently decided to accompany Kellen's party.

Including, of course, Shalkan.

"Why not?" Shalkan had said, when Kellen asked him about it on the first night of their journey. "Spring is a good time for traveling."

Knowing he would get no better answer, Kellen had left it at that.

And spring *was* a good time for traveling, especially this spring. The mountain air was crisp and clean, the forest they rode through once they left Girizethiel was filled with radiant new life. There were times when Kellen could almost convince himself that the past several moonturns had been some horrible dream.

He was not the only Knight with the convoy, of course. Four Twelves rode with him, Elves with family members at the Crowned Horns, who would be escorting them back to their homes. It would take time to empty the Fortress completely, but Sentarshadeen was not the only Elven city that would be sending wagons, only the first.

On the fourteenth day of their journey, they left the forest and rode out onto the plain below the Fortress. It was no longer the ice-covered plain that it had been the last time Kellen had seen it, but a meadow; with spring, the snows had retreated to the mountain slopes. All sign of the terrible battle that had once taken place here was gone, ice and snow had been replaced by a field of flowers, pink and white and blue, stretching as far as the eye could see.

Kellen and Vestakia were riding at the head of the convoy. It was peaceful to ride beside Vestakia. She was the last of his comrades who remained, the one who had been with him almost from the beginning. And while Kellen knew that she missed Idalia as much as he did, he also took delight in her constant wonder in everything new—and everything about the lushness of spring in the Elven Lands was new to Vestakia, since she had grown up in the harsh and nearly-barren Lostlands.

Suddenly she stiffened and leaned forward in her saddle.

Kellen put a hand on his sword.

"No! Kellen—look! It's Ancaladar!"

Kellen stared where she was pointing.

At the foot of the causeway that led up to the entrance to the Fortress of the Crowned Horns, there was a familiar black shape.

Ancaladar.

Kellen turned to Ornentuile, one of the Elven Knights who rode just behind them. "We're riding on ahead. You have command."

He spurred Firareth forward, racing across the meadow.

Vestakia followed.

⌘

"IT is good to see you again, Kellen, Vestakia," Ancaladar said politely.

The dragon lay basking in the sunlight, his great wings spread.

"What are you *doing* here?" Kellen demanded. "Didn't you know we were all worried about you?"

"We've been busy," Ancaladar said calmly, not at all distressed by Kellen's exasperation and anger. "You should go and see Jermayan. You'll understand."

Kellen glanced up the causeway. Master Tyrvin stood at the bronze gates that guarded the entrance to the Fortress—open now—waiting for them.

Kellen gestured to Vestakia.

"Oh, I'll go," she said, sounding exasperated, "but be sure that when I come back, Ancaladar, I'm going to give you the scolding of your life!"

"Oh, I don't think so," the dragon said, sounding amused.

⌘

"WELL met," Master Tyrvin said, when Kellen and Vestakia reached the top of the causeway.

"We've come to bring you news," Kellen said. "But I think you may already have gotten it." He nodded back to where Ancaladar lay.

"That *Their* power has been swept from the land is word that has perhaps come to us indeed." Tyrvin smiled. "But come. There is news you will wish to have as well, perhaps equally joyous, and I shall bring you to Ashaniel so that she may deliver it to you."

He led Kellen and Vestakia inside, and through a maze of corridors down a path Kellen had not taken on his previous visit to the Fortress. Though he heard the sound of scurrying feet many times—indicating that the corridor was being hastily vacated—Kellen saw none of what must, by now, be the many inhabitants of the Fortress.

Tyrvin paused before a door and knocked.

Sandalon opened it.

The boy seemed to have grown at least a head taller in the moonturns that had passed since Kellen had seen him last. He flung himself into Kellen's arms with a glad cry of joy.

"Kellen! You've come back for us! And Vestakia is here, too! *Mother!* Kellen and Vestakia are here! *Oh!*" Suddenly the boy remembered his manners. He stepped back and bowed. "Please be welcome—in our home and at our hearth, Kellen Wildmage, Lady Vestakia."

Kellen reached down and ruffled the boy's hair. "And I See you too, Sandalon," he teased, stepping inside.

The first thing his eyes went to in the room was Jermayan.

The Elven Knight was sitting beneath a window—it wasn't a real window, for there were no windows anywhere in the Fortress of the Crowned Horns—but Ashaniel's chamber had been painted in the likeness of a tower room, with mock paintings of windows upon all four walls.

He was sitting beside a cradle, a look of utter peace upon his face.

Ashaniel sat at the other side of the cradle, gazing down into it with a fond smile upon her face.

"I have a new sister," Sandalon announced importantly. "She is very special."

Kellen and Vestakia walked over to the cradle and looked down.

The baby was very tiny indeed. She lay beneath her blankets, regarding the world with calm curiosity.

Her eyes were not Elven black, but violet.

And she had a birthmark—a silvery eight-pointed star in the hollow of her throat.

"By the Good Goddess!" Vestakia gasped. "It's Idalia!"

The baby gurgled with laughter, waving her tiny fists. Jermayan reached out a hand, and she grabbed his finger, clutching strongly.

No wonder Ancaladar sounded so . . . smug, Kellen thought.

"But . . ." he said.

Jermayan looked up, met his eyes, and smiled.

"I can wait," he said serenely. "I have centuries—what is a mere eighteen years to that? I think—should I begin to grow impatient—that Ancaladar and I shall go in search of other dragons, to tell them that their need to hide from the world has passed. That is a task of years that will keep me from too much impatience. But when I return . . ."

He looked meaningfully at Ashaniel, who simply smiled.

"It will not be the first time a child has been betrothed in her cradle, Jermayan. And I can see already how stubborn she is. Not for all the treasure of the Nine Cities—or a dragon's magic—would I do anything to keep the two of you apart."

"So she is not dead," Vestakia said joyfully.

"No," Kellen said, still stunned by what he was seeing. Nor would Idalia's greatest fear—that Jermayan would be forced to live out long centuries of his life without her—ever come to pass. Not now. For as a last gift of the Wild Magic, in payment for her ultimate sacrifice, Idalia had been reborn among the Elves, possessed, now, of the gift of their long years.

Suddenly Vestakia put her arms around him. He hugged her back without thinking—and as he did, he realized that it was almost summer.

His bond with Shalkan—a bond of chastity and celibacy—had been formed in early spring, to run for a year and a day.

That time was over now. Well over.

He was free.

He could look at Vestakia now. He could *think* about Vestakia now.

"I—" he said, suddenly feeling terribly awkward.

"I always knew," she said gravely. Suddenly she smiled, and an irrepressible dimple appeared at the corner of her mouth. "Kellen, you worked *so* hard to avoid me!"

Kellen laughed with sheer relief. It was true.

But no longer.

⮑

THERE were formalities, of course. He had to speak to Tyrvin, and formally relieve him of his duties at the Fortress, something Jermayan had not been able to do. With that, the preparations for leave-taking could at last begin.

Once they were underway, Kellen and Vestakia went back down the causeway, this time walking hand-in-hand. For the first time in nearly a year, the children of the Elves were out in the fresh air once more, laughing and playing in the meadow among the watchful unicorns. He saw Sandalon among them, running in circles among the meadow flowers for sheer joy at being able to do so.

Where was Shalkan?

He'd said he wouldn't leave without saying goodbye.

Kellen located him at last, at the edge of the ring of unicorns that was watching the children. He was standing next to another unicorn, rubbing his neck against hers. Kellen recognized her at once—Calmeren, the only survivor from the first Crowned Horns convoy.

As he started to approach, Shalkan raised his head. His nostrils flared warn-ingly. Kellen stopped.

Still celibate. But no longer chaste, I guess.

"I suppose this is goodbye, then," Kellen said.

"You knew the time would come," Shalkan said, sounding more than a little cross at having been interrupted. "Some of it was fun. All of it was necessary. But now it's time for you to get on with your own life and let others tend to theirs. Goodbye, Kellen."

"Goodbye, Shalkan." Kellen turned away.

"And one last piece of advice," Shalkan called after him.

Kellen stopped and turned back. "What is it?"

"Kiss the girl."

Kellen grinned in spite of himself. Trust Shalkan to get in the last word.

Kellen turned to Vestakia. "Shalkan's advice is usually pretty good," he said.

"I think we should follow it," she agreed.

And so they did.